To Caroline

My thanks to Dave Morris, friend, reader and adviser, whose inspiration made the book possible. Thanks also to Steve Foster and Ian Marsh who rescued the book from computer discs older than the Ark. And to John Jarrold and to Dave Gemmell for their generous and unstinting advice over the years.

. . . Ere Babylon was dust,
The magus Zoroaster, my dear child,
Met his own image walking in the garden.
That apparition, sole of men, he saw.
For know there are two worlds of life and death:
One that which thou beholdest; but the other
Is underneath the grave, where do inhabit
The shadows of all forms that think and live
Till death unite them and they part no more;
Dreams and the light imaginings of men,
And all that faith creates or love desires,
Terrible, strange, sublime and beauteous shapes.

—Percy Bysshe Shelley,
Prometheus Unbound

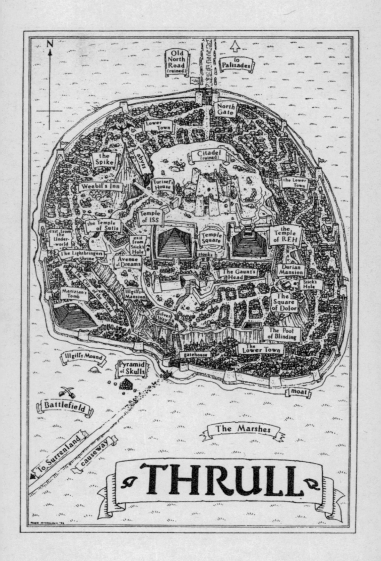

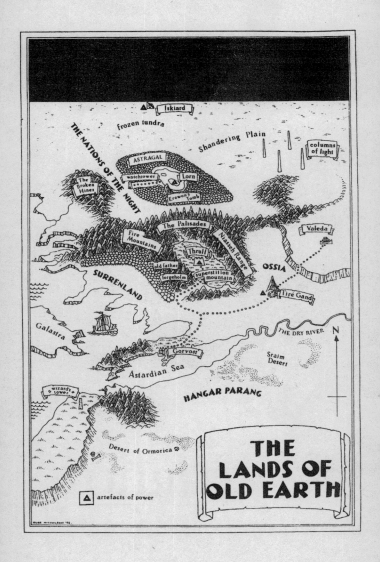

THE LANDS OF OLD EARTH

CHAPTER ONE

Under Superstition Mountain

A mountain pass—the peaks above it were old, sloop-shouldered and bald, without a scrap of vegetation. Ancient screes clung to the side of the mountains beneath fractured buttresses. The path, distinguished only by piles of stones built into cairns, threaded its way through the lunar waste of rock towards a looming peak. Overhead a red gibbous sun, its bottom half lost in the mists of the mauve-blue sky, hung in the heavens. The light was the red light of dusk, though it was only midafternoon.

In common with many of the high lonely places, there was a particular quality to the silence here, a silence so intense and all-enveloping that it seemed to take on substance and form, seemed to become the mountains and the sky, to fill both with a barely audible hum. The slightest sound seemed trebly magnified: an eagle was gliding on the thermals, its single cry defining and deepening the humming silence even further.

Then more movement and sound challenged the silence of the rocks. Lower down, the path switchbacked through the boulders, clawing its way to the top of the pass. A rock slipped from its old resting place, rattled down the slope, before settling for another millennium of rest. Then, like a small bent beetle with an oversized shell, a man appeared from that direction, dragging a hand cart behind him. The cart was as big as he was, seemingly having a mind of its own, jumping and bucking on the uneven surface.

The man moved slowly, with a pronounced limp. His bald head was liver-spotted, as old, it seemed, as the lichen-stained rocks of the pass. He was singing, breathlessly and tunelessly: an old man's voice, reedy and high. The song only had four lines, which he repeated over and over, in time with his feeble footsteps.

> White as white the hairs of your head,
> Your eyes they flame as fire.
> O lord of light, of love, of life,
> Protect me in this hour.

He stopped, his face tilted to the red sun, his teeth clenched in pain, as if suddenly aware of the terrifying silence of the place, of how feeble his voice was against it. The silence quickly filled the small place where his voice had been. Quickly the old man started off again, a small trickle of sweat on his brow.

The old man's name was Zacharias. By next summer he would have reached his sixtieth year, but that sixtieth birthday seemed as far away to him as the distant peak towards which he travelled so painfully and slowly. He had been walking for eight hours and was by now quite far into the Fire Mountains. He had left behind the desolate levels of the marshes at midday, five hours out from the city, since when his progress had all been uphill, steeper and steeper as the switchbacks cut into the mountainside. As he'd ascended, the hand cart had dragged more and more on his weary arms. Now his consciousness was subsumed by the struggle with the cart and with the fiery ache of his limbs. Only the hymn was good, fitting in with his trancelike state and the all-consuming necessity of putting one foot in front of another.

He had not expected to live these last eight hours. That he had done so seemed nothing short of a miracle bestowed on him by the deity to which he sang: Reh, Lord of Light, the Sun, God of Flame and the fiery Cohorts of the Second Coming. As long as the sun shone, however weakly, on the dying earth, he had a chance of life. He stared at his feet; each footstep nearer his destination before nightfall was a small triumph of the will, a small reason for joy. By sunset, with Reh's blessing, he might still be alive. By a miracle, he might even be at the top of the pass that led over Superstition Mountain.

Then a clatter of falling rocks above him told him that his blessings had run out. His voice trailed off and he looked up from the path. He had reached a narrow gully between two rocks precariously hanging on to the side of the mountainside: a perfect ambush spot. The gap was occupied by two men. One was immense, almost giant in stature, the other small and slight. Both were unshaven, their hair tied up in rags, their legs bare, their sleeves rolled up, exposing whipcord arms that looked to be made of wood rather than flesh. The larger one carried a sword, hefting it idly in his hand as if it were a wand rather than solid metal weighing several pounds. The giant's hand hardly wavered each time he tossed and caught it. The smaller man made do with a curved knife and a dangerous smile; he seemed to be the leader.

Zacharias took in the weapons—armament enough to deal with one defenceless old man. He let the handles of the cart fall to the ground with a sigh, the hymn forgotten. His wife Saman, whose remains he dragged behind him in the cart, had believed in Reh. He had only really been singing the hymn in deference to her memory. Now it was irrelevant. No god could save him now.

The larger of the two men climbed slowly down the path. He was nearly seven feet in height, his skin bone white, his hair flame red. There were many such as him in the lands of the old Empire: crossbred descendants of those who had built Thrull, the city that Zacharias had just come from. No doubt both of the bandits had lived there once but had fled when their world had ended seven years ago. Zacharias's nose wrinkled as he came closer; the giant's acrid scent was beyond farmyard. The man ignored Zacharias and leant over the cart, pushing a thick finger contemptuously through the assortment of rags and bundles at the bottom of it. He found the chest almost instantly. His eyes settled on its large brass lock, then sought Zacharias's. The old man noticed they were flat and dull; the light of intellect extinguished.

"What's in here?" he said, pointing. The voice sounded like rocks being rolled together.

Zacharias looked up the mountainside: the snowcapped peak of Superstition Mountain glimmered in the purple sky. He thought of the life he was about to lose, but he had no regrets; he had done what he had had to do.

The smaller man had joined his friend: "Deaf as well as stupid?" he asked, shoving Zacharias back into the side of the cart. The old man rebounded off it and fell to his knees, rubbing his shoulder where it had hit the cart handle. The pain didn't matter, he thought, he would soon be dead. Dead, and his bones carried by the sacred eagles up to the sun, where Reh would hold them in his fiery hands until the last day of the world. And, if Saman his wife had been right, he would see her again there, in the white light of Paradise. And then they would be together until the end of time.

The big man was lifting the chest out of the cart, with the bemused expression of a child who had discovered a toy puzzle. Zacharias felt a stab of mental anguish. The chest contained his dead wife's ashes: he'd thought to scatter them somewhere up here in the mountains; the wind would have done the rest, carrying them up to heaven. Also in the chest was the casket with the lock of her hair. Would the robbers trample it into the dust, burying it? Would the birds of Reh ever find each black gossamer strand of it? Zacharias thought of Saman at the Last Day, resurrected without the beautiful flowing locks which had been her pride and joy. His heart spasmed with grief.

"Leave it," he begged, struggling to his feet.

The small one effortlessly blocked his attempts to grab back the chest with one hand. "Today's our day, Birbran; this old usurer has brought us his gold," he said, yellow incisors bared in a smile. He took a step closer so Zacharias could smell the spirits on his breath. "How much is in there, stick bones? A hundred gold? Two hundred?" His eyes flicked down to the old man's chest. Zacharias followed the line of his sight. His cloak had fallen open when he'd staggered back against the cart, revealing a rusted key tied to a hemp cord resting on his undershirt.

"So, what's this?" The man reached forward and grabbed the cord. He snapped it off Zacharias's neck with a savage yank. The old man fell to the ground, choking and nursing the raw mark left on his neck. The robber studied the key, then nodded at Birbran. The giant lifted the chest from the cart and balanced it precariously on the top of the tumblehome. The smaller man thrust the key into the brass lock. The giant stared in dumb fascination as his friend jiggled with it, seeking the catch.

Zacharias struggled to his knees, his frail body wracked by a coughing fit. He raised his hand feebly to try to stop them but was rewarded by a savage kick from the smaller man that knocked him back into the wheel of the cart. There was nothing he could do: unable to watch, he looked away at the distant peaks.

It was then he saw the figure. It was standing between the boulders above him, where the robbers had been, the body silhouetted by the sun, the face in deep shadow. A tall, lanky figure. Orange-and-red robes fluttered in the chilly breeze. The colours of a priest of Reh. Zacharias had a moment to notice that there was something strange about the man's face and hands, then the stranger stepped from the shadows of the boulders into one of the red beams of light from the afternoon sun.

Zacharias gasped and scrambled backwards, knocking into the little man's knees. The bandit swung round on Zacharias, his eyes blazing with fury.

"Damn you, you . . ." His words were choked off. He, too, stared at the figure on the path above them.

"What is that?" he managed to hiss. Birbran turned, confused by the sudden fear in his partner's voice. When he, too, saw the man he let out an animal grunt of surprise.

Zacharias had already had a heartbeat to take in the vision which had appeared out of the sun. A face out of nightmares, of sick dreams, beggaring even the Mummer's costumes of two-nosed hags and one-eyed freaks. A face though human, only so in rough approximation and nothing more.

A demon of the God of Flame was come; the face a criss-crossed mass of scar tissue and fiery whirls of black, red and yellow flesh, the nose a hollow slit, from which a fire-blackened flesh-coloured tunnel plunged down towards the throat, the teeth exposed in a lipless rictus to which shreds of flesh still clung, white gleams of bone shining at the jaw. The eye sockets were blind hollows that seemed to suck in the light.

Zacharias grabbed the side of the cart and levered himself up into a half-standing position, but there he stopped, frozen. Behind him the two robbers had taken a step back. The precariously balanced chest tumbled to the ground with a crash.

A silent moment passed. Then the vision, having taken in the scene with one sweep of the voids of its eyes, stepped forward, full into a beam of stronger sunlight. It was then Zacharias saw that the face was only a mask. But what a mask! A craftsman had laboured for a long time to carve the face from wood, to paint each detail with such care so that every small scar in that livid beating mass of flesh seemed to shriek out in pain.

Time was frozen, the only sound the cry of the eagle further up the mountainside.

The smaller of the two robbers recovered his wits first.

"It's only a mask," he whispered, needlessly, since the priest was so close he must hear every word. "Take him, Birbran!" His voice lacked conviction. The giant was making his own judgements. His small eyes took in the priest. The man's mask would only come up to his chest, but even Birbran could sense the animal menace that seemed to radiate out from behind it. He'd heard of such men, wild sorcerers, fugitives like him, who exercised their power without prejudice or mercy. But seven years of hard struggle in the barren mountains—seven years of eating desert coyote and wild birds' eggs—of living hard between the rare slave caravans—had made him desperate enough. Desperate enough to kill the priest and the old man for whatever was in the chest.

His fleshy features contorted into a sneer of disgust as he forced himself to look at the mask again. He took a step forward, the old iron of his sword a reassuring weight though dwarfed in his fist. The priest and he were now thirty feet apart, but Birbran got no further. The priest's hands had been hanging loosely by his side, but at Birbran's forward step, they flew up, palms outward. Birbran had a moment to notice that the man wore strange gloves, leather gauntlets with metal protruding from their fingers, but even as he did so the air before the gloves began to warp and shimmer, as if an oven door had suddenly been opened. The mountain air had been cool on the giant's limbs a moment before, but suddenly he felt an intense, scalding heat on his sword arm. He glanced down: the red arm hairs were curling and blackening, and his skin began to pucker and blister. He smelled the acrid stink of singeing flesh at the same moment as the pain registered, and he let out a bellow of agony. The sword fell from his hand. He staggered back, then turned and ran down the path as fast as his lumbering frame could take him.

His friend stared at the giant's retreating form, then back to the priest. The man's gloves were now pointed at him. It was enough: he took off after the giant. His foot slipped on some loose shale and he fell. He scrambled back to his feet and bounded away down the mountainside as fast as he could go. The bandits had soon dwindled to small specks leaping down the distant scree slopes. The sound of falling rocks disturbed by their flying feet echoed up the pass for a minute or so, then faded away.

Zacharias had not moved, but had remained pinned to the side of the cart during the bandits' flight. Now his eyes switched back to the priest. The black sockets of the mask seemed to gather him into their voids. There was no respite: one source of his death had simply been replaced by another. The little gold he owned would be enough; the priest would kill him. He wondered how it would be done—the man carried no weapons. With a spell, or with his bare hands? The priest hadn't moved—his masked head was tilted slightly as he examined the gloves, turning them one way then another, as if the power that had been unleashed from them had surprised him in some way. Zacharias's eyes also fixed on the gloves. They were made of a hardened leather, with small sharpened metal claws at their ends. It was easy imagining them rending and gouging, like talons. Thin metal ridges ran from the tips back towards the wrist, where they disappeared under the folds of the orange-and-red robes. The ridges bunched into metallic knuckles at the joints like an outer skeleton to the hand. Zacharias watched the metal rods contracting, drawing the hand up into an even more clawlike shape. Then the priest stepped towards him.

Now it's coming, Zacharias thought, closing his eyes and offering up a silent prayer to Reh.

He heard pebbles rattling on the path as the priest approached.

Then nothing, save the repeated cry of the eagle and the faint keening of the wind through the rocks.

Zacharias cracked his eyes open again. The priest now stood next to him—his breath coming heavy through the nose slit of the mask, the threatening claws of the gloves delicately adjusting one of the thin leather straps that held the mask to his face. The man's face was slightly averted, taking in the view down the mountain. A section of his neck between the collar of his cloak and the mask was exposed. It was a mass of white scar tissue and livid weals.

Zacharias looked away, a dark suspicion sending a shudder through him.

Though death was so near, his eyes inadvertently followed the priest's line of sight, back towards the city that he had promised himself he would never look at again.

The great bowl of the plain unfolded beneath them, cupped by the mountain ranges that ringed it. Below them, the road zigzagged down the mountainside, disappearing over a ridge, to reappear far below on the flat expanse of the marsh as a thin white line which disappeared arrow straight into the heart of the dull haze which hung over the vastness of the plain.

"Is it far to the city?" the priest asked flatly. His voice was hollow, impersonal beneath the wood and lacquer of the mask. As he spoke he turned, revealing the full horror of the mask again. Zacharias could not help but stare. He sensed eye movement in the dark sockets.

"The city?" he repeated, confused.

"Is there more than one on the plains?" There was an edge of irritation in the voice. Zacharias shook his head rapidly.

"No," he said, recovering his wits and pointing. "See, over yonder, that's Thrull."

The priest leaned forward, following the line of Zacharias's trembling finger. It was possible to see, just where the road disappeared into the mist at the centre of the plain, the dim outline of a granite knoll rearing out of the tablelike flatness all around it. Even at this distance it was possible to make out the vague outlines of buildings clinging to the knoll's summit and sides.

The priest gave a grunt of satisfaction and took a step forward down the path towards the far-off speck.

The words escaped Zacharias's mouth before he could stop them.

"You're not going there, are you?"

The priest stopped short and turned. The dark eye pits of the mask looked the old man up and down. "Why shouldn't I?" he asked hollowly.

The old man hesitated, regretting his words. But the priest had saved, then spared, his life: he must warn him.

"No one wants to go to Thrull. . . . It's a bad place," he said, somewhat lamely.

The priest snorted in amusement: "What place isn't bad? The whole Empire has gone to wrack and ruin."

Zacharias shook his head in vigorous denial: "No, Thrull is worse . . . far worse."

"In what way?"

Zacharias swallowed hard, struggling for words: "If there were a place where the dead are more happy than the living, that place would be Thrull," he managed finally.

The priest had taken a step closer to Zacharias as he'd been saying this.

"Tell me," he whispered.

As he stepped closer, the fear returned, but Zacharias tried to control the tremor he felt beginning in his voice.

He took a deep breath. "Seven years ago, there was a great battle on the plain, the priests of Iss won it . . ."

But before he could get into his stride, the priest had held up his clawed hand, silencing him. "All this I know—speak of more recent events."

Having been tongue-tied for so long, Zacharias's words now came in a torrent. "So you know who rules there now? What he has brought to Thrull?" The priest's continued silence was further encouragement. "Then the rest is easy to imagine. At day you may pass freely, but at night you must lock yourself into your house. Even there you are not safe . . ." He hesitated, gulping down the bile in his throat. ". . . They got my wife, took her one night, I found her on the doorstep in the morning. Pale as snow. I helped her in, but she just looked at me with those black-rimmed eyes. Then I saw them, the bite marks in her neck, her flesh hectic from the fever. Her eyes full of hate and pain, like she was about to scratch and claw at me any moment . . ." His voice broke, remembering. "I lashed her down on the bed. Then went to get the priest, one of your own, that was, a priest of the Flame. He told me there was only one thing that could be done. I waited outside while . . ." Zacharias twisted away, leaving the rest unsaid, his heart like ice. He blinked away his tears before continuing. "Her ashes are in the chest; her hair, too. She had beautiful hair . . ." He bowed his head.

"Go on," said the priest, quietly.

"What more is there to say? Every night of every year, locked in our houses, the vampires howling and swearing outside, running their nails over the wood of the door, or the shutters. Each door, each window, each chimney piece blocked against them, and still they took us, when we were least expecting them. If in the day you chanced to step into a shadow, there they would be, hundreds of them, waiting for you to step from the sun."

"Then why did you stay so long?"

The old man glanced round at the barren mountains. "There was nowhere else, except across the marshes and the mountains, and crossing them is death."

"Yet you are doing it."

Zacharias shook his head. "I am old: I expect to die. Those younger than I still have hope; they cling to it, praying that sanity will return." He looked away at the city on the plains. "It never will; Thrull is a city of the dead. That is why I'm travelling, priest. And with Reh's blessing, I will make Superstition Mountain by dark."

The priest looked up at the mountain peaks, nodding slowly. "Aye, you may get there, with the God's blessing. But be careful: between here and Surrenland there are many enemies."

The old man smiled. "Where you go, you will find even more, but thanks."

"Then go in peace," the priest said, turning back to the path.

"You're still going?"

The priest turned for the last time. "I have to."

The old man shook his head. "Every day more and more of your fellow priests are rounded up; they will kill you if you go there."

The priest laughed, a savage, hollow laugh. "Old man, that is exactly the reason why I must go: to correct the balance." He turned and strode off down the mountain, his sandals kicking up small clouds of dust from the path.

Zacharias watched him, relief and pity contending within him. The lanky figure grew smaller and smaller until it seemed but an orange-and-red ant labouring on the side of the mountain far below. Then it reached the ridge over which the path disappeared and the green brooding plains seemed to swallow it like a toad sucking up a brightly hued insect.

Zacharias shook his head. Today had been a day of miracles. He had lived for eight hours longer than he could have dreamed. Once he got the chest back on the cart, he might live a few hours more. By evening he might be at the pass beneath Superstition Mountain. He was that much nearer a place of safety.

Unlike the priest, he thought, as he hefted the chest onto the cart. He looked back over the plains. Already they seemed to be darkening, taking on a late-afternoon hue. Already the feeble beams of the sun had ceased to warm the earth, and the air was cold.

"The Flame go with you," he whispered, then lifted the handles of his cart from the ground and resumed his painful hobble towards freedom.

CHAPTER TWO

"Keep from the Shadows"

I t took the priest most of the three hours before sunset to reach the city. In all that time he had stopped only once, briefly, on the causeway across the marshes. The road was deserted and he had leisure to inspect the city before him. From the mountains, the granite cliffs of Thrull had seemed an insignificant speck in the middle of the brooding plains. Now they towered over his head, a thousand feet tall. Massive curtain walls, built from the same granite as the cliffs, obscured the lower part of the city, but higher up roofs clustered thickly together on the precipitous slopes.

At the very top of the granite mountain, silhouetted against the washed-out sky of late afternoon, he could see the black towers of the inner citadel and the tops of the pyramids of the twin temples of the city. From that dedicated to Reh, God of Light, a thick plume of smoke from the sacrificial fire soared into the air. From that of Iss, God of Worms and Death, there was nothing.

Light and Death: eternal opposites. Once the two factions had been able to live together peacefully. But since the sun had begun to die, all had changed. Brother had fallen on brother; persecution, war and butchery had followed all over the Empire. But no place worse than here, in Thrull. Seven years to the day which had sent fifty thousand to their deaths, including his master, Manichee.

Then he did what he'd been avoiding doing up to that moment: he turned his gaze from the city to a small hillock fifty yards to his left in the marshes. Even in the inconsequential light of late afternoon, the mound glowed white against the dun green of the swamp. Already mosses and lichen covered half its fifty-foot height, but even at this distance, it was clear what it was made of: course upon course of human skulls, the heads of those killed in the battle of Thrull, now picked clean of flesh. Lord Faran would not let anyone entering Thrull forget the events of that fateful day seven years before. Yet though fifty thousand had died, the priest had known only one of them: Manichee.

It was said that Manichee's head had been placed right at the top of the pyramid. The priest craned his head back, but the summit of the mound was too far away for him to distinguish anything there. At this distance, all the ivory grins seemed all the same: votive offerings to Iss, God of Death.

He bowed his masked head rapidly, then set off with his brisk, loping stride down the causeway, pulling the hood of his cloak over his head as he did so. But as he approached closer to the city, the dead of the battle were once more thrust into his consciousness. A hundred yards from the city gate the surface of the causeway, packed earth to this point, became encrusted with white rocks. They appeared to be pieces of chalk; but the priest knew better. The bones of the dead had been scattered over the last stretch before the gate. Seven years' traffic had pulverised them into dust and small pieces, yet the priest could see humeri and femora bristling from both sides of the causeway like porcupine spines.

He lengthened his stride, his feet crunching down on the white fragments. At last he reached the bridge spanning the stagnant moat that ringed the outer walls. Across its span of moss-covered stone he could see the massive weather-stained gateway that was the only entrance to the city. He pulled his hood low over his mask. Priests of Reh still came here to visit their temple, but all were under suspicion. He stepped forward again, the sound of his sandals echoing off the looming walls in front. The cavernous gateway reared up in front of him, and he could see guards wearing the purple-and-brown surcoats of Iss' legions stationed in its shadows. They stirred slightly when they saw the colour of his cloak. One detached himself from the others, and came slowly forward, his halberd held by his side. His face was sallow and unshaven. He peered curiously at the priest's cowled face in the dying light.

"Who are you, stranger?" he asked, trying to get a better angle on the priest's face.

"One who follows Reh," came the reply.

"That I can see; but what is your business here?"

"To visit my temple: I was told that Lord Faran still permits this."

"He does," the guard sneered. "Though there are not many of your kind who avail themselves of it."

"Then I may pass?"

"Not before I get a look at your face—my guard captain likes to know who comes and goes here."

"I wear a mask," the priest replied, "as all our order do when we're abroad."

The guard took a threatening step forward; the halberd now slightly raised. "Mask or not, I will see your face," he growled.

The priest had retreated a foot, and held up one of his gloved hands. The guard's eyes went from the metal talons back to the man's hooded head, but before he could utter another word, the priest spoke again. "Very well—look at my face, though I warn you, you will not like what you see." He inched aside a corner of the hood at his chin, allowing the guard a partial glimpse of his mask.

The guard's face wrinkled in distaste. "Gods! What is that?" he spat.

"It's what I wear," the priest replied simply. "Now may I pass?"

"Pass all you like," the guard replied, turning his head away in disgust. "And keep that thing to yourself, in Iss' name!"

The priest waited for no second invitation and brushed past, hurrying through the postern gate. The other guards seemed not to have noticed the interchange between the two men and continued warming themselves around a brazier, oblivious of everything apart from the dank chill of the afternoon and the swiftly fading light. He pressed on into the streets of the Lower Town. The houses were gutted, ivy-hung ruins. Their blackened rafters, poking up into sky, stood witness to the fire which had swept through them seven years before. Deep shadows hung in the cold air in the twisting alleyways that threaded their way up to the beetling crags. Here the streets were deserted. Remembering Zacharias's warning, the priest hurried upwards, his sandalled feet slipping on the slick cobblestones. As he climbed his eyes darted through the eye slits of the mask, scouring the gloom of the buildings on either side. Empty porticoes, empty windows, their lights without a surviving pane, caved-in roofs, fire-blackened walls, where weeds grew in the sickly alley sun.

Ahead, a figure scurried into a house where there were still doors and barred windows. As he passed bolts were drawn and chains attached. His feeling of isolation, acute from a month's solitary journeying in the Fire Mountains, grew even more intense, as if he were the pariah who stalked these streets and terrorised the inhabitants. A ghost city; as he climbed further, even the sight of the fugitive a moment before would have been welcome. Twenty minutes into his climb he stopped to regain his breath on a terrace overlooking the plains. The great globe of the sun, a huge flat purple oval, hung above the mountain peaks to the west. Its rays cast no warmth and his breath came in a thick stream through the nosepiece of the mask. A shudder ran through him and he pressed on quickly.

His mind raced with fear and excitement. The encounter with the gate guard had been a warning: every servant of Reh was under suspicion in this city. But soon he would be safe with his brother at the temple, and then he would know why he had been summoned here; summoned from eight years of isolation, in seven of which he had not once seen the face of another human being.

Now he entered the last curtain wall, built twenty feet thick. Water dripped down from the arched roofway of the gateway tunnel. It was unguarded. He hurried through, to the dying light of the day on the other side.

Here on the flat plateau of granite on top of its cliffs was the most ancient part of the city. A large area, some hundred yards square, opened up in front of him. Its surface was made up of concentric patterns of cobblestones, each forming a whirling pattern taking as its central point a low obelisk set on a low mound at the exact centre. To his right stood the pyramid dedicated to Reh. Its dark steps climbed up to the greying sky, where birds of prey lazily circled the column of smoke issuing from the summit. Ahead of him to the north, the ruined curtain walls and fire-blackened towers of the inner citadel were silhouetted against the evening. On his left, a mirror to the Temple of Reh, the stepped pyramid dedicated to Iss rose up towards the darkening air from behind high walls. The last rays of the sun bathed the square, glinting off the cobbles. Apart from himself, it seemed utterly deserted. He puzzled at this; surely there would be life here, where the sun still shone?

Somewhere from the Temple of Reh he heard the sonorous note of a gong calling the faithful to prayer. Then another sound broke in on that of the gong.

The voice was feeble, but piercing enough to cut through the reverberation of the gong.

"Keep from the shadows, Brother Mask," it said, quaveringly.

The priest swung round in surprise. He hadn't noticed a line of stocks which lay at the edge of the dark shadows on the western side of the square, just where he had entered. There were fourteen of them. Every one of them was occupied, but the voice that had stopped him had come from the nearest. The priest stepped closer. The man in it was bone thin. The joints of his wrists and ankles, protruding from the wooden fetters, seemed huge in contrast to the wasted arms and legs. His face was sallow, the eyes purple-rimmed, his hair was like a fever victim's, falling out in clumps. He was dressed in the same orange-and-red robes as the priest, though his were stained and torn and rent so that the bare flesh showed through. He took in the hideousness of the priest's mask with the unflinching frankness of one who knows he will shortly be dead. The priest estimated the man's age at about his own, twenty.

Behind the row of stocks, thick evening shadows fell on the jumble of semiderelict buildings lining the side of the square.

Dark alleyways, overhung by leaning walls and roofs snaked off into the evening half-light.

Then he saw why the man in the stocks had warned him.

There was movement in the gloom of the buildings right behind the stocks. The figures were human in shape, stalking slowly towards the captives, their faces half-averted, as if the dim sunlight was a fiercely burning furnace. But they came on inexorably, hugging the shadows, and as they came closer the slightest scent wafted through the visor of his mask to his nostrils. It was a complex scent: mildew, grave soil and dead meat.

The priest took a step back towards the centre of the square. No need for the man's warning now: he knew what they were. Vampires. The Dead in Life. Creatures who hated the sun. For a moment he stood paralysed, his body utterly still save for the hammering of his heart. Never before had he been so close. Never before had he stood on the edge of the dead light of late afternoon and seen their dead white faces. But now the red glow of their eyes reached out to him, and he heard them, heard them whining like hungry dogs begging for a taste of blood.

The sun was falling rapidly now, the shadows lengthening from the buildings into the square. And as each second passed and the shadows got longer, so did the vampires, like a black tide, creep closer to the stocks. He knew he must run, run quickly to the Temple of Reh.

He looked back at his brother priest; the man's head and wrists were trapped between the two stout spars of wood. There was just enough room for him to breathe, but his wrists dangled uselessly. The spars were bound together by iron rings secured by massive bronze padlocks.

The priest swallowed his fear of the creeping shadows and stepped forward again. He seized one of the locks, wrenching at it with all the might of his gloves. The metal claws were like vices on the lock, and the metal squealed in protest, but the nails holding the lock to the wood held firm. Never since they were first made had anything defied the strength of his gloves. The priest heaved again, with all his might, but the hasps of the lock were immovable.

"Save your breath, brother, and your life," the dying man managed to rasp, though the sound that emerged from his voice box was so hoarse that the priest could barely hear him. He ignored his warning, wrenching again at the lock; again a squeal of metal, but no sudden explosion of nails from the hasps.

"You're wasting your time, the locks are enchanted," the dying man breathed. The priest paused for a second, conscious of the creeping shadows and a creeping chill, mirroring the movement in the shadows, a chill that froze his spine.

The man spoke truth, the locks must be enchanted: the gloves on his hands could crush rock, yet this feeble bronze padlock seemed to writhe and slip away from his claws as if it were made of quicksilver.

"Go," the man urged. "Save yourself." A white froth flecked his mouth. But his words only made the priest more determined. Out of the corner of his eye he glimpsed a figure reaching the shadow of the nearest building. He knelt by the man, trying to find a weak spot in the metal bonds holding the spars together. It was then he noticed the several puncture marks around the man's neck; he counted one, two, three bites before giving up; the neck was one livid, upraised weal, the skin inflamed with infection. The priest's hands stopped moving.

"How many nights has it been, brother?" he asked in a quiet voice.

"Just one." He managed to croak, but his vocal cords must have swollen to twice their normal size, and his voice was squeezed with pain at the effort.

The priest looked back into the shadows. There was a gleam of light from glinting incisors and a rustling from a pool of shadows under a ruined archway only three yards away. The shadows were now reaching the condemned man's legs stretched out behind the stocks. Five minutes at most, he thought, then the undead would be on the man's neck again like wasps on a scrap of rotten meat. The priest's heart spasmed in his throat, the blood sang in his veins. Danger was so close he could feel it like a physical presence to be reached out to and touched. A coil of tension wound within him. Suddenly a form lurched towards the stock with a snarl.

The claws of the priest's taloned right hand glinted in the light as he swept them up in a scything motion. The air warped in front of it, then a gout of flame materialised, like a dragon's breath rolling forward in an orange wave.

The vampire was frozen in mid-stride in the orange light, its white face stretched in a scream; then the blanket of fire rushed over it, and its cloak burst into flame. It spun round like a top, its hands beating ineffectually as its flesh ignited like old papyrus. It flapped its arms once, then twice, as pieces of burning matter fell from it to the ground. Then it collapsed. The flames subsided with a hiss, leaving a bundle of smouldering rags and a faint mist lying on the cobblestones.

The dying man had seen the wall of flame igniting the gloom. "The Fist of Fire," he whispered. "Who taught you that spell?"

"My master Manichee," the priest said, kneeling beside him once more and heaving at the lock.

"Then I know you," the man managed through lips clenched with pain. "You are Urthred, Randel's brother."

The priest stopped his movements. "You know me?"

The man didn't reply directly; his voice was becoming more and more feeble and he fought to get the next words out through the thick mucus blocking his mouth. "Urthred," he whispered, "go now for Reh's sake! The city gate is still open, save yourself."

"What do you mean?" the priest asked, hauling back with all his might on one of the padlocks. "I can take sanctuary in the temple; you will be with me, my friend."

"They have taken your brother."

The priest stopped dead. "They've taken Randel?" He looked wildly around at the other stocks, deep in the shadows.

But the man, seeing the direction of his gaze, shook his head as best he could. "The Temple of Reh, our own people. They've betrayed us all."

The priest had forgotten the threat around him, so engrossed had he been with the dying man's words. There was a sudden rush of air and a fluttering of cloaks. Too late the priest spun round, realising that the shadows now covered the stocks and he was in deep gloom. Before he had a chance to react, the vampire struck him full on, bearing him to the ground, his shoulders pinned by the creature's knees. He saw the saliva-streaked incisors like the red mouth of hell opening above him, then with a superhuman effort he rolled over, throwing the vampire over his back. It rolled once, its head in the light. It tried to raise itself on its elbows, but fell back, letting out a piteous wail. A thin white vapour, quickly changing to smoke, burst from the sallow skin of its face. It sagged and melted like wax parchment paper set to flame. The vampire rolled against the feet of the man in the stocks, thrashed once, then became utterly still.

The priest scrambled to his feet and knelt once more by the man; he could see he was fading fast.

"My brother," the priest asked. "Where is my brother?" The man tried to reply, but the froth at his mouth killed his words. The priest hauled the water bottle from his belt, unscrewed the top and applied it to his fellow priest's lips. Water ran down the man's chin. ". . . the temple . . . his own people hold him . . . he will be sacrificed . . ." he managed.

"When?"

The man's eyes closed and he shook his head, lost in a world of pain. "I don't know . . . soon . . ." he whispered.

A flapping as of a crow's wings, a billowing cloak outspread—now another vampire was crouched on a buttress of one of the buildings overhanging the stocks. It glared down at Urthred with malevolent red eyes, but it had seen what had happened to its fellows—it was looking for easier prey. It launched itself through the air, landing on the pinioned man's back with a hollow thump, its teeth tearing at his neck.

The priest's hand shot out, wrenching the vampire's head around by its lank hair. Its neck bones cracked. He twisted remorselessly; the vampire's face screwed round so it faced him, spitting and cursing, its teeth blood-streaked, its eyes alive with blood-crazed fever. Its breath smelt of old blood on a butcher's block. The mad light of its eyes was not extinguished even when the priest had wrenched the neck right round and every vertebra had broken with a dusty pop.

He pushed the body away so that the thing fell on its chest. It stirred, lifting itself on hands and knees, then began to crawl, the neck twisted around onto its back, lolling obscenely, into the shadows.

Urthred knelt again; but the last attack had finished his fellow priest: his eyes, when he lifted his head, were vacant. He was dead.

Urthred lowered the man's head and stood. The priest's words of warning and the information about his brother rang in his ears, disorienting him. He stared blankly around the square, uncertain what to do. Too late he saw that the shadows had now crept beyond the stocks, surrounding him and extending well back into the square. He had taken too long: five more vampires had appeared; one had worked its way behind him by the stocks, the other four were to the front, in the square. They were closing slowly but inexorably. Then with a sudden rush they flung themselves forward.

The one behind him was closest, but he didn't turn, waiting until he could almost smell its decayed breath on his neck. Then he jabbed backwards, clenching his fist on a stud on the inside of his right glove as he did so. Inside the leather gauntlet covering his lower arm, the stud activated a spring-loaded knife. The blade burst through the folds of his cloak at his elbow, smashing straight into the vampire's sternum. Its rib cage cracked open with the sound of breaking rotten wood, and it staggered back, its lung cavity, like the insides of a purple bellows, revealed. It rocked on its heels, then lurched back towards the priest.

They feel no pain, Urthred thought, but even as he thought he was in motion, plucking the dagger from its elbow harness with his left hand while aiming his right fist towards the vampires in front of him. He opened out his fist. The air over his hand shimmered and then burst into flame. With a chopping motion he sent the wall of flame rolling towards the creatures. The middle two of the four didn't have time to get away; their bodies exploded with flame. One pirouetted away, colliding with one of its fellows, igniting its cloak. The last vampire skipped around its blazing companions but was met by the priest's left hand. The long flensing knife drove through its face, crushing its nose and forehead like an eggshell. The vampire spun away, temporarily blinded. There was a whoosh of air as the wounded vampire behind him rushed him again, but Urthred ducked under the blow, swung round and drove his right fist in return right through its battered chest cavity. The creature snapped at his face as Urthred desperately tried to drag back his fist from its chest. Its teeth glanced off the lacquer and wood of his mask, just as he managed to free his hand enough to grab one of the vampire's splintered ribs and fling it to one side. It spun a couple of times before it crashed into one of the stocks and fell to its knees. Behind the stocks, Urthred could see at least two dozen more stepping from the shadows of the buildings.

He backed away hurriedly, into the sunlight, and looked about him. The square was still silent and empty, the temple pyramids stark against the darkening sky. For the briefest of seconds his gaze fixed on the birds of prey circling around the pillar of smoke ascending from the Temple of Reh. Then he ran as fast as his sandalled feet could take him across the cobblestones of the square.

CHAPTER THREE

The Sacrifice

The gateway leading to the inner courtyard of the Temple of Reh had once been famous throughout the Empire. So wide was it that two bullock teams could have been driven through it simultaneously, and it was some thirty feet in height. Statues had once stood in the niches in the moulding over its arch and over the keystone there was a relief of the God Reh himself, represented as an old man with fiercely jutting beard clutching in one hand the orb of the sun, from which radiated the beams of life, and in the other a bolt of lightning, which he flung contemptuously down to the earth from the layer of clouds upon which he sat.

But now Reh's features were disfigured by the lichen that flourished in Thrull's damp marsh climate, his face mottled grey like the victim of a plague. The precious stones that had once been set in his eyes had been gouged out by the men who had sacked Thrull. The statues of Reh's twenty-four aspects, which had once filled the niches in the moulding, were also gone, carried off to Surrenland, Ossia, Hangar Parang, and the other countries where Lord Faran's army had come from. Once the mighty twin gates of the temple had been left open day and night, but reflecting the fall from grace that had overtaken the gateway, the gates themselves were now shut and had not been opened these several years. Only a small postern was open, and it was towards this that Urthred ran as fast as he could.

The fight in the square and his approach had not gone unnoticed: two guards, liveried in the orange-and-red robes of the temple, were watching him from the postern of the gate as he ran towards them. They stepped forward in unison as he neared, but then caught sight of Urthred's mask. They stopped, rooted to the spot; Urthred swerved past them and jumped through the gate. He had only seconds before the guards recovered their wits.

He was in the inner courtyard of the temple, the cobblestones of which gave onto a series of broad flights of steps which formed the lowest courses of the temple pyramid. The pyramid itself reared high above in stepped progressions of ancient cracked basalt. Each step was a man's height in size, and only a smaller stairway, cut into the larger steps, gave access to the higher reaches. One hundred and fifty feet up, on the temple's truncated roof, statues of Reh, Lord of Light, and Soron, Bringer of Fire, were silhouetted against the virulent sky. Between the statues, the air appeared to shift and warp where the flames of the temple's Hearth Fire melded invisibly with the redness of the evening. Birds of prey circled the roof.

Halfway up the side of the pyramid, he could see a large portico: the entrance to the inner sanctuary of the temple. He took the steps two at a time, conscious now of the shouts of the guards behind him.

As he climbed higher and higher, he heard over the mournful croaking of the circling birds and the hammering of his heart a groundswell of excited voices. The hubbub grew louder. Finally, straining for breath, he reached the flat space under the portico.

There must have been a thousand people gathered there, crowding the dark entrance to the temple at its rear, taking refuge against the coming dark. He hurried towards them, plunging into the heart of the teeming throng, barely noticing the merchants, soldiers, artisans, priests, women and children wearing every conceivable hue of clothing. The colour, noise and smell were bewildering after a month's solitary travel and the silence of the Lower Town, not to mention the seven years he'd spent alone in Manichee's tower. He weaved through the pressing humanity, trying to avoid the tattered bundles of their possessions, wicker baskets full of shrieking fowls, hessian sacks filled with vegetables and mounds of coloured spices, all spread on gaily hued cloth laid over the crimson rugs covering the flagstones.

The crowd thickened towards the back of the vestibule, where the gates to the Inner Temple stood. The necks of the people there craned towards the gloom, their voices high with excitement. They barely noticed as Urthred plunged into their midst like an arrow aimed at the dark entranceway. Behind him he sensed rather than saw the red disc of the sun dropping lower and lower onto the western mountains. His heart was heavy with premonitory dread.

Now he was deep in the shadow of the portico where, if possible, the crowd was even thicker. As he pushed on, soldiers stepped aside with a clatter of armour, moneylenders laid down their stacks of coin on their counting desks to stare as the force of his passing set their balances swaying. A labourer's adze tumbled to the ground as the hem of Urthred's cloak brushed it. Sacrificial hawks in gilded cages shrieked and flapped. Priests flinched from the tripod-held censers which they tended as his speed sent up a great cloud of incense into their faces.

Now he was in the very centre of the mass of people around the entrance, using his elbows to force a way. Cries of protest and anger were stifled when those pushed aside saw his mask, the babble of voices hushed as the crowds around felt the disturbance running through their ranks. He was nearing the entranceway to the inner sanctuary. To either side, heavy red damask drapes hung in folds like frozen red waterfalls. Between them, a narrow gap revealed a huge hallway, forty yards across, rising in stepped progression towards an opening at the top through which the westering rays of the sun slanted. The walls were doused in a dull bronze ambient light cast from the raging fire pit at the centre of the pyramid.

Urthred broke past the last line of people blocking his way, oblivious to the near silence that had replaced the humming noise in the outer court, oblivious, too, of the several hundred pairs of eyes that stared at his back. He hardly heard their horrified whispers above the pounding of his heart; for the moment Urthred felt invulnerable behind the horror of his mask.

Another guard, dressed like the two at the gate, stood before him, barring the entranceway to the temple. The man was staring in horrified fascination at him, his body frozen with surprise and fear. As Urthred stepped up he belatedly recovered his wits and levelled his six-foot-long halberd at his chest.

It was too late for Urthred to stop his forward progress, even if he'd wanted to. He hardly felt the sudden pain as the halberd tip pricked through the thick felt of his cloak into the naked flesh beneath. He was in a trance, his eyes fixed on the middle distance, in the direction of the Sanctuary Flame. Without glancing at it, he seized the wooden haft of the weapon just below its blade and twisted it to one side. The wood splintered with a loud crack.

He tried to push forward, but other guards had materialised from curtained alcoves off to each side, their halberds lowered at Urthred's heaving chest. He looked around: there were half a dozen guards in front, and the densely packed mob behind him, the back rank of which, hearing the commotion, redoubled their efforts to push to the front and see what was happening.

"Let me past!" he growled, his gloved hands sweeping up to knock aside the semicircle of halberds, but the guards were too quick, drawing their weapons away from his flailing gloves, then thrusting them back again. Urthred retreated, into the mob of people behind him who were desperately trying to escape from the fight. There were several shrieks of terror before Urthred was pushed back towards the guards. He stumbled towards them, off-balance, a blow from a halberd shaft knocking him against a wall. Instantly he found his chest pinned there by a bristling hedge of weapons. He knew he would die if he moved. The guards stood uncertainly a few feet away, their eyes flinching away from the terrible spectacle of his mask, but their weapons reasonably steady. They were a mixture of countrymen and races: narrow-faced Astardians, dark Ormirocans, olive-skinned Parangians—mercenaries all. They seemed unsure of what to do, waiting for the arrival of an officer of the guard. Those injured by the crush were screaming and yelling, while their companions fought to get away from the confrontation. The situation looked to be getting out of hand, but then, as if by magic, a sudden hush fell over the crowd. A flicker of movement from deep within the gloomy recesses of the temple caught Urthred's eye.

Figures were moving in front of the fierce orange light of the Sanctuary Flame. He could only see their silhouettes, but he saw that the leader of the procession wore a cockaded hat with a fringe of tinkling bells: a High Priest of the Temple of Reh. Behind him two men dragged a figure bound in chains. The figure stumbled but was wrenched back to his feet by a savage jerk from one of the men. Even at this distance and in the dim light, Urthred knew that the man in chains was his brother.

"Randel!" he screamed, springing forward. He saw the head of the chained figure swing towards him, then a vicious stab in his chest as a halberd tip bore him back against the wall. He looked down; there was a dark red stain spreading on his red cloak and he felt a warm trickle inside his undershirt from the wound. Curiously, he felt no pain. His mind disassociated from his body. He wrenched his eyes back towards his brother.

It had been twelve years since he had last seen him, and now it was only seconds before Randel would die.

Urthred watched helplessly as the procession leading his brother reached the centre of the pyramid, where they halted, silhouetted by the Sanctuary Flame. They had stopped by the low black shape of an altar. The chained figure of Randel was thrust down onto the slab; attendants came out of the gloom, pinioning his arms and legs. A dark helplessness welled up from deep down in Urthred's throat and escaped as a howl of despair. Again a halberd tip drove him back into the wall; his blood-soaked cloak flapped wetly against his chest. In the distance, the High Priest now stood over the body, a curved dagger upraised in one hand; it glittered in the light of the Sanctuary Flame with a nacreous, unearthly light.

Then the dagger was curving down in a fast arc, as swift as a falling star into the heart of the chained figure. Even at this distance Urthred heard the surprised grunt, a noise more of sexual fulfillment than death.

Then Urthred howled again, smashing away the weapon at his chest with his taloned gloves, and leapt forward. His mask restricted his view. He didn't see the flat of a sword blade swinging in towards his temple. There was a sharp crack and an explosion of lights in his head. He had a vague thought that he was falling, then the earth rushed up to smash into his mask. Arms bound his hands behind him with a metal chain as he shook his head, trying to clear it of the whirling lights.

But though he couldn't see, he could hear. A gong sounded in the far recesses of the temple. Somewhere a choir of tenor voices rang out, soaring in a descant upwards to the skies, one voice tumbling over another like waves, washing upwards to the shores of heaven itself: then a ringing silence.

He was jerked to his feet by the chain and thrust forward towards the temple interior.

Inside, the heat from the Sanctuary Flame was furnace-hot, hitting him like a physical wave. He opened his eyes a fraction. The flames from the fire pit were reflected inwards by the ashlar blocks of the temple walls, warping the air. Sweat mixed with his blood in seconds, soaking his cloak further. His head throbbed from the sword blow, yet his vision had cleared.

The guards were leading him close to the altar: his eyes could not help being drawn to the sacrificial block. A group hovered about the prone body, cutting carefully at it with what looked like butcher's knives. One of them removed a squirming organ from the chest cavity; a still fitfully pumping heart. Others stood ready with dishes and jars ready to preserve the vital organs. Urthred looked away, sickened, closing his eyes.

His brother, sacrificed. He'd read about, but never seen such an event; they had been unheard of in the Empire for several hundred years. But darkness had returned to this age, darkness in the form of the vampires out in the square, and darkness in the hearts of his fellow priests of Reh.

Now the remains of Randel's body would be taken to the roof of the pyramid, where its scattered pieces would be torn apart further by the birds of prey. Each tiny morsel would be carried up to the orange halls of the sun, where Reh sat on his golden throne. Each tiny part would be stored against the day the sun would be reborn, and all dead things would reknit together in the forms they once inhabited on earth, and the souls of all the dead would come from Paradise and reinhabit their bodies.

Randel had summoned him here to Thrull after an absence of twelve years. Now he, like his brother, would be sacrificed, and without knowing why his brother had broken the twelve-year silence. As he was marched towards a door at the far side of the Sanctuary Flame, he felt the chains binding his gloved hands. Mere metal, metal that could not withstand his gloves or his rage. Intuitively, he knew the guards were leading him to the man who had condemned his brother to death.

CHAPTER FOUR

The Black Chalice

A large latticed window overlooked the moat which separated the temple pyramid from the ruined citadel. The sun, flat and purple, hung over the distant peaks of the Fire Mountains, throwing its last weak rays through the window into a room richly furnished with wall hangings and oak furniture. Though the rays were those of a dying sun, their light made the colours of the ancient tapestries and carpets glow with life.

An old man in a linen undershirt, the robes of his office cast in an untidy heap to one side, sat in a carved wooden throne. The throne had been placed in the shadows, and he averted his face from the rays of the sun, staring instead into the glowing embers of a brazier which heated the room. His expression, at odds with the radiance of the light and the luxury of his surroundings, was sour and contemplative.

His name was Varash and he was the High Priest of the Temple of Reh in Thrull. The events of the day, culminating in the sacrifice, had exhausted him. It had begun at dawn, when he had risen for the ritual of Purification by Flame. As always he'd intoned the words of the prayer perfectly as the sun had heaved its dying orb above the eastern mountains: "Let the flesh be perfected, like impure metal refined by the refiner's fire. Let us be as gold in the sight of Reh, Lord of Light: pure, unsullied, as shining as the disc of the newborn sun will be at the Second Tomorrow!" He'd hoped that none of those attending the ceremony had noticed how he had hung back from the glowing light, his eyes narrowed against the pain it inflicted on them. Though he had spoken the words of the ritual loudly, there had been a corresponding silence in his heart as he'd uttered them. Nor had the pure springwater with which his servers had washed him seemed to cleanse him; afterwards he was still conscious of an oily patina clinging to him, as if his self-loathing had become corporeal, a self-loathing which no washing could rid him of. The robes of office, freshly laundered and pressed, had, when the servers had helped him into them, given him no sense of uplift; rather they had seemed but a further unnecessary burden for his old shoulders to bear.

He sighed; his weariness was not just physical: long ago he'd given up looking directly into men's eyes lest they saw reflected back the darkness that had collected there over the years of his life: the compromises, the lies, the killings. The evil that can be concealed from other men until one set of eyes meets another and, in a split-second, all manner of hidden things are suddenly revealed.

So it was that Varash was not looking directly at the young acolyte who'd entered the room moments before, but into the glowing embers of the brazier.

He repeated the boy's message out of old habit, though he'd heard it well.

"A priest causing a ruckus you say?"

"Aye, lord, he tried to break past the guards at the temple entrance during the ceremony." The acolyte's voice had risen an octave or two in the excitement of delivering his message to as important a person as the High Priest.

"And where is he now?"

"Out—outside, bound in chains."

Varash cursed inwardly. Another troublemaker like the one he'd just sent to his Maker? Where would it end? His duty, anyway, was clear. However tired he was, he would have to question this person.

"Very well, bring him in," he said wearily. But the young man hesitated: "Well?"

"So—so please you, Venerated, the priest . . ." The acolyte came to a stuttering halt.

"What about him?"

"He—he is—uncommon-looking . . ." The acolyte's voice trailed off again.

"What, has he two heads, three hands, the tail of a dog?"

"N-no, sir, he has a mask . . ."

"A mask? Why do you think a mask should terrify me, boy, I who see a thousand masks a day? Bring him in!" The acolyte moved to speak again, but then he thought better of it and fled the room. The slap-slap of retreating sandals on the flagstones of the corridor echoed back into the chamber. Varash bent slowly and pulled up the heavy ceremonial garb from the floor. He looked at the sweat-stained robes, the outward mark of his office, without affection, before standing and wearily slipping them back on. Something made him wrinkle up his nose, and he sniffed at one of the sleeves. The faint whiff of blood, of the charnel house, of death. Also the stale smell of an old man. His own smell. A shiver wracked him. He sank back into the carved oaken chair and reached over to where some Ruby Viridium wine glinted in a crystal carafe; his hand trembled as he poured some of the liquid into a glass. He threw back his head, drinking so deep that some of the berry red liquid ran down his chin, then wiped his hand over his mouth and resumed his gloomy stare at the embers in the brazier.

His domed forehead creased in thought as he contemplated the state of the city of which for seven years he had been High Priest of Reh.

Things had been going badly even before the Civil War. Long before his birth the sun had weakened day by day, year by year in the sky, its rays too feeble to melt the winter snows or ripen the harvests. The waters had risen inexorably on the plains so what had once been prosperous fields were now a brown, stinking marsh, the smell of its rot hanging about the city like a wraith. Even before the revolt, it had been a dying place, with fewer and fewer worshippers at the temple of Reh, the flow of pilgrims that once had made this the most wealthy of all the temples in the Empire had years ago thinned to a trickle.

As for the Empire which had so long maintained the religious tolerance of former years, little could be said. It had once taken in the lands of Thrull, Ossia and Surrenland, but now order in those countries had broken down. Local warlords, such as Baron Illgill, the man who had ruled Thrull seven years ago, vied for local dominance over small areas of land. Trade had ceased in many parts, and famine was widespread, exacerbated by a string of failed harvests.

Many waited for the Emperor himself to come from his capital, Valeda, and put an end to the bloodshed and starvation. But they hoped for the impossible. Five hundred years ago, when the veil that obscured the sun had been first noticed, the then Emperor had retired with his concubines and astronomers to his Hidden Palace on the High Plains above his capital, there to study the mystery of the dying sun. Since that day, no one had been seen entering or leaving the palace, though Imperial messengers, with less and less frequency over the years, had come with messages from the Emperor's vassals, pinning them to the wooden gates of the palace when no answer came to their calls. The brief history of the last five hundred years could once have been read on those gates: the appeals for aid and guidance from the provincial governors which became more and more urgent as anarchy broke out, the demands from one temple or another for a religious wrong to be righted, letters from the warriors pledging fealty to the invisible Emperor as they plundered his Empire in his name. The history of a disintegrating world was there, but no one had read it: the messages had been blown to tatters by the icy winds that blew over the High Plains and around the grey walls of the palace. No one now travelled to the Hidden Palace: it was shunned as a haunted place where the Emperor and his Empire had died.

This was the world into which Varash was born—one of warfare and uncertainty and growing factionalism, none more in the religious divide between the Flame and the Worm. He had followed his father's career and become a Server here at the temple. He had never travelled further than Thrull, fearing the chaos of the world outside.

Yet in all the sixty years of his life, one temple had prospered in Thrull. The Temple of Iss had always stood across the

square from that of Reh. But at the time of his birth it had been
a mere weed-grown mound, its entrance choked by vegetation.
Pale gaunt fanatics had once or twice been seen flitting about
its ruins. Occasionally the dead had been carried into its
gloomy depths, to the catacombs that lay beneath the pyramid.
But as the sun had grown weaker year by year, so more and
more men were seen lingering by the gloomy edifice. The rubble and weeds of years had been slowly cleared, priests arrived
out of the east, rekindling the worship of Iss, God of Life in
Death. They patrolled the city, proselytising to any who would
listen to them, pointing at the dying sun, telling how Iss had
imprisoned his brother Reh in his land of darkness as the latter
had journeyed through his kingdom, how man would soon
know nothing else except an endless night.

It had not been long before the killings started: priests of Iss
knifed in back alleys, then the reprisals; citizens disappearing at
night and rumours abounded of the dead reborn as vampires in
the catacombs. The city had been ruled by Baron Illgill then, a
Hearth Priest of Reh: bitter punishments were laid on the priest-
hood of the Worm, and soldiers were sent into the catacombs to
root out the Dead in Life. Many had not returned, and those that
did spoke of thousands of the undead, woken from centuries-
old slumber, reanimated by the magic of the Worm's priests, fed
by the living blood of those snatched at night. Illgill sent more
men into the Temple of Iss, slaughtering the priests, burning all
the corpses they could find in the catacombs. The undead who
survived had fled to even lower levels of the tunnels that honeycombed the cliffs on which the city was built.

The survivors had sent messengers to the east, to Tiré Gand,
the capital of the undead in far off Ossia. The Elders there in
turn had sent Lord Faran Gaton Nekron. The rest was history:
the arrival of Faran Gaton's army, covering the plains like a
dark tide. Illgill's proud army marching out, banners ablaze
with colour, the vibrancy of all those who marched proclaiming
the victory of life over death. Then the battle: the gaily coloured
banners of Illgill's forces driven further and further back to
their inevitable defeat. The sack of Thrull had followed that
night, the undead in an orgy of bloodletting, half the city
ablaze. Then a period of respite as Faran calmed the situation.

Edicts were posted in the squares, telling the living they would be safe from the undead if they obeyed his laws, telling the surviving populace that all he wished was equal freedom to worship for the followers of Iss, and that they were free to go to the temple of Reh. It had been an empty promise: Thrull was worthless to Faran without their living blood. Furthermore, the temple of Reh was only permitted to remain open so that Faran could learn more easily what his enemies were plotting. Soon the living had realised the hollowness of their new ruler's words. But by then they were stranded in the city, the lonely marshes all around a barrier to freedom.

Now, seven years later, the priests in Varash's charge were growing rebellious; soon there would be another bloody civil war in the city, the Flame cast against the Temple of Iss. Varash had done his best to keep control. This latest infraction, bloodily dealt with by him, had been only one of several over the past few months. His priests no longer trusted him when he spoke of the continuing worship of Reh in the city being more important than an armed rebellion against Faran. Information, once volunteered by trusting fellow worshippers, had dried up. Then, a month before, something had changed completely. Many of the priests had become openly insulting to him, as if they knew something he didn't. Only at the last moment had he been able to discover the plotters, led by Randel, and execute them, but there was still a mystery attaching to the episode: what had happened a month before to make the priest's rebellion so open? Try as he might, Varash could not find out.

Varash cursed inwardly; didn't the fools realise that their religion was dead, that day by day, as the sun died, more and more of the worshippers of Reh fled from the city or joined the swelling ranks of those who worshiped Iss? Iss, a god who promised a life even in death, of a life that could continue even when the sun had finally been snuffed like a tapering candle, and man was left ever after in the permanent darkness and cold of the endless night to come?

Varash's faith had been lost before the Civil War, his service at the Temple of Reh an empty sham. It had been natural for Faran to single him out, a relatively junior Server, and elevate him to High Priest after the death of his predecessor in the sack of the city. Varash could still remember the fear and the dark promise of his first interview with the undead lord deep in the catacombs of the Temple of Iss. Thrull had still been burning all around them and Varash had feared for his life. He needn't have worried: Faran had been more than accommodating. They had made a covenant, that Varash would betray his fellow priests if they plotted against Faran. In return he had received not only the luxury of his current position, but what his soul had yearned for since he had lost his faith: a life after death.

That night Varash had pledged Faran his loyalty. That night and every night after, he had been led through the labyrinthine tunnels under the square to the Temple of Iss, and there had drunk of the Black Chalice from which an everlasting Life in Death sprung.

That first night he'd been repelled at the thick black blood in the chalice; a coppery liquid the taste of which would not leave him afterwards even when he'd washed it down with flagon after flagon of water. He'd vomited his dinner. So too, in time, he had lost his conscience, and his soul, as he'd drunk more and more of the blood. Every day he'd awoken, his eyes ever more sensitive to the light of the sun, and gone about his sham duties, hearing the priests talk, making mental notes of who had or would shortly be overstepping the mark; whose name would be tipped to Faran for assassination or for the stocks on the great square outside.

And each night the blood of the chalice had wrought a strange alchemy; already he could feel the vitality drying in his veins, his heart slowing, his flesh achieving a parchmentlike quality, his bones taking on the consistency of old mahogany. The first signs of atrophy, the beginning of that imperishable state by which man could enjoy a life of the flesh after death. A state in which darkness and shadows were to be preferred to the light of the sun. He would achieve in time what few others would achieve: a type of immortality. But the betrayals and killings by which he had achieved that state had meant that, rather than enjoying the prospect of an everlasting life in the flesh, the endless life to come was no more pleasant a thought than the idea of drinking a cup of ashes.

He needed to forget, to soothe the anguish within him. He

picked up a handful of small pods from a dish on the side table. He looked at them for a minute: Lethe buds, the smoke of which could transport a man to a paradise far from this dying world. He threw them onto the embers in the brazier. The pods cracked and the room filled with a pungent, musty, cloying smell much like cinnamon. The smell of blood and of stale old age seemed to vanish and his mind went with the drug, eddying up into the dark shadowy spaces of the rafters, losing itself in the dark shadows where centuries-old dust, from when the sun had been young, lay on ragged banners placed there by long-dead hands.

The bustle at the door snapped him out of his reverie. He had been dreaming of ancient times, of the Age of Gold, when the sun had still burned down upon ripe fields and men had smiled as they worked in them, harvesting the fruit of their abundance. . . . He glanced up at the figure looming in the doorway, then started back with an involuntary gasp. The un-flinching horror of the mask was brutal after the trance into which he'd sunk. For a moment all he could do was stare at it, mesmerised. Then he became conscious of the shadowy figures of temple guards behind the man, holding the chains which pinioned his arms.

He grunted and one of the guards pushed the prisoner forward so that he fell on the floor before Varash's throne. The man was dressed in the robes of a priest of Reh. But unlike the heavily embroidered robes that Varash wore, this man's were threadbare and travel-stained. Wet patches of blood showed through the material at his chest. A chain had been looped round the man's gloved hands, pinning them to his back.

The priest raised his head and regarded Varash through the lidless holes of the mask's sockets. Varash sensed the man's eyes scrutinising him from the deep shadows. He did his best to return the stare, assuming as best he could a look of cool indifference.

"Not a pretty sight is it, Venerated?" The voice, amplified by the wood of the mask, was full of hollow mockery. The words earned the kneeling man a kick from one of the guards. The priest gasped in pain; in contrast the expression of the mask remained frozen, an alien thing divorced from the mortal world of pain and suffering, infinitely alien.

The High Priest fought to keep any sign of emotion from his voice. "You have little servility, priest. Don't you recognise these robes?" he said, lifting one of the elaborately embroidered sleeves of his regalia.

"Oh, I recognise them well enough." Again mockery.

"So?"

"They are the robes of a High Priest."

"Then you will remember your duty and show respect to the god."

"Ah, it is not the robes that make a man, as the old saw goes."

At a gesture from Varash, two of the guards launched a series of kicks to the priest's back. Again the man gasped in pain, but the mask stared back impassively, a thing that had gone beyond pain into another realm of sensation.

A chill crept up the High Priest's back. Again he fought to control the quaver in his voice. "Now you see what happens to those who speak out of turn! If you enjoy pain, speak on; my men are as generous in giving as you will be in receiving." Varash cocked his head expectantly, but was gratified to see the priest had fallen silent.

"Good, now we progress. Your name?"

Now the silence was unbidden, until another kick from a guard elicited a muttered response.

"Louder, man!" Varash ordered.

This time he heard the man's reply clearly, and it sent another shudder through him.

"Urthred, Urthred of Ravenspur."

The old man's mind raced. Ravenspur! The same name as the rebel Randel. But though he had searched long and hard through the libraries of the temple, Varash had never been able to find any family of that name or a place called it on a map. One thing was sure: the two of them had been related, maybe even brothers. Things began to fall into place! This would explain the commotion during the sacrifice.

"Which temple are you from?"

"No temple," the man replied in a surly voice.

"So, no temple: which monastery?" The priest's silence was rewarded with another blow.

"Answer the question, dog!" one of the guards growled.

The priest twisted his neck, trying to ease the pain in his back. "Forgeholm," the priest said finally, his words muffled by the mask.

So, Varash thought, Forgeholm Monastery. Now things became even more interesting. Randel had come from Forgeholm twelve years before. The place was a hotbed of fanatics, isolated in the Fire Mountains, they of all the worshippers of the Flame kept the old religion alive. . . .

Varash made a snap decision. If he was to learn more about these men's activities, he didn't want to be overheard by the guards.

He gestured to them. "You are dismissed."

The guards looked at one another in surprise, before one of them had the courage to speak. "But, Venerated, the man may be dangerous . . ."

"Is he not bound in chains?" Varash snapped. "Leave us." The guards shuffled backwards out of the room, bowing. One laid the end of the chain gently on the red carpet behind the priest. The door closed silently behind them.

Now there was a chance, thought Urthred, a heaven-sent chance. The guards were gone, and all that prevented him from slashing his brother's murderer to ribbons were the chains twisted behind his back. He flexed the claws of his gloves again, trying to force a link apart, but the ironsmith who had made them had known his trade. The links remained rock solid. The High Priest was scrutinising him in the gloom. Urthred stilled the motion of his hands, careful not to give away his intentions.

"So, why have you come here, priest?" Varash asked.

Urthred was silent. The man who had brought Randel's message had taken a risk, crossing the marshes and the mountains to Forgeholm. Now an injudicious word from Urthred might condemn him, and all of Randel's other friends. He remained silent.

Varash shook his head, a thin smile playing over his chapped purple lips. "So you think your silence will save you, do you?" He rose stiffly from his chair and hobbled to a chest set against a wall, the heavy robes rustling on the floor behind him. He extracted a key and opened it, pulling out a drawer and choosing an object from it. He turned and held it up to the light from the brazier so that Urthred could see it. It was a pair of iron pliers, with a bloodied human tooth still stuck in them.

"Your friend, the one who died, needed a tooth pulling; it seemed to be stopping his speech," he said, waving the bloody molar up and down in front of the mask. "It worked; your friend spoke, as you will speak, when I invite the guards back in. But you can save yourself a lot of pain, priest, by telling me what I want to know."

Whilst Varash had been occupied in the chest, Urthred had worked one of the claws between two of the links of the chain. He was now trying to twist them apart. It was not an easy pass. The metal claw was fitted by a cap over the stump of his finger and despite the extra leverage of the mechanism, each twist of the link brought a searing pain to his mutilated digit, as the nail was torn out. He only hoped the High Priest could not hear the faint squeak of tortured metal.

His silence seemed to enrage Varash. "Very well," he spat. "We'll have the guards in a minute, but first I'll see what you look like." He put the pliers down on a table and dropped to one knee, reaching for the front of the mask. In that split second Urthred's talon broke the link in the chain with a metallic crack. His clawed fists swung round in a blinding arc underneath Varash's outstretched arms, stopping within an inch of the old man's throat. The High Priest's hands were frozen, his eyes rolling to either side as the razor-sharp claws scratched against his wrinkled neck.

"One sound and you're dead," Urthred growled. Varash's hands fell nervelessly to his sides. Urthred stood, the clawed hands ready to rip open Varash's face.

"Come," he said, lifting Varash's head up with one metal index finger, forcing Varash to rise uncertainly from his knee. He thrust him back into the chair, the ceremonial robes seeming to explode with dusty particles in the dim red light. His hands clamped down on the armrests to either side of the High Priest.

Varash could now see more clearly the flickering, lizardlike movements of eyes behind the holes of the mask. The coldness of the eyes told him he was going to die; the wasted years, the betrayals—all had been futile. He would die, wretchedly, at the hands of this maniac. He opened his mouth to scream, but one of the gloved hands clamped over it like an iron vice. He felt his jaws being pushed inwards as his mouth formed an O of pain. "Do you understand me now?" the priest hissed. Varash could only nod his head minusculely, so tightly did the hand hold his jaw.

"Now it's my turn for some questions," Urthred said. "First question—why did Randel die?"

"B-Because he was a heretic," Varash managed to mumble despite the vice clamping his jaw.

"No!" Urthred snarled, squeezing tighter, so Varash's mind reeled with the pain. "Randel was no heretic; it's you, you who have betrayed your religion. Here, Varash, look at the sun!" He swung Varash's head round to face directly the window through which the dying light of the sun shone like liquid blood. Varash flinched back as if he was being forced to stare into a white-hot inferno.

"I thought as much; light is hateful to you!" Urthred spat. "You've become one of them, haven't you? Dead in your heart and mind. Dead to life. How many good men have you killed? Answer me!" Urthred shook the old man's jaw, but even if he could have, Varash didn't answer. His silence spoke eloquently enough. The sunlight seemed to be burning his skin and his eyes, and he squirmed in its light, but Urthred's grip was relentless.

"Please," Varash pleaded. "Let me back into the shadows."

"What? And let another snatch his soul from God? Doesn't the cycle of the sun, its rising and its setting tell you something? All men must die. The only life after death will be at the Second Dawn."

The pain in Varash's head was excruciating, he shut his eyes tightly. But inexplicably the taste of the Black Chalice welled up into his mouth. Then he realised why; he'd bitten his tongue and was tasting his own coppery blood.

"Enough!" Urthred snarled. "Why speak of Reh to someone

with so little grace? Preaching to a dog would be better. Open your eyes." Varash felt the prick of the man's claws at his throat. "Open them!" Urthred repeated vehemently. Varash did so. Though the sun was low in the sky, the light exploded into his mind. He shook his head from side to side in agony.

"You wanted to see my face? Now look, look on the face of a true believer, one who has given everything for his god!" Dextrously, Urthred unlatched the two clasps holding one side of his mask to its leather frame while keeping his other gloved hand firmly clasped on Varash's jaw.

The mask swung to one side like a flap of flesh.

At first Varash thought he must have imagined that the mask had been removed. The same livid weal of scarred tissue shrieked back at him, the same hollow slit of a nose, the ragged lips exposing teeth and gums burned yellow and black.

Then he knew.

And knowing caused a scream to rise from the depths of his soul. But the glove was still clamping his jaw and the scream could not escape from his throat. Instead it exploded in his heart with a flash of white light that swiftly turned black. Then he fell over and over. Into the depthless void.

Urthred dropped the dead body to the ground, relatching the mask swiftly. A fierce heat burned his chest, a fire that was of anger and joy. Of pure revenge. He had not expected the chance, but he had taken it; now his own heart seemed to be about to burst, just as the old man's had.

He knew he would die. Whether on the sacrificial block or by the weapons of the guards he didn't know, but this knowledge for the moment was nothing compared to the overpowering sense of joy.

He waited, looking at the lowering beams of the sun, muttering a prayer. Slowly the frantic beating of his heart stilled, and the roaring in his ears diminished. A bird of prey swooped low past the window, silhouetted against the crimson sky, the single flap of its wings loud in the silence. He listened, waiting for the sound of the guards returning. Nothing. But they would come: he was certain of that.

He looked at the High Priest's corpse. Varash's dead eyes stared into the gloom of the raftered ceiling. In the moments

Urthred had been watching, a light film seemed to have formed over them. He was already far away on his journey, but Urthred wouldn't say a prayer to light his way through Iss' realm: the man belonged there, and there alone, not in Reh's fiery paradise.

The roaring in his ears had now almost completely gone, the sound of far-distant surf. The fierce joy of seconds before was dying, too, leaving behind an emptiness, a void. Outside the sun seemed frozen on the peaks. An immense hush hung over the temple and the city as if the world held its breath at the dying spectacle of the evening. No sound from outside where he had expected shouts from the guards and running feet: no one had heard the death struggle. The fact that no one had heard left him feeling even emptier. Now he would have to act. He knew what he must do.

He looked about him distractedly. For the first time he noticed the luxury of the room, the ancient tapestries from Hangar Parang, delicate crystal ware from Surrenland, the furniture carved from the cedar woods of Galastra; everything was of the finest taste, save the crumpled heap of the High Priest's body lying by the throne.

The richness of the furnishings added to the weight on his mind. Twenty years a virtual prisoner in a bare, whitewashed cell had made any ostentation sickening to him. Never before had he been in a room like this. Nor had he ever seen a city before today. For eight years before the summons from his brother he had never left the top of the tower where he had lived at Forgeholm Monastery. His isolation the result of his disfigurement, a disfigurement that only one other man had ever seen apart from the dead High Priest on the floor before him. A disfigurement he bore proudly, for it was a sign that he was one of the God's Elect, and to be one of Reh's Elect had been all his care ever since his infancy at Forgeholm Monastery.

That monastic life had been a life far harder than any city dweller could ever contemplate: of cold, of near starvation, of harsh discipline. A life which could strip the humanity from a man, let alone a boy, and drive him inwards on himself. A life which would make him seek that inner spark of life, the secret soul of magic, of fire, that was beyond flesh, implanted there by Reh at the beginning of time.

Punishment, mortification: these had been the daily lot of all who sheltered under Forgeholm's roof. Beatings, floggings, immersion in freezing cold water. Each day's pain had only been preparatory to the greatest day of mortification of them all: the Day of the Birch. The shortest, darkest day of the year when the sun barely peeped above the mountain tops at midday, then vanished again. The day when the noviciates stripped to the waists and laid their backs open with switches of wood, their blood running as they offered up prayers to the vanishing Sun God to pass safely through the kingdom of his brother, Iss, King of the Night, the Worm and Death in Life. No one who had suffered the icy cold and the frozen blood of that day could be the same again. Urthred guessed that Varash had not undergone this mortification for these last several years. The luxury of the apartment told him what type of man he'd been.

Why had Varash forsaken his god? Urthred himself had fought long and hard against the tug of fleshly pleasures, of luxury, of ease. In the outer world temptation was there; the sun was dying, soon all might be dead. All of Urthred's prayers, all the scars on his back, the disfigurement of his face, had not altered that. Why not give up to temptation and enjoy the last years in fornication and drink? Harvests failed, and dark storms rose and passed over the land, washing away plants and drowning villages. In the north, where the Palisade Mountains heaved up to the sky, it was always frozen, even when the summer season ought to have come. Surely the end would be soon?

Since Urthred's first conscious thoughts, the world had gradually slipped towards an eternal darkness, and mankind had slid with it. Seeing the death of the sun, many had turned to despair, or the treachery of such as Varash, accepting the Worm's promises, of the inevitability of the half-life to come when the sun would never rise again, and the world would be lost in everlasting darkness. Throughout the Empire the once grand edifices of the Temples of Reh crumbled, the peaked roofs collapsing in on weed-choked courtyards as his worshippers forsook him.

But where the sign of the horned Worm was displayed, new

believers swarmed, eating the dried blood of slaves in the God's dark rituals. They would have a life when the sun went out. Why not join them then? Deep down, Urthred knew why—it would have been too easy to abandon this life of denial, to have followed the others.

Now he would die and join his brother—a fitting end. The dying light of the sun outside mirrored his inner mood. He knelt on the thick-piled carpet, bowing his head in devotion, composing himself; though there was no noise from the corridor outside, it was better if he acted now and made peace with himself and the blood he'd spilled.

He pushed a stud on his gloved palm, and a blade snapped out from a sheath at the side of his left index finger; six inches of razor-sharp steel that could slice flesh to the bone with the slightest pressure. He thanked his master, Manichee, the artificer of these gloves and the mask. Now the gloves which should have preserved his life would end it. Then he would be with Randel and Manichee once more. He rested the blade just under the chin of his mask, above his Adam's apple. The cold tingle of the steel spoke of an easy separation, of a gout of blood, then a blackness in which he would seek the light of Reh. He would follow the light right into the heart of the fiery furnace, then all things would be subsumed in that white light of heaven.

He knelt, facing the wall to the east, where the sun would rise tomorrow. A length of burnished copper which served as a mirror leaned there. In it he saw what had killed Varash. The mirror image of the mask, but in the flesh. The bald ruin of his face, the raised whirls of scar tissue, the scorched lips, the dark sockets of the ears and nose. A horror made even more real by the brown, soulful eyes, the only point of reference to humanity in the whole sorry mess.

The eyes looked back mournfully. Minutes passed thus, and still there was no noise from outside. The reflection of the room began to blacken around the edges, and he was sucked into the darkness of the eyes, sucked back into the past, to years long gone when he had last seen his brother. For a moment he was lost to the realities of the present. He was with Randel again on a summer's day tending the monastery's sheep, free for a bit from the rigours of the monks, the harsh regime which had no letup except at precious times like these. He smiled in his heart, the smile dissipating slightly the horror of his face. The movement brought him back to the present. He relatched the mask abruptly, the grimace of his smile suddenly replaced by the set line of the mask's lips.

Then he heard dimly through the muffled, tapestry-covered walls the temple gong sounding the evening vespers. The chamber was diffused by the red light of the setting sun. Night was coming; soon Varash's men would fetch the High Priest for evening prayer. He looked once more at Varash's babylike head, its downy white hair, the now strangely uncreased features, then the blade he held to his throat. Was his life worth as little as this traitor's? Hadn't Manichee his teacher all those years ago foreseen him coming to Thrull? Told him that this was the beginning of his journey, and not its end? And lastly, had he not heard the God's voice again today? First, in the mountain pass. That moment of revelation as he'd stood before the bandits and heard the eagle calling and knew that the power had returned—the power that Manichee had promised him would once more be his. There, listening to Reh's sacred bird, the seed of fire had blossomed in his veins again, as it last had eight years before, and flame had burst from his hands. And later there had been magic enough to destroy the undead.

Varash would not be the first priest of Flame to die at his hand: he had killed one before; Midian, the man who had brought about the scars that ruined his face, had not survived that day when he had brought destruction on both of them. He had avenged himself twice. But vengeance was not enough. There was still work to do, though Randel was dead.

Now there came the sound of voices and footsteps approaching. There was a knock, then the door of the chamber was pushed open. He saw acolytes carrying washing basins and towels. They stopped abruptly when they saw him kneeling before Varash's body. Their mouths opened in screams.

Urthred barely heard them. He sprang to his feet, grasping Varash's chair with both gloved hands. In one swift movement he brought it up over his head and ran towards the bay window at the edge of the chamber, hurling it through it. The glass and metal lights exploded outwards in a thousand fragments. He rushed to the sill, to see the chair and the falling glass still tumbling through the air, the glass a red rain in the last beams of the sun. Then the throne hit the bottom of the dry ditch a hundred feet below and flew into whirling splinters. He spun around: guards were pushing their way past the acolytes. They would have him within seconds. He jumped onto the sill and, without a backward glance, launched himself into the void.

CHAPTER FIVE

If Fog Were a Thing

Down from the steep granite knoll on which the city was built, through a myriad of canyonlike streets overtopped by the dripping gables of old town houses, a flat area stretched between the city's inner wall and the curtain wall to the southwest. A gateway hung open on broken hinges on the city side, entangled with weeds, and polyped by fungus growths. The gateway gave on to an eerie scene. Beyond it, the tops of funerary monuments stretched away an arrow flight, breaking through the thick blanket of fog that had arisen there like spectral islands in a sea: black granite pyramids rising fifty feet into the air: low mastabas, their sides painted with frescoes on peeling stucco. Other, more modest, monuments in the form of single stones or plain piles of earth filled up the crowded avenues between the larger ones. The white fog filled up the spaces between the tombs, a fog so thick it seemed squeezed out of the sodden ground.

This was the City of the Dead, the ancient burial ground of Thrull. All those whose bodies were not consigned to the birds of Reh or to the sacred flames were buried here, their souls wandering Shades to the end of time.

Nothing stirred in the dense tangle of stone, thornbush and grass save the sable rooks in the trees shifting from one foot to another, their malignant yellow eyes seeking out one last prey before the night and the mists blotted out everything.

A lonely figure knelt in the midst of the desolate scene in spite of the fog and the coming darkness: an old, bent woman, on her hands and knees, plucking up weeds from a mound of earth next to an undistinguished headstone. It was the grave of her husband, killed in the great battle. In all this vast, gloomy expanse, only she lingered, daring what the night might bring, tending this, the poorest of graves. As she worked she continuously muttered under her breath, until, as if she heard something moving behind her, she turned, revealing her face: deep lines ran from her mouth and chin, the area around her eyes was a latticework of creases, the mouth thin and purple, a frail white lock of hair dropping from her forehead. The hands that clutched the weeds were blue-veined and liver-spotted. It was only the eyes that betrayed her: a startling diamond blue in which a hundred summer skies blazed with light and told anyone who saw her that, despite the crumbling of her outer defences, inside burned a fierce and undiminished soul.

The old woman's eyes darted amongst the shadows, challenging whatever was there to reveal itself. The noise came again and she peered intently through the wreathes of mist. Then her shoulders relaxed as a line of a dozen men appeared out of the whiteness. They moved cautiously, careful not to make any noise. They carried lanterns and picks and shovels and there was the slight squeak of leather armour from under their dark coats. Hilts of swords protruded from their belts. Their faces were unshaven and haggard and their wild eyes appeared to look in all directions at once: conspirators.

The old woman didn't seem surprised by their sudden appearance. She seemed to have been expecting them, even acting as a lookout. Her voice, if anything, was admonitory as she addressed the man leading them.

"You're late tonight, Zaraman." The sharpness in her tone was betrayed by a small smile at the corner of her mouth.

Zaraman halted, gesturing for his men to do the same. He was a pinch-faced man of about thirty years, with sallow cheeks and a hawk nose. "It wasn't easy to get here," he said shortly. His dark eyes continued to probe the mist and the darkness for hidden threats. "Something happened at the Temple of Flame;

the acolytes have left the sanctuary and are searching the town."

They both glanced at the dark cliffs looming out of the mists, topped by the temple roofs bathed in an eerie crimson light from the Sanctuary Flame of the Temple of Reh.

"Then it must be important," the old lady replied. "Not many of them have ventured out after dark these last few years."

"I thought at first we'd been betrayed," Zaraman said. "But they would have come straight to the house and taken us, just as they took Randel and the others."

"Then who are they looking for?"

Zaraman shrugged. "Whoever it is, let the True Flame have mercy on their soul, for soon the acolytes will be joined by the undead." The old lady added an "amen" to this sentiment.

"It's been quiet here?" he asked.

"As ever. Nothing save rooks and rats."

He nodded, apparently satisfied. "Well then, to work! We're nearly there."

"You're still going to the tomb?" the old lady asked.

Zaraman nodded. "We have to finish now: none of us are safe in Thrull anymore." His eyes wandered to the far end of the graveyard, where a large pyramid reared out of the mist. "You best get home. Make sure you and the girl are ready; Seresh will be with you before midnight."

"Zaraman, be careful. Don't forget what Illgill found in that place. How many people died because of it? How many may still die?" She, too, was now looking at the gloomy-looking pyramid. Its gaunt, weed-choked sides were sinister in the purple light of late evening. One or two rooks circled its top, emitting forlorn cries.

"It is our last chance, Alanda," he said dourly, as if he were more than aware of the dangers that awaited him.

She shook her head. "Go then, take my blessing."

Zaraman smiled mournfully. "The last of Illgill's men expect nothing, but thanks for the blessing. Remember, Seresh will come for you; be prepared, it will be a long journey." He gestured to his men and they followed him into the mists. *"The Flame be with you."* Zaraman's voice came to her after a few seconds, like a ghost's, but when the old lady strained her eyes through the fog, there was no sign of him or his men.

"The Flame go with you, too," she murmured quietly in return. "Though I will never see you alive again, my friend." She said this with finality, as if she had seen the future and knew what it held.

Heedless of the threatening gloom of the cemetery, she went back to clearing the weeds from the grave in front of her. As she worked, she spoke to the simple headstone, as if she were addressing a living person.

"Should I have warned them, Theodric? Should I have told them what I have seen, in the future . . . that they will soon wander in the Shades with you?" The stone, naturally, was mute, but this didn't deter the old woman.

She shook her head. "No, what the God gave me I cannot utter to a living man, lest the visions be forever cut . . ." She threw down a handful of weeds in frustration. "The curse of a seer, to know the secrets of the future but never be able to utter them.

"Better you're dead, my dear. Much better. You were right to fight. Right to die even. Seven years—since then the world only gets worse. It's as if this is the only place left where there is quiet, where there's no threat, even at night; they don't come here at night; they only need a grave when the sun is up."

She looked away into the fog, her blue eyes misty with tears. "No, the undead will find better blood than Alanda's in Thrull tonight," she said, shaking the tears away. "And tomorrow I'll be gone. The girl is ready, and I will find the Herald. I've searched the prophecies. He is here now in the city: I sense him. All we need now is what Zaraman will find, and we will be ready to journey into the north, to the Nations . . ." She patted the headstone like the shoulder of an old friend. "Be patient: one day I'll return and carry your bones to the temple roof and the birds will take you to heaven.

"Until then . . ." She took a small gold amulet from the tattered sleeve of her cloak. "Take back your wedding gift." She dug a small hole in the mound and buried it. "Take it: it is my heart, Theodric. Keep it safe. I will return." She kissed the headstone, then rose slowly to her feet. Her eyes took in the grave one last time. Then she turned abruptly into the bank of fog. Within seconds she was out of sight behind the rolling mist and the tombs.

It was now almost totally dark. On the causeway that ran through the marshes, the sun's light had already gone. Now only the mountain peaks to the west and the tops of the temple pyramids shared its last crimson glow. The mist began to rise up from the marshes to the level of the causeway. The local people called it Iss' cloak, the mantle the God of Death cast about him the better to stalk the city. As it reached higher and higher, supplanting the space where the light had been half an hour earlier, it brought with it the sulphurous stench of decaying marsh plants and the breath of the plague.

From the one gatehouse into the city, all that was visible over the marshes were some approaching lamps dancing over the causeway like luminous moths, and, off to one side of the causeway, a furlong away, the pyramid of skulls which, though the sun had gone, still glowed phosphorescently, like a rose glowing at dusk.

It was at this time of the evening that the monument began to take on a sinister life of its own. Fifty thousand skulls: brother, husband, son, sister, wife, daughter: they all looked alike now, though once their faces held those features which people loved: eyes that sparkled, cheeks that glowed, lips cherry-ripe. Now the anonymity of decay covered them all, and their grins mocked the efforts of the living to guess who they once were.

The bones on the causeway also glowed in the deep purple dusk; here was the aggregate of the dead: tibia and fibula, femora, humeri; the rib cages interlatticed and crushed together; small fragments of spine; all ground to powder by the passing feet of itinerants and cattle.

In the lamplit postern of the gatehouse, soldiers, their leather hauberks and jerkins cast to one side, struggled with two huge wooden winches, their bodies red in the light, gleaming with sweat from their exertion despite the growing chill. These were the human mercenaries that Faran employed to guard the city by day. The noisy ratcheting of the mechanism was like a series of small explosions in the confined space of the gatehouse. At the slow revolution of the winches one or other of the gates crept fractionally inwards, and the gap between them became less and less. Every day it was the same: but whether the city gates were closed to keep enemies out or the living in, no one knew. One of the gates had got in front of the other and finished its journey with a mighty boom. Two men stood just inside the other gate, peering out through the remaining gap over the bone white causeway stretching like a finger into the fog-shrouded marshes.

The men's faces could have been carved from grey granite—both had stern jaws with a week's worth of growth and bloodshot eyes that surveyed the world with disdain. The life of Thrull quickly brutalised a man—life was cheap and the nights long. Faran paid his human servants well, but not many stayed if they could help it. These two had both survived the battle seven years before. Neither had known a life outside Thrull. They had adapted to the new regime as they had to the one before, with an outward duty that concealed their ruthless self-interest. Neither would risk his life unnecessarily.

Their eyes creased in concentration as they tried to make out through the mist how many travellers were still heading towards the gate.

"Five of them, aren't there, Sorkin?" asked one of them, spitting reflexively in front.

His companion shifted his halberd from one hand to the other and likewise spat. "Less than that, Dob: don't you be fooled by them will-o'wisps again, like last time."

The other man stared hard again. Now he saw that two or three of the shapes in the fog glowed with an eerie blue light, wandering far from the line of the causeway. Writhing, dancing blue shapes: false fires, burning marsh gas exhaled from the sulphuric bosom of the bubbling morass. The shapes twisted and pirouetted like dancers, drifting slowly on the almost breezeless air. There were many stories of travellers leaving the causeway thinking them to be friendly lights, only to be lost in the treacherous marshes. It was easy to imagine a man floundering out there in the swamp, the muddy waters closing over his head like a brown caul.

Dob shivered: the marsh and the mountains beyond were almost as dangerous as the city behind. "Aye, false lights, but what's that yonder?"

Sorkin peered along the line of his pointing finger into the gloom once more. Now he could see two peatcutters, bent under the loads on their backs, approaching with a curious hobbling gait, their lanterns hanging from hooks over their eyes. But beyond them, another white shape began to materialise from the shroud of fog; twice the size of a man or more, it seemed to drift rather than walk towards them.

A shiver ran up Sorkin's back: his mind conjured up images of huge walking skeletons, ice creatures buried for aeons in the frozen north, or of any number of monstrous creatures commensurate with the terror of their surroundings.

But now it was Dob's turn to let out a grunt of amusement: "Well, Iss keep my skin, it's a horse!"

Now Sorkin, too, could see a dappled grey gelding, a bowshot away, its legs lost in the layer of fog so it seemed to glide like a vessel on top of it. Its legs, up to now invisible, appeared, giving the floating thing an earthly reference which it had lacked before. A figure clad in a dark cloak sat astride it with the proud upright bearing of a man born in the saddle.

Now they saw a mere human rider rather than a creature from the frozen north, Sorkin and Dob relaxed a little.

"Three coming," came a call from a watchman positioned on the gate tower.

The officer supervising the winching didn't even look up. His orders were explicit. When the last beam of sunlight was gone from the western mountains, the gates must be shut. The snow-covered peaks still glowed faintly in the purple light of dusk, but it would be totally dark in seconds. Then those still on the causeway would be left out on the marshes for the night.

The peatcutters, seeing how close the gates were to being shut, increased their painfully slow, spiderlike scuttling. Even so, the horseman, with no obvious pressure from his reins or stirrups, caught them effortlessly. Now Dob and Sorkin could see the swaybacked gelding's age, its white mane braided and knotted, its knees knocked, its movements not fluid as in a colt, but halting, tentative as one hoof after another felt its way on the causeway of bone. Now the horse came up to the gate, its head jerking from side to side as its hooves crunched down on the bone, its breath condensing in the chilling air. But, on the very threshold of the gate, the rider tugged back on the reins, pulling the horse up abruptly.

The two guards got a good look at him. He was dressed in the purple-and-brown robes of an acolyte of Iss, a not unusual sight; Worm God fanatics made up most of the numbers of those who traveled to Thrull these days. A deep pilgrim's hood hid his face. The horse snorted and stamped, impatient to be through the gates. A dry powder of bone meal eddied up from the causeway. But the rider kept a tight hold on the reins, his eyes fixed on an inscription carved in a stone set above the gatehouse.

Like the pyramid of skulls, the inscription had been here for seven years. Though they couldn't see it—even if they could, they lacked the skill to read it—Sorkin and Dob knew the words inscribed there by Faran Gaton those years before as if they were carved on their hearts: "Stranger: know this city is the dominion of the Lord of Worms, and his Master, the Prince of Death."

The ratchets of the winch exploded with sound again and the great oak gate groaned on its hinges: now the gap was down to a couple of yards. The peatcutters had caught up with the rider, their sweat-stained faces betraying amazement at his having stopped so close to the gate. Then they brushed past him through the narrow gap and into the lamplit gatehouse, gasping for breath. Another ratchet and now it was surely too late for the rider to get through the remaining space. But with one twitch of his reins and a nudge to the gelding's flanks he pushed through, riding through the gatehouse and out into the street outside.

Normally the soldiers might have called him or the peatcutters back, but the second the gates had swung to, their officer and the winching party had begun to assemble on the street outside, their halberds at port arms, each second man carrying a blazing torch. Sorkin and Dob were in danger of being left behind on the dangerous march to their night quarters. The man had been just another pilgrim—as harmless as the peatcutters.

They hurried to complete their last task, fear adding a spur to their actions. Dob seized the winch of a small wooden crane from which dangled a great oak spar. Sorkin swiftly manoeuvred the bar over the brackets on each side of the gate, then Dob released a lever. The beam fell into place with a mighty boom. Some rooks, settled for the night in a nearby ruin, were disturbed by the noise and launched into a croaking exchange.

The two men grabbed their weapons and a lantern and hurried out of the gatehouse. They found themselves already alone; the stranger and his mount, the peatcutters, and the rest of the gate guards had already vanished into the dark canyons of the streets leading up to the top of the city. Without a backward glance they hurried after them.

The rider was making the best haste he could. He had dismounted because of the steep incline and now led the horse, which, even without the burden of its master, slithered and slipped on the slick cobblestones.

He'd planned to pass through the gateway as quickly as he could, hoping his face would not be visible, hoping, too, as it had been proven, that the lateness of the hour would make the guards careless. The disguise of a pilgrim had helped, too. But he cursed himself for nearly giving himself away. He had been away for seven years, but on his journey from the south he had heard plenty about the city. He had steeled himself for the sight of the pyramid of skulls and the causeway of bones, had passed by these grim memorials stoically, though his horse had dashed the bones of his comrades, and the head of nearly every childhood friend he had ever had lay stacked in the pyramid of skulls. But the arrogance of the inscription over the gate had caught him by surprise. His family had ruled here for centuries. But now the city was lost: so, too, the cause of Reh. He would have to be more careful; everyone in this city was potentially his enemy.

It was now completely dark: the fog and the gloom of the overhanging houses relieved only by guttering watchfires at the intersection of streets. There was no sign of the gate guards behind him. Piles of rubble and the bowed gable ends of burned-out buildings spoke of the inferno that had consumed most of the Lower Town seven years before. Though he was no stranger to it, the changes to the city disoriented him, and he had to think carefully about his route.

The darkness was now both his friend and his enemy—as he'd always known it would be when he'd settled on his plan.

The horse's hooves slipped slightly on the damp cobbles as it balked at a tendril of ivy that swung out from the cavernous gloom of a ruined portico, but he pulled its head round, and led it on, muttering a soothing phrase into its ear, though his own heart had jumped into his mouth at the movement.

Up and up they went, their breath thick in the misty air. As they progressed and the minutes passed, the untended watch-fires at each crossroad burned lower and lower. The stranger peered anxiously into the gloom: not a sound. Suddenly the horse balked again, and his hand flashed to his sword hilt. Then he smelled it—the stench of decay: a pile of bodies lay heaped to one side of the street. Plague victims. He gave them a wide berth, pulling his cloak right back, so that his sword was free.

As he did so a curious thing happened: tiny pinpricks of light blazed from the stitch holes in the elaborately worked leather scabbard, lighting the area around him and the side of his face. He was a young man, in his mid-twenties with a sandy-coloured moustache, a ragged blonde beard and clear blue eyes fringed by light hair. His demeanour was distant, haughty, proud; the upper lip, puckered by a small scar, seemed slightly turned up, as if in a permanent sneer. But the eyes un-dermined this impression: if anything they were soft, filled with the melancholy light of one who knows the days of honour and pride are gone, and that one must do the best one can in an im-perfect world. Under the purple and brown of his pilgrim's cloak he wore leather vambraces and a cuirass, lacquered with a family crest and stylised whorls of flame and lightning bolts; the latter the symbols of Reh, contradicting his outer disguise. The scabbard through which the light shone was worked with a complicated pattern of entwined mythical creatures—basilisks, fire-spitting salamanders and scaly dragons—the work of a master craftsman. So, too, was the sword hilt: it was gold, fash-ioned like a salamander's head breathing fire; ingeniously wrought to form an interlatticed guard. Purple amethysts glinted in the creature's eye sockets.

He continued the upward ascent, the overhanging streets switchbacking one way and then another around tight corners, the horse continuously slipping on the slick cobbles and snorting with fear.

It took twenty minutes to reach the first sizeable level place. Here the road passed along a cliff edge overlooking the marshes. At this height, the fog was thinner, and the stranger had a perfect view of the white sea of thicker fog below and the distant ring of mountains. Dark storm clouds were gathering ominously over the mountains. To the east, the Niasseh Range was silhouetted by a rising moon. Erewon: the oldest god, who looked upon the faces of both Reh and Iss. The God of old secrets and mysteries.

The moon was full: the stranger knew what this portended: the vampires had to feed each lunar cycle lest their blood desiccate and they sink into a second, eternal sleep. This was the last night of the cycle. They would be desperate.

To his left a road passed behind the face of the cliff. The space in between was occupied by a crumbling twin-towered mansion partly hidden by a ten-foot wall on the side of the road. To his right, another road almost doubled back on the one he was on, continuing its crazy ascent up to where the red glow of the Heart Fire faintly illuminated the tops of the Temples of Reh and Iss, and the ruined citadel.

The stranger halted, contradictory emotions playing over his face. The ruined mansion to the left clearly held some attraction to him and he absentmindedly pulled out an object hitherto hidden below the leather throat of his cuirass. It was a golden key, which glowed in the light of the sword and the moon. He glanced from it back to the house, indecision marked on his face. The horse whinnied impatiently, and, still undecided, he walked it down the left-hand street for a few paces till they stood in front of a wooden, ivy-covered gate in the wall. The mansion and its grounds were hidden from view save for the tiled roof, turrets and the tops of two poplar trees pointing lonely fingers into the purple night air.

The man patted his horse's neck, and it responded with another impatient whinny. Like its master, it knew the significance of this place. Unlike its master, though, it wanted to enter the gate. Even from seven years ago, it could remember the thick hay of the stables and the stiff brushing that the ostler, Hacer, used to give it after a hard ride over the marshes.

The young man stood frozen before the gate. It was seven years to the day since he'd last passed through it, on the morning of the battle. He had wondered then whether he would ever return to the house and had looked back one last time, the eighteen years of his life to that date enshrined in its memories.

He had left two notes on the desk in his room: to be opened in the event of his death. In the first he'd detailed where he wanted his few personal trinkets to go. The other, imbued with all the sacred ardour of youth, was a letter to his betrothed, Thalassa. In the intervening years he'd thought of the swaggering words in the second of the two notes; that he had died for the Flame, that it was a just cause. . . . The early-morning sun through the latticed window had cast diamond-shaped patterns of light over the papers as he'd sealed them. He remembered pressing his lips to the one addressed to Thalassa. He wondered if the letters still lay there where he'd placed them, by now faded by the rays of the sun and covered with dust.

And Thalassa? He had returned for her, though he didn't know whether she was alive or dead. The chances were that hers had been one of the skulls on the pyramid out on the marshes. So few had survived the sack of the city. . . . But her memory, enhanced by seven years' solitary wandering, had burned purer and purer in his heart. He had dared not think of her dead in all those long years. What would he discover: a living woman or a ghost?

The house in front of him, though ruined, brought back such intense memories that for a moment it seemed that the seven years had been but a dream: that he was still eighteen, returning weary after the battle. Thalassa would be there, the sunlight streaming through the apple tree, its leaves turned an autumnal gold, shining on her light brown hair, on her white dress, her skin so fair . . .

He shook his head. Ghosts—ghosts and memories. Seven years had passed. No one was here. Seven years in which he'd passed through strange lands, the lands of men and creatures, alone and in misery. Fought battles with creatures and wizards that would have credited the pages of fairy stories; battled with the worst demon of all, himself.

For a few days after the battle, he hadn't been able to remember how he'd survived it. His memory of that time was a complete blank, and he'd tortured himself with the thought that he had fled in fear, abandoning his father and his friends. Only some letters in his saddlebag had brought back his sanity: letters from his father that told him why he travelled to the south. Letters that had reminded him who he was: Jayal, Baron Illgill's only son.

The horse whinnied again: it didn't realise that the stables it longed for were now in ruins, and Hacer most likely dead: his head no doubt was lodged somewhere on the pyramid of skulls.

"Steady, Cloud," Jayal said, running his hands over the creature's withers.

A flash of lightning suddenly stabbed down over the mountains to the north revealing an elaborate coat of arms carved into the stone above the gate. Though it was moss-covered, its details were still plain to see: a salamander entwined with a serpent, a gout of flame enveloping its victim. The Illgill family crest, the same that was embossed on the young man's faded leather cuirass. The lightning seemed to have resolved the indecision in his mind; he pushed at the gate and it swung open with a groan, a cascade of dust falling from the lintel. Inside a tangle of overgrown bushes, grasses and blighted dog roses choked a flagged pathway leading to the front of the mansion some hundred feet away. There stood the apple tree: its limbs blackened and leafless. The house itself stood in near ruins. The tiles on its steeply canted roof had fallen off in shoals exposing roof timbers which showed like the ribs of a corpse. A fire had gutted much of one wing, on the other side shutters hung at crazy angles by windows which had lost every pane of glass from their frames. Beyond the house, a huge vista of the brooding marshlands opened up, suddenly illuminated by another flash of lightning over the northern mountains.

The gelding whickered, pushing its snout against Jayal's shoulder as if encouraging him to enter the gate. But Illgill smiled grimly, shaking off the deep thought in which he'd been lost. He patted the horse again.

"Yes, we're home, Cloud, but it's too early. I must find Thalassa first, then return here." He tugged at the reins, and the horse reluctantly turned its head. He led it back to where the road rose up to the heights.

At the right-angled bend of the road, they entered a gatehouse piled with more corpses, the livid splotches on their faces showing them to be victims of the plague. Jayal threw the corner of his cloak over his mouth, gagging at the stench. Now the cobblestones were replaced by broad flagstoned steps. He passed buildings even more ancient than the fire-blackened ones of the Lower Town. A hiss off to one side, and the sword was halfway out of its scabbard in the blinking of an eye. A brilliant white light coruscated from the blade, stabbing into the dark entrance from where the sudden noise had come. Jayal caught a glimpse of yellow incisors and a drawn white face which vanished with a shriek as soon as the light hit it. Then he was struggling with the reins as the horse reared in terror. He was pulled hither and thither before he gradually calmed it. When he turned to the entranceway again it was empty. He slid the sword back into its scabbard.

"Come," he whispered, patting the gelding's neck. "It's not far now."

Above them, outlining the hulking ruins of the citadel, the Sanctuary Flame of the temple of Reh lit the sky like a false dawn. The black forms of carrion birds sluggishly circled the flat roof of the temple, too bloated to fly away to their eyries in the faraway mountains.

Jayal's limbs had begun to ache from his long journey, and he began to yearn for a warm, safe bed. But before that there was the seven-year vow he must honour; he put thoughts of weariness behind him. He plodded upwards, half-dozing in spite of the danger. A twinkling of lights in front of him woke him from his reverie. A score of torches were descending the steps towards him, their movement erratic as their bearers negotiated the steep steps. He stopped, cursing his luck. The dark alleyways that snaked away on either side might conceal him and his horse, but the vampire had been warning enough that only those who kept to the centre of the streets could hope to live.

He stood his ground as the torchbearers came into view, a jumble of orange-and-red and purple-and-brown robes showing them to be acolytes from both the Temples of Reh and Iss—a curious sight to one who had fought for the Flame against the Worm those seven years ago. But here they were together, the two factions apparently cooperating with one another.

Some of the acolytes were coming straight towards him, others branching off to the left and right in order to thrust their burning brands into darkened doorways and side entrances. Those in front were approaching him rapidly. At the last moment Jayal remembered to throw the flap of his cloak over the scabbard by his side and pull the hood firmly over his face. The men came to a slithering stop when they saw his horse blocking the way, the ones behind barging inadvertently into the backs of those in front. His sudden appearance caused an explosion of shouts and challenges from them and they thrust forward their flaring torches, causing the gelding to rear up in wild-eyed panic. Jayal turned, wrestling with the horse's reins as he fought to control it once more. Out of the corner of his eye he saw another figure making its way through the throng; he was dressed in the purple-and-brown robes of a priest of the Temple of Iss and seemed to be in charge.

He halted in front of the acolytes, looking Jayal up and down. Jayal had by now calmed the gelding and reluctantly turned to face the man. He was immediately struck by the priest's strange looks. His head was utterly shaven, revealing unnaturally large protuberances on his temporal lobes. The eyes were yellow, the skin sallow, the curiously shaped head framed by elfin ears, high and pointed, which added to the eeriness of the man's appearance. His look was full of suspicion and calculation.

"You are a pilgrim?" he asked brusquely.

Fortunately, Jayal was still too occupied with Cloud to feel nervous. He merely nodded.

"Then you should know that the streets are unsafe—unless, that is, you intend to give yourself to the Brethren?"

"No, I'm looking for some lodgings . . ."

The priest of Iss nodded slowly, his suspicions obviously not assuaged. "Have you seen anyone on the streets?"

"No one."

"Are you sure—a priest of Reh, wearing a mask?"

"No one but the gate guards in the Lower Town."

His interrogator still seemed to be dissatisfied with his answers, but clearly in a hurry. "What's your name?" he barked.

"P-Pengor of Surrenland."

"Well, Pengor, report to me at first light at the temple—otherwise expect me to come looking for you."

Jayal bowed slightly, but the priest had apparently lost interest in him and shouted out a series of orders. The acolytes started streaming past Jayal in the direction of the Lower Town. The priest made to follow them, but then suddenly stopped, just as Jayal was about to set off for the citadel once more.

"Wait."

Jayal froze as the priest walked back up to him.

"Where are you seeking lodgings?"

"I was told there is an inn near the citadel gates."

"Then you'd better hurry—the Brethren are already on the streets."

Jayal thanked him and moved off, trying to still the frantic beating of his heart. If he'd been recognised, he'd have been a dead man. Now this nosy priest had ensured he had only till dawn to complete the tasks he'd set himself. They would send out another search party for him if he failed to turn up at the Temple of Iss tomorrow. It was out of the question that he go there in daylight: then, he knew, he would definitely be recognised.

He coaxed the horse upwards towards the light of the Temple of Reh. Now he could see the third and final wall of the city, the wall which enclosed the temples and the citadel. A ramshackle inn, the one he'd mentioned to the priest, stood next to the gate, its eaves sagging nearly into the street, and its twisted chimney pots reaching almost to the top of the inner city wall. The doors to the main building and the stable yard were close barred, but Jayal fancied that he could detect a gleam of light from behind one of the shuttered windows on the ground floor. The place had been an inn for centuries, catering for visitors to the temples or citadel. By a miracle it had been spared the destruction all about it, probably because its looters had been too drunk on the wine in its cellars to burn it down.

He led his horse rapidly to the door and tethered it to a post, then rapped urgently on the broken-down shutter from which the light was shining.

After a minute or two a gruff voice called from inside. "Who is it?"

"A pilgrim. I want lodging for the night."

"Well, you're the brave one, aren't you? There's not many that wander these streets at night. Anyway, there's no room here, and never will be for them that come after dark."

Here was a problem he hadn't expected: he couldn't search the city with Cloud, and there were no other inns with stabling he knew of. "I have gold," he said desperately, jingling the money pouch at his belt.

"Ah! Gold you say? Now that's a word that might change old Skerrib's flinty heart! Let me see this gold. Hold it up to the light here." Jayal hastily undid the drawstrings of the purse and fished out a coin, holding it up to a crack in the shutters. Within the blink of an eye the shutter was thrown open and a hand had shot out and snatched it from his fingers. He caught sight of an old grizzled face wearing a bizarre form of headdress which resembled a pillowcase tied over one ear. Then the shutter slammed, and he could hear the old man chuckling inside.

"Damned if it isn't gold as well, heh, heh!"

Enraged, Jayal smashed his fists against the shutters. "If you don't let me in, I'll break your door down," he thundered.

"Ha! I'd like to see you try, me lad," came the landlord's mocking voice from within. "That door has resisted more buffets from the creatures outside as you'll be able to give it in a night . . . but me, I'm softhearted, and since you've got what pleases old Skerrib, namely gold, I'll let you in for a couple more of these beauties."

"Three gold pieces for one night's lodging? That's robbery!" Jayal exclaimed.

"Nevertheless, it's the price you'll have to pay if you don't want to share a pillow with a Vampir."

Jayal ground his teeth in rage; his purse had been light

enough, but this would leave him with only two gold pieces and some copper. But he had no other option.

"Very well, but I'll want stabling for my horse," he replied.

"I'm not fussy, my lad, the horse can kip down with you as far as I'm concerned. Now let's be having them two other coins, before I take the bar off the door."

"How do I know I can trust you?"

"You can't, my friend; but I'd advise you to give it a try!"

Jayal sighed in exasperation; he couldn't stand here all night arguing with the man. "All right then, but no tricks!"

"Heh, heh! Tricks from Skerrib? Just show me the colour of your money!" Reluctantly Jayal pulled the two gold coins from his fob and held them up to the shutter. It opened with the same alacrity as the first time, and the coins were seized equally quickly. The sight of the coins must have soothed the old man, for after a few seconds the shutter was thrown open again and he tossed something down at Jayal's feet.

"What's this?" he asked, though it was plain enough to see.

"What does it look like? A string of garlic. Now pick it up and hang it round your neck!" Reluctantly Jayal did so, his nose wrinkling at the pungent smell. The landlord nodded approvingly.

"Aye, you'll muster—none of them Vampirs can abide the stuff. Blood is the only scent they like. Come, pass around to the side door, and I'll find you stabling for your horse."

Jayal unhitched Cloud and made his way round to a high wooden gate set into a stone wall. The landlord appeared at it after a few seconds, fairly dragging Jayal inside before slamming the gate shut behind them. Jayal found himself in an inner courtyard, well protected on one side by the beetling inner walls and on the other by the bulk of the inn and the stables.

Jayal had no words of reproach left for the avaricious landlord. He would need the man's help. He had only the remaining hours of the night to find Thalassa and carry out his father's instructions. After that, if he lingered in the city, he was as good as a dead man.

CHAPTER SIX

A Diet of Worms

There was a throne chamber deep in the lower levels of the Temple of Iss. It was some forty feet square and forty tall. At each and every hour of the day a deep hush presided here, undisturbed by sudden movement or noise. Two shuttered lamps were set at its north and south corners—these, with a glowing bed of coals set into a pit in the floor, were the only illumination. The lamps cast weak beams into the room and onto the throne which sat at its far end, the main feature of the room's otherwise bare expanse.

The throne had been carved out of a solid slab of black marble as big as a cottage. Fire-blackened skulls were set at the end of each of its massive armrests. In the dim light their eye sockets glittered with bloodred rubies, and their teeth, painted with gold leaf, glowed sinisterly. The symbol of Iss, a serpent eating its own tail, was carved in a great round onto the backrest of the chair.

The man who sat on the throne was dwarfed by its black immensity, though if he had stood he would have been over six feet tall. As it was, he reclined torpidly against the backrest, his feet on a footrest of bones in front of him, his hands clutched under his chin, his eyes staring intently at the scene in front of him. His face had the yellowed parchment quality of age, his lips were purple, his hair reduced to wisps over a freckled scalp, his neck a turkey's croup of wrinkled flesh. Only his arms and legs, protruding from his black cloak, belied the impression of frailty. Though painfully white, they were powerfully muscled. Strength was apparent in the man's eyes: power radiated from their hooded depths, a power that could burn a man's gaze.

He was Lord Faran Gaton Nekron, conqueror of Thrull, High Priest of the Temple of Iss, and the leader of the Dead in Life. He had first supped from the Black Chalice 150 years before. In the intervening years he had never looked on the sun again.

The room was in near darkness; around the throne the walls of the chamber gave back an ivory glow from the dim light, its supporting piers and walls made up of tier after tier of bone rising up into the blackness of the domed ceiling and the further reaches of the chamber. The lamps and the glow from the bed of burning coal in the floor gave only a muted light suitable for his weakened eyesight. The lamplight gleamed in the rubies in the armrests and the golden teeth of the skulls, and underlit Faran's face and that of the man who stood before him, the subject of his dark gaze.

The man was one of the slaves brought by the last caravan that had visited the city earlier in the year. He hung from chains suspended from the ceiling, his arms stretched to either side, his ankles bound together with further chains. The man was naked; a score or more dark blemishes hung from his white, gleaming skin. He was shaking uncontrollably. His mouth was tied with a leather gag through which inarticulate grunts of terror could only dimly be heard. Despite the lowering gaze of Faran, the slave rolled his eyes in their sockets, straining to look behind him, but he couldn't twist his body round far enough to see what was happening.

If he could have, his terror would have been doubled. Another man stood there, bending over the bed of coal, heating a knife. He held a high-sided metal dish in his other hand. This man's name was Calabas. He was Faran's body servant, a man who had joined his master in the Life in Death 150 years before. His gaze was impassive as he watched the knife grow red-hot. Finally it glowed to his satisfaction.

"My lord?" he asked interrogatively, showing the red-hot tip to Faran.

Faran nodded, and Calabas moved to the side of the chained figure. The man thrashed from one side to another as Calabas came into view with the knife, the noises from behind the gag becoming even more desperate, but his movements were futile; the chains held him fast. Calabas crouched slightly, and applied the knife to one of the dangling black blemishes on the man's chest. There was a faint hiss, and something fell off onto the dish which Calabas had waiting underneath it. The man calmed when he saw that the knife wasn't intended for him. His bulging eyes followed Calabas as he went slowly around his body, repeating the process until all the black objects had fallen from his skin. Satisfied, Calabas replaced the knife by the edge of the fire, and knelt in front of the throne, his head bowed, his hands holding up the dish. Faran leant forward, his torpor forgotten. The bottom of the dish was full of the slowly writhing bodies of blood-engorged leeches. He took the dish from Calabas' hand and picked up the first of the wriggling black creatures and placed it between his lips, his yellow teeth champing down on the leech so that the blood burst in his mouth and down his chin like the juice of an overripe grape. He swallowed eagerly, seizing another, only just noticing before forcing it down his mouth that the chained man was watching him with sick fascination.

"Take him away," he said in a dry husky rasp from vocal cords which sounded as if they were made of sand and leather rather than flesh. Calabas snapped his fingers, and two attendants wearing the skull mask of the temple appeared from the shadows. "Back to the tanks," Calabas said, nodding at the chained man. There was a rattling of chains, and the sound of a small commotion, but already Faran's eyes were closed in pleasure as he picked through the dish. He forced one leech, then two at a time through his chapped purple lips, until the blood covered his chin. Then they were all gone. He slumped back in satiation, the plate falling from his hands with a clatter.

But he was only partly satisfied; leeches could supply him with blood, but there was never enough, though the tanks were full of men such as these. Only blood drunk directly from the veins and arteries of a living human being could truly satisfy. But the leeches contained some magic which thinned the blood. This had been known even at the time of his birth nearly two hundred years before. He was safe for another day; his blood would not dry and coagulate, forcing him into that endless sleep feared by all the undead.

Calabas sensed Faran's restlessness. "Master, let me bring you a slave to drink from; why should you, of all of us, deny yourself?"

Faran closed his eyes wearily. "You know why, Calabas, as well as I do." The croup of his neck shivered as he spoke. "There are over two thousand of our brothers in Thrull; and now there are fewer traitors and slaves left alive to feed them, whether they be in the stocks outside or in the catacombs here. Before Erewon next sets all those brothers must have drunk of living blood, or their veins will dry up, and they will die the last death. Every month we lose more and more, and the drought gets worse. I have to set an example to the others: if I can eat of these leeches, why not them?"

"But, master, why not round up all the city folk? There is enough blood in those left living to satisfy all of us."

Faran waved this suggestion away, "You know why: while the sun still burns in the sky we need the living to do our work for us during the day; otherwise, our enemies from afar will come and destroy us. The creatures from beyond the Palisades already roam the world of men. They will be here soon. When the sun burns, who will guard our ramparts and our gates? Only the living will do this, so we must keep them alive, give them hope that they may become like us. That they will live when the sun is snuffed out forever."

"May it come soon," Calabas murmured fervently.

"Every day the sun grows dimmer; it will not be long now." Then, unaccustomed to such loquaciousness, Faran fell silent, lost in thought, and Calabas withdrew respectfully into the shadows.

Faran's thoughts were not happy ones. Though happiness had always been a stranger to him, his current worries were pressing, and he needed a solution fast.

The situation in Thrull was desperate for the Temple of Iss.

Underground, each lunar month more and more of the brotherhood, starved of blood, faded back into everlasting sleep. There was not enough blood; it was as simple as that. Not enough slave caravans risking the long journey to Thrull. His masters back in Tiré Gand, where the slaves from a hundred wars kept the undead in constant supply, had not honoured the promises they had made to him seven years before: that if he should take Thrull, he should never lack blood for the Brethren.

Instead, what was he left with? Blood from leeches drained from slaves such as these, at the mercy of mercenaries who might desert at any time as more rumours came from the north: that the Nations were marching south; had already crossed the Palisades. And even if Thrull were not taken by the inhuman forces? The plague, starvation and the vampire's bite would mean that only a few hundred of the once-teeming population would survive into the next year. Then the heart of the city would barely beat. Soon after, even these few would die, and only the Brethren would be left. Without blood, they would fall into eternal slumber. In years to come Thrull would stand tenantless, alone in its vigil on the marshes, a place of bats and crumbling ivy-hung walls, of empty weed-choked streets. A ghost city.

That is not what the Elders in Tiré Gand had wanted when they'd sent him here to crush Illgill. He was but young in relation to his masters: many of them had lived over a thousand years. He had been eager to prove himself. Seven years to this very day he had defeated the baron's army on the marshes. But the taking of Thrull had not solved anything. Isolated for centuries since the marsh waters rose and drowned the fields, Thrull was of no commercial value. Even before the battle, its only attraction had been as a place of pilgrimage for the Temples of Iss and Reh.

Worshippers of Reh had practically ceased coming here seven years ago. The Iss pilgrims were another matter: fanatics to a man, they clamoured to be given the Life in Death. If denied this, many of them sacrificed themselves to the vampires, sending them into the blood frenzy in which no one was safe. Either way they were a nuisance, another burden on the few resources of the city.

And there would be more trouble tonight: he had learnt that many of the acolytes had taken to the streets, believing an ancient prophecy in the *Book of Worms*: that all the dead would rise up and destroy all the living this very evening. Faran half believed the prophecy himself. It was seven years to the day since Thrull had fallen to his advancing army. It would be a symmetry truly worthy of the Scriptures if all life in the city should cease this very night. If the prophecy was true, not even the blood of the acolytes would satisfy the Brethren. Every last drop would be scented out and drunk dry.

He'd hoped to have stayed here until the sun went out, but now he knew he must leave, abandon the temple, travel to where human blood was cheap. It might be this prophecy was true, or that the inhuman armies already marching from the north would conquer the city. In either case Thrull was finished and would have to be abandoned. In doing this he would defy the Elders in Tiré Gand, but Faran had not lived two hundred years to give up his immortal life for this wretched block of rock in the middle of nowhere. He would leave the Brethren to gorge themselves on the little living blood that was left. Surrenland was but two weeks' march; there the living still thronged, and he could prosper once more. . . . And then, in a hundred years or so, he would one day return to Tiré Gand as its master, ruler of the undead. But first, he must deal with the events of the day.

"Has Golon returned?" he asked the hanging gloom around him. Calabas reappeared like an attendant ghost.

"No, master, he is still out on the streets."

Faran cursed: Varash killed in his own temple, and the murderer still free. The news would be all about Thrull tomorrow: Faran's puppet had been killed, and he, Faran, had been powerless to act. Soon the news might reach Tiré Gand itself, bringing a reprimand from the Elders. If his authority was eroded, there might be an armed uprising, and, as they had during Illgill's day, the living might storm the catacombs, burning all those they found there. Faran sighed—the situation needed settling this night; if anyone could find the priest who had killed Varash, it would be Golon. With his sorcery he could find a man anywhere in the city. Thrull was large, but Golon would succeed.

The sound of approaching footsteps interrupted his train of thought. Faran scented the air. Although the approaching person was not yet visible, he could smell his living blood even at this distance. After a few seconds Golon appeared, as if summoned by his master's thoughts.

"Well?" he asked.

Golon shook his head, slumping unbidden onto a chair. Only he amongst the living would dare take such a liberty. "The acolytes are searching the Lower Town. The man seems to have no scent; we've tried every building, ruined or intact, near the temples—nothing."

"Both temples searching and still he evades us!" Faran rose from the throne and started pacing the flagstones of the vault. He came to an abrupt halt in front of Golon's chair. "How did the man escape the temple in the first place?"

Golon shrugged. "He jumped through a window—he was lucky—he grabbed hold of something and climbed down."

"You must go out again, keep searching until dawn if necessary. The brothers will help."

"The brothers? The priests of Reh won't like that."

"Then they shouldn't have let this man escape in the first place! Quick, we haven't much time." Spittle appeared on Faran's chapped lips as he fought to control his temper.

"It will be done, my lord," Golon whispered, cowed by the venom in his master's voice. He rose to his feet.

"See that it is."

Faran watched Golon leave. Another example of the erosion of power; even the most faithful questioned him. What if the vampires slew some of the turncoat priests of Reh who were looking for Varash's murderer? The time to leave Thrull was coming soon. Faran had used the traitors in the Temple of Reh like Varash; now they could serve one last purpose by their deaths. . . . And if they couldn't find the priest? Perhaps he would leave this very night if he couldn't be found. He would have to make arrangements.

"Calabas!"

"Yes, lord."

"Send some guards to the Temple of Sutis; tell them to bring the girl here."

"Yes, lord."

"Give them gold: a hundred pieces should be enough; they are to tell the High Priestess not to expect the girl's return. The money is final payment."

Calabas bowed low, and backed off into the gloom. Faran slumped back onto the throne. Tonight at least he would finally have the girl. So many times he had wavered over that milk white neck, pulling himself back at the last moment. But tonight would be different. Tonight he would drink of her blood—it would be a fitting farewell to the city. A small smile of anticipation played over his lips. Things might yet work out for the best.

CHAPTER SEVEN

The Palace of Pleasure

Night settled over Thrull; its black shadows, welling up from cellars and crypts and overspilling into the streets, swept into every nook and cranny of the city like an unconquerable tide. With its arrival, more and more of the undead had risen from the dark places where they had slept all day long. They joined their brothers and sisters, rustling their mould-stiffened cloaks, their black blood slowly churning through their atrophied bodies. Their need was great, for they would fall into a second sleep if they did not drink living blood between now and the setting of the moon.

But those that went to the temple square were disappointed; the victims in the stocks were drained already. With animal-like moans of disappointment the late arrivals split up and went about the city, sniffing at the air, seeking out houses where they sensed the presence of living beings.

The storm was coming closer, sweeping down from the far-off peaks of the Palisades. Lightning flashed, and those vampires in the open froze in mid-motion in the white light, their hands flying to their eyes in pain. Then they hurried about their task, knowing their hunting tonight would be curtailed when the lightning drove them underground once more.

Apart from the vampires, the streets were utterly deserted. The watchfires, which had been roaring bonfires in the late afternoon, now burned down unattended. All the guards on the ramparts were locked in their dark watchtowers, not knowing whether they should be looking out onto the fog-robed plains, or behind them, where any moment there might come a scratching at the door and a piteous wail, and the sound of a rasping voice begging for blood, for a little taste of blood . . .

But there was one place where night was not accorded the respect that it had become accustomed to. Lights blazed from a large mansion, hidden behind high walls in a side street off the temple square. In its courtyard, a thousand lanterns, their wicks scented with Lethe, twinkled in the chill, their aroma dispelling the smell of the sulphury marsh fog that infected the city; lights so bright and welcoming that the undead might think that the sun had just risen rather than set. They gave this place a wide berth, hissing as the light reached out from it, stabbing their fragile optic nerves with red-hot filaments of pain.

The building might have been a large town house, but there was an air of functionality about it, as if the design of a private house had been combined with that of a business, or a place of worship. Grey walls, made from the local granite, streaked with lichen and moss, surrounded a gravel courtyard and an extensive garden. The building itself was three storeys high. Its lower courses consisted of blocks of granite, but its two upper storeys were made of old wood and plaster, rotted with age. On each floor, front and back, wooden balconies held up by wooden brackets sagged precariously over the courtyard and garden. Further lanterns burned on these, and behind them most of the windows were illuminated by even more light shining through brightly coloured curtains. The eaves of a tiled roof overtopped the upper storey, its surface warped and undulating from the effects of age. The sound of tinkling laughter came from within, reflecting the gay abandonment that the whole building seemed to radiate.

A fire had been set in a brazier on the portico, sending out welcome heat into the chilly air. Beyond it, a set of cedarwood doors stood open, revealing a hall, some thirty feet high, its ceiling the rafters of the roof. Two sets of galleries ran around its walls, giving access to the balconied rooms. More lights illuminated the exotic carpets, the colours of which resembled a

field of wildflowers in the spring. Low tables laden with exquisite silverware were scattered around a raised platform in
the middle of the hall. Next to them were couches, strewn with
plump cushions in every colour under the rainbow; coral blue,
ochre, purple, the deepest red. Warmth, colour; this building, of
all the buildings in the whole of the city, held vitality, a beating
heart.

A statue stood at the end of the hall opposite the entrance. It
represented a well-muscled, naked man, a man so lovingly
carved that his marble surface gleamed like freshly oiled skin.
He was shown kneeling, swaying back. Wrapped round his
waist, not the article of clothing that decency might have dictated, but another body, a woman, her legs wrapped around his
hips, her arms around his shoulders, her pelvis thrust down as
his thrust up, her head thrown back in ecstasy.

An old man entered the chamber, shuffling his slippers over
the thick-piled carpet, holding his cloak up with one hand, and
a lute in the other. His name was Furtal. He was a slave employed as a musician and singer. Once he'd been Illgill's
favourite poet, but that had been before the battle seven years
ago. Like many of Illgill's favourites, fortune had been harsh to
him since—but, unlike so many of his peers, he had at least
lived. He seemed aware of his luck, for his face habitually wore
a wry smile never far from open laughter. As he passed he gave
the rump of the female part of the statue a familiar pat, then sat
down with the slow caution of age on a low dais right underneath her posterior. He began to tune his instrument. As he did
so, he looked up at the statue wistfully, the empty whiteness in
his eye sockets revealing his utter blindness. He strummed a series of chords, then, seemingly satisfied that all was in order,
began to pick out a gentle refrain on the strings of the pear-
shaped instrument. Then his voice cut in; it came from his lips
as pure as the bell-like voice of a young girl, revealing that he
had lost not only his sight but also his manhood seven years before. The song echoed down the side corridors and up into the
galleries.

It spoke of a jilted woman remembering dalliances on the
banks of summer rivers and in haylofts thick with spinning
motes.

"Ah, gentle love, come back to me,
Come back into my arms;
The soft moons are shining down
And my soft heart spreads the balm.
Evening incense and maidenhood,
The rapt mystery of a flower;
Oh come once more in the warmth of dusk,
Like a fierce wind to my bower."

His voice trailed off on a high note, leaving a faint after-ring in the air as when a finger is run across the lip of a glass. He plucked the lute, plangently, a series of dying falls that spoke of the death of hope and of love once taken, then cast aside.

As the final notes died out, doors began opening in the galleries, women appeared, clad in thin, diaphanous robes that revealed the curve of their legs and breasts in the lights of the lanterns. Their hair to a one was heaped in elaborate buns, or coiled in exotic plaits. Jewellery gleamed from their ears, their throats, their wrists and their ankles. Their chatter and laughter was gay, and, as they met on the galleries and stairs, they embraced one another with soft cooing noises, like doves coming home to roost. Some stopped and adjusted their hair and robes in the mirrors liberally sprinkled about the walls before stepping down the carpeted stairway to the hall.

The old man leaned his head to one side, smiling wistfully at the tide of femininity that now flooded around him into the hall. Some of the women congregated round him, planting little kisses on his bald head, and chucking him under the chin with peals of laughter. He leered back, an old blind turtle, starting a new tune with a bawdy lilt, his fingers racing ever faster over the frets of his instrument. Two of the women began to jig about him, circling faster and faster, until the lutanist finished with an elaborate flourish, and they fell panting through lack of breath and laughter onto one of the divans.

Now all but two of the doors leading into the house were open. One was on the ground floor, down a short passage leading towards the garden. It was a set of double doors, etched with a scene of entwined lovers copied from the *Book of Houris*; a lascivious scene of licking tongues and intertwined body parts which seemed supernumerary to the participants in the crazed orgy that the etching represented; it was a fitting cousin of the statue in the hall.

The other was upstairs on the first floor; all the other women's doors stood wantonly ajar, revealing gaily damasked rooms, gleaming bronzeware, glowing lamplight. But this door remained resolutely shut, as if its occupant wanted nothing to do with the gaiety outside.

At the end of the gallery was the head of a rickety backstairs. This was the servants' means of ascent from the service floors beneath. A hunched old lady emerged at the top of it, bearing a steaming pewter bowl. She moved as rapidly as possible without spilling the liquid inside the bowl. Pausing outside the shut door, she balanced the bowl in one hand and rapped quickly with the knuckles of her other one. Her eyes roved up and down the balcony as she did so. They were startling blue eyes, the same eyes that had stared through the fog of the graveyard at twilight; the eyes of the widow Alanda.

The door swung open after a moment. A girl of about twenty stood there, a girl of uncommon beauty, but beauty weighed down by care. A helmet of gold brown hair surrounded a high forehead, lightly freckled but otherwise an almost luminous grey-white. Set in this perfect frame under pale brown brows were eyes of the most startling grey. The chin was delicate as if set by a master craftsman in porcelain, tapering perfectly. The nose straight, long, but not haughty; the mouth the only place where one might find a fault, slightly apart, bruised and full, disconsonant with the delicacy of the rest. It was almost as if her creator had added it as an afterthought knowing that this flaw would admit an air of humanity and hence vulnerability to something which was otherwise too perfect. Like the other young women, she was dressed in a gossamer-thin peignoir, over which she had thrown a shawl. Her pale brow was furrowed with worry, and her eyes showed a faint dark ring.

"Alanda, where have you been?" she asked, the grey eyes rapidly taking in the old woman's damp cloak.

"Hush!" Alanda replied, casting another nervous glance up and down the balcony before passing rapidly into the room. The young woman closed the door behind her. The room was warm from a glowing fire and, like the others, decked in swathes and swathes of luxurious material; wall hangings, drapes, cushions, the curtains that framed a crooked casement window and the sagging balcony outside—everything oozed an air of luxury at odds with the girl's careworn face. A stool stood in front of a dressing mirror. A recently abandoned silver-handled hairbrush lay there, one strand of golden brown hair waving in the light.

Alanda set down the heavy dish of steaming water with a groan, straightening her back with a sigh of relief.

"You've been in the City of the Dead, haven't you?" the girl said accusingly. It was as if their ages had been reversed and she was the worried mother interrogating a wayward child.

"Yes, I was there," Alanda said, her eyes fixed sadly on the pewter bowl. "And you know why."

The girl came up and put her arms round the older woman's shoulders.

"I'm sorry," she said, "but you were out so late I feared the worst."

"Tush, it will take more than the undead to catch old Alanda —I know the ways of the city as well as any of them." She paused, looking intently at the girl, her blue eyes so charged that it seemed to her young companion that she could see right through her. "Thalassa, Zaraman and his men have nearly broken into the tomb—we will leave tonight, at midnight: you must be ready."

"I've been ready for seven years," Thalassa replied ardently, though her grey eyes searched Alanda's, as if seeking a catch in the old lady's words. "Are Zaraman and the others safe?" she added, as if she had intuited the old lady's knowledge of their future.

Alanda fought to maintain her eye contact with the girl: her prescience was sometimes as frightening as her own. But she wouldn't tell her of her friends' fates. Besides, her vows as a seeress precluded it. Those of her kind who gave up the secrets of the future swiftly found the God's gift of prophecy closed to them.

"They were fine when I left them," she said eventually, almost unable to endure the look of hope and expectancy which suddenly shone from the girl's face. Alanda's heart felt like ice.

She turned away and busied herself tidying up the scattered elements of Thalassa's day wear, which had been dropped as she dressed for the evening.

It was a familiar ritual: every evening had been the same for the last seven years since both of them had been given as slaves to the temple: the preparations; the chatter to mask the girl's dread of the coming night; Alanda's long vigil in the kitchen as she waited for Thalassa's duties to end for the night. Then the return to this room after the last of the men was gone. Those times in the dead of night were the hardest for the old woman: all she could do was watch as Thalassa silently prepared for bed—watching her absentmindedly contemplate herself in the mirror. Then she would sometimes touch her face as if not quite believing that here was the same Thalassa who had endured what she had endured in the last few hours. Such had been the girl's life since she was thirteen. Alanda could only guess at the inner damage those seven years had caused.

Thalassa had suffered so much already: she would never enjoy a bridal day or the hopes which that brought for the future. Never would her bridesmaids place on her pillow the three marriage crowns, as they had, all those years before, when Alanda had married Theodoric. A crown of thorns, for long life and endurance. A crown of myrtle and orange leaves, for sweetness and everlasting love. And a plaited round of bread, for peace and plenty. Alanda had had all these blessings for most of her life. But seven years before they'd been rudely taken from her. Thalassa would never enjoy what she had had. She might not enjoy anything beyond tonight, so real were the dangers in front of them.

Her preoccupation must have betrayed some of her inner thoughts.

"Is there something wrong?" Thalassa asked.

"No," Alanda replied, turning and patting her cheek. She noticed that the girl had not advanced at all in her preparations for the evening; her makeup and hairbrush lay on the dressing table, unused. "Come, you must hurry! We have to act normally; tonight of all nights!" She made herself busy again, bustling about the room. "I'll pack what's necessary for later;

some warm clothes, a little food, your jewels. You get ready for this evening."

Thalassa seemed to start from her reverie and quickly sat down at the dressing table, picking up the silver hairbrush. But even then Alanda could see the girl looking at her in the mirror as she pulled the brush through her tresses.

"Tell me about the north," Thalassa said.

Alanda stopped her activity and met the girl's eyes in the mirror. "You've never left Thrull, have you?"

Thalassa shook her head. "Never. Even as a girl everything seemed to be in the city. There was no need to leave. Besides, what else was out there besides the marshes?"

Alanda nodded towards the north. A flash of lightning silhouetted the latticing of the window. "My people came from there in the old days of the world. In these Southern Lands they called us witches because we had the second sight, but all my ancestors had it. Now only a few of us remain. But I have read the old books of my people, and know what lies there, though I've never been there myself.

"Two days' ride from here are the foothills of the Palisades. As you ride towards them the books say you will see white clouds hanging high in the sky. You'll ask yourself: where are the mountains, the fearful Palisades that I have heard of that no man or woman has ever passed? Then you grow closer. Faint lines appear beneath the clouds in the purple sky. The purple is not sky, but the mountains themselves, and the clouds their snow-covered peaks."

Thalassa stared out the window, trying to imagine the sight. Apparently it was too much; she shook her head slightly, her lips parted in wonderment. "Go on," she whispered.

"Then you come to the mountains themselves. Snow and ice, howling winds that could deafen you, heights and precipices beyond imagination, banshees and snow creatures that hate men. Crossing the Palisades is the job of an army."

"Yet we will do it?"

"Yes, Reh willing, we will do it with Zaraman and Seresh and the others."

"And Furtal will come, too?"

"Yes, he too."

"What is after the mountains?"

"The ground falls away in sheer cliffs thousands of feet high. Below, a glass-strewn plain where the gods used to live in the early times of the world."

"Your people travelled through these lands?"

Alanda smiled, pleased that for the moment Thalassa was distracted from her worries. "Only a handful of men through the ages have passed over the Palisades and seen Shandering Plain."

"You know so much!"

"The old books have taught me."

"I wish I had read them, too."

"They are written in the Fire Tongue of the Witches of the North."

"I've seen those books," Thalassa said impishly, her eyes straying towards an old leather satchel resting by the old lady's couch. She knew this was where the old lady kept her precious volumes, for she had dipped into them once or twice in Alanda's absence, trying to learn the strange language of her ancient race.

Alanda smiled. "They were the only books I saved when Faran's men looted Theodric's house. I had so many once."

"And is it true those witches had blue eyes, just like yours?" Thalassa asked slyly, her full lips puckering in a smile.

The old lady's blue eyes twinkled in the lamplight. "So the books say."

"Then you have the power—to see the future!" Thalassa continued, trying to tease further information from Alanda.

"Now, you know I never talk of those things."

"Use the power; tell us whether we're going to get to the north!"

Alanda hesitated for a moment, and the girl's face paled, the animation of a few moments before completely gone. She put the hairbrush down with a shaking hand.

"We will get there, won't we?"

"Of course we will." Not for the first time, Alanda felt tempted to tell Thalassa all she knew about the future, but once more, the unspoken vows she had made to herself at her first divination stopped her. Instead she decided to speak of what was written in Reh's holy Scriptures. "The *Book of Light* tells us that this very night, seven years exactly after the battle, great events will take place in the city. It will be a night of arrivals and departures and of a new destiny for those who believe in Reh. A night of magic long hidden, which will be revealed. They speak of a man called the Herald who will arrive and bring forth the Lightbringer, the person who will reignite the sun. Can our fortune be bad with all these portents?"

"And who is this Lightbringer?" Thalassa asked.

"Who or what—let the evening reveal its mysteries," Alanda said as lightly as she could, as if all these prophecies were but an average evening's fare in the *Book of Light*.

"But this prophecy is why Zaraman is intending to break into the tomb tonight?" Thalassa persisted.

"Hush!" Alanda cautioned, looking around her wildly, as if the walls had ears, as she was reasonably confident they did.

"It's safe now," Thalassa said. "They'll all be in the Greeting Room."

"As you should be, too. This night of all nights we don't want to draw attention to ourselves."

"I'll be gone in a minute. Let me finish my hair." She took up the brush again, and began to pull it languidly through her golden brown tresses. For a moment the girl's eyes took on a dreamy abstraction as her thoughts flew to freedom and the far north. Then she shuddered. "They'll come after us, won't they?" she said, her hand suspended in mid-stroke.

"If they can catch us."

"But there's only one road to the north. With horses they'll catch us before dawn."

"If they know where we have gone. Have faith in me."

Thalassa bit her lip, and began slowly to draw the brush through her hair again. Alanda set down the small bundle of clothes she had been drawing from a brimming chest and took the brush from the girl's trembling fingers.

"The world is large, Thalassa; there are many places to hide."

"Hide from Lord Faran?" Thalassa shook her head. "There's nowhere in this land where he couldn't find me, however long it took." She gave a small bitter laugh. "After all, he has eternity."

Alanda paused, and looked at the girl's reflection in the mirror. Such beauty, such innocence, yet such sorrow in one so young.

Thalassa had been born for higher things, the daughter of Soron Eaglestone, one of the Hearth Knights of the Temple of Flame. Engaged at the age of thirteen to Baron Illgill's son, Jayal, the very year that civil war broke out in Thrull and Lord Faran Gaton's army had crushed Illgill's forces out on the plains. With that defeat, Thalassa's fortunes had changed all too cruelly, as had Alanda's.

For this harbour of light in the sea of darkness was no ordinary building, but the temple dedicated to Sutis, Goddess of the Flesh. Its mistress, and High Priestess, a faded madame called Malliana, oversaw her domain with an unremitting devotion to a faith which, unlike the creeds of other religions, had no interest in the preservation of the soul, or other metaphysical concern: the delight of the flesh in the here and now was Sutis's only pursuit and pleasure. The young ladies of the building were dedicated priestesses of the Goddess: by providing a service which brought the temple wealth, and themselves comfort in a city where most people lived in rags and ate the meagrest scraps, they had escaped the darkness, living like princesses in a fairytale world.

Fairytale, if the occupation of the denizens of this place could be forgotten during the daylight hours when the women lay idle, waiting for the evening. Only in the evening were the temple gates opened, and men, their desires perversely spurred by the dangers of the night, would come to seek their pleasure with them. The threat of death and the end of time were powerful aphrodisiacs. If anything, the numbers of nocturnal visitors had increased since the undead had reappeared on the nighttime streets. Here, idling away the night in the luxury of the galleried rooms, they were able to forget for a moment the terror outside. At night the temple was akin to a luxurious prison from which no one would wish to escape until dawn made the city safe once more. There were many stories of how those who served here had come to their current occupation. But none had fallen as far as Alanda, Thalassa, and Furtal, the musician. All of them had been part of Illgill's court. All had been captured and sold into slavery. It was a bond that held them together, and made them work as best they could for the resistance that had opposed Faran these last seven years.

Of the three of them, it had been the thirteen-year-old Thalassa who had at first adapted best, keeping an inner core of her former life intact despite the demands of the temple. For a while she'd inspired her two older friends. But then disaster had struck, a disaster that had dispelled her false sense of security and had meant that from one month to the next she had lived under the threat of death.

Thalassa's beauty went beyond the flesh; looking at her it was as if a pearly light glowed from deep within her. And because her beauty was more than skin deep, a beauty that no casual blemish could mar for a day, she had attracted a deep envy from the other women of the palace from the time she was first led here in chains by Faran's troops. And no one had disliked her more than the High Priestess Malliana, the very woman who had bought her life in order only, it would seem, to destroy it. For Thalassa she had chosen a special fate, a fate she had visited on her every month for these past four years . . .

It had been in the middle of the night, some three years after their arrival. The sound of heavy feet outside in the corridor had woken the old lady on the small couch by the door of Thalassa's chamber. She had reached out for a flint and tinder to light a candle, but there had been no need. The door burst open and the room had been suddenly bathed with light from guttering torches. The High Priestess stood in the doorway, holding one of them over her head. The light did nothing for the harsh severity of her features. No doubt she had been a beauty once, but whatever she had once had was now disguised under the thick plasterwork of foundation and rouge on her cheeks and the thick ring of kohl under her eyes, which merely accentuated the fierceness of her glance. This glance was now directed at Thalassa and Alanda, her eyes daring them to make any sound of defiance.

Two men stood outside on the balcony, holding torches.

They wore the leather greaves, vambraces and cuirasses of the temple guards of Iss, their faces covered by copper masks shaped like skulls. Malliana gestured for them to enter. Thalassa had sat up in bed with a cry of fear, covering herself with the blankets.

A small hard smile had played on the High Priestess's face as she regarded the trembling girl. Then she picked up a dress from a divan and threw it at her.

"Get dressed quickly; these men are in a hurry," she had ordered abruptly.

Alanda had leapt up from her couch, throwing herself in front of Malliana. "Where are you taking her?" she demanded, grabbing at the High Priestess's sleeve. Malliana twisted round, beating away the old lady's hand with a clenched fist.

"You again, you interfering, blue-eyed witch!" she had hissed, her own green eyes blazing with fury. "Next time you touch me, you'll be out in the streets begging." Alanda had shrunk back; Malliana's threat was not an idle one, she'd seen a dozen or more women thrown out in this way in the last three years. And no one lasted long on the streets.

"Now, Thalassa," she said, turning back to the girl whose face had drained of all colour, "are you going to get dressed, or shall I ask these gentlemen to do it for you?" The men stepped forward with a squeak of leather armour, their skull masks gleaming in the flickering torchlight.

Thalassa nodded her head mutely.

"Good," Malliana purred. "We'll wait outside."

The door shut once more.

Alanda rushed over to Thalassa, who still sat on the bed, her chest rising and falling with emotion. But Thalassa fended her off and rose abruptly. In a single, angry gesture she pulled off her nightdress and, naked, seized the gown she had laid aside earlier.

"What do they want with you?" Alanda asked, trying to help her.

But Thalassa shrugged her off again, dropping the gown over her head. She turned to Alanda as she fumbled with the laces of the bodice. "Faran wants me—it's as simple as that."

"You can't go!"

Thalassa, tight-lipped, drew the drawstring of her bodice tight. Her eyes were set in shock. She looked around the room for her underclothes. Alanda already had them. Thalassa took them, her anger dissipating. "I must go; it's certain death if I don't . . ." She might have said "certain death if I do," but the unstated words were pregnant enough unuttered.

She looked at Alanda for the first time since the guards had entered. "Here," she said, reaching behind her white marble neck and unclasping a pendant necklace, placing it in Alanda's unresisting hand. "Take this. It was given to me by my father. Remember me by it if I don't return." Alanda opened her mouth to protest, but Thalassa laid her fingers on the old lady's lips. Her resolve was shaky enough without further words. She knew if she remained a moment longer Faran's men would return and drag her from here. She turned and opened the door. Alanda caught one glimpse of the skull-masked guards before the door slammed to and the girl was gone.

Alanda slumped down on a chair and sat there the rest of the night, immobile, clutching the necklace in nerveless hands. She stared at the wall, unconscious of the passing of the night, a vague belief that if she didn't move, Thalassa would be miraculously restored to her.

It was in the first light of dawn that Thalassa reappeared. Opening the door to the chamber almost soundlessly. She was pale and gaunt, her gown torn at the collar, her hair dishevelled. As she came closer Alanda detected a faint air of mildew clinging to her clothes. There were also red marks about her wrists and ankles. But none on her neck. She'd passed Alanda without acknowledgement and sat down softly on the edge of her bed, her eyes focusing on a point a thousand miles in front of her.

She'd not spoken for two days. And when she did, she never referred to the events of that night.

The pattern was repeated that month and every month after. The guards at midnight, the torches, the rough hands. Every month Alanda could see Thalassa steeling herself, looking up at the night sky to see how near it was to a new moon, for this was when the guards always appeared. And when the night finally came, she'd sit, fully clothed, waiting for the guards. They

...ever failed to arrive. But Thalassa amazingly always returned, pale and shivering in the cold light of dawn . . .

A sharp rap at the door brought Alanda back to the present with a shock of surprise; for a moment she was confused; the knock had sounded exactly like the noise of Thalassa's monthly summons. The hairbrush clattered from her hands onto the table. Thalassa stared at her, wide-eyed with fear; the last summons had been only two weeks ago. The moon was nearly full; it was too early. Both women glanced back at the door before Alanda, recovering herself, went to it. As she opened it, a tide of music and laughter flooded in from the hall below. One of the other priestesses was leaning insolently against the jamb, playing with some beads on a necklace.

"The High Priestess wishes to see Thalassa," she said, affecting boredom, though the crooked smile on her rouged lips showed that she thought this summons wouldn't be good news for its recipient.

"But Thalassa has to go to the Greeting Room."

The priestess shrugged indifferently. "She said it was urgent."

Alanda glanced back into the room; Thalassa stared back at her, her face draining colour.

"I'll come," she said finally. She shrugged off the shawl, swiftly attaching an earring to each lobe before walking to the door. The priestess had already wandered off down the balcony, humming a tune to herself.

The two women exchanged looks.

"Until midnight," Alanda whispered.

"Until then." Thalassa squeezed Alanda's hand before striding gracefully out onto the gallery overlooking the hall.

CHAPTER EIGHT

The Gaunt's Head

The landlord of the Gaunt's Head did not improve on closer acquaintance, Jayal decided. The smell of his clothing as he'd brushed past him to close the courtyard gates had overcome even the stink of the garlic necklace. He'd detached that item from his neck as soon as possible and it now lay on the ground, being trampled by one of his horse's hooves.

He now had a better opportunity to study his host—he was not the same man who had run the inn seven years before. The Falarn family had owned it then, letting it to a tenant innkeeper. The innkeeper had been with Jayal on the battlefield, and Jayal was reasonably certain he was dead, like so many others, including the man's masters, the Falarns.

Skerrib came clumping back from bolting the gate, his nightcap lolling preposterously off the side of his head. His face broke into an avaricious grin.

"You'll be wanting stabling for the horse then?" he offered, suddenly all jocularity.

"That was part of the agreement," Jayal replied cautiously, wondering what further extortion the old miser was about to attempt.

"Good, I'll get the boy." The landlord leant his head back like a cock about to crow and let out a call that would have woken the dead, if they had not in fact already risen. "Fazad!"

he bellowed in the general direction of the dilapidated inn, and again when after a couple of seconds no reply had come. "Damn young 'uns, never here when you want them," he muttered bitterly. Just then a thin stripling of a boy, not above twelve years old, emerged from the tumbledown door of the inn, his brown eyes wide with terror. "There you are, you skulking rat!" the cheerful innkeeper greeted him. "Get out here and stable this man's horse," he said, giving the boy a good push, so he stumbled on his way with greater speed than he might have wished. "And mind that old nag don't kick some sense into your head." The boy looked in terror at the darkness all around, his body trembling slightly.

"Move yerself," the old innkeeper shouted, a dangerous edge of impatience apparent in his voice which did not bode well for Fazad. Fazad clutched the gelding's rein and led it towards the half-ruined stables.

"He seemed reluctant to discharge his duties," Jayal observed.

"Oh aye, slovenly fellows is all you can get these days. Who wishes to serve when the sun is dying and tomorrow could be the last? Any roads, enough of this! No doubt you must be weary from your travel and would take a drink, or some vittles, or even both?"

"The road has been hard," Jayal agreed, wary of further questions and pecuniary demands. They entered the front room of the inn through a side door. It was lit by a single tallow candle, the light which he had seen through the shutters. Low beams warped with age held up a sagging roof. These in turn were supported by crooked wooden pillars. The dust of ages choked the surfaces of tables and chairs. An engraved coat of arms lay over the blackened fireplace: the arms of the Falarn family.

Jayal remembered the Gaunt's Head on the morning of the battle; the bustling activity of the room as the knights had toasted each other in Viridium wine before riding out to the marshes, the air of anticipation and nervous jokes of his companions, now all dead. He even remembered with guilt the pretty serving girl who had run out to the courtyard as he mounted his horse; how she had undone the handkerchief from her brown flowing hair and, with a look of open invitation in her eyes, eyes as brown as her hair, given him the scarf. He'd carried it that day next to his betrothed's. His face screwed up in embarrassment at the memory: unfaithful in his heart, to his betrothed, and to the Hearth vows he'd made when his father had made him a commander.

The innkeeper had followed his glance and seen it rest on the coat of arms. "Ah! The arms of the Falarn family. They owned this place before the Civil War," he remarked.

Jayal turned to him, his eyes distant with memories as it seemed to the crafty old man. "Yes, the Falarn family," he said, nodding slowly. "They would all be dead now I suppose?"

A knowing look passed over Skerrib's face, his nose wrinkling conspiratorially. "Well, not exactly . . ." He nodded his head out towards the stables. "You see, when I moved from the east and bought this place, all the goods and chattels of the Falarns fell under duress to me, them being rebels and all. Including that child, the only survivor as I understand."

"The only survivor," Jayal repeated in a reverie.

Skerrib, fancying perhaps that his guest was upset by this arrangement, cantered on as quickly as he could. "Of course, I was not likely to turn out a mite from what used to be his own property, given that the Falarn mansion was burned to the ground. I could see that lad's quality when I took over his place. And I use him well, a lot better than others in my circumstances would."

The stranger eyed him up and down glacially. "Very commendable," he enunciated after a distinct pause in which a look of dangerous anger flitted across his face. He composed himself. "You spoke of food?"

"Aye, sir, follow me to the refectory," Skerrib said quickly, leading him down an oak-panelled corridor. As they neared the back of the inn, Jayal heard the sound of voices coming from a back parlour.

"Are there many such as Fazad?" he enquired of the old man's hunched back as they walked along.

The old man stopped and leered up at him from a squinty eye. "Aye, a right many, all the orphans of the Flame Lords that died in the final battle. The Worm seized all their property and goods. You wouldn't recognise them now, beggars most of them. Or dead."

"Indeed," the stranger said stiffly. "And is this true of even the greatest of the families?"

"What sir: the Pavises, the Curshaws, the Gallampogons?" the old man asked, trying to figure where this line of questioning was leading.

"No . . . higher yet," the stranger said hesitantly.

Skerrib made sure his face remained its habitual mask of veniality and sourness, but inside his mind was racing—Golon at the Temple of Iss paid him well to inform on his guests. He would no doubt be intrigued by the stranger's dangerous line of questioning.

"You mean the family of . . ." He paused and looked theatrically up and down the deserted corridor. "Illgill?"

The stranger blinked in surprise, or so it seemed to Skerrib, as if this was not the name he'd been expecting. There was a slight catch in his voice when he replied. "Yes . . . yes, what of them?"

Skerrib faithfully memorised the young man's interest for his report to Golon before scratching his unshaven chin. "Well . . . rumour has it that he fled to the north . . ."

"Ha!" Jayal interjected. "It doesn't take a man to travel here from the Southern Lands to discover that rumour."

"Well, no it doesn't, sir," agreed Skerrib quickly. "As for the others, his son was killed in the battle, it's said, and the mother died some years before. However . . ." He hesitated for a few beats, waiting to gauge his guest's reaction to his next bit of information.

"Yes?"

"Some say that Illgill made a pact with the World Beyond, that his son lives, indeed travelled"—he waved his hands apologetically, as if discounting the coincidence—"to the Southern Lands." His eyes ran over the stranger's tall body as if gauging every sinew for its potential similarity to the rebel's son. The glare he received in return didn't encourage him to continue his inspection for long. "However," he went on, "I've it on best authority that the son, Jayal his name was, never went to the south. Changed his name and has been hiding out in the city these last seven years . . ."

A look of puzzlement crossed the stranger's face. "Jayal . . . in the city?"

"Aye, sir, but it's only a rumour, mind . . ." The look of confusion that occupied the stranger's face was intriguing enough for Skerrib: this was certainly worth reporting to the Temple of Iss. Maybe the man was one of Illgill's agents returned to spy out the state of the city.

"Enough of Illgill now," the stranger growled, breaking in on the innkeeper's thoughts. "What of the Eaglestones?"

Skerrib had begun his crabbed progression up the dimly lit corridor again, and the stranger addressed this last question to his retreating back. "The Eaglestones?" he replied, halting briefly before the threshold of the chamber at its end. "You'll have to excuse me of them: can't say as I've heard much of them these past years. Perhaps one of the fellows here knows something."

They entered the low, timber-ceilinged room. It was similar to the front parlour, except half of it, from about head high to the rafters, was covered with a thick blue mist of Lethe smoke; the sickly-sweet smell of it was nearly overpowering. A dozen or so men were seated on the hard wooden benches drinking beer out of wooden flagons. One group was dressed in the same purple-and-brown pilgrim's robes as Jayal: they sat to one side, poring over a dusty volume which lay open before them on a table. Jayal's unease increased: no doubt they would greet him as a fellow worshipper of Iss and ask awkward questions.

As a man the pilgrims looked up from the big leather-bound book and stared at him with cadaverous eyes. Jayal ignored them and studied the rest of the clientele. Two or three of the patrons were hunched over pipes, their glazed expression telling him they were addicts of the Lethe smoke that choked the room. The other men steadfastly stared into their pots, ignoring the stranger.

Whatever conversation had existed before their entrance had died out. Seemingly unaware of the silence, Skerrib continued his crabbed progress to a bar made of ancient oak beams hastily tacked together, no doubt from one or other of the Falarn family's priceless antique tables. He seized on an earthenware pitcher and poured a muddy-looking concoction into a wooden beaker. Jayal recognised the "beer" that the other patrons were drinking.

"Here you are then, brewed it myself," the landlord said cheerily.

"Aye, from the contents of your pisspot!" one of the previously silent men volunteered in a drunken voice. This elicited a volley of guffaws from the man's companions.

The landlord showed no indignation at this remark; instead it provoked a look of twinkling amusement in his eyes.

"Piss or not, you still pay your durcals and murcals for it." He turned to the stranger once more. "Drink, sir, the finest ale as you'll find in the whole of this fair city, and all for but one gold piece extra!"

"But we agreed on three gold!" Jayal protested.

"Ah, the intemperate nature of youth, thinking as you understand matters in your overhaste, when, as it happens you do not. The three gold were for the lodging of your horse and yourself; your victuals are extra!"

"Why, this is robbery!"

"Call it what you will, sir; would you rather be here or out there in the mists?"

Some of the other men in the common room might be thugs hired by the landlord to keep the peace. Jayal couldn't afford an argument now.

"The choice is a difficult one," he conceded, sitting at a trestle table as far as possible from the Iss worshippers.

"Well, come then; eat and drink!" said Skerrib, laying a plate of grey stew next to the tankard of vinegary beer. He wrung his greasy hands through his stained apron as Jayal extracted another gold coin from his purse. He palmed the coin and hurried off to his position behind the bar.

Jayal turned his attention to the food and drink, his nose wrinkling in distaste. It was true that he was famished, but even if the food had been more palatable he couldn't have eaten: his stomach was churning with anxiety. He'd risked everything to come here, and still there were awkward questions he had to ask; questions that could only elicit more suspicion. Everything he had done in the last seven years could be in jeopardy.

A shadow fell across his table, and he looked up quickly. The Iss worshippers had got up noiselessly from their table and were now congregated around his. He noticed for the first time their ragged clothing and their emaciated, starved faces. One of them still held the book, open at the place where they had been studying it.

The tallest of them, his cheeks shrunken and sallow, sporting a grey stubble, was obviously their leader. He spoke first. "You have arrived this evening?"

Jayal nodded his head noncommittally.

"Then you've come for the ceremony?"

Jayal wracked his brains. What ceremony? In his childhood had he noticed the Temple of Worms celebrate any anniversary on this day? Seven years to the day of the battle, the third day of winter. He would never forget it. Maybe the ceremony was something to do with the battle?

But his look of confusion must have already registered on his face, for the man set the massive leather-bound book on the table in front of him with a thump. The pages were yellowed, and riddled with wormholes. Spiky script flowed across the pages in inky waves. It took only a cursory glance to establish what it was: the *Book of Worms,* the Holy Book of Iss. He saw today's date written in the margin. The acolyte was pointing to it.

"It is the date of the battle of the marshes," Jayal said, looking up, hoping to end the matter.

The man organised his thin lips into a grim smile: "That and something else—read the text." Jayal's eyes moved to the main body of the writing. It was a prophecy, written in the riddling style that pervaded both the *Book of Worms* and the Scripture that he had studied all his youth: the *Book of Light.*

He read the indicated passage:

"You that live in later times will see the power of the Worm rise up from the east, from the Tiré Gand, the capital, and the Worm will fall on the sputtering Flame in Thrull and crush it on this day. Seven years more the Worm will live,

and the power of the Dead in Life will multiply until, seven years to the day, the gong will summon the Sleepers from the grave and they will feast before the dying of the moon. And thus will die the city of Thrull."

"A heavy prophecy!" muttered Jayal.

"Then you hadn't heard of it?" demanded the leader of the acolytes suspiciously.

"Of course I'd heard. . . . I had just forgotten it was today . . ." Jayal tailed off lamely.

The leader shut the book with a clap, and looked round at his fellows before returning his stare to Jayal. "We are going now to the mouth of some catacombs nearby: will you join us?"

"What for?"

"Why to offer our blood to the risen dead, what else?"

"But how can you be so sure this gong will be rung?"

The leader sneered. "Did not the battle occur exactly as it is written? The gong exists, stranger; we have seen it with our eyes in a vault in the temple. Someone will ring it tonight, and the dead will be with us once more."

Jayal's brain spun: the last thing he'd been expecting was an invitation such as this. A refusal could only excite further suspicion. But he couldn't waste a night waiting with these fanatics on a foolhardy mission, however compromised he might be by his refusal.

"I will join you later," he said eventually. "In truth I came to the city looking for someone: after that I'll join you." The leader frowned, dissatisfied by what he had heard, but nevertheless grunted instructions to Jayal where to find them. Jayal recognised the place, a gloomy entrance to the catacombs halfway down the cliffs. He promised to join them there before midnight, reasoning internally that it was unlikely that any of the acolytes would live that long in the vampire-haunted night and that his absence would therefore not be missed.

It looked like the leader was about to say something else, but just at this moment the landlord came stumping up again with a pitcher of beer, no doubt hoping to extort more money from Jayal. The Iss worshippers moved away quickly, obviously familiar with their host's endless pecuniary demands.

Skerrib gave them a withering look as they went—they were obviously not his best-paying customers. He turned an ingratiating smile on Jayal. "More beer?" he asked.

"No," Jayal answered firmly. The tension was getting to him. He would have to get his information quickly and somehow escape this place: it was too dangerous to remain here for long. He lowered his voice. "But there may be payment yet. You remember I asked you a question?"

"And so you did!" the landlord exclaimed, louder than Jayal would have wished. Before he could stop him, Skerrib had turned to his other customers. "Now, lads," he said, jerking his head towards the stranger. "Friend here," as he uttered the word "friend" he rubbed his fingers together suggesting graft, "has been asking for information." At this the men still sober enough looked up from their beer. The acolytes, who had resumed their seats, were staring at him with undiminished suspicion.

"What sort of information?" one of the drunkards asked, fixing his red-rimmed eyes on Jayal.

He paused to think, discretion contesting with an urgent need to know. The battle and the events preceding it had taken place a long time before. It was unlikely any of those in the room would have anything but the dimmest recollection of Thalassa being Jayal's betrothed. Besides, if Skerrib knew who he'd been asking for, it could hardly matter if his customers knew also. "The Eaglestones," he said finally, "I'm seeking 'information' on the Eaglestone family . . . the daughter particularly."

The small buzz of conversation that had started up again now died out. The man who had joked about Skerrib's beer stared at Jayal. The levity was gone from his voice when he spoke. "That's a heavy name, that Eaglestone is." He glanced around the room at his companions, seeking agreement. One or two of them nodded. Encouraged by this, he went on, "Even if we knew what happened to the daughter, or any of them, it would be too heavy to speak of it. Beware, a name as heavy as that might put a man's neck in the stocks. So ask elsewhere, stranger." His companions nodded their heads in assent and went back to the avid contemplation of their beer mugs. The Iss worshippers continued to stare fixedly at him.

"Well, Iss pinch me cheeks, this must be the first time that one of you skinflints ever balked at selling information!" Skerrib exclaimed.

The humorist looked up from his beer beaker. "That may well be true, Skerrib, but you weren't here when Thrull burned, and with it most of them who lived here. Many of our closest, too. The Worm has a long memory, and the Eaglestones are some of the most hated of all." He glanced nervously at the Iss people as he mentioned the Worm.

The pilgrims had begun muttering excitedly amongst themselves, casting Jayal quick glances. He must leave quickly, notwithstanding the vampires outside. Jayal placed his untasted beer down on the counter and began to relace the front of his cloak.

"What? Going so soon?" Skerrib asked him querulously.

The young man fixed him with his blue eyes. "Yes, where the company's friendlier and the information freer." With this he rose and strode down the dimly lit corridor to the front of the tavern.

Skerrib followed hard at his heels. "But what about your beer, your viands?"

"Keep them, and keep my horse well until I return."

"But where are you going?" Jayal had now reached the barred door.

"Why, where does it look but out?" he asked, turning to Skerrib.

Skerrib cursed himself inwardly that he hadn't already sent Fazad off to the authorities. If this was the man he thought it was, the temple of Iss would pay him handsomely. "It's dangerous out there," he blurted out. "You don't know what walks the street at night . . ."

As if in confirmation of his warning, there came a sudden scratching sound at the front door.

"Hark at that!"

"What is it?" Jayal asked.

"Don't you hear it? It's one of them!"

The scratching intensified, now accompanied by a piteous mewling, like a lost cat clamouring for admittance.

"What in Hel's name is it?"

"One of them Vampirs hungering after blood," Skerrib answered grimly. "Shh! Listen awhile, it'll get going in a minute." Sure enough, the mewling increased in intensity until it became a wail, and then the wail a shriek that threatened to pierce Jayal's eardrums. He could barely hear the landlord's words over the noise.

"That's that one's trick: he thinks to drive my custom out by his banshee racket. Little does he know that they're too drunk to hear him most of the time." Skerrib clumped to the door, putting his mouth to the keyhole. "Shut your noise!" he roared as if hailing the topmast of a ship in a storm. The noise instantly died to a plaintive hiss.

"That's enough of that," Skerrib continued, winking at Jayal. "There's none that will be leaving this inn tonight for you to feast on, so be off with you."

A dry, husky rasp responded through the door. "I'll be gone for now, Skerrib, but I'll be back; I know your wife sleeps in the loft."

"Hoh, blackguard, you think old Skerrib hasn't thought of that route? The skylight is nailed as tight as a coffin, as are all the doors and windows. Be off to the temple square with you."

The thing let off a tiny hiss of hate, and Jayal heard a dry rustling as it crept off.

"He'll be back," Skerrib said, thumping his fist against the door grimly in valediction. "So you see," he said, turning to Jayal, "there's no safe way to be leaving this inn tonight."

"That may be the case," Jayal replied. He turned and found himself being scrutinised by one of the pilgrims from the shadows of the corridor. "Nevertheless, I must check on my horse."

Skerrib saw his chances of sending Fazad to the temple of Iss immediately evaporating fast. "Your horse will be fine. Come, have a drink; you've paid after all!"

But the stranger had brushed past him and unlocked the door to the stable yard before he had a chance to speak again. The door closed behind him with a crash, sending small clouds of dust from the ancient rafters of the house onto Skerrib's head.

Never mind, I'll send Fazad the moment he returns, he reflected. He locked the door, and went off back down the corridor, rubbing his hands together at the thought of the huge fee that would be his when Fazad got to the Temple of Worms. He reentered the common room in a cheerful mood. "Come, drink up, you fellows, do you think I run this place as a charity? Let's see the colour of your durcals!"

Outside in the cold dark Jayal was surrounded by the mist, which by now had risen to cover most of the city. Its sulphury fumes pricked at his nose. At first he thought not a single light showed, but then he made out a thin line of lamplight around the stable door across the courtyard. He made his way towards this, nervously fingering the pommel of his sword.

As he pushed at it, the stable door gave way with a creak, and Fazad, who had been busy brushing at the old grey's flank, leapt up in wide-eyed alarm.

"Calm yourself, boy, it's only me," Jayal said, stepping quickly into the light. He looked around the stable at the empty stalls. They were black with dust and overhung with cobwebs, the straw now old and greying, the harbour of a thousand mice. "My lord?" the boy asked querulously.

At this the stranger in front of him seemed to wake from his reverie. He fixed the boy with as kindly a look as he could. "Do you know who you are? Whose inn this is?"

"Why sir, I am Fazad, an orphan and, and this is the house of my master Skerrib," he replied, a puzzled look on his face at the odd question.

"No!" Jayal shook his head vehemently. "Remember this: you are the son and heir of Count Falarn! You will never bow to these men again: do you promise me that?" He had seized the boy's shoulders, gripping him fiercely, but was rewarded by a look of complete bafflement on Fazad's part. It was obvious that the boy remembered nothing of his family.

"Never mind," he said, turning away. "I need some information that Skerrib and his fellows couldn't supply. Where else in the city could I make enquiries?"

If possible the boy's eyes widened even more. "Information? What sort of information?" he asked quaveringly.

"Best you don't know, boy; your master is suspicious enough as it is."

Fazad thought for a moment. "The few guests we get here tend to go to the Temple of Worms . . ."

Jayal broke in. "That is too dangerous."

"The Temple of Reh?"

"No, the gates will be locked for the night; there must be somewhere else."

"Well, there's a place up on the Spike. . . . It's where all the city guards spend the night."

Jayal thought for a moment: the city guard! He had had enough trouble getting past them at the gates. Now he would have to go voluntarily to an inn where there were going to be a number of them and where it would be even more difficult to conceal his true identity. His courage and his sword would have to suffice. He had only until dawn to find Thalassa; if, that was, she was still alive. "Tell me: which is the safest route to get there," he said, returning his gaze to the boy.

"But, surely you won't venture out after dark, sir? The un-dead will be in the streets," Fazad said stridently.

Jayal smiled, trying to hide his fear with the semblance of amusement. "You think anything out there is likely to bother me?"

"It's not just the vampires—the city guards are bad men, sir!"

"This place isn't so friendly either. The pilgrims for one."

"But you're a pilgrim, sir!"

Jayal smiled thinly. "Don't be taken in by appearances, boy: I'm not what I seem—I serve the Flame, and I need help. Is there another way out of here apart from the front door?"

Fazad thought for a moment. "There is the skylight at the top of the inn. It gives onto the battlements."

"But Skerrib just said that it is nailed shut."

"That's what he puts out." The boy shuddered. "But it's open. He's going to use it as a bolt-hole if the vampires ever get into the front of the inn."

"Even better!" Jayal exclaimed, patting him on the shoulder. "But I have to get past Skerrib; I don't trust him."

The boy nodded knowingly. "He's an informer at the Temple of Worms."

Jayal swore under his breath. "I should have guessed. Can

you get me to the skylight without being seen by him?" The boy nodded and scampered into the musty recesses of a stall. He returned clutching a verdigrised lantern. He took a light off the already burning one and applied it to the wick. The ancient copper glowed with a reddish gleam as the old wick finally caught light. Fazad trimmed it off, so it cast a more even brilliance.

"I have to leave one lamp burning; otherwise, my master will know I've gone," he explained. He went to the stable door and opened it a crack. He peered out. He gestured at Jayal—the coast was clear. They recrossed the courtyard quietly. But this time Fazad led them to a side door Jayal hadn't noticed before. Fazad slipped through it, followed by Jayal. They were in a dusty stairwell, the stairs zigzagging up into the darkness.

Fazad led the way, creeping upwards on tiptoe. The steps and banisters were rickety, festooned with cobwebs and scattered with broken furniture. The lantern cast long shadows. Rats scuttled away in the dark. They had nearly reached the upper storeys when a large mound of clothes lying on the floor of one of the landings suddenly stirred with an indignant sigh at their noise.

"What in Hel was that?" Jayal exclaimed, grabbing for his sword as the thing subsided again onto the floor.

"Shh! It's the master's wife," Fazad whispered. "Come! It's not far now."

They were now in the attic of the inn, crouching under low ceiling beams. They arrived underneath a barred shutter set into the roof of the inn. Fazad cautiously unbolted it, letting in a gust of cold night wind, wisped with fog.

"Go, quickly now," he said, giving Jayal a helping hand. Jayal hauled himself up through the opening, scrambling to keep his feet on the slick tiles of the inn's roof. He looked back at the lanternlit face of the boy.

"Take this for your pains," he said, handing him some of his last copper coins. The boy's face beamed with gratitude, but Jayal's heart froze over wondering if it would prove adequate compensation if Skerrib found out his part in his escape. "Look after Cloud," he whispered. "I'll be back at dawn." With that he grabbed at a crooked chimney pot, and started climbing up it to the battlements above. The bricks of the chimney were slick with moisture, but were so crooked that his booted feet found numerous toeholds.

Progress was relatively easy until he reached a flue which formed a ledge. He rested, looking back to the skylight. The boy had already shut it. He looked around, just as a flash of lightning illuminated the scene. The view was spectacular and eerie. Over the top of the battlements twenty feet above him he could see the red glow of the Sanctuary Flame in the mist-laden sky. Though the chimney stopped some ten feet short of the machicolations, the ancient wall seemed pitted with toeholds and liberally studded with sturdy-looking bushes growing from crevasses. Upwards there was no problem.

Below was another matter. The eaves of the inn seemed to plunge straight into a sea of mist, broken here and there by the tiled roofs of the Lower Town some five hundred feet below. The sea of mist looked like a bed of down that he could throw himself onto and be absorbed safely in a feathery embrace. . . . His head swam with vertigo.

He wrenched his eyes back up, level with the horizon. The moon Erewon shone wanly from the heavens, just in front of a black mass of storm clouds rolling in from the north. The moon threw the stickleback peaks of the mountains into sinister relief. Lightning flickered and, a few seconds later, there came a distant boom like the closing of a giant's door.

Feeling for footholds carefully in the dull red light from above, he resumed his climb up to the battlements.

CHAPTER NINE

The Man Who Came After Dark

Thalassa descended the stairs slowly, the train of her peignoir silkily pouring over the steps in a white waterfall behind her, her hair a dull burnished orange under the lights of the thousand flickering candles below. But though her step was measured, her mind was in turmoil at the prospect of the coming meeting with the High Priestess Malliana. The woman hated her, had victimised her ever since she had first come to the temple at the age of thirteen. As she had grown to womanhood things had only got worse until that fateful night when she had been summoned for the first time to Lord Faran.

She had made it her business to avoid the High Priestess, for bad only came of it when they met. Sometimes whole weeks passed without the two encountering each other. That it was this night of all nights that she had been called for struck her overexcited mind as more than coincidence. Had the plot been discovered? Yesterday evening there had been rumours that a number of Reh worshippers had been condemned to the stocks. But as yet she didn't know the men's names. Could it have been Randel and the others? Once more she was overcome by a feeling of powerlessness over her own fate—Malliana's pawn, Faran's pawn; the pawn of any man who would pay her hire. The escape had been her only chance of reclaiming her life.

The heaviness of her heart slowed her feet, then finally she stopped moving altogether, halfway down the wooden steps to the Greeting Room. She stood, one hand on the wooden banister of the staircase, staring abstractedly into the hall below.

Right below her she saw Furtal on his dais, bathed in the amber light of the candles, his hands moving over the lute, conjuring a melancholy air, which struck a chord with the weight of her thoughts. The notes seemed to fly upwards, towards the gloomy ceiling rafters; it was as if the music wished for escape from this place as much as she did. Furtal, too, had once known better times. He had been Illgill's court musician and poet: now he had to make do with the demands of the bawdy house, his masculinity gone along with his eyesight at the hands of Faran's torturers. But there was still freedom in his music. She began to step downwards again.

As if in response to her silent thoughts, Furtal's hand swept once more over the strings in a final, plangent chord, and he turned his unseeing eyes up to her just as she drew level with his dais. Despite his blindness, he had an uncanny knack of sensing her presence.

His high, reedy voice carried over the babble of the women. "Mistress, I greet you, and your beauty."

Thalassa had to smile at his archaic phraseology, despite the fear in her heart. She stopped, letting the woman who had come to fetch her disappear through the High Priestess's door below her. She had to speak to Furtal.

"Malliana wants to see me," she whispered, staring ahead at the door through which she would have to pass any minute.

"I know," Furtal said, likewise not looking at her, his blind eyes staring into the mid distance. "Have courage, midnight is not far away."

"Until then," Thalassa said, some strength returning to her limbs.

Furtal immediately struck up another tune. This one was bawdy and racing, fitting in with the ribald persona he adopted for the other acolytes.

Some of the other women had stared at them during their brief exchange. Thalassa ignored them, concentrating on the door to her right, with its vivid depiction of intertwined limbs. None of the looks of the other women were friendly, and never

had been in the seven years she had been in the temple. After
all, she was an aristocrat, an Eaglestone, one who had enjoyed
privileges before the war that none of these others had ever had.
Like the High Priestess, they rejoiced in her downfall. For the
moment she didn't care. After tonight she would either be dead
or free, and this gilded prison would be behind her forever.

The thought of it lifted her heart; finally, after seven years
the moment of truth had arrived. Whichever way the events of
the next few hours went, nothing would be the same again.
Freedom or death were the only options.

Just as she reached the bottom step there came a distant
boom of thunder from outside and with it came a gust of fresher
air which caused the candlelight to shift suddenly before settling again. Her eyes went to the open doorway through which
the brazier burned, welcoming any of those brave enough to
risk the streets after dark.

Thalassa stopped, a chill of premonition seizing her. There
came an almighty flash of light from outside as the night was
split apart by a filigree of lightning playing over the skies; another roll of thunder echoed about the hall, accompanied by a
gust of wind which set the candles flickering once more.

Then a figure, dressed in a dark hooded cape, stepped into
the pool of light cast by the brazier. His appearance, so soon
after the lightning, caused shrieks of alarm from the other
acolytes, but the man ignored them, stepping into the hallway,
shaking rainwater from his dark cloak. His head flicked from
side to side. Then he saw Thalassa and his gaze, partly concealed by the hood, came to rest on her. The man held himself
in a hunched position as if his back was cricked, so that his
head was at an odd angle. Despite the shadows of the hood that
concealed his face, only one eye glimmered out at her, an eye
that was fever bright. It seemed to drink in her form as eagerly
as a man dying of thirst drinks the ice-cold water of a well. Thalassa knew the look well: the man had been an irregular visitor
to the temple for the last three years. He must have come some
dozen times in that period, never removing his hood on any of
those occasions. And every time he had asked for her.

She remembered the first time, a stormy night not unlike this
one. Then, as now, the hall had fallen silent at his entrance. He

had whispered something to one of the priestesses at the door, and they had turned, pointing Thalassa out. But already the man's single eye had sought and found her, and the priestess's words went unheeded. He must have somehow guessed that this was the woman he was looking for. Or maybe he had already known what she looked like. Certainly there was nothing visible under his hood and in his hunched posture that reminded Thalassa of anyone she had known in her past life. Nor could she find out easily who he was, because the temple respected those who wished to hide their identities; he could remain hidden by his hood for as long as he cared.

He'd retired to a shadowy corner of the room, his single eye never leaving her during the dancing. Afterwards he'd placed a heavy bag of gold in front of the High Priestess, pointing her out as the one he wanted. But for some reason Malliana had refused. The man had showed anger, his hand reaching for his sword. But he'd stopped himself and, with a mocking laugh, walked out into the night, as if he had no fear of the vampires, or a care for the gold he'd left behind. At first Thalassa had thought Malliana's strategy a cunning ruse to increase her asking price, for the High Priestess often did this with her top women, refusing once and then taking more the second time. But when the man had returned with an even heavier bag of gold months later, Malliana had refused again. This scenario had been repeated time and time again, on each occasion the man had contemptuously left his purse and strode out into the night.

Now the enigma stared at her, and she wondered what had possessed him to brave the night all those times, when Thrull was locked up against the vampires and no one wandered the streets. And why had he chosen this night of portents particularly? Other guests arrived long before sunset and waited for the dancing in a separate room. Only he had ever come after dark.

Just as she had these thoughts the door to the right of the staircase opened and the High Priestess appeared. Her face was creased in its perpetual scowl of displeasure. She wore a green satin dress which threw off the near emerald green of her eyes. It was cut low at front and back, revealing leathery expanses of flesh. Her black hair was tied back in a severe bun, her painted eyebrows arched in haughty interrogation. As always, her green eyes were ringed by sooty circles of kohl; her lips were heavily rouged, and turned down in disdain, riding a proudly elevated chin. To complement her attire she wore a black fur stole around her neck. She seemed to carry another stole in her arms, but then it stirred its black head, revealing itself as a cat. Its green eyes surveyed the intruder with the same malevolent calculation as its mistress.

"So, you have come again," she said archly.

"Yes, I have come," the newcomer replied with a dangerous growl in his voice. "And you know why." He pointed a gloved finger at Thalassa. "I have come for her."

A frozen smile played over Malliana's lips. "Then my answer has to be the same as it was when you came last: no. Thalassa has been engaged elsewhere tonight."

"I have gold."

"As you have said before, and for that gold there are plenty of others, but not Thalassa."

"So you cross me again?" The response was edged with menace.

"Anyone who braves the night to come here is welcome," the High Priestess responded. "But Thalassa is engaged for other things."

But the man was remorseless. "No other will suffice. I will wait and see whether you have a change of heart. Ten gold says you will." He tossed a clinking purse into a copper tray by the entrance. He bent himself awkwardly into a cramped bow, and retreated into the shadows.

Malliana ignored the offering. "Your gold buys you sanctuary from the night, and any of the others; but not Thalassa." She snapped her fingers. "Let the other men enter," she ordered, sending some of the women hurrying to the side door, behind which customers were waiting. "You come with me," she said, gesturing imperiously at Thalassa. Thalassa came down the last steps, shuddering as she passed the figure.

She followed Malliana through the doors of her chambers, conscious of the man's gaze on her back. The doors were shut emphatically behind her by Viri, the woman who had fetched her from her room, one of Malliana's most loyal acolytes.

Once more Thalassa was conscious of her life being out of control and for others to command. And she wondered again whether the plot had been discovered. Surely not. She tried to calm herself, thinking of the promise of freedom at midnight. That couldn't be taken away now, could it? She avoided the High Priestess' eyes, looking around the familiar room, the very sight of which filled her heart with gloom. It was bedecked with swathes of red satin which covered the ceiling, walls and most of the furniture. Gold and gold leaf glinted from the arms and legs of every stick of furniture. A fire roared in the grate. Any warmth in the effect was swiftly dispelled when her eyes returned to Malliana's icy gaze.

"Who is that man?" the High Priestess demanded.

The question, out of all the possible ones, was almost a relief, for Thalassa genuinely didn't know the answer to it. She shook her head. "I've told you before; I never saw him before he came to the temple."

Malliana advanced on her menacingly, the cat tossed idly to one side with a piteous meow. "You're lying of course, lying like all your kind." She stood eyeball to eyeball with Thalassa, a complex scent of old perfume and stale breath wafting over the girl's face. "Clients don't ask for the same woman time and time—unless they have a reason. So tell me quickly. Who is he and what does he want?"

She had bent one of her hands back as if she were about to slap Thalassa round the face. The girl threw up her arms to ward off the expected blow.

"I tell you, I don't know. There are some men who're like that—they fix on you . . . won't let you go."

Malliana let her hand fall back to her side, nodding sarcastically. "Lies again; men don't 'fix' upon people so casually, even the likes of you, particularly if it means risking the streets at night." She swept around, so her back was turned to Thalassa. "Never mind, I have taken his gold. After tonight he won't come again."

Thalassa looked at her in confusion: what did she mean? Would the High Priestess summon the temple guards and have the man thrown out for the vampires? That would hardly encourage the other guests. Malliana turned to her again. There was an unusual sparkle in her eyes—a sparkle that didn't bode well. She crossed her arms, her mouth creasing in a small smile as if anticipating the reaction to her next words.

"You will be leaving here tonight. Prepare yourself."

"Leaving?" Thalassa asked, her mind suddenly reeling. It must be the plot; they *had* been discovered.

Again, Malliana paused as if savouring the moment. "Yes, Faran has bought you; you will belong to him after midnight."

All the colour drained from Thalassa's already pale face. She fought the giddiness that made her legs tremble and nearly give way. "No," she muttered. "It can't be." Anger gave her strength, and she stumbled forward, lashing out at the High Priestess with her fists. But before she could land a blow, she was seized from behind by Viri. Malliana had chosen her well—she was strong-thewed and muscled: more than a match for the painfully thin Thalassa. Viri pinned her arms. Thalassa struggled ineffectually against her iron grip.

Malliana's green eyes glinted in the dim lighting of the room, enjoying the tussle. "A hundred gold is not the sum I would have once expected for you, but it is all I can expect since you have become so pale and wan and pinched. Luckily you are going to the man who has made you so; otherwise, I'd expect him to ask for his money back." She squeezed Thalassa's bare arm as if to illustrate how thin and valueless she was. The girl struggled some more, but Viri was too strong.

"Let me go!" she screamed, but her discomfort only further added to Malliana's pleasure.

"So, Thalassa, you had your chance: you could have been amenable. But, no, you still had that blue blood in your veins, even when you came here as a slave. I wish Faran had known about you before you came here, then I would have saved the food I've wasted on you."

"What, and have lost Faran's gold?" Thalassa replied defiantly.

But her defiance only amused Malliana. "Speak your mind. It will be the last time you have the chance. And it won't help your damnable old nurse."

At this Thalassa stilled. "What do you intend to do with Alanda?"

"Why, what do you think? Throw her out for the vampires. She won't be any use to me when you're gone."

In an instant Thalassa had forgotten her anger in anxiety over her friend. Alanda would die on the streets; she was too old. "Do what you like with me, but spare her," she begged.

Malliana smiled frigidly again. "Maybe I will, maybe I will; but in return I'll want something more from you." She paused, finger on lip, as if she were thinking of a particular treat for Thalassa, rather than something which would undoubtedly turn out to be another extreme humiliation.

Thalassa closed her eyes. Given to Faran and soon to receive the fatal bite; what more could she give?

"You will serve me as normal up to midnight," Malliana said eventually. "Then you will go to Faran."

"And Alanda?" Thalassa asked.

"If you serve me well, I'll spare her. She can be made useful carrying out the scullery slops."

Barely knowing what she was doing, Thalassa nodded her assent. She had little hope of the High Priestess's keeping her word, but she would do anything to give Alanda the slightest chance. Seresh might still rescue her.

She allowed herself to be led from the room. Her head was ringing, and she didn't hear the babble of voices or Furtal's music, though she saw the room was now filling with the men who had been waiting in the antechamber. Young and old, priests of Reh and Iss, city guards, faded merchants, they eyed her curiously, her pale face at odds with the gaiety of the painted women who crowded around them, soliciting their attention. Thalassa barely noticed them. Her eyes swept the room, seeking out Alanda. But the old lady was nowhere to be seen—she must be in Thalassa's room still. Instead her gaze came to rest on the hooded man sitting apart, an untasted goblet in front of him on a wooden table. He rose when he saw her. She stared at him, wondering whether he could help her. But she shook her head: Malliana had already refused him. Her guest for tonight would be a further surprise of the High Priestess's: a man dying of the plague would most likely be her lot, then Faran.

Furtal began to pluck the strings of his lute in a stately pavane. The women detached themselves from the men and stepped up onto the dais, shedding diaphanous throws and shawls as they did so, looking over their shoulders to see what effect the naked limbs beneath had on their guests. All of the men's eyes apart from the stranger's were locked on them, their noisy chatter silenced as they drank in the sight of the women. Thalassa had a few seconds only, then she too would have to join the others.

There, finally, was Alanda, standing at the head of the stairs. She was staring hard at Thalassa, clearly sensing something was wrong.

Thalassa broke away from Viri and ran up towards her. Viri watched her go: enjoying the look of surprise and horror that crossed the old woman's face as Thalassa whispered urgently to her, then turned on her heels, throwing off her shawl as she descended the stairs once more. She stepped up onto the dais to join the others.

The dancing had started, but Thalassa quickly joined in with the steps of the other women, moving robotically, but keeping time, her eyes gazing vacantly in front of her. There were five hours before midnight. Seresh would come then, but so too Faran's guards. Who would be first?

Her feet moved unconsciously as outside there came another flash of lightning and a boom of thunder which for a moment drowned out the noise of Furtal's lute. She prayed that Seresh would hurry, before it was too late.

CHAPTER TEN

The Pool of Blinding

Darkness.

Urthred sat alone on the stone parapet at the edge of the Pool of Blinding: sat, it seemed, on the very edge of the world. Below him the cliffs fell straight down to the roiling mists of the plain a thousand feet below. The newly risen moon hung in the hazy night sky. Lightning flashed. A storm was approaching.

The pool was behind him, some fifty yards square, its surface matt black and unruffled by the coming storm; the only lights showing on it were the hazy reflection of the moon and the red of the Sanctuary Flame. Itinerant monks like him had once come here when the city was a place of pilgrimage for the worshippers of Reh. He'd heard the stories: how the most fanatical had stared into the sun from dawn to dusk until they were utterly blind and the glory of Reh was forever more imprinted on their minds.

Urthred, like them, had sacrificed much for Reh, but, unlike the blinded monks, Urthred had given everything but his sight. The hands he'd flung up to protect his eyes eight years ago had saved them, but little else. The hands themselves were now no more than charred stumps, only given movement and articulation by his gloves.

"Blinded by the glory of Reh": so the monks at Forgeholm

had spoken of those men. Once, before the Burning, he would have actually envied those men their unhappy state. Now his scarred body was penalty enough. He had given enough to his god.

He guessed from the weed-grown pavement all around him that not many of his fellow worshippers came here now; in these last days of the sun a man could look deep into its red orb from hour to hour and his sight would be unharmed, Reh's power was so diminished.

Surely the world would end soon. Surely Reh was lost in his brother Iss' dark labyrinth, the golden thread that Galadrian gave him to find the dawn broken on one of the pillars of his dark hall.

And surely he, Urthred, would die, with the sun, at this place where devout men had prayed in the zenith of the world.

For the moment there was no sign of pursuit. His heart had stilled after his pell-mell flight. Now anger and sorrow settled on him in almost equal measure. First, his brother: killed in front of him. He'd had his revenge, but was it enough? He would have liked to have killed all the traitors at the temple. Urthred ground his teeth. With Randel's death, the explanation of why he'd been summoned to Thrull had been lost. He didn't know another living soul in the city. Without friends, there was no escape. He was certain he would be dead before dawn.

Behind him the inky blackness of the pool stretched back to the city. The pool was built on a promontory, with open views to the east, south and west. No one could get to this parapet on its far side before first immersing themselves in its waters. This was an advantage, for the undead would not willingly endure water. Their flesh, dried after centuries of dusty internment, sloughed away with any contact with it. No, it would have to be the living who came to kill him. All the better: he would fight and die without risking the vampire's bite. He would not be bitten, would not become one of the undead, a soul without fire, forever harnessed to the decay of the body.

The wind was getting up, plucking streamers of mist from the plains and throwing them up to his vantage point. The moisture-laden air whistled past him, settling on his cloak, but it was soaking wet from the pool anyway. Now he barely noticed the chattering of his teeth. He wondered how long it would be before hypothermia set in. He braced himself mentally for a cold death: he'd been told by the monks at Forgeholm that such a death was often accompanied by strange visions and dreams. He would know the end had come when he began to have them.

But, as he settled once more and his mind replayed the events of the day, what had just passed seemed as strange as any cold-induced hallucination: first the old man and the robbers on the mountain path, the return of his magic after eight empty years, then the gruelling march to the city, the temple square, the stocks, the vampires, then the sacrifice, his brother's and then Varash's death, the arrival of the acolytes for the evening ritual. Finally, his dive through the windows at the back of the chamber.

It should have ended there: the glass breaking outwards in an explosion of multicoloured shards. The hard rock of the dry stone moat a hundred feet below hurrying up to him, hurrying the impact which would have broken every bone in his body.

But his instinct for life had conquered any wish for death; in the split second he began to fall he had seen to one side a gargoyle head butting out of the cornice just below the level of the window. His hand had shot out and grabbed it. Curiously, he had time to take in the details of the sculpture down to the tiniest pockmark in the ancient stonework: a dragon crossed with a dog, spouting a tiny tongue of flame. All this he saw in the split second it took for his right hand to clamp down onto the creature's neck and for his left to swing up also and take it in a strong embrace, his arm sockets nearly popping out as his downward force was checked. He'd swung, one way and then another, his legs dangling into space. He'd stared up at the stone effigy; its hideous bulging eyes, its snake-like tongue, its fiery scales. Now the wide arc of his swinging feet was checked, and the metal claws of the glove gouged grooves into the pitted stone of the statue.

He should have rested, but his arms were on fire, and his heartbeat exploding in his chest, and he could hear the cries of the acolytes from within the chamber. He dared the God and the

infinite space beneath him again and reached out to his left, to the
edge of the cornice, an even flimsier handhold than the one he
had at the moment. His hand caught the curved lip of the cornice,
but then carried straight through it as the rotted lip of the stone
gave way, sending a shower of dust spiralling down to the bottom
of the moat. His other hand was losing its grip on the statue's
neck; he wrenched up his left hand onto the cornice again, and
this time the stone didn't give way. He kicked his sandalled feet
into its crumbling surface. He hung thus, his arms outstretched
and burning, and turned his head in the direction of the High
Priest's window.

The massive body of the gargoyle now hid him from view.
Soon one of the acolytes might work out what had happened,
but he had time. He glanced down; the void pulsed up, urging
him to let go, to join the pull of gravity. He fought the vertigo,
blinking his eyes. Now he looked again, seeing what he had
hoped for in the gathering gloom of the evening: a thick, knotted vine which crept up and over the cornice to his left. He
clamped one hand over another and then another, crosswise, his
legs spinning, the cornice beginning to crumble again. Just one
more movement and he would be there. . . .

The cornice gave just as his left hand grabbed the foot-thick
vine. It took his weight, its ancient grip on the temple stone
strong enough to hold him. He swayed out as the parapet
plunged down and smashed into a thousand fragments in the
moat below. Another excited cry from the watchers at the window: now they would know how he'd got away. Not sparing a
moment he began to climb down the vine, the metal claws digging deep, ripping it away from the lichen-covered stone, the
thick cords of the vine sending down more dust. His body was
now soaked in sweat, but at last his feet touched solid ground.
A pile of ancient rubble lay in the moat, and he scrambled up it,
reaching level ground. In front of him stood the shattered, fire-
blackened ruins of the citadel. Behind him the stepped mass of
the pyramid, and, at its base, the fifty-foot sheer drop into the
moat, and the broken window from which he could see the frantic gesticulations of the acolytes as they at last saw him. Over to
his right, a group of orange-and-red-cloaked pursuers bundled

out of the main gate, looking about them wildly. They spotted him almost immediately and set off towards him at a run.

But Urthred was already moving, plunging into the dark, ivy-hung ruins of the citadel. Ten thousand men had once been garrisoned here—its ruins stretched over nearly half the summit of the rock. Bats erupted from the shadows as he rushed through a succession of rubble-strewn courtyards, the cries of his pursuers nearing by the second.

He came to the entrance of a passageway that slanted downwards; its sides were pierced at regular intervals with arrow slits through which the evening light spread like a red fan. He hurled himself down it and stopped in the darkness, listening as his pursuers ran past it. He paused for a second to regain his breath, then moved on, finding an old postern gate, ripped from its hinges and lying on its side, giving onto a gloomy, cobbled side alley at its end. The cries of pursuit got fainter and fainter in the ruins behind him. Then they were swallowed up by the great hush that settled over the city as the darkness fell. Now he heard new noises: strange screeches and chittering sounds coming from the citadel's underground cellars. Vampires? He didn't stay to find out but moved on through the gate. It exited from the citadel wall into a dank alleyway that might never have seen the light of the sun. Moss grew everywhere and there was the stink of vegetal decay.

He got to the end of the alley and looked left and right down a broader avenue leading to the east under the lee of the pyramid of Reh. He'd almost doubled back on himself, and he was confident that, for the moment at least, he had lost his pursuers. He screwed up his eyes made doubly blind by the restrictive eye slits of the mask and moved off down the alley. It soon joined the inner curtain wall, then ran parallel to it towards the southeast. He found himself in a ghost city: ivy-hung, windowless houses, their roofs collapsed, their shadows dark and sinister. Even at this height, wreaths of fog were already beginning to form. He kept moving in a circular movement to the south, towards the last glimmer of light from the setting sun. Then a lightening of the gloom told him he was nearing the edge of the cliffs overlooking the plain. There, glimmering in the lychlight of the newly risen moon, he saw the edge of the pool, dark cypress trees ringed round it standing up like dark sentinels into the darkening sky.

He'd crept up on the spot, keeping to the sides of the ruined buildings. He'd got to an ironwork gate overlooking the expanse of water. There was a splashing and he saw a stream issuing from a fountainhead into the inky black pool. Beyond the pool he could see the edge of the world; the last fire-streaked line of sunset over the mountains to the right, the rising blanket of mists from the plains far beyond, the bone white causeway glimmering through the mist, the pyramid of skulls, its whiteness seeming to grow with the darkness.

He'd taken stock of his situation. Soon all of Faran's men and the traitors at the temple of Reh would be looking for him. Some of Faran's men would be the undead, and he'd heard tell how the vampires could smell human blood from fifty yards away. And fifty yards seemed the width of the pool in front of him. A narrow margin of safety, but a chance he'd have to take. Returning through the streets meant death; here he might be safe until the morning.

He climbed the gate, then hitched up his robes and stepped into the pool. He felt the icy chill of the pool envelop first his calves and then his waist. The water seemed to get deeper and deeper; now he was up to his chest, the darkness like a helmet over his head, the mist coiling about his upper body. Then his feet lost touch with the bottom of the pool and he sank, twisting down, deeper and deeper, into the dark bottomless depths. He felt the pressure of the water pushing up from deep beneath the ancient rock, from the arteries of the great swampy plain, from the roaring torrents of the mountains. . . . Then, as his lungs were about to burst, he was hurled back to the surface. His gloves found themselves holding on to the far edge of the platform, and he heaved himself up, gasping for breath.

He found himself on the very lip of the cliffs. The darkling plain lay a thousand feet beneath him, the blue lights that roamed over its vastness no bigger than fireflies. He lay back on the cold stone, watching Erewon rise, watching the sweep of the sky across the great amphitheatre of the mountains and the red glow of the temple fires, the circling birds of prey silhouetted by their light.

That had been two hours before. Then he prayed through teeth chattering with the cold for his brother, for the safe harbouring of his bones in the fiery Paradise of the Sun. Then, when his prayers ran out, he repeated, over and over, one of the sacred mantras.

> Oh sacred seed of fire,
> Kindle in me warm desire:
> Let not night and evil force
> Conquer your eternal laws.

They were words that he had not thought much of since the Burning at Forgeholm, but, as if in answer to his hour of greatest need, it was as if the God heard him and brought a fiery tingle to his veins—he was alive, and active, the desire for revenge on this city burning fiercely in his soul. The city which had killed Randel. Deep within him he felt the God had woken after eight years' slumber. Despite the chill, warmth flooded through him, and a corresponding tingling of energy brushed through his fingertips—energy that had been lost to him since the Burning; energy he'd not expected to return to him. Yet today, first in the mountains and then in the square, fire had burst from his gloved hands for the first time in all those years.

Where had it come from? Manichee had promised that his powers would return, but even when he'd left Forgeholm he'd had no hope that this would ever be so. Only when confronted by the bandits in the pass had he felt that long-forgotten sensation—the savage song in his veins, and the magma of righteous anger exploding from his heart and through his fingertips before his own astonished eyes. Then he'd felt the power of those early days once more. It was just as Manichee had prophesied.

He sat by the pool in silent contemplation of the miracle, in a state half between waking and dreaming; never since the Burning had he felt Reh so close. He watched the moon rising and the flicker and swirl of the blue lights through the mists on the plains below, then, with ever greater frequency, the distant flash of lightning over the peaks.

Now the cold began to gnaw away at his fleeting mood of exultation. His teeth began chattering more and more from the cold. He waited for the visions which would presage death.

What had the monks told him all those years before? First the cold-induced hallucinations, then one's life, replayed with painstaking acuity. As if on cue, his mind took him back, to his first conscious thoughts and then beyond, to before memory, to what he had recreated from what the monks had told him of his strange arrival at Forgeholm Monastery, on a day even colder than this twenty years before . . .

CHAPTER ELEVEN

The Burning

A day twenty years before—the depths of winter.
Forgeholm Monastery, high in the Fire Mountains,
where the tree line ended and the snows began. Concealed in a
hidden valley, its walls, buried in the drifts, were nearly invisible in the white wilderness of crags and peaks which surrounded it. Lowering over the whole scene was the massive
volcanic crater that the monks called The Old Father. A column
of smoke issued from the top of its twenty-thousand-foot peak,
mingling with the clouds which swathed its summit. The Old
Father had been quiet in living memory, but history told of
eruptions which had buried the land for miles about in ash.
Some said the monastery had been founded so that the priests
of Reh could intercede with the God not to punish the poor
farmers on the plains. But if the story was true, it was now
mostly forgotten, and so for the most part was Forgeholm, in its
isolated valley.

The passes up to the monastery had been blocked by man-
high drifts for several weeks. But the stranger came, he and his
horse appearing out of the winter landscape like ghosts. He
came not by the west road that led to the plains of Surrenland—
the only one ever used by the monks and the few pilgrims that
made their way to Forgeholm—but by the old road to the north
that looped around the base of The Old Father and disappeared

in the direction of the far-distant peaks of the Palisades. At first the monk at the gate, whose eyes had been fixed on the road to Surrenland, couldn't understand how the man had got there. But then he saw the line of hoofprints leading over the virgin snow to the north.

He turned to the rider, many questions on his lips. The man's face was partly hidden by a coarse woollen hood, hoared with ice. The monk caught a glimpse of a frozen white beard and a hint of dark, coal-like eyes. There was something menacing in the look, and the monk's questions dried on his lips. The horse stamped impatiently in the snow outside the gate, and the monk saw that it wore a mailed surcoat over its flank and back as he had heard knight's horses sometimes wore. A wickerwork basket was slung across the front of the saddle. The man hauled it up and the monk saw that it was a crib. The rider handed it down to him. He was too surprised to refuse it, staggering slightly under its weight. He saw two infants inside it swathed in layer after layer of blankets. One was only a few months old, the other about two.

When he spoke, the stranger did so in accent unfamiliar to the monk. He told him the children's names, Randel and Urthred; also their family name, Ravenspur, a place neither the monk nor, when he told them it later, any of his colleagues had heard of. Then without another word, and before the monk regained enough of his wits to stop him, the stranger had turned his horse and rode off into the snowbound landscape. The monk had watched him, his ears deafened by the wailing of the babies, as he got smaller and smaller in the whiteness until he was a mere speck against the side of The Old Father. Then horse and rider had disappeared from view. If it had not been for the crib which he held in his hands, he would have believed the whole incident a dream.

He had bustled into the main courtyard of the monastery, calling out to the other monks. Gradually, they assembled in the snow, peering at the children in the crib. No one so young had been seen at the monastery for centuries: all the noviciates were twelve or more when they came. They chattered uncertainly about what to do with the children. Some were for leaving them for the birds of prey—food was short, the winter long. But others argued that in time here were two fine boys who one day would tend the herds and chop wood for the ageing population of the monastery. The opinions of these last prevailed, but only just.

If the stranger had cared for his charges, he could not have delivered them to a harsher place for their upbringing. The monks had been coarsened by the rigour of their calling and the harshness of their surroundings and had no sentiment for young infants.

In the first days Urthred had been weaned with goat's milk fed through a punctured sheep's intestine by a blind monk. By a miracle, he had survived. But, with the cold, the beatings and the lack of food, he had grown over the years into a thin, ethereal child. The monks, used to backbreaking physical exertion, cursed his weakness, and redoubled their beatings with the stout sticks they called their correctors. In those early years, Urthred had learned to be strong in spirit at least, for being strong was the only way of cheating the birds of prey which circled the flat roof of the monastery waiting for the next corpse to be laid out. And every month in the winter there was likely to be another one, dead through exhaustion, disease or the cold. To begin with the two brothers had been inseparable, protecting each other as best they could, but soon Urthred had had to learn to survive without his brother, who was sent away to the temple at Thrull when he was eight and Urthred six.

With Randel's departure from the monastery, Urthred lost his only friend. The other boys were cowed and sullen, eager to betray their schoolmates to gain small favours from the monks. In this, they studied well for their futures, for the older monks were as mean-spirited and unyielding as the mountain goats they tended. They swooped down on any spark of liveliness or joy in their young charges like sparrowhawks on prey. Many compensated for the hardship of their lives by drinking deep of the corn liquor Viseg. The spirit set fire to the men's veins. When drunk on it their cruelty was boundless. Many of them could not read, or had forgotten how to, their lessons punctuated by the sound of the rod striking flesh as much as by the Holy Writs being recited.

The hardship of the monastery threw Urthred in upon himself. As he grew he became more and more withdrawn and introverted. He began to hear strange voices, voices so real he often mistook them for the actual voices of the monks. And beneath these other voices, in a barely audible bass note, he heard another sound. It seemed to come from deep within the monastery, where the Sanctuary Flame burned in a shrine buried deep in the rock. Sometimes he wondered whether it was the voice of the God who dwelt there. As he got older, he became more and more convinced that it was.

The voice spoke to him alone of all the pupils, of this he was sure. He felt its pull wherever he was: in the seminary or in the boulder-filled fields on the mountainside. He decided he must get nearer to it. The desire was like a persistent itch he could not rid himself of, even in his dreams. And the more he heard the voice, the more convinced he was that it came from the depths of the earth under the monastery, where the sacred fire burned. One day when he was twelve he gathered his courage and descended the rock-cut steps into the bowels of the monastery, where the foundation stones blended with the rock of the mountains. His sandals echoed back to him as he cautiously made his way downwards until he reached a large cave hung with stalactites. He had only seen it on high feast days before. Otherwise, it was a forbidden place, off-limits to any but the Elder of the Monastery.

It was silent and very dark save for the orange Hearth Flame flickering deep down in its fissure at the back of the cave. He felt a cold fear creeping through him. The place was said to be a haunted place from the time, in the early days of the temple, novitiates like him had been sacrificed to the Flame.

The pool where the High Priest washed himself on days of Absolution steamed faintly in the heat of the fire. As he got closer to it, the very rocks seemed to sweat, while the roaring Flame concealed in the deep fissure filled his mind with an echo of the sound he had been hearing for the past months. It was the sound of a furnace when its door is opened—for the first time in days the other voices in his mind were silenced. The heat permeated through him, filling his veins with an energy he had never felt before.

Never in a scripture lesson in the schoolrooms above had he

felt the presence of the God. But here he felt it, and the glowing grew within him as if Reh had leant down and with one of his fiery beams lit up his heart. On a whim, he stretched out his hand: he felt a strange tingling in his veins, and a shimmering in the air in front of him. Then fire blossomed from his fingertips before his astonished eyes, filling the cavern with roiling orange flame. He staggered back from what he had conjured, as awed by what he had summoned as if another had brought it to life.

At once he knew what this meant: he was a conjuror of flame, a pyromancer. Everything that Reh had created at the beginning of time had a seed of fire implanted in it. But only one or two men every generation knew the secret of how to tease it out, to make fire blossom from the air and the earth.

Gradually, his courage returned. He swept his right hand in a wide arc. A dragon of flame, conjured from the supercharged air, exploded into being, swooping through the cavern, gouting flame, throwing wild shadows over the ancient walls. His fear forgotten, the boy shrieked in delight and the knowledge of his power. The dragon raced round and round, high and low, its glittering eyes gold, its body beneath its wings slick and red with fire, its beak opening to let out huge gouts of flame. The boy danced with it, abandoned in the joy of his power.

Then, in one of the blossoms of fire, Urthred saw movement back where the steps descended into the cavern, and a coweled figure running back up them. One of the monks. The moment Urthred saw him, the conjured being was snuffed in the instant, leaving only a wispy band of smoke in the air.

He had been discovered, and life was never the same afterwards. Soon all the monks knew; an Adept, a sorcerer, in the whole Empire only one every generation was given this gift. But they didn't tell what they knew to the monastery Elder. They were jealous of the boy's powers, powers they would never have.

The Elder's name was Manichee, another of those who could summon the fire from air and stone. A man who could see the shadow world as clearly as this one. The monks held him in awe: what he thought of them was unknown—he led the life of a virtual recluse in a high tower of the monastery, only appearing every few days to listen to Tenebrae and take a frugal supper in the chilly Great Hall where the monks and the boys ate each night, or on days of oblation, descending alone to the pool in the Sanctuary to wash himself. Some said that he had been banished here by the temple hierarchy, his knowledge too deep for the shallow bureaucrats who ran the Temple of Reh. The Elder kept to his tower all that week of Urthred's discovery, whilst, unbeknownst to him, the monks conspired to destroy the young boy.

The Day of the Burning: the monastery's seminary, high in the eaves of the many-storeyed building. The peaks had been obscured by grey banks of cloud, the wind bitter and cold through the window opening where the panes of alabaster glass had been broken by last year's storms and never replaced. The forty pupils, aged from twelve years upwards, shivered in their tattered cloaks, wrapping them ever closer round their thin frames as their breath sent great clouds of condensation out into the chilly room. Their teacher, Midian, stood in front of them, mounted on a stone pulpit, which once had been carved like the phoenix arising from the ashes, but was now so defaced by the graffiti of a hundred generations of students that the mythical bird was hardly recognisable.

Midian suddenly shut the sacred text he'd been reading aloud with a great clap of leather-bound boards. A small haze of dusty particles flew up from the ancient pages. His reading had been a stilted affair anyway: he was barely literate and only remembered the words by rote as they had been instilled in him when he had been as young as his current pupils. Midian was as mean-spirited as the worst of the monks: his thinning thatch of red hair accentuated the red blood vessels of his nose and his bloodshot eyes. He was a drunk, an addict of Viseg.

His character was all too apparent to his pupils, who shied away from him, a fact which only further enraged him. His character had become progressively more vicious the forty years he'd been at the monastery. He seized on any opportunity to bully the children in his classes. Now, bored with his sham reading, he was looking for someone to vent his anger on.

But beatings alone would have exhausted his pleasure too

quickly: mental degradation and humiliation always preceded the use of his corrector. The schoolroom was his theatre, and, like an accomplished actor, he would play the room full of boys, enlisting some of the weaker ones, encouraging them to join him in the mockery of one of their fellows, changing his favourites at whim, keeping the shivering boys guessing on whom the beating would descend.

The pupils knew this, and were careful to avoid Midian's bloodshot eyes as the teacher stepped down from the lectern, the corrector clutched in one gnarled hand, his eyes darting hither and thither under his hooded lids.

As was customary, his tormenting began with an oblique question:

"We all have qualities, do we not, boys, things at which we're exceptional?" he croaked, his eyes darting inquisitorially about the room, inflamed with the inextinguishable anger of a drunk. "And you, my lambs"—spittle on his lips meant that the words came out with a curious hissing noise—"have all been chosen by the God for hidden qualities. Only time will bring them out: time and the rod!" He thwacked the corrector, a three-foot length of hazelwood, solidly against the palm of his hand. He was now in front of the first rank of wooden desks, his head rotating slowly like a lizard in search of prey.

"You!" he said, suddenly rapping his corrector down on the rough-hewn desk in front of him. The boy seated there nearly jumped off his seat in his fright, but Midian's eyes were not fixed on him: they were focused further back in the gloom at the far end of the room. "Kevar. Is that not your name?" Though he addressed him, his eyes stared right past the child like a blind man's. "Y-Yes sir," Kevar replied, shaking like a leaf. He was a new arrival, unused to the game. "So, Kevar, why don't you tell us what your village priest found so wonderful in your runty little body that he sent you here?"

Kevar's mouth opened once or twice, but terror had silenced him, and only an uninterpretable moan came out, much like the sound of a yawning dog. Other boys, fancying that Kevar now would get the brunt of Midian's anger, snickered, siding against their new companion. "What? What, boy? Speak up, I can't hear!" Midian said, cupping his hand to his ear, feigning deafness. He brought the corrector down on the desktop again with a sharp crack, but only elicited another inarticulate moan from Kevar. "So, we're all going to have to study farmyard noises to make anything of your piglike grunts, boy . . ." A feeble laugh came from Kevar's classmates at this jest. "Never mind," he said tetchily, disappointed with the poor sport, his bloodshot eyes already seeking another victim. "Wait outside, and I'll deal with you later."

Kevar got up and scuttled towards the heavy oak door to the schoolroom, but not before Midian's heavy hand had thickened his ear with a resounding slap.

"Now, lad," he said when Kevar was gone, pointing to the next in line, a swarthy southern boy who, if the teacher had been a constant man, might have been called one of his favourites. "You're to be a temple guard, are you not?"

The boy gulped nervously at being singled out. "Yes, sir," he managed to reply. "I was wrestling champion of my village . . ."

"Wrestling champion?" Midian's eyes rolled in mock admiration, bringing out another snicker from the class.

"Then, boy"—with one pantherlike movement he'd grabbed the boy's ear—"why did you lose your wrestling bout with Haldor yesterday?" He gave the ear a savage twist, eliciting a yelp of pain. "Learn to be a man, boy, not a mouse!" He spun on his heel and stalked down the aisle between the desks, his eyes still locked on the back of the room. "Next, you," he said, pointing the corrector to a small wiry boy newly arrived with Kevar. "Your name?"

"So please you sir, Taldon."

"Learn quickly, Taldon, that nothing 'pleases me' as you quaintly put it," Midian hissed. "Now what is it that you have to offer this monastery, since it's evidently not any intelligence!" More snickers.

"So pl . . . I mean, I . . ."

"Speak, boy!" Midian raged, the corrector hovering over Taldon's head.

"I was a p-potter."

"Was a potter, boy? Why, what has changed? Have you forgotten your skill in a day? What's in that sack?" He asked, glancing down to a burlap bag lying by the youngster's foot.

"So . . . a p-pot," the boy spluttered.

"A pot *and* a potter! Excellent!" Midian snarled, his voice thick with sarcasm. "Why don't you show me this pot then?" Hurriedly, the boy opened the drawstring of the bag with trembling fingers and brought out an elegant, high-necked clay jug, which he held out to Midian. "Why this is good," Midian said, turning it in his hands. "Just as the Lord of Flame fashioned the world on the wheel of his will, so have you fashioned this thing of beauty." He looked at the pot again cradling it almost gently, as if it were a small child. Then, abruptly, he let it go. It shattered into a hundred pieces on the flagstoned floor.

"Now learn another lesson, Taldon," he snarled. "How the great god destroys as easily as he creates! Learn humility before you start boasting of your insignificant baubles."

But he didn't address these words to the snivelling Taldon, rather to the back of the room, where his eyes had been rooted since the beginning. For all the time he'd been addressing his other victims, his eyes had been locked on Urthred's in a rigid stare. And Urthred knew that everything that had gone before had merely been a prelude to what was about to happen.

Midian walked slowly down the aisle between the desks, the corrector thwacking rhythmically against the palm of his hand. The pupils on either side cringed away from him as he went past. They needn't have worried; Midian's eyes never left Urthred's. He stopped in front of him, blotting out the dim light from the windows.

"Now, Urthred," he said, his breath sour and hot on the boy's face. "It is an open secret why you were brought here, is it not?" He looked around the classroom with a conspiratorial smirk before turning his inflamed eyes back on his victim. "You and your brother are the bastard sons of a whore, are you not?" There was a small intake of breath at this from Urthred's classmates; the strict code of celibacy forbade any mention of sexual acts, however oblique.

"You understand the word 'whore,' don't you, boy?" Midian was in full flight now, but Urthred remained silent, staring down at the top of the desk in front of him.

"So, Urthred, tell us, are you, or are you not, the son of a whore?" As he asked this he fixed the tip of the corrector under Urthred's chin, lifting it up.

Urthred might have controlled his temper had it not been for the tip of the corrector forcing up his head. He'd seen boys humiliated by Midian a thousand times with words that could not be forgotten or forgiven but were all too commonplace in Forgeholm. Words uttered in an attempt to make the acolytes react to them, show a pride that the monks would not permit, and would punish severely. He might have forgiven the snickering of his classmates, boys too cowardly not to join in Midian's game, but that slight, teasing pressure under his chin made white light explode in his forehead. And a roaring, like the sound of the rushing flames of the sanctuary, filled his mind.

In one swift movement he brushed aside the corrector and thrust himself to his feet. Though slender, he was tall for his age, and for one gratifying split second he saw Midian flinch away from him. Seeing the monk's fear helped dispel his own. Distantly he wondered at his own courage; this defiance might end in the most savage beating yet. But the roaring in his ears was everything—nothing could alter what was about to happen.

His voice came through the noise in his mind like a stranger's voice, confident and bold: "What you said is a lie." He met Midian's bloodshot gaze squarely.

"What, boy, insolence?" the older man roared. He swung the corrector at Urthred's face, but the boy had anticipated this. His left arm was already moving up, grabbing at the hazel stick as it swung at him, trying to twist it away. But years of alcoholic abuse had not weakened Midian enough to make a twelve-year-old a match for him in strength. He wrenched the corrector from Urthred's grasp and brought it round in a scything motion which Urthred only just managed to block with his upraised arm. It was a stinging blow. He staggered back against the desk behind him. Midian was breathing hard. "Well, boy," he said, "you're full of pride, I'd grant you. Pride and vanity and deep ignorance. Well, then, so be it, take a blow as a lesson for each of your vices!" He raised the corrector over his head, and brought it crashing down again on Urthred's upraised arms.

"Like this, and this, and this!" Midian fairly shrieked at the

effort of each blow. They cracked into Urthred's arms, smashing them back onto his head, the hazel rod nearly bending in half as each blow impacted. Urthred fell back, falling over the desk behind him.

The other boys had got up and now formed a semicircle on the edges of the room. They stared with a mixture of horror and fascination at the scene: no one had ever fought back against one of the monks before. Now they watched to see what would happen.

Urthred was struggling to get to his feet from behind the fallen desk, but before he was completely up, Midian had thrown away the corrector and hurled himself with all his body weight on the boy. The air was pushed from Urthred's lungs with an almighty whoosh as he was crushed between Midian and the floor. The monk's breath was hot in his ear. "How do you like this, then?" he asked, spittle flying into Urthred's face as he twisted his head round by the hair. Urthred felt the sudden pressure of Midian's hand on the back of his head and the floor rising towards his face with terrifying speed. His nose impacted with the splintered boards with a dull crack, and his teeth bit halfway through his tongue. Immediately he tasted the salty tang of blood. He twisted with a howl of rage and pain, grabbing the monk's right wrist. Hot anger welled inside him, a molten flood of energy which burned down his veins and from the ends of his fingertips.

Midian smelt burning flesh before he even felt the pain in his wrist. He looked down. Flames licked from Urthred's fingertips, flames that scorched away the hair and skin of his arm and set the sleeve of his robes smouldering. Then he felt the pain, as if his wrist was being held by a red-hot vice. He tried to rip his arm away, but the power within Urthred made his grip that of two fully grown men. Midian began to shriek, and the room began to fill with the smell of burning meat.

There came a sharp intake of breath from the circle of onlookers, and they took a step back, amazed. They had never seen an adult in pain before, much less one who was usually the inflictor of pain. Urthred pushed Midian off and the teacher rolled across the floor, screaming, cradling his scorched wrist. But the boy hadn't finished; the roaring in his mind wouldn't let him. Through the mist of pain from his broken nose, he saw the corrector lying on the floor and picked it up, getting unsteadily to his feet at the same time. The boys surrounding him flinched even further until they lined the edges of the room. Urthred stood motionless for a moment, the heat pounding through his veins. Then smoke started coming off the hazel stick like mist, its surface charring where it came into contact with his fingers. Within a second, it burst into flame like a torch.

Urthred surveyed the boys, his face underlit by the flickering flames, then with one vicious blow he brought the blazing stick down on the teacher's balding head. And then again and again, each blow being accompanied by a gasp of shock from his classmates. Midian groaned, then lay still.

But Urthred had not heard the gasps of his classmates. The roaring still filled his mind—half furnace, half waterfall. He threw the burning brand down onto Midian's body. The monk's robe began to smoulder, but Urthred was already turning away.

The roaring would not leave him, a sound of inextinguishable pain and fury. He would become one with it, join it in the fiery bowels of the earth.

He seemed to drift rather than walk toward the door of the room. Everything seemed distant, as if viewed in a dream. The door appeared to open of its own volition, untouched by his hand. A cold gust of wind hurtled into the schoolroom, blowing papers from the desk and shaking the cloaks of the other students, but not a fold of Urthred's cloak nor a lock of his hair were disturbed.

He drifted out into the hallway. He saw the low, level winter light bursting through the oriel window at its far end, and in the beams of light he saw the boy Kevar cowering, waiting for his punishment. He opened his mouth to speak to him, to tell him that he was safe; but, if he did speak, he didn't hear, for the roaring occupied everything in his mind. And now he was past Kevar, descending the great stairway, with the light shining through the huge window to the south, a ragged light, coruscating through the panes broken by the winter gales.

He went down and down, each step seeming to take an age. Eventually he was at the dark stairwell at the bottom, the worn flagstones cool on his feet, and the cave of the Sanctuary Flame opening up before him. And there was the man-high fissure, its entrance bathed in the molten orange glow which lit the cave. Holy symbols of the Flame were carved all around the fissure; a passageway led inwards from the entrance to the furnace, doglegging to the right, so that the Flame itself was hidden. He walked towards it, not even pausing at its entrance. He felt the heat strike him like a wall. Through the roaring he could dimly hear angry shouts from behind—the monks were coming after him. He knew he must hurry. The orange-red glow intensified around the bend in front. He had never been this close, maybe no one else had ever been this close, he would see the God.

Then he turned the corner to the sanctuary, and saw the vision of Hel; the blackened bones lying scattered on the red-hot rock, bones which his feet crushed to ash; the towering fire-blackened ceiling of the cavern, the great gout of orange-red flame.

The heat was beyond heat, was sheer incandescent energy that warped the air and the rock. He flung his hands up over his eyes to protect them. His hair and his eyebrows went in a second, blown off like gossamer. The flesh on his hands split apart and matter welled up through the suppurating blisters. He staggered back, hearing a scream and only dimly realising that it was his own voice, and that he had turned from the Flame and was fleeing back down the corridor, his whole body on fire. Then he felt hands beating at the waves of flame that were washing over him, but already unconsciousness was sucking him down into the darkness where pain heaved and crashed like a mighty sea on a lonely rock in mid-ocean.

CHAPTER TWELVE

Manichee

He came back slowly to the present, surprised to find himself still sitting by the Pool of Blinding, so vivid had been his recollection of that day eight years ago. The wind was now howling over the cliff tops of Thrull. The sky was ugly and black, obscuring the light of the full moon. His teeth were chattering uncontrollably from the cold. A killing cold. He knew he had to move, keep warm, fight the hold of these memories, these heralds of death. But the pull of the past was vertiginous, and he seemed to have no control over where his thoughts wandered. Unbidden images began tumbling through his mind again. He found himself slipping back again, to the days after the Burning. . . .

The chamber where he had spent the last eight years, at the top of the Elder's high tower at Forgeholm, was suddenly there in front of him, more real than the ledge of rock upon which he sat or the lightning-streaked sky. The stone ceiling which he had watched from the bed where he had lain for all the year after the Burning was instantly before him. The mere remembrance of the moods of the mountains reflected there in light or passing shadow were more actual than the scudding clouds of this night sky. . . . So was the hard wooden bed; the bed in which he dared not move because if he did his charred skin, preserved by a layer of animal fats, would slough off like a lizard's skin. Morning, noon and night he had lain there. Only his eyes, where he had flung up his hands, had survived undamaged. The pain had been unbearable. Only the small core of separateness within him preserved him; that part that the flames could not reach, that the pain could not touch.

Only Manichee had attended him as he'd hovered between life and death. During the day, the Elder pressed dark compresses over his face, muttering charms. When all the monks were abed he still ministered to the boy, the light of the solitary lantern throwing long shadows, a beacon of light in the desolation of the boy's heart. The charms worked, the pain ceased at these moments; Manichee's soft voice took him to woodland glades and rippling green streams. But in the early light of dawn he'd wake again, alone, his mind filled with his recent nightmare of roaring flames and burning skulls, and with his body once more on fire.

Gradually, his wounds had healed. Manichee had let him look at his face in a metal mirror after a year. Wordlessly, he'd put his hand on the boy's shoulder as Urthred had stared at the ruin of livid tissue. Though his eyes took in the horror, Urthred felt disassociated from it, as if he was staring at a Mummer's demon mask, rather than his own living flesh. It had taken time for the association to form in his mind; that the face belonged to him. Then the madness had washed over him, and the monks in their cells had heard his howls in the cold night as he'd cursed his fate. They avoided the tower with its one solitary midnight light, for fear of what they might glimpse at its windows: a creature half-human, half-demon.

Urthred saw too clearly what he had become, lower than a creature; he could not feed or defecate, could not walk, could barely talk, his ears were filled with a continuous roaring as if the fire was still consuming them. He listened to his efforts at speech, mere grunts, but could not understand them, as if they were made by another being distinct from himself, a leering monster that was not the living, breathing creature that once had been Urthred of Ravenspur. Only this illusion of otherness, that he was not the scarred monster which looked back at him from the mirror, had sustained him in the eight years since the Burning.

Nor were the other monks of Forgeholm forced to endure the sight of the monster in their midst. He had never left the tower or seen any face but the Elder's in eight years. But though he had been totally immobile for the first few months, his mind had not been stationary. It sought escape from what he had become. He travelled further into himself than he had ever gone before, seeking for the soul of magic with which he had conjured fire dragons from the air in the cave under the monastery that day when he'd been betrayed.

Manichee taught him the names of the Disciplines of Flame, the Pyromancer's Art. Creation: the basic skill, being the conjuring of fire from the sparks that resided in even inanimate objects. Light: the bringing forth of the fiery ethers of the air to lighten darkness. Refinement: the alchemical lore of treating base metals to produce the pure essences. Guarding: the creation of offensive spells such as the Fist of Flame and the Wall of Fire. Spirits: the summoning from the air of mythical beings sacred to Reh, like the fire dragon he had summoned in the cave.

But only disappointment lay that way; the magic was gone, gone with his flesh. The God had deserted him. No fire blossomed from his fire-blackened hands, no responding tingle of energy came in answer to his prayers. Yet the Elder persisted: for many months he sat by Urthred's bedside reciting his charms one by one, and as the boy recovered he began instructing him in the holy texts and spell books from his library, ignoring the fact that the magic had gone, that the boy was now no more than a cripple that the God had deserted. He showed him illuminated books from when the world had been young, blazing colours, and curlicued script, red, blues and golds flowing like waves across the yellow vellum. But still the magic would not return. Urthred could not heal his loss—only time could.

Manichee had discovered Urthred's magical gift, but too late. The power with which Urthred had conjured dragons and scorched Midian's flesh was gone, evaporated with the curses that he'd rained on the God for leaving him alive. No more did he hear the roaring in his ears; the agony of his body shut out all sound of that. The books contained empty words that Midian rather than Manichee might have recited for all the grace they brought to Urthred.

Still, in his beautiful, modulated reading voice, Manichee had recited the lessons of the ages aloud, hoping to seed once more the soul of magic in his charge. And a trust grew between them. For Manichee was not like the brutish monks of whom he was spiritual head. He cursed himself for failing to take proper care of the boy, who once might have been—might still be—his successor.

So, despite the silence which greeted each lesson, and each healing charm, Manichee persisted, and at night, whilst his charge slept, he descended the tower to his workshop, and the sound of hammering could be heard as he worked long into the night, making the gloves and the mask which Urthred now wore.

Soon the gloves had been finished, and the Elder helped slip them over Urthred's charred hands. Each finger fitted neatly over the burned stumps. Gingerly, Urthred had flexed his hand, and felt the power of the steel rods working in the harnesses fixed to his arms. Feeling their power, his ragged lips had formed a smile for the first time in several months.

But the fragile bond between the Elder and the boy was about to be severed. Rumours of war had already reached the monastery. Illgill's defiance, the undead army marching on Thrull; these had been circulating for some time, unknown to Urthred. But one day there was a visitor in the courtyard below the tower. Urthred caught a glimpse of a rider, decked out in the orange-and-gold robes of the temple, his horse stamping on the cobblestones, its flanks slick with sweat from the hectic ride up the switchback path to the monastery.

The man stayed only about an hour before he rode off again. Soon after, Manichee had climbed the steps to the top of the tower. He looked at the boy with his soulful grey eyes, and an inexpressible sadness welled up in Urthred's heart, for he knew, without him speaking, that Manichee was leaving. The Elder had explained: he was Illgill's oldest friend. He must be at his side before Faran's army reached Thrull.

Two days later he was gone. At first light, he'd come into the room at the top of the tower. Urthred struggled to rise from his bed, but his body only allowed him to raise himself feebly on his elbows. He noticed that Manichee was carrying something. The Elder approached and laid it gently on the side of the bed. In the dim light he reached out to take it, then flinched back when he saw what it was: the mask, an exact replica of Urthred's ruined face. Urthred reached out for it again, gingerly, touching its lacquered surface, a mirror of what he now was. . . . A tingling of energy, much like the power he had felt when he had made the dragons in the air, glowed from the mask and into his fingertips. The boy looked up at Manichee, confused.

Manichee smiled. "You feel the power?" he'd asked. Urthred had merely nodded. "Good, then use it well, Urthred, for your own energies will not return for many years—what I have placed in the mask is all you will have to rely on."

The boy made to say something, but Manichee held up his hand, silencing him. He gazed out at the mountains covered by scudding clouds. "The mask is a gift, a strange one, I'd warrant, but a gift nevertheless." He turned his grey eyes on the boy. "Urthred, I will never return here; you must learn to face the world, for one day you, too, will have to leave," he said kindly. "When that time comes you must be used to the way people look at you. This mask will ease that pain. Not only because it gives you back the magic that you have lost, but because people will see it is only a mask, and by accepting it may one day accept your real face."

"That will never be!" Urthred muttered through his ravaged lips.

Manichee shook his head sadly. "Trust me: the day will come when you go out into the world again. From the safety of the mask you will be able to judge how the world will treat you when it is finally removed. Then you will know yourself better, and will be able to follow me to Thrull."

"I will go to Thrull?"

The old man nodded. "Yes, you will follow me, but not until the world has grown much worse, and they will need you there. There will be long years before I see you again, long years when your body and spirit will start to mend, and you will learn the power of the mask."

"I will cast the Dragon, and the Fist of Fire and the Burning Hand again?"

"And many more forms from the *Book of Reh*. Look!" he said, pointing to the worm-eaten desk sitting in the shadows. There were three leather-bound books lying on it, all three a different shape and size.

"I leave you my books," Manichee continued. "The largest is the *Book of Light*. Pray from it every day; pray that the sun won't go out, pray for the New Dawn and for Reh's return from the dark halls."

"I will do so, master."

"Next, the smaller book. Learn it well. For in it is every form of pyromancy known to the Flame. With it you will summon fire even from wind and ice, and bring lightning from the heavens."

"But it is such a small book!"

"The skill is not in the words but in the interpretation of them. That is why I leave you the third book. It is my own—a kind of diary and a history of these lands of the old Empire. You will find much about Thrull in it, and how it was founded by Marizian the lawgiver. The building of the temples of Reh and Iss—everything. Read it well: one day you will need the information."

The gift was no small one, and Urthred was at a loss for words. What Manichee was entrusting him with was beyond value, a storehouse of information built up over a lifetime.

"You won't be coming back here?" he managed eventually.

"No. The books are yours to keep."

"But I will see you again in Thrull?"

The old man smiled faintly, as if relishing a private joke that Urthred was too young to understand. "Oh, yes, you'll see me again, Urthred, never fear."

"How will I know where to find you?"

"A message will come when the time is right. Remember, whatever happens after, it is the beginning of your journey and not the end."

"You speak in riddles."

"Because I speak of the future. Farewell, and may the Flame be with you . . ." He leant over the bed as Urthred struggled to rise, squeezing the boy's shoulder affectionately. Then, with a swish of his travelling cloak, he had gone before Urthred could speak again. Minutes later, Urthred had heard horseshoes ringing against the cobblestones outside, gradually growing fainter. Then just the wind moaning through the eaves of the tower. The boy had stared at the mask and the books in a stunned silence for several hours after, wondering at his teacher's words. He had stared so hard that reality had seemed to peel away, and he stared into the heart of darkness. His own darkness. He was utterly alone, abandoned in the tower. He would have wept if he had known then how much longer he was going to live there, utterly alone, cut off from all contact. But thankfully he didn't then see the seven lonely years in front of him in which the walls of his cell and the lonely mountains were to be his only companionship.

Manichee had been wrong; they would never meet again. The old man had died at the battle of Thrull. Lord Faran, cheated of the head of Baron Illgill, had crowned the pyramid of skulls outside the city with Manichee's instead. Maybe that was what Manichee had meant about seeing him one more time, the sight of that pyramid far away on the lonely marshes? Was that why he had smiled so enigmatically that last day?

The news of the Elder's death a few months after his departure had sent panic sweeping through the monks at Forgeholm. Many fled, expecting Faran's undead legions to be at their gates within days. Those who remained had sat in resigned passivity, waiting for the end. But the Worm's troops had never come. Days had turned to months, then to years. Urthred had continued his solitary occupation of the dead Elder's tower. Amongst the dozen or so monks who remained, there must have been one or two kind souls, or those who feared the boy who had killed Midian. Every day there was some food and water lying in a basket attached by a simple pulley to the top of the tower. And every day Urthred winched up the meagre scraps which kept him alive, wondering whether the effort of winching was worth it, whether he wouldn't be better off dead.

The books that Manichee had left were his only companions. The first, the *Book of Light,* was his psalter: he prayed and sang from it every day. The second, the book of pyromancy, he

learnt well, but in a dark despair, for he knew that his magic was now gone and the instructions he learnt were as useful to him as a book on painting techniques to the blind. But he nevertheless memorised the Five Disciplines, so that all the summonings and gestures of the rituals were engraved on his heart and mind for whatever future purpose they might serve when and if his powers returned.

The third book, Manichee's notes, were his favourite, for through them he was afforded a glimpse of an unseen world outside the tower—of all the men and creatures who dwelt on the Old Earth, of the old gods, and of the founding of the religions of Reh and Iss by Marizian; of the Golden Age, now vanished, and the height of the Empire up to the Emperor's retirement from the world five hundred years ago. He learnt of the dying of the sun, the first dark veil cast over the sky, and the failure thereafter of crops and cattle. Then he read of the divisions that had persisted ever since, and understood how the battle of Thrull had come about, and he began to suspect what role he would have to play in the world if, as Manichee's heir, his powers ever returned.

After a time, notes had started appearing with the food winched up to his eyrie. Notes begging for healings or charms, those things which Manichee might once have supplied to pilgrims. He became dimly aware that a legend was growing of the Adept of the tower, a legend which had spread all over the Fire Mountains, a legend of the sorcerer of Forgeholm, Manichee's heir. As time went by the faithful came from all over the country, hoping for healings or miracles at the foot of his tower.

He heard their voices, but never descended to the doorway at the tower's base. He pitied their folly: hadn't they heard? That he had lost his powers, that there was no successor to Manichee in the tower, merely a hopeless cripple? He stayed way back from the slit windows, fearing that the pilgrims might see him, see the monster who dwelt within, and seeing, go into a frenzy of frustration and despair.

The years passed; no miracles occurred. The numbers of those waiting in the courtyard had gradually decreased, until only one or two persisted, waiting patiently in the ever-present

snow. He had been left his solitary reign of tower, forgotten for
the most part . . . until just over a month ago.

Painfully, Urthred returned to the present, and the windswept
ledge. He shook his head in the freezing dark. This wouldn't
do. He would be dead before long with this dreaming of the
past; the heat was slowly ebbing from his body. He stood, beating his arms against his sides for warmth. But as he did so, his
mind was once more drawn inexorably to the past, to the arrival
of the messenger from Thrull forty days ago.

He had not heard from his brother for nearly fourteen years.
He hadn't known whether Randel had died in the battle for
Thrull, didn't know whether his brother had heard of the Burning. But the letter, winched up with his food, had sent his mind
racing; for the first time in many long months he felt joy. At last
he felt contact with another being. Each word of the letter was
etched into his mind:

> *"Dear Brother—"* it had started,

> *You might, in the long years since we last saw one an-*
> *other, think that I had forgotten you. This is not so. I have*
> *heard much of you, from the Elder Manichee before his*
> *death, and from other friends who have come from Forge-*
> *holm. I have been with you in spirit, though I could not write*
> *or journey to be with you. The Worm holds the power here in*
> *Thrull, and it is risky to send letters such as these. The rea-*
> *son why I do so now is that I have urgent need of you.*
> *Manichee told me before he died that you would come if I*
> *wrote to you. He said to tell you when that time had come.*
>
> *Dear Brother, that time has come. Things stir in the city*
> *which I cannot write of in a letter but which you will see for*
> *yourself when you come here.*
>
> *Travel carefully, for the Worm hates the monks of Forge-*
> *holm. Announce yourself merely as the Herald when you*
> *come here to the Temple, I or my friends will find you.*
>
> *Until then, may Reh speed your travels—Randel.*

So Manichee had been right—he would, after all, travel to Thrull. Urthred had steeled himself to meet the outside world for the first time in eight years. He'd meditated a whole day, staring at the scudding clouds and the snowcapped cone of The Old Father, the scrawny pine trees clinging to the scree slopes, the familiar grey buildings of the monastery far below; now he would leave his prison at last and find his destiny.

He'd risen at dawn and descended the dust-choked staircase, his legs uncertain, though much strengthened over the years. To his surprise, the boys of his youth, Kevar and Taldon and some others, now grown to men, had been waiting as the oak door had groaned open on its rusty hinges: somehow they'd known he was leaving. He'd stepped from the shadows into the light of day for the first time in eight years. But if he'd expected the world to be an easier place, the gasps of horror from the waiting monks had soon reminded him of what he bore on his face: Manichee's mask. They'd stepped back from him, their parting gifts forgotten in their hands.

Urthred had wanted to say something to them: did Kevar remember how he'd stood outside in the corridor that day so long ago? Had Taldon ever returned to the potter's wheel? He'd wanted to talk, to reach out to them; but no words had come. How to explain that he was still a man, despite the mask? Instead, he'd walked past them and through the gate, the gate through which he'd been borne nearly twenty years before.

He'd never looked back once.

He had been wrong not to leave Forgeholm the very day he received Randel's message. Even this one day delay had been enough: his brother was dead and he himself had only escaped his pursuers by a miracle. Now, sitting on the ledge by the pool in the freezing wind, he was dying slowly of the cold. His limbs felt like ice. The visions would start soon, the visions that the monks used to have on the Day of the Birch, when they had been out in the snows all day.

He would not help or cure the wounds of the world, if that had been his destiny. His brother and Manichee were gone, and so presumably was the cause which they had both wanted him to serve. In any case the introspection of eight years in the tower had made him unsuited to whatever task they'd had in mind for him. He was unused to communicating with others, even if they could have borne the ruin of his face. He was not a leader. He was a man who saw too far, beyond the flesh that was no use to him. His hands were blackened claws, which only Manichee's gloves had saved from permanent uselessness, his chest and torso a mass of scar tissue. Pleasure and hope had been stripped away by years of suffering and asceticism. Instead his seven years' study of Manichee's books had led him beyond the world of flesh, into the abstract world beyond the shadows of earth to search for that fire that he once possessed in his veins and which he could enjoy only through the mask left him by his teacher.

The soul, prayer, self-doubt and intellectual rigour had taken over his life. The outer trappings, so important to others, were of no significance to him, a burden to be dismissed with scorn.

But in the darkness of this freezing night, there was one ray of hope. Today in the mountains and the square, when the flame had once more sung in his veins and blossomed from his hands, he had known the power of the mask. Or had it been his own power returned? Only Manichee himself could have answered the question. Yet in this return of his magic there seemed evidence of Reh at work: the God had not forgotten him in the long darkness. Maybe his spirit had begun to heal.

But even if it had, was it now too late? He had ridden the whirlwind for a few brief hours. Slain the undead, avenged his brother's death. Now there was nowhere for him to go, and he would surely die.

He turned towards the north: thick black clouds covered half the moonlit sky over the temple pyramids and citadel, their undersides rolling inexorably towards Thrull. He waited for the lightning to come, the same lightning that Manichee had once promised him he would be able to conjure from the skies. He waited for it to fork down onto the ledge where he stood and end it all.

CHAPTER THIRTEEN

The Vision

Now the lightning came ever closer, the intervals between its flash and its roar ever shorter; the wind had got up over the marshes, the mist began to shred and form exotic shapes, which flew up from under the lip of the cliff, soaring into the air like wraith dragons of Elder Times. And with it came the music of that old time: the wind moaning as if in pain over the water and through the cypress trees. Then, with a bending of the trees, the wind and the storm were upon him; a bolt of white electricity shot down to the earth, throwing every grain of the stone in front of him into momentary relief. Then the thunder came, seeming to rock the very parapet on which he stood.

Another flash, right overhead, but the lightning forked down into the plain below, striking the summit of the pyramid of skulls with a sharp explosion. Half-blinded by the flash, Urthred shut his eyes, waiting for the accompanying roar of thunder.

But none came.

It was suddenly absolutely quiet all around him. A shiver played up his spine. He opened his eyes cautiously, focusing on where the lightning had struck the pyramid. It seemed altered. The blackness of the marshes around it pulsed with energy, an inkiness even darker than the sable of the night, like ripples from a pool. But the pyramid itself glowed with an unearthly white light that seemed to burn at its very core. As he watched, the light source seemed to move upwards to the very summit, which flared up like a pitch torch. The light warped and shivered, as if something fought to assume shape, an embryo of light breaking through a shell of darkness. Then it was free, a floating, dazzling ether, slowly drifting upwards to the city.

Then sound came back, and, with it, the rain, so solid that it seemed metal lines were falling out of the sky. Within seconds his cloak and the inside of his mask were sodden once more; the mists were replaced by vapour as the deluge struck the surface of the pool with a hiss. Visibility had sunk to a few yards, the plain was lost, as was the floating white form.

But he knew it was coming towards him. An icy trickle played on the nape of his neck, but it was not a rivulet of water, but the ice of fear.

Then he saw it.

The white form floated towards him through the downpour, its shape rapidly assuming that of a figure striding through the dark air over the marshes, floating over the black emptiness, a thing of winnowing light and incandescence, the edges of which wavered and reformed with each pulse of energy from its core. He watched as it approached, his limbs once more frozen, the magic of the last two hours frozen, too, in his ice-cold limbs. Remorselessly it strode on, white light shining from its eye sockets, until it came to rest hovering at the edge of the pool in front of him. Through the blaze of light Urthred saw who it was, and seeing made him even more afraid.

The rain hissed down unheeded and there was a sudden cold stillness in his soul, for shining from the pool of light he could now make out the features and the bent body of Manichee, the long dead Elder of Forgeholm Monastery, just as he had been in life. The world was full of tales of unquiet spirits which returned from Shades where they awaited Reh's second coming, but never had Urthred expected to see one, and one who resembled so closely the form of his late master.

The white light pouring from the old man's eye sockets hypnotised him, and he stood paralysed as the thing floated to within touching distance.

His bowels turned to ice. Now he would die, as quickly as if the lightning itself had struck him down. But then another emotion swept through him, a madcap daring, a courage which he had lost years before. What had he to fear? Hadn't Manichee promised to return? Was this, while not actually him in body, his spirit? Yet still he flinched back from the blazing white light, as if it would suck up the fire of his soul and leave him a senseless husk.

As if in answer to his fear, Manichee raised his hands in a peacock's blaze of incandescent light, a sad smile playing over his face. And Urthred heard his master's voice for the first time in over seven years.

"See, Urthred, I have summoned the lightning and the fire, as I promised you. Do you remember?" The voice was gentle, as Manichee's had been in life, but muffled as if he spoke through a heavy door. But Urthred could hear every syllable, and with his voice every word that his master had spoken to him that last morning at the monastery came back to him again. As Manichee had commanded him, he had read the book of spells: he had read of summonings that could bring lightning and fire, but of no spell that could bring back the dead. Only Manichee could bring down lightning and, with it, himself.

He bowed his head. "Master . . ." he began.

But Manichee held up his blazing hand again, quieting him. "There's no need to tell me, Urthred; the world is but shadow and form. I've been in the shadows, watching you these seven years: I know it all."

"Then why have you come?" Urthred managed to chatter through his frozen lips.

Again the smile. "You have forgotten, then, my promise, that you would see me once more? Life is short, Urthred, but blood oaths are long; even from Shades a man's solemn promise calls him back, though he must summon the wings of the storm to bring him!"

It was as if an invisible force was pushing him down. Urthred knelt on the rain-soaked flagstones, his body by now trembling uncontrollably. "Master, I did not forget, though I doubted."

"Doubt is good, Urthred, for we see every day how the credulous fall, then flock to the Temple of Iss. But you, you were always one to question even that which seemed as clear as a beam of light; that's why I chose you, why I promised that one day I would return to you." The blue eyes blazed, penetrating even the dark recesses of Urthred's mask.

"It was always going to be like this, Urthred, this journey of yours, your brother, Varash. . . . But time is short; the energy I have will only last a few minutes, and I will be gone once more."

"You knew what would happen?"

"Yes, I saw: I saw my death and the death of thousands of others, the sacking of Thrull, the passing of power from Reh to Iss, and I saw the future that stretched ahead of you from this moment; that is why I have come." The eyes closed, shutting off the light, and Urthred dared to look up at the figure again. He suddenly saw in the diminished glow the tired lines of age webbing Manichee's face, each line etched, it seemed, from the translucent flame that burned within him.

"Time is short, so I must be as well. The storm will pass, even in this benighted city. This," he said, gesturing at the glowing orb that enclosed him, "will be seen: only the storm hides us. Urthred, we will never talk again until Reh returns at the Second Dawn to heal the world." The apparition paused, as if summoning energy from a far-off place.

"You will be as I once was, Urthred, then you will understand those things that are mysteries to you; you will grow tolerant of that which you now hate, gain humane understanding; you will see the fire of every man's soul and respect it. . . . Once you didn't respect yourself enough, you burned yourself nearly to death . . ."

"But it was a holy act!" Urthred protested.

"Which burned the magic from you?" Manichee retorted. "Which meant for these last several years you have been the master of the book of spells, but not the spells themselves?"

"But, master, the spells returned today . . ." Urthred began, but Manichee silenced him with another gesture from his glowing arm.

"Yes, they returned, but from where? Remember, Urthred, your own magic will not return while you wear that mask. Look into your soul, Urthred, see the barren years stretching behind, think of your despair, your solitude, your pride which made you think yourself better than any other man who has crawled the earth under the light of Reh."

And there they were, conjured up by the old man's words, the barren years like a desert, stretching in the confines of Urthred's mind from the Day of the Burning, through the empty years in the tower, to this very moment, years in which not a single solitary human act or word had penetrated his soul, which had brought back that living breathing fire that once had informed his every day. He had known it all this while, but for the first time acknowledged it; the Burning had not raised him up, made him better than his peers; the voice he had heard roaring from far below the monastery had not been the voice of the God, but the voice of an uncontrollable rage which had nearly destroyed him. Until this man had saved him.

But Manichee continued, his tone gentle, but the rebuke in his voice unmistakable:

"When you were a child, you judged like a canting hypocrite what was holy and what was not; where did your force, your flame go? With those vanities, with your rage? Now today you have killed a man, his spirit is already in Hel. But today is a day of turning, of transformation. It is good you are here at the pool—the fire and the water may purify you like an impure ore refined to gold."

Urthred bent his head, once more unable to look at the presence. "Varash killed my brother; I couldn't let his crime go unpunished. . . ."

"There are many crimes which men commit in so-called just causes, but no crime is right. Varash would have found a higher justice: let heaven assign his reward!"

"But you fought, master: against the Worm, against Iss; I did only that which Reh instructed me . . ."

"You have much to learn. The *Book of Light* has not taught you because you lack an inner light to comprehend it. Reh is distant in the sun, his divinity merely imparts a knowledge of reflected fire in our souls, a shadow of his presence. We cannot hope to be like him, nor understand his motives, for he is distant, far removed. Only the sacred birds which will carry our bones to him at death know his nature; how can we, then, who have no power of flight, comprehend him?"

Another mighty fork of lightning crashed down—a trident from the heavens. But again there was no sound, merely a buzzing as of a million bees in Urthred's head.

The old man's words continued over the strange sound: "Look into your heart, Urthred; find your destiny there. You have already undergone the first stage."

"The first stage?"

"The burning away of your pride, the destruction of your anger; don't you regret Varash's death now?"

Urthred remembered the man's babylike face in death, how frail, and defeated he'd looked. His heart felt like iron. It was up to the gods to exact revenge, not mere mortals.

"That is the first step," continued Manichee. "Tonight you will find out much more about yourself: some of it will surprise you. Finally you may succeed in discovering who you are, but this is hidden in a faraway place."

Urthred puzzled over these words. "Where is this place? I've never learnt where I came from, or who my parents were."

"Nor do you want to know—yet. But I will tell you where that place is."

"Where?"

Manichee gestured with his hands, through the driving rain, back to the north, to the distant, invisible peaks of the Palisades.

"The Nations of the Night?" Urthred asked, confused: no human had willingly stepped there since the gods left the earth ten thousand years before.

Manichee nodded: "Yes, in the Nations you'll discover your origins and your destiny. Today is the beginning of a great journey for you, but your thread will be short, unless you escape this city, and to do that you will need friends."

"Friends? I saw what happened to the Flame's friends: the stocks, then night . . ."

But Manichee held up one of his blazing hands, stopping him. "Time is short; fate brought you here on this day. The last of the true Hearth Brethren are leaving tonight; leaving this accursed city to its fate. You will find them, and go with them."

"But where will I find them?"

"For the moment they are scattered, but at midnight they will be gathered once more. You will be there."

"How? The vampires will be in the streets."

"The lightning blinds them. Besides, do you not feel the power of the mask returning? Return into the city. Go to Stick's Hole, in the square of Dolor—see, the lightning shows the way!" A bolt shot through the downpour, illuminating the cliffs off to their right. Urthred could just see a dark, forbidding entranceway nestling at their feet. From here it resembled the gloomy gateway of Iss' Underworld.

"There is a palace next to it," Manichee continued. "It is the keep of the Durian family, though it is now mostly ruins. There are friends there; tell them whose brother you are, tell them you know of the Lightbringer—they will admit you, and take you to a place of safety."

"Who is this Lightbringer?"

"It was for the Lightbringer that Randel summoned you here. The Lightbringer will be revealed to you tonight. It is the force by which the shadows will be banished from the world, but that only after many adventures and the regathering of magic long lost to men. But you must find out who the Lightbringer is yourself; otherwise, you will not believe, and thus not help the cause."

"You speak as if I'll have some sway over events."

"It's your destiny—don't betray it. Now I must say farewell, for the storm is passing. Never again will I speak with you until the end of time has come: and only once more will I be of service to you. Remember the cause of the world's sorrow, for it will fall on you to right it."

"What is the cause? Is it the sun's dying?"

"The sun began to die when the gods left the earth, and the wizardry of the north came upon us like a curse. Remember who brought it: Marizian."

"But he brought us the laws: the Book of the Light and the Worm!"

"Yes, but he built this city and founded the two temples. With the help of giants and leviathans, he threw up these cliffs in gouts of molten rock, and like those who followed him in the Flame he brought fire from heaven to crush his enemies. But Marizian had far greater weapons, ones which he'd stolen from a city in the far north."

"What is the name of the city, master?"

"Its name is Iskiard, but do not look for it on any map. Marizian unleashed a curse which killed all those who dwelt in that place and reduced it to a rubble in a day. Now it stands in its ruined walls far from human eye and from memory."

"So what was the sorcery that he brought with him that has doomed us?"

The ghost looked at him, the shining eyes dimming as its energies dissipated. "Three objects: a magical sword, a man of bronze, and, lastly, the very thing that consigned me to Shades rather than Reh's fiery paradise: the Rod of the Shadows."

"What is it?"

"It opens the way between the two planes of shadow and light. This is the world of light, though the sun dies. But there in the shadow the opposite of what is true here pertains. Our dark halves are there—our Doppelgängers. And the more virtuous a man is on this plane, the greater the horror of his shadow self. Saints are nervous men, Urthred, for they see the evil just out of reach on the other side."

"Tell me how to find this Rod: I'll take off your curse!"

Manichee smiled sadly. "Too late for that. But quickly—the storm passes. I must tell you its history. After the gods had left the world in their flaming chariots, Marizian took what was left of their magic, and the curse they left behind in the soil. This world was too little for him. He would have followed after the gods, but that magic had gone with them to the stars. Hence he contented himself dabbling in the secrets they left buried behind."

"So what happened to this Rod?"

"Listen to the tale—five thousand years ago Marizian left that cursed city Iskiard and fled south pursued by demons and the creatures who live about Shandering Plain. Finally he came to this spot and built this citadel. Impregnable against any assault: even the engines of the giants could not reduce Thrull within a year, for it was built by a giant, Adamanstor. So he prospered, forgetting the curse he'd brought upon the world; for the unleashing of the Rod was the beginning of the dying of Reh in the sky, though it took thousands more years to show itself. He lived two hundred years and died, the Rod buried with him, there!" Manichee's arm shot out to the southwest, and in the direction of the blazing finger a flash of lightning stabbed down far below, where Urthred could just make out the edge of the city's curtain wall and the tombs of the City of the Dead. One building, a stepped pyramid built right against the city wall, stood out above all the rest.

"Behold Marizian's tomb! Illgill delved there, having discovered ancient texts which he little understood. For days he laboured deep beneath the earth in the Maze in which Marizian had hidden his secrets all those aeons ago. Many of his helpers died, but he won through, bringing the Rod from the tomb, but incapable of using its powers—for that he needed me."

"You used the Rod?"

"Yes, and brought a shadow into this dying world: for that I am cursed."

"Cannot one slay the shadow?"

"Not without killing the substance, too. You must find the Rod: only by using it will you be able to return the shadow to its own plane."

"And where will I find the shadow and the Rod?"

"Oh, the shadow you will meet this very night. The Rod is in the far north, beyond the Palisades."

"And you were cursed for this?"

Manichee nodded. "Yes, and rightly, too: I brought a soul back from extinction, from the world of Shades—only my love for Illgill could have done it. Now the world will suffer once more for a monster is amongst us—he goes in human form, but he is part of that forging of the shadows that began those centuries ago in that far-off city from whence Marizian came. He will be your greatest foe, Urthred, though you will account him your greatest friend. I cannot tell you more: divine retribution already hangs over me. Only by the powers of death have I returned to warn you. Put aright what I have done wrong; you will discover how." He smiled gently once more. "Be patient, you will heal. Don't forget that I will return to help you once more, but once more only. Now it is time for me to return to the place of shadows."

The figure began to fade away, and Urthred reached out desperately trying to stop it, but instead grasped empty air as the vision disappeared like mist before his eyes. He looked around wildly. Nothing: just the rain-streaked pool, and the departing flashes of lightning over the black monolith of the city.

Manichee's words echoed in his mind. He remained kneeling on the rain-soaked flagstones in a trance, wondering whether what he had just seen had been one of the cold-induced visions he had heard of, heralding his own death.

Another flash of lightning. Again he saw in its light the dark entranceway across from his vantage point: Manichee had called it Stick's Hole. Next to it he could see a broken line of large mansions. One of them would be the place that Manichee had told him to go to. It was not far, but to go there meant plunging himself back into danger.

He might be safe here by the pool until dawn. But what then? The city was policed by Faran's living stooges. They would find him at daybreak even if the vampires didn't get him before then. He needed friends to help him escape the city. Manichee's words had filled him with purpose, and he again felt the tingling of energy humming through his veins.

He put aside his doubts: it had been no waking dream, he was convinced; Manichee had appeared, once more his master was guiding him, as he had done years before at Forgeholm. What's more he had promised to come one more time to help him.

With Reh's blessing he would live another night and find out the mystery behind the apparition's words.

Without further thought he lowered himself over the side of the dark pool into the chill waters and began wading back towards the city.

CHAPTER FOURTEEN

Dragonstooth

The storm had caught Jayal on the narrow cornice of a building overlooking the temple square.

It had taken him only a few minutes to climb to the top of the walls surrounding the citadel. From there he had made slow progress through the fog that now choked the highest reaches of the city, jumping from rooftop to rooftop over dark alleyways, snatching brief glimpses of the streets far below. His handholds had been the ivy which choked the buildings and the ancient statuary which graced nearly every one of their roofs; gorgons, basilisks, fire-spitting dragons: each in turn had saved him as he'd slipped and slithered on the slick tiles.

But then lightning had punctured the white gloom, and the thunder rolled over the plains from the north. One moment he'd been inching along the narrow width of the ledge, his back flat against a wall, his eyes fixed on the long drop at his feet, then there was a dazzling flash of lightning which threw the temple square beneath him into harsh relief: for a split second he saw the vampires congregated around the stocks, their arms thrown up to protect their eyes, then all was darkness again.

He was still pinned to the wall when the first curtain of rain hissed across the square, each drop beating a mad tattoo on his cloak. He was soaked in seconds. He flicked his head, trying to clear the water out of his eyes, clutching desperately at his handhold. As he had several times before in the last half hour, he cursed himself for his recklessness; returning to the city at all had been dangerous enough, but his rooftop journey had proven near suicidal on several occasions. Now the rain would make the stones and slates even more treacherous.

Another flash of lightning, and for an instant he could see his destination. Ahead and below a cobbled street branched off at the foot of the high wall surrounding the Temple of Iss; beyond the temple pyramid he could see for an instant, silhouetted against the flash, a spire of rock protruding like a fang from the side of the cliff. The place called the Spike.

He remembered it well; even seven years ago it had had an evil reputation. It was a honeycombed tower leaning out from the cliff face, invulnerable to attack from the city; its many levels had harboured lawless men over the centuries as well as, it was said, a creature chained at its top which no man had seen but whose cries had echoed over the city in the darkness when he had been a boy. His nurse had made the sign of Reh whenever she had heard its mournful hoot echoing through the night air, for the creature of the Spike was considered a harbinger of death.

The lightning forked all around the Spike and the temple pyramids. Far off, in a gap between two buildings, he saw the vast expanse of the plain showing ghostly white in the lightning, then fading from view again. He looked up, the rain stinging his eyes just as another bolt of lightning came crashing down in a crooked jag, striking the truncated pyramid roof of the Temple of Reh. The lightning made up his mind; he would be safer on the ground. He inched his way along the ledge to where there was a window opening, its glass and shutters long gone.

He swung himself through it, his nostrils immediately assailed by the smell of rot and mould. Another flash of lightning revealed an empty bedroom, its four-poster bed crumpled into a tangle of mildewed curtains and poles. There was a mound at its centre, a hint of a sleeping figure cocooned in a tangle of sheets and spiderwebs. He didn't stay to investigate, but passed swiftly through into another room filled with shattered furniture and fallen drapes, the nest of a thousand mice, judging by the piles of droppings on the floor revealed by the lightning. Cobwebs hung like thick gossamer in veils across the room. No one had passed this way for some time. Still he must be cautious; the vampires had fled from the square and might have taken shelter in the buildings around it.

He drew his sword from its scabbard. Green light filled the room, a green faery light like the colour at the bottom of a deep pool of water when a summer sun plays on its surface and its mysterious depths are reflected up; so the light played in ripples over the walls and ceiling, burning whitely from the blade so that its surface was indistinct, a white shaft of energy and not a physical thing. Only one thing showed against the white brilliance: halfway down the blade there was a crescent-shaped sigil etched into the face of the metal. It was black against the surrounding white. The symbol of the Old Moon; inimical to the servants of Iss, for the moon governed the cycle of their blood drinking.

Dragonstooth: his father had sent him halfway around the world to find this sword. How many deaths in the getting of it; how many deaths since? Forged in the Elder Times from the iron incisor of one of the God's scaly steeds, imbued with magic by Marizian the Mage, lost for centuries to the people of the Empire. He had found it, in a wizard's tower in the swamplands on the coast of Hangar Parang, as his father had ordered. But only after seven long years of doubt and delay, years in which he'd begun to wonder at his sanity. Now the light of the sword gave him courage.

He pushed on through the dark house, the light of the blade showing the way. In front a dust-covered stairway curved down into the darkness. He heard a rustle and a moan from its foot; the glow of the blade caught the movement of a figure crossing the hallway. It flinched back from the light and then was gone. He progressed more cautiously until he reached the broken-down front door of the mansion. It gave onto a side alley, shrouded in the darkness of the overhanging roofs. Rain sluiced down the central sewer of the street; nothing else moved.

He took a deep breath, then launched himself into the alley. A few steps and he would be in the square. Then it would be but a few seconds to reach the street leading to the Spike and he would be safe. His booted feet slipped on the wet cobbles as he hurried forward through the rain. Now he could see the opening into the temple square, the glow of red light framing the alleyway in front. He quickened his step.

Then a body leapt out of a side entrance in front of him, harshly underlit by the light of the sword. He caught a glimpse of a dark cloak outstretched like a bat's wings, a pale and haggard face, the long incisors bone white in the darkness, the chin flecked with blood. Before his brain could respond, his shoulder smashed into the vampire's chest, bowling it over. He lost his footing, and fell to his knees, struggling back up as he sensed the creature trying to grapple his legs from behind him. He swung the sword, a graceful arc of blazing light, behind with one hand, feeling only a slight jar as the blade sliced through the creature's clavicle. There was a sizzling sound as the white heat of the sword burned through damp cloth, skin and bone.

The creature jerked spasmodically, its severed arm socket smoking where the sword had cleaved straight through it. The blow would have killed a man, but the creature's eyes never left Jayal's. He felt a vertiginous pull as if his mind was being drawn slowly into their depths.

For a near fatal moment he felt pity for the creature, sorrow for its wound. Then he blinked hard, fighting against the vampire's mesmerism. He stepped back and brought the sword down on its head in a swift cross stroke. The head exploded like a dried walnut crushed by a hammer.

Without waiting to see whether there were more vampires, he turned on his heels and raced into the square. The forbidding temples, their gates closed, loomed to either side, but their details were only a blur through the rain. His feet flew over the cobblestones and suddenly he was at the mouth of the alley on the other side. Its darkness swallowed him, Dragonstooth casting long, jumping shadows in front of him. A long avenue of ruined houses flashed by, then he slid to a halt in front of his objective.

On the other side of a dark chasm stood the spire of rock rising up two hundred feet into the air, higher even than the temple pyramids. Its jagged peak was lost in the driving rain, but at its lower levels the Spike showed evidence of centuries of human habitation. Bridges at different levels spanned the chasm, reached from other ledges in the cliff face. Some looked to be in crumbling disrepair, but the one he needed looked solid enough. It was right in front of him, its arched stone span vaulting over the chasm to an old, worm-eaten oak door into which was fixed a rusted iron ring and a metal spyhole. Far below in the lightning flashes he could see the gleaming roofs of the Lower Town glimmering in the rain.

But instead of pushing straight across the bridge and getting out of the vampire-haunted streets, he paused to think, a crawling sensation at the back of his neck. The dangers of the place in front could be even greater than those behind. The men inside were Faran's militia, no doubt recruited from mercenaries and Thrull's own criminal classes. The chances of a warm welcome were slim. The chances of being recognised even greater. There might be some who had known him who now worked for their onetime enemy.

It was a risk he had to take. He needed information about Thalassa. She might have died seven years ago: if that was the case, so be it. He would mourn her later, after he had done what his father had ordered him to do. But, for the next hour or two at least he would do what his duty to his betrothed dictated.

Besides, who would recognise him after seven years? The scraggly blonde beard concealed his lower jaw—seven years ago he had been a fresh-faced youth. The crinkles of weariness and care round his eyes were new as well, as was the small scar on his upper lip. The pilgrim's cloak was large and voluminous, and the hood, which he now pulled over his eyes, would add further to the disguise.

Casting one more furtive look behind him, he scuttled over the stone arch of the bridge. He seized the rusted iron knocker and crashed it repeatedly against the metal clapper beneath it with all his might. Then he waited, holding his breath. No sound came as moments that seemed like months passed. He hammered away again, casting anxious eyes behind him for signs of the undead, but the lightning that flickered over the city seemed momentarily to be holding them at bay.

He turned, relieved to see at last the light of a torch playing under the door. He quickly remembered the sword, sheathing it and concealing it beneath his cloak. Now he could hear a tetchy voice as the bearer of the light drew nearer.

"Knock, knock, knock!" it muttered. With the voice came a heavy tread, then a curse, and then the metal spyhole in the door was thrown open with a squeal of rust. A bloodshot eye surveyed him from it.

"Who the devil is it?" the man growled.

"A stranger," he replied quickly. "For the love of what you hold holy let me in!"

The man behind the door let out a guffaw. "What I hold holy? Methinks that would be gold, whores and drink, so get back where you've come from, for I don't see none of them about your person."

"I have gold," Jayal said, perhaps overeagerly, remembering Skerrib's avarice, and that now only one gold piece was left in his purse. The owner of the eye snorted contemptuously.

"You're a pilgrim are you?"

"Yes, by Iss! I need shelter!"

"And I thought your kind was all for giving yerselves to the Vampirs."

"Not I, I assure you!"

"Well, you're as persuasive as a leech, I'd swear. Come then, and make it quick."

Bolts were undone, then a hairy arm, out of all proportion to the voice, snaked out and grabbed the collar of Jayal's sodden cloak. He was not an inconsequential man, but he was powerless to resist the strength of the arm that lifted him bodily off the ground and dragged him in. The door was slammed to, followed by the drawing of bolts. Then the torch was thrust nearly into his face as the doorkeeper inspected him. Gradually, Jayal's eyes became accustomed to the blazing light held in front of him.

What he saw made him tug against the prehensile grip on his cloak. But no amount of struggling would have helped him: the innkeeper was a descendant of the giants of the north—seven feet tall or more, still bearing the gnarled features of one of those who had built the city centuries before. His face was gnarled and skewed from generations of interbreeding with human stock, but his ancestry was in no doubt. Flaming orange hair exploded from his head and from the bulging muscles of his arms. He had to bend himself almost double in the low passageway, his breath filling the musty confines with the stink of spirits.

And, with a jolt, Jayal recognised the man. Weebil. His father had impressed some of these half-castes into his army, rounding them up from the shanties where they lived in the Lower Town. Weebil had been one of them. Jayal might not have remembered him if it hadn't been for the fact that Weebil had served in his very own company, the Elicitors of Flame. He remembered Weebil's sullen character, how he had been flogged for insubordination, a lash in front of each of the fifty companies in the temple square, a day or two before the battle.

The man was eyeing him suspiciously, and already Jayal fancied there was an element of mutual recognition. Then drunken laughter echoed down an ill-lit passage from a back room. If Jayal had hoped that this would distract the giant, he was to be disappointed—Weebil's eyes never left his.

"Don't I know you?" Weebil growled, knitting his thick furrowed brows together.

Jayal shook his head rapidly. "I don't think so—I arrived only today from Hangar Parang."

"'Arrived only today from Hangar Parang,'" the giant replied, mimicking him; the years had evidently not improved his disposition. He leaned closer, giving Jayal the benefit of his foetid breath again, his face a sullen scowl. "No, I never forget a whoreson's face, and yours is beyond passing familiar."

"I told you, I'm a stranger . . . a pilgrim . . ."

The man scowled again, as if Jayal had by his innocuous statement admitted to a heinous murder. "So, 'pilgrim,' what business has brought you to Weebil's Inn? Not a roof, for we don't take in travellers here."

Jayal knew there was neither going forward nor back in the situation he found himself in. He would somehow have to bluff his way through.

"I'm . . . looking for someone," was the best answer he could muster.

"Looking for someone? At dead of night with the Vampirs all about?"

"The storm seems to have driven them off for the moment. It gave me time to get here." He pulled his last gold piece from his purse and held it out. "Take it. All I want is to talk for five minutes with one of the city guards, then I'll be gone."

"A durcal for five minutes with one of 'em? Hah!" The giant swept up the gold coin in his massive fist. "Come, a gold might buy you more than you bargained for." He propelled Jayal in front of him down the low, foul-smelling corridor, squeezing past a weapons rack crammed with halberds and other weapons as he did so.

The room at the end of the corridor into which he was pushed was lit by the ruddy glow of a fire. It was furnished with plain wooden trestle tables, on which were set jugs of ale and the remnants of a meal. As in Skerrib's Inn, a haze of Lethe smoke hung in a solid band just under the rafters. The benches were half-filled with some ten or so men, while two or three more lay on straw palliasses around the fringes of the room, asleep or unconscious. By the close smell of the room it was clear that all the men stayed here during the hours of darkness.

Those still with their senses were arguing fiercely over a game of dice going on at one of the tables. But despite the fierceness of the argument, they all shut up the second they saw Weebil ushering a stranger into the room. Their sudden silence transmitted to some of the others, who lifted their heads from their drug- or drink-induced stupor and stared uninvitingly at the new guest.

"What's this that you've dragged in from the rain?" one of them asked. Jayal sensed he'd seen this man as well somewhere before.

Then he remembered; he was one of the soldiers who had been guarding the gate when he'd ridden into the city but three hours ago. Having avoided their questions then, he was irked to find himself voluntarily in their midst.

The innkeeper ignored the soldier's question, lumbering towards the back of the room, where various barrels and bottles were stacked. He seized one of the bottles, biting the cork out of its opening and pouring some of the liquid into an earthenware beaker, all the time his hooded eyes glowering at the drip-ping stranger. Jayal in turn stood where he was, uncomfortable under the scrutiny of so many eyes.

Weebil refilled the mug and thrust it out towards him. "A gold will buy you a drink, stranger, so drink," he growled, shak-ing the small beaker in his massive paw. "Then we can talk about what brought you here."

Jayal stood, frozen for a moment. Should he take the drink or flee down the corridor? There was no going back now, he de-cided. He stepped forward and took the beaker with shaking hands, avoiding the giant's gaze. Any moment now the man might challenge him, call him Jayal Illgill and his seven-year quest would be over.

"So, stranger," Weebil asked, "what brought you here?"

Jayal looked around him warily. He didn't detect any signs of recognition from the other men. He had come this far, he might as well get his question over with.

"I'm looking for a woman . . ." One of the men let out a knowing guffaw, but was silenced by a lowering look from Weebil.

"Go on," the giant said, returning his gaze to Jayal.

"Her name is Thalassa . . . Thalassa Eaglestone."

Jayal fancied the men around him had stirred at the mention of the name, but Weebil's expression, which was what he was watching most closely, didn't change.

"Thalassa Eaglestone," the giant said ponderously, scratch-ing at his bearded chin. "That name is familiar. Where might I have heard it before?" He turned interrogatively to his compan-ions.

One of the others now spoke.

"I've seen her, but last week! Least I was sure it were her."

"Oh?" replied Weebil. "And where might that have been?"

"Why when I had that gold durcal off that Surren noble and I thought to have some sport with the ladies. There she was, as plain as day, at the Temple of Sutis."

Jayal jerked forward angrily, caution forgotten. "You're lying!" he snarled.

"Temper, temper," Weebil said, laying a restraining hand on his arm. "Drink; it will calm you," he said, indicating the untasted beaker in Jayal's hand. The pressure from his grip indicated that there was little choice in the matter. Jayal looked at the drink, fighting his anger. He must get a rein on his emotions. He tilted his head back and poured the liquid down his throat as well as he could while keeping the hood over his head.

At first the liquor merely numbed his teeth, then an excruciating burning sensation erupted in his mouth, and his throat constricted as if he was being throttled. The burning carried down his chest and into his stomach. He coughed, his eyes bulging from the fire in his throat and belly. He could hear the laughter of the company, amused by his gagging and gasping. When his eyes could focus again through the tears filling them, he saw Weebil's face, cracked in a sinister grin.

"Not much of a drinker, are you, stranger? A small drop of Rak enough to lay you on your beam ends?"

So that was it: Rak, the thrice-distilled lees of a foul-smelling berry found on the marshes, often said to have narcotic properties. Weebil was evidently almost immune to it, but already the edges of the room had begun to bend and warp in the periphery of Jayal's vision.

"Dizzy are you?" Weebil asked with evil solicitude. With a push of a couple of his giant fingers, he sent Jayal reeling back onto a bench set against the wall. He sat abruptly, momentarily stunned, the hood flying back off his face. The room distorted and bent even more, so the faces of the other guests, now crowding round him, looked oddly distended.

"Now, 'Stranger,' since you're sitting comfortably, maybe we can learn something about you . . ." The giant loomed over him, the voice, far away but unmistakably sinister, ". . . though I fancy I already know enough."

"Do you recognise him, then?" Jayal heard one of the others ask, again as if from a great distance.

"As a tick the hide it burrows under: here, Dob, you fought in the battle; don't you recognise your old captain, Baron Ill-gill's son?" There was a gasp of surprise from the assembled company, and they crowded in even closer.

An icy chill had now permanently settled on Jayal's spine; the nightmare was starting. He struggled to rise, grabbing for his sheathed sword, but Weebil's huge hand had seized his arm in a second, holding it like a vice.

"Easy now; wouldn't want you injuring yourself, would we?" he spat. "Seeing how the Flame burns true and quick in your rascally soul!"

"What do you mean to do with him, Weebil?" one of the crowd asked.

"First we'll draw this viper's fangs . . ." said Weebil. Jayal watched helplessly as Weebil threw aside the flaps of his cloak, revealing the tell-all armour. The giant nodded his head slowly as he looked at the holy sigils of Reh embossed on it, then whipped open the belt holding his money bag and scabbarded sword and sent it skidding off into the darkness under one of the tables.

". . . and now the fangs are drawn, we'll make the creature talk." Weebil's free hand seized Jayal's jaw and squeezed it. Jayal had only the vaguest impression of the giant's gnarled face thrust up to his through the haze of alcohol and pain.

"Remember me, Captain? Seven years it's been. Remember how you led us to the Worm that day? A man never forgets the one that leads him to his death. But I was near death anyway from the flogging, and I didn't fear anything Faran had to offer. I'd show you my back, Captain, flayed to the bone it was, but you forced me to fight." He laughed bitterly at the memory. "It was by a miracle I lived," he continued, "when those whose skeins seemed longer than the Golden Thread were cut down either side. Ah, it makes a man glory in Providence to find you here, Captain. The gods must exist after all, to let me have this revenge."

Jayal's eyes were beginning to focus, but this didn't help. Weebil's bloodshot orbs were alight with murderous excitement in the gloomy room.

"Will you kill him?" one of the men asked.

"Not as yet, not until I learn what has brought him back here." He squeezed hard on Jayal's jaw again. "Now, Illgill's son, let's hear you sing. Why are you here?"

Jayal had finally found his tongue as the effects of Rak wore off. "You're mistaken . . . I've never set foot in Thrull before today!" But his plea was only met by the tightening of the vice-like grip on his jaw.

"Don't lie to me, whoreson; Dob, isn't this Jayal Illgill as you and I stand here?"

"That it is!" answered Dob, the man Jayal recognised from the gatehouse, spitting on the floor.

"See, Captain," said Weebil. "It's no use lying, and hiding behind that scrawny beard of yours. Now tell me, why did you return?"

Once Jayal's father and he had been thronged by adulatory crowds made up of men such as these. Now there was only hatred and a cruel malice in the resentful eyes of those around him. Even though his mind was befuddled, he realised the only chance of survival was to try to win them round, promise them gold. The men were mercenaries after all. Once they were blinded by gold, he might still have a chance, though only a slight one.

"Very well," he said. "I am Jayal Illgill, returned after seven years. I'm sorry for the wrongs, the wounds you suffered in the wars, it was a righteous cause . . ."

"Enough!" broke in Weebil, squeezing his jaw again. "No more cant. It's time we handed you to the Worm: Lord Faran will pay us well."

"I have gold!" Jayal protested.

"Not enough," Weebil growled, holding up the now-empty purse. "You'll have to do better than that. . . . Tell us where your father hid his treasures, something of that nature. We're not too greedy, are we, boys?" he asked, turning to the others.

Jayal thought quickly. He must escape now. He had one last chance. "Very well," he said. "Bring me pen and paper, I'll show you on a map. It's yours if you let me free."

"Bring him paper," the giant growled. Immediately, one of the men brought a tattered piece of vellum and a piece of charcoal.

"You'll have to let me go if you want me to draw," Jayal said, glancing at the giant's hand that held him down to the bench. Reluctantly, the giant eased his grip.

Jayal glanced from him to the paper.

Not yet, he thought. He must show them something first. He drew some lines that might have been buildings on the paper, and scratched a large X at their centre.

"Here!" he said, thrusting it forward. The giant grabbed it immediately and the others crowded round, momentarily distracted.

In a split second, Jayal was on his feet, knocking one of the men surrounding him out of the way. He vaulted the table behind which his sword had been thrown. In the darkness next to the wall he could see the faint glow of its light through the stitch holes of the scabbard. Too late he realised that he was not going to get to it in time.

Then his face was hurtling at speed towards the wall, propelled by a mighty shove from behind. His forehead cracked into the stonework and bright lights exploded in his head, followed by blackness.

He came to in agony, brief explosions of pain playing up his back and on his arm and legs. He opened his eyes a crack. The table had been dragged aside and now Weebil and his guests were administering a good kicking to his prone body. Luckily, in his semiconscious state, he had curled his body into a foetal ball. Weebil held up his hand when he saw him stirring.

"Look, we've woken the beauty!" He knelt in front of Jayal's bloody face. "You're not much of a draughtsman, are you, Illgill? That map doesn't bear any relation to any place hereabouts, and you know it." He picked up Jayal's head and slammed it down onto the flagstones of the floor. Sparks filled Jayal's vision.

He barely heard Weebil's voice through the buzzing in his ears. "No, you'll not be helping us to any gold, Illgill. All that went with your father when he fled to the north. You're no better than a dog's carcass to us. Worse in fact, for me and the boys will have to carry you out to the Vampires."

"We're not taking him to the Temple of Iss, then?" one of the men asked.

"No, it'll be locked tighter than a witch's arse at this time of night. Besides, do you think Golon would trust us as have kept someone like him for a night? They'd kill us as well, as sure as corpses stink." There was a general murmur of agreement at this from the others: they were obviously no more trusting of the new masters of Thrull than they had been of the old ones. But now Weebil was leaning down towards him again, the Rak on his breath making Jayal's gorge rise.

"So you came back for your betrothed, did you? That's rich! A pillar of virtue you are, that would kill men like flies, but save a strumpet's worthless life." Jayal tried to rise angrily, but was thrust back peremptorily by the giant's hand. "There's no need to rush—you'll soon be outside, Illgill. First let us tell you all about your betrothed. Eaglestone's daughter! She was a looker all right! The difference is now any of us can have her, not just the men of quality, such as you."

Jayal tried to spit in Weebil's face, but only earned a severe shaking of his head so that it felt as if his eyeballs were about to pop from their sockets.

"Temper, lad," Weebil cautioned sarcastically. "Now, Quig," he said without taking his eyes off Jayal's face, "where do you think young Illgill's son here might find his long-lost betrothed?"

The man called Quig scratched at his beard, a malicious glint in his eye. "Why, as I've said, where any man can have her for a durcal or two. The Temple of Sutis."

This time, Jayal managed to spit. Weebil drew back one of his hands and backhanded him savagely. Jayal's head jerked back, smashing into the wall behind. He sat there dazed, dimly aware of the other voices in the room.

"Shall we kill him now?" one of them said.

"Yes," another replied. "Them aristocrats never brought any of us joy; let's kill him."

Now still another voice joined the debate. "No, we ought to give him over to the Worm tomorrow; Lord Faran will pay gold for him."

"Aye, that's our duty," said another, no doubt more inspired by the gold than duty.

Weebil's bass voice broke through the hubbub. "Fools: I've told you already: what good is it to hand him over tomorrow? By then we'll have had him a whole night; you know what happens to anyone the Worm suspects of treachery; look at them stocks out in the temple square." There was a general murmur of assent at this.

"So what's to be done?" one of the voices asked. Jayal's vision was a grey fuzz, but he sensed someone leaning over him, and then the stench of Rak wafted over him, and he knew it was Weebil.

"Believe me it would please me more than sin to kill him now, nice and slow. A drop of blood for every living soul that he and his father consigned to Hel. A broken bone for every lash of my flogging and every wound I took on Thrull field. But where's the terror in that?" He looked around the room at his guests. "Remember, you who lived here, how your families died like rats in a hole when the Vampirs ran amok after the battle? Bled dry they were, screaming for mercy. They died slowly, like he will. The storm's over, the Brethren will be out in the streets—let them bleed him dry." The onlookers roared their approval.

Jayal felt the giant's massive hands bunching at the mouth of his collar. "Do you hear me, Illgill's son? I could kill you as easy as breathing, I could, but that's too good for you. You're going to go back out there with the Vampirs—that's where you're going to go. You'll feel their bite, feel the blood flowing away. They'll carry you down, into the catacombs, where it's dark, and they'll keep you there as you get weaker and weaker as they suck you dry. We'll hear you screaming as they take you. Is that justice? Answer me!" His collar was shaken again and Jayal's head wobbled backwards and forwards. But Weebil had not bothered to get an answer; already he felt cords being tied around his wrists and ankles. He was bundled to his feet and dragged down the corridor.

He desperately tried to look behind at Dragonstooth lying in the far corner of the room. Seven years wasted. His whole life wasted. . . .

Now they were at the door, and the peephole was thrust open. "All clear," he heard one of the men say.

"Not for long. The storm's over—they'll be here soon," Weebil growled. "Right lads— Out with him!" The bolts were drawn back with a series of sharp retorts. Jayal smelt the cool, rain-scented air, then his feet left the ground. He landed heavily on the cobbles of the bridge, blacking out.

The door was slammed shut even as his trussed body rolled once, then twice, then came to a rest. A last lightning flash illuminated the bridge, and dull thunder reverberated over the city, but sight and sound seemed powerless to raise Jayal to consciousness.

Across the bridge, a round stone covering some steps leading to the sewers was thrust up by a preternaturally strong arm, and a dark head and torso appeared. Its eyes stared intently at where Jayal's body lay.

CHAPTER FIFTEEN

Before Stick's Hole

Count Durian sat in his study in the old Durian mansion. The fire glowing in the grate imparted a red hue to his normally pale features. His hand rested on his chin, and his eyes soaked up the light of the embers unconsciously, for he was in deep thought and appeared quite oblivious of his guest, a man of some thirty years, who sat on a stool on the other side of the fire.

The count was an old man, his head liver-spotted with age, his hair, what was left of it, wispy and white, drawn over the pink of his scalp. A white beard tapered from his chin, but despite his advancing years, he still bore the features of one habituated to command. A lofty brow hung over an aristocratic nose and might have made his features appear stern were it not for the warmth and intelligence in his eyes. The man opposite, though some forty years the count's junior, shared many of the same features, but his eyes were cold and calculating where the count's were warm. The younger man cleared his throat, as if anxious to attract Durian's attention, but it seemed that the count had temporarily forgotten his existence, so deep was he in thought.

The count had once been a member of Baron Illgill's court, one of the Hearth Brethren who had ruled the city since its founding thousands of years before. He had been too old to fight in the battle of the marshes and, as a consequence, was the only one of the Brethren left alive. Faran had allowed him to live, no doubt as a comforting gesture to the townsfolk, who believed retribution would be meted out on all the servitors of Flame after the fall of the city.

But the seven years since the battle had brought no joy to the count, merely a weary incarceration in his mansion, spiced only by visits from some of the people he'd known from Illgill's court, the old woman, Alanda, being the chief of them. He'd seen the town population whittled away night by night, seen the defiance grow in the Temple of Reh, and the plotting. Now all those conspirators who were left were going to leave the city. He was too old to go, and the years in front presented to his mind a weary prospect.

At this moment, he was reflecting on the fate of all the old people like him in the city, waiting for the young to leave, waiting for the time when it didn't seem worthwhile barricading the doors at night. His servants had left one by one, the last but this morning. The man's name was Zacharias, a good man whose life had been destroyed when the vampires had taken his wife. The count would miss Zacharias. He hoped he had made it over Superstition Mountain before nightfall.

The freedom of the mountain passes! It was years since he'd seen them, and his soul longed for the untinctured air and the bare mountain crags. But he was older still than Zacharias and knew that he would have broken down on the first steep slope if he had gone with him. He sent a prayer after his departed servant, wishing him a safe passage to Surrenland.

No, a man as old as he could only wait. Tonight he waited with a purpose. The first person he'd waited for sat across from him in the dimly lit study: Seresh, his only surviving son. He had arrived outside the Durian mansion an hour ago when the storm had been at its height, but he'd had to wait in the downpour, watching from the mouth of Stick's Hole, because the count had had a prior visit: a search party from the Temple of Reh. The High Priest had been killed, they told him; they were looking for the murderer, a masked priest. They had been almost apologetic as they'd ransacked the house, overturning furniture, peering into every nook and cranny.

They'd found nothing, of course, for the masked priest was the second person the old count was waiting for this night.

He knew he would come: like so many others of the old baron's court he had dabbled in prophecy: an astrolabe and the *Book of Light* lay on top of his desk. But, after years of study, he no longer had to consult them. Since the battle, the events of the future had been his obsession. He'd pored for hour after hour over the clues that book and astrolabe gave him. Now he knew them off by heart: every verse, every conjunction. Now, on this night, seven years to the day since Faran had marched victoriously into the city, the time had come.

His son stirred uneasily in his seat. He didn't know why they waited, and he was anxious to leave. The count had kept his purpose deliberately from him, for his son was headstrong and had little faith in his father's divinations. It was better if the count waited for the priest to arrive, as he knew he would, for if he mentioned him before his arrival, he suspected that his son would scoff at him, and leave anyway. It was essential Seresh take this stranger to the Temple of Sutis so he could join the other conspirators. Seresh had come to say farewell: the count blessed the fate which had meant that his son had not been one of those rounded up at the temple two days ago. He had been a fugitive since the battle and had lived in many places in the city, but never in the Temple of Reh, where traitors like Varash mingled with good men. Seresh's task was to take Alanda and the young girl to the City of the Dead, where Zaraman was waiting.

Marizian's tomb: his friend Illgill had stolen the wizard's last great magical artefact from it: the Rod of Shadows. Now three of the objects that had once been buried there were scattered, and only one remained. It was the key to all the others: the magical Orb in which all the other items could be descried.

It was this Orb that Zaraman was trying to reach. From the tomb, he and the others would travel north, trying to find Baron Illgill. Only what they found in the Orb would help with this task. What they didn't know yet was how much they would need this priest. Was he not the one called the Herald in the *Book of Light*? For the prophecies to come true, his son and Zaraman would require his aid. Where was he? The storm had ended, the night was passing, and still he hadn't arrived.

The count sighed again and stared sightlessly at the flames in the hearth.

Now the uneasy silence between father and son deepened: their valedictions had taken all of fifteen minutes, then they had both run out of things to say. His son knew, he suspected, that this was the last time he would ever see his father. The circumstances made words difficult. Seresh had lost the rest of his family in the sack of Thrull. Only this house, and his father, who had stayed behind to protect it, had survived. All the others had died seeking sanctuary in the Temple of Reh.

Now his son was anxious to be off. He wasn't due at the Temple of Sutis for a while yet, but the silence was clearly oppressive to him. Once more he made as if to rise from his seat, but for at least the fourth time that hour, his father held up a hand staying him:

"Wait," he commanded.

"But father . . . my duties . . ." Seresh said.

The old man shook his head. "So anxious to leave? Alanda is an old friend. She knows you are coming. Stay a little time. I'm alone now Zacharias has gone. It's good we have these moments together."

Seresh fell back into his seat with a sigh. "The search party will be back soon," he muttered.

"Not for a while," his father replied. "Thrull is a large city. It will take them many hours to search every building."

Seresh resumed his moody stare at the embers of the fire, and the two remained in a silence punctuated only by the patter of rainwater falling from the gutter outside.

A faint penumbra of hazy light ringed the moon Erewon as it shone down wanly upon the wet cobbles of the street. Urthred kept in the lee of the shadows. He was nearing Stick's Hole. A last sluice of rain fell from the guttering of an overhanging gable, landing with a startling impact. The sudden noise made him stop in mid-stride, one foot suspended in the air. He listened: nothing save the pattering of raindrops falling from the eaves and then the distant roar of thunder as the storm made its way south towards the Astardian Sea.

With the dying of the wind, the mists were beginning to

form again in the canyons between the buildings. Urthred shivered in his sodden clothing and his teeth chattered uncontrollably. But the cold was more bearable now he was moving. The blood was circulating in his veins, and Manichee's ghostly appearance had filled him with purpose once more.

In front, the street descended steeply, passing through a moss-covered archway. He could see an irregular square beyond. To the right were the top of the ramparts of the inner curtain wall, the cliff face, then empty air, with the roofs of the Lower Town barely appearing through the regathering mist five hundred feet below. Across the square and directly in front was the thirty-foot-high cave entrance in the granite cliff that he'd seen earlier. In the darkness of the night it represented an area of an even greater darkness, a void into which all light was sucked. Even from this distance Urthred could hear the squeaking of bats from deep within it. Trailers of ivy hung over its entrance like decaying green teeth. Pillars of rock within illuminated by the moonlight reinforced the impression of a gaping human mouth. Stick's Hole. He had read about it in Manichee's book. For centuries the dead of Thrull had been taken through it to be buried in the catacombs below. Now, Urthred guessed, the undead swarmed up it at night, reversing the course of their funeral journeys. Any moment he expected to see one of them emerge from its gloom.

To the left of the cave was a row of weather-beaten mansions, their stone fronts grey and leeched, and stained with streaks of rain. There was just enough light from the moon for him to see his destination: a three-storeyed building with its windows boarded up. The only visible entrance was a worm-eaten double doorway, with one side hanging lopsidedly in relation to the other, a sun symbol carved into the keystone of its arch. The Durian mansion. A leafless tree stood in front of it, its melancholy branches dripping droplets of water. No light whatsoever shone from the building, and once more Urthred questioned whether the vision by the pool had been a feverish hallucination. But now he was committed, as safe in trying the house as going back to the pool to await the coming of dawn.

He hurried across the square, his eyes glued to the yawning cavern mouth. There was no movement from its shadows, and the only sound was the noise of his sandals on the cobblestones and the squeaking of bats from within its depths. Then he was at the doorway.

The sound of his fists beating on the worm-eaten wood of the panels sounded unnaturally loud, and the echo which came back to him spoke of empty, long-abandoned rooms which had not heard a human tread in years. He looked about him nervously, expecting the knocking to have brought a crowd of shambling figures from out of Stick's Hole, but there was still no movement from there. He hammered with his gloved fist again with a bravado which he himself found terrifying. Surely, in the deadly hush of the night, all Thrull could hear him? His fist stilled, and now he thought he detected the faintest of sounds within, as if a door far away in the depths of the building had opened. Then he heard the shuffling of feet as someone or something approached. The footsteps ceased, then a pregnant pause, and then a challenge. The voice when it came was older and milder than he had expected.

"Who is it who calls upon the Durian house? It is long past the curfew."

"A friend," Urthred said as confidently as he could.

There was mild amusement in the reply. "If you are so, you had better identify yourself. What is your name, who sent you? These things are of interest to an old man who wants to keep the little blood he still has."

"Sir, I wish you no harm. I'm a stranger here, a priest from Forgeholm."

"Then you are a long way from your monastery. What is your name?"

Urthred thought. Should he announce himself as Randel's brother? There was too much risk in that. But then he remembered his brother's letter and the password he had given him. "The Herald": wasn't that it?

"The Herald," he said tentatively, not expecting any response.

"Ah," the voice returned with a mild suspiration. Then, to his surprise, he heard the sound of a lock being turned and bolts being drawn. One of the doors opened and light spilled out from a guttering torch held in the gnarled hand of an old man.

His rheumy eyes focused weakly on Urthred's cloak and worked up to his face. His leathery face creased in pain when he saw the mask.

"Come," he said, averting his gaze, his hitherto mild voice suddenly hard. He gestured for Urthred to enter quickly and the priest did so, the old man hastily bolting the door behind him.

"That mask!" the old man spat, as if he had just eaten something vile.

"It was made for me by a monk at Forgeholm—Manichee," Urthred explained defensively.

The old man stopped. "Manichee?"

"Yes, he was my teacher."

"I knew him well when he was alive. But why did he make that mask? As a penance, or a protection?" the old man asked. He held up his hand abruptly. "Don't answer, I don't wish to know; my friend Manichee was wiser than any man, deeper, too." He paused. "Wiser and dead."

Urthred nodded his head. "He was like a father to me."

The old man looked him up and down quizzically. "I think I know who you are, but how did you come by that name, 'the Herald'?"

"My brother, Randel, told me to use it."

"So you're Randel's brother . . ." The count hesitated for a moment, his brow creasing as if he didn't know how to phrase what he had to say next.

Urthred made it easy for him: "My brother is dead, Count. . . . I saw him sacrificed."

The count shook his head sadly. "I only heard an hour or so ago. A search party came from the temple, looking for you."

"I killed the High Priest," Urthred replied, almost defiantly, as if he expected the count to eject him from the house when he heard this news.

"That is why the search party came," the count agreed, but without the terror that Urthred might have expected from someone in the presence of a murderer.

"It doesn't trouble you?" he asked.

The count shook his head. "Varash was a traitor; he caused the death of many good men, not only your brother." He looked at Urthred's mask again. "Tonight has been a bitter one for you, but I'm afraid your dangers are not yet over. The search party will return in a while, and it would be best if you weren't here when they come."

Urthred's shoulders slumped at the prospect of wandering the dark city once more. "Then I will go now—I'm sorry if I've put you at risk."

He turned to the door, but the count held up his hand. "I said they would return; but not yet. Come, we have things to discuss." He flourished the tattered, ermine-trimmed robes he wore, in an antique courtly gesture.

He led Urthred away from the door. A large hallway was revealed in the dim light of the torch, its chequerboard floor covered with dust. Furniture hung with dusty veils of cobwebs was arranged in the gloomy recesses of the room and the features of dead ancestors stared from portraits on the dark, oak-panelled walls like the faces of ghosts peering down disapprovingly at the intruder.

But as Urthred watched, one of the figures proved itself to be more vital than ancient paint and varnish by detaching itself from the shadows and advancing into the light of the torch. Urthred saw a young man, balding, with a long nose that had a familial resemblance to the older man's. He carried a two-handed iron sword in front of him. His nose was wrinkled in disgust at the mask.

"What in Hel is that thing?" he spat, his loathing undisguised.

The old man spoke for the priest. "Seresh, this is a friend, one of the Flame like us: Manichee's pupil."

The younger man's gaze was still hooded with suspicion. "Manichee died seven years ago on the Plains. . . ."

The old man chuckled. "Forgive my son," he said, addressing Urthred. "He forgets his manners sometimes, as do many of the hotbloods of this day and age. He is a wanted man, and the visit of the acolytes was a shock to both of us. I think you are going to tell us a little more about how you found this house?"

Urthred swallowed hard: now he would have to come out with an unlikely story, which would scarcely be believed, no matter how credulous or superstitious the old man and his son were.

"He came—in a vision, during the storm," he said hesitantly. "He told me I would find friends here, at the old Durian mansion . . ."

"Who came?" Seresh asked.

"Manichee."

The younger man snorted contemptuously. "You expect us to believe a story like that? Father, he's told us already that Randel has been killed. How many more of our other friends have been taken as well? He's a traitor and the mask is a disguise!" He took a step forward, the sword, despite its weight, whipped behind his shoulder in one sudden movement.

But the old man interposed his frail body. "Hold your hand, Seresh: where is your faith? You of all must know the difference between Light and Shades, that Manichee travelled between them as easily as we amongst the rooms of this house. There was no greater sorcerer. Even in death his powers may live on." He looked inquisitively at Urthred. "Was it not so, priest?"

Urthred nodded his head, keeping a wary eye on Seresh. "A vision—it seemed to come from the pyramid on the marshes. . . ."

The old man's rheumy eyes lit up with excitement—at least he seemed to have no difficulty with Urthred's story.

"Manichee, returned in a vision! This is good. It's just as the *Book of Light* tells us! The Lightbringer is amongst us! Thrull will fall—it will be the end of Faran." The old man nearly danced a jig, despite the infirmity of his limbs.

Urthred puzzled over the old man's cryptic words. Manichee had mentioned the Lightbringer, told him that he would find out the identity of this person, or thing. He cast his mind back over the *Book of Light,* Reh's holy text. Passages of the Scriptures came back to mind, learnt by heart under Midian's stern tutelage all those years before. Passages concerning the Holy City, Thrull, which would fall to the Worm in a dark age, but from which would spring the hope of mankind, the Lightbringer. This would coincide with a time of great visions, of the dead returned to life. There was even mention of a Herald somewhere in the text, but his memory failed him at this juncture. Surely the old man was getting carried away? Compelling though the vision had been, Urthred himself had still been wondering whether it was merely a product of the intense cold until it had led him directly to this spot.

"You lay great weight on this vision," he said cautiously.

The old man stopped his jigging and looked at him, the rheumy eyes twinkling in the lantern light. "It gives me hope, and hope is good. Randel called you the Herald, you said? This is a good omen. Not all is lost; though your brother is dead, there are still friends around the city, friends who will help—"

"Father!" Seresh protested, obviously still mistrustful of Urthred.

"Forgive my son," Count Durian said. "He has lived with his fear for a long time—we all have . . ." Count Durian lapsed into a silence. Paradoxically, it was the drip of water from the hem of Urthred's coat on the tiled floor that seemed to bring him back to himself.

"Forgive my lack of manners. You are cold," he said quickly. "Come to the back of the house; there is a fire and some simple food."

"But what of the search party?" Urthred protested.

"As I said, they won't be back for a little while, we still have time," the count said. He led them off, lighting the way with the torch down a dust-choked corridor; the passageway was wide, wide enough for six people to walk abreast, as perhaps they once did when the Durian mansion had known better times. But here as in the hall, the evidence of decay was all too eloquent testimony of the family's decline. As they passed along, Urthred took note of the oak furniture veiled in cobwebs, weapons racks filled with rusting iron, silver candles and plates dull and tarnished, the fly-specked wall-length mirrors that reflected their ghostly passing, the oak panelling riddled with wormholes. Count Durian must have noticed his glance, for he stopped in the middle of the corridor, holding the torch high over his head, so the melancholy ruins of the hallway cast long shadows.

"Not much to look at, is it? If you knew what this place was once like . . . it had a fine mistress, my wife Elea, two daughters, and another son besides. They are all gone, butchered in the Temple of Reh when the city fell. I was here in the house, protecting it. What an irony! I thought it was I who was taking the risk. They killed everyone they could find in the temple that day, and no looter even thought to come here. I would have given them everything willingly, in exchange for my family. . . ." He shook his head sadly. "Now only Seresh and I are left. I was pardoned as I was too old even then to bear arms. But Seresh fought on the marshes and has been a fugitive ever since."

"But why did Faran grant an amnesty to you?" Urthred asked.

Count Durian smiled a small, bitter smile. "What good would this city have been if everyone in it had been slaughtered? An empty shell where no living blood flowed. Blood is what they want. At first there were only the vampires which he brought with him, two or three hundred strong. They fed on slaves and the captives from the battle. But then they went into the catacombs below the Temple of Iss. There their necromancy raised the long-sleeping dead. The need for blood grew greater. More and more people vanished from the streets, plucked from their beds, sucked dry. Faran has tried to control it, but his followers now run amok. All those who still can, have fled. Only the very old, or very strong, remain. I am one of the former, my son one of the latter; but there are not many of either left."

At this he turned once more and continued slowly down the passageway, turning into an oak-panelled study. Leather-bound books and yellowing parchments were littered on every shelf and every tabletop. An astrolabe leaned drunkenly in one corner, a straw mattress lay in another in the place where the old man evidently slept. A fire, slightly burned down, glowed redly in a huge hearth big enough to roast an ox. The old man placed the torch in a bracket over the hearth and threw some more logs on the fire. It erupted into sparks and tongues of flame, and Urthred felt a welcome warmth penetrating his wet clothes. Seresh, who had followed them silently all this time, hung back at the entrance.

"Sit," Count Durian ordered, gesturing to the one oak chair free of books which stood before the fire. Urthred did so, contemplating removing the gloves from his hands, knowing that soon he would have to grease their metal joints else they would rust and leave his hands useless and crabbed. He saw that

Seresh was eyeing him suspiciously from where he leaned against the doorjamb. The younger Durian held the pommel of his sword by one hand, its tip resting on the wooden floorboards. Seresh clearly did not share his father's complete trust in him; and why should he? Within minutes he might be captured and made ready for the stocks and the vampires in the temple square. The old man came up with a pewter dish. There was a heel of bread and some grey meat on it. "It is all we have," Count Durian said apologetically, "but eat."

Urthred felt the stirrings of hunger within him: he had not eaten since dawn, when he had set out from the pass under Superstition Mountain, but nevertheless he shook his head. Just as he couldn't remove his gloves to expose his scarred hands to his hosts, he realised revealing what lay beneath the mask was even more impossible.

"I'm not hungry," he said stoically, "but thanks anyway."

The old man tutted and set the dish aside. "Now," he said, "perhaps you could tell us how you came to be here in the city; it is a long way from Forgeholm."

Urthred sighed; his mind whirled with fatigue, hunger and the cold, but explain he must if he was to gain the two men's trust.

"Randel sent me a letter telling me that I should come here: great things were afoot. I came as swiftly as I could, but I was too late . . ." He paused to take a breath, then launched into an account of everything that had befallen him since he'd entered the city. As the tale progressed, he felt he had both men's undivided attention. The stocks, the temple, his brother's sacrifice, Varash's death and his own escape, then the storm, the vision, Manichee's ghostly words amidst the lightning bolts, Illgill's Rod and Marizian's tomb, how he had come to the Durian mansion; all rushed from him in a torrent.

When he had finished he caught father and son exchanging a glance.

Once more, it was the count who spoke first. "An interesting story—you know some of what is happening in Thrull tonight, and I would tell you more, but now time is running out. The searchers will be back here soon and you must leave." He nodded at Seresh. "My son came here to bid me farewell. A group of his friends have broken into Marizian's tomb, where Illgill found the Rod. There is an object there called the Orb. Its sole purpose is to reveal where Marizian's three other magic items are in the world. Since Baron Illgill took with him the Rod of Shadows, it must necessarily show us where Illgill is as well, if he's still alive." He paused, wheezing for breath. "Tonight is a momentous night: I'm glad you came. The vision, the password—it all adds up—I believe the Scriptures, that the Lightbringer is somewhere here amongst us. The two of you must go together and find him."

"But what about you?"

"I will stay here. If the acolytes return and find me gone, they will become suspicious. Besides, they won't harm me. Hasn't Faran guaranteed my safety?" He held up his hand to still any further argument and turned to address his son.

"You know which way to go?"

Seresh nodded. "Aye, Stick's Hole." He looked at Urthred without pleasure once more. "But, Father, can we trust this man . . . ?"

Once more Count Durian cut off his words with a curt gesture: "He is who he says he is. Now, sir," he said, turning to Urthred, "I wonder whether you would be good enough to wait for my son in the hall? We must say our good-byes. We will not see each other again for a while, maybe not until we meet again in Shades, or in Paradise." Urthred rose quickly from the chair.

"I thank you from the bottom of my heart for your trust—"

But Durian stopped his words by handing him the torch from the bracket over the fire. "No thanks are needed, now go with Reh."

Urthred bowed stiffly, and, with the torch smouldering in his hands, made his way down the dust-choked corridor to the hallway.

CHAPTER SIXTEEN

The Leech Gatherer

It only took a few seconds for the count to say good-bye to his son. From where he waited down the corridor, Urthred heard some low, muttered exchanges, then Seresh's voice raised, he fancied, in anger. A second later the younger man came to the door, a nasty scowl on his face. His sword was sheathed in a leather scabbard on his back. He held a lantern in one hand and a cloak in the other.

"Here," he said, tossing the garment peremptorily at Urthred. It was made of black cloth. Urthred thought to protest. The orange-and-red robes of a priest of Reh were sacred vestments and not to be idly thrown aside. But despite the warmth of the count's fire, he was still wet through. He undid the clasp of his own cloak and let it drop to the floor.

"What shall I do with it?" he asked, nodding at the sodden bundle.

"My father will burn it after we've left," Seresh answered shortly. He was already donning a cloak similar to the one he had thrown Urthred. Urthred glanced back at the study. Though the count was out of sight, his shadow was thrown by the light onto one of the walls. The hunched figure made a lonely spectacle: an old, sad giant.

"What about your father?" he asked.

But Seresh merely jerked his head back at the library. "You heard his decision; he'll stay here."

He took the torch from Urthred's hand and lit the wick of the lantern. The ancient furnishings of the hallway were suddenly thrown into relief as light flooded from it. Looking up, Urthred saw two galleries running round the hall and a high, raftered ceiling, hitherto invisible. Then the view was lost as Seresh shuttered the lantern so that only a narrow beam of light exited from a metal slot at its front.

Wordlessly they passed to the front of the mansion. Urthred looked back down the corridor; the giant shadow of the hunched old count still remained where it was. Then Seresh threw open the door and, after a quick glance to left and right, motioned Urthred to follow. They hurried across the square to the mouth of Stick's Hole.

As they approached a damp exhalation came from the depths of the cave and with it an acrid smell of guano. Seresh seemed undeterred by the smell and pushed his way through the fronds of ivy which hung over the mouth of the cavern entrance. They progressed slowly through a winding passageway of tumbled rocks until the last glimmerings of Erewon faded and the darkness of the cave closed around them. Urthred could almost feel the weight of the ancient granite of Thrull pushing down on him like a physical presence.

Seresh paused, unlatching the front of the lantern. As the sudden light penetrated the ancient blackness, the squeaking of the bats reached a crescendo. Then, in an explosion of sound, Urthred was in the middle of a blizzard of leathery wings. The shrieking and weaving lasted for all of five seconds, then the bats were gone, a shifting mass of blackness disappearing into the darkness at the cave mouth. One or two stragglers zigzagged round, trying to find their bearings, before fluttering off after the others.

Now that the noise and the movement had finished, Urthred could take in the scale of the cavern. The light of the lantern revealed a forty-foot-high tunnel with roughly hewn granite walls. Water dripped down from cracks in the ceiling onto the guano-splashed floor. Green fungus hung in large fronds from the damp stone.

He felt Seresh's gaze upon him. The younger Durian's face showed ghastly white and elongated in the light. The undershadowed eyes made him look like a spirit returned from Hel.

"Aren't there vampires in the caverns?" Urthred asked, as much to break the oppressive stare as his fear of what lay in the catacombs below. Seresh's expression did not waver: resentment and distrust were there, maybe even hatred. He didn't answer, but, instead, jerked his head, motioning Urthred to follow.

He strode to the back of the cave. Here, the walls were made up of asymmetrical blocks of granite. A set of rough-hewn granite steps led downwards through a fissure at the back. That, apparently, was the way.

Seresh went down, the lantern casting long shadows forward into the gloom. Urthred followed, stooping under the low ceiling. Immediately he felt an intense claustrophobia: the passage was as dark as the abyss, with most of the lantern light being blocked out by Seresh's body. He had to use his gloved hands to find the way, and even then sharp protrusions of rock barked at his shins and shoulders. After five minutes of painful descent he saw that Seresh had stopped, his lantern held out in front of him.

From where Urthred was standing it looked like the passageway in front ended in midair. Beyond the round opening there was just a sheer black void. He caught up with Seresh and peered over his shoulder into the gloom. The sight revealed by the light of the lantern made him gasp in amazement.

The ledge they were standing on opened onto a cavern a thousand times larger than the one they had just left: it was as if the whole interior of the rock of Thrull had been hollowed out. Cliff faces reared up and fell away into the darkness, a hundred feet or more, the top and bottom hidden from the lantern light which, so dazzling a moment before, was ineffectual against the weight of darkness that seemed to brood in the cave. Thousands of drops of water fell slowly from the invisible ceiling above, through the lantern's light, then vanished as abruptly as they had appeared into the darkness below.

Seresh gestured to his left. A narrow path had been carved into the cliff face. Looking down, Urthred could see it zigzagging almost vertically into the gloom. Urthred felt his spirit tugged by the abyss, as if the path had been placed there not as a route down but as an enticement for the traveller to throw himself off the edge into the chasm beneath him. It was so steep; the sort of path that a man would be better to scramble down on his hands and knees, if at all. But Seresh had already set off down it, standing upright, the lantern waving erratically in his hand. Urthred scrambled after, his sandals slipping on the loose rock and sending scatterings of stone bouncing down into the blackness below, the void below tugging at his sleeve. An outcropping at the side of the path buffeted him and he teetered, his arms flailing for balance, the blackness beckoning him. He fought to control his vertigo.

Seresh waited for him impatiently, then set off again. Urthred gradually began to find his balance and made better progress. He started to take notice of what he could see of the cavern itself, rather than just the precipitous path. There were small rectangular entranceways carved into the rock face off the path. He guessed these were the tombs of the ancient inhabitants of Thrull, from before Marizian, from the time when the gods still lived on earth. Their entrances had once been blocked by round stone coverings, but for the most part these had been broken down or rolled away, either by tomb robbers, or, a more sinister thought, by the occupants themselves. Inside he glimpsed the remains of coffins and even the mouldy palanquins in which the dead had been brought to this place centuries before. Of the tomb occupants there was no sign. Further down, they passed what appeared to be the entrance to an underground palace. A larger opening some twenty feet high had been carved into the cliff face by the path, flanked by fluted pillars painted purple and brown, the colours of Iss. He saw in the lantern light the glimmer of gold leaf glinting off wall frescoes, copper furniture, and a mould-covered couch set on a dais, empty save for a skull that grinned back at him with golden teeth. Seresh went past without sparing the place a second glance, and Urthred hurried after him.

Below the gap between the cliff faces narrowed, and he saw a deep ravine where the two joined two hundred feet below. The patter of the water from the ceiling intensified, falling heavily on the coarse fabric of Urthred's cloak. Now yellowed bones littered the narrow pathway, washed here by the rills which had

formed from the rain from the ceiling. Then, his foot came down
with a splintering impact, and Urthred fell heavily onto his back,
his face right next to the shattered human skull on which he'd
slipped. He scrambled up hastily, sending scatterings of rock
and bone down the path.

Seresh had stopped and was looking back without sympathy,
his face even more sinister in the underlighting of the lantern.

"It's only a skull," he said, as if habituated to the bones and
the gloom.

At least he had spoken, and Urthred was anxious to keep him
talking. Anything was better than the oppressive silence that he
had maintained so far. "The bones are from the tombs?" he
asked.

Seresh glanced up at the tomb entrances above them. "Ancient burials, older than the city itself. Some say the bones of the
gods are lodged here." He nodded up towards the palace entrance, which they'd left far above them. "But you should know,
priest, if you are a priest: the gods didn't die; they flew up to
Reh's fiery paradise."

"What of the vampires? Don't they come here?"

Seresh smiled knowingly again, casting his head up to where
the droplets of water fell from the invisible ceiling. "Too much
water in this season. Their flesh sloughs away in the wet. When
it's dry the priests of their temple come and bring out those who
sleep." He nodded at a broken-down tomb entrance. "For the
moment we're safe."

Urthred saw they were nearly at the bottom of the vast cavern. On the other side, a path like the one they were descending
zigzagged up the face of the opposite cliff.

"Is that where we're going?" he asked. Seresh followed his
glance.

"Yes, and a bit further." He fixed Urthred with his angry
stare. "There are some caves we'll have to pass through on the
other side. Some creatures live over there—let me deal with
them."

Urthred opened his mouth to ask further questions, but
Seresh had already set off again, striding away, if anything, even
faster than before. Urthred followed, brushing bone fragments
off his damp cloak.

The rattle of displaced stones and the water hissing off the hot metal of Seresh's lantern were the only sounds as they progressed further and further down. Soon the trickles of water from the cliff face joined, and they had to step from stone to stone over small rivulets. The sense of oppression grew heavier and heavier as the space between the cliff faces narrowed. Now the rivulets were becoming streams, and the streams, torrents, until the whole frothy mass spilt into a wide man-made channel which split the ravine in two.

As the waters congregated, the noise had increased exponentially: first a drip, then a patter, then a roar which obliterated all other sound. At the bottom of the ravine the water rushed between two canal banks towards a huge archway carved into the cliff face to their left. A smooth, thirty-foot-wide bridge spanned the canal in front of them. Seresh pointed to the archway.

"That way leads to the City of the Dead," he shouted over the din. In the gloom where the waterway disappeared Urthred could now make out huge stone structures, which looked like huge granaries, built out of the sheer rock face, and a rubble-strewn jetty alongside the canal. Nothing like this had been mentioned even in Manichee's books: what he saw must have been built when the gods still dwelt on the earth. Now he was at the bottom of the ravine; he thought to look up the way they had come. The switchback path disappeared into the gloom, the cliffs above were looming, invisible presences, pressing down into the bottom of the ravine. He felt crushed, insignificant in contrast to the ancient vastness of the place. Then he saw a light moving amongst the rocks slightly higher up on the other side of the gorge. Seresh saw it at the same instant and shuttered the lantern with an adroit twist of his wrist. They were immediately enveloped in darkness. The other light continued moving, apparently aimlessly. A figure could be seen silhouetted against it now that Seresh's own lantern was shuttered. A rope hung from a circular cavern entrance fifty feet up in the cliff face down to the rubble-strewn area where the figure was moving.

"What is it?" Urthred shouted.

"One of those that I told you about—" Seresh replied, squinting into the dark. "—a leech gatherer."

"A what?"

"Come, you will see," said Seresh. Apparently satisfied that the shape in front posed no threat, he unshuttered the lantern once more and crossed over the bridge spanning the canal. The water roared whitely below them, then they began climbing the cliff on the other side of the ravine, the noise of the torrent fading behind them.

The light above them continued to move about in the same aimless pattern, its bearer seemingly heedless of their approach. Urthred could now see that the figure was crouched by a rock, as if recovering something from beneath it. After a while it straightened and moved onto the next rock, repeating the process.

Then he lost sight of it as the path switchbacked under an overhang. They emerged onto the scree slope, and suddenly the figure had vanished. The two men looked around them. Nothing. Then as abruptly as it had vanished, the lantern was unshuttered right next to them. Urthred leapt back in surprise. But Seresh apparently had been expecting something like this, and held his own lantern firm so it shone into the face of the creature sitting on a rock next to the path.

The first thing Urthred noticed were the creature's red eyes, which glimmered like coals in the dark. Next its face, diamond-shaped like a snake's, its skin a patchwork of green and grey scales. Its nose was two hollow slits, its mouth a lipless seam from which its forked tongue darted lazily. Though its body was covered by a tattered grey robe, and from a distance it had looked vaguely humanoid, he could now see its thick scale-covered hind legs and small arms which ended in tripodal hands with one longer central claw, and two shorter talons to either side.

Two bags, manufactured from the same material as the thing's cloak, hung from a rough cord that served as its belt. The bags heaved and twitched with hidden life. Something moved in one of the creature's claws—a thick, black, finger-sized object which he had evidently just removed from the underside of the rock. Looking closely, Urthred recognised it as a leech.

The creature stared straight into the eye slits of Urthred's mask as if it were the most commonplace object in the world. For his own part, Urthred was struck both by fear and amazement simultaneously. A salamander! One of the fire-inhabiting creatures of the ancient times. A creature sacred to Reh, one of the first to inhabit the world when its surface was but a molten lake of lava and they had swum the torrents of fire like fish in an ocean. He had thought they had died out aeons ago, but here was one, right under the rock of Thrull. But this sense of awe had clearly not transferred to his companion.

"Ho, Sashel," Seresh said, greeting the salamander as if their meeting was a common event.

"It has a name?" Urthred asked, even more surprised.

The creature inclined its head, its unblinking eyes never leaving Urthred's mask for a second.

"The creature cannot speak," Seresh said, "but it can communicate in other ways."

"How?" Urthred asked. But even as he uttered the question, he heard a voice whispering in his brain. A hissing, sibilant noise, but one recognisable as human speech. Telepathy! The creature could speak with other minds. The creature's mouth hadn't moved, nor had its red eyes left his face. But here was its voice, frighteningly close.

"So," the voice said, "two of you tonight. Who is your friend, Seresh?"

Seresh glanced at Urthred, unperturbed by the creature's mode of communication. "One who needs our help."

"Then I know who he is, if his mask didn't already tell me."

"You had heard?"

"Some priests of the Worm came earlier to the mouth of the catacombs. They told the guard there that there would be a good reward for anyone who delivered over the masked one." He looked significantly at Urthred, and the priest felt a chill, a chill which the creature seemed to pick up on, for the red of its eyes intensified, and he felt it probing his every thought.

Seresh glanced at Urthred, then back to the creature. "And will you hand him over?"

The red eyes never wavered from Urthred's mask. "As you know, Seresh, we trade these," he said, holding up the wriggling leech, "for medicine. But the priests of Iss are not our friends."

Seresh nodded. "We need your help to cross over to the other side."

The creature inclined its head once. "I will guide you and your friend through the catacombs, but first you must talk with my Elder."

"What catacombs are those?" Urthred asked.

"The ones beneath the Temple of Iss," Seresh said. "Sashel has led me many times. His people are on our side, though they are forced to trade with the Worm."

"Why?"

"You will see when we pass through their caves."

Sashel seemed unbothered by their open discussion of his people; the ease with which he accessed others' minds must have made most of what humans called secrets open to him. He tugged the drawstrings of his sacks together, lifted the lantern from the rock on which it had been resting and set off towards the rope hanging from the cavern mouth above them.

They reached the rope in silence. Sashel seized it with his talons and gave it a tug. Immediately, several more reptilian heads appeared above them, their eyes glinting redly in the lantern light. No obvious signal was given by Sashel, but two rope baskets, big enough to lift a man, were lowered down towards them.

"Get in." The creature's words once more came into Urthred's mind, unbidden. Seresh was already doing so, and Urthred followed, settling his lanky form uncomfortably in the basket. Immediately it was jerked upwards. Below he could see Sashel effortlessly scrambling up the rope after them. He reached the ledge at the same time as the basket.

Urthred stepped out of it gingerly. A cavern mouth snaked back into the darkness, but at its far end he could see a strong white glow of light. Some twenty or so of Sashel's fellow creatures surrounded him. They were armed with rusted spears and swords, which they held awkwardly in their three-clawed hands. Their breath hissed through their nosepieces, and their tongues flicked lazily backwards and forwards. His mind hummed with their unspoken discourse. The babble stopped immediately at a sign from Sashel, who gestured to Urthred and Seresh.

"Follow me," he said abruptly, leading them forward into the cave towards the white glow.

As they approached, they saw a tattered hessian awning covering the entrance to an inner cave. Sashel pulled this aside and immediately a dazzling white light flooded back down the passageway, temporarily blinding Urthred. When his eyes had adjusted again, he saw a circular chamber in front of him, with subsidiary passages leading off from it. The light came from several pots of ancient design leaning at odd angles on the floor. They were filled with glowing stones that gave off both a fiercesome light and furnacelike heat. Already Urthred could feel the sweat trickling down his back. More salamanders lay on rough hessian sacks around the glowing pots, but Urthred immediately saw that these were not healthy like the ones outside. Greymottled patches covered their skin, and their forked tongues hung from their mouths.

"These are the victims of the mould," Sashel explained. "My people love the Flame; the damp of the caves kills them. We have no option but to remain underground now, and take what solace we can from the fire pots."

"Where does their magic come from?" Urthred asked.

"We found them after the gods left the earth: it is the only flame that exists that is as strong as the fire with which Reh created the world."

"Yet your people die?"

"More and more as the sun gets weaker. Only the medicine that the Worm gives us in return for the leeches keeps them alive."

"What is this medicine?" Urthred asked.

Sashel indicated a bag full of a white powder lying next to one of the sick creatures. "These powders alleviate the rot, as does the white light of the pots. But once we were many, now only a hundred or so remain." There was a finality in the voice hissing in Urthred's ear, as if no further questions or explanations were appropriate. "Come," Sashel said. "You must see the Elder before I take you through the catacombs."

"Wait," Urthred said. In the light of the pots, the tingling in his veins had returned. He felt the old power returning into his limbs, the power that Manichee had given him through the mask. He felt sorry for these creatures: they, too, were the chosen ones of Reh. He stooped by the bag of powder, running his gloves through it. It was some crystalline substance, dry and brittle to the touch. But a stink of mould hovered over the bag, reminding him of the smell of the vampires he had fought in the temple square. The crystals were the sort that the Temple of Worms would use to absorb moisture during the embalming process. The smell told him why the medicine was not working. He looked at the dying creature in front of him. Its scales were moulting off in great swathes, a grey fungus spreading in large patches over its face and its upper body. Its skin gave off a stink of decay. It would not live long.

Urthred made up his mind in a second. If the God had returned his powers, he must use them for the benefit of his creatures. He detached the metal rods from the brace which kept his gloves attached to his arm, then tugged off the gloves themselves, revealing what lay beneath.

Not a hand but an alien thing, as much like a claw as a hand. A scorched lump of scar tissue, the fingers burned away above the middle joint of each finger. He heard Seresh gasp in surprise at the sight. But Urthred had no ears for him. He closed his eyes, summoning the power from the seed of Flame inside him, and from the mask. Then he felt the heat burning down the veins in his arms into the stumps of his fingers. When he opened his eyes again a white energy was playing in a complex latticework in the air around his hand, an energy even brighter than that of the blazing pots. He held his hand over the creature's mottled face. Immediately the grey mould began to pulse and sizzle at the edges, boiling away in a white mist within seconds. An open, clean wound was left behind. For the first time since he'd been in the cavern, the creature stirred. Emboldened by his success, Urthred passed around the other figures. There were twenty or more of them. The mould burned away on these others in the same miraculous fashion. As he finished the last of them, he felt his powers begin to die. He rehitched his glove and stood up.

There was another of the creatures standing next to Sashel now, slightly stooped, supporting itself with a gnarled stick, its eyes red and rheumy with age. The Elder that Sashel had spoken of. It must have seen the whole performance.

Its voice came into Urthred's mind. "You command the Flame, you are a priest of Reh?"

Urthred nodded.

"You have saved my people, when all the medicine of the Worm has failed."

"The medicine was infected with decay."

"Yes, I know this now, having seen your magic at work." The creature said this as if it were no great surprise, that the machinations of humans were a regrettable evil which he had long recognised. "They hate us, for we swam in the molten fire of Reh at the beginning of time."

"Then I have brought you into further danger; they are looking for me."

"They came earlier, with more of this medicine, offering rewards."

"So I have heard."

The creature ruminated for a moment. "I have seen the past and the future. Even the undead lord who rules here now has not seen as many human years as I. We were here when the gods lived on the earth. They buried their dead here when the marshes were a huge inland sea. We saw their golden barques rowed from far-off Niasseh, and heard their funeral drums like thunder over the waters. We let the gods come, for then it seemed there was room enough for both our kinds under the sun. But the plains dried out and became fields. The gods departed, and many humans came to the rock of Thrull. Finally Marizian came five thousand of your years ago, just as the first veil was drawn over the sun. You humans had not noticed it then, but we had. We fled under the ground as Marizian's giants and fire-spitting dragons hewed and melted the living rock. The rock was made a fortress and a prison, and the people who lived here enslaved by the chains of religion." Urthred made as if to protest, but the creature had already picked up on his thoughts, for it raised its claws and fixed him with its glittering eyes. "Reh is not what you think, priest. He is not a god entombed in dusty books, but a living, beating fire which even a great wizard like Marizian could never capture."

He paused, as he watched Urthred struggling with his words. But when no vocal protest was made, he continued, "Now, after five thousand years, the human time is ending in Thrull. This ancient rock will be ours once more and you will be gone. But you will live, masked priest, and I will help you as you have helped us."

Urthred bowed his head.

"Here, take this staff," the creature said. "Should you ever lose your way, one of my people will find you, wherever you are."

Urthred took the proffered item and immediately felt a flow of energy commensurate with what he'd just used entering his limbs. He looked at the Elder.

"This is magic."

"It is old—older than your race. It is a branch from an ancient tree which lies far to the North, in what you humans call the Forest of Lorn. It is called the Dedication Tree: it was the first plant that the Lord of Light infused with his sacred seed. Guard it well. Help will never be far away while you walk with Reh."

"That I shall always do. My thanks," Urthred mumbled.

"Now it is time for you to go. Remember, leave this city soon; its end is coming. Maybe this very night."

"That may be easier said than done," Seresh said. "We still have to pass through the catacombs."

"Sashel will lead you, as he's done before," the Elder said.

Sashel stood forward. The Elder bowed low, and retreated into one of the gloomy side chambers.

"Come," Sashel said, leading off down a side corridor. Seresh and Urthred followed, leaving the glowing cave behind them. Urthred looked at the staff in his hands. It seemed to be just a rough branch cut from a tree, but the energies within tingled even through his thick gloves.

They passed another group of the creatures guarding a rock-cut passageway. Urthred noticed that it was much drier here. The dryness seemed to increase Seresh's tension.

"This is the beginning of the catacombs under the Temple of Iss," he explained. Urthred peered into the gloom. The corridor in front didn't seem too different from the ones they'd passed before, but here there were several side passages leading off. He felt a warning tingle in his spine.

Sashel went forward, his lantern held aloft. Seresh drew the two-handed sword and followed. Urthred fell in behind after casting a quick look back in the direction of Stick's Hole. Already the other salamanders had disappeared. He followed the others, even more conscious of the great weight of rock pressing down all around. The corridor divided, then divided again, and they swiftly became lost in a bewildering maze of passageways. But Sashel moved forward unerringly. He ducked under a low opening, and they entered a new series of dusty corridors, so ancient that the floors were broken and cracked, so much so that frequently they had had to climb a scree of stones where a rock slip had cracked the passageway in two. Piles of bones spilling out from alcoves and mouldered leather stretchers partially blocked their way.

Sashel paused, allowing them to catch up. Urthred welcomed the rest; the pace had been unremitting, and he was dizzy with hunger and fatigue.

Seresh was staring down the dust-filled passageway up which they had just come. Something in his eyes caused another icy tingle to run up Urthred's spine.

"What is it?" he whispered, his voice even to his own ears oddly muffled by his mask and the close atmosphere of the corridor.

"Don't you feel it? They're coming now!" Seresh said.

"Who?"

"Why, who but they who are buried here, rising to the moon as we would to the sun?"

A small avalanche of white powdery dust fell from the ceiling, perhaps precipitated by the vibration of their voices. Or perhaps by something else.

Urthred listened intently, but the mask muffled sound, and he was conscious only of the exaggerated beating of his own heart. The only object in the winding passageway was an abandoned catafalque. It was robed round with mouldering tapestries, a small pile of yellowing bones fallen half out of it. They'd already passed many such hearses in this part of the underworld, ancient burials from a forgotten age. Why should he be afraid of these bones? Surely even Iss could not breathe life into such pitiful offerings, dead for millennia? As he watched, a small black-and-white viper slid from the eye socket of the yellow skull and wormed away into the darkness, away from the lanterns. As it went, Urthred's feeling of dread alleviated slightly. But then he felt the light at his shoulder begin to fade, the chill returned, and he swung round. Through the eye slits of his mask he could see Seresh and Sashel already making progress up the corridor. He hurried after them.

But as abruptly as they had moved off, they stopped again, their heads cocked, listening.

"What is it?" Urthred whispered.

"Hssst!" hissed Seresh, holding a finger to his lips. He nodded his head onwards down the corridor. Now Urthred could hear it as well, the rustle of dried leaves followed by a breath of fresh air. They were at the mouth of the catacombs. They had traversed the centre of the mountain and were now about to exit on its other side. He estimated that it had taken them just over an hour.

Sashel's voice came into Urthred's mind, the noise breaking the oppressive hush. "Now I must leave you. Guard the staff well, priest, for you may need it before the night is out."

Urthred made as if to speak, but Seresh held up his hand, cautioning him to silence. Sashel's red eyes stared for a second more into the eye slits of Urthred's mask, then he glided back down the corridor. He and his lantern had disappeared into the darkness within seconds.

Seresh jerked his head forward. "Come," he whispered. "We're nearly there." They advanced cautiously, Seresh leading. They rounded a corner and now Urthred could see a dim rectangle of light, a rough-hewn entranceway carved from the side of the granite knoll. Beyond, in Erewon's scant light, he could see a sunken courtyard filled with dead leaves and fragments of ancient pottery shards, steep steps leading upwards from it to street level.

But they'd got there too late: already the way was blocked.

"Look!" Seresh hissed. Down a side passageway which also led to the courtyard, two figures draped in white winding sheets had appeared, gliding towards them, their legs invisible under their graveclothes. Seresh tried to close the front of the iron lantern, but it was too late. The two vampires saw them well enough with or without the lamp. They hesitated for the briefest of seconds then came on, making a curious hissing noise, much like a cat hissing at a dog. Even by the fitful light of the half-shuttered lantern Urthred could see yellow fangs exposed in their emaciated faces, their inflamed red eyes.

When they spoke, the sound that emanated from their dried voice boxes conveyed a dialect so ancient that Urthred could barely understand what they said.

"Ho, I smell the blood of a couple of ripe ones here! Shall it be ours to drink, Fayal?" said the first, his words but a throaty croak.

"That and more, for the streets will be full of the living tonight."

"Then we will live another moon?"

"And a thousand more after!"

"Well spoken," said the first. They were past the entrance to the courtyard and were closing fast. "Come, sweets, why do you languish so, when your last embrace awaits you?" he said, addressing Seresh and Urthred.

"Quick, let us go back," said Seresh, opening the lantern again so its harsh glare shone full into the face of the two vampires. But the light merely served to illustrate further the horror of them: two men, with lank white hair, mottled purpled skin which had begun to flake, purple gums, their eyes all bunged up with rheum, their hands outstretched much like chicken claws, the protrusion of sharp canines over their bottom lips giving menace to their macabre appearance, as did the bulging muscles of their arms and upper torsos, which stretched the stained material of their winding sheets.

The panic in Seresh's voice nearly unnerved Urthred, but he knew that to run back into the labyrinth behind them would be suicidal.

"No, stay!" he said. He'd fought off the others in the square, and though the power of his mask had been used up in healing the salamanders, he could still fight them with his gloves.

"Well said, master," said the creature named Fayal. "For the sooner you come to us, the sooner that Flame shall evermore be extinguished in Iss' glory."

"In his rot and disintegration, you mean, for your master knows not of glory, only of the grave, and winding sheets and human misery," replied Urthred, laying the staff on the ground, and bringing his gloved fists up in front of him.

The creatures seemed content to swap badinage as they crept ever closer. "Time grows short, and I would not miss other opportunities to drink the red, red blood of living ones: lean close to me, let me embrace you," entreated the first, taking another step forward.

"Remember how they mesmerise, look away!" warned Seresh, stepping back and playing the lantern from side to side so the vampires seemed to dance in the shifting light.

"Yes, lean close," whispered Fayal as he drew near Urthred. "Think of it, no more striving, the ease of death, but a sweet dream, all you need is blood to live forever . . ."

Urthred took one step closer, then another. Seresh yelled a warning, believing him mesmerised by the vampire's words and its hypnotic red eyes.

But it was too late. Fayal was reaching out a white hand to Urthred's neck, his mouth widening, strings of saliva glistening between his distended incisors. . . .

It happened in a second: Urthred's right hand flew out and seized the vampire's throat, just as the jaw champed down in a bite. The incisors snapped down on empty air, splintering, a bluish blood burst from the purpled lips, the vampire's arms thrashed in the air as Urthred lifted it up off the ground, his other hand reaching round and grabbing a fistful of winding sheet, lifting the body even higher. Its brittle neck vertebrae cracked like rotten wood. The vampire gagged, its black tongue hanging out between the yellow teeth, a thick black bile running out of its nose and where its spinal column had broken through its neck. The other vampire darted to one side, trying to get a clear bite at Urthred, but Urthred shielded himself with the thrashing body of its companion. Then Seresh ran forward, the inside of the lantern open and ablaze with light. The creature cowered back, its hands shielding its eyes. Seresh played the lantern one way and then the other, the thing backing slowly down the passage, its teeth exposed in a savage rictus. Then it turned and rushed away into the darkness.

Seresh turned the light on Urthred; the priest threw the injured vampire to the ground. More bones splintered in its ravaged body, but it still struggled to rise despite its terrible injuries.

"They never die, do they?" he said flatly; the blood still

pounding his ears, deafening him. Seresh didn't answer, but opened the bottom of the lantern, pouring the smoking oil on the vampire before flinging the whole apparatus down on its back. The oil exploded in yellow flame, engulfing the creature. It flapped once, then twice, then lay still. The corridor was now filling with a black, acrid smoke.

"Fire kills them," Seresh said, half-choking on the oily smoke. "Quick, before others come," he ordered. Urthred hurriedly picked up the staff and followed him into the courtyard.

After the smoke, the air outside, though thick with the sulphurous marsh mist, seemed fresh as crystal. They both took in great gulps of air. "Well, Randel's brother, I will give you one thing. You don't lack courage!" Seresh said, in a voice not altogether unfriendly. Then he led them up the steps. They emerged into a quarter that Urthred identified by the lowering presence of the ruined citadel and the red glow of the Hearth Fire of the Temple of Reh. The whole journey had taken them only about a mile laterally, though it might have been thousands if he'd paid attention to the message of his aching limbs. Seresh took his bearings and set off quickly, down a street overhung by sagging eaves, his sword at the ready. Their feet splashed noisily in the puddles left by the storm. A distant flash of lightning to the north forced them to hide for a moment in the doorway of a ruined warehouse, its rotten wood spicing the air with decay.

Another glimmer of distant lightning threw the old lichen-pocked stonework of the buildings around them into sharp relief, just as a lamp might give an unwelcome glimpse of a pitted human face. "Where to next?" Urthred asked.

Seresh wrapped his cloak closer about him. "Follow me, and keep a sharp lookout—it's not far to go now!"

They set off once more keeping to the dark shadows, relying on the fitful light of the moon through the mists. Suddenly Seresh stopped and they darted into the cover of an empty doorway. The sound of voices came to them from further up the street. Four pale figures arrayed in dark cloaks were congregated around an old wooden door. They made low keening noises, and scratched pitifully at the door, like dogs left out in the rain. More vampires.

"They smell the blood of the living," Seresh whispered, inch-

ing backwards. They detoured, working their way ever upwards
in a wide-arcing curve.

They emerged out onto a broad avenue at the end of which, it
seemed, a million brightly coloured lights blazed from an open
courtyard in defiance of the gloom of the night. It was the scent
that struck him first, the very same scent he'd smelled in
Varash's study: the heavy musk of the Lethe bud. The scent
seemed to be coming from the candles themselves, lending the
chill night air a strange, heady warmth.

"What is this place?" he whispered.

"It's where we're going," said Seresh. Then, without further
explanation, he crept forward, Urthred close behind. Now
Urthred could make out the stone frieze over the entranceway to
the courtyard; a series of naked bodies, intertwined and writhing
in extraordinary positions. Though he had never seen one before, he recognised what the building was: a temple dedicated to
the Goddess of Flesh, Sutis.

"You're taking me there?" he asked incredulously.

"Where else? You're a holy man; the Worm will hardly look
for you here!" Seresh replied. Urthred opened his mouth to
protest again, but no words came out. He had to concede the
logic of Seresh's argument: this would be the last place in the
whole of Thrull his enemies would expect him to hide.

"Not for us the front entrance," whispered Seresh. "That
mask of yours stands out like a beacon. Follow me!" He hopped
over a puddle and, crouching low, moved towards a narrow side
alley that ran along the side of the temple wall. Urthred followed, wondering what new experiences would be added to the
many others this strange night.

CHAPTER SEVENTEEN

In the Realm of the Senses

Since her interview with Thalassa, Malliana had roamed her domain like a feral cat. She prowled the corridors of the temple ready to pounce on any slip or solecism she detected in the behaviour or words of her women. But they, accustomed to years of the High Priestess's moods, stayed well clear of her. Sensing this, Malliana's temper only worsened. Her black cloak swished out behind her like a sinister wave as she moved down the corridor towards the rear of the building.

Oblivious of her mistress's frame of mind, her cat stalked behind her, crouching and then making playful runs at the trailing edge of the cloak, bounding away at the last moment. But now the animal seemed to reach a critical phase of its fantasy hunt and leapt at it, its claws outstretched. Malliana felt the tug as it landed and then held on to the hem for grim life as it was carried forward along the ground. She swept round in an instant, yanking the cloak away, and sending the cat tumbling into the wall with an audible thock! She strode off, the look of thunder even deeper set on her brows. The cat, a sadder and wiser creature, followed her more circumspectly than before, mewing piteously. But if by this display of distress it hoped to win over its mistress's affections, it was to be disappointed.

One of the women flitted past the High Priestess, keeping well out of her path. There was a small twist of satisfaction in

the High Priestess's heart as she saw how she held her wrists,
stilling the rattling of her bangles lest it irritate her. The feeling
was short-lived; she reached the end of the corridor leading to
her study, her feeling of dissatisfaction mounting.

All was silent save the patter of the dripping eaves outside
and in the distance the sound of lute music from the Greeting
Room. All was as it ever would be at the Temple of Sutis: nothing had ever changed in the fifty years she had remained incarcerated in these walls. All was subjected to the necessity of
giving pleasure and receiving the god's tithe. Yet as Malliana
had aged, and her looks had decayed, every wile, every strata-
gem, every lie, all seemed as dust in her mouth—fifty years of
dust and disappointment.

She knew she would never leave this place, but would still
be here when her heart gave out or the sun finally decided to
die. In the meantime power and the exercise of power was all
her pleasure, the loss of it her greatest anguish. And this
evening it was the prospect of losing power forever over Thalassa that particularly rankled her. Her only comfort was that at
midnight, unless a miracle saved her, the young woman would
be given over to Lord Faran. She'd seen enough of his actions
in the last seven years to know that this was a man who
breathed cruelty as most men breathed air. Yes, she reflected,
Faran would soon remove from Thalassa all those things that
Malliana had once had and lost—youth, beauty and hope—all
those daughters of Innocence, which, when their dam dies,
struggle to live off the bitter milk of human nature alone.

But was it enough just to give over Thalassa? Would it not
be better to stamp on her once and for all time the loss of her innocence? What could be so extreme and so memorable after
everything she had experienced over the last seven years? The
young, the old, crippled and disfigured, diseased men; all had
been endured, not willingly, but without complaint.

Except, that was, the nights when Lord Faran had summoned her. The first time Malliana had gone herself, excited by
the night trip to the temple of the Worm, believing she would
see that bite which would end Thalassa's life, which would in-
fect her with the fever for which only living blood or death
were the cures.

But the messenger who had summoned them had warned her—the undead lord did not want to bite, only to touch. Malliana had shrugged at the improbability of it; what undead lord would wish such a thing, to stop at mere touching? Faran's palanquin had arrived at dead of night. Thalassa hadn't even screamed when the guards had come to take her—a disappointment—though her nurse had tried to raise a hue and cry. But Alanda was old and weak, and easy to subdue.

The scene in the crypt beneath the temple: the tomb of the Grey Mould, far underground. There had been one or two flickering torches, nothing more, and Malliana had grown afraid in the dark, so close to those who drank the blood of the living— would they take her, too? But they left her alone in the shadows, tolerant, it seemed, of her voyeuristic interest in the spectacle. Faran entered: the dark figure and his shadowy attendants appeared like spectres from a hidden door lost in the dark shadows; the smell of mildew filled the air. The attendants left as quickly as possible, having stripped Thalassa and used the chains. Then there was only the naked, shivering girl hanging from the restraints, her feet dragging on the floor slabs as she spun this way and that, her body inert, lifeless as if she had already crossed over. The High Priestess held her breath, watching from her position in the shadows, wondering what would happen next.

Faran flung aside his cloak like a bat unfurling its wings, revealing a thick-thewed, bone white body, still perfectly proportioned save the absolute desiccation of the skin, stretched tight like leather at a tannery over muscles set hard as wood. Yet out of proportion with the rest of the body was the tiny, shrivelled, white member, very much like a worm peeping from between the marbled thighs. Faran had approached Thalassa then, pushing one of his knees between her legs, forcing them apart. Thalassa was as responsive as a corpse, as he placed his hands on her breasts, tracing her milk white skin with his desiccated hands, the vampire's breath close in her ear.

And as she swung helplessly from the chain, Malliana heard him muttering.

"I know my breath is not sweet, but kiss me once." At this, the girl, hitherto so inert, flailed her head from side to side, so her golden brown hair swung in the dim torchlight until Faran grabbed a lock of it, stilling the movement, and pulled her head back, exposing her throat, his mouth flecked with saliva. It was then that two attendants had materialised suddenly from the darkness and had pulled him away as gently as possible. Faran's eyes were still locked on where the blue veins showed like rivers to a parched man in the desert on Thalassa's neck as he was dragged back and the attendants once more furled him in the voluminous black cloak. Then they and Faran melted back into the darkness as abruptly as they'd arrived.

Malliana had been confused: she had come to enjoy the spectacle, to see humiliation, then perhaps the fatal bite. Instead an attendant had come and given her a weighty purse of gold. She'd asked him whether Faran was displeased with what had happened, but the man shooed her away, telling her the arrangement would be renewed the next month.

But Malliana felt sullied by the incident: it was as if she had been the one bound to the chains, and not the girl, who, on the instant she wrapped her in her cloak had lapsed into a distant state of near catatonia. It was as if she, the High Priestess, had been abused. Surely the Temples of Sutis and Iss were linked: both put a premium on the flesh, one its pleasures, the other its preservation. Yet all flesh was fallible, and as Malliana grew older she had recognised it was only those who seemed to live outside its prison house who were really free. It was this freedom which Malliana hated Thalassa most for.

Now, on this evening of her bitterest gall, Malliana thought once more of Lord Faran; would the lord, after months of abstinence, finally take that fatal bite that would inject the poison into Thalassa's pure blue veins? Or would he keep her in luxury, like a parched man who looks at a ruby red cup of wine, hesitating from drinking, for the anticipation was more pleasurable than the slaking? Malliana had begun to suspect that this was the real reason for this infatuation with Thalassa: his restraint was the only thing which after two hundred years of arid existence kept him alive. He kept himself always teetering on the edge of satiation, but never drinking to the lees.

She sighed impatiently, exasperated by the emptiness of everything that surrounded her; Thalassa would serve her last few hours at the temple as she had promised; but what horror, greater than Lord Faran, could she visit on her which she had not experienced a hundred times already? What horror indeed could there be, besides this final summons to the Temple of Worms? There was the dark-hooded stranger, with his exorbitant offers to buy Thalassa's term of service. What secrets lay behind the cowl that masked his face? Already he had offered ten times what Malliana would have asked for any other of her girls, yet the perverse spirit which ruled her meant she had not let Thalassa go. Maybe she would seek him out now, strike a bargain before it was too late. Defy Faran.

As she had been thinking in this way she had been eyeing the cloistered garden at the back of the temple through the mullioned windows which gave onto it. As at the front, garish, multicoloured lanterns glimmered in the dark amongst the rain-streaked trees. Lightning flashed distantly, throwing the boughs of the trees into sharp relief: madman's arms, groping. Just then she saw movement. Two interlopers, climbing ponderously over the vine-entangled wall. She watched as they dropped down and headed towards a side entrance near the kitchens. Her curiosity was piqued. There were guards who could deal with any intruders or any guests reluctant to pay, but tonight she wanted more than a summary ejection. She would investigate herself. She turned and pushed a panel in the wall behind her. It swung open silently on a hinge. Beyond was a musty and utterly imperetrable darkness. She passed through, closing the door quietly behind her. Cobwebs brushed at her face as she pushed down the hidden passageway, her hand tracing the rough render of the flimsy lathe walls that divided the interior of the temple. Finally she came to the place she was looking for. She reached up and found a covered spy hole at eye level. She pushed the hinged wooden flap to one side and looked through.

In front of her was the stone-flagged kitchen area. The scene was lit by the dim glow of a single lantern and the dying embers of a brick oven set into the far wall. Dark cooking utensils hung from the low oak beams of the ceiling. Here she expected the two intruders to have arrived.

She was not disappointed. The two strangers were there: one

with a pinched face, the other with a mask which was a vision of horror. Both were shaking rainwater from cloaks sodden by the wet vines on the wall outside. The masked man leant the curiously shaped staff he'd been carrying against a wall. In front of them she saw Thalassa's damnable old nurse, Alanda, who must have let them in. The old lady stood at a distance from the man with the hideous mask, evidently taken aback by its singular appearance. As Malliana watched Alanda asked a sharp question of the pinched-face one. Malliana quickly applied her ear to the hole in the wall in order to hear better:

"You took a risk coming here early," she heard the old woman say.

"There was nowhere else," came a voice, one which Malliana deduced must belong to the first man. "Our friend here was in trouble, and I knew we'd find you alone at this hour."

"It's lucky you did," retorted Alanda, "for the mistress has had a to-do with the High Priestess tonight."

"A to-do?"

"Aye, the worst has happened: she has been summoned to the Temple of Iss."

"When?"

"This very night, at midnight. But this time Faran means to keep her."

"And tomorrow she would have been safe!" mused the intruder.

"Well, there's nothing for it; she will serve as normal until midnight, then she will be gone." Despite the fortitude of her words, Alanda's voice cracked with emotion.

"No! The plan can go ahead—we'll just have to put it into action a little earlier," continued the first voice. Malliana smiled in the dark; this was becoming more interesting than she could have ever dreamt.

"Who is this?" Alanda enquired, meaning the masked priest.

"Suffice to say the enemy would like to find him. Tomorrow I intended to take him from the city, with you and Thalassa."

So a plot had been afoot all along, Malliana thought, and she had not guessed it. She fairly writhed with pleasure at the prospect of imminent action. Now not only would Thalassa be handed over to the Temple of Iss, but Alanda and the two intruders as well.

The pinched-face one was talking again. "We'll get her out, but we'll have to wait until just before midnight. Zaraman and the others won't be ready until then. We'll have to act like guests in the meantime. Do you have another mask? He can't go into the chamber wearing that one."

"Masks aplenty, but what do you intend?"

"We'll mingle with the other guests. When the time comes, the priest here will choose Thalassa: it's better if he's with a friend. I'll come to her chamber before midnight, then we'll go together. But first a mask, one of the masks of the Worm acolytes would be best."

"There are enough of those abandoned in their drunken revels. I'll be back in an instant." The old lady shuffled from the room, leaving the two strangers alone.

"Is this a good plan?" For the first time she heard the masked priest speak; his voice seemed to droop with fatigue.

"It's the only plan we have."

The priest nodded his head in resigned agreement. "How will I tell who this Thalassa is?"

"Oh, she is not too difficult to spot: men are drawn to her easily—golden brown hair, pale, tall . . ." He lapsed into a silence, as if himself somewhat infatuated with the woman he described. "You won't miss her, priest: she is the most beautiful woman here."

"Won't the other guests vie for her favours?"

"No, she is promised to Lord Faran. The worshippers of Iss will stay clear of her. The High Priestess gives her to others occasionally. She may refuse you. Then go with one of the others, and try to act as if you're familiar with the rites of the Goddess."

"That may be difficult."

"You'll have to do your best. . . . One last thing."

"Yes?"

"If you do go with Thalassa, remember who she is."

The sneer was audible in the priest's voice. "You think I would be tempted?"

"No, but she is beautiful . . ."

"The world of flesh is nothing to me."

"Many have said that, but have fallen. Here, here is money for the fee to the priestesses." Malliana heard the clink of coins and applied her eye once more to the hole in the wall. Just at this moment, Alanda returned, a grey skull mask of the priests of Iss clutched in her hand.

"Here, this should do," she said, handing it to the priest.

"Good," said the first man. "Go to your chambers and pack up all your possessions and your lady's. You must be ready to leave by midnight."

"That we have already done. I'll be at my lady's chamber within the hour. You know your way from here, should anyone challenge you, just say you're lost." With that she was gone.

Now the first man turned to the priest.

"Put it on and throw that thing in the fire here," he said, gesturing to the glowing brick oven set into the wall. "You won't be needing it from now on."

The priest looked from him to the mask in his hand. Though his features were obscured, Malliana still felt his reluctance.

"No, I can't wilfully destroy it, but I can hide it under my cloak."

"Whatever you wish," replied the other. "But remember, if the Worm catches you, that thing will put you in the stocks."

"That's a risk I'll take; now turn your back, my face is not . . . pretty." His companion shrugged and turned away. The priest reached up and with a deep breath unlatched the mask. Malliana nearly gasped in horror when she saw the ruined face, but managed to stifle the sound as she took in the hideousness of the scarred features. Here was a face from Hel itself, a face she could wish on her worst enemy. And a man she could certainly wish on Thalassa as her last lover at the temple, a just reward for her airs and graces, her pride. And what was more it seemed that it would be ridiculously easy to arrange: the intruders had played into her hands. The priest had the other mask on his face in a trice, stuffing the first under his cloak. At the movement his companion turned around.

"Come, follow me," he said, taking in the priest's new appearance with apparent satisfaction.

"And the staff?" the masked man asked.

His companion looked at the object leaning against one of the walls. "We'll have to leave it here until we return," he said. "Hide it there." He pointed at an alcove to one side of the brick oven which was filled with brooms and mops and other paraphernalia. The priest did as he was bidden and then they exited to the left, out of the line of Malliana's sight.

Malliana thought for a moment. The priest and his friend were no doubt outlaws, and the Worm would pay for information on their whereabouts. Even tonight she had heard from one of the guests how Golon, Lord Faran's sorcerer, was out scouring the streets for a man who had slain the High Priest of Flame. A man who had been wearing a demon mask. There was no doubt that this was the murderer. Political expediency dictated that she should send a messenger to the Temple of Iss immediately. But for Thalassa to have to suffer this man's face on her last night would be better even than the knowledge of an eternity of Faran's fumbling advances. No, the messenger could wait. First she would arrange Thalassa's last assignation at the Temple of Sutis. She glided silently back down the secret passageway.

Seresh opened the heavy, panelled door leading from the kitchen. The corridor outside was empty: all the acolytes who normally served in this area of the temple had gone to greet the evening's guests in the reception rooms. Together, the two of them glided down the thickly carpeted passage towards the sound of heavy, plangent, lute music which came from the depths of the building.

Through the eye slits of his new mask, Urthred could see the statuary that lined the corridor: a shiver of repugnance ran down his spine. Here was a place dedicated to the pursuits of the flesh, pursuits which he despised. A feeling of self-disgust washed over him, and he wondered again whether it would have been better if he'd just surrendered himself to the Flame priests after he'd killed Varash. He felt naked without Manichee's mask, certain that any magical powers he had had earlier were now hidden with the mask under his cloak.

The sound of the music was louder now: a courtly air, played slowly, with pregnant hushes between each bar. A chamber some fifty feet across opened in front of them, dimly lit by more multicoloured lanterns hanging from brackets on the wall, or suspended from the galleries that ran round the four walls. Thick swags of a luscious velvet satin hung down from the balconies of the galleries. Divans, covered with multicoloured rugs, were artfully arranged about the wood parquet floor, a raised dais at its centre. Men, young and old, lounged sybaritically on them, being waited on by women clad in the flimsiest of materials, which revealed the curve of well-shaped limbs, and more, as they stooped to pour ruby wine from long-necked serving vessels.

There was a low dais at the end of the room, dwarfed by another statue, even more lascivious in its subject matter than those they had already passed. Upon it an old bald man sat cross-legged, plucking at a lute, the whites of his eyes showing that he'd lost the sight of them many years before. Just as well, for in front of him on the central dais were some twenty women, if anything, more scantily clad than the servingwomen. They were stepping slowly and languorously in time to the tune he was playing. Like the servingwomen, they were dressed in thin, gauzy costumes which left very little to the imagination.

To Urthred, who had been incarcerated in the harsh confines of Forgeholm Monastery all his life, the dancers' beauty had the power to wound. All were perfect of face and limb, their movements absolutely in accord with each passage of the music as it unfurled, as if the blind lutanist's hands stroked them and not his instrument: they responded in kind, pirouetting with every grace and agility that youth gives to a body. His eyes moved up from perfectly shaped ankles, with thin golden bangles flashing in the dim light, to calves flexed slightly in movement. The thighs revealed through the slits in the flimsy dresses were almost salmon-coloured, smooth, firm. His eyes moved up, flicking momentarily at what was revealed beneath the girdle of the dresses, all too new and strange to him, to slightly curved bellies, and exquisitely tipped breasts which showed through the thin fabric which covered them.

Then the faces: it was as if a dictionary of female beauty was revealed to him: here was the dark, flashing welcoming one, her mouth wide and sensual, the eyes knowing under fluttering dark lashes, then the pale blondes, grown in a field of golden lilies, so straight and natural did they seem; then two well-thewed women, taller than most men, leather greaves and vambraces giving them the domineering, disdainful looks that some men craved. But most were slight, mere wands swaying to the music; Urthred's mind seemed to sway with them, and he realised that he felt dizzy.

Dimly, he became aware of a tugging at his sleeve. Seresh was whispering to him, leading him over to a pair of divans. His scorched face burned even redder with shame as he realised he'd been staring, albeit from the concealment of his mask, for several seconds. *Sot,* he muttered to himself, *your Flame soul lost to the shadows of the flesh in seconds.* But now Seresh was pressing him down on one of the divans. He reclined and saw Seresh do likewise on an adjacent one. A girl dressed in the flimsy material ubiquitous to the temple came up to his companion's divan. With an easy smile Seresh pulled a handful of golden durcals from his money pouch and put them on the silver tray she was holding out to him. The girl bent and whispered into his ear, and Urthred saw a thin, crooked smile break over Seresh's hawklike features. If he was feigning enjoyment, Urthred thought, he was an accomplished actor. Now the woman was coming to him and he watched her as if in a dream. A sly smile played on her lips as she held out the tray.

Urthred willed himself to throw off the allure of her fresh round face and the dancing eyes, telling himself to look beneath the contempt of the flesh, to the beating heart, the coils of the intestine, the skull. But that face kept swimming back into focus, the cruel, anatomic disciplines of his temple past lost in the sheer voluptuary of the moment. The girl smiled again, waving the tray slightly playfully so that Seresh's coins swished backwards and forwards.

"A contribution, sir, and may your worm find a safe nest tonight." She giggled. Suddenly Urthred remembered the Worm mask, the plan—he hastily pulled out Seresh's coins from one of the pockets of his cloak, the gloves making him momentarily clumsy, and scattered them noisily on the tray, not knowing whether he gave too much or too little. But the girl seemed satisfied and gave him a warm smile before sweeping on. Meanwhile he saw another woman filling a golden beaker that Seresh held before him with wine. Now she came towards him, but Urthred shook his head, he felt intoxicated enough with the sight of the women dancing on the dais in front of him. Besides, to drink would have meant removing his mask. His eyes found their way back to the dancing women. It was as if they became rooted there, and the more he looked, the more the rest of the dancers faded away, and his eyes, already focused through the eye slits of his mask, became more and more concentrated on only one of them.

He hadn't noticed her at first, as one doesn't an exotic orchid in a bed of multicoloured flowers, but the more his eyes travelled over the company of dancers, she alone stood out with a rarity, a singularity which the others lacked. A helmet of golden brown hair and an exquisite pale face, incongruous, slightly sulky lips that made him want to wipe away the cause of their mistress's disaffection with, the Flame help him, with a lingering kiss. . . .

With a lurch to his heart he saw her return his stare, not overtly, but from the corner of her eyes as her head moved from side to side with the steps of the dance. This must be the woman Seresh had spoken of. A shiver ran down his spine, half in anticipation, half in dread. Then he remembered Seresh's warning, and his own, angry rejoinder. How was it that only minutes later his heart had turned from purity to lust, and that after a day and night of travel and pursuit, and a whole lifetime of celibacy? He shook his head, hoping to clear it, hoping that this wasn't the woman that Seresh had meant: lust would only further complicate the situation.

Thalassa danced only because the steps of the ritual were, after seven years, so ingrained that her feet and arms moved automatically. Her mind was elsewhere. She thought of midnight and death, and her throat felt like lead.

She'd seen Alanda trying to attract her attention from a darkened corner of the room, but her heart was too low to take comfort from her friend. She'd looked away from her, lest tears had filled her eyes. A tearful acolyte was not what the visitors to the Temple of Sutis expected, or paid for.

Now Seresh was here: she'd seen him enter the room moments before. For some reason he was with a priest of Iss. Seresh was meant to fetch her and Alanda and Furtal away from the temple, but in her overexcited imagination it seemed that he, too, conspired with the agents of the Worm. She'd looked hard at Seresh's companion. Masked, like all the other priests who came here. But he would soon abandon the mask when he drank or ate. Then she'd see who he was. Maybe someone who had seen her during her monthly ordeals at the Temple of Iss. The man was certainly staring at her, the skull mask an eerie warning of death.

As she watched, she saw Malliana enter the Greeting Room. A spasm of hatred tightened her chest, and she had to remind herself that she must do the High Priestess's bidding. That way Alanda might still have a chance. Malliana walked straight over to the divan where the masked priest was sitting, as if this had all been planned. As if she knew something that Thalassa didn't. Had she been right to trust Seresh all these years? She had wondered at the man's ease at the brothel; he was worldly, the sort who would betray his friends for a price. She turned to Seresh, but he was talking familiarly with another guest, as if he were a regular guest here, blending in seamlessly with the ambience of the temple. The High Priestess was now by the stranger's couch. Thalassa had a dark premonition as she leant down to speak to him.

The girl had been staring at him for several minutes and Urthred felt waves of hot and cold pass successively through him. When would the dancing end? How would he pick her out? As he wrestled with these thoughts, a new emotion obtruded into his consciousness: unease, a prickling at the back of his neck. Then a black cat jumped up onto the divan beside him and ran its flank down one of his outstretched legs. He turned to find a woman standing right behind him, as if she had been following the direction of his gaze all this time. He blushed furiously under his mask, for the knowing look that the woman cast him suggested that she had already fathomed every thought he had had since he'd entered the chamber. As she favoured him with this look he had time to study her face: the parchment white makeup, hiding imperfectly the lines of middle age, her wide mouth curved slightly as if in wry amusement, the high-peaked black hair, the beetling eyebrows, the black-and-purple robes and the silver amulets of office, and the knowing look, darted through the eye slits of his mask from heavily kohled eyes. He knew instinctively that this was the High Priestess of the temple. Behind her, he could see Seresh turned towards them, a look of concern on his face.

Urthred felt his heart beating ever faster: he expected words of accusation, of discovery, running feet, brusque hands dragging him off. But the only hand he felt was that of the High Priestess: beautifully thin, tapered hands which she placed on his thigh as she swung herself onto the edge of the divan, squeezing him ever so slightly, in a playful way.

"Why, priest, are you new here? By the feel of this"—she squeezed his thigh once more—"you're young and lithe, and fit; fit enough even for a night of love with me when I was as young as you." A chill went up Urthred's spine; he felt unable to deal with the conflicting emotions that the priestess's hands were inspiring. But the woman was continuing with her banter.

"Well, goose, Malliana is now too old to take on any but your patriarch. Never fear—I know your heart is on younger flesh than mine!" She glanced mischievously up at the girls dancing on the dais: one or two smiled shyly back, courting her favour. But Urthred noticed that the girl he'd been staring at before had turned her head away and was looking at another part of the room. Malliana's eyes darted from one girl to another as if mentally selecting who best would suit him. But each of the girls seemed to displease her in some way, until she locked onto the one who had been staring at Urthred.

"Ah yes," she said, giving his thigh another squeeze, "Thalassa! Just the one for you!" She was on her feet and onto the dais in a second, reaching out her hand to clutch the girl's arm. She, as Urthred would have expected from her aloof beauty, swung round angrily at the touch, and for a moment Urthred thought she was going to resist, but then the anger passed from her face and she allowed the older woman to lead her down the step towards him. Urthred's gaze swept over the flowing form as it approached, devouring every moulded sweep of thigh and breast and ankle revealed, and the heart-shaped face and the grey eyes . . .

He wrenched his head away, trying to clear his mind. As he did so, Urthred caught one of the other men lounging on the divans staring intently at him. Though his face was partly hidden by the hood of his cape, Urthred could quite clearly see the curious mixture of fascination and jealousy stamped on his face. And what a face! Used to the ruin of his own features, Urthred saw that this man must pass as a pariah amongst his fellows. The scar which seemed to pull up the entire side of the face down which it ran gave him the appearance of a permanent leer. Certainly the look he was giving Urthred didn't excite any welcoming thoughts in the young priest's mind. Perhaps he'd singled out the woman for himself? Urthred hadn't time to wonder because the High Priestess was talking to him again.

"Here we are then," she said brightly. "I think the priest has taken a fancy to you already, don't you, Thalassa?" The girl stood silent, her head downcast, and Urthred found himself at a loss for words and unable to look at her, contrary emotions warring in his chest.

"Well come, then, the night was made for love, be off with you to the chambers," Malliana said, handing him from the couch and fairly thrusting him at Thalassa.

Urthred looked round desperately for Seresh, but he realised that the High Priestess's action had precipitated the end of the dancing. The other dancers were stepping down from the dais and heading towards whichever of the clients seemed to have given them most encouragement. Seresh was already accommodating two of the women on his divan.

For a moment Urthred felt helpless and abandoned, blown by the winds of the High Priestess' whim and the plot that his companion had orchestrated in the temple kitchen. It was all so easy; but maybe it was always this way? A plot which unexpectedly had delivered to him the very woman he'd been told to look out for. Now he found the girl's soft, slight hand on his arm, leading him to the stairs. Urthred found that he'd gone quite deaf. Then he realised he was holding his breath, and all he could hear was the beating of his heart. Though she still kept her pale, grey eyes averted from him, the softness of the touch sent a bolt of electricity through him, and he shivered.

But before they had gone two steps, the High Priestess had once more laid a restraining hand on Thalassa's arm. She leant close to her and whispered something that he couldn't make out. Once more Urthred's gaze was drawn to where the scar-faced man sat alone in a corner. Was the man an agent? As he watched, the man lifted a goblet to his lips, a wry smile playing over the puckered mouth where the scar ran through it. He toasted Urthred with a sneer, revealing yellowing teeth, before throwing the wine back in a single gulp. Then the light pressure of Thalassa's hand came on Urthred's arm again, and he felt himself being led from the room.

CHAPTER EIGHTEEN

The Battle of Thrull

Outside Weebil's Inn.

The storm had passed—the last growl of thunder faded as it died across the plains—a cannonball rolling in a wooden barrel.

Then silence save for the pattering of water from the rain-soaked eaves of the surrounding buildings.

Jayal lay motionless on the cobbles, a livid contusion on his temple where Weebil had sent him crashing into the inn wall. Blood caked the right side of his face.

Body and soul were divided. His soul circled, not certain whether to fly or stay. But his body, through the pain and the darkness, listened, and heard the sound of shuffling footsteps coming nearer. Then a pause, then hands lifting his feet and dragging him from the place where he lay, his head bumping over the hard cobblestones of the streets. Each of the bumps made the world progressively blacker: black . . . black . . . black . . .

Then his soul was flying, falling away down to the Plains of Grey in giddy circles. He left his body far behind, for the Plains were where the souls of the dead went to await the end of time and the resurrection of the body. He fell over and over, staring down at the Plains, but they were empty and featureless. And the further he fell, the darker and darker they became. Then all was night. His soul had alighted, but it was blind. He sensed he was moving in the darkness. A strong current was pulling him along.

Now the darkness was full of a mighty roar, and at last he could see. Grey forms flew past, hurrying forward like twigs whirled on a current before a waterfall. He knew he was in the land of Shades near the lip of the abyss over which all unaneled souls were sucked into Hel, tumbling slowly with infinite slowness of revolution into the darkness from which no light could ever save them. Was he damned, too? Pale shadows on either side, souls of those who would never return but would be cursed to an eternity of darkness.

His mind and soul were being drawn forward swiftly by the current. This is where it would all end, his worthless existence. He'd failed his father and Thalassa, the sword was lost, and he was damned. For what? Too many years of recrimination and guilt to account for now, the waters roaring so loudly that thought was almost impossible. He would go with it into the maelstrom and the half world beyond.

Now he could see faces surrounding him, the skin on the faces stretched, the mouths open in a piercing howl beyond human pitch, a noise that horrified but enticed, and always the current got stronger. Then, suddenly, the drop opened out below and the roar became stupendously loud, and wraiths of mists and spirit vapours roiled up and the dark chasm that led to Hel stood revealed.

But on the very lip of the abyss an invisible force held him back as if his soul were a twig held by a boulder on the edge of a waterfall.

He was not to be damned—not yet, anyway. His soul wavered this way and that, part of the flow but distinct from it.

The fear of the river was with him, the mighty, invincible river bearing him ineluctably to the dark, underground sea where all is lost—mind, identity, hope.

Ghosts swept past his dream-fevered mind: familiar ones, men who had fought and died with him on the battle of the marshes seven years before. There were Vortumin, and Jadshasi, Edric and Poluso, their mouths stretched voicelessly as they were swept past into the abyss. Jayal reached out to touch them, but he had no hands, only his disembodied being floated on the void. He screamed, but no sound came.

Now his spirit circled back, through the rings of the past, seeking answers, memories.

And memories did come back, memories that his conscious mind had suppressed these last seven years, but which now were liberated.

The battle. For a long time after it his memory of that day had been a complete blank. For a long time he had thought he'd fled out of cowardice, deserting his comrades. Only some hastily scribbled notes from his father in the saddlebags of his horse had persuaded him otherwise. But now the memories of that day came back strong and irresistible, for the first time in seven years.

Once more he was back on that field of death as it had been in the late afternoon of the battle. The barren grey-and-brown marshes stretched far away to the black-toothed mountains that ringed the plains. Behind was Thrull, its jagged, black, citadel-topped peak the only feature in the marshes. The sun was low in the sky, and a grey drizzle had begun to fall. Red-and-black clouds of smoke hung over the lines: burning flares illuminated the scene.

The two armies faced one another. On Jayal's side on a slight rise were stretched the lines of his father's, Illgill's, army. Four divisions, left, right and centre, with Illgill's Hearth Brethren as a reserve. All the lines were ragged from the casualties of a hard day's fighting. Already, the militiamen conscripted into the ranks had begun to mutiny, cursing the baron and their wounds in the same breath. Some already slunk off in the growing shadows, making good their escape. Even the regular troops had begun to mutter. What madness made the baron face Faran's hordes on the level terms of the marshes when the walls of Thrull would have survived six months of siege? It was a good question, the answer to which Jayal knew too well: simple hubris and pride forced his father to beat the enemy in an open battle. He wanted a clear victory for the Flame over the Worm so all the Empire could marvel at the glory of Reh. This devout wish held no comfort now for the troops: their nerve

would hold for a little while longer, but not beyond the night,
when the undead would rise and slay them.

On either side of Jayal, the murmuring and the desertions
were infecting the ranks; one, then two, then a whole clump of
men detached themselves from the lines and scuttled back
through the growing dusk. But in the centre, where Jayal stood,
there was still a show of blazing colour, the same colour that
had dazzled the townsfolk early that morning. The standards of
the Ancient Flame Lords flapped in the wind—yellow, red and
orange, the surcoats that covered the chainmail armour of his
men still showing the proud, fire-spewing salamander of the
family crest on a field of white, though many of the surcoats
were muddied and torn from combat.

That morning there had been twenty thousand in Illgill's
army: every able-bodied man from Thrull, and from the surrounding mountains. Even some mercenaries from Surrenland.
But twice they had been beaten back, right to the brightly hued
headquarters tents. Now it was difficult to know how many remained. Half? The field in front was carpeted with the dead and
dying, the latter's screams encouragement enough for the deserters to leave in an ever-increasing flow. Jayal saw an officer
on his flank try to bar the way of one desperate group. The man
was trampled in their mad rush. His own men, two hundred in
all, remained steady. They were the Elicitors of Flame, the elite.
They stood in grim-faced silence.

Across from him, separated by a hundred yards of trampled
marsh and the carpet of the dead and dying, stood the ranks of
Faran's army. Unlike the Servants of Flame, their colours were
muted blacks, browns and purples, and the face masks of the
elite troops that faced Jayal were fashioned as skulls. The
masks gleamed bone white in the dying light, all too potent re-
minders of the death promised by their gleaming copper swords
and maces. The melancholy call of their bone horns sounded
over the field again. As he watched, the black tide of Faran's
army advanced on the wings, pushing back the already demor-
alised militiamen. The line of a moment before became a half
circle, pressing back on the headquarters tents.

Bitterly Jayal remembered the optimism of the morning,
how he'd ridden out in the dawn, a feeling of invincibility in his

heart. But the marsh had levelled them; the black, sucking marsh through which no progress could be made as the arrows crashed into their ranks, and the copper swords fell. His horse had died with an arrow in its withers during the first charge, a slow-motion affair where no matter how hard he'd spurred the gelding, the ranks of Faran's men had never seemed to draw any closer. He'd struggled back to his feet despite the weight of his chainmail and limped back to his lines, muddied and bruised, knowing already that the battle was lost. From that moment, the tide of the battle had only flowed in one direction: back towards Thrull. Now the situation was beyond repair. Behind him, his legion's lancers placed the tips of their weapons against the outstretched hands of a priest. The weapons suddenly flared with an incandescent light, throwing the old man's face into a ghostly undershadow. Jayal recognised the man, his father's friend, the sorcerer Manichee. Apart from the lancers no one else stirred, the once proud army of Baron Illgill were too exhausted to move, their armour battered and stained, their weapons chipped from dozens of strokes. Their weariness was as much mental as physical; soon night would come and the odds would be turned irrevocably against them. Only in the day did they stand a chance of victory; their hopes would die with the day's waning; soon the undead, who hated the sight of the sun, would rise with the darkness from the shallow pits in the marshes where they had been hidden all day. Jayal knew then the battle would be over. For the undead felt no pain, unlike their human foe.

Jayal's chainmail was suffocatingly hot; the weight of his helm bent his head to the ground, and his gaze was fixed at where his mailed feet rested on the oozing slime that bubbled up from the marsh's surface. Another dull fear came to him: Faran had occupied the battlefield overnight. It could be that he stood now upon one of the shallow graves in which the undead had been buried. And as his gaze lifted he saw, not far off, a pale limb snaking up from the ground, looking for all the world like a white, withered arm. Then his eyes, adjusting to the half-light, recognised it as nothing more than the root of a marsh plant.

He looked across at where the army of the Worm stood, their

ranks disappearing off into the gloom on either side. How many
were left? Fifteen thousand? Their numbers seemed immaterial
now that his mind was bowed with weariness. It seemed to him
that such a large number of enemies could not be killed in a
thousand years of battle. And at that moment, that was all he
knew. A humming filled the air, as it had all day—the Reapers'
Death Chant, rising and falling, an ever-present wail of despair
which reminded him of his own frail mortality, and of his terrible tiredness. A volley of arrows, some trailing plumes of black
sorcerous smoke, whistled from the enemy ranks, cutting
through the orange-and-red-cloaked lines of his fellows, and
into the tents behind him. The tents were in tatters, ripped to
shreds by a thousand similar arrows to those in this volley. No
longer were they full of laughing, confident men, as they had
been this morning, toasting one another in Selenium wine. Now
half of them lay dead. Now the tents were filled with different
sounds; the groans of the wounded. More screams were heard
as the arrows impacted. The ragged sides of the tents offered no
protection from this mortal rain from the darkening sky.

   Jayal saw that his father had left his own tent and was standing on a small hillock surrounded by his generals. Illgill seemed
outwardly unperturbed, as confident as he had appeared all day,
his fierce eyes under their beetling brows and jutting black
beard and his red-and-black armour giving him an air of utter
invincibility. Though they stood fifty or so feet apart, and three
ragged lines of infantrymen separated them, Jayal realised that
his father's eyes were fixed on him. Even at this distance, he
recognised the challenge in that glance, daring him to fail, to
disgrace the Illgill line which had stretched through generations, back to the first father of the city, Marizian. His father
lived for that history, and all his short life, Jayal had strived to
honour it as well, but never to his stringent father's satisfaction.
Despite his bone weariness, Jayal once more questioned his
own worthiness, and wondered whether he had not failed in his
father's eyes every day of his existence.

   The latest volley of arrows had wrought destruction all
around; men screamed in agony, horses twitched in death
throes, the side of one tent had erupted in flame. Jayal saw it all

as if through a red prism, distantly, in an altered light, as if none of the arrows could touch him.

Through the gloom he saw his friend Vortumin staggering towards him, a broken arrow shaft in his hand. He was trying to speak, but his other hand clawed at something stuck in his throat. Then Jayal saw that it was the other half of the arrow and that bright red blood stained the man's red tunic an ever-deeper red. He reached forward to help him, but before he could touch him, Vortumin's eyes had turned up in his head and he'd sunk to his knees. There was a curious rattle in his mangled voice box, then he keeled over slowly to one side.

Jayal knelt beside him, his hands fluttering ineffectually, not knowing what to do. Like a bird of prey, a priest materialised from the gloom. He wore the silver bicorn hat of his office, peaked like a long-prowed rowing boat rimmed with small silver bells. His orders were to despatch all the badly wounded before the undead reached them. But Jayal glared at him so fiercely that the man backed away, scuttling off to find another dying sacrifice for the God.

Jayal raised Vortumin's head and tried to make him drink from his water bottle, but the man couldn't swallow and he gagged, some of the water flowing out of the terrible wound in his neck in a pink froth. His brown eyes looked at Jayal sadly, croaking something, something that was nearly audible. Jayal leaned closer, and Vortumin repeated the words, "See you in Hel, my friend."

Then his throat gave off another protracted rattle, his body heaved once and was still. Jayal let Vortumin's head sink back onto the ground and stood shakily. It was now quite dark, and the eerie chant of the Reapers of Sorrow sounded again, this time accompanied by the call of their bone cow horns: a single mournful note, as dry and as empty as death to Jayal's ears.

Now his sergeant, Furisel, was hurrying up to him.

"Well?" he snarled, his frustration and anger boiling insanely inside him.

"It's Talien, sir—he's hit bad."

"Then you know what must be done," Jayal said, staring down at Vortumin's corpse.

"But, sir, he might live. . . ."

Jayal looked up angrily at the sergeant. "You heard me—you must give the badly wounded to the priests—you, or I, or anyone, the rule is the same."

Furisel stared back at him with cold hatred. He and Talien had been raised as boys together. His eyes went to the carrion pyres being built behind the lines.

"Damn your rules, Jayal Illgill. And damn your soul as well." At this he turned and hurried back to where a huddle of men surrounded the writhing form of Talien. Jayal thought to stop the sergeant. His father would have had him killed on the spot for his insolence. But the rigidity of purpose which made his father such a cruel man was lacking in his son. Just as Jayal knew the battle could not be won, he also knew he could not kill Furisel. It was as if his whole life had been a compromise between the strict inflexibility of his father's codes and this softness in his heart, a weakness which made him see every side to an argument, which made him allow the justice in Furisel's request, and yet still deny it, so that he neither had the discipline on one hand or the humanity on the other, and having neither made him a nothing, a nullity, and recognising his state of worthlessness, made him yearn for extinction.

That extinction would surely not be long in coming. The same priest he had seen a few seconds ago was approaching Furisel's group, encouraging forward his young acolyte who carried a copy of the *Book of Light* almost as big as he. The men turned fiercely on them and Jayal saw angry gestures. Just then another volley of arrows ripped through the ranks, the priest whirled in his magnificent cloaks, like a cock hit by a slingshot, and fell to the ground. The acolyte stared in horror at where another arrow had impaled the heavy leather-bound book in his hands. He dropped it and ran as fast as he could towards Thrull. Jayal looked back towards Faran's lines, a dark rain cloud passed over the battlefield, sending a sudden torrent through which the last beams of the sun passed in yellow shafts. Strangely a rainbow appeared over the top of one of the carrion piles, then the slate grey cloud moved over the face of the sun and the battlefield was swallowed up in darkness. Now, in the no-man's-land between them, he saw the black marsh earth churning up in the gloom, as if a hundred moles worked there.

White, white hands, slick with worms and slime, broke out, followed by snarling white heads, yellow teeth bared in hatred. The undead had been maddened by the damp earth they had had to lie in all day, for the dampness rotted their atrophied bodies. They sprung up, growling like maddened dogs.

The lancers ran forward to meet them, their lance points phosphorescent in the gloom, hissing in the rain. Another volley of arrows, tipped with dark fire, exploded amongst them. Many dropped, but others struggled on, lunging at the creatures bursting from the graves. The light forced some of the vampires back, but others ran onto the lancetips, which exploded with incandescent light. Several of the undead burst into flame, and sank back to the ground. The survivors roared their defiance, clawing at the lancers. Behind the vampires, another melancholy note from the cow horns sounded, and the serried grey ranks of the Reapers advanced against the centre, their copper maces and shields glowing dully in the phosphorescent glow of the smouldering flares. The remnant of the lancers threw down their weapons and stumbled back towards Illgill's lines—more arrows catching some of them.

The undead joined the front ranks of the advancing infantry, roaring in a berserk rage born of blood starvation. One or two of them fell onto their own men or the wounded lancers, so maddened for the taste of blood had they become, but apart from these one or two small eddies, their front as it came towards Jayal's men appeared if anything like a monstrous tidal wave. Behind Illgill's front rank, ballistae hurled flaming fireballs into the advancing mass: holes appeared momentarily where they struck home, but their gaps were immediately filled by more skull-masked warriors.

Jayal looked once more behind him to his father, standing erect and proud in front of his brightly coloured tents, surrounded by his generals. Beside him stood the remnants of the Hearth Brethren, holding the standards of the Flame Legions. When he had been a child how he had admired the standards hanging bold and proud in his father's hall, emblazoned with the sigils of the Hundred Clans of Fire wrought in thick gold thread. Now they, too, hung in shreds, flapping disconsolately in the rain-filled wind. For a moment it seemed as if his father looked his way, once more, and Jayal tried to interpret the glance: encouragement, or a farewell?

The moment was gone in a second and now he was once more facing the grey hordes advancing remorselessly towards him. There were too many of them: as when a swimmer who has swum for hours, in sight of a far-distant shore, finally discovers that the shore is no closer, that his hours of effort have been in vain, that for every stroke forward the tide pushes him back the same distance, so for each sword blow he had struck this day, Jayal felt another of Faran's men had magically reappeared to replace the slain, that there were as many of them now as there had been at dawn. Now he realised that his strength was nearly spent, that the force against him was invincible, that nothing could now stop the wall of purple-and-black-cloaked warriors sweeping right through their lines.

Frustration at his impotence burned in his heart, for though he was not the man his father was, all the Illgills were prouder than eagles, untameable, and would never bow to anyone, least of all the Worm. He let out a scream, not ignited by courage but by sheer helpless rage.

Now he was running slowly, floundering in his heavy armour in the mire, urging his men forward. The bloodred sun broke momentarily through the band of black cloud, and the level beams washed over the battlefield, striking the undead. Steam hissed from their dissolving flesh and they howled like dogs. Then Jayal was amongst them, the smell of grave cerements strong in his nostrils. The surviving vampires lashed out at him blindly, one landing a lucky blow on his breastplate which halted him for a moment. But then he was pushing forward again, the last beam of the sun filling him with the haunting music of the Flame. Then it was hidden by another band of cloud and more of the undead burst from the ground. He struck to the left and to the right, at undead and living foe alike. Screams, his enemies, his own men, his own—he no longer cared, the sword finding a rhythm now, eating at hard flesh and sinew, arteries that spouted geysers of blood, skulls that cracked through helmets. However thick the armour, nothing could prevent his blows from cleaving, and sundering and destroying, for that was the way of the Flame, and was he not one of the Hearth Brethren?

He would prove by his death that he was one of the Elect, that the years of training and harsh discipline, the blows from his father's heavy mailed fist, his dismissive words, all had stoked the incandescent rage which now consumed him: he would die a creature of anger, he would die Illgill's son. He sensed rather than saw how his companions were whittled away by the rain of blows from the enemy. Each one was like a part of him torn away: Jadshasi, Edric, Poluso, companions of his youth. Men screamed and flailed and died as if they were monstrous clockwork engines that once started on the path of destruction could do nothing except rattle themselves into a million fragments. Now it was only he and one or two others who waded on, swinging their weapons to right and left, heedless of the blows rained back on them.

There beside Poluso was the seven-foot giant Weebil, with a shock of orange hair sticking up from the bloodied bandage that was wrapped round his head, his two-handed blade flashing to left and right with a strength no ordinary man could have mastered. Next to him stood his sergeant, Furisel, hacking and thrusting as if he were threshing corn, oblivious of the blows that rained down on him.

But just as the light of the sun died, so did Jayal's vision begin to dim and waver. Everything was happening much slower, as if the passion of the battle was ebbing away to be replaced by a dark finality.

He saw the weapon that killed him: a mace swung towards his face, its flanged edges engraved on his memory.

A split second before it struck home, his whole life passed in a vivid flash of green like sunset over a polar cap, a whirlwind of filigreed colour. Then the jagged edges of the mace's four-bladed haft smashed into the side of his helmet, crushing it like paper, tearing a great gouge from eyebrow to mouth and destroying half his face. Every detail of the mace glistening now with traceries of his blood as it was withdrawn for another downward blow was etched onto his mind. But he was losing consciousness. He heard the howling of the void. And distantly, beyond that, a far-off horn call, the horn call of his father's Hearth Brethren, calling the advance.

Too late, too late they come to rescue him, he would die in the Flame. . . . Consciousness drained from him, but the second mace blow never came. Instead he felt the thrust of a spear into his side, a bee sting compared to the gaping wound in his head, then, as light from a candle dropped into the water from a barque off the Astardian Sea, the light was snuffed. All was darkness, and he was carried over the lip, to the ineluctable depths, where all is changed except the sea itself.

CHAPTER NINETEEN

Ghosts

Like a fugitive red moth, the flickering light of a candle was burning through Jayal's closed eyelids as he swam back to consciousness. Was he alive after all? He clenched his eyes shut. The crushing pain in his head seemed to tell him he was. For a moment he was confused: the vision of the battle had been so real . . . but hadn't it been just that: a vision? Yet the pain of the wound lingered. Then he remembered: Weebil shoving him into the wall, his hands being tied, then the cold air as he was thrown outside.

Then what was the light? He tried to open his eyes a fraction. The light was still there, persistent, rotating in front of his eyelids, which were glued together by blood. He forced them open—a butterfly breaking through a chrysalis—and his vision returned.

And with it, a ghost.

The candle was actually there, held by a wrinkled, gnarled hand that trembled slightly in the pool of light which it shed. Another hand cupped the candle which had evidently only just been lit. On the periphery of the pool of light, and underlit by it, hovering, was a face, as brown and gnarled as the tree stump of the hand which held the candle. The face was missing several front teeth. Only the eyes, warm and brown in the impassive, chiselled features showed signs of life, squinting down at Jayal.

It was a face from the vision of the battlefield. The face of his sergeant, Furisel, but now grown older—seven years older.

Jayal realised that he was lying on the floor, on his right side, his head lying in the shadows. His hands were free of the ties that he could vaguely remember being fastened in Weebil's Inn. He took in what he could see of his surroundings: a packed-earth floor, a jumble of ancient and cobwebby furniture off in one corner, a high, arched window above them, just beginning to admit the light of the moon. Erewon, riding like a galleon through the clouds of the departing storm. His gaze travelled back to that hauntingly familiar face in front of him. Despite the blood clogging his mouth he tried to speak, but only an inarticulate "Whhh—" came out. The man held up the hand cupping the candle, admonishing him to silence.

"Hush," he said. "You're safe here. Drink from this." He held up a battered old leather drinking bottle to Jayal's lips. It seemed all the dust of the Sraim Desert was clogging Jayal's tongue; he rose with a superhuman effort onto one elbow and applied his lips with enthusiasm to the mouth of the bottle. As he did so, the man tipped it up, facilitating the flow.

Fire. Fire in his lungs and in his guts, burning. Not the cool water he'd expected, but firewater, Rak, the potent distillate of the marsh berries. Now the recent past came flooding back with greater clarity—Weebil's Inn, his mind distorted by the liquor, the struggle. . . . As the thoughts whirled round his mind he gagged and spluttered, unable to breathe. He felt Furisel's free hand thumping him on the back, helping him clear his windpipe.

"There, there," the old man said, beating away lustily. "You'll live, though no thanks to Weebil and his friends."

Now Jayal had his breath:

"What happened?" he gasped.

"What happened?" the old fellow snorted. "I saw you running from the temple square, through the rain. And I thought, what is this? Jayal Illgill, on his own, and heading for the Spike?"

"You recognised me so easily?" Jayal asked.

But Furisel merely smiled condescendingly, as if Jayal's mind had been affected by the blow. "Sure enough," he continued, "you went straight to Weebil's Inn. I'd followed, sensing trouble. Got down a sewer hole and waited. Lucky for you that I did. A few minutes later they threw you out, and without that fancy sword you were carrying."

Dragonstooth: it was gone. This took a moment to register in Jayal's throbbing head. "Where are we?" he asked, attempting to sit up.

"Just down the street from the Spike—the usual place."

"The usual?"

"My, Weebil's hand is as strong as ever, your brains have gone awalking with that there wound." He laughed dryly. "Yes, the same place that you send to when you want some dirty work done."

"I send for you? But I haven't seen you in seven years!"

The old man chuckled. "Now I know your head is addled. Weebil may not have seen you in a while, but I have. Why, you sent one of your men here only yesterday."

Jayal wondered whether he was slowly taking leave of his senses. "Yesterday? But I wasn't even in Thrull yesterday!"

But the old man paid him no heed.

"Well, I grant you that the City of the Dead is not strictly part of Thrull . . ." he continued.

"I wasn't in the City of the Dead either!" Jayal protested.

Furisel sighed. "Well, have it as you wish, but at least let me get you home; Kazaris will reward me well, even though his master doesn't remember who he is, or where he's been."

"Who is this Kazaris?"

"Hah! That's another good one. Why, who else but your sorcerer?"

But now Jayal had grabbed the old man's forearm and was squeezing it remarkably tightly, for he was a very strong young man. The pressure of his fingers and the determined cast to his mouth soon stilled the old fellow's chuckling.

"Now listen," he said through clenched teeth. "This is all an amusing tale you have told me thus far, this business with this Kazaris. But first tell me why you think you saw me yesterday when I was miles away in the Fire Mountains and have not been back in this city for seven years."

As he'd leant forward to grab Furisel's arm, the right side of

Jayal's face had fallen into the light for the first time. The
effect on the old man was startling; he sprung back with a half-
suppressed scream. His efforts to escape were useless. Jayal's
grip was unrelenting.

"Your face . . ." Furisel wailed.

"What of it?"

"The scar—it's gone!"

"What scar?"

"Why the one you got at Thrull field!"

The vision of a moment before came flooding back to Jayal,
the descending mace blow . . . then the blackness. It was as if
he was waking from a dream of seven years ago, rather than
one only a few minutes old.

"Please, sir, spare me!" Furisel sobbed, breaking in on his
thoughts.

But now, despite the throbbing head, Jayal lunged forward,
his hands roughly bunching at the collar of Furisel's ragged
tunic. "Tell me, what is it you see?" he snarled. The horror in
the man's stare was enough to send icy waves marching up his
spine. In that look, Jayal saw a reflection of himself, a devil's
face in a mirror, imperfectly glimpsed, which chilled him to the
marrow. He freed a hand from Furisel's collar and rubbed at his
blood-caked face, wincing at the pain of the wound. It was in
the same place as the crushing mace below. Had it actually been
struck? For seven years he'd forgotten everything about the last
moments of the battle. But as he'd been unconscious, the memories had come back with painful acuity. The blow had fallen,
so it must have killed him. What was he doing here? Shouldn't
he be another wailing spirit in the abyss or a lost soul wandering Shades? Should his skull not be fixed into the pyramid of
skulls, and should not his bones be pulverised by the feet of
beast and man on the causeway?

To add to which Furisel was looking at him as if he were a
ghost.

His veins were full of ice.

"Tell me what you see!" he repeated, grabbing hold of the
man's collar again as if grasping the last vestige of reality itself.

"Your eye—" Furisel mumbled.

"Yes?"

"The eye!" he cried, his voice rising to a plaintive wail. "The eye . . ."

"Why, don't men have two eyes?" he shouted. The old man shook his head dumbly. "Then what? Damn your bones, where has that tongue of yours got to?"

"Why the one you lost on Thrull plain—you have it back. And the scar is gone."

Then the feverish vision of a few minutes ago came hastening back to Jayal in its full intensity, and the blood rushed away from his head, as if once more he was falling away from the light rapidly. The final blow, the spear in his side, the darkness, the edge of the void . . . a terrific shudder coursed through his body. He was a ghost, wandering the earth. A ghost who had returned, as ghosts will, to the place which holds their fondest memories. Was all life a dream, inhabited by ghosts like himself? Was this room, with its illusion of a risen moon, but a minor illusion in the endless mirrored halls of Hel, where nothing was as it seems, even the torments thrust upon the unshriven? He blinked his eyes once, then twice, trying to dispel the artifice, to see the whirlpool of the vision again, the souls borne down into the dark depths. But when his eyes opened each time the light had not fled; the moon Erewon still beamed through the high-arched window, and Furisel, for there was no doubting it was he, still crouched by him, the old leathery features creased in fear.

But wait; had not Furisel survived the bloodbath of the battle, and Weebil, too; had not his father's horns sounded to the charge as he fell? Could they all have been saved? Had he not just lost his memory and some vital recollection which would solve everything?

The old man had found his voice once more, talking as if in a trance. "You are a demon—a demon from the abyss. Tell me it is not true, that Kazaris has used some sorcery to take off your wound. Then I'll rejoice, believe me, sir, no one happier than old Furisel. . . ."

"I'm no demon," Jayal said, interrupting and giving Furisel's collar a shaking for good measure. "Don't you see? I'm flesh and blood like you!"

But the old man didn't seem to hear him, flinching away,

trying to curl himself into a tight ball. "It was the blood on your face, and the darkness . . . I didn't realise the scar was not there anymore . . ."

But Jayal barely heard him; his thoughts were racing back. If that blow had landed, then at least he would have been permanently scarred. Once more he touched his hand to his temple: under the hair there was only the laceration of the wall in Weebil's Inn.

He could not be a ghost, for ghosts felt no pain. This wound throbbed. The Rak had choked him. A ghost felt no physical sensation, suffered neither heat nor cold, nor saddle sore, nor insect bites. He'd suffered all these and more these seven years. He was alive; that was all there was to it. Jayal realised that whilst his thoughts had been drifting, Furisel had wriggled out of his grip. With his eyes still fixed on Jayal's face he put a hand inside the inner fold of his cloak and drew from it a wickedly curved dagger. The blade gleamed in the candlelight. He stood shakily, the dagger pointed at Jayal's chest.

Jayal stood, too, his head spinning, but his eyes never leaving Furisel's.

"No further, or I'll kill you, demon!" Furisel said in an unsteady voice.

The remark struck Jayal as absurd. Why threaten a ghost or a demon with death? They were imperishable. He leant his head back and let out a dry, wheezing laugh that shook his whole body. He was on the verge of hysteria, in a world turned upside down. Yes, things had changed. Once he'd ordered this man to let his best friend die, and he'd obeyed. And now he was being threatened by him. How much had he lost in the last seven years? The sacred anger that had made him strong, the authority he'd once wielded, the woman he had loved, his home, and now Dragonstooth, the sword he'd journeyed halfway round the world to find. And on top of that, this man looked at him as he were a spirit returned from the abyss to haunt him. His laughter seemed to have unnerved Furisel even further; the dagger fairly shook in the veteran sergeant's hand. Jayal reached forward and took it from him as easily as taking a toy from a child.

The fight had gone from Furisel as rapidly as it had arrived.

His body trembled, and he stared at the floor. "Sit," Jayal commanded, and, after a moment's hesitation, the old man did so, squatting uncomfortably. Jayal did likewise, so their eyes were once more level.

"Now tell me," he said. "Tell me of this other person, the one who looks like me."

Furisel looked away. "He is the mirror image, in every respect. Save the scar . . ."

"Then he must be some impostor."

"No! I carried him, this same person, all the way back from Thrull field. The spitting image, except the wound to his head."

"And he goes by my name?"

"No—he has a new name, for the Worm would do anything to take Jayal Illgill."

"What is it?"

"Setten—he took it soon after the battle, thinking that and his scar would throw them off the scent."

Jayal remembered the rumours he'd heard earlier at the Gaunt's Head: that he, Jayal, had been alive and living in the city ever since the battle. This man who called himself Setten must be an impostor who had gulled his old sergeant into taking pity on him, then used the Illgill name to wield authority over a gang of cutthroats.

"Whoever this man was, he only masqueraded as me," he said as evenly as he could. "I've been away these seven years, in the Southern Lands. I've seen for the first time in seven years the old house on the Silver Way, empty, abandoned . . ." But Furisel was shaking his head rapidly. ". . . What is it, man?"

"But that is where you—I mean the other has lived all these years!"

"In that ruin?"

Furisel nodded his head.

"But it seemed abandoned when I passed it!"

"Did you go in?"

Jayal shook his head no.

"That is where he lives, with his band."

"Band?"

"Aye, he and twenty others, including the sorcerer

Kazaris—a black-hearted bunch who would murder you for one durcal."

"And you work for them?"

"I don't kill—others do that. I help just enough to keep alive."

Jayal sneered. "You're a rogue; you made up this tale because I came round before you could rob me."

"Then wouldn't I have robbed you and left you for the Vampirs instead of dragging you here?"

True, reflected Jayal. He'd have to piece together Furisel's story from the beginning. "Tell me about the battle—I barely remember it. The blow to my head made me forget . . ."

". . . the battle?" Furisel laughed bitterly, his fear for the moment lost in his memories.

"Yes, the end, the evening . . ."

Furisel swallowed hard, his eyes roving about the room. The memories were still evidently painful. He took a quick pull of Rak, then turned his gaze back to Jayal. "Only those who had miracles stored survived it. All those in your cohort would have died if it hadn't been for that final charge of your father's. The Reapers fell back, beaten hither and thither by him and the Hearth Knights. I had already fallen, with a wound to my chest, but I remember Baron Illgill. A brave sight! His eyes glowing like carbuncles in the dark, his beard jutting out from his chin as if he were too proud to die." The memory seemed to rouse him from his terror for the first time: fire glinted in his eyes. Jayal sat motionless, knowing that the tale would now unfurl.

"Oh fierce he was, unconquerable," Furisel continued, "though a dozen or more wounds laced his black armour with blood." But then the faraway gleam faded, and the light seemed to go from his eyes and he hung his head, his shoulders hunched.

"But then . . ." he whispered, lapsing into silence.

"Then what . . . ?" pressed Jayal.

Furisel let out a queer sob from the back of his throat, looking now firmly out the window to where the amber face of the moon beamed down into the chamber.

"Then . . . then your father saw your body lying there. Crushed by a mace blow to the head and a spear in your side. It was as if all the fight went from him, standing there in the twilight, the Reapers fleeing away, a carpet of dead at his feet . . ."

The agony of the wounds came back to Jayal—how had he forgotten them? It was all he could do to clench his teeth to prevent himself from crying out at the memory of them. He forced himself to concentrate on the old man, despite the phantom pain which wracked his body. "Yes, and then . . . ?" he prompted, his voice wounded and hoarse. Furisel shook his head, his eyes misty.

"And then what happened?" he repeated gently.

"As I said, the fight went out of the baron. One minute he was roaring berserk, then his shoulders fell . . ."

Jayal shook his head. This wasn't the father he remembered. "Go on," he whispered.

Furisel now regarded him in a strange way, as one who has some difficult news to impart to his audience, and seems reluctant to pursue the matter any further. Jayal tried to help him again, gentler in his manner.

"The time after my wound is a blank. Only tonight, for the first time in seven years, did I remember that I had been wounded at all."

"It was a grievous wound; your head was split from here to here," he said, drawing a line from the right eye socket to the chin. "There was no doubt about it—you were gone."

"Gone?"

"Dying—soon to be dead as a nail. Later, on the carrion piles, I couldn't believe that anyone could have survived a blow like that."

Jayal remembered the blow, remembered the blows he had himself inflicted: it had been a deadly wound he'd suffered. What had happened?

"Tell me what you saw," he said as encouragingly as he could.

"I only know a bit of what happened, but I'll tell you that . . ." Furisel put the candle slowly on the floor and wrapped his cloak around his shoulders against the cold night air.

"I was lying next to you, a sucking wound to my chest, when I heard your father's trumpets sound, and the crash of steel. I knew that charge was too late for me, though the Reapers were swept back like sheaves of grain. Then it grew quiet. I was waiting for the priests to come and finish me. It makes a man concentrate that does, when death beckons you with his iron claw. Then I heard your father give out orders: all the dying were to be removed, with special care for his son. Here's luck I thought, the orders being for the priest to sacrifice us and all. Two of the Hearth Knights came forward and grabbed me, one my arms, the other my legs: they were quick and clumsy and I passed out. That was the last I saw of you till later . . ."

"Later?"

"Aye, later, but it is a long story . . ." said Furisel, huddling against the chill of the night. He took hold of the flask of Rak and took another long pull, as if preparing to exorcise some demon of the past.

He began to speak, hesitantly at first, but as the Rak worked its way through his system and Jayal didn't interrupt him, he became more confident. And as he spoke it was as if the spirits of the dead issued from Hel once more, and came pressing in at the windows and the doors like the fog, which, now the storm had passed, was returning to the streets outside. But Jayal barely heard his tale as it unfurled. It was as if the past once more had come alive and the old man's words were a mere accompaniment to the images that he saw once more before him. Images that had not come for seven years, but which tonight had decided to revisit him, the very night he had returned to Thrull for the first time in so long. Then even the noise of Furisel's words faded; each accent, nuance, taste, scent of those events of seven years past was delivered back to him with total acuity. . . .

The world had begun to spin, that was his first thought as he had lain on the ground, his mind full of the vision of his lifeblood lacing the mace that had struck his head. Slowly at first, then with ever-increasing rapidity, he was being dragged forward into the darkness. But then, miraculously he had come back to consciousness. The world still spun: only he was stationary. Everything else whirled round and round in such a blur, now he was the whirlpool, the dark centre, sucking in everything else.

He felt hands lift him, and then he was being carried swiftly by willing arms. Where, he didn't care, for the darkness would come soon and with it the end of this useless motion. Then the voices, a babble of contradictory sound of which he could make out only fragments.

"It is the lord's son!"—"Dead?"—"A hairsbreadth away"— "The Flame have mercy in the final days"—"Out of the way, you whoreson. Carry him into the tent!"

Then his father's voice. "There is nothing we can do?"

"Not a thing, lord, but your prayers . . ."

"Prayers be damned, he is my son!"

"Sire, the battle is lost, your crusade is lost, the Worm carries the field, this is but another wound you must carry into exile."

"Wound? Carry? Carry my soul to Hel! My only son dying, and you have no words of comfort?"

"My lord, there is only one remedy, but it is beyond us . . ." The surgeon's voice now, urgent. "He's slipping away; let the priest say the final absolution."

"Stay! No cavilling priests while my son dies!"

"But what if he goes into the next world unaneled?" The voice of the priest, cutting in.

"Harken to me, I have not fought and lost so my only hope dies with the sun: I will use the Rod!"

"The Rod?" the priest's voice again.

"You heard me, grey-haired dog! Go now, fetch Manichee; he was tending to the wounded last I saw him." The sound of rustling silk as the Adept departed. A silence in which Jayal's mind circulated, toying with the edge of the whirlpool of nothingness. Then a soldier's voice from outside the tent.

"My lord, the Worm attacks again!"

Now his father's voice, soft in his ear, softer than it had ever been in the eighteen years of Jayal's life. "So, the end of time has tripped us up like an errant boy, our ankles knocked together before we fall in useless rage. The final attack, and we must all die. But not you. You were born for the light and not Hel's grave!" Another noise as the tent flap was pushed aside. Jayal became conscious of another presence besides his father's.

"So, Manichee, you have finally come, when it's too late."

"The battle is lost," the other voice said, agreeing.

He heard his father command, "The rest of you, get out!" Dimly he heard the surgeon and the other priest depart. The wind howled through the rents in the side of the tent. Now the three of them were alone.

"Jayal is going to die," his father said quietly. "You know why I've called you."

"You want me to use the Rod." Manichee's voice was hushed, too, despite the noise of the wind and the clamour of battle which resumed outside.

The tone of his father's voice turned from despair to anger. "All day I've asked you to use it. The battle would have been won by noon if you had. But no, you refused me; and now the Worm will rule this city, and the Flame will be extinguished in the Hearth."

"I warned you when I came from Forgeholm that I wouldn't use it—that it was cursed."

"You don't think I am cursed anyway? The battle is lost, and my son's dying!"

"I told you my reasons; the Rod was not for you or me to wield, but for another man who would come soon and rid this world of ours of its woes. A man who will rekindle the sun, Illgill. Think of it."

"Think of it, while my son dies? Listen! They attack again. We have only moments left. By all our friendship, Manichee, save my son!" Outside the clash of arms and screams could be heard. Inside a strange stillness had settled over the three men—Illgill, Manichee and the dying boy.

Finally Manichee let out a deep sigh. "And I saw this too—years ago. Why didn't I give way to you earlier? I could have saved a thousand souls by now, not just your son. Now I will suffer Reh's curse for just one life."

"Hold him while I fetch the Rod, we haven't much time." Jayal felt his father's hand on his shoulder, and the warmth of it gave him a last strength to fight against the whirlpool sucking him down.

His one good eye opened.

Above him his father looked down. Across the tent, bathed a

deep red by the burning pyres outside, he could see Manichee, the High Priest, the long cocked hat, its bells jingling as he bent over a lead casket. The priest reached in and brought out of it an object which glowed with blue-white eldritch fire, the priest's gaunt features underlit by its light. He held the object up reverentially, intoning a mantra in a language which Jayal only dimly recognised as the Fire Tongue of the Old Ones. Now he was carrying it over to the bier, the thing held out in his outstretched hands.

"Have you got him?" Manichee asked.

"Aye, and look, he is conscious."

"Let me see!" The priest's cocked hat hung over him, the bells jingling faintly, the flaring white light hurting Jayal's eye, sending shooting splinters of pain into his head.

"He is with us still, but the shadow of death is on him. Hold him so he can't struggle—we've work to do."

"Do it, Manichee, and I will be grateful for as long as we both live."

"Then I will not expect much thanks, for Faran's men are nearly upon us. Let us begin."

The light blazed into incandescence. Jayal shut his eye—but the Rod still shone in the darkness, casting a pillar of light upwards into that darkness. Jayal's soul lifted from his body, he saw it being left behind, below in the tent, his father and Manichee with the blazing Rod standing over it, unaware that he had gone. He sped upwards, the world left far behind. This was death, he thought. There was no returning from this flight.

But then, hurtling towards him through the gloom of space, over an arcing bridge of light which stretched from the shadow world to the land of the living, he saw a figure. At first he couldn't make out its features, but then in an instant it was upon him. Sandy hair, a blonde moustache, blue eyes: the mirror image of himself, but snarling with fear, flecks of foam on its lips, as if being dragged through the air by invisible demons. It was as if the two were being pulled together by an irresistible magnetic force. Their beings collided with an incandescent flash. Immediately Jayal's forward progress was halted and he felt himself sliding back down the bridge of light towards the land of the living, entangled with the other body. His soul shot away from his body into the other's. He felt life again, and watched as his other half began to die, blood streaming from its head wound. Back and back he fell, watching the body stuck to him heave and convulse in its death throes, blood and brains welling out of the smashed head . . .

His eyes snapped open, wide with terror. He had remembered. Remembered why he was still alive, did not carry a scar, had both eyes. Another had taken on his wound. Another dark self pulled from Shades to die for him. A creature of shadows who was his mirror image, who had suffered horribly and died.

But had not died.

Who was alive in this city. This very night. The creature that hated him more than anything in the world. His Doppelgänger.

CHAPTER TWENTY

The Second Lighting

The Temple of Sutis.

It was two hours before midnight. Guests and acolytes had disappeared into the rooms on the upper floors. After the noise of the dancing and the rowdiness of the visitors, the Greeting Room was strangely silent. Now only the High Priestess and Furtal remained. The old man stretched his cramped limbs then stepped down from the dais and, one hand stretched in front of him to feel the way, limped off in the direction of the kitchens.

Malliana watched him go impatiently; she had things to do, and she had to do them quickly. There was a small secret chamber next to Thalassa's room. In a moment she would go to it, not too early, not before the priest and Thalassa had started their business. Their sounds would muffle the sound of her own movements. She already knew him to be the man that Faran was searching for, the one who had killed Varash, but the element of danger in what she was about to do merely added to her excitement.

But first she would see Thalassa's reaction when she removed the man's mask as she had been ordered to do. Her screams would no doubt bring the guards running. But if not, Malliana would fetch them herself. Then, not only Thalassa, but the others would be dragged to the Temple of Iss.

She would be rewarded for this by Faran, and not before time. Though many of the acolytes and priests of Iss came here, they, she knew, despised the trade of the flesh she dealt in. Hypocrites to a man: despite their yearning for the Life in Death, they yearned for Life as well. These pale acolytes and their priests, whose yellowed skin told of many sunless hours waiting for Faran to offer them the Black Chalice, were her main customers. Yet they sneered at their desires, and at her. Things would be different after tonight.

Then the temple which she'd inherited twenty-two years ago would finally be recognized as such, not just a mere brothel. The Worm and the Flesh, after all, were closely allied: one could not exist without the other. Faran knew this already; why else did he pursue Thalassa? He wanted her lifeblood just as the living wanted another's body; it was only a degree of possession. No one was born without the desires of the flesh. The Goddess had primacy, and only after her would Prince Iss claim his due in the grave. Malliana's face creased into a tight little smile at the thought.

She'd given Thalassa instructions in the brief seconds before she'd led the masked man upstairs. There, too, was satisfaction, a neat rounding off of the two interrelated problems. She'd told Thalassa that if she did her job well and enticed the man into revealing who he was, she would keep her promise to spare Alanda. Malliana knew that Thalassa would do anything for the old lady. The next half hour or so in her spy hole were going to be fascinating. After that both Thalassa and the masked stranger would be dragged away to the Temple of Iss. As for Alanda . . . she would end up on the streets anyway. The High Priestess had had enough of the blue-eyed witch.

The cat by now had returned from an impromptu meal amongst the guests' leftovers and was mewing piteously. She swept it up onto her copious bosom in a spasm of anticipation. She felt her old powers returning: intrigue and manipulation. Sensing her mood, the creature purred with astonishing enthusiasm, its furry sides heaving with delight.

But something was still troubling Malliana. She looked about the room and realised that the light was growing progressively dimmer as the candles burned low. It was the time of the Second

Lighting, when every single one of the thousand candles that turned night to day were relit. Where were the slaves whose job it was to keep them permanently alight? and where were the guards who should have kept them at their duties? Normally the Greeting Room would have been bustling with activity by now. Instead, an air of eerie quiet hung over the swiftly darkening hall. She glanced past the brazier in the entranceway to the gardens. The candles were burning down out there as well. Soon the vampires would be in the grounds.

She strode rapidly towards the slave quarters. She expected to find the men drunk on wine; slaves had an infinite cunning in the matter of stealing alcohol. She would rouse them soon enough. They would have to be whipped, then sold to the Temple of Iss; a shame, there were not many left of the captives from the battle of Thrull, and few merchants came this way with slave caravans. But something had to be done. Her velvet dress swished over the floor behind her as the cat's metronomic purring grew, if anything, more intense, as if it sensed its mistress's anger.

Then a figure rose up from where it had been sitting in one of the pools of shadows at the edge of the room. The sudden appearance in the gathering gloom of the hall made Malliana stop dead in her tracks with surprise. Then she saw who it was—the hooded stranger, the one who had come for Thalassa. The man's features were still concealed in the deep shadows of his cowl. As they stood facing each other wordlessly, Malliana thought she could detect his body swaying slightly from side to side. Certainly she smelt the stink of Rak on his breath. This was another nuisance she hadn't expected. The guards would have to be reprimanded for leaving him alone: and with Rak, the most intoxicating of all liquors! Maybe the guards, too, would have to be sent to the Temple of Iss. She tried to brush past him, but the man snaked out a hand, stopping her roughly.

"What do you want?" she snarled, struggling against his grip, the cat adding a warning hiss to the menace of its mistress's voice.

The man didn't relax his hold, though Malliana's spittle must have struck him on his face. Now she was nearer, the High Priestess could make out more of his features, particularly a heavy scar that ran down the right side of his face. "Why, mistress, nothing . . . that isn't my due," he said menacingly. Though his voice was rough, it seemed to bear vestiges of a superior accent, as if his current unprepossessing appearance was not in accord with his natural station in life. There were many who went under disguises in Thrull, many of them dangerous men with nothing to lose. The sooner she got the guards to eject this one, the better. She tried to dodge around him to the servants' quarters, but he was quick, interposing his body between her and the door.

"You've had my answer," she said curtly, "as you've had it a hundred times before: Thalassa is otherwise engaged."

"As I've noticed, lady, since I saw you fitting her up with that priest."

"So? Drink your wine. One of the other women will become available at the Third Lighting; you will have to wait." She moved forward again, but he still blocked her way.

"There won't be a Second Lighting, let alone a third," he said easily.

"What do you mean?" Malliana asked.

He drew closer. She saw that his right eye socket was a puckered hole where the scar she'd noticed before ended. The stink of spirits became even more noticeable. Malliana wrinkled her nose in distaste. The man favoured her with a lopsided smile where the scar pulled up the side of his face.

"Where are the slaves, the guards?" he asked, as if he already knew the answer.

"They'll be here in a minute," she replied, less certainly now.

He shook his head. "No, mistress; your guards won't help you anymore; in fact no one can." He pulled a small black phial from one of the folds of his cloak. Even from two feet away and through the stink of Rak she caught a rotting, vegetal odour— the smell of the root of the Dendil plant, the most potent poison known in Old Earth. "Dropped it in their beer: funny how slaves and guards all drink beer: you'd have thought one or two wouldn't but, no." He shook his head. "They all drank—and they're all dead."

"You're lying!" Malliana shouted, trying to break past him to the kitchen, but the man's free hand swept up over her mouth in a second, stifling sound. Malliana lashed out with her fist, but the intruder grabbed her wrist and forced it up behind her back. Phial and cat went spinning to the floor.

"You don't believe me?" the intruder asked, panting with exertion. Malliana let out a muffled cry of pain as he forced her arm even higher up her back. "Come, let me show you your servants."

He pushed her in the direction of the slave quarters, kicking open the door. The first thing Malliana saw was the staring eyes of a guard. He appeared to have been asphyxiated, his face puce, his head lying in a pool of vomit on one of the refectory tables. The floor was carpeted with other bodies. Enough bodies to account for all the guards and all the slaves. The stench of death made Malliana gag.

"As I told you," the stranger said evenly, "all dead."

Malliana stared at the bodies for a few seconds, unable to believe what she saw. How could one man have killed so many? Then the stench of the dead reached her nostrils again, and with it the reality of the situation: without the Second Lighting and without the guards the temple was helpless. She jerked her head free and spat out the foul taste in her mouth.

"What have you done?" she moaned.

The man laughed, throwing back the hood of his cloak with his free hand, revealing his features in the flickering light of the fire. The scar was more obscene than she could have imagined: a ragged, puckered wound that twisted and pulled one side of his face into a frozen mask and made a mockery of the other half, which showed what might have been a handsome youth in his early twenties had it not been for its darker hemisphere.

He laughed at the expression on her face. "You don't recognise me, then?" Malliana could only let out a dry retching sound from her throat; she was incapable of speech.

He shook his head in mock exasperation. "Ah, lady! The wrongs you have done me; but I have been patient, have left you gold. . . . Now, though, my patience has gone." He twisted her arm again, eliciting another yelp of pain.

"Why do you think I have returned time and time again for Thalassa when I might have had any drab in the place?"

Malliana, encouraged by another twist of her arm, shook her head.

"A tale then, and a short one. Do you remember before the war, who Thalassa was betrothed to?"

Again Malliana made as if to shake her head, but she stopped short as more pain flooded up her arm.

"Oh yes you do! Why else have you employed her all these years? She was engaged to Illgill's son. Isn't that right?"

"Yes, yes . . ." Malliana managed through the pain.

"Good—then have you guessed who I am?"

But Malliana shook her head again. The man lifted his solitary eye to the smoky ceiling in exasperation, before returning his gaze to her kohl-streaked face.

"I have been here seven years, lady, but not many have recognised me. This is why I have risked discovery at this brothel time and time again. The scar has changed my appearance, but I am still Jayal Illgill!"

Malliana would have flinched back again, but the arm behind her back restrained her. She averted her gaze from the scarred face. She could vaguely remember Illgill's son from the past. Certainly there was a vague resemblance despite the disfigurement. But he had never come here all those years ago, and she couldn't be sure. But there was something hauntingly familiar in the man's face, scar or not.

"You're mad!" she managed. "The vampires will be here in seconds."

"Don't worry about them, lady," he said savagely. "Vampires won't harm me. If you're lucky, and cooperative, they might not harm you either."

"Why, what do you want me to do?"

"Oh, just lead me to Thalassa's room, and quickly." He pulled a dagger from his belt. "Then we'll see how things develop." He prodded her towards the servants' staircase with the tip of the weapon.

Malliana thought to cry out for help. But who would hear her now? The guards were dead, and all the women would be occupied with their guests. And this man, this shadow of the baron's son, was clearly insane. With the prompting of his knife, she picked her way forward over the dead bodies towards the staircase leading to the upper rooms.

Alanda and Furtal sat alone in the temple kitchen on the opposite side of the building. The old man, who had been eating from a bowl of stew, was groping about the table trying to find a pitcher of wine with which to replenish his beaker. Unbeknownst to him it sat on a sideboard well out of reach. The old lady was clearly unconscious of his efforts, staring abstractedly at the fire. Furtal's patience finally ran out.

"Where is the wine?" he said, getting to his feet.

There was still no response from Alanda. She was utterly still, her mind lost in the sifting of past and future events. She probably wouldn't have noticed if Furtal had shaken her.

She had the power of the second sight: events of the past and future came to her in still moments such as these. But the visions never came with any clarity when they directly related to her. Thus she hadn't foreseen her husband's death. Nor that Thalassa should be taken from her this very night, just when it seemed their escape was a possibility.

Her mind conjured fragmented images of the future: surely she saw Thalassa there somewhere? She journeyed long and far in a kaleidoscopic blur of colour and movement; occasionally she glimpsed substance and form in it. One image kept returning. A city covered by snow—early evening—its ruby towers glinting in the sunset—the snow stretching to infinity—she was in a grand courtyard in the centre of the city, the wind threw up will-o'-the-wisps—a form was taking shape, coming towards her through the snow blizzard—a heart-shaped face as white as snow—Thalassa, and someone behind her—she glimpsed the mask of the priest: he was there too. But what was the place? Was it Shades? No, it seemed to be a location in this world. . . . But the images weren't clear; she groaned in frustration. Then the vision disappeared: once more all she saw were the flickering flames of the fire. If only she had been able to talk to Seresh before he had gone upstairs, tried to deduce what his plans were. Seresh it was who had been delegated to take them away from here—but now what was he doing? Nothing more or less than all the other men who visited this place—and midnight was so close!

Alanda didn't hear Furtal drawing near her. The flames of the fire occupied her whole mind. She conjured up once more the hideous mask of the stranger: the vision of it seemed to hang there in the flames, a thing of the flames, as seemed the person who wore it. She sensed anger, rage, destruction in his being, yet also a fragility, a wound that would not die. There was power and vulnerability in him: she sensed a parallel with Thalassa.

Thalassa was just a woman now, a whore in the Temple of Sutis, but when she had first met her as a little girl wandering the gardens of Illgill's mansion, Alanda had seen her destiny so clearly that for a while she couldn't speak but could only look wonderingly at the child. She remembered the moment: the sun dappled by the leaves of the orchard where they'd met, the sunlight playing patterns of light over the girl's face, the face itself numinous, shining with power. Alanda had seen it, but no one else had. She was the one the Scriptures spoke of, the Lightbringer who would bring the people out of the time of darkness.

Now she had glimpsed in a few minutes that he'd stood in the kitchen with Seresh a similar power in the priest. Who was he? Seresh had referred to him as a friend. But he had not come from Thrull: Alanda knew all the Hearth Brethren in the city. This man was a stranger, had travelled far, and, what's more, had arrived on the very evening when the *Book of Light* prophesied that the time of darkness would begin to wane.

The *Book* spoke of a Herald, the man who would come before the Lightbringer, a man with no face. Was the priest the Herald? A masked man. But there were many masked men in Thrull: all priests wore masks, though this man's had certainly been unusual. But to Alanda his arrival seemed fated. She felt the weight of future events building up, crushing her down, so the weight of her bones seemed too heavy for her to carry . . . yet still she couldn't see what was about to happen, just that gossamer-thin vision of the snowbound city. . . .

Her thoughts circled back to the masked priest. He had gone with Thalassa, as planned. But it had been Malliana who had encouraged it. There was something amiss here. Seresh would not reappear until the Third Lighting, just before midnight; then, surely, it would be too late . . .

She felt a hand on her shoulder. She looked up. There was Furtal leaning over her. She realised that she had been sunk in reverie for several minutes, maybe even longer. She hadn't said a word to Furtal since he'd come in from the Greeting Room: he wouldn't know what had happened to Thalassa.

They were the oldest of friends, having both served in Illgill's court, but sometimes, at moments like these, she forgot his presence.

"Furtal," she said, "Faran wants Thalassa—tonight."

The old man nodded his bald, gnomic head as if he already knew this. "Yes, I guessed as much. Seresh came, did he not?"

"Yes, with a masked stranger."

"I heard them both, even above the lute—you hear everything when you're blind."

"What should we do?"

"There's nothing to be done. Seresh will have to think of something. In the meantime fetch me some wine, the singing left me with a thirst."

She stood up in a trance, as if the visions of the future had cramped her limbs and added each of the years she had glimpsed onto her stooped shoulders. She fetched the wine, pouring it into his beaker with shaking hands. He had sat down again and drank greedily. Then he set to once more at the bowl of stew on the table, his nose almost at a level with the vessel as he methodically shovelled food into his toothless mouth with his spoon.

"You don't seem worried," she remarked.

"A man has to keep up his strength."

"What for? We're all likely to die here."

At this Furtal laid down his spoon, turning his blind eyes towards Alanda. "You would know when a man's time was come, wouldn't you?"

She looked away; she kept her powers from her friends lest the knowledge of their deaths break her. But sometimes she glimpsed the skull beneath the face, just as she had glimpsed Zaraman's this evening. A premonitory chill seized her, she fought against it, but Furtal had already snaked out a hand, grabbing her wrist.

"It will come soon, for all of us," he said, his customary jocularity quite gone from his voice. "But we must have faith. Seresh will think of something, the plan will go ahead." Alanda stared around at the familiar fixtures of the temple kitchen: the worn, flagstoned floor, the low-timbered ceiling with its huge, fire-blackened hearths, the burnished copper cooking pots hanging from hooks in the wall, gleaming in the candlelight: all the familiar sights of her service for the last seven years. A domestic enough scene, certainly, but one which she had hoped to have left behind forever at midnight.

But Furtal was right: there was nothing she could do for the moment. She gave the old man a smile, though he couldn't see her face. He had always been here—in the seven years of their slavery they had bolstered each other against the petty tyrannies of the temple.

Things had been different once. Illgill's mansion on the Silver Way, filled with the nobility of Thrull. Perhaps she had been arrogant, had looked down on servants, uttered harsh words. In truth she couldn't remember. All she knew now was that things would be different if she was ever free again. She would treat everyone with unflinching impartiality. Only slaves knew the value of freedom.

"Do you remember playing for Baron Illgill?" she said wistfully.

"Yes, I remember," he said, gesturing at the empty hollows of his eyes, "though I can't see, I can remember. I remember the young lady visiting after their betrothal. There was a banquet, I played the 'Lay of the Love of Idras and Iconoclas.' It went down well. The baron gave me a purse of ten durcals, though I missed two or three notes . . ."

Alanda cut in. "I remember it well; you sang like an angel that day."

"And now I sing like a eunuch; such is time."

"But it's only seven years."

"Why should I weep, lady? They took my sight and my manhood, but now I'm surrounded by beauty that cannot wound, by flesh that I don't desire . . . and tonight I will have my freedom again."

"Amen to that. Seresh will be back soon, as you said; he will have a plan."

"Reh willing. Meanwhile we must act normally. What time is it?"

"They will have finished the Second Lighting."

"Then I'd better get back to the dais—the lovers will want to hear my music as they disport themselves."

"Lull them to sleep, old friend—the fewer enemies awake at midnight the better."

"We'll save Thalassa, don't worry." He squeezed her hand again, his fingers, despite his age, surprisingly delicate and tapered, decorated with old family rings depicting the sacred creatures of the fire: the gryphon, the salamander, the dragon.

She kissed it. "Bless you, Furtal. Better times are in front of us again."

"In front of you, lady, not me: my skein is coming to an end. Blind people have the sight, too, you know."

Alanda was silent. She had felt the chill again: surely she wouldn't lose Furtal now? She looked across at the ringed candle burning on the windowsill. Each part of the night was measured by the rings burning down. It was time.

Furtal groped for the neck of the lute leaning against the bench. Alanda guided his hand to it and he smiled his thanks.

"Have cheer. Reh works his way for the good, even in these last days," he said, his voice cheerful despite the heaviness of his soul.

"May the Flame make it so," whispered Alanda. "Now go, or you will get another thrashing from Malliana."

"Oh, I am used to those! Be careful and things will work out before midnight." Alanda helped him to the heavy wooden door, and pulled it open. Immediately she was aware of something wrong. The corridor and the hallway beyond it were lost in darkness, the small amount of illumination offered by the one or two candles still burning merely accentuating the gloom. Furtal had been about to step down the corridor unaware of the darkness, when Alanda dragged him back into the kitchen.

"What is it?" he asked, as Alanda threw the bolts on the door.

"The lights," she said breathlessly as she thrust home the last of the bolts. "They've all gone out!"

CHAPTER TWENTY-ONE

The Temple of the
Flesh Consumed

It had taken some time for Thalassa and the masked stranger
to reach the door to her second-floor room. Her mind had
been in turmoil during their ascent. Malliana had told her to
find out the man's identity, promising that if she did so, she
might yet spare Alanda. But the man was Seresh's friend. They
had entered the Greeting Room together. If only she had been
able to speak to Seresh after the dancing, to find out what was
going on. . . . But Malliana had been too quick. Now Seresh
had disappeared, leaving her with the masked priest. Was he a
friend in disguise, or what he seemed, a priest of Iss? Surely
Seresh was trustworthy. He was Count Durian's son, a wanted
man who'd risked much coming here. . . . But then what had he
been doing with a priest of Iss? And what had Alanda been trying to signal her during the dancing?

Faran. Nothing in Thrull could escape his influence. Maybe
this was one last trick which he had concocted with Malliana.
She knew only a miracle could save her from him, and midnight seemed to be hastening towards her at an alarming speed.
She could already imagine the gongs that announced the dead-
est time of night ringing out from the Temple of Iss as they did
every night. It would be the last time she would ever hear them
from outside the Temple of Worms.

She would just have to do the High Priestess's bidding for

the while. That way whatever happened, Alanda might still be safe. She had played a role for years, an hour or two more could not harm, might do good.

They were at her chamber door. She was a woman, with a woman's feelings; once she had longed for tenderness, had sought for it in the luxurious surroundings of this place. Lethe smoke had given everything a softer edge, where it had been easy to sink into a state of luxury, to do things which she now regretted, where the flesh and not the mind had been paramount. When she had first come here with Alanda, near starvation, having been brutalised by the soldiers outside, she had hoped for little. Luxury, warmth, light, shelter: her body had seemed a small tithe to pay for life.

All that had changed for her on that first midnight visit to the Temple of Iss—the rough hands, the passage through the cold streets, the blue flares lighting the way, the mist thick in the damp, heavy air, the guards exhaling streams of smoke through the nose slits of their skull masks. Then the ossuary deep beneath the Temple of Iss, the hands that had stripped her bare, Faran with his spreading cloak, like bat's wings, smelling of mildew . . .

Since then her life had been one of denial: the small blandishments she had offered to the guests were now too hateful for her to give: she had become withdrawn and cold. She was seldom chosen a second time.

But with this priest she would have to remember how she had once been, when she was still relatively innocent, when she had almost wanted to please the succession of vain, selfish men who had come to this room. Malliana would be watching, she was sure. And she would have to do the High Priestess's bidding with the knowledge that at midnight, even if she did as Malliana instructed, she would be given over to Faran forever anyway. Faran, a man who only treasured that which he could ultimately destroy.

Her hand was on the doorknob now, and she prayed silently, as she had prayed every day of her time at the Temple of Sutis: a prayer from the *Book of Light*, the jewelled, leather-bound book which she had opened every morning of her life as the sun rose over the mountains. The *Book of Reh, of Life, of Light*—

the fire which shone within, the fire which she had first let die when she had come here and forgotten herself in the luxury of the temple. Every morning she still opened it, and the amethysts and emeralds on its cover sparkled in the early-morning sun on her balcony, and she read, washing away the memories of the night with the sacred words that took her back to better times:

> *"Herein is inscribed the Way of Reh; the Way of Light which triumphs over the Way of Darkness, which is the Way of his brother, Iss, Lord of Worms—listen to the words of Light, and you will never fear the night."*

Her fingers would trace the illuminated words, the vellum yellowed with time, and her lips would whisper the words, and a soothing fire would flow through her veins.

> *"I will rise with you in the morning. I will set with you in the evening. My blood is fire, and your fire is blood, and joy is in your appearing."*

After she had read, she would look up at the mountains. Often Alanda would be there as well, smiling with those blue, blue eyes, and the world would seem tolerable again, and the night would be banished from her mind.

But now the fear could not be shrugged off so easily: midnight was so near. Would she betray this man? Ask him to remove the mask as Malliana had ordered her? It was the skull mask of her persecutors, the Temple of Iss, after all.

Even the touch of his palm through the soft inner leather of the glove didn't seem right. Though her fingers encountered soft leather here, she could feel the flexing of the steel talons in the exoskeleton of the hand—steel as inflexible and mute as the man himself. They had not exchanged a single word in all this time. The man's skull mask was turned to her—he was wondering why she delayed at the door so long. Another wave of panic swept over her as she hurriedly pushed it open. The room was diffused with orange light from the veiled lanterns. She wondered where the spy hole was: she had always suspected there to be such a thing in her room, but she had thrust the fact of its existence to the back of her mind. The High Priestess was no doubt already stationed behind it.

A plan was forming: she would perform her role up to a certain point at least, try to find out who this man was. If he was a friend, there might still be time to warn him . . .

Just at this moment, as if tired of the pretence of what he'd been doing, the priest brushed away her hand. Thalassa sensed hostility and violence behind the mask. With a heart full of trepidation, she closed the door behind her.

Urthred looked at the decoration of the whore's room through the eye slits of his mask. Nothing he saw impressed him: the tapestry wall hangings depicting the Goddess Sutis in a series of erotic adventures with the other gods was a blasphemy in itself. The furniture of the room was decked out to reflect the ambience of the lascivious Goddess; heavy red damask drapes hung from the rail around the four poster bed, carved with figures achieving acrobatic feats in the pursuit of copulation and fellatio. The nestlike qualities of the bed were enhanced by what seemed like a hundred multicoloured cushions. Bronze drinking vessels stood glinting in the orange lantern light. Scented candles further added to the muted lighting, their smell speaking of far southern climes where the sun teased the scent from exotic blooms, and a warm breeze, an almost forgotten memory in the lands of Old Earth, blew across the desert sands. If he had ever imagined a room in a bordello, it would have been exactly like this.

He suddenly felt trapped. In his conscious memory he had never been alone with a woman. The featherlike touch of her hand, even through the leather of his glove, as she'd led him up the stairs, had excited feelings which he had long suppressed; the warmth had spread from that touch, to his heart and then to a growing pressure at his groin. Feelings he'd fought against, but which the beguiling atmosphere of the temple had only stoked.

Now that he no longer held Thalassa's hand, he tried to get his beating heart under control by walking over to the casement window, which, half-open, admitted the chill night air. Outside, the outer walls of the temple were still streaked with rain, but, in the light of the rising moon, Urthred could see the dark bands of storm clouds rolling away to the south. The lightning flashes were distant now, and their thunder a dying growl. Of the earlier mist which had partly hidden his flight from the citadel, only one or two wisps hung like wraiths in sheltered spots untouched by the fierce winds of two hours before. The candles, protected in their vases from the rain, twinkled away in the garden like stars shining in the night sky. But even as he watched first one, then another went out. He puzzled at this: surely the temple didn't rely on only the internal lights to ward off the undead?

In the diminishing light he could see the main gatehouse of the temple, its entranceway lost in the shadows. Outside lay doubt and uncertainty. Here, too, the same emotions reigned. He could not trust this woman, whoever she might be. He would have to be on his guard. But when he analysed his emotions further, he found, to his chagrin, it was the woman waiting for him across the room who was causing him more anxiety than all the dangers outside. As if to bring back to his mind the purpose of the building, a tinkle of laughter echoed from down the corridor. A provoking, flirtatious sound, as beguilingly feminine as every scrap of fabric and every curve of statuary in the whole temple. His jaw tightened, and he resolved to be stern.

The touch on his arm was electric: featherlight, but so unexpected that he jumped forward nearly a foot, bumping into the wall. He swung round on the girl, who had backed away at his sudden movement, her hands held in front of her as if to ward off a blow. They stood thus for a moment, her grey eyes wide with fear, his fists clenched within their gloves, his heart beating a mad tattoo in his chest. Then his shoulders slumped, and he unbunched his hands.

"You shouldn't have touched me," he muttered through partially clenched teeth.

"I'm sorry—" the girl began, but Urthred cut her short.

"Never mind," he said, though the fierce hammering of his heart nearly deafened him, and the room had begun to spin slowly round him. He turned his back on her again, breathing in deeply at the open window, the Lethe blossom scent from the garden beneath, blown in by the cold air, almost overwhelming.

But Urthred barely noticed the scent. He tried to think of neutral things. Though he was no coward, the situation seemed to rob him of all ability to speak or even make the simplest of decisions. He was angry with himself: half the city was out looking for him, the murderer of the High Priest of Reh, yet here he was going pale at the touch of a girl! The inanity struck him so peculiarly that he let out a strangled gasp of laughter through his mask. When he turned from the window again he found the girl's eyes, saucer-wide, staring at him, evidently trying to decide whether his laughter had been that of a sane man or the cackle of a lunatic.

Her fear brought him enough confidence to speak. If he spoke and she replied, he reasoned, her human qualities would be revealed; he would see her flesh for what it was, mere flesh, the curtain of the bones, the obscurer of the burning coal of the spirit. Besides, he must tell her Seresh's plan.

"I'm a friend," he began hesitantly. "Seresh told me to pick you out . . ."

At this, it seemed to him that she started nervously, her eyes wandering around the room. He looked around as well. They were alone. Or so it seemed. He would have to take the risk and trust her. She seemed a bundle of nerves, the coquetry of a moment before evaporated, her eyes set in a demure, downcast stare, as if she didn't wish him to continue speaking. Urthred found this silence made him more confident. Maybe it had only been Seresh's warning to him which had put him so much on his guard? How he had steeled himself against the advances of this onetime princess; he, a chosen one of Reh, who had never touched a woman's flesh before! She wouldn't touch him again. The hours would pass and Seresh would come and he would be free of her and temptation. The thought gave him comfort, and he spoke again.

"Seresh told me he will come at midnight. Is my money good until then?" Once more the girl's eyes darted nervously from side to side.

"What's the matter?" he asked.

"Nothing," she said. "Come sit with me. We can talk. . . ." She sat on the divan, patting a cushion by her side.

"I prefer to stand," Urthred replied, fighting a lump in his throat.

Reluctantly, she stood again. He noticed that her paint was not as thickly applied on her cheeks as the other women's; only the faintest application of a pale hue which delicately accentuated her pale colouring. . . .

Her eyes were now focused on his mask, grey eyes that seemed to look beyond the mask: eyes which looked and didn't judge. Again he felt the impulse to speak, to break the spell . . . "Tell me about yourself," he said, despite himself, his voice sounding to him unnaturally loud.

"What's there to tell?" she replied, smiling shyly. For a moment Urthred wondered whether this shyness was a ruse to lead him on, but suddenly he couldn't resist knowing more about her. "Everyone has a history," he said. His reason told him the more he knew about this woman, the harder things would be in the next few hours. But with the inevitability of fate he was already sliding towards temptation as Thalassa looked away, her brow slightly creased, her eyes taking on a faraway look which told him of a past which, for better or worse, would now become part of his future.

"My father and brothers were killed in the Civil War . . ." she began, without self-pity, if anything with dignity, as if her suffering had ennobled her. ". . . My mother was an invalid, she died not long after. Our house was burned to the ground after the battle." She looked out of a casement window at the rising moon. "I was found wandering the city by some of Faran's soldiers." She turned and met the eye slits of his mask defiantly. "They used me for a day or two, then sold me as a slave to this place. I had one advantage that not many other women had: I was a noblewoman, and it amused the new rulers of Thrull to sell me to a brothel." She paused, as if allowing him to weigh this information. "You may not know it, priest, but necessity makes anything acceptable. I could have killed myself: the battlements are high. Many chose to jump rather than be enslaved. But I chose life; life with a price; life in the Temple of Sutis; which would you have chosen?"

Urthred looked away, uncomfortable under the scrutiny of her clear grey eyes. "So," she continued, "I was lucky: many others starved . . . or were taken by the undead." At the mention of the undead, she shivered, and she pulled the flimsy material of her dress closer around her.

Urthred by now thoroughly regretted his curiosity. The undertow of her voice seemed a physical force, pulling him closer to her. As if in response to his silence, she stepped in closer to him, so her head was just level with his chin.

"What is your name?" she asked, whispering so quietly that Urthred could barely hear her words. He could feel her breath, sweetened by cardamom, blowing in through the mouthpiece of his mask, suffusing the confined space behind it with a heady scent.

"Urthred . . . Urthred of Ravenspur," he replied, unconsciously lowering his voice to a whisper as well.

"I've never heard of that place . . ." If it hadn't been so quiet outside, he wouldn't have heard the words—her voice was now just a gentle suspiration.

"No one knows where it is . . . the name was given me."

"And you're a priest of Iss?"

The close proximity of their bodies was eroding the boundaries of reserve he'd erected only a few seconds before. "No," he whispered, "a priest of Reh; the mask is a disguise."

Thalassa didn't know why—perhaps because she had so little to lose—but she trusted the masked priest. His nervousness, his jumpiness struck her not as the guilty signs of a traitor, but those of someone who had never been in one of these places before. Yet already she suspected he was betrayed. Malliana would be watching, taking note of everything that had been said before she had got close enough to whisper. She would have to play her role so that the High Priestess, although unable to hear their words, would think she was performing her duties.

The girl was very close to Urthred, her breathing almost part of his. Her hand came up gently and pressed on the sleeve of his still damp cloak. It was as if his senses were in thrall to some succubus who, when he woke in a moment, would be revealed as a monstrous snake sucking his lifeblood dry. Her honeyed breath seemed to progressively drug him.

His hand went out to brush away her grip, but now her body seemed to be melting into his: he felt her head lean gently into his chest and the perfume of her hazel hair, sandy and sweet like a desert flower, seemed, along with her breath, to fill his mind with a heady wine. He looked desperately about him, but the very room itself seemed to give off an almost palpable air of softness, of seduction; his senses swam just standing in it: Thalassa's birdlike nestling at his chest, the touch of her hands so featherlight . . .

In his heightened state of physical awareness, it seemed that his tunic had vanished, that his skin touched hers directly. He felt the press of her body, the tips of her breasts just touching his chest, the slight swell of her abdomen pressed against his upper groin, her thighs almost melting in their silkiness against his own legs. He looked down at her to find that she was looking up at him with a frankness and directness which made his senses reel. Somehow he'd imagined the look of a woman would have been different from this; alien somehow, less human, the gaze of some marble statue to be worshipped for its cold beauty rather than its beating pulse and fluttering eyes. The flesh, he thought, desperately trying to rekindle the dying flame of his iron discipline, mere animal warmth. . . .

Just as he thought he was going to melt away under her gaze, she whispered something so low that he took it to be an endearment, but then, as if sensing he hadn't heard it the first time, she repeated it, slightly louder. "We're being watched." Urthred froze, his mind suddenly spinning as desire turned to fear.

"Don't move away, priest. Trust me and follow my actions," Thalassa continued, and then in a louder voice, as she held one of his gloved fingers up to the tip of one of her breasts: "Come, priest, take off your gloves, don't be ashamed." She drew closer. "We have to act normally, otherwise the High Priestess will call the guards," she whispered.

So it was the High Priestess who watched. His fear had now turned to anger. How to go through with this charade? His gloves. If he took them off, he would be powerless. And what lay beneath? Five scorched digits which resembled the blackened chitterlings served at a peasant's supper, the claws of some monstrous crow, in a permanent clutch? The girl was trying to go through the motions, allaying the suspicions of the High Priestess. But what would happen when she removed the mask? The sight of what lay beneath had killed Varash; what would it do to her?

He broke away from her abruptly.

"What's the matter?" Thalassa said, following him, looking around nervously at the edges of the room. Urthred followed her eyes. Were his enemies at the door, or at a spy hole drilled through one of the lathe walls?

"Don't touch me, or come near me again," he said loudly, circling the room, his eyes searching for a sign of where the watcher might be stationed. He would fight his way out, team up with Seresh and flee . . .

And here it was, right in front of him, a small black circle drilled through the ancient rotting plaster at eye level. His gloved fist drove through the wall as if it were only paper, but Urthred's hope that someone's face would be behind it was frustrated; it met only empty air.

The noise of the impact nearly disguised another sound from behind him. He whirled round to find that the door had been opened. Two struggling figures were framed within the opening. The High Priestess, writhing in the grip of the cloaked man who had saluted him in the Greeting Room. The stranger bundled Malliana into the room and kicked the door shut. Urthred now saw that he was holding the point of a dagger to the small of the High Priestess's back.

The four of them stared at one another for several heartbeats: the High Priestess too scared to speak, the cowled man listening to hear whether Urthred's destruction of the wall would bring any inquisitive acolytes, Urthred wondering whether this man was friend or foe. Thalassa's expression was the most dramatic of all of them. For the first time she had had a good look at the man's face. As she had done so her own face had drained of colour and she had staggered back a step, her hands covering her mouth as if stifling a scream.

Apparently satisfied that no one was coming, the cowled

man pushed Malliana further into the room. "An interesting show," he said, smirking. "No wonder the High Priestess has spy holes throughout the temple: no doubt it is more interesting than the act itself . . ."

"What do you want?" growled Urthred. The man's tone irritated him, though it was clear he was not on the High Priestess's side.

"All business, aren't you?" the man said, pushing Malliana even further forward. As his cowled face came into the light, Urthred could see the scarring on the side of his bearded face even more clearly than before. The man looked at Thalassa, then back at Urthred. "I think your whore can tell you well enough." Urthred turned to Thalassa and was shocked by what he saw. All the blood had now drained from her already pale face so that the veins stuck out on her temples like a fretwork of blue rivers. Then her eyes turned up in her head and she sank to the floor in a dead faint.

"What in Hel . . ." Urthred muttered, taking a step towards her, but the man hushed him.

"Some explanations are in order, but my time is limited. Faran will want his woman at midnight, and I believe your friend will be returning soon as well. Besides," he added with an evil smile, "the lights are going out all over the temple." Urthred thought of springing forward, but the dagger was rock steady in the man's hand, and it didn't take too much imagination to see the blade sliding smoothly between his ribs. The man smiled easily at the bunching of Urthred's gloved hands.

"Temper, temper; what can you expect from the Temple of Sutis: discretion?" He gave off a high-pitched laugh tinged with hysteria. Malliana winced again as the dagger pierced her flesh through her flimsy dress. The man let out another short laugh, enjoying Malliana's pain, his one eye rolling in its socket like the gimbral ring of a compass. "Ah yes, I'm sorry; I'd quite forgotten: the introductions. You know how one can forget these little details in the excitement. I've already told the High Priestess why I've come." He made a mock bow at Thalassa's unconscious body.

"As for my lady here, I believe she has recognised me at last. All these years I have come, but she has never glimpsed my face until tonight. And what does she do? Faints away like I was a ghost. And well she might, since she left me for dead on Thrull field. Other women came and sought their loved ones: not my Thalassa. No, she was too eager to take up this profession to bother with that!" A flick of spittle appeared on the man's chin as he fairly spat these words out. "See!" he said, finally whipping back the hood of his cloak so that his face was fully revealed to Thalassa's motionless body. "It is I, your betrothed—Jayal Illgill!" His theatrics were ill rewarded, Thalassa's body didn't stir an inch.

He laughed contemptuously, then turned his attention to Urthred. "I'd kill you, priest," he said, "but then I'd have to kill all of those she'd been with. Instead, I'll give you a chance. I'll tie you and the High Priestess up, gag you. You never know— the vampires might miss you."

"I'll be damned if you'll so much as touch me!" snarled Urthred, stepping forward threateningly. It was enough for the man to whip his dagger round at him. Once the weapon was no longer at her back, Malliana reacted with surprising speed. Her hand snaked out, grabbing him by the wrist, momentarily immobilising the dagger.

"Quick!" she shrieked at Urthred.

He had no weapon, only his gloves, but they were enough. He bunched his right fist into an iron ball and hit the stranger on the shoulder with a sledgehammer blow. The dagger jarred out of the man's hand and spun away across the room. Urthred needed no other invitation; his left hand came over in a roundhouse blow that glanced across the stranger's temple. It was enough to send him reeling back onto the carpet unconscious.

Malliana stood for a moment eyeing Urthred uneasily, then suddenly lunged at the door. Urthred sprang after her, catching the frail material of her dress. It ripped away in his grasp, leaving him with only a handful of gauzy fabric. He fell, catching a glimpse of her bone white back as she lunged at the door, pulling it open. Urthred got up too late; the High Priestess was gone, screaming for help as she went.

He thought of running after her, but he had the unconscious Thalassa to deal with. She was stirring slightly as he knelt beside her. He shook her gently and her eyes opened. At first she clearly didn't know where she was, then her eyes opened wide in recognition. She scrambled to her hands and knees to get a better look at the body of the cowled man.

Urthred had other worries. The High Priestess's yells would by now have alerted the guards. They would have to move quickly.

He ran out into the corridor; it was gloomy, with only a few of the candles still alight in their pewter dishes on the stone floor. He remembered the lights going out in the garden. What was happening? The undead could be in the grounds any minute. He heard Malliana's cries for help coming from somewhere downstairs. Doors along the corridor started opening and anxious faces peered out. Urthred ducked back into the room.

"Malliana's gone, and the lights are going out. We'd better hurry," he said.

But Thalassa was still kneeling by the body on the floor, her face paler even than usual. She was breathing shallowly, her chest rising in short, spasmodic heaves as if she had been taken by a sudden attack of asthma. The scarred face and shock of blond hair of the man who called himself Jayal Illgill lay in plain view, blood caking the sides of his head where the ridges of Urthred's metal gloves had torn open his skull. The blood evinced no pity in Urthred: his heart was still full of fury.

"Come," Urthred said, roughly helping her to her feet. The gloves would rend and rip and bruise more tonight, and he was heedless of the pain he did her. She stared at him blankly. "The lights are going out; we have to find Seresh."

Thalassa's eyes returned to the body on the floor.

"It's him, it's really him," she whispered.

Urthred saw she was in another world. He pulled her through the door, Thalassa's head craning back all the time at the body. Urthred cursed as he struggled with her. Outside there was now a scene of turmoil; men and women ran hither and thither, some heading for the stairways, others desperately trying to relight the burned-out candles. No one seemed interested in him or Thalassa.

Urthred pulled at her, but she was rooted to the spot, her eyes wide with shock as she stared at the body on the floor.

"Whoever he is, or whoever he was, we must leave now,"

Urthred whispered urgently. Still no response from Thalassa. "Didn't you hear him?" Urthred insisted. "He spied on us . . . Whatever he might once have been, he's not the same man; leave him!"

"He looks just like Jayal, except for the scar . . ." she said eventually, her eyes not leaving off their staring.

"Did he act like your betrothed? He's changed, and for the worst."

"Yes, you're right," she said slowly.

"So, then come with me!" Urthred urged her, tugging her towards the stairs. But she broke free of his grasp.

"I must get our bundles," she said hollowly. She hurried back into the room, skirting round the body, which still seemed to exert a magnetic attraction on her gaze, and lifted up one of the hangings covering a side table. Underneath were two tallow-covered skin packs. She dragged them out and, with a surprising show of strength, hefted one onto each shoulder. "Lead the way, priest." Her voice betrayed a tremor, but she seemed to have composed herself somewhat. The packs looked to weigh more than her slender strength could bear, and Urthred reached out for one of them, but Thalassa shook her head. "Take the dagger," she said, nodding at the stranger's fallen weapon glinting in the lamplight on the floor. Her voice was suddenly firm, the indecision and shock of a moment before forgotten. Urthred knelt and picked up the weapon. The blade looked razor-sharp, but no match for his gloves. He slid it into his belt. With one glance at Thalassa, he stepped once more into the corridor.

Only one priestess remained there, desperately trying to light a candle with a taper though the candle had burned down to the wick. She screamed when she saw Urthred in the gloom and fled down the corridor, the abandoned taper guttering on the floor.

For the first time Thalassa seemed to notice the situation.

"The lights . . ." she whispered.

"We'll have to find Seresh," Urthred said. He looked around him uncertainly, but saw nothing in the near total darkness. Which room had Seresh gone to? From downstairs came the sound of screams and the banging of doors, but the upper levels of the temple were quiet. "Come," he said, leading the way to the head of the stairs.

The first scream paralysed him. A shriek of horror, and of anguish, of the death of a soul. It came from a room but ten paces down the corridor.

The door of the chamber crashed open, and a half-naked woman struggled out, a geyser of blood shooting from her neck, spraying the opposite wall of the corridor. Before she had taken one step she was abruptly hauled back into the interior and the door slammed to. Urthred took a step forward, but then another scream came from behind him.

"They're all around us!" Thalassa shouted. Urthred grabbed her hand and pulled her down the corridor after him, eyeing the door from which the priestess had emerged. A low moan came from within, then a low sobbing sound and a noise very much like someone sucking on a moist gourd. He felt a sick pity, but knew it was too late; the woman's blood would by now be infected. They must escape. He led Thalassa along to the head of the stairs leading down to the Greeting Room. Below, a fire still blazed in the grate, and a whirling mass of figures milled around it, their pale faces pointing up to him in the half-light. Amongst them he could see the old woman from the kitchen, and the old blind lutanist. Thalassa stumbled past him down the stairs and reached the first landing, looking back to see if he was following. But Urthred stood motionless, a crawling sensation working at the back of his neck. He looked to the side. The light from the fire below was the only illumination, casting a huge shadow of himself onto the wall behind. Then another shadow joined his, a shadow that held something high over its head.

He spun around. There was Illgill, blood masking the side of his face. He was holding a cast-iron candle holder nearly as tall as himself raised over his shoulder. In the split second of Urthred's turning, Illgill brought the end hurtling towards Urthred's head. Action came before thought. Urthred swept up his left hand and caught Illgill's right wrist. The candle holder juddered to a stop barely an inch from Urthred's temple. He squeezed hard as he stared into Illgill's bloodshot eye, and heard the satisfying crunch as his opponent's metacarpals broke. Illgill's face contorted in agony and the candle holder fell to the ground.

"Sorcery," he whispered. Urthred swept the taloned fingertip of his right-hand glove up to the man's throat, touching its razor-sharp edge to Illgill's Adam's apple, pushing his head back. Illgill's one eye stared back with burning hatred.

"Kill me, wizard," he growled. "I can only return to Shades and be plucked forth again to haunt you."

He might have saved his breath; Urthred heard nothing. Every ounce of blood in his veins was shrieking for him to kill this man, as fierce as the fire of the Hearth itself, compelling and irresistible, wholly destructive. He pulled the glove back, ready to slash the man's throat. Illgill held his free hand up in a futile attempt to avert the coming blow.

But though the Fire sang in Urthred's veins, he heard another voice; it was Thalassa's voice, imploring him to stop. Then came the soft electric touch of her hand on his arm, and the room spun back into focus.

"Don't kill him!" she pleaded. "He has wronged you, but he doesn't deserve to die. He was a good man once."

"Once too long ago," growled Urthred, but the anger had passed and he was already unconsciously lowering his hand. He looked at the man who had rolled onto his side and was now nursing his broken wrist under his armpit. Surely he was no threat now. "Live then," Urthred said.

But the man only gave him a look of undiminished hatred.

"You will be dead before dawn; I'll see to it personally that you die finger by finger, inch by inch," he spat.

Urthred might have replied if there had not come a splintering crash from near at hand and another scream of terror. Wordlessly he turned on his heels and followed Thalassa down the two series of stairs to the Greeting Room.

About a dozen of the women were huddled there, the firelight and the few candles they'd salvaged giving them the illusion of safety. There was no sign of the rest of the guests and acolytes, but the cold air blowing through the open front door suggested that they had risked the invisible dangers of the night rather than the palpable ones within the temple itself.

But now Urthred heard a voice moaning outside, and a vampire stumbled through the doorway into the light. The face was desiccated and cracked, showing huge purple fissures where the skin had split apart. It stopped for a moment, its eyes adjusting to the glare, then advanced, menacing the women with clawed fingers.

The women screamed at the creature's sudden appearance, fleeing to the back of the room. But Thalassa threw down the packs and stood her ground. She grabbed a burning brand from the fireplace, flung it at the vampire as it closed with her. But the burning log merely glanced off its shoulder without impeding its progress. It fell at the foot of one of the towering velvet drapes hung from the balconies above. The material erupted with a whoosh of flame as the creature lunged towards Thalassa. She desperately sidestepped it, and Alanda hauled Furtal out of its path as it stumbled towards the back of the room.

Urthred sought within himself for the conjury of fire which he had used in the temple square, and flung out an arm. But the fire in his veins was absent, and he felt but a hollow tingling rather than an explosion of flames from his fingertips. Then he remembered—the mask was under his cloak. He wore the borrowed one of Iss. The vampire turned on him, hissing its hate.

Just then Urthred noticed movement on the balcony above him. There finally was Seresh, his gaunt face taking in the scene below him in one glance. He was standing just above where the burning drape was attached to the balcony rail. He ripped off its fastenings and dropped it down on top of the vampire in a scattering of sparks and flame. The thing screamed and struggled in the blazing caul of material, then sank to its knees, the flames spreading from it to the carpets and the overstuffed furniture. The room began filling with a choking smoke.

Now another vampire had materialised next to Seresh on the balcony. They struggled for a moment, then Seresh's sword arm flashed and the creature crashed through the balcony rail to the floor below.

Seresh reached ground level in seconds. He strode over to the fallen vampire and severed its head with one fierce blow of his sword; the thing crawled off towards the shadows like a broken beetle.

By now the fire was out of control, racing up the side of the rotten plaster and lathe walls and wooden balconies. The heat and smoke were unbearable. There were only five of them left: Urthred, Thalassa, Alanda, Furtal, and Seresh. The other women had disappeared. The five of them looked at one another, then Seresh took command, yelling at them to go to the kitchen. Urthred found Thalassa staring once more at the balcony, where Illgill had fallen. But the landing was now a mass of flame and there was no sign of him.

As the others hurried towards the kitchen, Urthred quickly snatched Manichee's mask from where he had hidden it in his cloak. He let the others go on, averting his face as he latched it on. If he was to die, he would rather die as he'd lived, with Manichee's gift. The others hadn't noticed his absence as he rejoined them; they were preparing themselves for the dash outside, snatching up cloaks and food from the table. Urthred remembered the leech gatherer's staff. It was still where he had left it, and he picked it up. Then they were ready. Seresh held a lantern in one hand and his sword in another.

"We'll fight our way out!" he yelled over the roar of the flames. Then came a crack and a roar as the entire first floor balcony surrounding the Greeting Room collapsed in a ball of flame. Sparks rolled down the corridor towards the kitchen, igniting the wooden walls. Alanda pulled open the door and they hurried out into the garden, gulping in the clean air. Urthred looked back. The whole temple was now a blaze of orange flame as the fire greedily consumed the old rotten wood and lath of the building. A figure appeared on a balcony and, like a human fireball, dropped to the courtyard below. Urthred turned and hurried towards the others huddled around the postern gate. Alanda had produced a key and was opening it. Seresh leapt through, quartering the alleyway behind with his sword. Nothing. He set off at a pace down the alleyway, Alanda and Thalassa helping the old blind lutanist along, Urthred taking up the rear.

*   *   *

None of them thought to look behind them as they hurried away. If they'd done so, they might have seen the scarred man appear at the postern gate, his face blackened by soot and his cloak smoking from the fire, his wounded wrist tied in a pilfered cloth. His one eye gleamed as he sought them, and seeing them hurrying down the alleyway, he scurried after them, keeping to the monstrous shadows cast by the burning temple.

CHAPTER TWENTY-TWO

Shades

The man who followed Urthred's party was the same who had fought with him in Thalassa's room and afterwards on the landing overlooking the greeting room. In Thrull, he went under several names: Setten, Jayal Illgill, the Doppelgänger. He had jumped through a back window of the burning temple adding a twisted ankle and a heavy limp to the list of injuries he had already acquired from Urthred.

But it was not the physical pain that hurt him most. It was mental anguish: anguish at being bested twice by the priest and for allowing Thalassa to escape his grasp. Maybe the Rak had clouded his judgement. But he was sober now.

Gritting his teeth, he hobbled after the five fugitives in front, silently hawking as he tasted the coppery gall of blood in his mouth where his teeth had bitten through his tongue.

Cold rage and hatred were like life's blood to him. To breathe was to be at war with the element of air itself. Each step upon the earth was not so much a step forward as a crushing of the ground beneath his feet. Since he'd been forced into this existence, revenge, and only revenge, had spurred his desire for action. Many had died at his hands, many women been forced by his lusts: torture had been an everyday occurrence. Each day for seven years he had had to seek new excesses so that the rage that inspirited him did not die. Each day he had stoked his fury to ever greater heights.

The party ahead moved in and out of the fog banks. As they went, he caught intermittent glimpses of his quarry: Thalassa Eaglestone.

In her he saw the apogee of his lust for revenge. That she was dishonoured by her time at the temple was not enough: he wished to possess her, rend her beauty and her spirit like paper and cast them to the uncaring skies. Then he might begin to be satisfied. Then, and only then, might he say that his vengeance on the Illgill clan had begun.

Thalassa's words begging the priest to save him burned in his gut like a furnace, adding to the bile in his mouth. He would feed those words back to her with inches of sharpened metal, prod and poke them back, into every orifice. He needed no mercy, no compassion. Not from someone who was no more than a chattel to be used by him, her rightful owner.

But despite his rage, he tracked the party with uttermost stealth, coming so close at times that it seemed he could have reached out and touched the priest at the back of the group.

In front of the priest, he could see Thalassa with the old lutanist whom he had listened to on many an evening when his suit had been refused at the temple. The man's music had been a mere jangling in his ears, for music meant nothing to such as he. As for the girl, she appeared an ethereal being, a ghost, a spirit from another world. The moon through the mist imparted an unearthly glow to her skin—a glow he longed to own—a light he would have liked to seize in his hand and squeeze into the smallest ball, as if it were a physical thing to be put away for ever.

But he knew he could never possess anything made of the light. He was made of light's opposite, a creature from another world—a creature of the shadows. All he could do with the light was destroy it.

For he had seen the two worlds of the here and now: the Mundane world and Shades, existing in a mirror image of one another. The latter place only glimpsed from the former by visionaries and ecstatics, poets and madmen; those who could see round the corner, see the twin worlds of light and dark, good and evil. In exterior view there was no difference between the two; a man might find his way as easily from Thrull to Surrenland in either—for Shades was as physically real as this world. There, if visions took you, you would find the same streets, the same houses, the same sky and road, the same trees in the mountains. Yet, being of this world, you would not be able to make the people you saw hear you, for your spirit would be elsewhere, back in the Mundane world. To them you would be a ghost.

For Shades was where the dispossessed lived—the unaneled wandering a world that seemed real, a world in which every day they, in turn, might see their loved ones, but their loved ones could not see them. This was where Manichee had been damned to wander, and all those others whose bones had not been taken up to Reh's Paradise or consigned to the abyss. But not only ghosts lived in the world of Shades. So did the evil spirits cast out by the priests and thrown into the void.

And this was what he was, this shadow of Jayal Illgill.

His mind took him back—over the years which fell away like a shadow before him to a time when he had been one with his twin. The young Illgill had been five when he first suffered mad fits and seizures, seizures which had become progressively more violent as he'd got older. It was as if two warring souls had been forced to inhabit the same body, each instructing the flesh to go the way of its desires. Good and evil, divided equally so that neither could attain their goal and volition, warring in the same body, leading to uncontrollable rage and violence. The dark side that had become the shadow wished for utter annihilation of the other contending soul, but to achieve this would have had to assure his body's and his own destruction.

In his teens Jayal, in his violent episodes, had required several grown men to restrain him. At sixteen his father had brought in the exorcist—that same Manichee who now shared his former damnation. The Flame priest had a reputation for driving out spirits that possessed, or laying to rest the souls of the undead. The examination had been brief: he'd seen at once how Jayal's soul was split in two—one half corrupt, the other pure. The man's face had changed in the instant of recognition, as if he had seen the mouth of Hel staring back at him from the boy. He'd called urgent instructions, and Jayal had been bound and dragged to a shuttered room. Black drapes had shut out the feeble light of the sun, candles burning in the pattern of a five-pointed star had been set around the table on which the boy was bound cruciform, his arms on either side of the table, his heaving chest exposed.

Jayal had heard himself speaking, but the words were not his; it was as if a stranger spoke, cursing the evil that was in him. Then he knew it was his other who spoke, and he cursed back, so now two different voices rang around the room, to the consternation of the bystanders.

The priest had re-entered, his bicorn hat with its little bells tinkling around the fringe. He had chanted some sacred words urgently, and then gestured, fashioning fiery spirits from the ether. A flaming sword appeared in the priest's hands, highlighting the man's gaunt face as he stepped up to the prostrate body of the boy. Then he raised up the burning sword, and brought it down in a blazing arc so it cleaved right through the centre line of his sternum. Jayal felt a flash of light commensurate with the fiery sword striking his skin, then the blackness of unconsciousness.

When he came to, he was still lying on the table, but his arms and legs were now free. Across the room he saw the priest and his father holding up a slack-faced boy who wobbled unsteadily between them. The boy was like him in every detail: height, colour of hair, every pore was the same! He rose to his feet angrily—was not he the one who was alive? He approached the group, and his hand went out to touch his father's arm, but it passed right through it, his father didn't turn, he hadn't felt the touch.

But the boy, the usurper, felt something, for he shivered as if someone had walked over his grave. The priest put his hand to his shoulder: "Evil spirits, boy—they have been driven out for now—but always be on your guard against them." Then he had led the boy off.

Anger had gnawed at Jayal's innards. Had not the priest spoken of him as an evil spirit? He opened his mouth to protest, but not a word he uttered was heard by the others. Nor later by his mother, or nurse, or any of the servants. He was worse than a stranger—a ghost whom no one saw.

He wandered about the house for days, then weeks, then months. Hoping desperately that there was one person who would be able to see him, acknowledge him and his existence. None did. Yet, strangely, other physical qualities of the world were here: he could touch and feel inanimate objects, even consume them, like the loaves of bread which he took from the kitchen, first making them float before the cook's eyes, or the chair he shifted in front of the hearth, causing all those who sat there on the dark winter's evening to flee, screaming out that there were poltergeists in the room. These and other pleasures had now become all his study. Often he would spy on the women: he could drift through the narrowest of gaps, through the tiniest crack in brickwork. Nothing was hidden from him, and nothing being hidden his soul became more corrupt, seeking greater and greater excesses to stimulate the appetite that would never know again true human congress.

But he could touch no one who possessed a soul, and make them feel his presence. Even his physical powers began to die as he drifted further and further from the Mundane World and became part of its shadow.

His other half, the slack-faced boy whom Manichee had led away from the room that day, was always before him, receiving all the good and bad a family can give. The Doppelgänger watched and smiled when his father was stern and forbidding to the milksop; the boy often wept in the solitude of his room. At this Jayal, for he still thought of himself as Jayal, felt scorn: what would he have given to have had the touch and contact with the living, however harsh, that this boy had, this spirit who had usurped his place?

There were other ghosts and spirits that haunted the place, whose punishments were such that they could never leave the house. Ghosts and spirits which even now, years later, he saw hovering in the shadows of the house on the Silver Way.

The ghosts had warned him then: "Get away from this place. Don't inhabit the old world. Leave! There are many other places where you can be free! These visions of what you will

never have will make you mad. We would leave if we weren't
bound."

And he had recognized the truth of their words, that the
madness of staying was greater than the madness of going and
that soon he would be unable to manifest himself as he had
done these last months with acts of malicious glee. Now the
furniture barely budged when he strained at it, candles did not
snuff at his blowing, valuable objects could not be stolen to the
consternation of their owners. Now he felt the real pain of being
a ghost in the living world.

He'd left Thrull. The shadow world thronged with such as
he: he would find rest somewhere. He'd travelled through the
mirror world to another place, always just round the corner
from mortal eye, to a place where ghosts, not memories, were
thickly congregated, ghosts he could touch and speak to.

Gorvost: a port by a wide estuary debouching into the Astardian Sea. It was a place of bitingly cold winters and mos-
quito-infested summers, but the seasons meant nothing to the
spirits who inhabited it. It was empty of living souls, abandoned when the estuary had silted up. The houses and ware-
houses lay empty. Only smugglers and itinerants from the real
world passed through, leaving it to the ghosts for the remainder
of the time.

Here Jayal found rest, far from the living world whose loss
could now only wound him. The place matched the desolation
of the spirits who roamed it: a ghost port under a flat grey sky,
the sea grey and lonely too, the featureless dunes sweeping
away as far as the eye could see. But the soulless could still
touch each other, or inanimate things. Debauchery and excess
in the spirit world! The ruins of a temple of Sutis existed here,
and there were always dispossessed women ready to take their
pleasure with him. To do anything, for they had no souls left to
be damned. Only pleasure existed, pleasure of the here and
now, for none of the dispossessed had meaning in the moral
universe.

He drank the wine of far-off Galastra purloined from a vint-
ner's long abandoned cellars. Its scent was beautiful, its taste
satin, just like the soft thighs of the dark-haired beauties. He
revelled in the pleasure of the senses, and for a moment forgot

the gall of Thrull and the endless grey of sea and sky and sand. Then the smoke of the Lethe bud captured him. Dark smugglers from the southern lands brought it here for the itinerants. They seemed to expect some of it to disappear, for things always disappeared in Gorvost, the ghost city. The Doppelgänger sat in a cloud of it: a shadowy being caught up in the web of a shadowy drug. The edges of reality began to peel back: he had flashes of his youth before he was separated from his other half by Manichee's sword.

Under the drug, strange edges and angles of the real world revealed themselves as he travelled back, round the corner. The laughing face of a whore he rode would suddenly become the face of one of his nurses scolding him; the smooth-talking priest of Worms transformed himself into an old tutor, his face turned into a demon mask of hate.

Inside out, upside down, the world was topsy-turvy; he couldn't shake off the memory of the life he had once had and the soul he had lost which his other half now had, which never more would be his. He decided to stop taking the drug, but it was too late; the visions continued, unabated, Janus-faced. The faces of the spirits and ghosts would warp and peel, changing to the faces of the people he'd known in Thrull. There were voices constantly in his ears, voices that he had left behind at the exorcism, conversations carried on just on the edge of audibility.

They had once had a god in Gorvost and the surrounding areas who was neither of the Flame nor the Worm; Arcos was his name. The locals had once believed he represented pure knowledge, the wisdom of the ages which was older than the knowledge of the gods which Marizian had brought to the southern lands. But now the marsh was empty, and few in the Empire worshipped him. One day a priest had come to the town, wearing the robes of the god. The ghosts sensed the presence of one who came from the Mundane World, for he passed through them heedlessly as they thronged the streets and wharves. He had gone to a small hut near the docks, relishing no doubt what he imagined to be the solitude of the place. It was dead of winter, the estuary was frozen over. To Jayal, it was a day, if there was ever a day, to test how far from the real world he had travelled. Surely this priest of ancient knowledge would sense his presence? Finally he would have contact with the real world again!

He'd stolen into the cold single room of the hut. A man sat cross-legged on the floor, staring deeply into the single candle on the floor. His appearance was singular: a monkey-like face which might have belonged to a man of thirty years, or a hundred. It was framed by a wispy white beard and the priest's eyes were milky in their orbs, as if he were blind, or on the edge of unconsciousness. The priest made no movement as the opening and closing of the door set the candle guttering, but merely sat, his eyes fixed on the flame, his hands outstretched to it. Jayal wondered if he knew he was there, or whether he believed that the wind which howled outside had opened and then shut the door.

He felt so empty in spirit, so near yet so far from the world this man inhabited. He needed to speak, to try to communicate, however futile the effort. He'd begun talking, knowing that the priest could not hear him. But better he should speak and not be heard than not speak at all.

The whole tale, the exorcism, everything, tumbled from his lips. All this time, the priest's eyes had remained staring emptily at the candle, his hands trembling slightly as he held them out in front of him as if he were warming them at the flame. It was obvious that he couldn't hear Jayal's tale. When he finished there was deep silence punctuated only by the moaning of the wind outside. Now Jayal noticed that the priest had closed his eyes, and had apparently fallen asleep. He turned to the door and pulled it open. The wind howled into the hut and the candle snuffed out in a greasy plume of tallow smoke. Jayal was about to leave the man in the darkness, when the priest's eyes suddenly snapped open, the white startlingly vivid in the gloom. He took in Jayal as if noticing him for the first time, but with a look that was utterly unsurprised at what he saw, as if seeing ghosts was a common occurrence. They remained thus, eyeing one another for a few seconds, then the priest spoke.

"You've crossed over," he said.

"Yes," Jayal acknowledged, mad hope stirring inside him for the first time in years. "I have been cast out."

"And now you wish to return."

Jayal merely nodded, barely believing that this man could see him, let alone talk to him.

"There is no returning for the damned," the priest intoned solemnly. "You are cursed to wander this earth until the end of time. Neither the pains of Hel nor the joys of Paradise are yours, nor the Purple Halls of Lord Iss. This is the greatest damnation of all—Shades, where all about you you see the world you have lost, that you never will be part of again."

"But you are speaking to me," Jayal said eagerly. "It must mean there is some way back?"

The priest didn't answer this directly. "Reach out your fingers to this candle," he said, striking a flint and tinder and re-lighting it. A chill had settled on Jayal's heart, but nevertheless he thrust forward one of his hands.

"Look," the priest said, nodding at the flame. Jayal looked: though the priest's body cast a shadow, his own hand didn't. "Because you have crossed from that world to this, what you do now, what you say now, what you think now—all these are but shadows dancing on the wall of a cave; no more will you touch a man's soul, or a woman's heart—you are dispossessed. Your true self, your mirror image, is elsewhere. But just as you lead a disenfranchised life where nothing you do will change a man's life, his is the opposite, laden with meaning and portents that will change much. Substance and shadow. Take heed: only if he should die will your existence here end and you be taken to another place of punishment."

"Then I will kill myself," Jayal said, "and he will die also!"

The priest shook his head: "Remember, you are only the shadow. Nothing you do will affect him. You cannot die."

Jayal shook his head. "So I will suffer like this for many more years, without hope?"

The priest smiled for the first time. "Great things are afoot in the lands of the old Empire. An army has come out of the east from Tiré Gand. They mean to destroy Thrull and all who dwell there. Maybe your twin will die and you will be released?"

"Thrull," whispered Jayal. Sad memories came, then anger. If his father and mother knew what torments he had suffered!

But it was as if the priest read his mind: "You are a dying spirit in the world of the living—no one remembers you as you once were. Your mother and father are happy that you've gone. You were the thing that perverted and twisted their child. As you die in the real world's memory, so too will you die in this shadow world, for only the memories of the living can keep a ghost alive. Now your existence has less and less meaning. Soon you will start passing through even this insubstantial world; the touch of a woman's flesh will be like making love to a wraith; you will have no pleasures left—this body you inhabit will merely melt away, vanish, disappear, and your soul will drift through Shades like an autumn leaf."

"But what would prevent me from going to Thrull now? I will haunt my father's house; they'll know that I have returned."

"Moving objects, causing accidents; all these things were once possible, but now you lack the power."

A thought occurred to the Doppelgänger: "How is it that you are here, talking to me, a spirit: in which plane do you exist?"

The priest shook his head. "I am enlightened; in thirty-three reincarnations my shadow soul has been integrated into me; it now lives in complete parity within me. This is the true knowledge, the exact meeting and joining of man's dark half with his good."

"And what happens to those who don't achieve this enlightenment?"

"Why, a man continues in the world, lacking the balance to make him a truly great man. His judgement will always be lacking, for he has thrown away the balance and self knowledge that would give him an insight into the minds of men: both good and evil. The other—the other becomes a Shade, as you have become, leading a shadowy dance to your dominant half. Only by the way I have explained or by a miracle will you return to the full light of day."

"By a miracle?"

But the priest had shut his eyes again. He was communing, travelling through the myriad corridors of the Palace of Grey, the many mirrored rooms where the shadow selves and the skeins of destiny interlaced in a thousand images, infinite reflections, echoes of a million voices calling to their lost selves. He sought there for a long time. That he knew this man to be a dark spirit didn't worry him a jot; it was his job to accept man's dark half with his good. As he had said to Jayal, only a man who could accept both halves of his life was worth anything in the final analysis. Eventually he found what he was looking for.

Jayal had relatched the door and had sat down impatiently for several minutes after the priest had withdrawn into himself. More than once, he had thought to rise and leave the hut, but the miracle of the man's seeing him held back his natural impatience. Then once more the priest's eye snapped open and he looked at Jayal so piercingly that it seemed that every fibre of his being was laid bare.

"Your father will bring you back to the Mundane World, but you won't thank him," he said cryptically.

"What do you mean?" blurted Jayal, but the priest had shaken his head.

"That is all I am allowed to bring from the Palace of Grey. If you want more information, travel there yourself."

"You know that is impossible," Jayal said, rising angrily. "Tell me what you've learned!"

But the priest merely favoured him with a small smile and kept silent. Jayal slid the sword from his scabbard and held it to the man's neck.

"Since you can see me, you can be hurt by me—tell me what you've seen!" he growled. But the priest still smiled absently, as at a fond memory. Jayal cursed, prodding the sword gently against the man's neck. It met no resistance, passing through the flesh as if it wasn't there.

What sorcery was this? Like a dog chasing its own tail, Jayal was filled with impotent rage. The sword flashed once, backhanded, then twice, thrusting; cavalry sabre blows he knew well. But the sword seemed to pass through the priest with no resistance. The man rose slowly to his feet.

"Now I will travel far from here," he said.

"Why did you come to torment me?" Jayal asked, the sword now hanging limply by his side.

"I didn't know until I travelled to the Plains of Grey what fate is in front of you. Be happy that you will return where so few of you can return. Take your revenge on the world, and not me."

"And you?"

"I have learned much: as much as I have learned in my thirty-three deaths. Now I will go to my next one in peace."

Then he opened the door and went out into the blizzard which had begun to rage outside. The Doppelgänger never saw him again.

In the days after the meeting with the priest, things got worse and worse in Gorvost: the faces of the people kept peeling back, revealing the faces of others in the Mundane World.

As for the time the priest had mentioned in his revelation, he was close to it, he knew. Something was having an effect on him which had not been there when this, his shadow self, had been sundered from his real self two years before. What it was, he had no idea, but he feared it with an icy chill which never left him.

In the spirit world of the town, his dissipation became wilder and wilder. At nights he would lie abed, two, three, four women with him. But their faces kept peeling back; his libido evaporated. Now he was too afraid to take Lethe, and alcohol made him wake in the middle of the night, sweat on his brow, his heart thudding painfully.

After a few nights spent thus in restless waking dreams, he had dismissed the spirit women and just lay there, sober, companionless, day after day, night after night. It was like waiting to be born, except this time he was fully conscious of the process.

Then it came. One night he must have dozed fitfully. He was woken by a shining light. It was as if a gateway had opened in the ceiling over his head: bright light was shining through, brighter and whiter than anything he had ever experienced before. The light was playing on him, covering his body from head to toe.

Suddenly an excruciating pain sliced through his head, over his right eye: his hand flashed up to cover it, and he felt something sticky. It came away covered in blood. There was an object which looked like a crushed red grape sticking to the smear of viscous blood covering his fingers. With a start he realised he could only see out of one eye. The pain in his head was unrelenting and he could feel cold air blowing through a flap of skin in the side of his face onto exposed back teeth. Then there came a terrible stabbing pain in his side. The room began to spin round the shaft of light from the ceiling; round and round, until he was sucked into the centre of the maelstrom of light and it seemed he flew through space, over a bridge of light, the wind deafening, the pain whiter than the whitest light.

Then he lost consciousness.

Next he found himself lying on his back—it was that time of the morning when dawn is but a faint hint of grey in the sky. In the ghostly light he saw the massive cliffs of Thrull rearing up in front of him. Somehow he was as unsurprised to see them as he would have been in his own bed back in Gorvost. Everything led back here. He had returned.

From his position, he guessed he was lying on a pyre of some sort. He moved his head slightly and saw what he rested on—bodies. Bodies upon bodies: grey-faced warriors in the cold light of dawn. He smelled the acrid scent of burning and the stench of the charnel house. There had been a battle. This was one of the carrion piles on which they laid the dead.

He watched, with his one eye, buzzards circling overhead, their silhouettes becoming more and more defined as the light grew in the sky. He concentrated on the birds fiercely. He knew if he thought of the pain in his head and back, he would scream. But it could not be ignored for long. He tried to open his mouth, vent some of his pain, however futile. But even this release was denied him because one side of his head was paralysed, and his jaw would not move, though he could still feel the cold wind blowing through the wound onto his teeth.

He had been reborn, merely to die.

Though he couldn't scream, he groaned, a strange sound that welled up from the back of his throat. It was then he felt the dark shadow looming over him. He saw a man he didn't recognise through the filmy vision of his one remaining eye. He expected him to finish him, at least make it easy for him to go. Instead, his perspective on the world changed radically as he was hoisted up onto the man's shoulders. Now he saw the man's legs and a corpse-littered battlefield stretching below him in the early light of dawn. The real world, he thought grimly, as littered with corpses and misery as the world of Shades. Then came a feeling of injustice, and then an absolute resolve to live.

He was carried down a ladder, the man breathing heavily and raggedly as he did so. He'd been but barely conscious, but something knitted together inside him despite the nature of his wounds and the jarring cross-country march which now began. Hours, possibly days passed, the blinding pain in his head an unremitting and constant companion that became so familiar that he was not sure how he had ever existed without it.

Then the motion stopped. He was aware of his body being laid on the floor of a damp cellar. He sank into the darkness.

Later, when he struggled back to consciousness again, he realised where he was: the cellar of the Illgill mansion. It was night, and forms materialised out of the darkness. Familiar forms: the ghosts who had haunted the mansion all those years before. But though they opened their mouths to speak to him, he could no longer hear them.

Once more he'd lost consciousness.

When he awoke the third time, the ghosts were gone and it was day once more. A small puddle of water had gathered on the flagstone by his side and he tentatively dipped his fingers into it, lifting the moisture feebly to his parched lips. The rancid drops tasted sweeter than the sweetest wines that he could see racked just beyond his reach in the gloomy recesses of the cellar.

He'd wavered on the edge of death several times: as the cold fog lifted off the marsh outside the city at evening, and he watched it rise up to the grille set in the cliff face, and the crows cawed their requiem to the light, many were the times that he didn't expect to wake in the morning. The silent ghosts would hover by his side all night, like mourners at a wake. But some indomitable spirit raised him up. The most powerful of all emotions, revenge, lit a fire that the cold marsh air could not extinguish.

Many days and many nights passed. He recovered slowly and surely, gaining enough strength to crawl about the cellar and collect some of the dry food and water that had been stored there. He fashioned poultices from dry marsh herbs which were hanging in bunches from the roof rafters. They drew the poison and the gangrene from his wounds.

Then he'd learned to walk again, with the same difficulty and pain as an infant. Many were the times he'd fallen and railed impotently at his weakness. But each time he had forced himself back to his feet by sheer force of will.

Finally, he'd made it to the head of the cellar stairs and out into the wan light of the sun. The garden into which he emerged was now overgrown with weeds. Dogs snuffled at mounds of cloth which he only slowly recognised as decomposing bodies. He squinted up into the unfamiliar sunlight and saw that, while he'd been sleeping, half the mansion had been burned down.

Later still, he'd left the house and taken his first, uncertain steps in the streets. Then he'd seen what a bitter world he'd been reborn into: the still smoking ruins, the pyramid of skulls, the skull-masked guards that patrolled the streets by day, and the vampires that came out at night.

He'd been reborn as the priest had promised. Reborn in a crippled body and into a ruined world. His only comfort was that his other half, the slack-jawed boy, still lived. Hadn't the priest told him that neither could live without the other? Something told him that they would meet again one day, and, when they did, he would be prepared. Magic had brought him back to this world, magic which he would discover, harness and use to banish his other half to the torments he himself had suffered so long.

He set about his preparations, passing by day amongst the survivors of Thrull, unrecognised by them because of his disfiguring scars. They knew him only as Setten. At night those whom he had seen in the daytime streets became his victims. He would force entry into houses where even the vampires had failed, slaughter or capture the occupants, steal all he could. The cellars were turned into a chamber of horrors—robbery, rape and torture.

Soon others heard of his exploits; they flocked to him. Months afterwards, he caught the man who had carried him from the battlefield sneaking into the cellar. Much of what he hadn't understood at the time was now made clear; the man's name was Furisel. He had been under Jayal's command at the battle. Furisel clearly thought him to be his twin. The Doppelgänger had enlisted him into his cause anyway, and the old sergeant had done his bidding ever since. Dotard! Didn't he realise that the master he had once served had changed?

But what of his other half? Where was he? There were stories that he'd last been seen fleeing the battle on a white horse. He'd gone west, the stories went, to the Fire Mountains. Yet the other Jayal knew that he would return, could feel it in his bones with an utter certainty.

Meanwhile the victims he and his new companions dragged back to the mansion were made to suffer for the years he had spent in Shades. Their cries were not heard outside, for no one passed the house in the Silver Way anymore. And once their bodies could no longer take the suffering, they were dropped from the mansion's oubliettes built into an overhang of the cliffs; five hundred feet to the marshes below; crow and lizard meat. Their ghosts would rise up to greet the Doppelgänger with the evening mist: but now he could no longer hear their words of recrimination. While others starved, he and his men fed well. Craftier and stealthier than vampires, they inhabited the night as well as the day, and none of the living were safe.

Yet though he was once more incarnate on this plane, there still was an emptiness in Jayal's life. A melancholy which drove him into the few dusty rooms of the mansion house which remained undamaged by the fire. In solitude, he meditated gloomily on his half-life, for everything was half and not whole with him: looking at the dim sunlight playing through the dirty windows, scenes from childhood came flooding over him, scenes from before he had "crossed over." He explored what remained of the house from top to bottom, looking for clues, for something palpable from his past he could build on and make himself whole with. The magic that had brought him back must be hidden here still.

One room he'd returned to time and time again. It might once have been a study; the floor was covered with scraps of yellowing paper, ripped from books. They were decorated by mouse droppings, and the ink had faded from the pages, but he'd knelt in the mote-filled room as the last light had come through the window, and remembered a scene. His father, also on his knees, in this room. The image persisted, like the after-image on the retina left after staring at the sun. He thought on it more. Why had his father been on his knees? He peered closely at the papers in his hand. Records of business deals, figures written out in neat ledgers, letters sent from foreign parts, tax notes . . . then a worm-eaten scroll, sealed with red wax, and tied with a dusty ribbon. He pulled it open, the paper crackling under his fingers. He squinted at the ornate court hand of the announcement. The betrothal bond between Jayal and Thalassa Eaglestone. So that was what his twin had been doing while he languished in the spirit world of Gorvost!

He was immediately seized by a desperate curiosity. Here was an anchor with which he could root his shiftless existence: this person, this woman who had belonged to his other half. If she were still alive, he would redeem his lost life through hers. First he would possess her, then destroy her.

On the instant, he called for his men; they stumbled in, wiping the sleep from their eyes. He issued commands; they should scour the city and find her. He caught secret glances exchanged between two of them. His temper was legendary: he stepped up and smashed one of the men to the ground with his mailed fist. The other told him readily enough: Thalassa served at the temple of Sutis; no further search was needed.

Jayal dismissed them and returned moodily to the betrothal document. To Jayal, the document was not a pledge of intent, or of love, merely the bill of sale: he owned this woman. If his shadow brother ever returned he would have taken her from him—this knowledge brought him comfort. That very night he had braved the streets of Thrull and visited the house where a thousand candles always burned. There he'd seen Thalassa, and seeing only increased his determination. The High Priestess's rebuff was merely a temporary setback. Meanwhile he contented himself with the knowledge that his shadow's honour was stained each evening by the long succession of men who made their way to Thalassa's chamber, and by Lord Faran himself, who summoned her to the temple every month.

He would wait until the time was right. Once he was ready

to leave the city, he would return and take her. And destroy the temple and the harlots who cheated men there.

Again and again he returned to the room where he had found the betrothal scroll. The shattered windows filled one entire side of the room and, as the cold wind howled in from the west, he looked over the mottled grey and green of the vast marshes below, out to the pyramid of skulls. As he stood in silent contemplation, watching the dying sun wobble across the sky, he asked many questions; not the least of which was by what device had he been plucked from the world of Shades back into this life? The silent room and its scattered documents gave him no clue. All he knew was that his shadow self still existed, for otherwise they would have both perished. Several days after his first visit, the image of his kneeling father came back to him again; kneeling, in prayer? No, it hadn't been like that. He rose from the broken chair he'd been sitting in and looked at the floor where the half-image had come to him. He knelt on the bare flags. In front of him was a stone wall, giving no clues. He rose and pushed at it: no hidden catches, or panels concealed in the stone. He walked back: it was then he saw the area where his feet had disturbed the thick dust on the floor. Faint traceries were now visible on it, hardly distinguishable from natural ridges in the flagstone. He knelt again, running his fingers along the barely perceptible pattern.

As he finished tracing the pattern, he thought he heard a distant thring, much like the noise of a finger passing over the crystal rim of a wine glass. He listened intently, his hand poised over the floor. There it was again, a thring, then the flagstone started rising up and a bright light shone from either side of the cracks, revealing a golden cage suspended underneath. The heavy flagstone rose further and came to rest, seeming to hover in midair.

He leant closer. The bars of the golden cage were thickly arranged so a hand could not pass through them. The interior glowed with otherworldly energy. A lock was set prominently within a gate at one of the sides. Within, through the golden haze, he saw jewels and money bags and some scrolls. He hesitantly put his hand forward: the bars rang with the far-off tintinnabulations of bells as he touched them. Where was the key? He looked vainly into the shadows of the room—in all the days he'd spent searching here, he'd surely have found such an object by now. He put out his hand again. Again the golden bars chimed, but the golden door remained resolutely closed.

Then he became aware of something else: shadows forming on the far side of the room. Something large and human-sized, arms crossed, upturned horns and red eyes that regarded him with an alien light. Its words were not spoken, but seemed to ring in his head like the distant tintinnabulations of the gate. "Do not summon the guardian of the cage a third time, unless you have the key," it said solemnly, then faded from view. Jayal was left staring at the place where it had appeared. After a few moments, the cage sank rapidly into the floor from whence it had come.

His visits to the study stopped abruptly thereafter. It was only weeks later, the next time Furisel came begging for work, that Jayal took courage and drew the older man down the dusty corridors to the room.

"Look in there," he demanded. Furisel did so, none the wiser. "What happened in here?" the Doppelgänger demanded.

"Why, lord, surely you know?"

"Call it a test," replied Jayal, cursing that he'd forgotten that, to the old man, he was Illgill's son.

Furisel thought for a moment. "Why, blessed if I know," the former sergeant replied. "I was brought down here only once; the lord kept books and such here . . ."

"That I can see!" Jayal snarled, gesturing at the worm-eaten books and paper littering the floor. "But who has come back here since the battle?"

"Why, the Lichlords came, soon after the battle, when I . . ." Furisel found it difficult to mouth the words "abandoned you," but this is what Jayal assumed he would have said, had he had the courage.

Jayal fixed the old man with his one eye: "They were looking for something, something I want as well . . . a golden key."

Furisel rubbed his grizzled chin reflectively. Then he glanced up, with a gleam of recollection. "Yes! On the day of the battle, don't you remember? Your father was wearing a golden key around his neck, as if it was a talisman to ward off blows or such like."

"This key, what happened to it?"

"What happened to anything? It must have gone with him to the north," the old man replied, shrugging as best he could. The Doppelgänger took a step forward and grabbed the front of his cloak angrily, his one eye burning into Furisel's face. "Remember, my lord, I was on the carrion heap with you when your father fled," the old man added hastily.

Jayal released his grip, allowing Furisel's feet to touch the floor once more.

After that, Furisel had seemed thankful to depart, leaving Jayal alone in the room. Here then was the mystery of the two Illgills. The younger fled to the west and to who knew what points thereafter. His fate was uncertain, but the Doppelgänger was sure of two things: first that he was still alive, and, second, that he would return one day to Thrull.

As for the elder Illgill, why had he fled to the north? Expediency? But expediency would have dictated a retreat to the west, following the footsteps of his son. To the west was Surrenland, with its ports and shipping to Galastra and Hangar Parang. The Flame still burned in those countries—he would have been well treated there. But no—he'd gone *north*. What was there? An ancient way, now virtually unused except by peatcutters and berry gatherers, stretched for the fifty miles to the foothills of the Palisades. There were ruined fortresses in those hills, fortresses built by an earlier race of men, but no man, let alone the remnants of an army, could live there for long without food. They would have all perished within a month. Unless, that was, they never intended to stop at the foothills, but were attempting what no man had attempted for centuries—the passage of the mountains themselves. This could be the only explanation, but what lay beyond? The Nations of the Night, Shandering Plain, the Forest of Lorn—all unknown and as dangerous as the mountains. Even if Illgill had survived the Palisades, where was he now? And, more important, where was the Rod, the Rod which he needed to repossess the body which had been stolen from him? The Rod with which he would consign the other Jayal Illgill to this cripple's frame in which he had been imprisoned these last seven years?

No more clues to any of these questions remained in the Illgill mansion, of that he was sure. And since that day with Furisel, though he had raised the golden box from the floor several times and gazed at the riches within it, he had never touched the golden bars again.

CHAPTER TWENTY-THREE

The Doppelgänger

The other Jayal was closer than the Doppelgänger could have imagined: only a fifteen-minute walk from the Illgill mansion on the Silver Way. He was still listening to his old sergeant's tale in the ruined house near the Spike. By now his limbs were numb from the length of time he had been sitting on the hard earth floor of the ruin. He suddenly came to himself and wondered how long he had been frozen in that position: an hour or more? He had no idea; though his eyes had been fixed on the moon, his mind had been full of another light: the blazing, incandescent light of the Rod, a light so great that its beams reached out to where man's shadow self dwelt on the plains beyond. A light so powerful that its force could drive a shadow into this world: a shadow with the very same body, in all appearances, to the one which he now inhabited. A light so powerful that his memory had been erased for seven years, so he knew not what had been done to save his life—until today.

But now he knew; he knew the world to be divided into light and shadow: the light of the fire and its shadow cast against the wall; one substantial, vital, the other a grey illusion. Thus was the world divided in two, reality and shadow, and each man had his real soul and the dark soul that dwelt apart. The dark soul: the polar opposite of the self that dwelt on this plain, a soul that dwelt in Shades.

But now his shadow was also here, in this city. The dark mirror of what he was. And they were inseparable.

Furisel had stopped speaking. Their eyes met. Jayal returned his stare blankly; he had no idea what the old sergeant had just been saying. Then he remembered—Furisel had been telling him about the end of the battle, how he'd found the body of the double.

That was it: Furisel had been badly wounded. The priests whose job it was to sacrifice the dying had mistaken him for one already dead, and he'd been carried to the top of one of the carrion piles at the back of their lines. Jayal remembered the piles well, thirty-foot-high stacks of alternate layers of spirit-soaked wood and corpses. At the end of the day the priests had needed long ladders to get to the tops of them, there had been so many dead. Several of them had already been set ablaze before he had been wounded, filling the dusky air with orange flame and a thick greasy smoke which lent further gloom to the battlefield.

"Please," he mumbled, gesturing at the old sergeant to continue. The candle was burning low, guttering slightly in the cold air that crept in through the makeshift door of the ruin. Furisel drew his ragged cloak tighter around his body, pulling at the flask of Rak again. He offered it to Jayal wordlessly, and this time the younger man took it uncomplainingly, taking a long pull, the fire of the liquor as nothing to the fierce pain that burned within his heart.

"Well, as I was saying," Furisel continued after a few seconds of reflection, "the priests carried me to the top of the last pyre. It was the only one not alight, and they were anxious to set it off before the battle was lost. You remember the orders: none of the dead to be left on the field. I could hear the sound of the battle and the dying, but, when I tried to speak to tell them I was alive, no sound came out. I could only see and hear. I could feel, too, feel the heat of the pyres they had already set alight, the smell of roasting meat, thick and oily it was; with the wound in me chest I nearly choked to death, but no such luck. The two fellows that brought me to the top threw me down like I was a bag of dung and hurried back down, hoping, no doubt, to save their carcasses from the Worm.

"I lay there for a while, waiting for them to light the fire at the bottom. I knew it was going to be a hard death, being roasted alive. I tried to compose myself for the flame. I could feel it almost, through the backplate of my armour. But it was my imagination. There were no flames: the priests must have run off without lighting it. Meanwhile the sound of the fighting came right up to the foot of the pyre, and all I could do was lie there, staring up at the last glimmer of sunset and the buzzards circling overhead. After a while things quietened down; just the groans of the wounded. It sounded like the Reapers had been driven off. The minutes went past, and the sky got darker and no flames came, and I began to think maybe I would see another dawn.

"I found I could move a bit, so I crooked my neck and saw another fellow from the company, Sanlang his name was. He was lying there, his hauberk laid right open by a mace, his guts hanging out, and his face grey. The priests had been overhasty with him too; he was still breathing, but only just. I didn't want to let him go without a word, so I says: 'No Rak for us in the mess tonight, Sanlang!' and he opens his eyes a fraction and smiles queerly, and whispers: 'Remember me in the halls of Flame.' He was looking right at me, then his eyes turned up in his head, and he gives a shudder, and I think, 'You'll be lucky to see me there tonight, my friend, because, if they don't light this pyre, I'll make it back to Thrull, me wound, the undead and all Faran's legions notwithstanding!' Just then, curse my luck, there comes another creaking on the ladder and I think, 'Sanlang, wait a while, they remembered after all.' But it's just one man coming up, very slowly, a body over his shoulder, and I see it's the Elder, Manichee himself, all bent and stooped under the weight of a naked body. Curious what you think when you're a gone 'un. I thought at least it's the Elder that will send my cinders off to Hel. The priest pauses for a moment, as if making a last effort, then tips this naked body down beside me, muttering something all the time, and shaking his head, then he's gone with a tinkling of his hat bells.

"I closed my eyes and waited for the flames again. Instead of which there comes another almighty blast from the Reapers' horns and now the battle is all about the pyre again and judging by the sound right through the tents and all, then the sound goes far away as if they've finally swept our lines away and they're in pursuit, and all I can hear are the groans of the dead and the dying, and after a while another sound . . ." He paused breathlessly, his eyes wild in the flickering candlelight. "It was the sound of gnawing, the undead feeding away at the wounded at the bottom of the pyre. I said to myself, Furisel, neither them vultures nor the undead will have your meat, no sir! I look across then, thinking how I'm going to get off the pyre, and then I see the body old Manichee has brought up with him and my poor wounded soul nearly goes tripping after Sanlang's." He paused again for a reaction from Jayal, but he just stared through him, knowing with a dull heaviness in his heart what would be coming next.

"Well, it was you: Jayal Illgill. What's left of your head resting on Sanlang's guts just where the Elder had thrown you. Even more curious, but what do I see in the light of the burning pyres all around, but that you're still breathing! Another one that the priests missed, the Elder himself what's more!" He smiled, but, if he was hoping for a response from Jayal, he was to be disappointed. Undeterred, he continued.

"Time to leave the worm perch, I thought, before the vampires down below sense more living flesh up the ladder, but my chest was on fire when I tried to move, and I lay back looking up at the twinkling stars and the croaking buzzards and thought maybe if I waited a bit I'd be all right. Punctured lung, cracked ribs; people had survived those before, I thought; maybe it would be all right if I just rested." Furisel shut his eyes, as if composing himself for the sleep of death. Then he suddenly shook his head, as if throwing off the pull of the Shadow world. "I must have blinked out then," he continued, "for the next thing I knew the grey light of dawn was upon us, and the old sun was heaving itself over the horizon above the far-off Spike of Thrull. I felt a bit of strength return with the light and crawled over the bodies to the edge of the pyre. There was a sight! A thick mist covered the battlefield, the legions' tattered standards hanging limp, the tents ripped to shreds, and below the ghostly gleam of bodies as far as I could see through the fog. But now it was silent, deathly silent. No one stirred, neither the dead nor the living.

"Best to get moving, I thought. By a miracle the ladder was still there and I said to myself, since the god had preserved me, I'd better use it before Faran's men returned. And so I had resolved when I heard a groan. I was about to ignore it, but then I thought, since the Dawn has blessed me, should I not try to help another? I crawled back and checked the bodies. Flies were already buzzing in and out of the wounds and the dead eyes, and no one stirred. I nearly gave up, but then I heard the groan again, and it was from you, your mouth half-open, your face a mass of blood. Just then one of them big buzzards came flapping down onto your chest. It looked about and fixed me with its big yellow eye. Then it turned its head back and took a peck from your cheek. I clapped my hands, bit feeble, mind, and the bird just turned and fixed me with its stare again as if it were thinking here's another likely carcass for me breakfast. But then I shouted at it and it hopped a bit, then flapped away. I think it must have had your eyeball in its beak."

The old fellow peered closely once more at Jayal's right side. "That one there," he said, pointing with his gnarled fingers. Jayal's hand went up to the eye socket as if to check that that orb indeed was still there. The movement seemed to break the spell which he'd been under for several minutes.

"And then?" he croaked, still holding the hand over his eye.

"Well, then I carried you, or who I thought was you, all the way back to the city. My wound wasn't as bad as I'd thought, just some cracked ribs and a pint or two of blood: average soldier's fare. It took two days to get back to Thrull and you were a deadweight all that time, groaning away like a door that needed oil: groan, groan, groan, groan. I should have left you, I swear, for what you'd ordered to be done to Talien. But a promise to the Dawn is a promise and I dragged you—cursing all the way, I was."

"And what happened after we got to Thrull?" Jayal asked.

"Lorks, you don't remember nothing, do you?"

"That's assuming this other person was me."

Furisel nodded his head, the uncertainty back in his eyes.

"Now I see you without the scar, I'm not sure. It might have been someone else . . ." His voice trailed off.

"Tell me about the city," Jayal demanded.

Furisel gathered his thoughts. "There was not much of it left, nothing but a half-smoking ruin, with the people standing about throwing the ashes of their houses over their heads, those that hadn't been slaughtered, that was. For most of the way I thought I dragged a corpse, but you'd come to and proved me wrong, and I'd given you water from the marsh, and you came round a bit more and there we were finally at the gate where the beggars always sit, except now there was just wounded soldiers who had dragged themselves into a tight semicircle. There were not many left. The vampires had come the two previous nights: most of them couldn't protect themselves and had been taken off. Some of the others begged me to help them into the city, but I was too tired and I sat and rested and looked at the smoke from the Lower Town still burning away and the piles of corpses and thought that the world had really ended. I knew without looking that my house was burned and my family with it.

"It was then that I got the idea of taking you back to your house on the Silver Way. The houses up there weren't still burning like in the Lower Town, and I thought there might be help up there. It was like a dream; I don't know why I did it, or how, but in the evening we were there. Half the house had been burned, and there were the dead lying in the gardens and in the house. The stink was fierce, but I was used to it by then. But I thought I'd made a mistake: here were your nearest and dearest, their guts pulled out, or mutilated, or drained dry by the vampires. But you looked at them as if you didn't know them. I told you you couldn't stay there, that you'd go mad staring at all the dead, but you just laughed and told me to carry you down to the cellars, and that's where we went. I found food and wine and bandages to bind your wounds. And you ate and drank and seemed better for a moment, but then went into a hot fever and I thought you would be dead by the morning. That night I heard the undead creeping about the house, searching, and it seemed as if they might come down to the cellar . . ." He hesitated.

"Then what?" asked Jayal.

Furisel seemed embarrassed. "I left you. You were near death anyway. I thought to finish you, in case the undead got you, but then I thought you still had a small chance. I sneaked out and didn't come back, not for many months. There were too many dead for my liking. I found this house by the Spike. There were still people holding out there, and the vampires didn't come at night. That was when I saw Weebil again. But instead of greeting me like an old comrade, he stole the food I'd found and sent me packing. Soon after he went over to the side of the Worm. By then I was desperate: there was no food left. I thought of the Illgill cellars; there had been enough victuals there when I was with you. And so I steeled myself to see your bones.

"I sneaked through the gates, and down the steps into the dark, feeling my way till I came to the cellar door. I got my courage, then twisted the handle and passed through. First I looked at the stretch of floor where you'd been laid out, but there was only the old bit of straw mattress you'd been lying on and I thought 'Oh, the vampires got him,' and said a little prayer. Then I think, well, the lord won't mind if I take some of the bottles. There they were winking at me prettier than a whore from their dusty racks. I went over and grabbed an armful. Just then a hand clamped down on me shoulder and I thought, here it is then, I'm vampire feed, and I screamed and twisted and fought, but was borne to the floor, the bottles smashing. Then I heard a voice. When I recovered my wits I saw it was you. Your face was healed and you were as strong as you'd ever been. I came over funny then and laughed and laughed and couldn't stop. You had to belt me one to get me to stop so as you could talk to me."

"Then what did 'I' say?"

"Lorks, you want your life in a nut, don't you? Why, you said, 'Hello, my old sergeant, what has the world done for you since I last saw you down here?' Then you came over sarcastic-like and pulled at the sacking I was wearing and admired my fine raiment, and tweaked my locks which were all dead and lank and complimented me on my barber, then said my chef was a good one because I had put on fat . . ."

"Enough, enough, what then?"

"Well, then you seemed to tire of the play, and gave me a cuff for my pains for leaving you and told me you were minded to kill me, but that you were feeling charitable. You said the whole city had gone to rack and ruin and the only way a man could live was by robbery and avoiding the Worm. You'd taken a new name: you were no longer Jayal Illgill, but Setten. That it was safe for you to remain because only I knew how your face was altered by the scar. Then you set me to work: you needed a good pair of eyes for that night, and I was just your man. That was the night we did the slaver's house."

"Did?"

"Reh preserve the Fire! 'Did,' as in stole from, burgled, took his wife, and slew his son an' all; a bad job, it was."

"The man masquerading as me did this?"

"As I said, the man who calls himself Setten."

Jayal was breathing hard, the scar on his upper lip twitching with rage. He brought himself under control after a minute.

"Then?" he asked shortly.

"Why, since then I've been to the old house every now and then when I was in need of a durcal or two, and this man has given me jobs like that—never safe ones, mind."

"And when was the last one?"

"Why, but two nights ago, watching again in the City of the Dead, that old tomb your father meddled with, Ma—Ma—"

"Marizian's?"

"The same. And damned dangerous it was too, with the un-dead shambling at the base of the tomb I was hidden in. What's more, I wasn't alone, for skulking in the shadows I saw one of the spies for the Worm watching as well, though he didn't see me."

"And who were you watching?"

"Why, the rebels, the Flame heretics, those that were arrested yesterday."

"Heretics? Have you taken leave of yourself?"

"That's what Setten called them."

"All right, so what did he want you to look for?"

"Why, when they broke through the stone floor of the tomb I was to run and tell you."

"And did they . . . break through?"

"Aye, and when I'd run, dodging all the dangers abroad in the city at night, and told him, he said, all mysterious, 'in two nights' time then.' Two nights from what I didn't think to ask, because for a change he seemed right pleased and paid me well, and since then I've been drinking Rak, that is until I spotted you tonight."

Jayal thought for a bit, before eyeing the old sergeant again: "Do you believe that I am Jayal Illgill?"

"Aye, now I do, but there is an uncanny resemblance."

"And do you believe this Setten is an impostor?"

Furisel nodded his head slowly, as if still doubting the evidence of his own eyes.

"Good, then will you serve me as you once did in the legion?"

"I will!" the old man said, smiting his thigh ardently with the flat of his hand. "Thieving and scavenging were never my trade. I served you well once, didn't I?"

Jayal remembered Furisel's insubordination on the battlefield: but he had little option but to trust him. Besides which, the old man seemed as frightened of him as of his double. The city had changed out of all recognition since he'd last been in it and he needed a guide. "Right. We'll go to the house on the Silver Way and deal with this man for good!" he said firmly.

"But what of Kazaris, and the other ruffians that he keeps there? You'll be hanging from your ankles on a butcher's hook before you can blink."

Once again, Jayal remembered that he'd lost Dragonstooth back at Weebil's Inn. As far as he could see, the old man had only the dagger, hardly enough to deal with an armed and desperate gang.

"We have to retrieve my sword," he said.

"But Weebil has it!" Furisel protested.

"That may be. But I didn't cross the world to get it so that he should have it. How far is it back to the inn?"

Furisel jerked his head behind him: "It's only a few minutes' walk."

Jayal thought. First the sword, then the impostor. Then Thalassa. But what had the man in Weebil's Inn said about her?

That she was now a common whore? His blood boiled. He would kill him for the insult. His heart had begun to race. Two hours to midnight, he calculated, and so much to do. Where could Thalassa be if she was still alive? Surely Furisel would know. He thought to ask him, but something held him back, something that told him that maybe he had been told the truth in the inn, a truth that he couldn't accept. "Come, let's go," he said, rising abruptly. He staggered a bit, still woozy from the bump on his head, but recovered himself.

Furisel looked at him doubtfully, still confused no doubt by the reality of what he saw: a man who seemed the exact double of his old commander. Jayal could have told him the truth, but the truth was too fantastic. It was up to him to track down this shadow and destroy it—even if by doing so he destroyed himself.

CHAPTER TWENTY-FOUR

Waking the Dead

Malliana clutched a fur rug close to her half-naked body. It was all she had managed to snatch to cover herself before fleeing the temple. The night air was chill, but chillier still was the knowledge of what surrounded her in the darkness.

In a matter of moments her empire had ceased to exist. Of all the women who had once served her, there was only one left: her favourite, Viri. There had been others with them as they'd fled the building, but the Avenue of Dreams had been full of vampires. Viri and Malliana had somehow fought their way through, but the others had been taken. Malliana could still hear their screams ringing in her ears. Viri showed signs of the struggle: a livid bruise on her temple, and blood from a cut on her lip. Her dress was rent and torn, but the look on her face was determined. In truth, Malliana was slightly in awe of her acolyte. She doubted whether either of them would have escaped the mêlée in the avenue if Viri hadn't tripped one of the other women, leaving her as bait for the vampires as they'd fled.

With the destruction of the temple there was only one place the two women could go: the Temple of Iss. Malliana had information that Faran could use. But at the same time she knew Faran would be enraged at the loss of Thalassa. Maybe she could tell him that one of the undead had taken her? Or that she'd died in the conflagration? Her story would have to be a good one, for Faran had lived long enough to see through most stratagems and lies.

She'd only been to the Temple of Worms once before, that first occasion when Faran had summoned Thalassa. The experience had been disturbing enough. This visit would be stranger and more dangerous still.

They'd detoured off the Avenue of Dreams and were now approaching the temple square in a wide arc that took them round the back of the Temple of Iss. The glow from the Hearth Fire of the Temple of Reh in front of them was now complemented by a savage glow from behind, which lit up the street like day. Malliana had seen the first flames licking around her temple; she knew it was doomed.

Suddenly a door opened to their right and the women dived into the shadows on the opposite side of the street. Two figures emerged from the gloom of the doorway. They were dressed in cowled cloaks, their faces averted from the light. They looked about them cautiously and, not noticing the women, slunk past their hiding place and headed up the alley towards the Spike. As they did so, Malliana got a good look at the left sides of their faces. The first was a handsome youth with sandy-coloured hair; the other was a gnarled old man, bald as a coot, his face as weather-beaten as mahogany. The younger man was encouraging the older man to follow him, something which the older man was evidently reluctant to do. They passed within a few feet of the women, arguing vehemently, then disappeared down one of the alleys.

Malliana let out a curse after they were out of earshot.

"It's him," she hissed.

"Who?" asked Viri.

"Who do you think? Jayal Illgill—he who poisoned the servants and destroyed the temple."

Though this was somewhat of an exaggeration, Viri accepted it at face value.

"How has he got in front of us?" mused Malliana, noting where the two men were going. There was only one place up that road that humans would venture to: Weebil's Inn, and she would bet her last durcal that this was where the two men were heading. If so, here was more information for Faran; something to compensate for the loss of Thalassa.

"Come on!" she urged Viri, breaking from their hiding place and hurrying down the street. Viri followed hard on her heels.

It took them only a couple of minutes to reach the temple square. They stopped at a ruined house by its edge. From here, the square was about a hundred yards across, the massive expanse of cobblestone broken up by the mound in the exact centre. The Temple of Iss was to their left, but there was no cover between where they stood and the uninviting copper gates. Tendrils of mist floated through the air. The stocks were to their right, the doll-like figures pinioned in them bone white in the light of the moon.

There were no vampires to be seen; they had evidently found better prey at the Temple of Sutis. It seemed as safe as it would ever be in Thrull after dark. Malliana jerked her head at Viri and they set off towards the gates at a fair clip, sending the mist swirling in their wake.

"Master, this is insane!" Furisel was tugging urgently at Jayal's sleeve. But the younger man didn't notice. His whole conscious thought was occupied by the idea of retrieving the lost sword. His personal safety, and Furisel's, were secondary. They had soon reached the stone bridge leading to the Spike. The narrow point of rock stuck up sinisterly into the air, silhouetted by the glow of the fires. Five hundred feet beneath them, the cliffs ended abruptly in a whirling sea of fog punctuated here and there by the higher roofs of the Lower Town. Jayal thought hard: his entrance to the Spike would have to be substantially different from his last one. Stealth and daring were required. He looked at the windows either side of the door at the end of the bridge, but these were covered by iron grilles. But there was an old doorway a few feet underneath the bridge. Once another bridge must have connected it to the main cliff, but this had tumbled into the chasm between the two a long time ago. The doorway was only barred by a few wooden spars . . . if he had a rope, he might be able to swing down to it. He whispered his plan to Furisel.

The old man was no more enthusiastic than he'd been when

they'd left their hideout a few minutes before. He was obviously still confused, doubtful even of his own senses. Who was this man he was with? And who was the other, who also claimed to be Jayal Illgill? But the young man's requests finally made an impression on him, and he took him over to the sewer hole where he'd been hiding when Jayal had been thrown out of the inn. He heaved the stone covering aside with a grunt. In the red glow of the fires Jayal could see a few slime-covered steps leading down into darkness. The steps ended abruptly at the lip of a dark hole. A rope was attached to a rusted ringbolt on the edge of the hole. Furisel crept gingerly down the slick steps and began heaving it up.

"Where does the shaft go?" whispered Jayal.

"Deep into the catacombs," Furisel answered, "to a place you wouldn't want to visit."

Jayal refrained from asking further questions as the old sergeant brought up the last of the rope, some thirty feet of it in all. He unhitched the end from the ringbolt.

"There goes our escape if things go amiss," he said grimly. Wordlessly they returned to the bridge, creeping along it until they reached its farther end.

Suddenly there came an awful screeching from far above them where the top of the Spike was hidden by the mist.

"Mercy!" gasped Furisel. "What in Shades is that?"

A damp cold had settled on Jayal's soul when he had heard the call. It was the harbinger of death that his childhood nurse had warned him of, the lone call of the Creature of the Spike echoing over the walls and the marshes. How many times had he heard it in his youth? And every time, the next morning, there would have been blacker smoke issuing from the top of the Temple of Reh, as accident or plague or war had carried off another of Thrull's inhabitants. The image of a fierce chained creature locked from mortal view in its hidden eyrie high above the temple pyramids came into his mind. The familiar of the city, its fate linked with those mortals it overlooked in its perch; for it was said that if the creature ever broke its adamantine chains and flew, that day would see the end of Thrull and its inhabitants. Now it was calling—a jackal's call, high and keening, louder than Jayal could remember it before. Was that time come? Would Thrull die tonight as the Iss pilgrims had predicted?

"It's nothing," he said, giving the lie to his own fear. "Just a night creature."

"No!" Furisel muttered. "You can't lie to me, Illgill—I know what it is."

"Courage, man," Jayal said, shaking his old sergeant's arm. "Just help me with this rope and you can go back to the sewers."

Jayal quickly looked around for somewhere to secure the end of the rope, and selected the lichen-covered statue of a basilisk which stood on the stone parapet. He looped the rope round the pediment of the statue, pulling a tight knot.

He signalled for Furisel to get back to the safety of the sewer hole, which the old man did with unseemly speed, glancing repeatedly up at the top of the Spike as he did so. Jayal swung out onto the parapet of the bridge, paying out the rope. A small shower of powdery dust broke off and fell into the void, then he was abseiling down the side of the cliff. In a second he was at the level of the door. He reached out, trying to get a handhold on the lintel, but it was fractionally out of his grasp. He spun, his feet dangling over the chasm, the rope swinging like a pendulum away from the door, then back again. He realised that the momentum of the swing was going to take him right up to it at some pace. He took a deep breath as the rope swung back over the void, and let his body weight carry him at breakneck speed towards the doorway.

Viri and Malliana stood breathlessly before the gates of the Temple of Iss. The matt black of the stepped pyramid reared up into the night sky like the blunt head of a huge earthworm. No sound came from within its walls. The silence was daunting, and neither of them knew what to do. Mastering her fear, Viri shouted once, then twice, then both the women yelled together, but there was no response; it was as if the temple were deserted. They looked at each other. The more noise they made, the more likely it was that they would attract the attention of some of the undead, but there was nowhere else for them to hide in the whole of Thrull. The priests of Reh would never admit them, nor did they know the houses of any of their patrons, for neither of the women had left the temple precincts except in extraordinary circumstances for the past seven years. The only way they were going to survive was by attracting the attention of the priests of Iss or by finding some alternative.

They shouted again, as loudly and for as long as they could. But only a ringing echo came back to them from the silent walls of the temple square and the ruined citadel from where a covey of rooks, wakened from sleep, set up a cackling exchange.

Now things were desperate. After they had finished with the Temple of Sutis, the vampires would no doubt return to the temple square. Malliana racked her brains. Was there another entrance to the Temple of Worms? A distant memory came back to her, of when she'd been a child. In those days, the temple had been nothing more than a weed-covered mound, surrounded by unscaleable walls and gates which never opened. But there had been one entrance, set into the forbidding outer walls, which her childhood friends and she had dared one another to go into. As far as she recalled, no one had ever done so, but now she seized on its continued existence as her last hope.

She grabbed Viri's arm and dragged her along the face of the south wall of the temple to where she recalled sitting with her companions over thirty years before. The place where she thought she remembered seeing the slit in the walls was now covered by a thicket of brambles and thornbushes. But she remembered the slight declivity in the ground in front of it. This must be the spot, she was sure.

"What are we doing here?" Viri whispered. Malliana hushed her, and began pulling at the screen of brambles. The thorns ripped at the gauzy fabric of her skirt and her bare arms. Viri, infected by her mistress's enthusiasm, her question forgotten, joined in. Her own clothing too was reduced to shreds in seconds. The noise of their struggle with the vegetation sounded deafening to the two women, but fear lent speed to their efforts and within ten minutes they had cleared enough to see a thin fissure between two of the ashlar blocks of the temple wall. At this point in the wall, it looked as if the fissure must go right into the base of the temple pyramid which reared above them in the night air.

With one last glance behind them, Malliana fought her way through the remaining undergrowth to the slit in the wall. Her hair caught in the brambles, and she felt it tearing from her scalp. She squeezed herself into the gap, mentally cursing the extra weight which she had gained over the years. For the moment, she didn't care whether she was blundering into a dead end from which she could not return. Anything was better than the vampire's bite. Viri followed, her slimmer frame making it easier for her to get into the crack.

Malliana groped blindly in front of her in the pitch-darkness, feeling the coarse edges of the ashlar blocks, and the gossamer threads of spiderwebs in front of her. There was no turning back now. The tunnel zigzagged left and right, following, she guessed, the cracks between the building blocks of the outer walls. After about twenty yards, the way in front opened up. She paused, scenting the air. It was musty with the smell of death and decay, and for the first time the terror of what lay ahead conquered that of what lay behind.

She forced herself forward. Immediately her foot struck something which rolled across the floor in front of her with the unnerving sound of bone on rock. A skull?

She continued onward, her hands her only guides. Now they met a rock wall and she felt around, seeking an exit. Instead she found an alcove at chest height. Her fingers explored within and suddenly touched a bony surface. Her hand darted back as if bitten, but then a curious thing happened. A white light sprang from within the alcove and she saw a skull. Light was pouring through its eye sockets and mouth.

Malliana and Viri flinched back to the centre of the room, which was now revealed in the light. They saw that the chamber they were in was surrounded by similar alcoves filled with skulls. Tunnels lined with even more skull-filled niches ran off in several directions. But, as they watched, a series of the skulls in one particular tunnel began to light up, one after another, so that they could see down its entire length.

"What does it mean?" whispered Viri.

"It seems that this magic was put here for a purpose," Malliana replied. "But why?"

"Vampires don't require light to find their way," Viri suggested, though without much confidence.

"But why would they wish the living to find their way into the temple?"

"Perhaps they wanted the living to go this way?"

"We'll soon find out," Malliana said; there was a certain logic in what Viri had said, and they had no other feasible options. She headed off down the corridor.

Now she had light, she found it easy to make good progress. Her feet kicked up clouds of dust: the passage had obviously not been used for aeons. The impression was confirmed by rock falls from the ceiling which partially blocked the corridor and over which they had to climb. But the light from the skulls remained constant as they went forward. Now they reached a junction, the corridor breaking right and left. On the left, the illuminated skulls continued. On the right a similar corridor, but with the skulls still dark.

Malliana paused, fearing a trap. But returning was impossible. She remembered too well the terror of the lightless outer passage. She took the left-hand way. After a few yards, it doglegged right in front of them. Malliana approached cautiously, her fear growing, then peeked round the corner.

What she saw froze her blood. A headless figure some eight feet tall blocked their way, dressed in armour, its cuirass heavily pointed and shaped in an ancient style, covered in a thick layer of grey dust. It held a mace in either hand, ready to strike. A desiccated head, well preserved despite its antiquity, sat on the floor a yard or so in front of the warrior's feet; it, in turn, was covered with dust and cobwebs. But as she watched, its eyes blinked open and stared at her. Behind, the body of the headless warrior shuddered into life, shedding a thick haze of dust from its armour. The women stepped back, too terrified to speak. But, even as they watched, the head's lips cracked open. Black bile spilled out from them with its question: "Who trespasses here, where no mortal has walked since the dark time of the world?" The words were slow, accompanied by a gurgling as more black blood flowed from its mouth. Malliana could only watch as the pool of black ichor formed around its chin, her own tongue forgotten.

But Viri still had her wits: "We wish to enter the Temple of Worms," she said in a trembling voice.

"You live, but wish for the temple of Death?"

Viri nodded.

"Then you have come a way that no one has dared to come since the High Priest set me here generations ago! Go back. The price you must pay to go on is too heavy for humankind and for the city."

Now Malliana had regained her own voice: "It is too dangerous to go back."

"And you think it not dangerous to go ahead?" the creature replied. As if in confirmation of his warning, the headless warrior stirred again, its arms creaking threateningly.

Viri was backing down the corridor, but Malliana held her ground: determination had replaced her earlier fear.

"We will go on."

"Very well: the priests will be satisfied. It was written in the *Book of Worms* that this should be: that one should come and strike the gong and wake the dead."

"What gong is this?"

"Pass on: I will not harm you unless you return without striking it. It will admit you to the Temple of Worms, much may it help you. The Worm have mercy on you, as it did not have on me." So saying, the eyes closed and the warrior became still once more.

Malliana and Viri stood indecisively. There was just room to squeeze past the figure and continue down the passageway, if they wished to.

"What shall we do?" whispered Viri.

Malliana was becoming irked by her acolyte's questions, but she had to appear to be strong.

"Why, we will go on. What else?" she said, as confidently as she could.

"But what about the curse?"

"Curse? What curse?" Malliana snapped back. "Don't you think we who have lost the temple tonight are not cursed enough?" So saying, she stepped somewhat gingerly over the head. It didn't move as her body passed over it. Next she approached the headless torso and slipped past it. Viri followed, her face frozen in terror.

In front of them the corridor ended in an unlit vault. Cautiously, Malliana stepped over a copper chain blocking the entrance. The interior of the vault was a solid wall of black. An icy trickle of sweat ran down Malliana's back. Behind her, Viri let out a whimper of terror. The sound echoed in the vault and, at the far end, Malliana sensed movement, a shimmering.

"What is it?" Viri asked querulously. The shimmering increased, as if in response to the vibration of the sound of her voice. Malliana's eyes were beginning to adjust to the darkness. She started hesitantly forward. Another shout and she saw a white shape moving towards her. She stopped and the figure stopped. Then she realised what she was looking at: her own reflection in the face of a huge copper gong, some six feet in diameter. It was moving slowly in a leather and wood frame, disturbed by the vibrations of Viri's words. Viri was close behind her, her reflection appearing with Malliana's in the face of the gong.

"What is it?" Viri breathed, the gong swaying slightly again. Their faces looked like skulls in the reflected surface.

"You heard the guardian: whoever rings the gong will summon the undead," Malliana said, her expansiveness revealing her fear.

"But it will slay us if we return," Viri whispered.

"There's no option," Malliana agreed.

"You would dare?"

Malliana turned to the younger woman. "And why not? The priests will surely come once it's been rung. And if it brings destruction, it cannot be any worse than that which has overtaken our temple."

"But it will wake the undead."

Malliana gave out a harsh laugh: "Then let them come; we'll all die soon anyway." At the noise of her laughter, the gong let out a quiet thrumming which increased in volume as the sound rebounded off the stone walls of the vault. "See, it's beginning to work already!" Then, before Viri could stop her, she lifted both her fists and brought them crashing down onto the surface of the gong.

The noise was deafening. The sound seemed to grow from some invisible point within the copper surface, sucking in all other sound, all thought, all consciousness. Wave after successive wave spread out, forcing Malliana and Viri to their knees as their hands flew to their ears.

But the noise was only beginning. It bounced from the walls of the vault and issued from the entranceway magnified a hundredfold. The sound was a physical force, lifting the women from their knees and sweeping them to the back of the chamber.

The wall of sound hurtled down the corridor, which acted as a funnel, amplifying it still further. The warrior and his head were blown aside in a second and the wave passed on, shattering each alcoved skull in succession. It burst from the entranceway to the square in a whirlwind of shredded bramble bushes, rebounding off the walls of the temple and the ruined houses, over the fire-blackened alleyways of the Lower Town, over the Spike and the walls of the city, over the marshes, where the ignes fatui still moved in the fog banks in a blue ghostly dance, over the pyramid of skulls, and onwards to the ring of far-distant mountains.

But it was not in the empty plains and mountains that it wrought its magic—for the purpose of its long-dead artificers in Tiré Gand had been to raise the dead by its sound. In the catacombs the noise flowed down and down into ancient passageways unseen by the living for centuries. There it rolled over the tombs where the dead who would never rise lay in rotting coffins, over the empty graves of those who had already risen, and then to those tombs where the undead had sunk into the second sleep, deprived of blood to liquefy the contents of their veins. The sound fibrillated through their beings, agitating the black sludge of their blood so it began to flow once more. The gong rang and rang, resonating in their atrophied bodies, and their eyes cracked open, and their mummified lips moved and their nostrils sucked in the dusty air and then their brains remembered: the thing that had kept them alive once and the promise of which had saved them from utter extinction: the scent of blood.

*   *   *

But Malliana knew nothing of this as she knelt in the vault, her hands clasped to her ears. She just hoped that the noise would not send her mad, or deafen her forever. And then, just when it seemed that it would never stop, that she would have to endure it until she went insane, it began to diminish and recede like an ebbing tide. Then it was gone, leaving only a distant ringing in the women's ears.

Malliana got to her feet shakily, followed by Viri. As their deafness receded, they heard a new sound—a massive granite block covering one wall had begun to groan open. Through the gap they could see a moonlit square which Malliana instantly recognised as the courtyard of the Temple of Iss. Now came the sound of feet running towards the opening. Two priests wearing the brown-and-purple cloaks and silver skull masks of their order emerged through it, followed by twenty or so of the temple guards.

The masked priests stared blankly at the two scantily clad women.

"Who was summoned the dead?" one of them asked hollowly from behind his mask. The words would have terrified anyone else, but Malliana, now she had an object for the rage within her, was not to be cowed.

"Do you know me?" she asked, stepping forward.

The skull mask who had spoken shook his head.

"I am Malliana, High Priestess of the Temple of Sutis. The temple is burning!" She flung her hand behind her dramatically in the direction of the fire, revealing her bare breasts as she did so.

The skull mask took in the breasts and the gesture with bony indifference. "You have rung the gong: that is enough. Seize them." The guards leapt forward and manhandled the women towards the temple.

"You don't understand," Malliana shouted. "I've important information for Lord Faran Gaton."

"Don't worry, my lady; our master will certainly want to meet the person who rang the gong."

Now Malliana could hear a sound over the rattle of the soldiers' armour. It came from the square outside. The sound of stone gratings being shoved aside; whatever the gong had summoned was already on the move.

The two women caught a glimpse of their surroundings as they were bundled forward. The courtyard was lit by watchfires which glowed with a purple nacreous light from its four corners. Pale bodies, tied to stakes, glowed in the dim light. In front of them the pyramid reared a hundred feet into the air. At its peak she could now see a ten-foot-high stone skull, purple fires burning in its twin eye sockets, a stone serpent of death coiled around its neck—Iss' symbol, a being that ate its own tail, representing life consuming life.

CHAPTER TWENTY-FIVE

Return to Weebil's Inn

Rats scuttled in the darkness as Jayal groped blindly amongst the splintered remains of the worm-eaten door. After a second his hands found purchase on a flagstone floor and he pushed himself to his feet. He strained his eyes in the darkness. All that was visible at first was the jagged hole he'd punched in the door, faintly outlined by the moon and the lights of the fires raging in the night sky.

For a moment, as he'd swung in towards it, his feet braced for the impact, he'd had the terrible thought that the door would prove to be more solid than it looked, that he would ricochet off it, lose his grip on the rope, and go spinning down to his death on the roofs of the Lower Town five hundred feet below. But woodworm had done its work; as his feet touched the door, there had been a brief explosion of dust and splinters, but he had swung through without any deceleration at all until the lintel had caught the rope and he had been jerked to the ground.

Now the rope had swung back out of sight. He thought of retrieving it immediately, but dismissed the idea. First he must see if anyone had been alerted by the door's being broken in. He listened intently, but there was no sound. Emboldened by the silence, he stepped through the wreckage of the door, blundering into an empty wine cask as he did so. He hastily grabbed its edge before it fell over.

His hands groped the darkness in front and found the outlines of a second door and then a door handle. He had taken a
pitch torch and flint and tinder from Furisel's house, and now
debated whether he should light it. He decided against. The
guests might expect strange noises from below where, judging
by the scuttling movements by his feet, the rats ran wild, but a
light coming up the stairs would be a different matter altogether.

He slid Furisel's dagger from his belt and, with his free
hand, twisted the ring of the handle. It gave with a faint squeak.
Still no sound from in front. The mad beating of his heart
calmed slightly. The swing over the abyss had been a mad gamble. But meeting Weebil again with only a dagger as protection
seemed an almost equal risk.

His eyes had now adjusted to the gloom as best they could.
Beyond the door, stone steps spiralled up to the higher reaches
of the inn. He crept up them, his hand guiding him along the
wall. Now there was another doorway in front of him, beyond
which he thought he could hear something. He leant his head
against the panels of the door. The sound was clearer—snoring,
then the sound of someone turning in their sleep. His fingers
found the ring bolt of the door and twisted it. The latch clicked
up with barely a sound.

In front he saw the dim glow of embers in a fireplace and a
guttering candle which was barely alight. It was the room he
had been in but two hours before. Two men were slumped over
a trestle table, drinking beakers still clutched in their hands.
The other men lay scattered amongst the straw mattresses on
the floor. The smell of urine and body odour was almost overpowering. Weebil sat in a chair directly opposite where Jayal
had entered. For a moment he thought the giant must have seen
him. But even in the dim light Jayal could see that Weebil's
head was nodding and his eyes were closed. In one hand he
held Dragonstooth, eldritch light seeping through the stitch
holes in the scabbard, in the other a flask of Rak.

Jayal crept forward, placing his feet carefully amongst the
broken fragments of crockery, which littered the floor. One
step, then another, careful that his riding boots made no sound
on the flagstones. He reached Weebil's sleeping form. Weebil's

lips were slightly parted and the sword hilt, which lay across his stomach, rose and fell in time with his breathing.

Holding his breath, Jayal slowly pushed the dagger into his belt and reached out his hand towards the sword. The salamander's head on the hilt, its jewelled eyes glinting in the firelight, seemed to regard him with an alien hatred, daring him to touch it. Jayal's hand faltered, and the giant suddenly grunted in his sleep. Jayal's heart stopped for an instant, but Weebil settled again, the sword slipping precariously to one side. Any moment one of the giant's snores would send it crashing to the floor. Jayal reached out his hand gingerly. There! His fingers closed on the gold plate of the salamander's head. He gripped it firmly as another seismic snore racked Weebil's body and would have tipped it off his stomach. Jayal lifted the sword slowly away. He'd done it!

Then the crashing wall of sound, the reverberation of a gong amplified a thousand times, hit the inn like a tidal wave. First there was a sudden vacuum in the air, an absence of other sound, then the wall of noise washed over him, the floor and the furniture seemed to leap in the air and he was nearly knocked off his feet. Crockery jumped off the shelves and tables and crashed to the floor. All this occurred as if silently; so all-enveloping was the noise of the gong that actions, as they unfolded, appeared to occur as if divorced from the sounds which normally defined them, thus lending an unreality to everything that followed.

The giant woke in an instant, and bellowed in surprise at seeing Jayal right in front of him. But no sound seemed to come from his mouth, nor from his chair as he pushed it back, so deafening was the noise of the gong. Jayal swung at him with the scabbarded sword. It made contact with Weebil's head, sending him reeling back into the chair.

Now Jayal had just enough time to wrench the sword from its scabbard. Light exploded from the blade as it came free, painting the chamber a magnesium white. But Weebil was already back on his feet, yanking the chair up from behind him and swinging it at Jayal. The young man ducked as the chair missed his head by inches. The sword was ineffectual against the great bulk of wood in Weebil's hands. The giant swung the

chair back and this time he had no option but to parry with the
sword. Its blade bit deep into the wood, but Jayal was carried
back into the wall by its momentum. He pushed off the wall, the
sword coming free as Weebil staggered back. But now hands
grabbed at Jayal's cloak, and he realised he was surrounded by
the other men. He twisted one way and then another, the sword
scattering his opponents.

Jayal only needed the second's respite granted him. He
turned and flung himself desperately towards the front door. A
man stumbled to his feet in front but fell as Jayal caught him
with the flat of the blade. He vaulted the body, conscious that
another of the guards was right behind him.

He flew down the corridor, the noise of the gong deafening
him, his eyes on the massive key hanging from the lock and the
bar across the door at the farther end. He wouldn't have time to
unfasten both before his pursuer got to him.

He whirled round, and there was the man, still dressed in the
stained leather armour of the city guard, his sword ready to run
him through. Jayal had just enough time to bring Dragonstooth
back, then swing it forward in an incandescent arc that ended
deep in his pursuer's shoulder. The man's mouth opened in a
scream, but no sound could be heard above that of the gong.
Jayal yanked the blade free, this time stabbing at another man
behind the first one. The sword tip passed through the man's rib
cage as his momentum carried him right onto it. The man
stopped dead in his tracks, the sword protruding from his back.
Jayal recognised the man called Dob. They held this position
for a moment, the man's mouth open in an O of surprise, his
eyes fixed on Jayal. Then he sank to his knees, bearing Jayal's
sword arm down with him.

All the time, the maddening sound of the gong echoed and
reechoed around the Inn. At least it served some purpose. for
apart from Weebil, who now came lumbering down the passage, the other guests appeared too frightened to pursue Jayal.
But the giant was uncowed. Seeing Jayal's sword still impaled
in Dob, he seized a two-handed axe from the wall bracket and
charged Jayal from the other end of the corridor.

Pull as he might, Jayal couldn't release the sword from
Dob's body; he was defenceless. He had only one option and

took it, throwing himself at Weebil's knees just as the giant swung the axe at him. The blade whistled a fraction over his head as Jayal's shoulder smashed into the giant's knees. Weebil's momentum did the rest; he pitched over Jayal, adding further force to the axe blow which, instead of Jayal's head, now smashed straight through the stout oak panels of the door. Weebil fell outside in a shower of splinters.

But Jayal had no time for him: he was still defenceless. He put his foot on the chest of Dob's corpse and pulled with all his might. Dragonstooth slid away, Dob's blood sizzling on its blade. He swung round, expecting to find Weebil charging back at him. But the giant was still outside, struggling to regain his feet.

Jayal stepped through the ruins of the door, his sword levelled, as the noise of the gong began to recede. Still Weebil struggled vainly to heave himself up. Jayal now saw that Weebil had landed on one of the blades of his axe; it was embedded deep in his chest. A trickle of blood flowed out of his mouth and down his beard. A large pool was forming around his chest.

He turned to look at Jayal, his bloodshot eyes like dying coals.

"So, Illgill's son, you were the death of me after all," he groaned. The great boughlike arms strained at the surface of the bridge but were incapable of lifting him more than an inch or two from the ground.

Jayal knelt by the man, his knees soaking in the pool of blood. "Tell me," he said, shaking his shoulder. "Tell me where Thalassa is!"

Weebil smiled faintly, as if, though he was a dead man, what he was about to say would bring him some pleasure. A bubble of blood formed on his lips, but no words came. His gaze went up over the parapet of the bridge to the citadel, beyond the red glare of the Sanctuary Flame, as if he sought inspiration here.

"I told you the truth, Illgill," he managed to croak at last. "She pulls a harlot's trick now. There," he said, nodding his head feebly, "where that other fire lights the sky, that's where you'll find your whore"—his face spasmed with pain—"and may you rot with her forever." With that his eyes rolled up in their sockets, and he slumped forward, back onto the axe blade, which, receiving his mass, exploded through his back in a shower of blood.

Jayal got to his feet unsteadily, barely taking notice of the blood that had spattered his cloak. He looked uncertainly at the new fire that illuminated the sky, his heart leaden. Though he hated him, surely Weebil wouldn't have repeated the story about Thalassa if there was no truth in it. The fire that the giant had indicated looked like a big one. What calamity had occurred there? He looked back at Weebil's corpse, wishing he could have asked him more.

But he had delayed too long; the noise of the gong had faded, there was movement within the inn. An object hurtled from the dim recesses. He ducked instinctively and a throwing dagger passed over his head. He turned and ran the length of the bridge, Dragonstooth lighting the way, calling out for Furisel.

But the end of the bridge was empty, as was the sewer hole when he knelt and inspected it. He looked around wildly. The street was empty of life.

Once more he was on his own.

A crowd of guards, acolytes and priests had been drawn out into the courtyard by the noise of the gong. They flocked around Malliana and Viri, jabbering and gesticulating. But the contingent who'd taken them from the vault dragged them off towards the main entrance of the temple, an opening right at the base of the pyramid. Torches guttered in wall brackets affixed to the ashlar blocks on either side. At the bottom of the steps a figure, silhouetted by another of the purple fires, awaited them. As they drew closer, they saw that he, too, wore the brown-and-purple robes of a priest, his mask held carelessly in one hand revealing a long gaunt face, pocked and sallowed by hours of dark study away from the sun. Malliana recognised the man from her previous visit to the temple; this was Golon, Faran Gaton's sorcerer.

Golon was looking at her nakedness with displeasure, his lips pursed into a pinched line. His look almost stilled the self-righteous anger in Malliana's heart. She opened her mouth to speak, but Golon took one step towards her and hit her backhanded across the mouth. The blow was so unexpected that she stood silently, her mouth hanging open in surprise.

"You have rung the gong!" Golon snarled. "Soon all the living in Thrull will die!"

"But why didn't anyone come when we called?" Malliana managed to spit back through the thick blood which filled her mouth.

"What? Are we at the beck and call of all the whores who come here at night?"

"The Temple of Sutis is burning!"

"Then let it burn, and everyone in it too," Golon replied bitterly. "All of Thrull will be destroyed tonight, not just your temple."

"What have we done?" moaned Viri; her earlier confidence had gone, and she was almost senseless with fear.

"Why, what else but summoned the dead?" Golon replied. "All those who slept, waiting for the call to awake and drink blood—thousands of them—all of them will now be stirring. Only the undead will survive this night." He spat in disgust. "Think on it, High Priestess, for your time will now be short." He gave her another withering look, before gesturing at the guards. "But first, Lord Faran—make your excuses to him, if you dare."

"I have information for him," Malliana volunteered.

"Nothing that you know will interest him now," Golon replied curtly, then turned and strode off down the shaft. The guards followed, pushing the women in front of them down the corridor towards the hidden depths of the temple. The women were too terrified to protest further.

Golon paused at another entranceway, covering his face with the skull mask and thus becoming almost indistinguishable from the two other priests whom they'd met in the courtyard. The way in front of them resembled the gaping mouth of a devil: long dripping spikes of stone hung like stalactites from the lintel of the thirty-foot-wide entrance. In the floor, tips of other stone spikes jutted up: these, when winched up, could join with the topmost ones to form an impenetrable barrier of stone. Above the lintel were two oriel windows shaped into oblique openings resembling the nasal passages of a skull. Deep within the centre of the mouth, a mauve pannier gave out a low purple light which threw the roughly shaped stone walls of the corridor into dim relief. If anything the interior looked like a human throat and the sensation, as they were pushed forward through the gateway, was that of being swallowed.

Viri looked nervously at her mistress, but Malliana's bruised face was imperturbable. Golon led them deeper and deeper. Red wall lanterns and ribbed arches in the circular tunnel once more gave the impression that they were being swallowed whole, as did now the single, insistent beat of a drum from down below as if a mighty heart throbbed there. Now the corridor divided left and right. In front stood another huge set of double doors, the height of three men, decorated in bas-relief by a vast panorama created of beaten copper. The metal mouldings, though verdigrised, were startlingly lifelike.

On the left-hand side were depicted skeletally thin human figures tending the fields under a huge engorged sun sinking from the skies; skull-masked priests were shown moving among the workers, pointing up at the dying orb. Beneath the line of the earth, crypts and catacombs were shown, stacked with piles of bones and coffins.

On the right hand, the scene was of the sun's ultimate dying as it finally sank from view. The artists had merely gouged out the surface of the mould at this point, so only a deep hollow represented the sky. The dead rising up from the graves, the priests rejoicing, the workers in the fields and orchards throwing away their now-useless implements and offering their necks in reverence to the reborn Dead in Life, all followed in successive tableaux. Scenes from the Death of the Sun, from the *Book of Worms,* the cornerstone of Iss' rituals. Behind the double doors the drumbeat slowed still further, like the dying of a heart, then expired in a sinister silence.

Golon and the guards bowed their heads reverentially, before leading the two women off to the left. Here the corridors were hung with black velvet drapes, and the lights were held in latticed lamp holders which gave out only the thinnest striated light.

Now they passed through a chamber where scribes dressed in the brown-and-purple robes of the Worm peered over ledgers and scrolls in the dim light of tallow candles. A vast gallery ran at two manheights around the room, old leather-bound books and scroll cases disappearing up into the tenebrous darkness: here was knowledge that one man could never hope to learn in a single lifetime. More knowledge than in any other place since the Time of Darkness.

Now Golon passed through a set of wooden double doors underneath the far wall of the gallery. They left the guards at the door and entered another room, a small stone chamber devoid of light save for a flickering candle burning on the stone-flagged floor. Then two figures appeared from the shadows at the far side of the room. They wore heavy black cloaks and their boots made no sound on the stone as they moved forward.

Two things occurred to the women almost simultaneously: first that the men in front of them were both nearly seven feet tall; second, from the mouldering scent of rot, they were un-dead. Viri's fingers clutched automatically at her neck as the two creatures closed on them. But they merely stopped silently in front of them, their arms akimbo, a white pallor now visible in the dark shadows of their cloaks, their breathing hoarse through their dessicated nasal passages.

Golon turned to Malliana, an unpleasant smile on his thin lips. "Some sorcery will be necessary if we are to proceed fur-ther."

Malliana merely glowered at him.

"I regret the sensation may not be exactly a pleasant one," Golon added, smirking in anticipation.

"Do what you must," Malliana said finally. "I think Lord Faran Gaton will be more than interested in what I have to say, and also . . ." she took a deep breath, "outraged at the way you have treated us."

"Very well." Like a conjuror he unfurled his cloak with a clap, throwing his arms wide as if throwing handfuls of seed. And even in the near total darkness of the room it was as if he did cast seed, black seed that flew towards the far side of the room but then disintegrated into vapours in midair, curling and intertwining until the seeds became whirling creatures of shadow. Golon stepped back, pulling the creatures towards Viri and Malliana as if he were a puppet master manipulating them by invisible strings. Prompted by his gestures, the creatures whirled and swooped towards the women.

Icy fingers seemed to penetrate through their flimsy garments, probing at their skin and their cavities, searching every crevice of their being. In a lifetime of erotic excess, Viri had never felt so probed and plumbed; a cold sweat broke out on her brow, and for a moment the room reeled around her. Then the probing stopped. She looked at her mistress; her face was even whiter than usual.

Golon smiled thinly. "Very interesting," he murmured. Then, at a snap of his fingers, the black vapours whirled into a ball, then disappeared into the folds of his cloak. A shaft of dim light had now appeared in the far wall. Viri realised that it was an ever-widening gap between two blocks of stone; she could hear the low grating sound as they were winched back.

In the room behind stood a dais with a throne set on it, the backrest a maze of Gothic spires and barnacle-like encrustations, handrests carved in the shape of entwined serpents, a chair of human skulls serving as the seat. A pannier burned close to the foot of the throne, throwing the face of the man sitting on it into a gaunt relief. The eyes were recessed and hooded, the dome-shaped skull perfectly bald, marked only where liver spots dappled the pure white. The lips a kind of purple blue, the chin utterly hairless, gleaming with a white pallor. The hands seemed physically thin and weak but Viri noticed how the fingers nevertheless clutched the armrests with a prehensile strength. A look of nervous energy and alertness informed the face as if an unquenchable fever burned behind the eyes, an impression reinforced by the eyes themselves which gleamed a dull red in their dark sockets.

Viri needed no introduction, though she had never seen him before: this was Lord Faran Gaton Nekron, High Priest of the Temple of Worms at Thrull, crusher of Illgill's crusade, the erector of the pyramid of fifty thousand skulls on the marshes. Some men spoke of Faran as being 150 years old, some two hundred: no one knew the truth save him.

He leant forward to take in the two women in a look which burned with menace. As he did so, a faint odour wafted to their nostrils, ill disguised by the scented wood burning on the pannier. The reek of death: of turpentine and tar and preserving liniments; what at the beginning of history had been used in the mummy's embalming room was now the stuff which patched up and preserved the decaying fabric of the Dead in Life. Viri flinched away, but noticed that her mistress's expression had not changed. She struggled to keep her own emotions in check.

Malliana bowed low before the throne, a compliment returned by Faran with only the slightest inclination of his head. Viri, too, abased herself, wondering in the pregnant silence which ensued which of the two would speak first. When she dared look up again she realised that Faran had been staring intently at Malliana for several seconds, a wry smile beginning to play over his desiccated features as if he had learned something in their silent exchange.

And it was as if this knowledge now prompted him to speak, the voice somewhat croaky and dry, strange clicks issuing forth from the parched epiglottis in the middle of sentences.

"You have come to tell me you have lost the girl," he said.

Malliana cleared her throat. "The girl has gone, abducted, and the temple is in flames, attacked by the Brethren . . ." Faran held up a hand, silencing her.

"The Brethren will not be stopped tonight, or tomorrow, or the next day. The gong has been sounded, the gong that gives this city in perpetuity to the hands of the dead. Don't tell me of your temple: think of your fate. Think how ten thousand of the Brethren will hunt every drop of blood tonight; think how many drops flow in your veins; how many bites it will take before you die! After all, it is only a fitting punishment for what you've done." Malliana was about to reply, but he held his hand up again, silencing her.

"But first, the girl: if she is dead, priestess, remember what I just said: count each drop of your blood, and, for each drop, then count the pain you will suffer!"

His words were almost too much for the women, both of whom were shaking uncontrollably, but Malliana finally found her tongue, and, in faltering tones, began to describe as best she could the events of the night, beginning with Faran's message, her talk with Thalassa, the two intruders, the hideously scarred face of one of them, then the appearance of the man who called himself Jayal Illgill.

Faran interrupted at this. "Illgill? Are you sure?"

"Yes, he came for Thalassa."

Faran turned to Golon. "So, it seems Illgill's whelp has been in Thrull all this time, making fools of us."

Golon stirred uneasily. "My lord, there are plenty of rumours, people who were robbed by someone they said looked like Illgill, but this is the first time we've had confirmation . . ."

Faran cursed. "If only we knew where he was now . . ."

"But I know where he went."

Both men stared at Malliana, who, emboldened by her knowledge, had interrupted. "Where?" Faran asked.

"My lord, there is the matter of my temple, my women . . ."

"I told you—it's too late for them. Now, if you want to live, tell me where Illgill is!"

Malliana's face sank. "Weebil's Inn," she whispered. "I saw him going there not half an hour ago."

Faran got rapidly to his feet. "We must get him before the Brethren find him. Then I will fetch Thalassa and the others. I know where they'll be going: spies have been watching the rebels these last few days. You," he said, pointing at Malliana, "will come too. I needn't mention the consequences if this story of yours is a lie."

He clapped his hands: attendants came running from the darkness and he issued a whirlwind of orders. The men departed as quickly as they'd arrived, Golon going with them.

Malliana and Viri were left alone in the gloom with Faran.

Viri was surprised to see Malliana sink to her knees in a supplicatory manner. She had never seen her mistress abase herself in any way in all her years at the temple. The sight scared her almost as much as everything which had gone before.

"Lord," the High Priestess began quaveringly, "we wouldn't have rung the gong if we'd known . . . spare us."

Faran stared at her impassively for a while before replying.

"Thrull will die tonight, but, if Thalassa and Illgill's son are captured, then, and only then, you might live, priestess."

Now Faran lapsed into silence, a silence which lasted several minutes until they heard footsteps in the anteroom outside. The doors grated open and Golon appeared.

"Well?" Faran asked, arching a brow.

Golon shrugged: "Weebil and his men are dead. Some were killed in a fight, others by the Brethren who got there before us. There was no sign of Illgill. No one without sorcery will survive outside tonight. The streets are thronged with the risen dead."

Faran turned to Malliana. "So, lady, there is no proof that Illgill was there."

Malliana's jaw quivered. "I told you: I saw him as clearly as I see you. First in the temple, then going up to the Spike."

"We'll wait and see whether you've told me the truth. First you'll help me get Thalassa back." He turned to Golon. "Tell all the guards to turn out."

"And what of the Brethren? I had trouble enough getting to the Spike: there will be even more of them now." There was real fear in Golon's voice.

"Your sorcery will have to keep them back until I have a chance to address them. They will obey me," Faran answered, rising imperiously from his throne as he did so, thus silencing further debate. He strode towards the entrance of the chamber. Golon followed, pushing Malliana and Viri in front of him.

CHAPTER TWENTY-SIX

The Lightbringer

The fog and darkness were punctuated every few feet by the glow of the moon shining down between the overhanging roofs of the city. Urthred and his party had been hurrying downhill for twenty minutes or more, their hands often having to do the part of eyes in guiding their way. They were breathless and barely able to continue, but at least they were safe. They had not stopped to light a lantern or a torch during their flight: either would have been like a beacon for the undead. The flames from the burning Temple of Sutis and red glow of the Hearth Fire illuminating the sky above them were the only indication that their direction was to the south—away from the centre of the city, towards the Lower Town.

Urthred had taken up a position at the rear of the other four: Seresh and Alanda led the way; Thalassa was leading Furtal along just in front of him.

He wished that instead of being at the back he had been at the front of the party. Now, when the fog and darkness allowed it, he couldn't avoid seeing Thalassa. Her body moved in and out of the bands of moonlight like a wraith's. Worse, he daren't take his eyes off her: for long periods she and Furtal were all that he could see. If he broke off contact for a second, he might find himself blundering down the wrong fog-choked alleyway, utterly lost. But, though he could barely bring himself to admit it, it was not mere necessity which kept his eyes glued to her body. The attraction he had felt to her at the temple had not been utterly dissipated by the dangers of the night. As they entered another patch of moonshine, he once more drank in the lines of her limbs outlined by the light through her thin dress. All rational thought seemed to desert him as he looked at her. She seemed a vision from another world, a faery cast down by a moonbeam to beguile the human race. And with the sight of her body came the memory of the touch of her skin. So strong was the sensation that it was as if he were back in her room again, the tips of her breasts touching him just below the heart, the small mound of her belly pressed against his groin . . .

As quickly as he had these thoughts, he fought them off. He was forgetting who he was: a priest of Reh. Besides, he was still distrustful of Thalassa's role in what had happened earlier in her chamber. It seemed to him that she had gone along with the High Priestess's plan with rather more enthusiasm than was necessary. He had to remember her profession, tell himself that enticement was this woman's way of life. He had nearly fallen, made a fool of himself, when years of asceticism had built up his defences against the ties of the flesh. . . .

And yet, his attempts to steel himself against her were futile. There was clearly a quality, a nobility in Thalassa which belied what she had later become. It had surfaced the minute she had left the temple grounds. She bore herself like a princess, her back erect, not bowed like a slattern's, her head held up high, her gaze, though demure, direct and unashamed.

Desire and duty pulled him in contrary directions. It was true what men wrote: one only desired that which was unobtainable. And for him to desire Thalassa was doubly impossible. First, there was his vow of celibacy. But second, even if he denied his vows, what woman would ever look upon his scarred face without revulsion? Now he had Manichee's mask back on his face, any woman would at least have a preview of what lay beneath.

At dawn, he reflected, things would be clearer. By then they might have escaped the city. He would be free to go—perhaps he'd return to Forgeholm, forgetting Manichee's words in the vision, of the lands of the north and his destiny there. Never again would he have to see Thalassa and her other companions.

Yet even this thought gave him a perverse pang: he wanted to be away from this woman and temptation; in the half hour since he had been with her, a new world had opened up to him; a world with an irresistible attraction that once glimpsed could not be denied. Attraction, revulsion: his mind was like a magnet forced from one pole to another.

All the time he found his eyes locked on the luminous white of Thalassa's skin in the gentle glow of the moon through the mist.

So preoccupied was he that Urthred nearly ran straight into the object of his scrutiny when she suddenly stopped. In front the mist had cleared slightly. Seresh had halted where their current alleyway descended sharply into a roadway running across it. He urgently waved his hand backwards and they quickly darted into the shadows of the doorways to either side.

Then Urthred heard voices, moaning softly, followed by the sound of shambling feet dragging slowly along the street running in front of them. A dozen or more of the undead emerged from the mist, coming down the street at right angles to their alleyway. They were already only thirty feet away, so close that he could see every detail: their faces were white and haggard in the moonlight, their teeth bare and yellow and dripping with saliva, their graveclothes in rags revealing jutting rib cages and bone-thin limbs. There were too many for Urthred and the others to fight off. He pressed back into the shadows of the doorway. They got closer and closer: so close that they must scent the living blood of the hiding humans. He remained utterly still as the undead stopped at the foot of the alley and peered up it, sniffing at the air, scenting it like hounds on a trail.

He held his breath, his bones chilled with fear.

Then it happened.

He sensed the noise of the gong before it reached them, a curious humming that grew and grew in intensity until it filled all thought to the exclusion of everything else, a sound that seemed to echo off one side of his skull and then the other and back again. He hunched down in the shelter of the doorway, helpless to stop the successive waves of sound from battering his ears.

Wave after wave, until his breathing stopped and he felt he was drowning in it. He twisted from side to side, unable to escape his torment. Only after half a minute or so did he remember to open his mouth and take in a great gulp of air. The effort eased the pressure on his eardrums slightly, but only a little. Just as he thought the noise would never stop, the power of the sound began to fade, then ebb slowly away as it dissipated on the night air. It left a ringing silence behind in which the very stones of the buildings seemed to hum like tuning forks.

Then that disappeared too and the flat silence of the fog-bound city returned.

For a second or two, Urthred had forgotten the vampires. He got quickly to his feet, bringing his gloves up in front of him; if they were coming he would take some of them with him.

But instead of their footsteps, there was only silence from the alleyway. He risked a glance out of the shadows of the door-way.

The place where the vampires had been was now empty. The only person visible was Seresh, who was peering out of another doorway on the other side of the street. As he, too, saw the coast was clear, he left his hiding place, gesturing for the others to do the same. They met in the centre of the alleyway, each apparently as wild-eyed with relief as Urthred. Even now the ringing had stopped, he still felt the aftershock of its echo in his ears.

"What in Hel's name was that noise?" he whispered so quietly that he could barely hear himself.

"It saved us, whatever it was. The undead have gone," Seresh said.

Furtal shook his head, his habitual cheerful look replaced by solemnity. "They will have gone to the Temple of Worms. Someone has rung Iss' gong."

"Iss' gong?" Urthred repeated.

Furtal nodded his head: "For all the years I have lived in this city, I have heard rumours of it. A gong that could summon the dead back to life, but which must be rung by a human hand."

"But what human would be mad enough to ring it?"

"Someone has," Seresh said, breaking in. "But at least it lured away the undead."

"There will be more of them; many more," Furtal replied grimly.

"Then we better hurry," Seresh said. He pointed at the sea of fog covering the Lower Town below them. "I'm going forward to scout—stay here for the moment." He drew his sword and slowly crept to the junction of the lane in front. He glanced back once, then disappeared into the mist.

Urthred took Furtal's arm and stepped back into the doorway in which he'd hidden from the vampires. Alanda and Thalassa were just visible on the other side of the street. They were talking quietly as they went through the contents of their travelling packs, which they'd just taken off their shoulders. They started pulling out warm clothes to protect themselves from the damp chill of the air. Urthred watched with a pang as Thalassa covered her beautiful back with a shawl.

He had been so taken up with the spectacle that it surprised him when Furtal spoke: "A close escape."

Urthred nodded noncommittally, his eyes still fixed on Thalassa.

"What time is it?" the old man asked. Urthred looked up at the moon glowing through the mist. It was difficult to tell how far it had moved across the sky, but by its position he guessed it to be two hours before midnight. He told the old man this.

"Ah, midnight!" Furtal breathed. "What will happen between now and then?"

"To know that, one would have to know the future," Urthred replied.

"Then we must listen to Alanda," Furtal said, nodding in the direction of the women. "She has the sight; she will help us if she can."

"The sight? You mean she can see the future?" Urthred answered, looking across at the old lady. He was pretty sure that neither of the women could hear the conversation on this side of the street, but he had lowered his voice to a whisper.

"Yes, and the past—nothing is hidden. I think she's been waiting for you," Furtal said cryptically.

"Why, because she was a friend of my brother's?"

"No, because she foresaw your coming. She believes that you and the girl have a destiny."

"An amusing thought: but don't forget that I am a priest and the girl is a . . ."

"A whore." The old man smiled, supplying the word that had stuck in Urthred's throat. "See—it doesn't trouble me to say it."

Urthred glanced nervously across the street. The two women continued to sort through their packs as if they hadn't heard. "You seem to know a lot," Urthred said flatly.

"I was once more than a musician at a bawdy house."

Just then there came an impatient hiss from farther down the street, and there was Seresh emerging from the mist. He gestured for them to join him.

They slipped out of the shadows. Seresh motioned them to silence. "Something strange is happening," he whispered. "Listen!" Urthred's mind had been occupied by his conversation with Furtal, but now he heard what Seresh had heard. A faint sound from below: a stony rumbling, as of gratings being thrust aside, stone doors being pushed down. The cobblestones under their feet moved slightly with the vibration.

"The gong has worked its magic," Alanda said. "Even the dead who have lain for thousands of years are waking."

"How many are there?" Thalassa asked.

"All those who worshipped Iss in the past; all those who did not wish to be quit of this life, but refused the final viaticum which would have despatched their souls to the Prince's Purple Halls. All these will rise."

"Thousands?"

"Thousands upon thousands," she replied grimly.

"Let's hurry then," Seresh said. "There's still time before they reach the streets."

He led them off down a side alley, at the same reckless pace as before, the buildings to either side a passing blur through the fog. The noise of the underground movement diminished the farther they got from the summit of the city. Down and down they went, the alleyway almost doubling back on itself as it descended the cliff face. Urthred tried to recall how long it had taken him to climb to the temple square from the gate. Half an hour? If so they must nearly be back at the bottom of the cliffs.

As if on cue, the steep gradient suddenly eased and they

found themselves on the flat. The houses around them, what could be seen of them, leant at crazy angles, their foundations having sunk into the marsh ground surrounding the granite cliffs. The fog was thick and dead. Not a stirring of wind. In the silence, Urthred thought he heard something behind them—a boot scraping on cobblestones? He turned, but there was only the mist and the darkness, sucking up all light, all movement.

They continued along the street, the alleyway curving around the bottom of the cliff face, the houses fading from view to their right as if on that side there now lay an open space.

Then there came a breeze, a gentle push of wind that whisked away the blanket of fog for a moment, revealing what had been concealed from view.

Vine-covered crumbling walls, broken gates, gravestones stretching off into the distance, where the crumbling towers of the outer city walls loomed in the fog.

The City of the Dead.

The place where they buried the bodies of those not dedicated to Reh or Iss, and the last resting place of Marizian. The inky mass of the founder's pyramid tomb could be seen half a mile away, abutting the outer walls. Even from this distance, the tomb looked enormous, easily dwarfing the temple pyramids of Reh and Iss in the citadel. In it Illgill had discovered the Rod, which had ultimately wrought destruction on Thrull and which had caused Manichee's damnation. A dangerous place, yet one which exerted an almost magnetic pull on Urthred as he looked at it. No one in the company had told him that this was their ultimate destination, but he had known it would be Marizian's tomb: hadn't Manichee shown him it in the vision?

But they were not going there immediately. Seresh was leading them off to the left towards the row of broken-down houses at the base of the cliff. There was a narrow fissure in the granite cliff face between two of the buildings. If Urthred had been alone, he would have missed the entrance, which was only indicated by a moss-covered sun symbol carved over its lintel. At one stage the doorway had evidently been higher, but, like the buildings around, it seemed to have gradually slipped downwards into the all-consuming marsh. Seresh stooped under its lintel without hesitation. Alanda, Thalassa, then Urthred and

Furtal followed. Inside, a tinderbox was scraped and a spark caught on the end of a pitch torch which burst sullenly into life, throwing the low corridor into a medley of dancing yellow light and dramatic shadows. The air smelt musty and unused. Seresh quickly lit another torch from the burning end of his and handed it to Alanda.

"What place is this?" Urthred asked.

It was Alanda who answered. "We call it the Lightbringer's Shrine. You know the *Book of Light* and the prophecies. The people of Thrull over the centuries believed that the Lightbringer would first be revealed here. But, since the war, not many come here to lay offerings at the shrine. We'll be safe here till midnight."

"What then?"

It was Seresh who answered this time. "Some friends of ours will come. We will go with them to Marizian's tomb."

So Manichee had spoken truthfully again. But he still wanted to know why his brother had risked everything for the tomb—was it for the objects of power that Manichee had told him about? Surely he'd said there was nothing buried there now?

"What will we do there?" he asked.

"There is something we have to find. The men who are coming have opened a way into the tomb."

It was as if Urthred had heard that they were intent on dousing the Hearth Fire in the temple. "But that's heresy!" he exclaimed. "Marizian was the founder of our religion."

"Baron Illgill dug there and took out an artefact. We're only doing the same. It's our last hope."

Now Alanda spoke again. "It may be so; but the priest is right: meddling with the past brought disaster on the city once before."

Seresh's face flushed in the torchlight. "We argued about it before. The remaining Hearth Brethren agreed to it, including this man's brother, Randel."

Urthred nodded his head slowly. Randel must have had good reasons to approve the plan, he reasoned. He was not going to question his dead brother's motives now.

"Let's go to the shrine," Seresh said, seeing that there was no further protest. He set off up the passageway, followed by Thalassa and Furtal.

Urthred was about to follow Seresh when the old woman snaked out a hand, stopping him.

He turned to face her and was once more struck by the amazing depths of her blue eyes, alien and frightening in their intensity.

"What is it?" he asked nervously.

She looked at the others disappearing up the corridor, making sure they were out of earshot before speaking. "You talked to Furtal back where we stopped, didn't you?"

He nodded.

"I know that you were talking about me, about my having the sight. Do you believe I have it?"

Anyone looking into those unsettling blue eyes would be hardpressed to believe that this woman didn't have some power beyond that of normal people. Urthred simply nodded again.

"Then listen to what I have to say."

"But the others will be at the shrine by now," Urthred protested, anxious to get away.

"It is as I intended—the girl must see for herself."

"See what?"

Alanda smiled enigmatically. "Tonight the shrine will be different from how it normally appears—quite transformed, in fact."

"And you have seen this without actually going there?"

"Yes, as Furtal says, I've seen the future. But the girl hasn't. She doesn't know what's waiting for her."

"Why didn't you tell her, if these visions are so certain?"

"So she can form her own opinion of what she sees. If I'd told her, she wouldn't have believed that what's waiting is for her."

"You speak in riddles—what has been waiting for her?"

"Come, priest. I know you spoke with Count Durian. Didn't he tell you of the prophecies, of his divinations?"

"A little."

"It is seven years to the day that Thrull fell: on this day the Lightbringer will be revealed."

"He told me that, but I can't see how some art as inexact as prophecy could be so accurate."

"You may doubt, priest, but the prophecies are based on the Scripture you follow: the *Book of Light*."

"But what has this got to do with Thalassa?"

"She is the Lightbringer."

"Her?" Urthred said incredulously. "A common whore? Now I've heard it all!"

"Scoff as much as you like—you will see!" There was a flash of anger in Alanda's blue eyes.

Urthred was not so easily put off. "Reh teaches us that we must keep from the sins of the body, lest our immortal flame be ever extinguished in its damp lusts. The girl has given herself a thousand times: how can she be one of the God's Elect?" He was conscious that he had raised his voice.

But Alanda's anger seemed a match for his. "Don't be too pure, priest—I know you were tempted by her."

Did she really read minds or was she just an accomplished guesser? "She used a whore's tricks," he said shortly.

"You show your heart in your anger, priest—your mask doesn't hide anything."

How true, Urthred thought; truer than she could have guessed.

Then Alanda smiled, a secret smile, her anger suddenly gone, as if she knew she would eventually persuade him that what she was telling him was true.

"Come," she said, "you'll see." She set off down the corridor, lighting the way with the torch. Urthred followed, only slightly mollified, but nevertheless intrigued as to what lay at the end of the passage.

The tunnel had rough stone walls carved deep into the granite. The floor had a slight incline and Urthred guessed that they were heading towards the granite core of the mountain. Maybe it was part of the system of ancient tunnels that riddled the interior of the massif. Perhaps, if he followed it long enough, the tunnel would take him back to Stick's Hole, and the strange creatures that lived there. But unlike the earlier journey with Seresh, the atmosphere of this part of the underworld seemed almost benign. The chill of the outside was swiftly being replaced by a gentle warmth which seemed to seep up from the very depths of the earth itself.

As he went farther along the passage, the unease which had plagued every footstep that he had taken in the city that evening slowly evaporated. Each stride took him farther from his pursuers, the undead and the sinister mist. Here, deep under the granite massif, everything seemed safe and secure.

As if in confirmation of this feeling of well-being, he could now see a golden glow emanating from the end of the tunnel ahead. As they approached, the dazzling light became even more intense until, after a few more steps, the tunnel abruptly gave way into a larger chamber.

They found the others standing at its entrance. The chamber was some fifty feet square and fifty feet high. It was bathed in golden light, a golden light which was given added refulgence by the gold shrine which lay at its end.

The shrine seemed to be made of precious metal, but in the dazzling light it was difficult to see whether it had physical form, or was merely an insubstantial vision from another world. It was constructed like an altar, with an altarpiece made of glowing panels from which the light itself seemed to blaze. The outline of images on the panels could be dimly seen through the glow. Pastoral scenes of men and beasts gambolling in golden fields and forest glades, shepherds taking their rest at the foot of a golden waterfall, mountains crowned with shining palaces. At the top a many-pointed sun symbol blazed in glory, irradiating the chamber with coruscating light.

But this was not the only thing strange about the room. Its floor and the foot of the altar were covered with a swarming mass of life—every conceivable creature, obviously drawn here by the light: snakes, frogs, birds, mice and rats, domestic cats and dogs—whatever ran loose in the city—all were here, and though many of the mammals were half-starved and mangy not one turned upon its natural prey, but stared, pacified, at the blazing star.

And not only physical creatures had come here; fiery shapes moved through the air like fireflies, winnowing back and forth, assuming myriad different shapes.

Seresh, Thalassa and Furtal stood before the golden light, as mesmerised by the spectacle as the creatures were.

Urthred glanced down at the gnarled branch that the Leech-gatherer had given him. It, too, burned with the golden light. As he watched, a small bud sprouted from a knot on its dead surface, then put forth a delicate leaf. He glanced at the others to see if they had noticed it, too, but they were too enraptured by the great spectacle all around them. After a few seconds he found his tongue.

"What does it mean?" he asked in a hushed whisper.

"These creatures and spirits are awaiting the arrival of the Lightbringer," Alanda answered calmly, seemingly less affected by the spectacle than any of the others, as indeed she must have been, if she'd foreseen it as she'd told Urthred.

"But yesterday the shrine didn't glow," Seresh said.

Alanda turned to Urthred, a small look of triumph on her face. "You know the *Book of Light,* priest: what does it say about the second time of darkness?"

" 'Seven years' subjection under those who hate the sun; Seven years of darkness before the redeemer comes.' "

The lines slipped from his lips before he had even thought of them. Of course. The words which he had never paid particular attention to among the thousands of others in the *Book of Light* suddenly came to his mind unwittingly, with the clarity of a prophecy realised before his very eyes.

What were the other verses?

Look for the Herald before the dawn:
He walks in darkness, without a face,
Yet all will know him when he comes.

A thrill ran through his body—"the Herald"—the code name his brother had given him in his letter!

Seven years to the day had passed since darkness had descended on Thrull.

A man, without a face, who walked in darkness, hidden from the sun by his mask, had come to the city . . .

"I can see the glow!" Furtal exclaimed, breaking in on Urthred's thoughts. He was reaching out a hand towards the

light source. Thalassa had relinquished her hold on the old
man's arm and stepped forward to where a small white mouse
had approached the hem of her dress. She tentatively bent and
petted it. The animal showed no sign of unease at this, suffering
the petting as if it were used to the touch of a human hand.

"Surely the Lightbringer will be here soon," Seresh muttered, in an apparent daze.

Alanda didn't reply—she, too, was lost in thought, gazing at
Thalassa.

"Perhaps the Lightbringer has already come," she murmured, but so quietly that Urthred was sure that only he could
have heard her.

"Will the spirits speak?" he asked her, nodding his masked
head at the glowing forms.

She shook her head. "No, these are creatures of the Flame.
They have no body or tongue. They follow the streams of fire
deep underground like fish in the deep currents of the ocean.
They go where the earth is pure fire and has not changed since
the world began in an explosion of flame millennia ago. They
are beyond our nature, and our understanding."

As they watched, the flickering forms began to congregate
around Thalassa, coming closer and closer in a whirling cloud
until they touched the hem of her skirt with fiery hands. But
there was no heat or burning. She stood slowly, the forms
whirling about her, throwing strange patterns of light over her
face and body. Then the spirits cloaked her in a sheen of pure
gold that was almost unbearable to look at, so dazzling was it.
Urthred averted this gaze. Yet Alanda, standing next to him,
drank in the spectacle in front of her, her old face suddenly
made young by the light. She turned to him, the triumphant
look in her eyes once more. Urthred glanced from her to Thalassa. Alanda had been right: the girl was transformed; it was as
if this place had been waiting for her presence all these years.
Thalassa was turning slowly, admiring the blazing light on her
clothes, the light coruscating as she moved.

They might have remained staring at Thalassa for hours, but
suddenly the sound of footsteps running up the corridor behind
them made them all snap out of their reverie back to the world
outside and its dangers. It was as if a spell had been broken.

They turned as one to the entrance to the chamber, the spirits whirling away from Thalassa at the sudden movement, skittering away to the other side of the room.

Two torches bobbed into view at the far end of the corridor. Two men appeared behind them. Their cloaks were matted with dirt, and their unshaven faces glistened with sweat. They both held swords in their free hands.

"Gadiel and Rath!" Seresh exclaimed, relaxing slightly.

The men were two of those who had been with Zaraman in the City of the Dead. They skidded to a halt at the chamber entrance, looking about with wild eyes momentarily dazzled by the light. They didn't even appear to notice the horror of Urthred's mask.

"Where are the others?" Seresh asked, taking a step towards them. "Where is Zaraman?" The men glanced at one another and then back at Seresh, as if unwilling to speak.

Alanda spoke. "Tell us," she asked Gadiel gently. "Where are the others?"

"Dead," the man called Gadiel said, swallowing hard. Urthred noticed for the first time that what he had taken to be lines of sweat running down his grime-streaked face were actually tears.

"Dead?" Seresh asked. "How can that be?"

Gadiel stared at the chamber wall, his head slowly shaking from side to side. "We had dug down to the tomb entrance, as we had been told. But Zaraman wasn't happy leaving it at that—he wanted to see what was farther on behind the entrance. We tried to argue him out of it—but he broke down the stone slab." He closed his eyes, as if not able to bear the memory of what followed. "We'd only got a little way along when . . ." He shook his head.

Rath now spoke. "There was an explosion—only Gadiel and I escaped." He, too, lapsed into an uncomfortable silence.

Urthred turned to see what impression these words had had on his companions. Thalassa held her head in her hands. Urthred, with a pang, saw tears welling from between her fingers. The spirits had returned to her, but now moved round her with less celerity than they had displayed a few moments before, as if their sluggishness mirrored her despair.

Urthred turned to Seresh. "What did you hope to find in the tomb?"

Seresh's face was downcast, and he only answered slowly. "Marizian was buried with three great artefacts. Illgill took one of them: a Rod that was said to have the power to open the way between this world and Shades. It was lost when he fled to the north. There were once two other items in the tomb. A metal warrior mightier than anything that has lived . . ."

"Its name was Talos," Urthred broke in, remembering the books that Manichee had left for him at Forgeholm. He held up his gloves. "My master Manichee modelled these on its hands."

Seresh nodded. "Manichee knew many things. But the Talos also is lost to us. Centuries ago during a violent thunderstorm the Talos burst from the tomb and disappeared. No man could follow it, for it was so swift that a galloping horse could not keep pace with it. Nor could any man bind it because of its strength. Like the baron, it went to the north, to the Nations. It has never been heard of since."

"You spoke of a third item?"

"Aye, a sword called Dragonstooth, forged from the metal tooth of one of the fiery beings that ruled this world before our race came from the skies. It is indestructible, and its cut is pure venom; it will burn a man to the bone. Millennia ago the tomb was breached by the Worm. It was they who took the sword. But, being a thing of the Flame rather than the Worm, it was inimical to them. Not being able to use it, they took it to a place far to the south, the fortress of a mighty wizard who has kept it safe from human hands for many years."

"Then there is nothing left in the tomb?"

"No, one thing remains—the key to all three of the other items. It is some form of scrying device that will reveal the location of all of the items, wherever they are in the world. It's name is the Orb."

"Your father spoke of it," Urthred said.

"It will tell us where the three artefacts are. We will find them, and, once we have them, we will rise up and crush the Worm!"

"You seem confident of their powers."

"You have read the books, priest: Marizian only brought

three objects to the dwellings of men, but with them he made the world as we know it—governed giants and trolls and dwarves; bent the very rocks of this mountain to his will; opened congress with the world beyond—can you doubt their power?"

"No—only whether a man is wise to meddle with them," Urthred replied, thinking of Manichee, cursed to wander Shades until the end of time.

"We have no option but to use them," Seresh said, his jaw set. "The Worm's armies reach from the High Plains of Valeda, where they camp outside the Hidden City, to the borders with Surrenland. Soon Galastra will fall and the Southern lands as well."

"The Worm's time has come," said Gadiel, reinforcing Seresh's point. "But there are so few of the Flame left—who will harness the powers of these devices, even if we can find them?"

"Randel sent for his brother," Rath said, nodding at Urthred. "We all heard the stories, how his powers were equal to Manichee's."

Now Seresh turned to Urthred. "It is said that if Manichee had used the Rod at the battle of the Plains, the day would have been ours—do you know anything of this?"

Urthred thought again of Manichee's damnation and shook his head, though, unlike Seresh, he knew full well that the Rod had been used at least once: "My brother had great confidence in me, but he never saw my magic. As for whether I or you or anyone else can use these three artefacts of Marizian's: that will have to be seen when we have them in our possession."

"But you have the knowledge—you are a pyromancer, like Manichee?" Seresh persisted.

"My powers are not a hundredth of what my master's were," Urthred replied, conscious now that the whole company was staring at him.

"So what are your powers?" Seresh asked.

"I have my faith—the rest is given me by Reh, when the time is right," Urthred said, looking round at the others.

"Then pray the good god gives you it when you most need

it, for the next few hours will be the most dangerous of your life."

"Are there magical devices protecting the tomb?" Urthred asked.

"Devices, creatures, traps," Seresh replied. "We don't know how many. The only person who knew the exact layout of the tomb was Illgill, and the knowledge was lost with him. Some say he hid a book with everything he knew somewhere in the city, but no one has been able to find it these last seven years."

"And my brother helped you?"

Seresh nodded. "He spent many hours with Zaraman and the others at the tomb, digging a new tunnel along the lines of the one Illgill excavated." His voice faltered. "But now there are only three of us left. . . ." He looked meaningfully at Urthred, evidently wondering whether he would join them.

A heavy silence fell over the group, as they realised the scale of the task in front of them.

But in contrast to their mood, the glow from the altar had grown and grown in intensity as the minutes had gone by, bleaching the chamber of colour so everything took on the sheen of pure gold.

Urthred looked at Thalassa: she seemed a golden statue of a young goddess, her eyes cast down in sadness, the spirits circling her head slowly, in respect for the golden tears which, like small beads of molten ore, ran down her cheeks. He stared so hard that he felt his eyes would never leave her.

"It is nearly midnight," Alanda said, breaking the silence that had fallen in the golden light, capturing even Gadiel and Rath in its spell.

Seresh nodded wearily. "It is time we left—though only three of us remain, we may still win through to the tomb."

Alanda shook her head. "No, Seresh; we will all go—whatever fate awaits there belongs to us all, not you alone."

"But you are old, and Thalassa . . ." He looked up at the girl. The light from the altar had begun to fade, and she had turned to face him. He had expected to find her as downcast as he, but the light had transformed her. Her whole being seemed irradiated with purpose and an inner light which belied the tears that beaded her cheek.

She spoke softly, but firmly. "We will all go, will we not, priest?" Urthred, too, had been stunned by the transformation. This direct appeal, the first words she had addressed to him since they'd left the temple, melted any of the suspicion which he still harboured about her previous actions. Before he knew he was doing it, he nodded his head, wondering how a creature so beautiful could contemplate the horror of his mask without flinching. She favoured him with a smile which seemed to send some of her own golden radiance to his heart.

"Furtal will come too: it will be all right—you'll see," she said. Her words seemed to comfort all of them.

No one spoke further; as if silently agreeing that there was nothing else for it, the others took one last look at the golden shrine, then filed from the room. Urthred hesitated for a moment, still unable to take his eyes from Thalassa. For the moment they were alone.

The golden light from the many-pointed star, the golden panes and the fiery spirits was now becoming muted, but her beauty still mesmerised him, piercing the eye slits of his mask, sending a tingling over the scar tissue of his face.

As if responding to the dying light, she stepped up to him, her eyes unperturbed by the horror of his mask, which must have seemed at cruel odds with the fading golden vision all around them.

"I'm sorry for what happened in the temple," she said. "The Iss mask confused me: I thought we'd been betrayed. If I'd known you were Randel's brother . . ."

Urthred held up a hand. "The fault was mine: I acted badly . . . I was tempted . . ."

She smiled. "It is human to be tempted, priest. But I'm sorry that it upset you. The Worm priests have none of the same scruples." To Urthred her smile seemed slightly enigmatic, as if, despite the transfiguration of the golden light of the shrine, the woman who had sold herself at the Temple of Sutis still shared the body of this goddess. The contrast set his mind reeling once more.

Thalassa reached up and touched him on the arm. The touch was electric, just as it had been in the temple. Then she brushed past him, leaving him alone in the shrine room.

The colours, once so golden, were now the bronze and copper of autumn. Shadows grew in the corners and the creatures carpeting the floor slithered away into them. As he watched, the fiery spirits melted into the rough rock walls and, with a final flash of glowing light which seemed to light up the rock from within, vanished.

Urthred turned and walked back down the corridor. His heart was heavy once more, confused by what he felt for Thalassa and filled with foreboding of what lay in front of them in the City of the Dead and Marizian's tomb.

CHAPTER TWENTY-SEVEN

The Man Whose Soul Was Grey

Two men had seen Seresh's band on its way to the City of the Dead.

The first of them had been amongst the tombstones since dusk. His name was Morula. He was one of the Worm acolytes, a fanatic willing to risk the night and the vampire's bite for the service of his god, and the chance of an everlasting Life in Death. He was the man that Furisel had seen during his own spying expedition on the excavations two nights earlier. Morula had arrived in the city a month before and had been pleasantly received at the temple. So pleased, it seemed, were the Elders of the temple with his devotion that they had given him this important job—this watch on Marizian's tomb. At first he had not queried why one of the more senior acolytes wasn't doing it instead of him. He had an unshakable faith in his superiors and had gone to his post willingly, seduced by the idea that, if he served faithfully, the Black Chalice would be his.

But night had succeeded night, out in the cold and damp, when the slightest sound in the suffocating fog might signal his end. His eyes had grown red and raw peering through the darkness. His heart had begun spasming painfully after the repeated climbs up the face of Marizian's pyramid to spy on the conspirators' excavation. Each dawn Morula had reported his findings to the skull-masked priests, but no offer of the Chalice had

come. Instead he had been sent back to his post in the City of
the Dead every evening without reward. Each night he had
dragged himself to his lonely perch on the side of the tomb.
And each night he had become more and more afraid, and more
determined that the next morning, when the Temple of Iss was
empty of life, he would slip away and return to his home in Surrenland and never see the graveyard again.

When the gong had echoed over the city, he hadn't known
what to do. His orders were to remain till dawn, but the noise
that swept down from the citadel was brutal, compelling, sending shock waves through the layers of mist like wind through
corn. Stunned, he'd scrambled down from his post and started
through the tombs towards the cliffs. He had had enough wits
left to hide himself when he'd heard the party heading towards
him through the mist. He watched them go past from the shadows, even caught a glimpse of Urthred's mask, which he mentally noted for his report. If he'd made it back to the temple,
there would be no doubt that Faran would have caught Urthred
and the others in the Lightbringer's Shrine and dragged them
back to the Temple of Iss.

But the acolyte never got as far as the temple.

A little way in his ascent, he heard the same underground
grating of stone that Seresh had heard earlier, and paused for a
moment, wondering what it meant. The fog was thick and damp
around him, and there was no telling where the noise was coming from. Then, along with the sulphur in the marsh air, he
sensed a new aroma.

The scent of mildew.

The fog blew away.

He was in a small square. There were hundreds of the undead around him, their winding-sheets trailing on the cobbles
as they silently came towards him. . . .

Morula was never heard of again after that night. But, then
again, neither were thousands of others.

The second man to have seen Seresh's group, and who had followed it ever since it had left the Temple of Sutis, was the other
Jayal Illgill, the Doppelgänger. He followed, marvelling that
the priest didn't turn round and see him there, but the man

seemed to be in a daze, unconscious of anything but the way ahead. This suited the Doppelgänger. He stopped when the party in front stopped for the undead, and when the noise of the gong washed over them. So focused was he on the task before him that he had barely registered the sound. His eyes had never left Thalassa: for years his revenge had been squeezed and concentrated so that the bitter grape of her destruction was all that would satisfy him. So many times he'd been to the Temple of Sutis and had received perverse pleasure from the High Priestess's refusals, caring little for the gold which he had wasted, or that he had been balked of what he had legitimately paid for. The High Priestess had suffered handsomely for her obduracy tonight; as for Thalassa, when he caught her, the frustration of his long wait would be offset by the realisation of his deferred pleasure many times over.

Now the party moved on, and the Doppelgänger became conscious of the undead stirring beneath the city streets: many more than he had ever known, and he had wandered these nighttime streets with impunity for seven years.

Unlike the other inhabitants of Thrull, the Doppelgänger had no terror of the undead. The dead only fed on Life. He was the opposite of Life—a thing of shadows. The undead could not even scent him; his blood was the opposite of what they craved. He passed through them as he did through the living, like a shadow—barely noticed, barely seen. Insidious yet all-powerful.

Thus, though he was alone, he followed the party without attention to the dangers that were growing all around, right to the mouth of the shrine at the edge of the City of the Dead. Here he stopped, noting the place, and resolved to return as soon as he could bring from the Silver Way the motley gang of men who served his needs in the city.

But on the second he thought this, and was in the act of turning on his heel, there came a sudden hiss from behind him, and he glimpsed, as he turned, saliva-streaked teeth framing a red mouth. A vampire had appeared out of the mists, its clawed hands stretching out to his neck as he flinched back. The thing teetered thus for a heartbeat or two, and for a split second the Doppelgänger thought that it would take even his poisoned blood. Its eyes bored into his single orb, trying to suck in his spirit with its mesmerism, trying, by its will, to make him part of its own dark desires.

But what it saw mirrored in the Doppelgänger's eye was a reflection of its own dark nature. It flailed ineffectually once or twice, then retreated back into the mists, whimpering like a dog.

The Doppelgänger laughed—a dry chuckle, a mirthless rattle at the back of his throat. He sensed other vampires around— but they, too, would be powerless to touch him. Only the blood of a living, breathing creature could give them sustenance and, though in outward appearance he was such, the vampires sensed, as surely as creatures sense poisoned food, that here walked a man whose soul was grey, whose breath of life had been extinguished, whose single blue eye encompassed a knowledge of death that even the dead could not command.

The Doppelgänger limped slowly through the streets of Thrull. He was now getting close to the house on the Silver Way. The roads were thronged with vampires, many more than he'd ever seen before. They approached him, plucking at his robes, simpering with excitement, but he brushed them aside as he would have brushed aside the hands of street urchins. They melted away into the darkness and the mist with disappointed cries. He had no scent, no existence that they could readily take. His thoughts were elsewhere: on the past, and on revenge. Revenge for his injured hand, and his hurt pride, revenge on the whore Thalassa, whom he owned, whom he had so nearly had within his power.

The mist-filled streets were dark; only the moon and the watchfires, unattended since dark, gave any light. The night was cold. Now he was nearly at the turnoff to the Silver Way. The darkness was full of movement; the smell of mildew and rot almost overpowering. He could hear vampires all around him, smashing down doors where they sensed living blood, letting out high-pitched shrieks of joy as they fastened onto new victims within.

For the first time the sheer number of them struck home. Why were there so many of them? Had it been the ringing of the gong? He watched as another victim was pulled bodily from the front door of a house. Surely there wouldn't be a living person left in Thrull by morning.

It was as he turned into the Silver Way that he saw the first of those that the vampires had already drunk dry. They were laid out on broken down doors as on trestles, like impromptu operating tables. And like the corpses left behind after the surgeon's art has failed, these too were white and drained of blood. But their wounds were confined to their necks: a mass of puncture marks. The Doppelgänger passed silently along the row of doors; then stopped abruptly as he heard his name called out feebly. He peered closely at the nearest body in the gloom. The bald, wizened head was recognisable even in the semidarkness: Furisel.

The man's face was white, and his throat bubbled with wounds, yet somehow he was still alive. As the Doppelgänger watched, his eyes opened once more and he looked up at his master. His eyes were glazing over and he was near death. The Doppelgänger knelt hastily, trying to catch the old man's words.

They were rambling, disconnected. It was as if Furisel had mistaken him for someone else. He was warning him not to go to the house on the Silver Way. It was too dangerous. He had warned him, back in the house . . .

A growing realisation came to the Doppelgänger. The old man's loyalties had changed. Something or someone had finally persuaded him that the Jayal Illgill he had served since the battle had not been the same man who had fought alongside him on the marshes. There was only one explanation—Jayal, the real Jayal Illgill, had returned: the man he had waited for for seven years.

And even as Furisel spoke a final word of warning and then choked slowly on his own blood, the Doppelgänger knew that his long wait was over: his other half was, at that moment, coming to the house in the Silver Way.

CHAPTER TWENTY-EIGHT

Shadow of My Shadow

Substance and shadow: both were very close now.

The moon was setting over the jagged-tooth peaks to the east in a red ball; the mists had risen to the city's heights. Jayal hid in the lee of the Illgill mansion, waiting. Sounds came to him from the streets outside—splintering wood, screams, the sound of shuffling footsteps in the Silver Way. He knew whose footsteps they were, and who occasioned the screams from the houses: since the gong had sounded, the undead had risen, generation upon generation, so the streets were thronged by revenants. He had fought his way here from the Spike. He'd been lucky: he'd met only one or two of them. Now it sounded as if the whole of the upper town was swarming with them.

Dragonstooth was concealed under his cloak; but though concealed, its light was still visible, shining even through the thick wool of the cloak as if it were only the flimsiest of garments. But the colour of the sword's light had changed: the fierce white fire that had burned from its blade earlier had been replaced by a coppery red glow, much like the colour of the setting moon.

Or blood.

Never before had the blade changed colour. Jayal wondered what it meant.

His heart was heavy with dread, filled with the memories of

the battle and the Rod. Whatever was waiting for him was part of that curse that Manichee had warned his father of in his headquarters tent. A mirror image of him? He shook off the idea. Maybe it was just an impostor after all; maybe Furisel had been lying. He wished that there was someone with him. Where was his old sergeant? But he already knew the answer to that question—Furisel had not been on his side, but on the side of this other, who now waited in the mansion. He had helped him only because Jayal had coerced him. He'd taken advantage of the first moment he was free of Jayal to sneak off. No doubt he had already warned the mansion's current occupant that he was on his way. If he was warned, Jayal thought grimly, so be it; this bloody gleam on the sword blade boded badly for those who stood in his way tonight.

But which way was best to enter? He scanned the ruined walls once again. Ahead was the inner courtyard of the building, its centre dominated by a statue which haunted his childhood dreams. The fiery demon Soron. Once its sculpted sides had been pointed with stony gouts of flame erupting from its skin, the artist capturing well the mad-eyed fury with which it stared at the struggling worm under its feet into whose neck it had plunged a fiery trident. But now the statue was overgrown and Faran Gaton's soldiers had done a thorough job of defacing it: the demon's eyes had been chiselled out, the trident broken at the hand, the fiery points ground to nothing. But the statue still held a half-life of menace as if all the mutilations could not destroy the avenging spirit which still lived in it.

Soron: the avenging spirit. Jayal knew the demon represented all that he lacked. Had it really taken six years to find Dragonstooth? Could he not have completed his task sooner? And if he had, how many more lives might have been saved? How much easier would it have been to find his father? Yet, even now, he delayed entering the mansion and dealing with this thing that had so disgraced the family name.

It was the past, he decided, the past and its memories which weighed him down. Earlier, when he'd stopped outside the gates with Cloud, it had been a small scruple that had restrained him from entering, a scruple about disturbing the ghosts of the past a minute before he had to. He had been so eager to get

away from this place with all its memories—finding Thalassa
had seemed an easier option.

He wouldn't be finding her now. In his heart, he knew Weebil had told him the truth. The thirteen-year-old child he had left
would now be nothing more than a streetwise drab, scabs and
sores covering her body, her eyes glazed over with Rak and
Lethe. She wouldn't even recognise him if she saw him, he
guessed. There was nothing left to wait for. Nothing, that was,
apart from the memories.

Seven long years to the day had passed since he'd left this
place on the morning of the great battle: he could remember the
streets in uproar, the gaudy pennants of the legions fluttering in
the breeze, the heavy wagons rolling over the cobblestones, the
tramp of the booted feet of the soldiers as all the fighting pride
of Illgill's army had spilled out onto Thrull plain to face the advancing hordes of the Worm. Then he'd been a prince from a
noble lineage: bowed to, deferred to . . .

Tonight he had returned like a thief, flitting into the city in
disguise, with the full ruin of what his father had done staring
him in the face.

He thanked Reh that he hadn't been in the city when it had
fallen. He must have already been in the Fire Mountains when
Faran's troops had finally broken down the gate and begun the
slaughter.

Maybe he should have died with the others who had fought
in the streets. For a while after the battle he had thought he'd
fled in cowardice. But now he knew the truth.

The battle. After the white light had flooded the tent with sorcerous fire he'd fallen unconscious, and his soul had journeyed
far, into the shadowland, or at least to its periphery. He remembered the creature arcing over the bridge of light towards him
and the collision of their bodies.

Then suddenly waking.

He had been lying on a blood-soaked litter, the funeral pyres
casting a deep red light over the interior of the tent. Outside he
heard the screams and clamour of the battle still raging. It was
as if he woke from a deep sleep; his limbs were heavy, his
blood slow in his veins. He wanted to slip back into uncon-

sciousness, but the hand shaking his shoulder had kept drawing him back. He'd forced himself to open his eyes once more.

There was his father, looking down, a curious, almost suspicious look on his black-browed face, as if he doubted the truth of what he saw before him on the litter. Guilty stirrings forced Jayal to try to sit up, but it was as if his limbs were not his own. He sank back exhausted.

His father continued to stare, and might have gone on doing so for a considerably longer time had not the jingle of hat bells announced that Manichee had returned to the tent.

"The enemy are rallying for another attack!" the Elder said urgently, though the sound of the bone horns from outside would have been warning enough.

The baron turned and looked at him for a moment without recognition, such was his state of stupefaction. Then he seemed to pull himself together.

"What of the body?"

"I carried it myself to the top of the pyre."

"Then light the pyre immediately!" The priest hesitated as the bone horns of the Reapers sounded once more, and a mighty call went up: the enemy attack was under way. He nodded his head slowly at father and son. Then he was gone.

But Illgill's attention was back on his son.

"Can you walk?" he asked.

Jayal nodded feebly; sensation was slowly creeping back into his limbs. Illgill helped him to his feet, where he wobbled precariously like a child learning to walk for the first time. Jayal had expected pain from the wounds to his head and his side, but there was none: he touched his hands to where the blows had been struck, but there was nothing, no feeling, as if the wounds had been covered by some nerveless tissue. All that was left was this terrible weakness in which sleep seemed as easy as breathing, and staying awake an impossibility. As these thoughts swept over him, his eyelids drooped. But duty still had a pull on him.

"I must return to my men . . ." he mumbled, staggering one step towards the flap of the tent before his knees buckled. The baron caught him.

"No, the battle is lost," he said in a hollow tone. Jayal slowly lifted his head to stare at him; had he heard aright?

The baron stared back at him. Jayal couldn't read his expression—the determination was still there, but also an unutterable sadness. "It's over: your men are dead. Only the Hearth Knights are left," the baron said. "There's one last thing I want you to do for me. Will you do it?" he asked, shaking Jayal's shoulders so his head flopped from one side to the other. The boy nodded feebly in reply.

Illgill helped him towards the back of the tent. It seemed to Jayal that he waded through a sea of molasses, each step only achieved with the greatest effort. His father's words came to him from a long way away.

"Your wounds are taken off, boy, by a great magic. Magic which may yet bring doom upon this house of ours. But it is done: never ask of it should we meet in this world again."

These words of death and defeat were so unlike his father that Jayal felt he must interject. "Not meet again, how so?" he asked weakly. The effort seemed too much, and he stumbled, but Illgill caught him and half carried him to the back of the tent. There was a ragged tear in the tent fabric where black fire had burned a man-sized hole. Illgill helped Jayal through it, stepping over a charred body as he did so. Outside, the noise and the evening chill woke Jayal slightly. Woozily, he noticed shadowy figures passing the tent, slipping off into the darkness in the direction of the causeway. The chink of abandoned weapons and armour harnesses told all too eloquently who these men were: deserters.

"You see," the baron said, nodding grimly after them. "The army's spirit is crushed, and with it the Flame is nearly extinguished." His eyes were filled with bitterness as he watched the men scurry away like rats. "I will fight and probably die; that is my duty. But you," he said, clamping his mailed fist to Jayal's shoulder, "you must live to finish the work we have begun here."

Jayal felt his throat constrict, struggling for words. All he could manage was a slight, affirmatory nod. "Good," said Illgill, clapping him once more on the shoulder. He gestured into the shadows. His ostler Hacer came forward leading Cloud, the baron's grey gelding; fifteen hands of thoroughbred war-horse, hung with its silver battle armour and its high, silver-studded saddle. Dark saddlebags hung down as low as its stirrups.

The horse nuzzled softly at Illgill's neck as Hacer led it up. A look much like a wound passed over Illgill's face at the horse's attention. He patted it once on its white-starred forehead in farewell. It was as if the animal understood the baron's gesture, for it whinnied slightly, shaking its maned head.

Hacer was now helping Jayal up into the saddle, while his father held the reins. Eventually Jayal was mounted, his mailed feet struggling to find their way into the stirrups.

Then the baron spoke again, but such was the clamour of the battle that Jayal had to lean forward over Cloud's withers to hear him.

"I have been a strict father, I know, but remember your trials have forged your spirit. You are my heir, a guardian of the Hearth, an Illgill!" His eyes blazed in the red of the corpse pyres. "Now, the final test." He pointed to the saddlebags. "Once you're safely away, read the documents in there. You will understand what you must do, and why you alone must do it."

He nodded towards the causeway across the marshes. "You must go to Hangar Parang."

"What is there?" asked Jayal in befuddlement.

"The papers will tell you everything," his father answered curtly.

But suddenly Jayal needed to know a lot more. He fought against his drowsiness. "What must I find there?" he repeated, his words coming as if in a dream.

The baron glared behind him at a roar from the battle lines: the enemy was getting nearer. He leant close, having to shout over the noise. "It is a sword of power, named Dragonstooth; its blade will cleave rock itself and no mortal can withstand its bite. Where you will find it is well detailed in the parchments, for it was taken there by the Worm in the Time of Darkness: find it and return." Another great cry came up from the battlefield, and the number of men running from the front line increased alarmingly.

A new note of urgency entered Illgill's voice. "I must return to rally the Guard." He pulled open the front of his black tunic. Something golden glowed there in the light of the blazing pyres. He lifted it over his head and motioned for Jayal to lean down farther. The young man did so and Illgill placed it around Jayal's neck. Only then could Jayal focus his eyes well enough to see what it was: a golden key.

"Guard this well," his father said. "When you have got the sword, however long it takes, return to Thrull, to my study. Look for a flagstone faintly marked with runes. Trace them with your fingers and you will see what you must do with the key."

"But what of you?"

"If I am alive, what you discover under the flagstone will tell you where I am gone and the best way of reaching me there. But don't come unless you come with the sword!" His expression and the roar of the battle as it came like surf upon the tents brooked no delay. Jayal held out a tentative arm and touched his father's shoulder lightly.

"I will return," he promised, sensing the hollowness of his words.

But his father had not heard him. "Now, Cloud, go like the wind!" he cried, slapping the gelding's hindquarters. The horse turned and set off at a gallop. Jayal hung on to the reins for dear life, his remaining strength focused on staying in the saddle as the gelding streaked over the sodden earth towards the causeway across the marshes, the fleeing soldiers peeling to left and right out of its way. Cloud reached the top of the causeway in two bounds, reared on its hind legs, so that for an instant Jayal caught a last glimpse of the black rock of Thrull, then turned and sped down the causeway.

They rode through the night, at first a gallop, then a canter, then a trot. The gelding was pretty well blown by the time they reached the foothills of the Fire Mountains and began the slow ascent. The fugitives had been left far behind, and with the coming of the dawn there was no sign of Faran Gaton's army either. As the grey light eased over the mountains, Jayal looked back towards Thrull. The plains were still covered in a thick mist, but the rock of Thrull thrust above it. A single column of black smoke rose up from the city, rose up and up, until it touched the cloud base.

Jayal noticed that snow was falling, though the season was early for it. He held out his hand. The snow was not cold to the touch and disintegrated as he kneaded it between his fingers. It was not snow, but ash from the burning city.

The key. He felt for it under his undershirt, checking that it was still there. It was his last connection to his father. Somewhere in his father's study, safe from any looters and the fire that had destroyed half the mansion, was the golden cage that the key would open. In it he would find what his father had left him. What it was, he had no idea. None of the papers he'd found in Cloud's saddlebags after he'd fled the battle gave him any clue. All he knew was that his father had planned it this way: that if the Flame lost the battle, he would send his son to the south for Dragonstooth, and that, if he returned, whatever it was that was waiting for him would help Jayal find him again.

Cloud had brought him back; though the horse was now old, it had made this last journey. Seven years to the day. Had his father known it would take so long? His attempts to wrest the sword from its owner had been arduous and full of danger. Days spent in dripping sewers under the mage's fortress, battles with creatures covered in slime that arose like nightmares before him. The battle with the sorcerer himself, the room filled with an unearthly fire that threatened to blind and burn him to the bone simultaneously.

Courage and an unflinching bravery had got him through that ordeal, a courage which had never left him until he had returned here, and memories once more flooded back, robbing him of his will.

Truly the past was the deadliest foe in the world, an enemy who could rob a man of all the courage which he had stored against its insidious pull.

Jayal realised he'd grown stiff crouching in his position by a fallen, weed-choked pillar. His eyes went back to the house, travelling over the facade, the half-remembered doors and windows. Any seemed a possible point of entry, but according to

Furisel, the place was crawling with the impostor's men. And no doubt, thanks to Furisel, they would be lying in wait for him. Crouching low, he made his way towards where a large oaken door leaned open drunkenly, its entrance overhung by tendrils of ivy. There he flung back his cloak, revealing the coppery red gleam of the sword. He glanced once at Erewon, setting over the roof of the mansion, then plunged into the darkness, the gleam of the sword his only illumination. There was a corridor running off to his left and right and a frayed tapestry hanging in moth-eaten shreds from a wall immediately in front of him. A rat scuttled away in the darkness. He stood still, getting his bearings: everything looked so different—the gloom, the smell of decay, the leaf-choked corridor.

The study was to the right, surely. He was just about to set off towards it when he heard a light rustling from the piles of leaves in the courtyard outside. He whirled round, but the only movement was the circling of the leaves on the flag-stones, caught in a momentary breath of wind. The blind statue of Soron stared back at him, as if daring him to go far-ther into the shadows of the mansion. His nerves were stretched as tight as lute strings as he set off into the darkness of the corridor. Ruined chests, weapons, armour stands with rusted cuirasses on them cluttered the way. Spiderwebs trailed over his face and hands; no one had been this way for a long time. It was several minutes before he saw another welcome glow of moonlight streaming into a much larger room ahead of him.

Jayal recognised it as the wood-panelled hall where his fa-ther had kept his court with the Hearth Knights of Thrull. Every important meeting that had ever taken place in the Illgill man-sion had occurred in this room, and the place had always been invested with a certain awe when he was a child. But now, in common with the rest of the building, a feeling of old time hung heavily in the air, the double doors in front of him hanging off their hinges at crazy angles, broken rotten floorboards scattered over the floor, leaving dark, gaping holes over which he had to step carefully. He edged into the room, emerging at the far end of the long hall. The scene was much as he remembered it: to his left a triple-arched window some thirty feet high overlooked the vast plain. The light of the setting moon poured through it. Below the windows, stretching towards him, was a long table, silvered with a thick coating of dust, with two huge, cobweb-covered candelabra at either end. The table was surrounded by high-backed chairs, many of them lying now in pieces on the floor. The largest chair was a thronelike structure at the window end where his father used to sit.

Twenty feet above him, along the other three sides of the room, ran an ornately carved gallery where musicians had once played. The minstrels' benches now stood empty in the moonlight. Underneath, framed by carved canopies of wood, were portraits of the Illgill family. The first had been painted when the hall had been built centuries before. The features of the ancestors staring out were lost in the gloom, and the varnish had blackened over the years, so the indistinct faces seemed skull-like, an appearance accentuated by those who had sacked the place seven years before: or like the statue of Soron outside, the portraits had been defaced, large holes having been carved where the sitters' eyes had once been. The eeriness of the hollow eyes was compounded by Jayal's knowledge that behind each of the panels lay a secret chamber in which the cremated ashes of each ancestor lay. At the far end of the hall, by the huge windows, was a door set into the wood panelling. Only those who knew it was there would be able to find it, so well concealed was it, but its location was fixed in Jayal's mind through a thousand exits and entrances that he had seen his father make through it in his childhood and young adult life. This was the door to the study, the place his father had told him to go with the key.

He stood uncertainly, creeping dread taking possession of his spine—where were the impostor's men?

Then he knew: something, someone was behind him. He whirled round.

And screamed.

Furisel stood behind the door, his dead eyes turned up in his head. Perhaps the sudden noise of Jayal's cry of alarm upset the delicate balance of the corpse, for it suddenly fell forward towards him.

He leapt back into the centre of the room, crashing into the table. The corpse fell with a dull thud and puff of dust onto the floor in front of him. It was then that the figure in Illgill's high-backed chair at the far end of the room stood up with an abrupt clap of its cloak.

Everything in Jayal's body stopped: his breathing, his heart, his guts were frozen into ice on the instant, his legs became lead trunks. There came a rustling from above and figures rose up above the level of the gallery. Then, at an abrupt gesture from the figure standing in front of the throne, the side panels on which the family portraits were painted burst open. More men emerged from them, carrying swords which gleamed in the moonlight and the glow of Dragonstooth. Jayal was now surrounded by some thirty antagonists.

He swung to the left and the right, conscious that, for the moment at least, his back was protected by the width of the table. Still there were eight men hemming him in on his side, and it would only take a moment for some of the men behind him to vault the table. . . . There were at least as many on the other side.

He thrust Dragonstooth at the nearest figure. The man brought his own sword up to parry and there was an explosion of red light, then the man screamed as his whole body was bathed in glowing red light which flowed up from Dragonstooth into the man's blade and down his arm. He fell to the floor, rolling from side to side as if he were on fire.

Undeterred, another man leapt at Jayal, and he had barely enough time to dart to one side, the attacker's sword passing through the lining of his cloak. He backhanded him into the table with Dragonstooth, then thrust up into the rib cage of another assailant, who ran onto his sword point. The sword slid easily between the links of his mail armour. A curious inner glow lit up the man's rib cage from within, as if his body was a paper lantern surrounding the eldritch fire that burned inside him. His eyes turned white and steam exploded from them. He opened his mouth to scream, but only red light poured out of it in a crimson exhalation. Jayal wrenched back the weapon and the steaming corpse fell to the floor. But even the second he had taken to do so had been too long.

He whirled round. There were two more opponents behind him standing on the table over his head, ready to bring their swords down on his neck. He waited for the killing blow.

"Wait!" The voice rang out from the end of the room. It sounded oddly familiar, and Jayal glanced round as the man who had been sitting in the high-backed chair moved towards him.

Surely this was the impostor; at least he might now take him with him. The man seemed to have anticipated this, for he drew his sword with a squeal of metal from its scabbard. The men around Jayal dropped back, waiting for their leader to fight it out single-handedly. Jayal crouched, ready, but the man kept on, his sword still dangling by his side. Jayal noticed that one of his wrists was bandaged and that he held the weapon clumsily in his left hand. For a moment Jayal hesitated: he could not kill a defenceless man. But then he remembered who this thing was that approached him. He drew Dragonstooth back over his shoulder, aiming to sever his enemy's head from his neck.

It was then the man's face entered the pool of coppery light cast by the sword.

Jayal's backward stroke stopped, his hands went limp and the weapon fell heavily onto the floor behind him. He would have screamed, had he been able to open his mouth, but his whole body, including his face, was frozen in terror.

In the split second before the sword dropped, he had glimpsed his own face staring back at him. His own face, but horribly scarred, as if a hideous parody of himself: the face ruined on one side, and the puckered eye socket.

His father's words at the end of the battle echoed in his mind: ". . . Magic which may yet bring doom upon this house of ours."

The vision had been true. This was the form he had met on the bridge of light, the one who had taken the pain of his wound. The one who should have died, but hadn't.

The double stepped right up to him, and stared piercingly with its single blue eye into his face. Then it threw back its head and laughed, a triumphant, crowing laugh which seemed to rack it in spasms to severe that it jackknifed forward, nearly bent double.

Jayal felt the men surrounding him move in and seize him, pinioning his arms behind his back. But the creature's laughter went on and on, in wave after wave, until, finally, a single tear rolled from its eye and down its ravaged cheek.

CHAPTER TWENTY-NINE

Leaving the Temple of Worms

In the courtyard of the Temple of Iss, there was a scene of controlled pandemonium as figures rushed hither and thither preparing for Lord Faran Gaton's departure. The copper gates blocked the view of the great square, but those within knew what awaited them outside. Some fifty of the temple guards, armed with maces and shields, were assembled in twin columns facing the gates. Their skull masks and copper armour gleamed in the light of the flares and the red light of the setting moon. Four musicians stood at the head of the column, dressed in the same skull masks, but naked otherwise apart from animal pelts thrown over their shoulders and loins. They carried a motley collection of instruments: a drum, a fife, a pair of cymbals and a cow horn.

A massive palanquin stood at the centre of the two columns. Four slaves stood at each of the four carrying poles, already trussed in their harnesses. The palanquin was more the shape and size of a boat than a simple carrying device. Its prow, which jutted forward from between the front two poles, was shaped like a serpent's head, the snake's eyes set with rubies so they glowed red in the patchy light, the armoured head set with small metal scales which also made up the undertray of the vehicle, ending in a tail which protruded from the rear two poles. On top of this structure was placed the curtained tent in which

Lord Faran and Malliana now sat, screened from view. Viri stood outside the conveyance, trembling with cold and fear, as the last preparations were made.

Golon walked down the lines of the men, inspecting them. Apparently satisfied with what he saw, he stationed himself at the head of one of the columns. A server came running up and handed him a censer. Golon held it up from its chain in one hand while motioning with his other. The interior of the censer exploded with blue light which filled the courtyard with a harsh glare. Then Golon barked an order, and the musicians struck up, a discordant clash of sound in which each instrument seemed to war against the others. The bar of the temple gates was thrown open, and the gates swung outwards into the night.

Now the vast temple square was revealed. The undead stood in the mist outside, rank upon rank of them, five thousand or more, thronging the square. They stood in the clothes they had been wearing when they had sunk into the first sleep of the dead. Those garments were now ragged and worm-eaten: some wore the gilt livery of the Empire, showing they had served the Emperor when Thrull had been a provincial capital, five hundred years before. Others wore the white smocks of the farmers' guilds that had once thrived on the plains, others still the military garb of the crusading era when armies set out for the Nations to subdue the creatures of the north. All Thrull's history lay in view in their ruined apparel, generation upon generation.

Though they came from so many different times that few would have known each other in life, yet they all had one thing in common. All those present had once drunk of the Black Chalice, or, infected by a vampire's bite, had then drunk of another's blood, spreading the infection until they were driven from the surface by their enemies. Then, in the maze of tunnels beneath Thrull, their blood supply had run out, the ichor in their veins had dried up and they had laid themselves in the catacombs in the dreamless sleep of the revenant. They had waited as year succeeded year, their bodies prey to weevils and rats, waiting for the gong to be rung. Waiting for their resurrection.

Though they had shambled here, many of them presented a fearful physical spectacle. On some, yellow bones jutted through grey skin, others' faces had been eaten away by mould so only a sunken skull could be seen. The vampires' hearts beat barely four times a minute, and their breath was slow, puffing out a musty exhalation from their dried throats. They waited in utter stillness, in their burial clothes, pale and haggard, expectant. The smell of their mildewed breath mixed with that of the sulphurous marsh air.

Golon stepped forward, holding the censer high, and the front rank of the vampires opened up, allowing the passage of the palanquin. The musicians, then the rest of the column, followed. Viri tried to melt back amongst the crowd of acolytes inside the temple courtyard, but one of the guards grabbed her arm as he went past and pulled her along. She struggled, but the man was much stronger than she. His hollow laugh at her resistance was in eerie accord with the grinning skull of his mask.

Successive ranks of the undead parted in front of them as they marched forward, the blue light illuminating the way and the music scratching away in disharmony with the jingle of the guards' mail armour and the squeak of the leather rigging of the palanquin. Golon reached the very centre of the square, where there was a small mound in the cobblestones. Here he halted, swinging the censer around his head in a mighty arc. The undead stepped back from the light, leaving a wide circle. He held up his hand, and the palanquin was brought to the top of the mound by the sweating slaves, who placed it carefully on the ground. The curtain was swept aside, and Faran Gaton stepped out.

He was now dressed in black leather armour from top to toe, his head bare. A buckler with a skull motif was on his arm and a sword sheathed at his belt. Malliana's white face appeared briefly at the gap in the curtains, then disappeared as the music stopped abruptly, and a total hush descended over the square.

From his vantage point, Faran Gaton looked around him slowly. The generations of the dead stood below him, rank upon rank, right to the far peripheries of the square. Here were all those who had been lost for centuries in the city's catacombs. He was lord of all of them, for he was Lord Iss' High Priest in the city. There were more than even he could have believed existed, each desperate for the drop of the redeeming, living blood that would free their veins once more and give them their last chance of eternal life. They hadn't got long, the moon was already waning. If they hadn't drunk before it set, they would die the second, irreparable death.

All had been summoned by the promise of the gong; all expected to drink. All those left with living blood in Thrull could be bled dry tonight, and still many of the Brethren in the square would go unsatisfied. For the moment the censer would keep them from his own entourage: its magic was strong enough to kill the scent of blood, thus protecting Golon and the guards. None of the others they came across would be so lucky. Thrull would be a dead city by dawn.

Maybe he should have let it happen after the battle: let the undead drink their fill. But he had stopped their excesses after a day. He had known Thrull couldn't survive without living guards while the undead slept. His Elders' orders had been to hold the city, but the wisdom of their strategy had been called into doubt right from the start. There was a drought of blood here, where no living man came apart from the whey-faced acolytes he'd come to despise. Then as now he should have defied the Elders and moved on to Surrenland, slaughtering everything in his path. Surrenland was far from the Elders in Tiré Gand: the land was still fertile and the living congregated thickly in the villages.

Not all Thrull would die tonight: he would save Thalassa, and the young Illgill, if what Malliana had told him was true. He would have uses for both. Malliana might live a little while, but only as an example to those who came after not to meddle with the ways of Iss.

He threw up an arm, an unnecessary gesture, for the throng in the square was already totally silent.

"Brethren," he cried, "Iss' gong has been sounded, the same that was placed here by the Elders of our religion generations ago. You have risen because of its promise; that there will be blood for all of you. All those of you who have not died the second death are here, and all Thrull awaits you. Drink now before the moon wanes. Many enemies are still in Thrull, enemies that will feed you so you may take the long-awaited journey to Tiré Gand. Brethren, you know where that enemy is lodged." He gestured dramatically at the temple pyramid of Reh across the square. "While you have slept the sleep of bloodlessness, they in that temple yonder have plotted against us. They have taken your friends' bodies from the catacombs and burned them, here in this very square. Those Brethren will never rise again, but you have. The moon is full: take your revenge!"

At this there came a great roar of approval from the desiccated throats of the throng. Already there was movement at the crowd's edges towards the Temple of Reh, as if the tide of the dead had suddenly turned and now flowed irrevocably in that direction. Gradually the crowd around the mound began to disperse as more and more of them turned towards it, their white faces drawn back in scowls of anger.

Faran watched them go expressionlessly. The time for agreements between the two temples had died with Varash. He did now only what Baron Illgill had tried to do to the Brethren seven years before. His action was a final one: if news of this ever got out, holy war would spread through the lands of the old Empire, maybe even to the gates of Tiré Gand itself. So be it: the die was cast.

"The way is clear now, Golon," he said, stepping back towards the palanquin. Now for Thalassa and the City of the Dead.

The sorcerer nodded his head, shouting out orders to the palanquin bearers and the guards. Faran reentered the palanquin, drawing the curtains so Malliana and he were left in impenetrable darkness. He heard the woman's dress rustling as she drew away from him. She needn't have worried: her blood smelt old and stale to him, he who had known the blood of a thousand younger than she. If he was to drink tonight it would be from the blue, blue veins at Thalassa's throat.

The column moved off again, heading towards the gate in the wall at the far side of the square. Some of the undead followed them at a distance, but most were even now swirling around the gates of the Temple of Reh. Those taking shelter there must have known what was about to happen. The tops of the walls were already occupied by a solid line of guards and priests. Flaming brands and burning oil suddenly started to rain down on the heads of the throng. Bodies erupted into flaming torches; the air was filled with a cacophony of screams of pain and hatred. Whether the efforts of those on the walls would save those within the temple was in some doubt, for already there came the booming sound of hundreds of shoulders smashing into the gates. Soon the undead would ransack stones and beams from the ruined houses around the square. Even the gates of the Temple of Reh could not sustain a battering for long. The sound of the struggle was suddenly muffled as Faran's palanquin passed under the gateway leading out of the square. The jangle of the column's mail armour echoed noisily off the tunnel walls, then abated as they passed out into the night air.

The palanquin suddenly stopped. Faran flicked back the curtain and looked out. Golon was standing outside looking up into the night sky, a look of irritation on his face. They were in the small square where the Gaunt's Head was situated. Brethren must have got here before they reached the main square; there were several corpses scattered on the cobblestones outside. Faran craned his neck out farther, following the direction of Golon's eyes. He saw two figures high up on the precipitously sloping roof. It was these that Golon was regarding so bad-temperedly.

"You know them?" Faran asked.

"Yes—one of my best informers, Skerrib, and his wife," Golon answered. "But he won't be doing any more informing now."

The two figures were silhouetted by the moon, trying to get away from a small knot of pursuing vampires, who were even now clambering up after them.

Faran was about to order the column not to delay any longer when there was a sudden commotion in the stable yard of the inn. There was a clatter of hooves, then a large grey gelding burst through the shattered gates. A boy was clinging to its neck, trying to keep his position on the horse's bare back. Horse and rider were pursued by an even larger group of vampires than that on the roof. The horse spun once, turning on them, its hooves striking sparks from the cobbles. Then with a touch of his feet to its flanks, the boy set the horse off at a gallop, running down one of the undead in its way.

Faran, watching from within the palanquin, caught the flash of a white star on the horse's forehead as it raced towards him. It slithered to a halt on the wet cobblestones in front of the column, then sheered away into the darkness, parting the mist with the speed of its passage.

He watched it go, the sluggish movement of his heart suddenly quickened by a stab of excitement. He was certain he had seen a horse like that once before, but where, and when?

Only when the echo of its hooves had nearly faded from the night air did he remember. Seven years to the day—at the battle of Thrull—Illgill's charger. He'd been watching from the shade of a palanquin very like this one as the baron's army had left the city gates and marched towards the line of his men. He had straightaway recognised the man he'd come to defeat. Baron Illgill had led the column of men personally, erect and proud in the saddle, his black-and-red armour in contrast to his mount's silvery grey coat, which seemed to glow in the light of the dawn. He had seen horse and rider many times that day, passing up and down the progressively more ragged line of soldiers opposing his own army.

What was the horse doing back here? Illgill could never have returned to Thrull without his knowledge. It must be the baron's son, as Malliana had claimed: the son who, like Illgill, had escaped him at the end of the battle.

But the boy riding the horse was too young to be Illgill's son, and it was too late to order his men to pursue him: at the rate at which he'd been going he would be in the Lower Town by now, or have been thrown and had his neck broken. The presence of the horse was merely further confirmation that tonight was a night of portents.

Seven years to the day of the battle. *The Book of Worms* had been right.

He barked another order and, without another glance at the hapless couple still stranded on the inn's roof, ducked his head back inside the palanquin. The column moved off again, following the horse into the bank of white fog which now blanketed the town. Soon they were lost in a white world in which the only sounds were the tramp of mailed feet and the distant clamour of battle from the Temple of Reh.

CHAPTER THIRTY

The Face in the Window

Once, when he was a child, Jayal had awoken in the middle of the night. It was the depths of winter. Outside, the wind was howling over the marshes. It came, screaming with banshee rage, all the way from the northern mountains, across the miles of frozen hills and barren levels right to his bedroom window without stay or hindrance. The whole of the Illgill mansion seemed to shake with its concussions as gust succeeded gust. It had been thus all day, and as dusk settled no one had had any doubt that it would blow a full gale by midnight. But the wind had not been the sound that had awoken him. No—the tap, tap, tap on the windowpanes, audible even over the noise of the wind, was the noise that had penetrated his dreams, teased him back to consciousness.

Tap, tap, tap.

The curtains hid the windows. With trembling hands he turned up the wick of the lamp that always burned in his room. It was suddenly full of a yellow, comforting light. He saw around him the familiar objects of childhood: books and toys scattered about the floor, his clothes untidily discarded on a chair. Immediately he felt safer, until the noise at the window came again, sending another chill through his lank body. Tap, tap, tap.

He sat up in his bed, frozen once more by the sound. Was it

the Creature of the Spike which had come for him, as his nurse had so often promised? In his mind he conjured its image hanging on the vine-covered wall outside, its fangs dripping venom, its eyes like coals.

The noise had stopped again. Had it gone? The lamplight gave him courage. The air was bitingly cold as he threw back the bed covers.

Tap, tap, tap. There again! He froze.

Now a new image came to his mind. The north wind might have blown one of the creatures from the Nations of the Night south from the Palisades. He imagined it riding the freezing blasts of air through leagues of blackness, a creature as big as this house, a manta ray that would block out the light of the moon. It passed over the land destroying all the light in the world until, finally, it spotted the Hearth Fire of the Temple of Reh. The only illumination in the whole desolate plain. It would fly in, slowly, its eyes darting, looking for prey. Then it would spot the tiny pinprick of light coming from the turret on the house on the Silver Way. . . . His light . . .

Tap, tap, tap. He would have remained motionless all the night, half in and half out of his bed. But then thoughts of his father came to him: how every day in the practice yards he had mocked him for his cowardice, and how that mockery had always made him angry, made him want to prove himself. . . . The light of the lamp would drive away whatever was out there; even creatures of the Nations hated the light. He stood, trembling in his nightshift, picked up the lamp and took the two steps to the curtain obscuring the window. No creature of the night could withstand light. He took a deep breath, then grasped the edge of the curtain and wrenched it back.

A demon face was at the window, looking in. Its eyes were undershadowed, its face long and drawn and etiolated in the yellow light as if it had been stretched. As Jayal opened his mouth to scream, it opened its mouth too, so it seemed to fill the whole window. And he felt himself being drawn forward with a feeling almost of vertigo into the abyss of its mouth. Time froze. All that existed was the screaming face. Then the tap, tap, tap started again. And he saw the branch of ivy, agitated by another gust of wind, striking the windowpane. And he saw how the glass was warped out of shape, so all reflected objects were distorted by it. And realised that the face in the window was his.

So now Jayal looked at the Doppelgänger, willing this face, which was his own except for its ragged scar, to disappear. He moved his head fractionally to the side, but the other's head remained utterly still, its single eye never leaving his face.

Rough hands were binding his hands behind him—the Doppelgänger's men. The image in front of him took all his power away. He was pushed to his knees and his head was yanked back by his hair so he was forced to stare again into the Doppelgänger's face.

The face in the window, the remembrance of which, thereafter, came to him every night of his childhood as he slept, had haunted him until the day of the exorcism. . . . Like so many things he had forgotten it, pushed it deep into his subconscious. But here was the nightmare made real: the demon returned.

A sour breath wafted over him as the creature leant closer, inspecting him, his mouth open in a crooked smile. And when he spoke, The Doppelgänger's voice was like his, though toughened somewhat by the street argot of Thrull. There was a dancing, lilting madness to it as well. And in time to it, the Doppelgänger moved about, prancing and jigging round Jayal's kneeling body. And the words he spoke were more like a song than speech, though he sang them to no tune that was recognisable:

> "Ghost of me,
> yet no ghost.
> Shadow,
> But no shadow.
> What I would have been,
> But am not.
> Brother that left me
> On the forking path.
> Shadow that walked away
> In the pale light of the sun."

The Doppelgänger's song came to an abrupt halt. Then he hawked and spat into Jayal's face. His single eye burned with hatred.

"You robbed me of life!" The spittle ran slowly down Jayal's cheek and onto his chest. The Doppelgänger was silent as he watched the passage of his bead of phlegm with avid interest.

Then his eye darted back to Jayal's. "Do you remember me?" he hissed. "Twice now"—again he fought with the spittle that leaked unbidden from the side of his ravaged face—"Twice now, you've tried to kill me. First, that priest thought he'd driven me into Shades. He thought his boy would be safe when I was gone. Snug you were, very snug: until Faran came. Then you needed me again: when your blood was washing your father's boots. The Rod, the Rod! they cry. Where is the Other, the dark half that we didn't want? Give him this dying body so my son can live! And you brought me back into this—this body!" He thumped his chest with his unbandaged hand, then threw his head back and laughed. "And now I've got you! I've dreamt—how shall I call you: brother, twin, cousin?—I've dreamt that you would return. And now you're here—perfect symmetry. The old fool Furisel told me everything before he died: everything!"

Jayal did not respond: his mind was frozen, his spirit, too. His father had spoken of a curse. What greater curse could there be than this?

But the Doppelgänger was unrelenting. He came closer again, the Rak breath getting through even to Jayal's frozen consciousness, making him flinch away.

The Doppelgänger took this as a sign of fear. "So you think I'll kill you, do you?" he said exultantly. Then he shook his head vigorously. "Too easy, too easy. That way we will both die. We're bound, you and me. Bound to live together, but with a difference: that body belongs to me. It is a body that women dream of, a body that could wrestle with tigers, that could drink a measure or two of Rak. Not this broken thing," he said, thumping his chest again. "No, we will find our father, the baron," he continued. "He is in the north. He has the Rod that will sunder you from that stolen body and return it to me!" This time he slammed both hands onto his chest. The pain from his injured wrist made him wince. He lashed out with his foot in his pain and rage, kicking Jayal in the midriff, then hopped from foot to foot, cursing.

"Bring me some Rak, whoresons!" he roared. One of the men hastened forward with a leather drinking pouch and applied it to the Doppelgänger's lips. The creature took a great draught of it so that the liquor ran over his chin. He wiped away the spillage with the bandage covering his broken wrist.

"Now, cousin," he chuckled, "can't have me beating my own body." He smiled lopsidedly, enjoying Jayal's grimace of pain. "Kazaris," he said, turning to a man who stood deep in the shadows, "remind me not to kick my brother again until we've found the Rod!"

Jayal had fallen slightly to one side at the kick, and the chain holding the key had fallen outside his shirt. The Doppelgänger now noticed the glint of gold at his chest.

"What is that?" he asked, suddenly very calm and still. Jayal struggled with the man who held him, but the grip was vicelike. Not waiting for an answer, the Doppelgänger stepped forward and pulled the key towards himself. The moon hung over the broken peaks of the Fire Mountains to the west, and its amber light flooded through the huge windows at the end of the hall, almost as strong as daylight. The key glowed more brightly still, with a dazzling, ultraplanar energy. At a nod from the Doppelgänger, the man behind grabbed the chain and lifted it from Jayal's neck, passing it to his leader.

The Doppelgänger held it gently in his unbroken hand.

"Well, the Mad God protect us!" he exclaimed. "What have we here?" He turned the key this way and that in the moonlight, his one eye glittering in its sparkling reflection. "A key, but no ordinary key, I'd warrant. But where is the lock? A vizier's treasure vault? A virgin's chastity belt? Tell me, brother—what is it for?"

Again, Jayal struggled, but the man behind him held him firm. The Doppelgänger bent and brushed the end of the key back and forth across the end of Jayal's nose.

"Tick, tock, the ticking of a clock," he sang, the same lopsided smile on his face. "And when the clock will stop, the head will drop," he said, suddenly ripping the tines of the key over the bridge of Jayal's nose. "So, tell me; what's this key for?"

Jayal clenched his teeth against the pain from his nose. He could feel blood dripping from it onto his chin, but he kept his silence. At a nod from the Doppelgänger, the man behind him shook his head violently from side to side, sending the blood spraying in every direction.

"Well?" the Doppelgänger repeated. There was still no answer from Jayal, and the Doppelgänger threw up his hands in mock disappointment.

"Don't know? Can't remember?" He turned to the watching men, shrugging his shoulders, then turned and kicked Jayal extremely hard in the solar plexus, once more forgetting his resolution of but a moment before. Jayal bent double, sinking to his knees despite the efforts of the man behind him to keep him upright.

The Doppelgänger got down on one knee before Jayal, ignoring Jayal's groans. His voice was more conciliatory. "Now, brother—don't expect me to kill you—that would be too easy, and inconvenient, as I've told you. I know what the key is for." He nodded his head at the study door at the far end of the room. "It's in there, isn't it?"

Jayal didn't favour him with a reply, but the creature merely smiled at his silence. "As I thought! We'll go to put it to use in a moment. But first, some other information, about the Rod. You know what I'm talking about, don't you, boy?" he said, thrusting his nose up to Jayal's. Jayal remained silent.

"Silent again!" the Doppelgänger crowed. "You know why I want it: so that you can have this broken body of yours back, and I can have the one that is rightfully mine!" He motioned, and the man behind pulled Jayal's head back: the single blue eye, so like his, burned brightly, madly. "So, where is it?"

"I don't know," Jayal managed to mumble.

"Not good enough," the Doppelgänger said, shaking his head, almost sorrowfully. Another kick from a henchman landed in Jayal's side. His face screwed up in pain.

"Easy, lads," the Doppelgänger ordered. "Don't forget whose body you're abusing! Now, let's go back, shall we?" he said, almost gently. "When was the last time you saw the Rod?"

"A-At the battle," Jayal managed through gritted teeth.

"Of course, at the battle; for how else would I awake on top of a carrion pile with your loyal sergeant over there"—he nodded at Furisel's corpse staring sightlessly up at the moon—"if it wasn't used at the battle? What I want to know is where is it now?"

Jayal shook his head: "I told you, I don't know." The Doppelgänger glanced at one of his henchmen, who stepped forward and backhanded Jayal across the face with a mailed fist. As his vision cleared, he found his enemy's bandaged hand clutching his collar, despite the obvious pain this caused the creature.

"Believe me, that hurt me as much as it did you, brother," he said with savage irony. "Next time, it will be harder. Now, what arrangements did you make to meet with your father?"

"None . . . no arrangements . . ." Jayal mumbled, earning himself another blow across the face.

"You didn't return to Thrull to find your father?" the Doppelgänger asked. "Then why did you return?"

"Thalassa—I came back for Thalassa . . ."

At this, the Doppelgänger tilted his head back and laughed. "You came back for your betrothed? Then you might like to know what trade she now pursues . . ."

"I've heard," Jayal interrupted, gritting his teeth.

"You have, have you? No doubt the good sergeant told you before his accident? Excellent! Though she's only a whore, I will have her, Illgill. Have her in more ways than you could imagine. Then give her to my men, and then I'll kill her in front of your eyes."

Jayal didn't respond, but remained with his head bowed. The Doppelgänger leaned in close, his breath sour on Jayal's face. "Enough of this charade—shall we see about the key now?" he asked, holding the golden object before Jayal's eyes. Jayal didn't answer. The Doppelgänger smiled again. "Never mind: you'll become more talkative, by and by. As I said, I know where we'll find the lock." He rose to his feet, gesturing at his men. "To the study with him!" Jayal was brought to his feet. He stood swaying groggily from side to side. "I'll take Kazaris and two guards," the Doppelgänger said, addressing the men. "The rest of you prepare yourself for some amusement."

"Where are we going?" one of them asked.

"Why, where but the City of the Dead? You heard the gong; the shambling undead issue forth from cellars and sewers, mewling like babies for their blood. What could be better than a midnight stroll?"

"We'll never get there," one of the men had the temerity to say.

The Doppelgänger stepped up to him. "So how did I make it?" he asked, turning to the other men. "Have I not just come from there? Am I not alive?"

"But you're different," another man said.

"Different enough to have courage! If yours is lacking, then the oubliettes are waiting." The man held up his hands placatingly. The creature's mad eye now swivelled over the rest of the men, daring any of them to defy him. No one spoke up or, indeed, met his gaze. "Good!" he crowed. "You men assemble in the yard. Bring the wretches from the dungeons; they can act as a lure for the undead."

All the men, apart from the two pinioning Jayal's arms, filed from the room.

The Doppelgänger's glance next fell on Dragonstooth, lying on the floor, along with the two burned corpses of the men that Jayal had slain. Its blade still gleamed coppery red. He stooped, as if about to pick it up, but then thought better of it. "Kazaris," he said, "take care of this until I have need of it."

Kazaris now stepped into the light of the moon. He was a young man with lank black hair and a hooked nose, who had the bookish and important air of one who had laboured long in study and would have the world know that those hours of cerebral toil had given him an importance in it.

He picked up the weapon gingerly, turning its blade hither and thither so the coppery glow reflected from Erewon's light.

The Doppelgänger regarded him shrewdly. "Well?" he asked.

"It is very old, and very powerful," Kazaris replied carefully.

"That I have already seen," the Doppelgänger snorted, jerk-

ing his head at the corpses of his men. He turned to Jayal.
"Where did you get this sword?"

"In the lands of the south," Jayal replied, staring at the floor.

"At our father's instigation, no doubt?"

Jayal didn't reply, but the Doppelgänger seemed to take his
silence as an affirmative.

"Very well, let's see what the study has to offer." He motioned to the two men pinioning Jayal's arms to drag him towards the side panel which concealed the study door. The
Doppelgänger preceded them, turning the key this way and that
in the moonlight.

He pushed at the hidden panel, and it squeaked open on
rusty hinges. Inside, a lantern burned on the floor and papers of
different descriptions were littered all over the flagstones.
There was a large wooden table at the centre of the room. On it
were alembics and retorts in which bubbled strange distillates
of many colours. The Doppelgänger surveyed these for a moment and then, with one swift motion, swept them off the table.
The sound of breaking glass was deafening in the confined
space. Kazaris made a murmur of protest, but the Doppelgänger
swung round on him fiercely. The young man flinched back.
With another lopsided grin, the Doppelgänger turned his attention to the table, which he sent crashing over on its side with a
swift kick of his boot.

He nodded in satisfaction at what he saw. Underneath, a
flagstone with faint runic signs carved on it was illuminated by
the lantern. Jayal knew immediately that this was the slab his
father had told him to look for.

"Bring him forward," the Doppelgänger ordered without
turning round. The two men dragged Jayal farther into the room
and threw him down amongst the broken glass and steaming
liquid. His bleeding nose was almost touching the flagstone,
and the carvings were even clearer.

"Release him," the Doppelgänger commanded, looking off
into the middle distance. The rope binding Jayal's arms behind
his back was unfastened by one of the men. "Now, what do you
see?"

"A stone," replied Jayal tonelessly through bruised lips.

The Doppelgänger turned suddenly. "And what do you know of it?"

Jayal swallowed hard. The Doppelgänger was obviously playing with him, and knew more than he did of what lay beneath it. There would be no shame in confessing as much.

"Something is hidden beneath it," he mumbled.

"Good! Now we're progressing." The Doppelgänger gestured at the traceries faintly scoring its surface. "Well, what are you waiting for? Feel the lines: see what our father has bequeathed us!" He nodded at the two minders, who stepped back.

Jayal rubbed his bruised arms, staring at the whirls and patterns etched on the floor for a few moments while he collected his wits. He thought briefly of escape, but the study had been built with all the rigour of a monk's cell: there was but a single window set high up on the wall on the side that faced directly onto the martin-haunted cliffs overlooking the marshes. Other than that there was just the one door where the Doppelgänger's unshaven thugs stood, their thigh-thick arms crossed in an uninviting way across their chests.

After seven years his quest was finally over, the sword returned to Thrull, the key brought back and the secret of his father's study revealed. But for what? Nothing. Yes, the curse his father had spoken of that night on Thrull plain had fully come to pass. His father could not have known that the Doppelgänger would survive the wounds and the carrion pyre, and return to take his revenge nor could his father have known that Jayal could not now live without his shadow, and vice versa.

But yet his father had felt it in his bones, had warned him before he'd ridden from the battle on Cloud. The use of the Rod would bring a curse on the Illgills. How right he had been.

Now the game was over. Seven years of danger and struggle for nothing. But after seven long years, Jayal's mind was not so benumbed by the events of the day that there was no vestigial curiosity in his mind as to what lay beneath the stone. Almost unconsciously, he reached forward his hand.

His fingers traced the runes. As he did so, a vision came, unbidden, to his mind: a vision of summer meadows bedecked with yellow and white flowers, a glorious orange sun burning in

the sky. A white charger pawed at the ground, snorting before a
pavilion. In the background, a thin tower rose up into the stun-
ning azure sky. Old magic and old signs, of when the Earth was
whole and not sick and in its dotage as it was now. The time of
Marizian and the Lost City of Iskiard. A time before ghosts and
the undead had come into the world and the sun had begun to
die.

As his finger traced the last curlicue of the ancient lettering,
there came a soft hiss, and the slab of stone rose up gently, and
came to rest, hovering in midair. Beneath it glowed a golden
cage, as much a part of that golden world he'd seen in the vision as the vision itself. A golden lock hung in the side of the
cage. Automatically, his hand moved to his breast, to where the
golden key had hung every day for the last seven years. Only
when his hands closed on empty air did he remember that it was
gone.

"Looking for something, brother?" He became conscious
of the Doppelgänger's voice breaking in on the beauty of what
he saw in front of him, reminding him of what he did here—
the devil's work, and not Reh's. He didn't look round though
he sensed the Doppelgänger taunting him with the key.

"Bad things happen to those who meddle with that cage—
unless, that is, they have a certain itsy-bitsy thing," the creature
said in a wheedling, baby voice.

"Damn you!" Jayal screamed, raising a fist and smashing it
into the golden bars of the cage.

A faint chiming came to his ears, and his fingers tingled, not
with pain but with energy. "Stop that!" he heard the Doppelgänger shout, a sudden panic in his voice. There came a sudden
breath of fetid air, its source untraceable, as if the chiming had
set off an invisible chain reaction. One that the Doppelgänger
feared . . . Jayal suddenly felt the power of his position. He
gave out an hysterical laugh and smashed his fist into the cage
again. Over in the gloom on the far side of the room, some of
the fallen papers whirled in sudden commotion, and the shadows there seemed suddenly to join together. Something was
taking form there, half-glimpsed. He sensed the onlooking
guards and Kazaris take a step back. Now he saw it, materialis-
ing out of the gloom, a creature of shadows. Its red eyes glim-

mering in the darkness. A cry of fear came from the two men behind him, then the door groaned as it was flung open. But he barely heard the sound of their feet running through the hall. His eyes were on the thing in the corner.

"Don't hit it again." The Doppelgänger's voice had lost its wheedling quality and was now very quiet. The creature wound towards them slowly, manifesting itself like a shadowy snake of giant proportions, its breath humid and hot even at this distance. It wavered between this world and the next like the tide just before it begins to ebb, contending with its own force. It slithered forward, interposing itself between the Doppelgänger and Jayal. In the far corner, Kazaris stood uneasily, the sword held out before him.

"Here," the Doppelgänger said, holding out the glimmering key, "take it, open the lock; before it strikes!" Then he threw the key across the room, the golden object passing right through the body of the shadow creature. Jayal fielded it in one movement. He looked at it for a moment, then back at the Doppelgänger, whose attention was divided between him and the creature between them. Somehow he knew that if he struck the cage again, all of them there would die. The secret of what lay in the cage would rest here until it was taken by someone else, possibly by one of the undead.

What would his father have wished? Surely it was better if he lived with a small chance of escape than certainly died? He slipped the key into the lock. The musical chiming, which he only just realised had been echoing in his ears ever since he'd struck the cage, ceased. The creature started melting away before his eyes in the flood of golden white light that poured from the now-open door of the cage. Then it was gone.

The interior of the cage was dazzling, almost blinding. Jayal screwed up his eyes. Inside, in a vista that seemed to open endlessly before his gaze, Jayal could see objects haloed by the burning furnace light. Things that belonged to the vision of the golden meadow, of the white champing horse, things that an older age had seen fit to guard with the creature of shadows. Piles of golden coins, and shining weapons, tapestries that were made of molten fire, drinking cups that overflowed with silver wine, mounds of jewellery that seemed glowing mountains. He knelt, bedazzled by this vision of a purer age.

Then a shadow came across the vision—the Doppelgänger had come closer. But unlike Jayal, he seemed to be totally blinded by the light. The creature averted his gaze with a curse.

Now Kazaris had drawn up, but he, too, shielded his eyes from the blaze. The Doppelgänger shouted something, and Jayal felt the prick of Dragonstooth at his neck.

"Take what is there, and shut out that damned light!" the Doppelgänger ordered, the menace in his voice unmistakable.

Jayal thought to shut the door and tell him that there had been nothing there, but just then his eye caught sight of the one object that was not surrounded by an aura of shimmering radiance. A small, leather-bound book which lay just within the door of the furnace of light. Was this what his father had left for him?

Without thinking further, he snatched it up, slamming to the door. The light faded in an instant, and the block sank back into the stone floor.

There was silence for a moment, as the three men's eyes readjusted to the gloom of the lanternlit room. After a moment, Jayal found himself staring at the cover of the book in the sudden gloom. It was only a hand long, its leather cover much rubbed and its corners bent out of shape. A faded likeness of a fire-breathing salamander was embossed on the cover: the Illgill family crest.

He opened it unconsciously. The pages within were yellowed and much thumbed. But despite this, Jayal had already seen what this book was. He knew all too well the handwriting which covered each page: it was the script of his father.

The Doppelgänger had seen it too: he snatched the book from Jayal's fingers. Jayal lunged after it, but then he felt the blade of the sword on his neck, and heard Kazaris's warning: he could do nothing.

The Doppelgänger started leafing clumsily through the pages with his injured hand, his eye darting hither and thither like a bird of prey's. Towards the end of the book he let out a triumphant yelp. He began to murmur the words as he read them: " '. . . besides the other minor dangers, the outer halls are protected by a demon of fire. Only a warding will save a man from being burned in a single second by his glare . . .'" He turned to Kazaris. "It's describing Marizian's tomb!"

"So it seems," the younger man agreed.

"'. . . Go down deeper,'" the Doppelgänger continued. "'The plants are voracious and will eat your flesh if you come too close. Then seek for the door which is not a door; look for the copper symbol, that will give you your way.'" He glanced up, a twinkle in his solitary eye, before looking back at the book. "'Next,'" he read, "'the maze. The ghost of the First Father will appear; woe to him who does not examine his soul and give a full account of himself, for otherwise, his earthly body will be carried to the dripping catacombs beneath the city and he will be lost there in darkness. There follows the tomb chamber. From here, the last day of Samen, before Lord Faran Gaton came from the east, I took the Rod which will open the gates of the Mundane World to the World of Shadows. It is this object, and this object alone, which, according to the writings examined by me and the Hearth Brethren, will save the world. So I have left the other object there, the Orb, merely noting where on its surface the sword Dragonstooth will be found, and where, too, the Man of Bronze. Both are an adventure. The sword lies in Hangar Parang. But the Man of Bronze, the Talos written about in the old books, will be found at the forge in the Nations of the Night. only a madman will travel there, but this may be my fate should the battle be lost tomorrow and the Worm victorious.'" The entry was dated, seven years and a day ago exactly.

The Doppelgänger lowered the book, a mad gleam in his eye. "The Orb!" he exclaimed, dancing a jig again. "The Orb will tell us where the Rod is!" He shook the book in the air. "All I need is the Rod, and I will be made whole again, and you"—he spat in Jayal's face—"will be returned to this, your rightful body!" He rubbed his chin thoughtfully. "Then I'll think of some brave tortures for you—up to your neck in a pit of lye, with hornets eating your eyes!"

"Damn you!" Jayal snarled, thinking of springing up at the Doppelgänger, but the point of Dragonstooth, held in Kazaris's rock-steady hand, deterred him. Instead the sorcerer encouraged him to get to his feet rather more slowly before prodding him towards the door. The Doppelgänger chuckled mirthlessly, tucking the book into the pocket of his cloak before following them. They exited thus, Jayal cursing himself for losing the initiative; once more he was in his shadow's power.

The Doppelgänger's men stood at the other end of the dark hall, weapons drawn, looking anxiously at what might emerge from the room. The Doppelgänger merely laughed at their frightened faces.

"It's only me, whoresons, so put up your blades for better sport. The City of the Dead, lads, and hurry, for mischief is afoot—mischief that we may profit by."

The men looked uneasily at one another. They clearly thought any excursion into the streets would be near suicidal. But their fear of the Doppelgänger got the better of their fear of the vampires, and they fell to as the Doppelgänger shouted a stream of instructions and invective. Jayal's hands were once more bound behind his back, and he was bundled forward, down the corridor he had entered by. He glanced back despairingly. The portraits of the Illgill ancestors stared back hollowed-eyed as the last of their line was dragged from the room to the front door of the ruined mansion.

CHAPTER THIRTY-ONE

The Man Nearly Immortal

By some curious meteorological occurrence, there was a clear band of air between the two layers of fog in the City of the Dead: one layer hung from the ground to about waist height, the other started some twenty feet in the air, masking the tops of some of the larger monuments. So it seemed that the seven members of Seresh's party glided over the mist without the benefit of legs or waists, wraiths sailing over a sea of fog. They were heading down a wide avenue, towards the building that dominated the whole of the City of the Dead: Marizian's tomb.

The sinking moon peeped over the outer walls of the city, silhouetting the pyramid. From here it appeared to be the same size as the Temples of Reh and Iss: a long strip of shadow reached out to them over the layer of undulating whiteness to the middle of the graveyard. On either side of them loomed the crumbling tombs and mastabas of the earlier generations of Thrull, overgrown with moss and lichen, their stonework scarred and pitted by time; the elaborate painted friezes which had once proclaimed the virtues of their incumbents had now peeled away in the damp marsh air and hung forlornly in rotting strips. But it was Marizian's tomb, fifty times the size of any of the other monuments, that dominated the scene.

Thalassa walked with Alanda, slightly apart from the others.

She was still in a daze from what had happened in the Light-bringer's Shrine. The light of the shrine still seemed to burn in her, warming her despite the chill of the air. She longed to take out the *Book of Light* from her backpack and stop and look at it: try to find meaning in what she had seen at the shrine in the ancient text. But the others were all desperate urgency, pressing on through the mist so quickly. . . . And Alanda had been deathly quiet ever since leaving the shrine, as if she wanted Thalassa to reach her own conclusions about what they had seen. She would look in the book later, when they were out of the city. But for the moment she wondered: wondered what the vision had meant, wondered what Alanda's looks had presaged, wondered at the feeling of warmth inside her, despite the fear that the fog and the night instilled.

Then something passed over the face of the setting moon: something whose shadow blocked out its light for a moment. Thalassa looked up: five hundred feet above her she saw a shape through the mist, huge, gliding slowly and inexorably on bat wings through the air over the City of the Dead. It could have been a bird of prey, but no bird of prey could obscure the light of the moon. . . . She watched it glide on through the mist, flapping its huge wings once to keep up its airspeed. A moment later the down pressure of its wings displaced the lower level of the mist, blowing it up in spirals. It circled once, its mist-obscured body now outlined by the medley of different lights burning at the top of the city: the orange blaze from the Temple of Sutis, the red glow of the Hearth Fire of the Temple of Reh, now augmented by a lower ring of orange fires that had seemed to flower all around its walls, and lastly, a blue light which had suddenly appeared at the top of one of the streets five hundred feet above them.

"What in Shades is that?" Urthred murmured, pointing at the huge shape which now flew slowly back towards the city.

"The Creature of the Spike," Alanda said. "It hasn't been seen in generations, but the gong must have disturbed it."

"It is the harbinger of death," Seresh said grimly.

"Another portent." Alanda looked at Urthred. "It is as I said: the city will be destroyed tonight."

Seresh was silent, but his thoughts were easy to guess: he

was looking up to where the Durian mansion was hidden from view by the fog. He was thinking of his father, and what might even now be happening to him.

No one spoke: they knew that Count Durian's chances were slim, as slim maybe as their own. Seven against the dangers of Marizian's tomb.

"What are those lights?" Urthred asked, breaking the silence.

"The Temple of Reh is under attack," Seresh replied grimly. "They're using burning oil to keep the undead back, but their supplies won't last long."

"Then may the Flame go with them."

"And the blue light?"

"I don't know—but look, it's heading this way!" Sure enough the blue light was descending the side of the cliffs in slow zigzags.

The spell cast by the lights and the giant flying creature was broken in a second. They no doubt had the same thought at the very same second: Faran was coming after them. Only he would risk the vampire-haunted streets. They hurried on.

Thalassa's thoughts were once more occupied by the dizzying succession of events that had overtaken her that evening. Alanda's prophecies were proving to be right: the city, where she had spent every one of her twenty years, good and bad, would be destroyed tonight. The vampires and the Creature of the Spike would surely see to that. For the last seven years she had barely thought about the poor unfortunates who eked out a living outside the walls of the Temple of Sutis. But she thought of them now, desperately waiting for the vampires in their houses, knowing tonight nothing would stop the undead in their bloodlust.

She prayed as she hurried along: prayed that their souls would be aneled, that someone would scatter their bones for Reh's sacred birds so that they might wake once more to a yellow sun burning in the sky, in a world where the flowers would return, and the bees, and the birdsong: all that was lost, in the Last Days of the Earth. As she prayed, the weight on her heart, the weight that had bowed her down these last seven years, seemed to be suddenly lifted as if borne off by the claws of mighty birds. She seemed to float momentarily. For the moment even the sudden appearance of her betrothed earlier at the temple failed to weigh on her, though she was full of curiosity as to what happened in the seven years since she had last seen him. What was the meaning of his rough words and actions at the temple? Everything that had been exposed to Thrull in the last seven years seemed to have been warped and perverted from its true nature. She had fallen, too, but now, even in the grim surroundings of the City of the Dead and with the dangers ahead, that past was almost forgotten, pushed to the back of her mind. Once more she felt her true age, twenty, rather than the age she had felt all that time in the temple.

She regarded her companions with a sudden stab of affection. Even the masked priest. What if he was the Herald? The priest must have suffered, must still suffer, to wear that hellish mask, a mask that alienated all who saw it.

The glow that filled her radiated throughout her body: she saw hope and a future. The priest held a fascination, despite the mask and his austerity. There was power there, power and stubbornness and bravery—bravery to have done what he had done today, bravery to have carried on when it would have been easier for him to give up, a bravery that the rest of them would need when they faced the mysteries of Marizian's tomb. For she doubted that Seresh, with all his outer confidence, really knew what to expect when they got there.

Urthred, too, had been pondering the lights, the winged creature and the fate of the living left in Thrull. Yet, above all these other things, and he once more marvelled at how it could be thus, it was Thalassa's glance which set his heart beating in expectation. He was a rational man: he could contend with these feelings. Tomorrow he would laugh at them, but for the moment, despite the danger, or maybe because of it, it felt as if spiked barbs of desire were lodged in his flesh and, shake and wriggle as he might, he couldn't get rid of them.

He tried to concentrate on what he had seen in the shrine and what Alanda had told him. He knew the *Book of Light* better than any other book. The prophecies were exactly as she'd said: Marizian had seen these events in the far distant past, had anticipated this moment of crisis, had foreseen the Lightbringer. The Lightbringer . . . Thalassa walked ahead of him, drifting over the mist. She looked like a goddess, or any of the other heroic women mentioned in the Scriptures, but she was none of these things. She was a whore who had slept with any number of men, serving a heretical god. No, that was not the whole truth. His brief exposure to the Temple of Sutis told him that Thalassa was not one of the typical acolytes. Her outer being was different from her inner core. . . .

Urthred's mind abandoned this train of thought; only madness lay along it. He must think of positive things—how his knowledge might help in the tomb. He must remember what he knew about Marizian from Manichee's book.

The pages of the volume covered by his master's spiky script, left behind in Forgeholm, sprang to his mind. There had been pages and pages about the ancient wizard. He had come from the Lost City of Iskiard at the dawn of time. He had borne magic to the people of the south. He had also brought the two holy books of Iss and Reh, so the people of the south would understand the sorcery of those gods. Had not Urthred learnt his pyromancy from the *Book of Light,* Reh's holy book? Marizian had also brought the three magical artefacts that Seresh had spoken of: a Warrior of Bronze, a Rod of Power and a mighty sword, Dragonstooth. He built the city of Thrull full on the plains, so all men could see it—from the Palisades to the Fire Mountains. Giants and trolls and dwarves hewed and hefted until the palaces reared to the sky and all was made good. And with him was buried the king of the giants, Adamanstor. The rest of the creatures who had built Thrull had been banished to the Nations. Or so it said in the book that Manichee had given him.

But though he brought learning to the south, no man spoke of the age of Marizian as a golden age. That age had come before. With Marizian had come the Age of Night when men first noted the pallor that crept over the face of the sun, and the diminishing of its light, and the gradually shorter growing seasons for their crops, and the bitter winters becoming ever more bitter. It was then that man first took solace in the *Book of Worms,* and the worship of the Flame had diminished: just as the sun had died year by year, so had the worship of the god. And some said, though those who still believed in the Scriptures thought them heretics, that it was Marizian who had first brought death to the lands of the south, and that Iskiard, that fabled city in the north, had fallen because he'd meddled with the sorcery that the gods had left behind them.

Whatever Marizian had done, it had not saved him from death. He had been nearly immortal, but after a thousand years he had died and been brought to this tomb, which had been made for him centuries before, and with him were buried the artefacts he'd brought with him.

Yet all the objects now were lost and the tomb pyramid an enigma which only one man had fathomed in the last century. Its secrets had gone with Illgill to the north: it was for them to discover and solve them anew.

They were now very close to it. It reared up in the night sky, its bulk looming out of the mist. Its entrance was like a palace: surrounded by a high wall, breached by a mighty gate on which once stood exquisite reliefs, now defaced by wind, weather and lichen. Then a flight of fifty giant steps, much like those on the Temples of Reh and Iss, rose to a porch set in the side of the tomb. The back of the pyramid abutted directly onto the outer city walls. Anyone who stood at its base and looked up at its four-hundred-foot-high structure would have been quite rightly amazed that this object, which had looked relatively inconsequential from a distance, should, close up, be of such mighty proportions.

Urthred stared at the giant steps with trepidation. Unlike those in the Temple of Reh, there was no smaller flight running down the middle of the steps: each of them was at least six feet high, covered by bushes and split by gullies where thousands of years of rain had carved channels in the monument's side.

It had taken them some twenty minutes to get this far, but, looking back, he could see that the blue light had already descended the cliffs and was in the Lower Town. Now it glowed through the band of mist at the edge of the graveyard. Whoever was following them was catching them rapidly.

"They must have wings for feet," Seresh said, looking in the same direction. Urthred knew the reason why they had lost so much ground. Alanda and Furtal were old, their pace had been slow. They would lose even more ground climbing the steps. Their pursuers would catch them halfway up the pyramid. Gadiel and Rath had been muttering together to one side. They had obviously come to this conclusion, too.

Now Gadiel stepped towards Seresh: "You go on," he said. "We'll keep off whoever is following."

"Don't be mad," Seresh replied. "There are only two of you—there could be hundreds of them."

"We'll hold them for a bit," Gadiel replied, his jaw set. The two men eyed one another in a silent battle of wills. In the end it was Gadiel's quiet determination that won out.

"Very well," Seresh said eventually. "Watch for us when we leave the tomb." He said this without conviction, as if the prospects of the two groups seeing each other again were remote. He was about to say something else, but no words came. They looked at one another for a second more, silently saying farewell to one another, then Gadiel turned to Rath and the two melted back into the layer of mist.

The rest turned and began scrambling up one of the many gullies in the pyramid face. They climbed grimly, Urthred leading, having slung the leech gatherer's staff, which still sprouted the single leaf which it had gained in the shrine, over his back. He helped Furtal, the power of the gloves making light of the work needed to pull up the old man. They were followed by Seresh and the women. The silence was only broken when Furtal slipped as he was being handed up the slope by Urthred, and the lute strapped over his back thrummed with the shock of the fall. The old man brushed off the concerned enquiries, and started climbing again. The two women came next, dirt falling on them from above, struggling with the thornbushes that snagged their dresses. Then Thalassa stopped, a branch having worked its way well into her dress. She couldn't move, but Urthred came back and, with the pincers of his gloves, snapped her free of the branch. She thanked him, and for a moment their gazes went back to the blue light, which was now much closer.

Thalassa shivered. "It is Faran. I know," she whispered.

Urthred thought to contradict her, but something about the light's inexorable pursuit of them seemed to suggest that it was being controlled by a power commensurate with Faran's own. "Come on," he said, turning his back, and grabbing for another handhold.

They continued the uphill struggle, dirt crumbling and falling from the feet of those above, a fine sweat covering Urthred's brow despite the chill of the night.

Looking back again, he saw that the blue light was even nearer, floating over the bottom surface of the fog. He could also hear eerie cries and ululations. Seresh had paused on the ledge above; his face was set.

"The death cry of the Reapers," he said. "I heard it enough during the battle of the marshes."

They tried to hurry, but once more their progress was impeded by the old woman and the blind man. Then they heard screams from behind them. Gadiel and Rath had found a target. But the fight was hidden by the fog. There were muffled sounds of combat, but the blue light forged on, undisturbed seemingly by the struggle going on so near it, the noise of which increased in a crescendo, then abruptly stopped. There could only be one conclusion: Gadiel and Rath were dead, and they had bought them very little time. Urthred renewed his upward scramble, hauling Furtal desperately behind him.

Minutes that seemed hours passed until Urthred was as wet with sweat as he had been with the waters of the Pool of the Blinding. But with one last effort he made the final step and found himself in the great shadow of the porch, two-thirds of the way up the face of the pyramid. He hauled Furtal up behind him. Then he saw Thalassa's face, her hair hanging in damp strands over her forehead, struggling up the last step. He leant down and handed her up as well. She stumbled forward and came to rest momentarily against his chest. Then Seresh appeared with Alanda. They all sank to their knees, gasping for breath.

The blue light was still approaching them through the band of fog. Urthred struggled back to his feet. The entranceway to the tomb stood behind them. Vines and creepers hung down from the pediment fifty feet above, partially masking the entrance. Inside, he could see a mosaic floor made up of black-and-white tiles. He pushed one of the creepers away, allowing the slanting rays of the moon to enter the gloom: the complexities of the mosaic were obscured by centuries of bat droppings. Halfway to the back of the room, he saw the beginning of a deep trench cut through the floor; piles of dirt and rubble had been heaped close to the near end of it.

The others by now had joined him. Seresh was busy lighting torches from his tinderbox, but damp had got into it and he was finding it difficult to obtain a spark. To Urthred, each second of his fumbling seemed intolerable. He felt the blue light at their backs getting ever closer. Then a chill went up his spine. Once more, he sensed the presence of the undead. He stepped outside onto the ledge: the blue light was there, burning below them at the gate in the wall. But whoever carried it was still hidden by the mist. It wouldn't take long for them to follow them up the side of the tomb.

The blue light—he knew whoever wielded it would follow them to the ends of the earth. Where was the fire that had burst from his hands on the temple square this afternoon? A fire that could contend with this light's sinister presence? Gone, since Varash's death. It had been as Manichee had told him, he had transgressed and the power, when he really needed it, had disappeared. He had never felt farther from the God. Now it was midnight, but two hours hence it would be Tenebrae, the darkest time of the night, when his brother monks at Forgeholm would rise from their pallets in the freezing dark and pray the sun would once more be released from the black chains that held it under the world.

He quickly prayed as they would pray then: to the atoms of fire that dwelt in everything on earth, animate and inanimate. Fish, fowl and mammal. Stone, earth and sky. All had been impregnated with the seed of fire at the beginning of time. To that seed they owed their origins and form. The whole world moved to the order of the sun, as a lodestone drew iron. All of it would die with its passing.

Tenebrae, he prayed silently: soon it will be the darkest hour of this world, but let me make a pledge to the god burning within me and to all living things—a pledge to take a torch from this darkness and reignite the sun.

Then, as he stared at the blue light, he felt once more the familiar tingling in his veins as if the God had heard him, and had answered.

As if on cue, Seresh's torch finally sputtered into life behind him, casting a pallid glow on the faces of his companions. Urthred brushed through the barrier of creepers and rejoined the others. The young warrior's eyes were shifty, scared in the torchlight.

"Remember, we don't know what lies beyond the excavation except that Zaraman and the others died there," he said, jerking his head towards the V-shaped tunnel dug into the floor of the mausoleum.

He set off towards it, the torch spluttering in a sickly manner.

"Wait!" Urthred's command stopped him dead.

"What is it?" he said impatiently.

"Gadiel and Rath told us that fire killed Zaraman and the others—we need wardings to keep off the curse of Reh."

"The priest's right," Alanda said, "but hurry—we haven't much time."

Urthred still had attached to his leather belt the small travelling pouch in which he'd stowed the paraphernalia of his craft. He opened it. Inside were some coloured wax sticks, undamaged by the immersion in the pool.

"I will draw the Form of the Flame on your foreheads: it will drive off the spirits." Seresh looked doubtful, but Alanda stepped forward with Furtal.

The old man inclined his bald head, ready for the mark. The priest laid his gloved hand gently on the back of it, steadying him, and, trying to control the slight shake in his hand, took one of the crayons between the pincers of the other glove and began carefully to inscribe the sign of the Flame Rune on Furtal's forehead.

"Hurry!" urged Seresh, who had stepped outside and was looking anxiously down the giant steps to the light which had now passed through the gates and was at the base of the tomb.

"May the Flame burn in you," Urthred murmured, finishing the sign with a flourish.

"And with you, priest," Furtal muttered.

Now Alanda stepped up, bowing her head. He reached up trembling hands, the crayon wavering. She fixed Urthred with her piercing blue eyes, one of her hands snaking up and grabbing his gloved fingers.

"There is a little time, priest; do it well." He felt a tingling of energy from her grip as her blue eyes bored into the eye slits of the mask. The grip steadied him, and he drew rapidly and surely.

Now it was Thalassa's turn; her eyes were fixed on his. Though he saw fear there, he also saw strength and confidence. Their greyness was as beguiling as Alanda's blue eyes had been frightening. He saw what she must see, the hideous demon face leering in a lipless grin. Yet she stooped her head, and with trembling hands he pushed aside the golden brown locks from her forehead, marvelling briefly at the marble-like perfection of her skin. Then he carefully drew the rune. When he was finished, her eyes flicked up again, assessing whatever lay behind the mask, not with horror, but with a gentle inquisitiveness. She squeezed his gloved hand briefly, then melted back into the shadows.

Now Seresh came up, with a grimace.

"Make it good, priest," he snarled, "if you know how!" Urthred finished the inscription with a savage twist of the crayon. Seresh glared at him, then strode towards the passage dug in the floor. The others followed, only hesitating at its entrance when they noticed that Urthred had not joined them.

"What is the matter, priest?" Alanda asked, her eyes reflecting eerily like a cat's in the light of the torch.

"I must draw the sign on myself," he answered, "and for that I must take off this mask."

"Then do so."

"I have vowed that no one will see my face; please, go on, I'll catch you."

"Leave the fool," Seresh urged. "Faran can have him for all I care." He dived down into the pit, and the light of the torch began to diminish. Alanda led Furtal after him, but Thalassa hesitated.

"Go," Urthred said in a strangled voice.

"Then hurry," she said. "We will wait." She was gone, like a sylph in the shadows, a mysterious, half-glimpsed wraith. Urthred was left alone in the gloom, staring after her. He shook himself out of his reverie and turned his face in case she still lingered in the shadows of the pit, and unlatched his mask. He brought up the crayon to his hideously ridged forehead. The unevenness of the skin and the fact that he now had to inscribe the rune in a mirror image made the job difficult, but at last it was done. He relatched the mask hurriedly, his heart hammering in panic.

But then a curious thing happened.

Glancing up, he saw the mist beyond the ledge glowing with the sinister blue light—their pursuers must be very close now. But instead of scuttling for the safety of the pit, a contradictory spirit entered him, a stillness, just as it had years ago on the day of the Burning. He felt impelled to go forward to danger, to self-destruction, rather than back, where there was safety.

Without thinking why, he strode through the frond of creepers to the edge of the step, and looked down the vast flight of stairs where the blue light now burned steadily, as if waiting for him. In its light he saw figures standing silently in a semicircle at the base of the pyramid. As he watched he saw one of them, much taller than the others, wade out of the bank of fog and look up at the pyramid. Even at this distance, Urthred's eyes locked with his. The two stood thus, for several seconds, in silent contemplation. A chill filled Urthred, a freezing glacier in every vein. But there also came a calmness, an acceptance of death which made him look in the face of the nemesis below with utter calmness.

Instinctively, Urthred knew who this distant figure was: Lord Faran Gaton Nekron.

With an effort he broke eye contact. The vampire's powers of mesmerism could stretch this far, but he was equal to it. The fire in his veins burned again. The battle to come would be a hard one, but he now felt he had the measure of Faran. He turned and followed the glimmer of the torch which faintly illuminated the mouth of the excavation.

Faran Gaton had seen the figure at the top of the steps. For decades he had lived in twilight places: dark crypts, subterranean passageways choked with dust, anywhere that complete darkness hung even at midday had been his home. And over those interminable years, like grains of sand trickled through a hand, slowly falling, the eyes that once, during his first life, could have spotted a sparrow at a mile's distance had become accustomed slowly to the absence of light. So now perfect darkness was the medium in which he saw perfectly, and raw sunlight the lance of fire that would shatter his retina into a thousand shards. Even though the figure was nearly three hundred feet above him, he had seen the Scar Mask clearly, glowing white in the setting light of Erewon through the mist, and known that this was the man he'd been pursuing all night—the priest who had killed Varash.

His guards stood by him as the first of the vampires who had followed them swarmed past them and began climbing up the side of the pyramid. Faran Gaton was happy to let them go; they were unlikely to get to Thalassa before him. The priest had sorcery, and there had been others with him, fighters who would no doubt put up a better struggle than the two they had just killed amongst the tombs. Half the undead from the square had stayed behind to drink from the corpses of the two men who'd ambushed them. But those vampires climbing the side of the tomb would be sufficient to take the brunt of the assault, clearing the way for him.

The speed with which the vampires were climbing the face of the pyramid attested to their thirst. Time was running out for all those who had not drunk their fill: Erewon was low in the sky, on the mountain peaks to the west. Two hours at the most until it set. And if the vampires didn't drink before it set, they knew they would sink into the second death.

Faran well knew their lust. The blood of a still-beating heart, this was all that could perfectly slake the thirst of the Dead in Life. The borrowed blood of the leeches was like dust to the sweet-flowing nectar of it. He sensed it now, even over the pungent smoke issuing from Golon's censer. It came from the two women. Faran marvelled how in the last hour Malliana's blood scent, which had seemed old and stale before, should have grown so much in allure.

They'd left the palanquin at the entrance to the City of the

Dead. Malliana was by his shoulder, shivering from the cold. She, too, had glimpsed the figure high on the tomb steps, but only as a muddied blur.

"That was the priest," Faran said, fighting the thirst that the scent had prompted in him.

Malliana caught the blood craze in his eyes and looked away. Faran was so close; the smell of mildew was very strong, like a drug. She was certain she was going to die at some stage of the evening. Only the mysterious blue light burning in Golon's censer kept the undead at bay, and this warding could be removed at any time, at Faran's whim. She huddled close to Viri: her acolyte was equally terrified, her face white, her eyes staring and wild.

Faran was frowning at them, a fleck of spittle on his lips.

"Lord," she started hesitantly, trying to distract him, "you have found the priest—please . . . let me and my servant go."

A dry rattle was emitted from Faran's throat: it might have been a laugh, or a grunt of contempt.

"No, priestess; that would be too easy. You rang the gong. The Brethren have awoken. You wouldn't get far."

She was trapped: by now not only the City of the Dead, but the whole of Thrull was crawling with the undead, aroused by the temple gong which she herself had struck. She had been the cause of her own destruction. She couldn't have known what its powers were. Only one thing was sure. Faran was right—there was no going back into the city.

Faran stepped forward, Golon with the censer at his shoulder. He surveyed the first granite step with distaste, as if the physical effort of climbing it was beneath him, then motioned two of the Reapers forward. They climbed the step, then leant back to pull him up it. Golon followed. The censer clanked against the steps as the Reapers now in turn helped him. A heavy cloud of blue-white smoke burst from it. Malliana came after, scrambling madly for footholds, the Reapers making no effort to assist her. She reached the first step and turned to reach down for Viri.

But Viri had had other ideas. The guards had released her in order to climb. As Malliana watched, Viri hesitated, first looking at the steps, then back into the graveyard. Then, her mind apparently made up, she took one step back, then two, then ran back towards the graves. Malliana was about to shout a warning, but Viri had already reached the tombs. It was then that the first vampires, barely slaked by the blood of Gadiel and Rath, shambled out of the shadows towards her.

CHAPTER THIRTY-TWO

Despair

Jayal had been tied to one of the Doppelgänger's other captives, a flaxen-haired youth sporting a pallor that would not have disgraced one of the undead. Not only were their wrists bound, but the same coarse hemp had been looped around their necks so he was attached to the youth and the two other prisoners in the train. One of the Doppelgänger's men held the front end of the rope, encouraging Jayal and the others to increase their speed every now and again with a sharp pull on it. Jayal's neck had already been rubbed raw by the friction.

The other captives had been entirely apathetic when they'd been brought up from the cellars. The only animation they showed was when the Doppelgänger approached them and they shrank away, no doubt expecting more of the punishment that had become their daily diet. But since the first two of them had been left for the vampires, they had shown more animation, their eyes darting from the Doppelgänger at the head of the column back to their remaining fellows, as if trying to calculate which of them would be next.

Though the Doppelgänger had led his party by the most circuitous route down the cliffs, they had nearly blundered right into the middle of a group of about fifty of the undead. The Doppelgänger's men had, as one, turned and fled into the night, the vampires close on their heels. Jayal had heard the rustling of their mould-stiffened cloaks as they'd come pounding down the streets after them, the shouts of alarm from his captors, the raw, burning pain in his neck and arms as the rope was yanked forward, then the ropemaster's voice cursing them to run as fast as they could. There had been a sudden slackening of the pull of the rope from behind as they'd run, but it was only five minutes later, when the vampires had miraculously melted back into the mist, that Jayal realised why. The two rearmost captives were gone, cut away as bait. When they'd regrouped five of the gang were missing as well, lost in the fog. Jayal winced as the rope sawed at the wound on his neck again.

They were still moving hurriedly through the streets, losing altitude rapidly. He had an idea that they were nearly in the Lower Town, but he couldn't be sure. He eyed the Doppelgänger's men through the mist. There were about twenty of them left. The Doppelgänger had chosen them well: they all seemed hewn from the same block of stone; lantern-jawed, muscled, unshaven and unwashed, they wore bright jewellery about their persons like trophies and swore like men possessed by the god of madness. Their eyes to a man were flinty and stripped of human sympathy. They looked at the captives with the interest of butchers staring at shortly to be slaughtered steers.

The guard gave the flaxen-haired youth a vicious tug, and Jayal was nearly pulled off his feet as the whiplash ran through the rope around his neck. He nearly choked, but was too busy trying to keep his feet as they set off at a run down the street in front. More vampires? Jayal tried to crane his neck round, but the rope stopped him. He had to continue jogging along, his eyes forced to the front.

Then they came to a sudden, jerking halt. Jayal took in ragged breaths of air through his bruised larynx. The Doppelgänger walked back down the line of men, smiling when he saw Jayal's discomfort.

"Enjoying the exercise, brother?" he said, apparently oblivious to the danger all around them. He laughed when he received no reply, merely passing to the rearmost captive. This one was a woman. Dark-haired and well built, she was probably only thirty or so, but the livid weals on her face disguised her age. The Doppelgänger now gently seized her chin and stared into her eyes. The effect on the woman was startling: she jerked her head back and forth savagely, the movements once more being transmitted down the rope to Jayal's raw neck.

"Atansha, Atansha," the Doppelgänger remonstrated, "have you forgotten all the good times we've had? Look at me: it is I, Setten!"

"You killed my husband and children!" She spat.

"Your husband was only a poor carter and your children noisy brats. Haven't you been happier with me?" he asked in a wheedling tone.

The only answer he got was another dry spit from the woman.

The Doppelgänger shook his head sadly: "So: we must end it all, Atansha. Sometimes a woman wants freedom; I understand that, applaud it in fact." The woman looked from the Doppelgänger to the ropemaster as the latter stepped up and sliced through the rope attaching her to the others. But before she could react to being released, he seized her and wrestled her over to where a post stood in the centre of the street. Atansha was thrust up against it, her hands tied behind her around the post. All this time she had not uttered a word, her face obscured by the dark mane of her hair. The ropemaster ripped at the front of the flimsy rags she was dressed in. They gave with barely a hint of resistance. Her breasts spilled out, and she was left shivering in the freezing air.

The Doppelgänger pulled a dagger from his belt and stepped up to her. "It's sad to lose you," he said almost wistfully. "But you'll have others—many more before the night is out." He laughed dryly as the woman struggled with the new bonds. Then, in the flash of an eye, he swept the point of his dagger across the top of her breasts twice, leaving a rough X mark from which blood immediately welled. The creature looked at his handiwork with satisfaction, then made a lascivious licking motion with his tongue and laughed. Atansha had fallen still for a second, staring at the wound on her chest, but now let out a soul-piercing scream. The Doppelgänger ignored her, hurrying back to the column. "Come, with luck she'll attract every vampire for a mile with those screams," he said, yanking at the rope.

Jayal's mind filled with the woman's piercing screams as they set off again. He hoped she wouldn't have to suffer long. A dark despair filled him. Not only at his situation, but at the acknowledgement that it was his own dark half, something that had once been integral to himself, something without which he could not now exist, which had done these terrible things to the woman.

Self-loathing almost choked him. If it meant that they would both die if he killed the Doppelgänger, so be it. Such evil couldn't be left to roam the earth. His spirit felt crushed, annihilated. He longed for oblivion, wished it had been he who had been left behind as bait. But he knew his end would be far, far worse.

He had felt despair like this before: for years after the battle he'd wandered on his quest through the lands of Hangar Parang. Though he couldn't remember any of the details of the battle, his dreams had been filled with the images of it. The face of Vortumin as he staggered towards him with the arrow in his throat, the carrion piles burning in the night, the tattered shreds of the once gaily coloured tents, the pall of smoke over Thrull as he looked back from the Fire Mountains. He'd ridden on, exhausted by self-torment, on most days more asleep than awake, waking nightmares coming to him in the saddle. There were Poluso and Edric as they had been on the day they died, walking down the dusty road in front of him. He would call out to them as he rode past, but their eyes were fixed ahead of them, their faces and hair caked with dust, their wounds red and raw, Poluso's entrails hanging like chains to his knees. Cloud would not stop, though in his dream he pulled at the reins and shouted and cursed. He looked back despairingly, Poluso and Edric becoming ever smaller dots on the road behind. Why had he lived, and all those he had known died? That had been his first lesson in the guilt of a survivor, a guilt so strong that even his waking hours were filled with the faces of the dead. A guilt so remorseless that self-destruction seemed preferable to suffering it any longer.

One night he had sat by a well in a village burned to the

ground by the bandits that wandered all over this region. He
could tell by the sickly-sweet stench coming from its bottom
that the dead had been thrown into it to poison the water. The
bandits needn't have bothered: Jayal threw a rock down it; it
fell for what he estimated were some fifty feet, hit something
soft, then rattled over stone. The well was empty. He was out of
water, and the desert stretched all around him.

It was then he determined to add his corpse to the others. His
life was gone—his home, his father, Thalassa. He had hung
rocks on a cord around his neck: he would throw himself down
the well as the sun rose the next morning. If the fall didn't kill
him, then the rocks would surely break his neck. He'd waited in
the darkness for the sun, for the return of Reh from his brother's
dark kingdom. He had waited thus for what had seemed an eternity, fighting off sleep.

Why was the night taking so long? Had Reh finally been imprisoned forever in Iss' dark labyrinth? Had time itself died?
Then the sky imperceptibly turned to a lighter shade of black, to
grey, then an edge of gold appeared as the sun heaved itself
slowly over the desert dunes. He'd flung his legs over the parapet of the well, ready to jump. He glanced at the sun for the last
time. Its upper half, engorged and red, hung on the ridge of the
farthermost dunes, turning the yellow sand to crimson all
around him. Then he'd seen it: a flash of fire erupting from its
surface. A sign? He'd hesitated, balanced on the edge of the
parapet. Behind him Cloud had neighed impatiently to be away
from this place of death, and it was as if he had suddenly
snapped awake from a dream. What was he doing? In that instant he'd learned his second lesson: it was too easy to take his
own life—it wouldn't bring back the dead.

He'd cut the rocks away from his neck and resaddled Cloud:
passing the day in a daze as they made their way slowly
through the barren rocks and dunes. His mind once more filled
with thirst-induced hallucinations. Then, in the afternoon,
Cloud had stopped and neighed once, rousing him from his stupor. He raised his head wearily. What had disturbed the gelding? He looked around. Nothing. But then he sniffed the air: a
salty tang: they were near the sea! The scent revived his senses.
He'd spurred the horse forward: there in the distance was a low

silver band of water. He rode towards it and soon stood on the beach. He listened to the gentle roar and ebb of the water rushing over the pebbles like a cascade of a million diamonds on the glistening stones. To his left he saw, beyond beetling cliffs that came right down to the sea, a marsh stretching away into the distance. In its midst he saw a far-off tower, the tower that he'd ridden over half the world to find, the tower where, according to the scrolls his father had given him, Dragonstooth had been hidden by the Worm millennia before. . . .

That had been a year before, in the Southern Lands, where the feeble sun actually warmed the earth. A place far warmer than this City of Skulls. Now he was filled with the old despair he'd known then—the triumph of recovering the sword mocked by its presence in Kazaris's belt, his father long gone, his secrets betrayed to this cruel mirror of himself, the Doppelgänger, his betrothed a whore, and he ignominiously trussed like a slave. The quest had taken too long: time had been the great enemy; any opportunity for the sword to do good was long gone. But the sword had been transformed: the light from its blade had turned from white to a coppery gleam, reflecting the sinking moon's colour. Never in the year it had been in his possession had it shone with this colour. What did it presage?

His speculation was rudely interrupted as the column halted once more. They were in a small square. The fog had cleared slightly, and he could see that the far side overlooked the City of the Dead.

The Doppelgänger was coming back down the line of men. "How are the tethered dogs?" he asked, as he came up to the captives. The two men tied to Jayal shifted uneasily, but the Doppelgänger was ignoring them, staring deep into Jayal's eyes. He gave a quick tug at the halter, burning Jayal's neck once more. "Good! You're awake at least," he crowed. "See yonder." He pointed back the way they'd come. "Fireworks in Hel!" Jayal looked back. The night sky around the citadel was livid with the colour of the flames raging around the Temple of Reh. "The Temple of Reh is burning, and all the priests as well with luck." The Doppelgänger chuckled mirthlessly. "But look again there!" Jayal followed the line of his finger forward across the square. A strange blue light burned through the fog bank in the City of the Dead.

He turned to find the Doppelgänger's one eye, a blue reflection of his own, staring intently at him as if examining his own features in a mirror with an unheathily propietorial interest. The creature's face broke into a lopsided grin, accentuated by his lip-splitting scar. "Fire from Hel," he spat gleefully. Spittle flecked Jayal's face and he winced away, but the Doppelgänger pushed his face even closer. "There lies our way, Jayal Illgill, so let's see you move." He wrenched on the halter again and sent Jayal stumbling a few feet down the cobbled street, to be stopped short when the slack of the rope jerked against the other captives' necks. Off-balance, he fell to the ground, unable to check his fall with his tethered arms.

"Tush, tush," the Doppelgänger clucked, stepping forward and hauling him to his feet, "I don't want that precious body hurt, seeing as it will be mine again once we find the Rod! More caution, less speed!" he chuckled, pushing Jayal in front of him down the cobbled slope. Kazaris and the others followed behind. Five of the gang had been lost, and the men's nerves were clearly stretched to breaking point. Their eyes were continuously on the move, trying to spot any danger in the shadows and fog. But they still followed the Doppelgänger, who exhibited nothing but a cold indifference to his surroundings, their motley collection of weapons, swords, axes, crossbows and halberds pointing out in all directions like the bristles of a porcupine. Only Kazaris seemed to have any of the sangfroid of their leader. He held a yellowing scroll in one hand and a long ritual dagger in the other. Jayal's eyes went to Dragonstooth again. Even in the five minutes since their last stop, its blade seemed to have become even redder-hued. Again, he wondered what it signified.

Just then they plunged into a thicker band of fog, and Jayal found himself immersed in a strange white world where visibility was reduced to two arms' lengths and all sound was muffled and distorted. They proceeded thus, past the guttering remains of the watchfires and along a dank, rubble-choked alleyway, long unused judging from the weeds which made the ground slippery underfoot. Burned-out buildings surrounded them.

Then the guards in front reached a broken-down section of wall which suddenly loomed out of the mist. They climbed over it, white toads, disturbed from their evening's rest, hopping away into the fog from under their feet.

Jayal was jerked forward. He hesitated at the top of the wall, wondering if he could make a quick break into the inviting fog all around him. But the two remaining slaves would have to come with him, and they seemed oblivious of everything except their fear. But the Doppelgänger was waiting for him at the top of the slope, as if he had read his mind. His sword pricked Jayal through the serge of his cloak, and he stumbled forward, down the loose scree of rock. The funerary monuments of the dead loomed up all around them from the mist: they were in the City of the Dead.

They blundered on, now totally blinded by the fog. There was a sudden noise in front, and the column came to another abrupt halt. There it was again: a distinctive crack as of a branch being broken over a knee. He looked behind him. The Doppelgänger's face was barely lit by the glow from the fires raging through the city a thousand feet above them. He was listening intently too, puzzled. He prodded Jayal and the other captives forward past the line of men.

Because of the muffling effect of the mist, Jayal nearly stumbled over the figure lying on the ground from which the cracking noises had come. It was a human warrior, its leather armour slashed to tatters, its skull half-bitten through. Two creatures crouched about it, one human, but undead, the other half-human, half-hyena. One chewed through the remaining part of the shattered cranium, sucking up the grey brains from the man's skull like porridge, the other gnawed with prehensile jaws at the bones of a leg. The bone cracked again as the creature came away with another mouthful of shattered bone, marrow and ragged flesh.

But the vampire had scented them. It let out a hissing noise from deep within its throat, revealing a mouthful of blood-flecked, sharpened teeth. Then its head was jerked back as if by an invisible string, cracking against the marble tomb behind it, a crossbow bolt planted exactly in the centre of its forehead. A

smear of black ichor was left on the white marble as it slid
down it, the front of its face now a fist-shaped hole.

The Doppelgänger danced round Jayal and swung at the
were-creature with his sword, but his left hand was feeble compared to his accustomed right one and the creature parried his
weak blow with the detached leg of the warrior, hissing like a
cornered cat. Jayal tried to drop back as more of the Doppelgänger's men pressed forward. The creature swung the leg
around madly, sending one of the swords spinning off into the
air, but this gave the Doppelgänger another opportunity, and his
quick thrust forward slid between the creature's emaciated rib
cage. It let out a screech and wriggled like a hooked fish on the
end of the sword. Then, sensing its impending doom, it dropped
the leg and flailed at the Doppelgänger's face with taloned
claws, but a double-handed axe crashed through its skull, sending fragments of bone into Jayal's face. He tasted the coppery
taint of corrupt blood on his lips, unable to wipe it away because of his bonds. He spat, trying to rid himself of it.

The Doppelgänger's men were raining blows down on the
vampire, which was trying to crawl away despite the gaping
hole in its head. Further fragments of bone and clotted blood
sprayed up from their blades, and eventually it lay still. But the
Doppelgänger had taken no part in the dismemberment: he was
staring at the strange hybrid that lay in front of him. Its body
was worthy of scrutiny. It was feline in appearance with well-
developed hind legs which looked capable of leaping great dis-
tances, yet the body skin was utterly smooth and without fur.
What was more, the thing's face, despite a pair of long, for-
ward-pointing ears, had appeared humanoid before it had been
reduced to pulp.

"I've never seen anything like it," Kazaris said softly. The
other men, finished with their sport with the vampire, seemed
equally perturbed as they gathered round.

"What in Hel's name was it?" cursed the Doppelgänger.

Kazaris shrugged his shoulders. He looked up at the flames
illuminating the mist-shrouded cliffs. "The gong has summoned more than we bargained for."

Jayal's mind was racing: strange portents, strange happen-
ings, strange creatures. Above all the sword at Kazaris's belt. It

glowed an even deeper red, the red of arterial blood. The sorcerer's whole body seemed bathed in its colour.

The Doppelgänger's men were now muttering uneasily to one another. It was clear that, if they had their way, they would be back in the safety of the Illgill mansion. The Doppelgänger rounded on them. "Never mind," he snarled, baring his teeth over his scar. "We've dealt with worse: let's keep our wits about us!"

He jerked his head and they continued through the avenues of eerie sepulchres, if anything even more subdued than they had been before. They disturbed another nest of feeding creatures, huddled round another body, but this time they gave them a wide berth.

Now the fog began to thin again and Marizian's tomb loomed vaster and vaster out of the mist in front of them. At its base they could see a blue light burning, and a group of figures congregated around it.

Jayal and the slaves were pushed into the gloomy entranceway of a house-sized tomb as the Doppelgänger and Kazaris crept forward to where a broken pillar gave them cover. In the gap between the two layers of mist they could see the mass of figures congregated around the tomb wall.

"Well, so it is the lord himself," whispered the Doppelgänger, squinting through his one eye at the tall figure silhouetted against the blue light in the gateway that led into the tomb. Faran Gaton was looking at the figures scurrying up the gigantic steps of the pyramid. He had provided well for his security: there must have been some fifty Reapers surrounding him, as well as Golon. Next to Lord Faran, the Doppelgänger recognised the figures of Malliana and Viri, shivering in their thin dresses.

The Doppelgänger cursed under his breath. Now he would have to deal with Faran as well as the man who had taken off with Thalassa. He wondered whether Kazaris would be a match for the abilities of the legendary Golon. All he could hope was that the dangers within the tomb would so whittle down the energies and powers of the two groups in front that his men would be on hand for easy pickings.

As he thought this, the first of the vampires reached the top of the pyramid and disappeared from view. Seeing this, Faran,

helped by two of his men, began to ascend slowly, Malliana following. But Viri clearly had other ideas: she took one step, then
two steps backwards, then ran towards the tombs. The Doppelgänger saw Golon shoot a question at Faran, but the vampire
lord shook his head, allowing her to go. They resumed their
climb as Viri came running pell-mell in the direction of the
Doppelgänger and Kazaris. As she came, she looked behind
fearfully as if expecting pursuit, but when she saw no one was
following her she slowed her pace, the expression on her face,
which they could see quite clearly, changing from relief to sudden doubt. She peered fearfully into the shadows of the tombs,
and then back towards the lights of Faran's party. A sudden
movement made her jump to one side. A vampire had materialised out of the shadows right next to her. It came at her hissing and spitting, a claw outstretched threateningly. She
staggered back, turning to run, but now two more appeared behind her, blocking her retreat. She screamed, and the Doppelgänger could see the white face of Malliana staring down from
the side of the tomb.

"Should we rescue her?" asked Kazaris, but the Doppelgänger shook his head.

"No, let her die; it will distract those things while we make
our move."

More vampires had now appeared: the creatures were playing with Viri, prodding her this way and that, so she ran
backwards and forwards around the ever-tightening ring surrounding her. Gradually she was lost to sight as the jostling
figures blocked her from view. She must have fainted quite
away before the first set of fangs ripped into her, for, strangely,
she didn't cry out again as the vampires set to work. The Doppelgänger gestured at the men behind, who dragged Jayal and
the two other captives from the shelter of the doorway. They
detoured around the knot of undead, keeping below the line of
the wall so that none of the figures working their way up the
side of the tomb could see them.

CHAPTER THIRTY-THREE

Marizian's Tomb

The tunnel was low and cramped; earth spattered down from its crumbling ceiling onto Urthred's cloak, and dirt worked its way down his neck, its coldness like fingers on his spine. Though it had only been recently dug by Zaraman's men, the tunnel was swiftly approaching a state of collapse, the vibration of each footstep causing another miniature cave-in. The air was close, with the scent of grave soil. A rat, disturbed by his approach, ran off in front of him squeaking frenetically. He kept his eyes rooted on the faint glow ahead of him down the shaft, praying it was Seresh's torchlight.

It was the only light in the darkness and Urthred cursed himself for not taking another of the torches for himself. But the light was getting fainter and fainter as the excavation wound to the left and right in front of him, and presently there was only the merest suggestion of grey far ahead. Then the grey was suddenly replaced with a violent flash of red that burned into his eyes. It was followed by the sound of a muffled explosion. Urthred stopped dead, every sense alert. There was silence and, now, total darkness. After a few seconds he smelt acrid smoke gradually flowing up the shaft from the direction of the explosion. What had happened? He hadn't time to think; Faran could not be too far behind now. He started feeling his way by running his gloved hands along the tunnel walls, the shadowy confines

of the mask reducing him to near blindness. Panic mounted as
the feeling of sightlessness increased as the afterimage of the explosion faded from his retinas and he became even more conscious of the all-enveloping blackness around him.

He cursed again, blaming himself for delaying so long outside. What had possessed him to confront Faran? Just as he
thought this, he stumbled over a wooden obstacle lying across
the floor. He fell forward, the breath driven from his lungs by the
impact. He kicked away the object entangled with his ankles, by
its feel one of the pit props which should have been shoring up
the ceiling, and struggled back to his feet.

Enough was enough. He unlatched the mask, feeling another
breath of smoke from the interior of the tomb on his ravaged
face as he did so. He breathed deeply once, choking slightly, but
the feeling of claustrophobia was retreating now the mask was
off. He set off again down the corridor.

More earth rained down from the ceiling onto his cloak, but
he carried on regardless, not caring now if he was crushed under
a ton of it. Anything was better than this darkness. It was nearly
impossible to judge, but he estimated he must have descended at
least fifty feet of the three hundred that he had ascended going
up the huge outer steps of the temple.

Then two things happened simultaneously: the tunnel suddenly widened out in front of him, and the chamber he found
himself in was bathed in sudden light. He was momentarily
blinded, his eyes trying to readjust to the brilliance. He caught a
glimpse of an open area wreathed in smoke and half-filled with
earth from the excavation spilling across its floors. He sank up
to his ankles in the dirt. Too late, he remembered the mask, desperately fumbling with the flap to cover his face. He turned to
the source of the light, an unshuttered lantern off to one side of
the chamber. He sensed a shadowy figure behind it. His lidless
eyes had no way of keeping out the light: he turned away, struggling with the mask. After a few seconds, he found the latch and
snapped it to.

When his eyes could focus again, he turned and saw that it
was Alanda standing, holding the lamp, every wrinkle of her
face outlined in the harsh light; her gaze was steady, unperturbed.

"You!" he muttered.

"I waited, knowing you had no light."

She had seen his face! Violent emotions: panic, anger, vulnerability, flowed through him, but whatever Alanda's reaction was, she kept it from her voice. "The others have gone on: Thalassa was upset by that," she said, jerking her head at the far end of the chamber.

Urthred looked in the direction indicated. There was a pile of what looked like charred logs just in front of an arched entranceway at the far side of the room. There was a wide ledge over the entranceway, partially lost in the shadows. A tingle of fear ran up Urthred's spine as he looked at it. He returned his gaze to the logs. As his eyes adjusted to the lantern light he recognised them for what they were, charred human limbs, fused together by an intense heat. The smell of scorched meat lingered in the room. Urthred had seen plenty of unpleasant sights in his twenty years, his own face included, but the burned flesh made the bile rise in his throat.

"Zaraman?" he asked.

"He and his friends—Reh has taken them."

Urthred looked away from the charred bodies. "What caused this?"

"Fire—another step into the room and you would see what happens."

Urthred didn't feel inclined to test Alanda's statement.

"My seal worked?"

"Yes," she replied. "Come, we have to hurry—Faran can't be far behind. Shield your eyes, the light is strong." With this she picked up the lantern and took a step towards the arched entrance.

It was as if a furnace door to another world had been opened. Orange-and-red flame blossomed from the floor and ceiling, enveloping her. Urthred was momentarily blown against the chamber wall by the blast of heat. He had averted his face, but now turned back to see what had become of Alanda.

She was struggling towards the archway as if against a strong wind. Never since the Hearth Fire at Forgeholm had Urthred known such heat. The room pulsated with red-and-orange light, its source apparently on the ledge above the arch. Squinting his

eyes, he could dimly make out the shape of a creature crouched
on the ledge, a stream of liquid fire pouring from its mouth, a
demon face, winged ruff around its gills, burning red: then it
was gone in another explosion of flame.

He saw that Alanda had reached the other side of the chamber, apparently unharmed, and was now waving him across. He
took a deep breath and flung himself forward into the maelstrom.

Immediately there was a great roaring and the air was full of
flames once more. He staggered forward, his cloak whirling up
in the heat, but untouched by the fire. It was as if he had plunged
back into the Hearth Fire at Forgeholm, but this time the sign
drawn on his forehead seemed to deflect the flames from his
body, so it was only the force of the burning hurricane and not
its heat that he struggled against as he staggered across to the
archway. He was fighting to breathe; all of the air had been
burned up by the flame, but then he burst through the final curtain of fire and he gulped in the cool air of the tomb once more.
Behind him the flames stopped as abruptly as they'd started.

He was unscathed, the rune had worked. But, even more curiously, all the scars on his body tingled with energy, as if meeting the element that had first caused them had effected some
healing on them. He suddenly wanted to scratch at all of them,
to rid himself of the thousand small itches that burst out around
his body.

Alanda watched his writhing with concern. "Are you
burned?"

"No—Reh's sign protected me. But there is a strange kind of
tingling in my skin."

"Maybe the fire has healed you."

In the excitement of passing through the fire, Urthred had
forgotten that Alanda had glimpsed his face when he'd first entered the chamber. Now her statement brought him up short.
"You saw my face."

"Yes," she said simply.

"Then you saw what Varash saw—it killed him."

"I had guessed already what lay beneath the mask. I spoke
with Manichee before the battle seven years ago. He told me a
little about what had happened to you, how you were one of the

chosen ones, that you would follow him. Since then I have waited for you, knowing you would come."

"I didn't realise that you knew him," Urthred said, wondering whether he should tell her of the vision of his old master he'd had earlier.

But Alanda had other things on her mind. She nodded her head at the chamber behind them. It was still and empty apart from some wisps of smoke being drawn steadily down the tunnel beyond. "There are many things that you don't know about me, but we must go now—Faran will struggle to get past this obstacle, but he won't be far behind."

"And the others?"

"They're some way ahead."

There was a set of steps in front, plunging into the darkness. She set off down them, the lantern held up high so Urthred could clearly see the damp grey steps spiralling down into the impenetrable gloom below. They went down as fast as they could, but, before long, Alanda stopped, her chest rising and falling as she struggled for breath: "I have to rest a moment," she panted. "I'm not as young as I used to be."

Urthred looked behind and up in the direction of the chamber. There was no sudden light indicating that Faran had run into the demon's lair. It might take him hours to figure out a way to get past it. He turned back to Alanda, wishing to continue the conversation about Manichee, but she spoke first. "So, priest—what did you make of the Lightbringer's Shrine?" she said hoarsely, still gasping for breath.

"It was as you said it would be," he said briefly.

"And the girl?"

"What of her?"

"Come, priest—you know what I mean. Didn't the spirits cleave to her, haven't you seen the transformation?"

Urthred had seen it—all too well. "Of one thing I'm sure—you have the sight."

"You are a difficult man to convince: but you will be persuaded, I know. Your fate and Thalassa's are inextricably linked."

Urthred's heart surprised him by giving a sudden lurch, as if this was what it had been secretly hoping to hear above all other things, despite his inbuilt caution. For the moment, however, he didn't say anything.

Alanda ignored his silence: "As I said, I was once more than a serving-woman in a brothel. You were still a boy when I was at Baron Illgill's court—he came to me for prophecy, divination. My husband, too, had the power. But not enough to save himself. He died in the battle. Now he rots in the City of the Dead; Reh will not take him to Paradise; his head is on the pyramid of skulls." Her eyes became remote, unfocused, as the memories kicked in. "Seven bitter years. I've waited a long time for you."

"You were so confident I would come?"

"As I said, Manichee told me you would. Then I saw you in my dreams. I spoke to your brother, who told me more about you." She looked faintly embarrassed for a moment. "I asked him to send that letter to you at Forgeholm."

"And now I'm here, and my brother is dead . . ."

"There was nothing any of us could have done to save him."

"But you see the future—did you know what was going to happen to Randel?"

Their eyes met: his shadowed by the eye sockets of the mask, hers electric blue and alien.

"I've recovered," she said briefly. "Let's go."

"You haven't answered my question," Urthred muttered. "Did you know that Randel was going to die?"

"Yes."

"And the other conspirators?"

"Them as well—it's a curse, priest," she said bitterly. "I see the future. I see the deaths of friends whom I could warn. But I cannot tell them: the skeins of fate would unravel, the earth would end in chaos, past and future would come undone like a ball of wool and I would be given up to Shades until the end of time . . ."

"You are a dangerous woman, Alanda," Urthred interrupted, "but I wouldn't be you even if I could have my face back—all those deaths in your mind, maybe even my own."

"I told you—you have a future, with Thalassa . . ."

"Then why can't you tell us of the dangers ahead?"

"Marizian didn't just leave demons here, Urthred: all magic

is warped and displaced here—there are hidden baffles against my art, maybe yours as well."

Urthred wondered. His power, since he'd stared down at Faran from the top of the steps, felt as if it were seeping back into his veins, and it didn't seem to be coming from his mask. His skin felt as if it was on fire, as if the Flame would erupt from it at any second as it had done in the square at dusk. He would see. Alanda had her breath back: Faran would be following. He motioned her forward.

They continued descending in silence, not of the most companionable kind. The ceiling and floor here were made of worked stone. Water dripped from the cracks in the blocks above them, and, below, the steps were moss-covered and slick. As they spiralled down he saw strange white ferns, starved of light, growing from crevices between the steps and the walls. As Urthred stepped past the first of them, one of the tendrils of the nearest plant unfurled and reached for his leg. He sprang back.

"Be careful," Alanda said. "They are attracted to heat and are poisonous."

"Thanks for your warning, though it comes rather late."

Alanda took him by the arm. "Remember everything beyond this point was put here for one purpose by Marizian: to keep out interlopers. Even the plants have minds of their own; as for the other things . . ."

"What other things?"

"We'll come across them soon enough. Illgill defeated them when he took the Rod of Power: let us hope we are as skillful as he was."

She led on, the lantern casting long shadows. Then the steps ended with a level platform. Three tunnels went off into the darkness in front, but Alanda took the central one, as if she knew where she was going.

They passed through it and came out by the side of an underground pool, about twenty feet across. On the other side they could see lights and Seresh, Thalassa and Furtal standing in a stone-cut chamber. Seresh and Thalassa were inspecting a rectangular entranceway to the right of the chamber, but looked up the second they spotted Alanda's lantern, their faces tense, expecting trouble. They immediately relaxed when they saw who it was. Thalassa called out a greeting which echoed in the empty vault.

Alanda waved back, stepping forward to the edge of the pool. It was as still and dark as ink, save where drops of water fell through the ceilings and landed with melancholy plops at its centre, sending out oily ripples over its surface. A narrow walkway led down one side, fringed by the same sinister white ferns which had embarrassed Urthred earlier.

He and Alanda set off down the walkway, picking their way through the ferns. He looked down with curiosity at the pool. What he saw made him stagger back—ghostly faces leered up from its depths, grimacing, emitting silent howls. He tripped and fell back into the bed of ferns. Immediately his cloak was gripped by white tendrils. He slashed to left and right, breaking the fronds away, but releasing a pale green juice from their stems which fizzled and frothed on contact with his cloak. Alanda bent swiftly and, with surprising strength, helped him back to his feet.

"Thanks," Urthred murmured, staring at where the plants' acid had burned holes in his cloak.

"Remember—everything is dangerous," Alanda said. Urthred kept his face averted from the surface of the pool as they hurried over to the other side.

"You've taken your time," Seresh muttered as they reached them. Alanda ignored him, preferring to inspect the stone block that barred the way forward.

"What do you make of this?" she asked Urthred. He stepped forward, catching a glimpse of Thalassa's face as he did so. It was white and tear-stained and she looked away under his scrutiny. The shock of seeing the burned bodies had affected her badly; gone was the early confidence she had shown after the Lightbringer's Shrine. It would be a kindness to her if they pressed on as quickly as possible.

But the way through the door was not apparent: no handle, or keyhole, or secret panel. . . . The stone block appeared solid and seamless. He pushed with his gloves at its centre, but nothing gave.

"I've already tried that," said Seresh, with a hint of irritation.

"There must be some way forward," mused Urthred.

Furtal spoke: "Sometimes a doorway is not what it seems."

"What do you mean?" Urthred asked.

Furtal fixed him with his milky white orbs. "Legend has it that this place was built with great cunning. Doors may be solid rock, and rock open doors. What is on the other side of the chamber?"

Urthred shrugged and went and looked. Nothing, just a plain granite wall. He was about to turn away when he noticed it: a small copper seal set into the rock at waist height. He inspected it more closely. The seal was ancient and verdigrised and clearly wasn't there by accident. He placed his gloved hand on it. Immediately there came a rumbling from deep within the wall. He feared he'd started an avalanche, but instead a five-foot-square section of the cavern wall swung open, grating on ancient hinges. A broad passageway was revealed beyond it in the torch-light.

"Well done, Furtal!" he exclaimed. He stooped under the lintel to get a better look at what lay beyond.

Ahead, there was a set of stairs plunging down into the dark depths of the tomb. Crumbling wall paintings proclaimed the antiquity of the place. They must have been here since the first founder had been buried centuries before. Compared to the paintings which Urthred was familiar with from Forgeholm, which followed a naturalistic style, these were in an unfamiliar manner which must have been popular even before the monastery had been founded seven hundred years before. The figures in them were stiff and etiolated, the stretched lengths of their bodies mimicking the human aspiration to reach up to the heavens where the gods had gone millennia ago. To Urthred, they were purer and more spiritual than anything he had ever seen.

He knew they were now near the ancient core of this most ancient place. There was no turning back: Faran had them caught in the tomb like a hound who has sent a hare to ground. Urthred prayed that whatever was waiting for them below would help balance the odds against the undead lord. He took a deep breath of the musty air and began to descend the stairs.

CHAPTER THIRTY-FOUR

A Trial of Fire

With a final leathery heave from his desiccated lungs, Faran reached the portico leading into the tomb pyramid. The steep climb had been punishing: the bones of his chest creaked, expanding and contracting like an ancient leather bellows, emitting a faint mustiness which even he could detect despite the guano-scented air. Time had slowly worn away his body, but, like a seasoned bit of wood, that which was left was strong, stronger than the soft flesh of the living.

A little at a time some of the gulps of air slowly percolated through his atrophied body, and the ragged hammering in his chest began to fade. Four beats a minute: that was all the dead needed to keep their sluggish blood creeping around their systems. Faran's heart must have accelerated to at least ten beats a minute. But there was no pain: none of the fire in the limbs which had plagued him during life. He checked himself—the yellow flesh of his hands, his armour-covered body—to see whether any of the falls and scrapes he'd suffered had ripped off any of his dried, nerveless flesh. Miraculously there were no rents or scrapes.

Malliana now appeared on the ledge, hauled up by two of the Reapers. She had fared less well in the journey to the top of the pyramid; her thin diaphanous skirt was in shreds, showing her white legs veined with blue varicose lines, her fur stole was dogged and ragged. Like his, her breath was strangled, her face a white, grime-streaked mask. He looked at her dispassionately. She still served some purpose: the remaining Brethren would remain close, hoping to drink her blood. As for his own urges, which were piqued more and more with the setting of the moon, he could resist them for the moment: the scent of living blood was beguiling, but he didn't desire hers—only Thalassa's.

When life had gone on so long, something more than empty physical satiation, represented in his mind by Malliana's stale blood, was required. He sought an inner beauty, an untouchable thing, which he could nevertheless probe and tear at until it gave itself up with the husk of the body. Thalassa's distant beauty promised this redemption. Only when he had attained her would he be able to feel again, would he be able to touch that invisible seed of life forever denied him through the centuries of his arid existence.

But, despite his fixation on Thalassa, he had not forgotten the role the High Priestess had played in this evening's events; how her folly had unleashed the Brethren before their time, when there was not enough blood in Thrull to satisfy a tenth of them. He would have his revenge on her. Though he believed the legends—that this day had been fated to be the end of Thrull—a gesture, a sacrifice was required to mark the occasion. The woman's acolyte was dead: the Brethren would have to satisfy themselves with her mistress.

There were at least forty of the undead left. They had hurried up the side of the pyramid and now waited in the shadows of the portico, kept at a distance by the musk of Golon's censer. The moon already cast long shadows over the City of the Dead even through the mist. The time before it set was getting short.

Despite their presence, Malliana appeared to have lost the fear that had kept her cowed during the journey from the temple square. Faran had no doubt that it was the killing that had thus emboldened her. Little did she know how close she was to the same fate. Her dark eyes were defiant as she glared at him.

"Your . . . creatures," she spat, "killed Viri."

Faran didn't immediately favour her with a reply. He turned and brushed away the creepers covering the entrance. His eyes quickly adjusted themselves to the near impenetrable gloom

within and he saw the mounds of earth and shattered tiles and
the deep trench dug into the centre of the floor. For weeks now,
every day until this evening, his spy had told him of the rebels'
activities here, so he was not surprised by what he saw; long
ago he had guessed that they were once more trying to reach
Marizian's tomb chamber. He wondered where the spy could be
now, one of Golon's trusted acolytes, one of the pale worshippers who had travelled here from Surrenland. No doubt he'd
paid with his blood, like all the other living would this night.

Now he saw the work that the rebels had done, he was thankful at least they had saved him the trouble of reopening the
tomb, something he would have hesitated to do himself. To the
followers of both Iss and Reh this was a holy site, a place not to
be idly tampered with. He let the creepers drop back into position and turned to face Malliana. He had given up trying to compose his sallow features in order to intimidate people long ago:
the drawn desiccation of his face was enough to cow the dead
and the living alike.

"I told you to keep close. Your servant panicked—only the
blue censer will protect you."

Malliana was not appeased. "You forgot the favours I have
done you these last seven years: did I not bring you the girl?"

"The girl is not with us now—she escaped because of your
carelessness."

He turned to the Reapers of Sorrow: he counted forty-eight
of the fifty he had brought with him. At a gesture from him, two
of them stepped forward and laid hands on Malliana. Her anger
was immediately replaced by terror.

"Get your hands off me . . ." she quavered, but then her
voice faded as she felt the strength of their grip and realised she
was powerless. The Reapers dragged her to one side.

Faran turned to Golon. His lieutenant was standing atten-
tively behind him, the censer gushing a blue-white mist which
bathed the scene in eerie light.

"What do you know of this place?" Faran asked.

"No more than you, my lord," the sorcerer replied. "The
tomb is dangerous to the Flame and the Worm alike." He took a
step forward, keeping his voice low. "It would be best to send
the Brethren on in front, in case of traps . . ."

Faran nodded. The undead lurked in the shadows of the tomb, some ancient superstition more potent than their blood-lust keeping them from entering. Most of them were too feeble to be of much use to Faran anyway. They were eyeing the shaking figure of Malliana with the covetousness of misers viewing a pot of gold. "Brethren!" he said. His words still had power to stir them. They turned their heads towards him.

"You know why I have brought you here. There is blood below, blood to satisfy all of you. Go on and drink, leave only the young girl—she is mine!"

A hubbub of approval rose from the undead, and they shuffled forward through the creepers at the entrance. Faran quickly divided the remaining Reapers—half to accompany him, the other half to stay on watch at the entrance. He gestured for some of his own group to precede him, then followed with Golon and Malliana. The undead were already clambering down into the trench in the middle of the floor. Faran and his entourage had to hurry to catch up with them. The creatures were in their element: a subterranean tunnel, without a hint of light.

They barrelled down the excavated tunnel, heedless of the earth that rained down from the crumbling ceiling. The soldiers, getting in each other's way, blundered into the tunnel walls, cursing as each cave-in rained dirt on them. The undead in front had none of the same difficulties, seeing well in the dark. They reached the first chamber a few yards ahead of Faran's group. Ignoring the charred bodies fused together on the floor in front of the archway, they were halfway across it when Golon, following just behind the first Reapers, emerged from the tunnel. His mouth opened to shout a warning, but he was too late.

A fireball exploded in the middle of the vampires. The leaders ignited like resin-soaked torches, pirouetting in a St. Vitus' dance. Some stumbled back into their comrades behind, setting them alight as well. The others, having not seen bright light for years, groped about, blinded by the flames, some of them stepping into the fire rather than away from it. A stampede of bodies, some ablaze, headed back towards Golon and Faran.

Golon had thrown himself in front of his master, but in the

split second before the explosion Faran had noticed his sorcerer's body stiffening and, sensing something amiss, covered his eyes with his hands. Now he felt the heat of the burning bodies stumbling towards him. He had barely enough time to fling himself against the wall before the tide of undead swept up. Golon barged one of them away but another fell at Faran's feet. He stared in terror at the flames licking at his leg before Golon, recovering his balance, kicked it away hurriedly.

Then it was over: a dozen bodies blazed in odd corners of the room, the rest of the vampires had fled, along with some of the guards. His eyes adjusted to the unaccustomed light of the flames. Only fourteen of the Reapers were left, along with Golon and Malliana.

The survivors were coughing and spluttering with the black oily smoke that filled their lungs, but it barely troubled Faran. The noise gradually subsided, leaving them with only the sound of the crackling bodies that were rapidly being reduced to tarry puddles.

Golon opened the top of the censer and snuffed it. "We won't be needing this now," he said hoarsely.

Faran blinked his eyes, irritated to find he was still half-blinded by the afterimage of the flames. "Can we go on?" he asked, peering as best he could into the chamber.

"Apart from the odds not being so favourable?" Golon stepped forward, inspecting the area just short of where the holocaust had appeared. "I may be able to cast the Protection against Flame, but you will all have to stand close to me."

Faran toyed with the idea of going back for more of his men, but he had already seen what confusion was bred by the dark claustrophobic conditions of the underworld. He would have to put up with the handicap for the moment. He gestured to the remaining Reapers. "Close up on the sorcerer," he ordered. The men looked as dazed as Malliana by the explosion, but they obeyed readily enough, leading Malliana up to Golon. They stood thus in a tight semicircle as the sorcerer began an incantation, his hands framing ancient symbols in the air, the shadows cast by the burning bodies dramatically leaping over the walls of the chamber. The air around Golon began to shift and warp in time with the elaborate gestures of his hands. Gradually a penumbra of light appeared and formed a shape much like a glass jar surrounding the group. The light intensified and thickened until it looked solid enough to touch.

"It would be best if you shield your eyes," he told Faran. Faran left off the futile rubbing of his eyes and did so. Golon then stepped forward, the others closely grouped around him. As his foot touched a spot just inside the chamber, the room once more exploded into flame, which roared into an orange blossom all around the circle of the spell's effect. But, inside the dome of light, the air remained cool.

They shuffled forward. One of the Reapers, entranced by the cold beauty of the flames, reached out a hand to touch the edge of the barrier. His hand passed through it as if it weren't there, right into the flames. The flesh immediately blistered and burned down to the bone, flaring into light like a torch. He staggered back, pushing one of his colleagues completely out of the circle. For a moment the man stared back at them from outside the protective barrier, his mouth open in surprise, then he ignited in a sheet of flame. His scream was lost in an explosive roar as the fire engulfed him.

Golon pressed forward, the others huddling still closer together. Then the flames suddenly died as abruptly as they'd started. The man with the burned hand stared stupidly at the blazing stump; the fire had now spread to his cloak and had caught his hair, which was burning like dry straw. He screamed, a heart-piercing scream of agony. But Faran made no attempt to intervene as he sank to the ground, his flesh and his clothing belching black fumes. He watched as the man beat ineffectually at the flames once, then twice, then lay still. The man's death throes would caution the others that this was the fate of the ill disciplined. A word was enough to break the others from their horrified stares. He nodded at two of the remaining guards, and they preceded him through the archway into the heart of the tomb.

The Doppelgänger had been hauling Jayal up one of the last steps of the pyramid when the first blazing body appeared at the top and came rolling towards them in a whirlwind of sparks and windmilling limbs. He ducked, releasing the hemp rope around Jayal's neck, letting him fall several feet into a thornbush. But the Doppelgänger was not bothered by the fate of his other half. He watched as two more bodies came tumbling down, followed by the scuttling forms of the other vampires. In their fear, many of them failed to notice the ledge, flying over it to tumble head over heels down the three hundred feet to the base of the pyramid, their limbs breaking like rotten wood as they fell. The Doppelgänger watched, his mind telling him that nothing could survive such a fall. But, even in the gloom at the bottom of the pyramid, he could see some of them rise to their hands and knees after a few seconds and begin to crawl away like broken cockroaches. Others, whom he guessed to be some of Faran's living guards, followed the vampires, hopping down the broken steps and gullies in a shower of falling stone. They were too intent on their escape to notice him or his band.

Something bad had happened up there, something which meant Faran was now without adequate protection, equalising the odds for the Doppelgänger. If so, he must hurry to catch him at a disadvantage. He waved his men on, reaching the ledge within minutes.

There was still a group of guards standing at the ledge outside the portico. They were talking agitatedly and peering into the gloom of the entrance, evidently not sure whether they should go in or remain where they'd been posted. At a gesture from the Doppelgänger, his men spread out to either side, the guards' noise drowning the noise of ratcheting crossbows and the sound of throwing knives being drawn from their sheaths. Then, at another sign from the Doppelgänger, they let fly. Some half dozen of the Reapers fell immediately. The others whirled around as the bandits leapt towards them. Steel rang on steel. More of the Reapers fell, though some fought on, their skull masks impassive as they were surrounded and hacked down. Then there was silence save for the groans of the wounded.

The Doppelgänger counted his men—only five lost, a good result. He guessed they were now on terms of parity with Faran's party in the tomb.

All was quiet as he pushed through the frond of creepers. He saw immediately where he must go: the deep notch dug into the floor. Kazaris came up next to him, dragging Jayal. His twin's face had been badly scratched in the fall into the thornbush: also one of the man's eyes was closing over a livid bruise. The Doppelgänger had a mild feeling of anguish, as if he was looking at a prized piece of furniture which had been scratched or broken. But the feeling passed. There would be plenty of time for Jayal to heal before they found his father and, the Darkness willing, the Rod, which would give him back the body that this usurper currently occupied.

The Doppelgänger jerked his head forward towards the notch. Two of his men advanced, one carrying a heavy winch crossbow strapped to a leather harness at his chest. A well-aimed shot from it could throw a man back ten feet; it would at least temporarily halt a vampire. One of the younger of the Doppelgänger's thugs, a callow youth, trembling with fear and excitement, went with the crossbow man. The Doppelgänger frowned: there was no place for cowardice in his organisation: he would have to get rid of the man, maybe as bait for the vampires. He followed with the others.

The tunnel was full of a black, choking smoke. The men began to cough and splutter, and the noise, compounded by their frequent falls on the uneven surface, would have warned any ambusher of their approach.

Fortunately there wasn't anyone waiting for them. They entered the chamber where the conflagration had taken place, noting the still-smouldering vampire bodies, but nothing else.

"Faran?" the Doppelgänger asked interrogatively. A couple of the men went forward, but Kazaris muttered a word of warning, and they stopped dead.

The Doppelgänger turned inquiringly to his henchman. Kazaris didn't deign to reply, merely picking up a pebble and tossing it into the room. There was a brief explosion of flame right in front of the men's startled eyes. An inch farther and they'd have been incinerated.

"The clue is in the book, master," Kazaris said. The Doppelgänger cursed, first for Kazaris's impudence and second for letting him inspect the book, however briefly. Kazaris's memory was perfect, and he had now gained knowledge which he had used to challenge his master's authority.

The Doppelgänger pulled out the tattered volume he'd brought with him from Illgill's study. He started leafing through it, until he found Illgill's description of the tomb. As he had suspected, Kazaris had memorised the passage.

" 'The first trial is by fire, in the first room,' " he read. " 'Do not enter until you have drawn the Form of the Flame upon your bodies, for the demon of Flame that dwells here will otherwise destroy you.' " The Doppelgänger glanced up as he finished, hoping to find a trace of smugness on Kazaris's sallow young face, but there was none. A pity: he'd have taken great pleasure in wiping it off.

"Whatever caused that is a demon?"

"Yes—look!" The sorcerer gestured. He threw his hands out wide as if casting a fishing net into the sea, and the object that appeared in front of him did resemble a net, a mesh of winding forms which flew forward. The flames roared once more into life. But the mesh of sorcerous light passed through it unharmed. As it struck the far wall, the form of a huge being crouching on the ledge over the doorway could be seen. It was some ten feet tall, with a leering face and a fanged mouth from which spewed gusts of fire. Though its body was shaped like a dragon's, its face was entirely human.

The Doppelgänger's men started back in horror. But Kazaris didn't seem to be perturbed by this hellish vision. Strands of the shining net were still attached to his fingers and he twisted them, tightening them around the creature. It bellowed, an unearthly roar that echoed deafeningly in the confines of the chamber. Then it exploded into activity, thrashing and writhing against the net. But Kazaris's grip on it was unrelenting: the tighter he twisted it, the less fierce the demon's activities became, until nothing, not an exhalation, could be heard from it, and the movement became less and less violent as when a fish, pulled out of the water, struggles less as it slowly suffocates in the air. Now Kazaris began pulling in the net, winding the ball of sorcerous energy smaller and smaller until it was only the size of a gourd, then a ball of wool, then a marble. Finally, he palmed the speck of writhing matter. It vanished with a faint popping sound.

"It's safe now," he said.

The men stared, gaping.

"But what about the Form of the Flame?" said the Doppelgänger, pointing to the passage in the book.

Kazaris arched an eyebrow. "We don't have to follow all of Illgill's instructions, do we?"

He stepped forward. No wall of flame greeted him. The others followed cautiously, staring around the gloomy chamber as if fearing an ambush.

The Doppelgänger stooped to check the charred corpses. They were now no more than bubbling pools of a tarry substance. There were no recognisable features visible in the remains: even if there had been, identification would have been difficult. Faran might be one of the burning bodies, but he doubted it: the conqueror of Thrull would have been more careful than to die like this. Next he looked for the remains of a lacquer mask like the one the priest had been wearing. He knew Thalassa and the priest would have had to come this way: everything indicated it. Again there was no fragment of a mask to give him hope. The two men he most wished dead had apparently survived to pass on to the next obstacle. So be it—he'd expected to have to fight. And he had two great advantages: the book and Kazaris.

Kazaris. The Doppelgänger winced with irritation. They might have died without the sorcerer. He could see now that his already terrified men respected Kazaris more than they respected him. In the past, in the many foolhardy outrages he had orchestrated in the city, not one of these desperadoes had dared question him. But now things had changed; within a half hour of setting out for the City of the Dead they looked to Kazaris and not him for their salvation. This would have to change and very shortly. His right-hand man was getting above himself.

He would deal with him, but later. For the moment Kazaris and the book gave him an advantage that neither Faran nor the scar-faced priest had. Only when he had discovered the secret of the tomb and had had his revenge on them would he settle scores with Kazaris. First was the mystery of what Marizian had left behind him; a mystery which had only once been unlocked in living memory, but now awaited him. He would find the Orb, and, by finding that, discover the location of the Rod.

He waved his men through the arch and they started their descent into the depths of the tomb.

CHAPTER THIRTY-FIVE

Marizian's Maze

They had descended the core of the pyramid for at least half an hour: down and down, following a damp stone staircase in bewildering spirals. Urthred wondered whether by now they had penetrated beneath the surface level of the City of the Dead. If they had, they could now be far beneath the ground.

The stairs were broad and relatively shallow, the sloping walls to either side decorated with more of the paintings he'd first noticed at the beginning of their downward journey. The original paintings had been badly damaged by water seepage, but those farther down were in better condition. A band of gold lettering which he hadn't noticed at first because of its poor condition ran along the top of the frescoes. The gold glittered attractively in the light from the torches. Just as Urthred was wondering whether they should stop and look at them, Seresh held up his hand. The stairs had ended abruptly, levelling out into a broad corridor from which branched several side passages.

"The tomb chamber must be near now," Alanda said in a hushed voice.

"That or we are going to the centre of the earth," Seresh muttered.

Meanwhile, Urthred was inspecting the frieze of golden lettering above the last of the frescoes.

"It's the Fire Tongue," a voice said by his shoulder. Thalassa had come to stand next to him, so close that he had felt her breath blowing gently on the nape of his neck.

"Yes," he managed, focusing desperately on the fresco underneath it. She knew the Ancient Tongue! Somehow this extra bit of information didn't surprise him. She might have learned it from Alanda, or as a child. But only a very few knew it. It marked her out once again. He tried to concentrate on the faded paintings. Each of the frescoes was divided into huge panels. This last one portrayed Marizian, a stern-visaged patrician, as he would have been in old age. Urthred had noticed that the hundreds of frescoes they had already passed represented a pictorial life of Marizian. The early scenes at the top of the tomb had depicted Marizian's first arrival at the cliffs of Thrull, the erection of the city, with giants heaving huge blocks of stone, halflings delving deep beneath the earth—this shown in crude cross section—the palaces and the temples gradually emerging. Then, in the pictures halfway through their descent, Marizian had been shown giving the two Books of Faith to the first priests of Reh and Iss. In the first scenes he had still been a relatively young man, but this last fresco showed him as white-haired and frail. Marizian had aged like all mortals, but over centuries rather than decades.

But there had been another progressive change in the frescoes: the colour of the sun. In all the early scenes there was a sun as yellow as egg yolk beaming from an azure sky. But the sun in the later pictures, as it was in the real world outside, was wan and washed out; the fields were shown as sere and brown, the branches of trees drooped, the fruit withered on the bough. All was melancholy. Urthred wondered at this: surely people had only noticed that the sun was beginning to die five hundred years ago, not at the time these pictures were painted? Had Marizian known what was going to befall the earth in the latter days and prefigured it in the paintings in his tomb?

In this final picture, the patriarch sat by a window, somewhere in the city, perhaps the now-ruined citadel, which looked over a panorama of the marshy plains and the saw-toothed peaks of the Fire Mountains drawn in crude perspective. But Marizian was not portrayed as looking at the scene; instead he stared into a hand mirror which he held in front of him. But the mirror, angled towards the viewer of the painting, was empty of Marizian's features, a perfect blank.

Urthred stepped closer. Something in the mirror moved! He approached still closer and saw that the mirror was not painted at all: it was real. His and Thalassa's reflection stared back dully from the age-tarnished surface: beauty and the demon mask.

"What does this mean?" Thalassa breathed.

Urthred squinted up into the gloom where the words of the Scriptures seemed to hang suspended in midair above the picture. He read them aloud, translating effortlessly from the Older Tongue:

> "The sun grows old in the sky,
> As I grow old in my tower.
> I seek truth in mirrors
> But find only lies and vanity.
> What I am, I stole.
> Now I never will be healed.
> Seeker of the truth:
> You who have passed the trial of fire
> And the trial of stone,
> Pass now the trial of truth.
> For truth alone
> Will give again
> The truth that was mine and yours."

"The words are hardly illuminating," Seresh said scornfully.

"They were not intended to be," Alanda replied, moving off down the corridor with the lantern.

"It speaks of a third trial," Thalassa said.

Furtal had remained silent throughout this entire interchange, but now he spoke, his voice subdued, ruminative: "You puzzle over riddles: then think of the greatest riddle of them all."

"What is that?" Urthred asked.

The old lutanist's blind orbs shone eerily in the flickering light of the torches. "It is said the sun began to die when Marizian came to these Southern Lands from the north."

"So it is said—though the change only became apparent five hundred years ago, at the same time the Emperor shut himself off in Valeda. But the frescoes show the world dying, and they were painted thousands of years ago. What does it mean?"

Furtal's blind eyes gazed off into nothingness. "Marizian brought Life and Death into this land: Reh and Iss. Before, in the Golden Age, the two went hand in hand. After his coming man and nature were split, became divided against one another. Everything that has followed has driven brother against brother, father against son, until the world has ended in two warring factions."

"If things are as you say, it is because the priests of Iss have made them so," Urthred replied, the heat rising to his scarred face. Marizian was the great lawgiver; no man should dare criticise him.

"I speak only what is true, as Marizian's own words seem to beseech us to do," Furtal replied mildly.

"That is a heresy! Marizian gave us the *Book of Light!*"

"And the *Book of Worms.*"

Urthred now felt the full flush of anger. His gloves clenched, and he heard their articulations grinding. But the man was old and incapacitated. He had been too long at the whorehouse—had become depraved. He would forgive him for now.

"Let's get going," Seresh said, glancing nervously up the dark stairs above them.

Then Alanda called from down the corridor, startling them. They had all forgotten she'd gone on alone.

"What is it?" Seresh shouted back.

"Something very strange."

They hurried on, their discussion forgotten. They passed various side passages from which Urthred could dimly hear the melancholy splashing of water. The corridor became black granite, with condensation dripping steadily from its ceiling. Further tunnels disappeared off to either side. After fifty feet there were four pillars holding up the ceiling; then the corridor opened into a huge chamber, the size, it appeared, of the entire base of the pyramid.

The whole breadth of the chamber was suffused by shifting shadows of light and dark, like the shadows of wind passing over cornfields. Light came from beneath the floor, which glowed a pearly white as if it were translucent marble in which a blinding sun had been imprisoned. In front of the shifting pattern of light, by the pillars at the entrance to the chamber, glowing motes filled the air, like a thousand fireflies, dodging here and there but maintaining a shimmering screen between Urthred's party and the room.

They advanced cautiously, their faces lit up by the light in front. They came to a halt by the pillars, the dancing particles of light before them reminiscent of those in the Lightbringer's Shrine.

"These are spirits," whispered Alanda. "Guardians of the tomb."

"But they don't look any bigger than glowworms!" scoffed Seresh.

He was about to take a step forward, but Alanda shot out a clawlike hand and pulled him back.

"Caution at all times," she hissed.

Seresh shrugged her off, readjusting his cloak in irritation.

The more Urthred studied the shifting patterns behind the glowing forms, the more he noticed how they formed what appeared to be walls and corridors of light, like a maze. Was this the room the fresco referred to: where the trial of truth would occur?

Alanda now spoke. "Marizian hid great secrets. Secrets that he wanted only a very few to discover. The Worm stole away Dragonstooth in the Time of Darkness. The Talos left under his own free will, and Illgill took the Rod from here. This is all we know of this place. I beg you all to be cautious; one false move and you may be killed."

"So how do you think we should proceed?" Urthred asked.

Alanda nodded her head back to the last fresco. "I think you were right, priest—that painting holds a clue."

"It spoke of the trial of fire, the trial of stone and the trial of truth," Thalassa said. "But what is the trial of truth?"

Alanda thought hard. "Marizian must have assumed that bad men would come here in later years to rob his tomb, men who would have no interest in reading the inscriptions on the walls, only in gold and treasure. To get to the tomb chamber, you evidently have to pass some test. Brigands, tomb robbers would lie, but those with a holy mission would not do so. One of us has to find out before Faran catches us!"

He didn't know why, whether because by a show of bravado he might impress Thalassa, or because he felt it was up to him to set an example, but Urthred spoke up instantly. "Then I will go!"

Alanda smiled. "You, priest? But you only arrived tonight. One of us others should go. After all, we've planned this for years."

"You said yourself my brother called me here for a purpose: he told me to take the name of the Herald—he who comes before the Lightbringer. If that is the case, I should go first, whoever the Lightbringer is." He consciously avoided catching Thalassa's eyes as he said this.

Alanda weighed his words. "Be true in your heart, priest," she said, accepting that he would go.

"You're going alone?" Seresh said incredulously.

"It's for the best," Urthred said steadily, amazed at his inner calm.

"I will go too!" Thalassa stood forward. Her cheeks were flushed, her chest rose and fell with excitement, but she, too, seemed possessed of the same strength of purpose as Urthred.

"Now I've heard it all!" Seresh exclaimed. "The priest I can understand, but what good can you do, Thalassa?"

"I just know I must go—you saw what happened in the shrine." She turned to appeal to Alanda. "Tell them."

Alanda nodded her head slowly, her eyes never leaving Thalassa's. "She's right—she should go with the priest."

"And what of the rest of us?" Seresh asked, apparently accepting the decision. "Faran must be nearly on top of us."

"There were tunnels back there," Alanda said, nodding back to the black granite corridor. "We will hide there and await events. Maybe there is a route that will take us out into the marshes."

"But what of Gadiel and Rath?" asked Urthred, knowing before he asked the question that he would get no reply. They all knew the two had died buying them time, that they would never see them again, whichever exit they took from the tomb.

There was a moment's silence as they all digested this fact. Then Alanda spoke again. "Are you ready?" she asked Urthred and Thalassa.

Thalassa turned to Urthred. Her grey eyes were full of the light he'd seen in her since the vision in the shrine. As her gaze caught his, his face tingled again—tingled as it had ever since he'd passed the barrier of flame, as if his face and his soul were healing, leaving a cocoon of the past behind from which he'd emerge: re-created, reborn.

"I'm ready," she said. He held out his gloved hand without thinking. She took it, as unselfconsciously. Once more he felt the slight electrical charge of the softness of her touch, pressing in against the thin leather at his palm. Then she stepped out onto the floor. For a second the hovering spirits spun in confusion, then hurtled towards her. She was surrounded by a penumbra of glittering, dancing light. Then she vanished right before Urthred's eyes, as he still clung to her hand.

He stepped after her. Immediately he sensed, rather than saw, rapid streaks of light as the spirits closed on him. Urthred cast his eyes behind him, but Alanda and Furtal were receding at an alarming pace, as if a tidal wave had snatched him up and was washing him far out to sea at a tremendous rate. He opened his mouth to speak, but no sound came, then the speed of his movement made him blank out temporarily.

When he came to himself, he was standing in the same vast hall, the white and black lights winnowing around him. He'd heard of how in the far north, where the sun never sets, lights like these appeared in the sky in the arctic dusk—curtains of light, shimmering across the sky in every hue that the world had ever known. But here the colours were all monochrome, black, white and grey—the last being the most dominant of the three. Several seconds or several years might have gone by since he blacked out; he had no way of telling. The spirits had disappeared, but so too had Thalassa. But there, at the end of one of the corridors of light and dark, he saw a figure approaching. Like the vision of Manichee, the being radiated a white light

from its eye sockets. Beyond the dazzle, he could make out the
same haggard patrician features that he had seen in the last
fresco on the stairs. Urthred shielded the slits in his mask with
his gloves, the blue-white light more blinding the nearer it got.

A spirit like Manichee, sent from Hel! But this one was not
the benign spirit of his mentor: this ancient spirit was alien,
possibly unpredictable, as likely to rip him to shreds as to help
him.

Then the vision vanished as abruptly as it had appeared. He
looked around. Though it was nowhere in sight, he sensed Marizian's presence. The patterns of light and dark seemed to form
walls and corridors. He was in a kind of maze. He took a step
forward towards what he thought was a corridor, but instead he
came across a barrier that stopped him as abruptly as a stone
wall.

"Who are you?" The voice echoed like a giant's in his mind.

Should he lie: try to trick his way into the tomb? Invoke the
name of Marizian, or of Illgill? Then he thought of Alanda's
words—only honesty would do.

"I am Urthred of Ravenspur," he said aloud. The patterns of
the corridors of light started shifting, and he felt that he was
walking down one of them, though his feet were not moving.
Distantly now, on the far side of the vast chamber, he sensed a
glow of light.

"Why have you come here?" The voice echoed in his head.

"I seek the truth . . ."

Again he flowed on as if carried by a wave that lifted him
from the floor. The glow in the distance intensified.

The voice again: "What truth?"

"The truth that was buried with Marizian."

"What truth is that?" The voice didn't change in resonance,
but Urthred sensed that this was the key question. The difference between life and death. Life and death.

What had Furtal's heretical words been? He spoke before he
could think. "I seek the truth of the sun's dying."

"And why have you come now?"

The scene in the Lightbringer's Shrine came to his mind.
What Alanda had told him then. Had she been right? Only now
would he find out.

"I—I am the Herald," he said hesitatingly.

Another surge and he seemed to be almost flying along the corridor, the walls to either side a blur of light.

"Will you serve the Lightbringer?"

Only now did Urthred hesitate. Was Thalassa the Lightbringer? It was as if his doubt was transferred to his forward movement. He suffered a sudden deceleration, as if he had suddenly, from full flight, been slammed into a stone wall. His eyeballs popped with the pressure, his limbs suddenly felt like lead.

"Will you serve?" The voice again, growing fainter.

Urthred felt a cold wash of panic. He would serve her. "Yes," he said in a whisper.

Again the forward motion began: now he saw that his body was twisting and turning down myriad corridors of light, the walls lashing past at frightening speed. Then the motion stilled. He stumbled forward, his feet once more on solid ground.

When he recovered himself, he found he stood before a huge archway from which blazed the same golden light as he'd seen coruscating from the Lightbringer's Shrine. This time the light came from a thousand candles burning at intervals along the sides of a long nave vaulted by a hundred arches. Candles that burned not with terrestrial light, but with an unearthly glow. Right at the far end of the nave he could just make out a huge, spinning orb, some twenty feet in diameter. It appeared to hang suspended in midair. It glowed with myriad colours: greens, reds, blues, white and black, changing slowly as he watched. Next to it was a solid mass of black basalt—Marizian's tomb. This end of the nave was lost in gloom. In the grey light he saw Thalassa standing in front of him. A taper from her backpack burned in her hand. She was staring at him, as if trying to see who or what had just appeared from the shining corridors. He stepped towards her, and he saw her shoulders relax as she recognised him.

"Are you all right?" he asked.

She nodded, though her body trembled. "You saw the vision, heard the voices . . . ?"

"Yes." He waved his gloved hand, as if trying to brush away how near he had come to failing. "I didn't know how to answer, but then words came to me unbidden." He hung his head, ashamed to admit to the words he'd spoken. "I said I came to seek the truth of the sun's dying."

"Just as Furtal said?"

"Just as he said."

"I too." Now it was her turn to hesitate. "Urthred . . ." she began, then stopped as if once again at a loss for words. It was the first time she had used his name.

"What is it?"

"Do you believe I am the Lightbringer?"

"Yes," he said simply.

"But earlier this evening . . ."

He shook his head. "Whatever you were then doesn't matter anymore: we've all changed."

They stood silently for a moment in the winnowing light, a strange feeling of calm settling on both of them, as if their fate was determined, and nothing could change it now. Eventually Thalassa spoke again. "The vision told me things."

"What things?"

"Of the past and the future, of the city he came from in the far north, lost in ice . . ."

"Iskiard?"

"The same: I must go there, Urthred."

"Then I will come, too."

She smiled. He looked away, down at her feet, his feelings confused. Tonight she had awoken twin emotions in him: the lust he regretted now, but the desire would never go away. Even her foot, encased in torn and scuffed satin slippers, seemed woundingly perfect. But then this woman of flesh was also a woman of legend, written of in the *Book of Light.* How to reconcile the two? He looked up; his expression, he guessed, would have been a curious one, but the horror of the mask would be all she would see: the hideous, indomitable mask that would forever hide his face. His heart felt as if it had been seized by an iron vice. Why had Manichee devised this cage? Had he meant to teach him something by this mask, make him join the world, but in such a way that everyone was forewarned as to what lay beneath? Or maybe it was as he had said: people habituated to the mask would one day accept Urthred's real face? He wondered grimly whether this ruse would work on Thalassa. At the moment she no doubt thought the mask a pretence, an affectation. It was best to keep it that way.

He knew this sudden awakening of feeling would ultimately destroy him. The solitude of his tower at Forgeholm was all he had wanted a month ago. Now, in the real world of give-and-take, he had already betrayed his inner thoughts time and time again. He felt exposed, scrutinised from all sides. Was there nothing sacred buried deep within which he could keep from the world?

Nothing. And once his heart was unlocked like a pantomime chest, all its wares on display, for all to look at, where would that leave him? A freak, a laughingstock, an object of mockery for trying to join a world from which he was forever excluded.

But then he felt a surge of defiance in his chest. He would risk everything. Derision and disgrace were nothing to him. He was set on his course, and nothing could deflect him now.

His flesh still tingled from the trial of fire; he felt empowered, just as he had when he'd conjured the dragon from the air as a boy at Forgeholm. The god was still with him, was closer than at any time since the Burning. This new openness had not harmed him yet.

He met her gaze again. Her smile was still unwavering. "Shall we go?" he asked, once more offering her his gloved hand, and once more his heart gave a small leap as she took it. Together they started off down the candlelit nave towards the Orb and the tomb.

CHAPTER THIRTY-SIX

Magic of the Moon, and the Grave

Outside, Seresh stood at the place where Thalassa and Urthred had vanished. One second they had been there, the next they were gone. And gone where? The curtain of whirling spirits, like a swarm of moths, was transparent, and he could see quite clearly into the mazelike corridors of light and dark beyond. The vast chamber eddied and shifted with light, as if the illumination that poured from its floor and ceiling were refracted by water. But there was no sign of the priest or the girl.

There had been close to a hundred conspirators against Faran a week before. But one calamity after another had whittled them down. Randel and the others had been rounded up two days ago, betrayed by Varash; then Zaraman and his band, now nothing more than a pile of charred limbs; he never expected to see Gadiel and Rath again; his father had been left to the mercy of the vampires, and only a prayer would suffice for the masked priest and Thalassa, wherever they were. Alanda, Furtal and he alone were left.

It was his father's fate which weighed most heavily on Seresh's mind. He thought of him sitting in his study waiting for the end. Had it been the vampires, or had it been the searchers from the temples who had got to him first? A feeling of doom had weighed on him ever since the arrival of the priest at the mansion, a man as ill omened as his mask. After that

Seresh's optimism had faded as one accident had succeeded another. Now there were only three of them left, and Faran could not be far behind.

He sighed, and the exhalation stirred Alanda from her own silent contemplation of the maze.

"We must go back and wait," she said.

He nodded his head. Their position was laughably bad. Only two old people and him, Faran in pursuit, and he didn't even have his weapon drawn yet! He pulled the two-handed sword from his back scabbard, feeling the weight of old iron.

He looked back towards the entrance corridor. Any moment now, the vampires might pour through it. During their pell-mell journey through the tomb, he hadn't really given much thought to how close their pursuers might be behind them. But now a cold chill crept up his spine. Some people, like the priest, could sense the presence of vampires, just as, in turn, vampires could scent living blood. Did he sense them now? How many would have got through the trial of fire? Every instinct shrieked in him not to go back towards the corridor, but to follow the priest and Thalassa into the mysterious lights of the maze. But he knew there was nothing for him in the maze—only death. But death was probably behind as well.

He took a deep breath to steady his nerve and, his sword at the ready, led Alanda and Furtal back towards the granite corridor.

They entered its silent depths. In the dim light of the maze and Alanda's lantern it seemed as empty as when they had left it a few moments before. Seven tunnels led off to either side, some twenty feet high and wide, spaced at twenty-foot intervals as if in purposeful symmetry. Seresh peered into the first one on the right, Alanda holding up the lantern so he could see better. After ten feet, it ended in a stone door.

He looked at Alanda.

"Try the next one," she whispered.

He crept forward as silently as possible, the utter quiet weighing heavily on him. Though the corridor was empty, the darkness was full of threat; the very walls themselves seemed to move in the winnowing light from the maze and the shifting illumination of the lantern.

He got up to the entrance to the next tunnel on the right and stopped to listen: the only sound was the melancholy dripping of water from the tunnel's ceiling. They had only passed this way five minutes before, but he knew something had changed. But, despite the heightened state of his senses, he couldn't tell exactly what. Nothing looked to be amiss. He gripped the sword more tightly and swung rapidly out in front of the next entrance, the sword poised behind his shoulder, ready to strike.

The side passage was empty: ten feet along its length it was blocked by an opaque amber block. As Alanda's lantern light played on it, he saw the skeleton of a massive creature imprisoned in it. He had never seen the like: it must have been some twelve feet tall, but appeared humanoid. Maybe one of the giants who had built the city, buried with its master? Perhaps all the side tunnels led to other, subsidiary burial sites. At least the dead offered no threat.

He let out his breath, and was turning to say something to Alanda and Furtal when he suddenly realised what it was that had changed in the corridor.

The air.

Charged with the scent of mildew.

Faran was here. He swung round. The Reapers had slipped from the tunnels farther up the corridor, their cloaks rustling slightly, their skull masks expressionless. The nearest was almost within the arc of his four-foot sword. He counted: twelve of them in all. And, behind them, three other figures: the tall, leather-armoured figure of Faran, standing next to a bald man in robes whom he recognised as the sorcerer Golon. Somehow he wasn't surprised to see that the third figure, held tightly by Golon, was Malliana. Seeing her merely added to his sense of fatefulness, of circularity. Things had started to go badly wrong in the Temple of Sutis; it was only fitting the High Priestess was here to see the cycle to its bitter end.

The sword felt heavy in his grip: two stone of deadweight. In the past he'd been in fights where the odds had been heavily against him; fights where, by a miracle, or Reh's blessing, he'd killed two or even three opponents, and lived. But he had never fought alone against fourteen.

The certainty of his death struck him full on; for a moment

his breathing and, it seemed, his heart stopped. Then his senses came rushing back; now was not the time to freeze.

Faran, waving the guards aside, stepped forward. So, it was to be single combat: the odds were shortened for the moment, but not by much. Faran towered over him. The vampire lord's eyes caught the wavering lantern light, and Seresh was instantly drawn to their hypnotic depths. He broke free from the gaze as Faran advanced, his leather armour squeaking slightly at each stride. Then, with a fluid motion, Faran unsheathed his sword, holding it to the light. Purple amethysts glinted from its pommel. He held a small buckler in the other hand, its face embossed with a copper skull. His voice, sandpaper dry, broke the silence.

"You can still save yourself," he said hollowly, the tone belying his message of hope. "Just lay down your sword and tell us where your friends are."

Despite himself, Seresh found his eyes meeting Faran's again. Again, he felt their dark, vertiginous pull. Surrendering suddenly seemed a pleasant option . . .

Mesmerism! Once again, he had almost forgotten the undead's power. He wrenched his gaze away and swung his sword, two-handed, putting his weight behind it. Faran ducked the blow effortlessly and sprang forward, the buckler raised up, his own sword darting under it towards Seresh's chest. The blow would have struck home had not Seresh, in the process of following the momentum of his blow, twisted to one side. The sword passed clean through his cloak between his arm and his body, barking the skin. He brought his own sword back in a cramped stroke, but he was off-balance, and Faran was too near. The guard cracked into the face of the smirking skull on Faran's buckler.

The two men were stuck thus, their swords too close to be effective. Though Seresh was tall, Faran was taller still. His breath, the scent of dried blood on a butcher's floor, wafted over Seresh. He thrashed his head from side to side, trying to avoid Faran's malevolent gaze. Then Faran thrust him back into the wall, his skull exploding with pain, stars filling his vision. He pushed back desperately, but Faran's sword still pinned him to the wall, and through his slowly clearing vision he glimpsed the vampire's saliva-stained teeth, preternaturally sharp, darting towards his exposed neck . . .

But then Faran's face was suddenly flooded by white light. The bite grazed Seresh's neck and ripped away a chunk of his cloak at his collarbone. Alanda stepped forward, the blazing lantern now unshuttered and aimed at Faran's face. The vampire clenched his eyes in pain, staggering back. Seresh helped him on his way with a push from his sword. Faran stumbled, trying to regain his balance, his own sword coming up to parry the expected blow from the front, but Seresh had already thrust away from the wall and moved to one side. Faran was blinded; for a split second he was defenceless.

Seresh's sword swept back, then in for the killing blow. He felt a mad jubilation as the razor-sharp blade swung towards Faran's head. Seven years of humiliation revenged!

It was the last thing he ever felt. In the split second it took for the sword to impact, he saw a gesture from the sorcerer farther up the corridor. Quicker than vision, something wet and sticky slapped into his head. His face was covered by a mass of writhing tentacles. His eyes, but not his mind, snatched a final glimpse of three wickedly barbed spikes that erupted from the creature's inner core before they plunged into his mouth and eyes, penetrating his brain instantly. He was dead before his body realised it, the sword spinning off into the air over Faran's head and clattering against the corridor wall. His body, weighed down by the obscenity wrapped around its head, swayed for a second, then fell forward onto the floor with a dull thud. There was silence save for a dull hiss as the body of the creature slowly inflated with his blood and brain matter.

The lantern light wavered, its purpose forgotten, as Alanda let her arm fall to her side, her eyes fixed on Seresh's corpse. The body gave a final twitch, then lay still. She was only dimly aware of Golon stepping forward and snatching the lantern from her hand. He levered its shutters tight, plunging her and the scene into semidarkness.

After a few seconds, she became aware of Furtal tugging desperately at her sleeve; all he could have heard was the sound of combat, then a sudden silence. No screams or words of triumph. The silence must have been terrifying.

"What is it, mistress?" he asked, but then he, too, became aware of the figures which had now closed in all around them. He looked about him desperately, as if his blind eyes could find a means of escape.

"So, now there are only two of you," Faran said, sheathing his sword. He looked down the corridor towards the maze. "And the others?" His gloved hand swept round and struck Alanda on the cheek, the studs on its knuckles gouging deep tracks through her wrinkled skin.

She fell back against the wall with a gasp, her hand holding the wounds. Furtal flung himself forward, but Faran's glove chopped him down, and he fell heavily onto the floor, the lute strapped to his back letting out a plaintive thrum as it smashed at the impact. He, like Seresh, lay ominously still.

Faran let out a dry rasp that might have been laughter. "Who are these wretches?" he asked, without turning, his question addressed to Malliana, who now cowered just behind him, her eyes rooted on the corpse.

Only slowly did Malliana's wits return to her, allowing her to move her eyes from Seresh's body. She blinked once, then stared at Alanda and Furtal as if waking from a deep sleep.

"Thalassa's maid, and a musician from the temple," she said slowly.

"Then Thalassa and the masked priest can't be far away," Faran said. He pulled Alanda from the wall and held her up so she could see his eyes.

"They're in that room, aren't they?" he spat at her, nodding towards the maze. Alanda said nothing, her blue eyes defiant, though one side of her face was running with blood. A look of displeasure passed over Faran's face as he realised that his gaze was not affecting her as it had Seresh. He relinquished his grip.

"Though you can look me in the face, witch, your blood is forfeit to the Brethren. Enjoy your last moments!" He turned to his men. "Look after these two and the priestess," he ordered four of them. Then, without a backward glance, he advanced on the shimmering lights of the maze.

The Reapers dragged Malliana forward towards Alanda and

Furtal, who still lay motionless on the ground. The High Priestess regarded the old woman bitterly, but she kept silent: revenge when both their lives were in jeopardy was clearly not feasible if she wanted to live a little longer. She contented herself with spitting in Alanda's face, her spittle mixing with the blood from Faran's blow.

"I hope you die badly," she hissed, "as badly as your friend!"

Alanda was too numb to reply: she had seen death before. Both in actuality and in her visions. But every time the abruptness with which a life ended startled her. Once more she had not seen this coming, though Seresh had been curiously absent from her dreams of the future. Were her visions worth anything if they didn't help her to protect her friends? Seresh, Zaraman, Gadiel, Rath and the others, all dead now.

Only let Thalassa be safe, she prayed silently.

Golon was studying the shifting patterns of light, a sour look etched on his already bad-tempered face. His scrutiny lasted several minutes, during which his brow furrowed in concentration. But even after this period, he turned away dissatisfied.

"I know there is a way through," he said. "When the Brethren took the sword aeons ago, they knew of a way."

"Then what was it?" asked Faran impatiently.

"Iss was stronger then—but the knowledge was lost in the ages that followed."

Faran cursed. Golon's response was one he could have thought of himself. "One of you must go first," he said, turning to the Reapers. "You," he said, pointing.

The man was completely impassive: those of the Reapers who had not fled from the fireball were the most courageous of Faran's elite guard, trained to the same blind obedience which had beaten Illgill and had kept Thrull for Faran for seven years. None of these elite ever questioned any of his orders, even if, as now, they would lead to almost certain death. He pulled a phial from his belt and handed it to one of his fellows. Faran recognised it: a small receptacle, containing a few drops drawn from the Black Chalice, saved for the day of his crossing over. He might never need it now—finding instead the total extinction of the one death. With a low bow to his master, the man stepped towards the barrier of white particles.

At that split second two things happened at once.

As the guard touched the light in front of the maze he, like Urthred and Thalassa before him, vanished in the blink of an eye.

But in the same split second there was an orange flash, a massive explosion, and the flagstones underfoot erupted upwards and went spinning through the air. Faran saw them quite clearly: squares of whirling masonry which must have weighed more than several hundred-weight. Yet one flashed past his ear as if it were made of air. With the same detachment he noticed that he was no longer standing, but was being carried through the air, as if he'd been plucked up by an invisible hand. Then the sound of the explosion hit him. A wall of noise that annihilated all other sensation. He landed heavily, still conscious, but deaf and half-blinded.

With curious dispassion he saw the floor around the hole blown by the explosion begin to peel away and fall into the abyss which had opened below. The lip of the hole seemed to be racing towards him. Suddenly, his legs were hanging over its edge. He lashed out for a handhold, but grabbed only empty air. Then he was falling, over and over, blocks of masonry tumbling with him, down into the depths.

The Doppelgänger's party had shadowed Faran's group during the descent of the pyramid's core. The Doppelgänger had scouted ahead, knowing that only he of all his party could not be detected by vampires. He had followed Faran to the corridor and seen him laying the ambush which had ended in Seresh's death. When he'd entered the tomb, he'd had confidence in his men's ability to finish off Faran's depleted party, but the one gesture from Golon which had killed Seresh had swiftly dispelled it. It was magic far beyond the capabilities of his own man, Kazaris.

So it was that his mood, a few minutes before verging on the manic, was sombre as he returned to his men.

His one eye met Kazaris's. "Faran has defeated the other party: he's at the maze."

The young man didn't seem impressed by this intelligence: "Then they were weak—we are strong."

The Doppelgänger's scarred lips twisted as much as they would ever do into a supercilious grin. "No, Kazaris, they have Golon, and he's stronger than any of us."

Anger flickered briefly in the younger man's eyes: it had been brewing the many years since the Doppelgänger had first found him, outcast from the Temple of Worms for some obscure heresy, a prey to the vampires that stalked the nighttime streets. He had thought Kazaris would follow him with unwavering loyalty from the moment he had given him shelter.

But he'd been wrong; Kazaris had always been headstrong, unbowed by his punishment by the temple. Now he was openly challenging him. He should have known better. But, as he had for these many years, the Doppelgänger showed a rare patience with the man. He still had his uses, for the moment. Above all, he had the sword which the Doppelgänger himself could not touch.

The light of Dragonstooth's blade had changed to an even angrier red than when he'd first seen it back in the mansion on the Silver Way. The Doppelgänger knew that its sullen red fire would bode no good to him.

"Have you asked him what this means?" he asked Kazaris, indicating Jayal. Jayal was still tied around the hands and neck with the hemp cord. But the slaves he'd been tied to had long gone, left at the top of the stairs as a decoy for the undead.

"He's said nothing," Kazaris replied, "but I have my own ideas."

Was that a tiny flicker of a smile on Kazaris's lips? Was he deliberately withholding information? Maybe he'd been speaking to the men as the Doppelgänger had scouted ahead, getting them on his side?

He stepped in close to the sorcerer. Kazaris would have seen him kill men with his bare hands, and though one of his wrists was bandaged now, the look on his face gave a clear enough indication of his intentions.

"What ideas?" the Doppelgänger growled.

"It is the moon . . ." Kazaris answered, rapidly, the blood draining from his face as he saw the look of psychotic menace on the Doppelgänger's. "The blade glows stronger the nearer it is to setting."

"Good—that is very good," the Doppelgänger said, nodding his head slowly, never taking his single eye off Kazaris. "There is a full moon tonight. How is this related to the sword?"

"Look," Kazaris said, summoning up enough courage to hold up the glowing sword for the Doppelgänger's inspection. "There is a sigil on the blade."

The Doppelgänger peered at the ruby red surface. There it was, etched onto the metal blade of the sword—the crescent moon symbol, from when the world had worshipped the old gods, Erewon above all of them.

"You know how to work the sword's magic?" he asked abruptly.

"A spell—in the Older Tongue, from when the world was young—"

"Go to it, then, we haven't all night!" he barked. The young man seemed glad now to have an excuse to break off eye contact with the Doppelgänger. He took a step back and composed himself, then raised the sword in two hands, so its tip pointed at the ceiling of the stairwell. He shut his eyes and began muttering some words. At first they were so quiet that the Doppelgänger could not work out what they were, but they increased in volume as he gathered confidence. They were words in the Ancient Tongue, beyond the Doppelgänger's skills to comprehend.

If the red light in the blade had been bright before, with the sorcerer's words it became more and more intense, so that, as he ended his incantation, it looked as if Kazaris held a brand of molten ore taken straight from a forge in his two hands. The light bathed the stairwell, undershadowing in red the faces of the astonished bandits, throwing their shadows along the corridor, making the ancient frescoes shift and warp as if they were alive. Then a crackling white energy exploded from the sword's blade.

The sorcerer looked as stunned as the men at what he had wrought. He looked at the Doppelgänger for instructions, his earlier confidence quite evaporated.

The Doppelgänger stepped up to him. Even from this distance he could feel that the power of the sword was inimical to him, to the world of Shades. He would never be able to touch it without suffering dire consequences. But for the moment Kazaris seemed biddable, more than willing to do everything he asked him, despite the power he now controlled.

"Use it well," was all his master said to him, before gesturing impatiently for him to precede the group. He took hold of the rope around Jayal's neck, waving on the men. Whatever the sword did, he was sure it could be as injurious to their own group as to Faran's.

The sword glowing like an icon before them, the motley group advanced slowly down the corridor into the entrance of the black granite tunnel. The Doppelgänger caught the glinting of light from the maze in front and, silhouetted against it, Faran's party.

Then everything happened at once: Kazaris started running down the corridor, the sword upraised, his cloak flapping around his heels as he ran. The sound alerted Faran's guards; they swung their heads in unison. Just as one of them shouted a warning, Kazaris swung the sword forward as if hurling something from its point, but his forward momentum was his undoing. One of his feet caught in his trailing robes and he stumbled. A bolt of incandescent energy surged from the tip of the sword, but instead of hitting Faran and Golon, as he intended, the bolt went slightly to one side, where a group of seven of the Reapers were bunched together staring at the maze. It exploded in a plume of coppery red sparks. The Reapers were outlined by the blast for a millisecond, then disappeared, as if vaporised. At the point of impact, the granite tiles of the floor punched upwards as if struck by a mighty fist from below.

Then the sound of the explosion was like thunder in the confined space. The whole corridor trembled, water and rock debris rained from the ceiling. Somehow the Doppelgänger managed to stay on his feet. He saw the floor open where the bolt had landed, and two of the remaining guards standing by Alanda disappeared into it. Faran, who had been nearest to them, had been blown to his knees and was struggling back up when another huge section gave way, and he, too, fell into the gaping hole.

Golon was luckier: he'd nearly been blown back into the maze, but had managed to snake out a hand and grab hold of the bottom of a pillar. His body spun around it, and he was thrown to one side, behind the group of captives and the two remaining guards.

Despite his fall and the concussion of the blast, Kazaris was back on his feet and running with the rest of the Doppelgänger's men towards the survivors. The Doppelgänger was frozen to the spot: he'd seen what Golon could do, and he knew he must move—quickly. But he still held Jayal by the halter around his neck; the man was deadweight. He tugged urgently at the rope with both hands, cursing the excruciating pain in his broken wrist.

As he hauled at Jayal, he saw Golon rise to his feet. His clothes had been blown to shreds by the explosion, and his face was black with soot, but already his hands were shaping the form of a spell. Suddenly the pain in his wrist became immaterial; he pulled Jayal towards a side tunnel by brute force just as Golon finished the ritual. A black vapour appeared in the smoke-choked corridor, rolling like a wave towards Kazaris and the others. Kazaris couldn't stop his forward momentum and stumbled into it, followed by two of the men. Immediately there was a bloodcurdling scream. Even in the dark of the vapour, Dragonstooth's glowing blade could be seen to flip over in the air and slide along the floor. There was another enormous explosion from the end of the corridor, further adding to the hellish noise and fumes.

Then Kazaris came staggering backwards, wreathed in the sticky coils of the vapour. His whole body was covered with wriggling maggots. He was clawing at his flesh, which had begun to slough away in handfuls, like a six-month-old corpse's. Then his face began to shrivel, his eyeballs bulging until they burst like ripe grapes. Then his limbs gave way, and he fell, as the roiling mist advanced over his body.

One of the other men, similarly draped in crawling worms, had stumbled out as well. He got a little farther down the corridor before colliding with another bandit. The blinded man

clutched his comrade and they both fell as the vapour rolled over
them; their screams were added to those of the other dying men.
The rest of the Doppelgänger's troupe were scrambling back
from the advancing tide of destruction, but it was rolling forward at more than running pace. They, too, disappeared as they
were overtaken.

The Doppelgänger didn't stay to hear their screams: he
had been momentarily paralysed, but now the tide of death
was nearly on him and Jayal. He yanked on Jayal's halter,
pulling him down into the impenetrable darkness of the side
passage.

He blundered along it blindly, praying that he wasn't going
into a dead end. Cobwebs brushed against his face, and a block
of stone barked his shin; but his whole consciousness was in his
flight, not in his pain. That was why when the ground gave way
beneath his feet he didn't have time to stop himself, but fell
with Jayal, crashing down several steps and rolling across the
floor at the bottom of them. The pain from the shattered bones
of his wrist ripped through him and he blacked out for a split
second. The rope was jerked from his hands. He felt Jayal
struggle to his feet in the darkness. He lunged out weakly,
barely conscious. Jayal must have lashed out with one of his
boots. It caught the Doppelgänger in the ribs, doubling him
over. Through the pain he heard Jayal stumbling away, then the
sound of his receding footsteps.

He would have stayed where he was, trying to recover his
breath, but he knew the vapour was racing towards him
through the blackness. He must get up. . . . He struggled to his
feet, despite the pain. He was disoriented, without any idea
which way led to safety and which to the invisible death
hurtling towards him. He stumbled forward till he touched the
chamber walls.

Jayal had found another passage: he must follow, before the
vapour caught up with him. He hugged the wall, feeling fever-
ishly for an opening in the stonework. He found one at last and
threw himself down the passageway beyond it. Something
brushed at his face: the vapour, cobwebs? But nothing could
impede his forward momentum now. The corridor twisted and
turned in the darkness, and he rebounded from the unexpected

blows from its walls, his hands his only protection. But he was part of the darkness now, indivisible from it, so each blow to his maimed hand, each shooting stab of agony, seemed merely part of the hell of the darkness. He smashed and ricocheted off its walls, oblivious of pain, only conscious of the vapour that followed him.

He ran until he could run no longer, his fear and energy expended, then fell to his knees. Through his ragged gasps for breath he became conscious that he was at another junction of the passageway. To his right he detected the faint glow of the maze and the winnowing lights of the spirits. By a miracle he had got behind Faran's sorcerer. He took in a great gulp of air. It was heavy with the acrid fumes of the explosion, but at least it was not the vapour. He had escaped the spell. As far as he could tell, the only one to do so of all his party.

Though his heart was racing, he took a moment to collect his thoughts. He looked to his left, in the opposite direction to the light. That way lay only darkness and the faint sound of dripping water. There was only one option: to go towards the light.

He inched his way along the right-hand corridor, the shimmering glow of the maze growing stronger and stronger. He paused and watched the light for a moment. No one stirred near it. He would have to enter the maze. The book had said that the location of the Rod could only be found by doing so.

The book . . . his uninjured hand darted down to his side. Finding what he wanted, he breathed a huge sigh of relief. By a miracle, Illgill's diary was still in his cloak pocket. He pulled it out and fumbled with his bandaged hands to find the place towards the end where Illgill had written his instructions to Jayal, screwing up his eye to read in the dim illumination. Yellowed pages with Illgill's handwriting flipped past until he had the passage he was looking for: a map of the pyramid and, next to it, words penned in Illgill's spiky script: *Approach the maze and let the spirits take you. The First Father will appear. Do not be afraid. Say boldly that you are the Herald, come to serve the Lightbringer. These words will suffice. The tomb chamber will be yours.*

*   *   *

The Doppelgänger smiled grimly. This mumbo jumbo was more than he would usually stake his life on, but, with Golon against him, he knew the maze would be a far safer place than anywhere else in the tomb.

He inched forward and poked his single eye cautiously out of the passage entranceway. It was the last before the end of the granite corridor. He was only thirty feet away from the edge of the maze. To his right, the two surviving Reapers and Golon were kneeling at the edge of the large crater in the floor into which their leader had disappeared. By luck, they had their backs turned to him. The High Priestess and Alanda stood against the wall a little away from him, their faces covered by grime from the explosion, their expressions slack and in shock. The body of the blind musician lay at their feet; alive or dead, the Doppelgänger couldn't tell. They wouldn't cause him any problems.

He took a deep breath and hurled himself towards the shimmering pattern of light. Malliana snapped out of her daze when she saw him and let out a screech of alarm. The Doppelgänger caught a glimpse of Golon rising to his feet by the edge of the crater, but, before he could act, the Doppelgänger had launched himself into a headlong dive towards the curtain of shimmering spirits guarding the way into the tomb.

He, like the others who had gone before him, vanished in an explosion of white light.

It seemed he was carried on the edge of a mighty wave. Lights streaked past on either side so fast they seemed a continuous blaze. But then his forward motion abruptly stopped, his neck arched back with the force of the deceleration, his teeth drawn back over his scarred lips. He blacked out momentarily.

When he came to, he was lying on the floor of the maze. He looked back towards the entrance, but there was no sign of Golon or Faran's men. Around him the grey, shimmering light put into his mind only one place he'd ever been: the Plains of Grey—that land of twilight through which he'd been dragged to be reborn in this crippled body.

He was sure of one thing: the tomb was not in that plane that men called the earth, but another, maybe in the Palace of Grey itself, guarded thus from the hands of desperate men come to steal the magic of olden times.

The thought didn't daunt him. Had he not lived and breathed in Shades since his exorcism? The Plains of Grey were a mere antechamber to that most damned of all places. He was near his objective: the Orb.

A white light was emerging out of the myriad corridors ahead. The First Father, Marizian. But though he was no creature of earth, the book had given him the answers he needed. He had nothing to fear. He got to his feet as the light grew and grew in front of him.

CHAPTER THIRTY-SEVEN

The Orb

Though it was thirty or more feet across, it spun languidly in midair as if weightless, a low keening hum accompanying each revolution. Its surface was irradiated by an inner light which cast patterns of variegated greens and browns and blues and white over its surface. Pastureland, mountains, ocean and tundra: the earth as if seen from the throne of the gods in the sky.

Urthred had seen a globe before, at Forgeholm, in Manichee's study, but that one had been much smaller. This sphere was inspired by ancient magic. It was a living, changing thing, the light of the ancient wizard who had created it still informing it a thousand years after his death.

The globe's colours were those of the soil, rock, sea and ice apart from three distinct red spots which burned brightly from its surface. They were all in the same hemisphere, and roughly in a north–south line.

Three points on the globe: three artefacts of power once buried with Marizian, now scattered over the world. Urthred had no doubt that this was the significance of the lights.

There were no cities or other human features marked on the Orb, but there was no mistaking the location of the bottom marker: contrary to all expectations, one of the artefacts was back in Thrull itself. The red point of light burned more brightly, as if it sensed the proximity of the artefact to its place of origin. Urthred could see quite clearly the surrounding ring of mountains: the Fire Mountains to the west, the Surren Range to the south, Niasseh to the east, and finally the Palisades to the north. The red spot was nestled in the small green area right in their midst. There was no mistaking it. One artefact was here, but which one? And how had it found its way back here?

His eye followed the imaginary line up to the next spot. The Palisades to the north were shown as a tangle of brown and white: glaciers and saw-toothed peaks, ravines and ridges, the barrier which had kept the Nations at bay throughout human history.

To the northwest of the mountains there was a green area, as innocuous-looking as many on the map, but to man the most dangerous: the Nations of the Night. Very little was known of it, only that the creatures who lived there hated mankind. To the northeast was a dun expanse: Shandering Plain. It was from there that the gods had departed the earth, riding their fiery steeds to the stars. To the east, columns of light broke from the globe's surface, reaching up into the air, no doubt representing the cloud-touching towers of legend formed at their departure. All that was left of the palaces of the deities were plains of glass and mounds of fused rock. In between the Nations and the plain was what looked like an extensive forest, with a sizable lake in its midst which shone as a blue jewel in the emerald of its surroundings. The lake held the second glowing spot like a ruby miraculously set into a sapphire.

His eyes travelled farther, much farther up the spinning Orb. He would have guessed that Thrull stood near halfway between pole and equator on the globe, the Nations a quarter of the way to the pole. All the rest of the globe north of Shandering Plain to the pole was covered in ice, ice that twinkled and sparkled in the light of the thousand candles burning in the nave behind him. In the very far north, so near the very top of the globe that it was only just visible from where Urthred stood below it, was the third red spot. Marizian's city, Iskiard, had been far to the north. Urthred suspected that the third red spot was at the Lost City: somehow the artefact marked by it had made its way to Marizian's original home.

The globe represented the sum of all that his brother and the others had given their lives for: with the three objects Randel had hoped to defeat the power of Iss and reestablish the worship of the Flame. Urthred had no idea how the three objects might work in congress with one another, or, indeed, much of their properties apart from what Manichee had told him of the Rod. Clearly the Rod was the most powerful of all of them, opening the way to Shades. A thing of huge power and huge danger to the wielder, for no one would willingly open the gateway into the mirror world where the darker side of humanity dwelt.

He wondered what Randel would have said looking at the globe now. One of the objects, amazingly, was in Thrull. Which of the three was it? The sword, The Warrior of Bronze or the Rod? By now the object might be lost once more, or, worse, fallen into the hands of the Worm.

Yet, despite the dangers of the city, that artefact would be the easiest of the three to recover. No one had ever returned from the Nations, and what lay in the arctic wastes of the north was completely unknown. Urthred wondered whether they could afford to leave the city without it. He doubted it.

Thalassa had been studying the Orb with the same rapt attention as Urthred and must have come to the same conclusion as he about its purpose.

"One of the artefacts is in Thrull," she said.

He nodded his head. "My brother thought to look for it in faraway places, but maybe it's been here all this time."

"Maybe, or maybe it has only just been returned here."

He became conscious of the hum of the Orb; time was passing with every revolution—their friends could very well be in danger outside.

But there was one last thing he wanted to do before they left. He looked at the sarcophagus again. It was beyond the globe, occupying nearly all the end of the nave. It was made of a single block of black basalt, some twenty feet high. The last resting place of Marizian, the founder of his religion. With a mixture of fear and curiosity, he approached it. There was no apparent way of getting into it: the whole block appeared seamless and impenetrable. Urthred could not even begin to guess at the magic which had gone into its construction. The treasures it contained were great, more valuable by far than the three objects of power marked out on the globe, for buried with Marizian were the two holy books of Reh and Iss as they had been written by the First Father five thousand years before. Only copies of them existed in the outside world: on the two occasions when the tomb had been breached by human hands, neither the priests of Reh nor those of Iss had dared try to enter the sarcophagus itself.

But the last fresco in the passage outside had implored the Seeker to discover the truth, which Furtal had interpreted as the secret of the sun's dying. The secret was not revealed by the Orb; it must be buried in the sarcophagus with Marizian.

Thalassa had followed him, but, when he had stopped, as if on a sudden impulse, had taken another step forward and then another until she was right next to the sarcophagus. Urthred was about to say something, but before he could even open his mouth she had held up her right hand and touched its side.

An explosion of white light filled the apse. A mighty wind followed, racing down the nave, extinguishing the thousand candles in series, one by one. Urthred clenched his eyes shut with pain. When he opened them again, the block of basalt that a second before had completely filled his vision had disappeared. The apse was cast into semidarkness. The place where the block had been was now just empty floor with some steps leading down into the ground. A glow came from the bottom of the steps, silhouetting Thalassa's thin body in front of him. She seemed totally untouched by the explosion, as was he, as he discovered when he looked down at his body—not a scratch. "Are you all right?" he managed.

Thalassa turned to him, her eyes were wide with excitement and fear. "I only touched it!" she marvelled, holding up the hand responsible as if it were an alien thing, rather than a part of her.

Urthred looked at the place where the basalt block had been, expecting what he'd witnessed to be an optical illusion and to find that the sarcophagus had reappeared. But there was no doubt about it: it had gone. Something that had existed for five thousand years disappeared in the blink of an eye.

He stepped up next to Thalassa and peered down the steps towards the glow of light which he had noticed earlier. He felt her very close, her arm brushing his, her breath shallow and quick from the sudden shock. But when he turned to her he saw that her eyes were staring intently down the steps. She wanted to go down them.

"We can't," Urthred protested. "The books are down there—the holy books."

She clutched his arm, sending a small trail of electricity up it. "We must, Urthred—don't you think I'd be dead if I hadn't been fated to go down there?"

"You may have just been lucky."

"No—you know it's more than that. Think of the prophecies, of the shrine." She took a step forward, still holding his arm.

He was going to protest again, but found instead that he was being led by her. They slowly descended the steps towards the glow of light. A terrible sense of foreboding filled his heart. But they were nearly at the bottom of the steps. Then the glow below suddenly disappeared and Thalassa's hand was gone from his arm. He was alone, in total darkness.

A familiar odour came to his nostrils: the smell of decay, of crypts which have once harboured bones, where the musty essence of the dead, like that of old books, still lingers though the flesh has crumbled to dust and the bones scattered to the birds. Such was the smell at the bottom of the stairs. He took another cautious step forward, an awful curiosity vying with his terror.

"Don't be afraid." It was Thalassa's voice, remarkably steady. "Look." With the last word, a beam of light shot down from a hole in the ceiling of the tomb onto a low plinth in front of them. Thalassa stood next to him, her hand upraised, as if conjuring the light.

A body lay on the plinth—the body, he presumed, of Marizian. He waited for the shining apparition they had met in the maze to suddenly rise up and destroy them, but nothing happened.

Gathering his courage, he stepped up onto the step surrounding the plinth and looked down.

The remains of Marizian lay before him wrapped in a simple white sheet. The face was a leather mask through which yellowed bone glinted. The hollows of the eyes were vacant, the white beard a mere gossamer wisp brown with age. Skeletal hands were crossed at the chest.

The man nearly immortal was now mere bones and dust like any other man who had run the natural course of his life.

Two metal-bound books had been propped inside the crook of the corpse's arms. One gold, one silver.

The *Book of Light* and the *Book of Worms*.

Except there were no books anymore: the paper between the metal covers had crumbled into a fine black powder which had pooled onto Marizian's chest.

Thalassa was now standing next to him. "The books are destroyed," he said in a strangled voice.

"Yes," she answered, "the books of law are dust, the books that divided men, set brother on brother—isn't that what Furtal said?"

"But you don't understand. Our religion, everything, was based on those!"

She stared evenly into the eye slits of his mask: "It may be for the best. Centuries of dogma and misunderstanding have been based on them. The world may be a better place for their loss."

Urthred's mind was too taken up with the destruction of the books for him to rebuke her. In any case, she was right: without the originals, every other copy of the *Book of Light* was unprovable, suspect. All the Scriptures and all the prophecies might have been the fabrications of a later age. No one now would know what Marizian had actually written.

He looked once more at the twin piles of fine dust: so many beliefs and aspirations had gone into the study of those books; his whole life to date had been predicated on the teachings of one of them. Had the secret of the sun's dying been hidden in these originals? Or had the calamity been brought about by another of Marizian's actions? Nothing was certain anymore. Only faith remained.

"Now we have to go back," Thalassa said. "We've left the others too long."

Urthred had lost track of time: minutes or hours might have passed since they went through the maze. The pitiful cadaver in front of him suddenly reminded him of his own mortality, and that outside the maze time was passing swiftly. He nodded his silent agreement and led them back to the stairs.

It was dark at the head of the steps, but Urthred nevertheless saw the figure peering down into the gloom from the top of them. He gave a grunt of surprise as the man's single eye glinted in the light. It was the man he had fought in the Temple of Sutis. The man Thalassa had called Jayal. Before Urthred could react, he had darted back out of sight.

How could anyone else have penetrated the maze? Before he gave himself time to consider this, Urthred was bounding up the steps. But when he got to the top, the figure was already halfway down the nave, running towards the distant lights. Urthred followed but was still far behind when the figure entered the area of shifting shadows and disappeared.

Thalassa caught up with him. "It was him again!" Her face was drawn, white.

"He came through the maze—and that means he came past our friends as well," Urthred said.

No further words were necessary. They both hurried forward, fear for their friends' safety obliterating everything they had just seen in the tomb chamber.

CHAPTER THIRTY-EIGHT

Into the Pit

Outside the maze, the dust powder and the vapour from the battle were beginning to clear. Golon had already inspected the yawning pit that had been blown into the floor by the bolt from the sword. If Faran was still conscious, there was little he could do for him yet. First he must see whether any threat still existed behind them.

He had been surprised when the figure had burst out of the side corridor and leapt into the maze: he had expected all their assailants to have been killed by the vapour. But he didn't worry himself unduly about the man. The Reaper that Faran had sent forward into the maze had not returned, and he expected the fugitive to have shared a similar fate. He paced down the corridor to the bodies littering the floor. Golon looked at his handiwork dispassionately. First the rebel who had fought with Faran. The octopoid creature that had flown into his face was now set like stone, and the young man's body was grey and leached, like the body of a statue. Farther up the corridor, the corpses of the Doppelgänger's men were still covered with a seething mass of maggots heaving whitely in the gloom. The sight would have been too much for most men, but Golon's interest was undimmed by the spectacle.

He counted the dead, tallying them with the number of men who'd attacked. Two of them were still missing, he calculated.

One had been the one he'd seen dive into the swirling light patterns of the maze. There was only one more of their enemies to worry about. Two of the Reapers remained alive. Golon guessed that their faces would show terror—their friends had been killed in a single instant—but their faces, as always, were covered by the skull masks. They stood by Malliana and the two other captives, shifting uneasily from foot to foot. The sorcerer beckoned them over and the three men advanced down the passage. Golon peered into each successive side corridor, but they were all empty. The man had got away, but he was only one man. There were other matters to attend to.

He backtracked slowly. His gaze came to rest on the sword that had caused all the trouble. It lay not far from the worm-eaten corpse of the man who'd led the charge. A sorcerer, Golon surmised, but one who had been but an apprentice, hardly worthy of the spell that had killed him. The sword's blade glowed a dull coppery red. He knelt, his hand outstretched. Even from the distance of a couple of feet, Golon felt the power radiating from it, the power of the Flame and not of the Worm, a power that would be inimical to him and the undead. He would have to leave it where it lay.

He stood and walked back to the three captives. The old lutanist still lay unconscious on the floor. The two women looked sufficiently cowed not to offer any trouble. He was about to pass them by when the High Priestess reached out a bony hand and seized his arm.

"It was him!" she exclaimed, her eyes wild.

"Who?" Golon asked, jerking his cloak away from her with repugnance.

"The man who ran into the lights. It was Jayal Illgill! I told you, I saw him earlier . . ."

"Enough of your fantasy; it won't save you!" Golon snarled. Malliana's mouth opened and closed as if she wanted to say more, but was too terrified to do so.

"Look after them well," Golon ordered the two remaining guards, "and make sure you capture anyone who comes out of there," he added, jerking his head at the maze.

He went to the edge of the hole blown in the floor by the sword. His eyes peered down into the darkness, from which dust still eddied up. The bolt from the sword must have hit the supporting arch of the corridor below, causing the sudden and unexpected collapse. Through the clouds of dust he could see the gloomy outlines of shattered masonry some fifty feet down. Faran would be down there somewhere, probably trapped. But not dead—two hundred years of existence could not be snuffed out so easily.

He spread the wings of his cloak out like a bat to either side and stepped into the void. Instead of plummeting, as gravity would have dictated, his body was buoyed up by the cloak and he fell gently downwards, like a leaf falling from an autumnal tree, towards the rubble in which Faran lay buried.

Alone, lost and blind, Jayal had blundered through the dark passages, the euphoria of having escaped the Doppelgänger quickly replaced by terror at the darkness and by the invisible objects that barked his shins in the dark. What was worse, his hands were still tied behind his back, and he was unable to brush off the cobwebs that draped over his mouth and eyes, or to flick away the water droplets that fell steadily from the ceiling onto his face.

He must have wandered in this way for twenty minutes or more, stopping every now and again to listen intently before moving on, not knowing whether he was getting more and more lost in the warren of passageways, or was heading towards some positive objective.

He continued in this manner for a while, his weariness and wounds forcing him to lean against the damp walls of the tunnel during his stops. In one such pause, he leant against what he thought was going to be another section of the wall: instead his back met no resistance and he fell, landing with a crash amongst a heap of jangling metal. Something ripped open the leather vambrace on his arm, and a sensation of wetness quickly spread over the sleeve of his cloak. He'd been cut, badly.

He struggled like a madman, his tethered hands scrambling frantically to boost himself to his feet. As he did so, they encountered something sharp and metallic: a sword blade. Despite the pain, his heart leapt. With this he could cut through the bonds tying his wrists. But how to get the leverage to do it? His hands reached out behind him and touched something wooden: a frame of some kind. Then, reaching up farther, they touched another blade, standing upright in what he now recognised to be a weapons stand. He inched his way backwards so the hemp cord was against the blade and began to saw away at the bonds, not caring when an injudicious movement cut his wrist. The bonds dropped away after some twelve or so lusty scrapes. The circulation throbbed back into his hands, and, with it, more welling of blood from his wounds.

He was still utterly blind, but feeling about in the dark, he now found the fallen pieces of metal all around him to be other weapons. His hands measured them. The blade that had cut his arm belonged to a giant sword: the hilt was some two feet long and its blade six feet: it had been made for some early race of supermen, of giants, long fled from the world.

His body was now shaking uncontrollably. The wounds must have been worse than he had thought. The invisible room spun and he fell to his knees. He wrenched at the linen shirt under his cloak, tearing it into strips. He bound his wounds clumsily, using his free hand and his teeth. He felt slightly better with the bleeding staunched. He got back to his feet and began once more to feel his way around the room. He touched more of the towering swords, then came to a stand that was filled with much shorter weapons: what must have been to the giants mere daggers, but which to him were still heavier than any weapon he had ever wielded, including Dragonstooth. He hefted one from the stand, its weight forcing down his arm. Though it was cumbersome, it was a weapon, one which he'd need if he came across any of his enemies. This thought gave him pause. And what if the enemy was the Doppelgänger? Jayal was not sure whether he would have the courage to kill him. Whatever his father's intentions in using the Rod, there were two Jayal Illgills alive in the world. The death of one of them would result in the death of the other. It was only the Rod that Manichee had taken from the lead chest as he'd lain dying at the battle that could banish this shadow of himself back to its own plane. And to find it, he also needed to find his father. But, first, the warren of corridors.

He set off again, leaving the armoury behind him, any momentary resolve fast dissolving as once more he blundered from object to object, wall to wall. But then, in the utter darkness, a small glimmer of grey. He headed towards it, a mad wave of joy seizing his heart. The light grew more and more pronounced until he saw the rectangular end of a corridor. As he neared, he heard a woman's voice, raised high, in anger.

"The temple's burned and the women dead; because of you, witch, because of you!"

Alanda was dabbing at the wound on Furtal's head with a dampened scrap of cloth, and barely registered Malliana's words. "The temple would have burned with or without me," she said without looking up, trying to keep her voice neutral. Her eyes were fixed on the maze, wondering when Thalassa and Urthred would reappear. Furtal moaned again: a large part of his skull was covered with a grey-and-black swelling. Alanda suspected that Faran's blow might have cracked it. He was half-conscious, muttering snatches of old songs and a name he repeated over and over: maybe the name of a woman he'd once loved. Above Furtal's moans, Malliana continued her litany of complaint, heedless of the old man's suffering.

Finally, one of the guards grew tired of the noise. He stepped up to her and uttered a curt warning. Malliana shut up immediately, her defiance evaporating in a moment. In the sudden silence they all heard the noise from up the side corridor nearest to them. The guards immediately turned towards the sound, their maces and shields at the ready.

Then the man stepped from the corridor.

Seven years had passed, but Alanda recognised him in an instant: it was Illgill's son, returned to Thrull, just as Thalassa had told her. The man who had wrought such havoc at the Temple of Sutis. She had only glimpsed him for a second when he'd fought with the priest on the staircase leading down to the Greeting Room and during his mad dive into the lights of the maze. How was it he'd now returned to this place by a different route? Surely there was only one way out of the maze?

For the moment he hadn't recognised her. He stood at the entrance of the corridor, his eyes warily taking in the two

guards and the sword lying in the middle of the corridor behind
them. He was wearing battered leather armour, showing the
whorls and sigils of the Flame. She noticed that his left arm was
bandaged with a bloodstained rag, as was his right wrist. He
held a curious weapon in his hands: cumbersome and badly balanced, the guard highly wrought and interlatticed, a sword
etched with ancient runes, more ancient than any of her own
learning. It didn't look as if it would be very useful in a fight.

The Reapers came forward, maces and shields held before
them, their skull masks concealing their expressions. Jayal circled round to one side, skirting the edge of the pit in the floor.
It was then Alanda saw what he was doing: he was heading for
the red glow of the other sword halfway up the passageway behind them. The Reapers must have realised this, too, for they
suddenly lunged forward, trying to cut him off from it.

Jayal reacted quickly. One of the two men had got slightly in
front of his colleague, and Jayal darted to one side of him, par-
rying the man's blow with his weapon, using the Reaper's body
to shield himself from his other antagonist. The first Reaper, his
weapon knocked to one side, tried to shield-barge Jayal, but he
twisted aside again, keeping the man between himself and his
comrade. Then he took the Reaper by surprise, flinging his
sword at his face. The weapon flew over his head, but the man
was momentarily thrown off-balance.

It gave Jayal the split second he needed: he turned and raced
up the corridor, skidding to a halt where Dragonstooth lay. The
guards were only a short distance behind him, but their movement was hampered by their heavier armour. Jayal seized the
hilt of the sword and drove savagely upwards at the first of
them. The man was off balance from the run and could only try
blocking the low blow as his impetus brought him into it.

But Dragonstooth had sheared thicker metal than the chainmail worn by the Reaper: its blade passed through the man's
shield arm just above the elbow, severing it and sending a gout
of blood over the walls and ceiling of the corridor. The
wounded man somersaulted over the point of impact and fell in
a heap on his back, the stump of his arm continuing to spray
Jayal and the walls red.

The other guard had managed to stop his forward momentum and waited as Jayal rose to his feet. They swayed one way and then back again, the guard's movements unsure, as if he was debating whether to flee or not, his comrade's twitching body giving him encouragement enough to do so. But he'd left it too late. Jayal swung the sword again, a roundhouse blow aimed at the man's neck. The Reaper flung up both his shield and mace to stop it, but mere metal could not stop the ancient blade. There was an explosion of sparks as it cut through both of them, then a dull thunk as it passed through the leather armour at the man's neck. The man's head spun through the air, landing neatly between Malliana's feet.

Malliana screamed and backed away, her face ashen. Her eyes went to the head rolling on the floor, then back to Jayal. He made a frightening spectacle: soaked in blood, covered with rough bandages, his eyes burning with maniacal rage.

But for the moment his gaze was occupied with the sword, which he looked at with a kind of rapture. It was only after a few moments that he seemed to become aware of their presence, and he looked at them.

Immediately his face lit up in recognition. "Lady Alanda?" he asked.

Though he was the spitting image of Illgill's son, Alanda was wary of him. She remembered Thalassa's account of what he had done at the temple. How he'd attacked the priest. She backed away. This man was either an impostor or a madman, or both.

"Keep your distance," she said, hoping that the fear was not too obvious in her voice.

"Don't you recognise me? It is I, Jayal Illgill!"

"Maybe, or maybe not," Alanda replied.

A look of puzzlement crossed Jayal's face. "Why do you think I could be anyone else?" He held his arms out so the light of the sword played on his face. "Come, seven years have passed, but I haven't changed that much."

The look on his face was so beseeching that Alanda was almost convinced. On a sudden impulse, she turned to Malliana, who had stood silently at her side all this time. For the moment, the two women were allies.

"Isn't this the man you saw at the temple?" she asked.

Malliana's features were creased in puzzlement. "He looks like him," she said, "but the other man had a scar, running down here." She traced a line down the right-hand side of her face.

"You've seen him?" Jayal said excitedly, his head swivelling around him as if he might spot his double hiding in the shadows.

Alanda took a step forward. "You mean there is another who looks like you?"

Jayal's features fell, as he realised that the chamber was empty and his enemy was nowhere near. He turned back to Alanda. "Aye, there is one just like me. Exactly like, though his nature is the reverse of mine. If he has hurt your friend," he said, glancing at Malliana, "I will be revenged on him soon."

"She's no friend of mine," Alanda answered, glancing contemptuously at the High Priestess. "But tell me, who is this double?"

"It is a long story, beggaring belief and the time we have. He brought me here as a captive. I was at the back of the group who attacked Faran. We became separated."

"Then it must have been he who went into the maze," Alanda said.

Jayal turned his attention to the flickering lights. "He went in there? Then I must follow."

Alanda held out a hand, restraining him. "It's too dangerous."

"I'll go anyway!" he said, shrugging away her hand.

"Then you'll die—there's ancient magic at work in there."

A strange look, of both defiance and despair, passed over Jayal's face. "He had my father's book, with the notes he'd taken when he came here seven years ago." He turned to her, his eyes blazing. "He'll find the Orb! He will gain its power and knowledge."

"There are two of our friends in there; they may stop him," Alanda said, trying to calm him.

"Who? Who are they?"

Alanda was silent. Golon might return any moment, and they had to get Furtal away from here. It was best for him not to hear about Thalassa now.

But Malliana had recovered her tongue and her sense of

mischief. "One is a priest of Reh, the other is someone well-known to you," she said with a small smile.

"Well-known—how so?"

"Your fiancée," she said, with a sneer of pleasure, "Thalassa."

"Thalassa is in there?"

"So near and yet so far, young man," Malliana said. "I doubt whether you'd recognise her after all these years."

"That's enough!" Alanda said, trying to stop the conversation before it had gone too far.

But Jayal held up his hand, silencing her. He was suddenly very still. "Who are you?" he asked Malliana.

"Why, only the woman who has kept Thalassa and this old hag here in bread when they might otherwise have starved—I'm the High Priestess of Sutis."

Jayal twitched slightly as if an unseen blow had struck him. He turned to Alanda. "You've been with Thalassa these last seven years?"

"All can be explained," Alanda said, desperate now for them to get away.

But Jayal was having none of it. "You've been at the Temple of Sutis all this time?"

Alanda nodded silent assent.

"All this night," Jayal said quietly, "I have heard rumours—Thalassa . . ." His voice broke off. ". . . Thalassa, these people told me, rogues and thieves all of them, was nothing better than a common drab at the temple."

"You heard right, Illgill," Malliana cut in, her rouged lips cracked in mirthless pleasure. Jayal whirled round on her, a look of such fury on his face that the High Priestess flinched away.

"In the God's name, man, give me time to explain," Alanda said, casting a filthy look at Malliana. "Faran's sorcerer may be back any moment: can't we at least go to a safer place?"

Jayal seemed suddenly to become aware of his surroundings again. "Faran's sorcerer? Where is he?"

"In the crater: he's trying to find his master."

Jayal glanced in that direction. "Then we'd better go," he said, his brow nevertheless furrowed with suspicion. "We can

wait for Thalassa somewhere safe, and see what she has to say
for herself when she comes out."

"*If* she comes out," Alanda corrected him. "Your double is in
there, don't forget." She looked down at Furtal. The old man
had been rambling deliriously all through the fight and the sub-
sequent interchanges, oblivious of what was happening. "Will
you at least help me with him?"

Jayal glanced at Furtal for the first time: his face, dark and
brooding before, lightened and then darkened again when first
he saw who it was, but then how grave his injury was. He knelt,
feeling for a pulse—it was weak and fitful. "My father's musician!" he murmured, as if this night's wonders would never
cease. He pulled the old man to his feet and, holding Dragonstooth in one hand, hauled him up over his shoulder. He followed Alanda, who had set off down the side passage from
which he had appeared a few minutes before, Malliana reluctantly in tow.

His head spun. He was only twenty-five, yet felt as old as
the burden he carried—the past had arrived, vengeful and not to
be placated. His past had been buried these last seven years, but
life had continued here in Thrull without him. Many changes
had occurred, crossing his expectations that, somehow, everything would be the same once he returned. Now he saw that
he'd preserved his memories in amber, while irrevocable
changes had happened without him. His dreams were nothing:
he knew now what Thalassa had been. The reality of it crushed
him: he could not weigh his ideal of her with what she now
must be like. She had been enslaved—she could have had no
choice but to serve at the temple. But then he felt terrible bitterness as he remembered all the dangers and near death he had
suffered. For what? For pride, the pride that his fiancée couldn't
muster when she should have chosen death, the noble escape
from disgrace. But had he chosen death that terrible day in the
desert? Hadn't Reh appeared in the dying sun and told him by
his sign that he must live, live to fight the Worm? Blessedly, for
the moment his mind refused to think any more of it, so incal-
culable seemed the chasm between his hopes and the bitter reality of what he had discovered that night. He plodded on in an

abject silence, the old man's weight and the pain of his wounds a counterpoint to the hurt of his soul.

The blade of Dragonstooth glowed like a red-hot brand, adding to the light of the old lady's lantern. Water dripped from the arched ceiling vault of the tunnel and their cloaks trailed through oily-looking puddles. Some two hundred paces in, Alanda brought them to a halt, evidently deciding that this was as safe a place to stop as any. The corridor ahead of them was black, the darkness impervious to the lantern light: it might conceal even greater dangers than those they had just left behind. The faintest glimmer of light came after them from the maze. At least they would be able to see anyone following them.

Jayal laid the wounded man carefully on the floor. Though Furtal was only a bundle of bones, Jayal's bruises and cuts had begun to ache from the exertion of carrying him and he was grateful to be rid of his burden.

He straightened slowly and met the gaze of the old woman. Seven years had not changed her: she looked exactly as she had done the last time he had seen her, in his father's house on the eve of the battle. Here at least was someone not a slave to the hurrying hours. Seven years to the day: it was as if the years and the fates had hastened them together to meet again, sweeping away the time in between.

Whatever she had been at the Temple of Sutis, and whatever part she'd had in Thalassa's downfall, he needed an ally—someone he could tell what he must now do. For Jayal's thoughts were now fixed on one purpose: he must kill the Doppelgänger. Shadow and substance, soul indivisible: if one should die, so too would the other. This was the magic of the Rod. Somehow he would cease to exist when he killed his other half; but whether his life would end in a flash of light, or a slow ebbing away, he could only speculate. In any event, he had to prepare himself. She would have to carry Dragonstooth to his father in the far north. She might seem to be only an old lady, but he knew her to be a seeress, and suspected her to have the powers of sorcery as well. He would give her the sword now, then fetch another weapon from the many littered about the floor in the chamber outside. This time his double wouldn't surprise him: one, or the other, or both would die. Then there would be an end to the curse.

She was looking at him evenly, as if expecting him to speak, explain what had happened to him in the last seven years. There was, in turn, much he once would have liked to have discovered about her. But he had to ready himself for the battle with the Doppelgänger. Her story would have to wait, perhaps forever.

But if Alanda was to have the sword, she had to know what it was, what purpose it might serve in the battle against the Worm. He would have to tell her the story from its beginning.

So it was, with one eye fixed on the entranceway down the corridor, Jayal began to recount the tale of all that had befallen him in the last seven years. He began reluctantly, his words slurred with tiredness, grudging each syllable. But gradually, as his tale unfolded, he began to speak with more animation. He had never told a living soul what had happened to him in all those years of wandering. And now he was doing it for the second time, on the same night. At first he could not meet the old lady's eyes as he spoke of the years of doubt and procrastination. Once or twice he stopped talking altogether, the words choking him as he fought back his emotions. The day of the battle, the hopelessness of the struggle, the charge against the Reapers, the wound, and then, that which had only flooded back into his consciousness when he'd seen Furisel again, the resurrection of his body through the Rod. Then the quest for the sword. Its discovery and then his return to the city. And then the darkest discovery of them all—his double. But when he glanced at her, her look was not altogether unsympathetic. His words by the end were a torrent. He was surprised to find that his anger had nearly vanished when he had finished, as if he had confessed himself to a priest, and now he waited for absolution of all the guilt and the self-doubt that he'd suffered in the past seven years.

Alanda reached out a hand and patted him consolingly on the shoulder. The touch was good, healing after so many arid years when he had felt no human contact at all.

"You have brought the sword—one of Marizian's treasures. Your father would be proud of you," she said.

"If he's still alive."

"I've a feeling that he is," she replied.

"I remember—you have the sight. My father listened to your advice. I remember, the night before the battle, he spoke with you in his study."

"Call my gift what you will, Jayal: it is both a blessing and a curse. As for your father—he didn't listen to what I told him. Otherwise, a lot of bloodshed might have been avoided."

"You saw what would happen?"

"Only dimly. Many things were too close to me. But I saw the pyramid of skulls, the widows weeping in the street; yet I didn't know that it would be I who would be weeping, nor that it would be my husband's head on the pyramid."

"We've all suffered," Jayal said quietly.

"Thalassa, too," Alanda interjected.

Jayal fell silent at the mention of her name. Alanda could only guess at what emotions were passing through him. But his next words surprised her.

"Take Dragonstooth," he said, proffering the hilt of the sword. "If the fates are kind, you'll be able to find my father. Tell him how I suffered getting it, how I didn't give up, though it took so long."

"You'll live to give it him yourself," Alanda said, waving it away.

"No! I told you—I must find the Doppelgänger. One or the other of us must die." His voice was loud, and they both became conscious of a dim echo from the mouth of the dark corridor in front of them.

They were silent for a few seconds before Alanda spoke again. "Wait for a little while; the others must return soon from the maze."

"If my double hasn't done his worst."

"We'll see," Alanda replied evenly.

The call took them both by surprise. It came from the direction of the lights. They turned and saw a flicker of movement at the end of the tunnel. "It's the priest!" Alanda said, hurrying forward with the lantern.

CHAPTER THIRTY-NINE

Reunion

Urthred and Thalassa had once more moved through the
flickering lights of the maze. Their slow progress was
maddening, given their state of anxiety over their friends. As
they went forward, they caught glimpses of the Doppelgänger
in the shifting grey light—one moment he looked far in front of
them, then suddenly he seemed close enough to touch, but
when Urthred held out his gloved hand the image disappeared,
only to reappear far behind them, dwindling by the moment in
the pearly light. Then the air began to shift and warp in front of
them: they were nearing the edge of the maze. As before, it
seemed that their feet suddenly grew wings and it was as if they
were borne up by a mighty wave and transported forward, now
at an alarming pace, towards the bright curtain of spirits. They
exploded from it in a flash of white light, stumbling slightly at
the sudden deceleration.

They barely recognised the place from which they'd departed. The gloomy tranquillity that had reigned there when
they'd left had been replaced by a scene of utter destruction.
Right in front of them stood the gaping hole in the floor blown
by Dragonstooth. Bodies skeletal, decapitated, leached of
colour, lay scattered up the corridor's length. Seresh's leather
armour was instantly recognisable, though his face was now
covered by the grey accretion from Golon's sorcery.

Thalassa looked away quickly, but all Urthred's senses were alert to any threatening presence in the shadows.

Nothing stirred in the gloom: they were safe for the moment. He forced himself to look again at the bodies, praying that Seresh would be the only one he recognised. To his relief, there was no sign of Alanda or Furtal.

He decided to risk calling out. For a moment, the sound of his shout echoed eerily down the side passage, bouncing back and forth from the ancient stone of the tomb. Then an answering call came from down the nearest of them. He recognised Alanda's voice. They both hurried towards it, through the darkness, noticing a lantern light far down it coming towards them, and after it, a reddish, sullen glow.

The first person they saw emerging from the darkness was the old lady herself, her cheek coated with blood.

"You're hurt!" Thalassa exclaimed.

Alanda hushed her. "It's nothing—Faran was closer than we thought—his sorcerer killed Seresh."

"And Furtal?"

"He's farther back down the corridor, wounded but alive."

"Where is Faran?" Urthred asked anxiously.

"He was blown into the pit. His sorcerer followed him."

"I hope that he's dead," Urthred said grimly. His eyes were adjusting to the lantern light and he could now make out the two figures standing behind Alanda. With a shock of recognition he identified Malliana. He was surprised to see that she, too, had survived the nighttime streets, even more surprised to see her with Alanda. But that surprise was as nothing when the figure next to her, the one carrying a redly glowing sword, materialised from the gloom. The man from the maze, the one who called himself Jayal Illgill! Alanda had been captured, that was the only explanation. He leapt forward, his gloves ready to strike. But Alanda jumped in his way.

"Steady now!" she exclaimed, wrestling with his arm.

"Don't you see? It's him! The man who attacked us in the temple," Urthred snarled.

"It's not him—it's another man," Alanda replied, clinging to Urthred with surprising tenaciousness.

Urthred was about to shrug the old lady away, but a cry from behind him stopped him in his tracks. He turned to see Thalassa standing motionless, her eyes fixed on the man farther down the corridor, her face a mask of surprise and fear.

"Alanda is right," she said, her lips trembling. "He looks the same, but he has no scar!"

Urthred looked back at the man. He was the very mirror image of the other Jayal, except he had both eyes and his face was smooth and unblemished. "And the other man?" he asked.

Jayal had flinched when he first saw Urthred's mask in the half-light of the passage. And raised Dragonstooth as the priest had closed with him. Now he spoke for the first time: "The other man is an impostor—whatever he did was nothing to do with me. I returned to the city only tonight: I learned what this other Jayal had done these last seven years and went to confront him. . . . Things didn't go the way I'd hoped. He led me down here with his men, but only the two of us escaped. He must have been the man you saw in the tomb."

"He looked just like you," Urthred replied, staring uncertainly at Jayal's face. So alike, and yet so dissimilar. The Jayal he'd fought with in the temple had been the epitome of malevolence. His carriage, his ravaged face, his speech had all declared an inner corruption. But where everything was crabbed and diseased with his shadow, this man had a nobility of carriage and speech that seemed to shine out of every gesture and word.

"I've explained everything to Lady Alanda," Jayal said. "The strange circumstances that brought me here, the discovery of my twin. The tale sounds strange even to my own ears, though I live it. I couldn't blame you if you doubted it, priest."

"If Alanda and Thalassa are convinced, that's enough for me," Urthred replied. He looked round at the two women. Alanda nodded her assent, but Thalassa had her face averted, unable, it seemed, after her initial identification of him, to look Jayal in the face. With a stab of jealousy, inappropriate to their danger, Urthred remembered she'd been engaged to this man. But that had been seven years before—their meeting now, unsurprisingly, was full of a silent tension.

"We can't remain here," he said briskly. He turned to Jayal: "This other man, this double of yours, was not far behind us."

"Then I'll wait for him by the maze," Illgill said, "but I must know what he saw in there."

"He would have seen what we did," Urthred said.

"And what was that?" Jayal asked anxiously. Urthred glanced at Alanda again. She gave him another encouraging nod.

"The Orb: the world like a many-coloured ball, turning in the air. On it were marked the three magical artefacts of Marizian."

"And?" Jayal asked.

Again, Urthred turned to Alanda to see whether he should continue, but she gestured impatiently for him to finish his description of the Orb.

"One of the items is here, in Thrull."

Jayal held up the sword, so his face was lit up by its coppery light. "Then you saw this: the sword stolen by the Worm millennia ago. My father sent me to the deserts of the south to recover it."

Urthred stared at it silently for a minute, trying to guess the weapon's powers. Whatever they were, they would be great. "Then you have had a long quest," he said eventually, "but a longer one lies ahead for those who wish to gain the other two: one of them is beyond the Palisades, and the other in the frozen north."

Jayal came closer, untroubled it would seem by close proximity to Urthred's mask. "Then find them, priest; find them and my father!"

"But what of you and the sword?"

"I've already told Alanda what I must do: I have to confront my double. The old lady has refused the sword—but you are a priest. Take it, with the God's blessing. You will put it to work, I know!"

"Why? Won't you have need of it?"

"Most likely I'll be dead, priest—that other you saw, that thing in the maze who has plucked out my father's secrets—he must die, and I must die with him."

"But why?"

"We are bound up, he and I," Jayal said with vehemence. "While he lives, my name will be dishonoured; my father, whom he hates, will be in danger. I must kill him now, and by doing so, end my own life."

"Strange words," Urthred said, turning to Alanda.

"Strange, but true, as I know," Alanda said. "The Rod has opened the way to the shadow world and let this other creature out."

"Who did such a thing?" Urthred asked, but he already suspected what the answer was going to be.

"My father and his priest," Jayal replied.

"Manichee?"

"The same."

"I saw him tonight," Urthred said after a slight pause.

Alanda seemed unsurprised to hear it: "A vision?" she asked.

"Yes, it came to me as I sat by the Pool of the Blinding. I was on my last legs. He came to help me, as he promised when he left Forgeholm."

"What did he say?" Alanda asked.

"He said he had been cursed to inhabit Shades for one terrible act . . ."

"He used the Rod to summon my shadow self from Shades," Jayal interjected. "The two bodies were exchanged as I lay dying. Manichee believed that this other would die, but he had forgotten—a man cannot live without his shadow. The creature had to survive, though penned in my former body. So Manichee was cursed, and so was I," Jayal continued bitterly. "Six years I spent looking for the sword, but for nothing. Here, take it, priest; you don't need a magical sword to kill a dog." But again, Urthred ignored the proffered hilt.

"Leave this double, this other," Alanda urged. "We have the information we need: we can leave now."

"And have him follow me to the world's end?" Jayal replied. "Believe me, lady, he will: maybe he won't catch me tomorrow or next week, but as the years trickle away he will always be near. Then, I may not be ready for him. Now, I am. As the priest says, he'll appear soon. I'll wait for him by the edge of the maze."

"I'll come with you," Urthred offered.

Jayal turned to him. "My thanks—but it's too dangerous:

Faran's sorcerer may return, and then we'd both be dead. Though I die, you must take the sword and what you have learnt in the tomb to my father."

There was such an air of entreaty, such pleading in his eyes, that Urthred hardly dared break contact with them.

He forced himself to look at Alanda again, and then at Thalassa. They were both silent; the old lady had seemingly voiced all her objections, and Thalassa had not said a word all this time, nor had she or Jayal looked at one another. Whatever lay between them could not be articulated in such a short period of time. She hung her head, not giving Urthred any indication of what he should do.

"Very well," he said, laying his gloved hand on the hilt of the sword. He felt an immediate surge of power running down the metal struts of his arm brace. Fire kindled in his veins. Jayal's eyes were still fixed on him. "This is strong magic," he said.

"Rare magic, drawn from the steed of a god," Jayal agreed.

"It is for a warrior to wield, not a priest," Urthred said.

"Carry it for a while, until the day you find my father," Jayal said, then, with a grim smile, he turned and brushed past them down the corridor, his eyes still averted from Thalassa. They saw him briefly silhouetted against the glow of the maze, then he disappeared.

Malliana had been silent all this time, as caught up in the unraveling of Jayal's story as the others, but now she couldn't resist a jibe at Thalassa: "It seems that he doesn't remember you," she said, smirking at her.

"Why is she here?" Urthred asked impatiently, suddenly reminded of the High Priestess's presence.

"Faran brought her," Alanda answered.

Urthred turned to the High Priestess. "You are not our friend: by choice, I'd leave you for Faran."

She smiled again. "You're too kind, Scarface. Remember, if I'd given you over to the Worm at the temple, none of this might have happened."

Urthred didn't favour her with a reply. The High Priestess was a problem they'd have to deal with later, he decided. There was enough to think about as it was.

"Where's Furtal?" he asked.

Alanda led them back a few steps to where the old man was propped up against a wall. Though his eyes were open, they were fixed and glazed: he was clearly in a bad way. They'd have to go soon. Faran's sorcerer would not be in the pit all night.

Alanda was obviously having the same thoughts. "We can't leave by the way we came in: we'll have to find another route out of the pyramid," she said.

"Do you know of any?"

She shook her head. "There are underground passages all over: if we go farther into the underworld, we might find one that leads to safety."

Urthred thought of the staff the leech gatherer had given him. He unlimbered it from his back where it had been all this time. The tiny green shoot and the single leaf which had appeared in the Lightbringer's Shrine were still there. "Seresh and I were given this by one of the creatures in Stick's Hole. I helped them: their Elder told me to call on its aid if I ever needed them."

"What is it?" asked Alanda, studying it closely.

"He told me it was a branch of an ancient tree. But how the leech gatherers will find it, I don't know."

"The creatures have great powers; maybe they already know we're in danger."

"Let's hope so," Urthred agreed. "The outside of the tomb will be crawling with the undead by now."

Alanda looked round at Thalassa. She was staring down the corridor in the direction that Jayal had gone, heedless of Malliana, who stood next to her like a malevolent shadow.

"We'd better go; I'll carry Furtal," Urthred said.

"What of him?" Alanda asked, nodding her head down the corridor towards Jayal.

"You heard what he said—his mind is made up."

"Let me talk to him," Thalassa said suddenly, surprising them all.

"Do you think that's a good idea?" Alanda asked.

"He knows, doesn't he?" Thalassa asked.

Alanda nodded mutely.

"It's best if we speak now; it may be our last chance," Thalassa said firmly, turning to follow Jayal.

"Hurry!" Urthred urged her. "Golon will be back soon." But he wasn't sure whether Thalassa had heard him; she was already several feet down the corridor.

Jayal had retrieved one of the swords from the ground and, having tested it for balance, had positioned himself at the end of the tunnel. Here he had a good view of the front of the maze. His fingers clenched and unclenched on the hilt of his new weapon. It wasn't Dragonstooth, but it would suffice. Any second now the Doppelgänger might emerge. Both their lives would be finished by one searing blow from the sword. It would be an end, an inglorious one, but an end nevertheless. . . . He was so preoccupied with his thoughts that he didn't hear the footsteps behind him until they were right next to him. He whirled round, then turned as rapidly back again when he saw it was Thalassa.

"What do you want?" he asked, his face set.

"The others want to go on, try to find a way out of the tomb."

"Good—it's as we discussed."

"You won't join us?"

"I told you, I'm waiting for my double."

"Faran and his sorcerer may reappear before he does."

"I'll take my chances."

Thalassa hesitated; there was so much more she wanted to say, but Jayal's face was turned away from her. Many years had passed. The summer they had spent together, laughing in the gardens of the Illgill mansion, seemed several lifetimes ago. The agony when she had thought him dead . . .

He had really died seven years ago, she decided. He was right: the past should have no hold over either of them.

"Good-bye," she said simply.

"Don't forget the sword," he said by way of valediction, but got no reply from her as she made her way towards the others.

Her blank look said everything when she emerged from the gloom.

"He won't come, then?" Alanda asked. Thalassa shook her

head. "Fate will throw us together again," Alanda said. "He's been gone seven years, yet he reappeared tonight. We haven't seen the last of Jayal Illgill, believe me."

"If you say so," Urthred said sceptically. But Alanda had been right about so many things already. . . . Maybe she was going to be right about this as well.

Without further debate, Alanda picked up her lantern and led the way into the gloom of the underworld.

CHAPTER FORTY

Nekron

Dust—the dust of ancient corridors—the millennia-old dust in which draughts over the years leave patterns on the deserted floors of tombs. This was his first sensation: the dust in his eyes and mouth—then came the tingling from where his left arm had once been—it was gone, but when? In the explosion, during the fall? Now there was just a terrible vacancy. A chill blew over the ragged stump: the exposed nerve ends still shrieked with pain at the coldness of that draught, though they were black and atrophied. The slow treacle of his blood ebbed from the stump.

He felt the slow slide to death; he had felt it once before, 150 years ago when the assassins had come for him. The night filled with the silver blades against the moon, his blood black in the light, black on the walls and the white sheets and the woman he slept with. There had been less pain then, more of a flowing away, the sensation of a dam burst far away leaching the river of his life. The killers had been thorough, but not thorough enough: it had taken a minute or two for dark extinction to come over his brain. In those last few seconds he had tasted death, and drunk of it for the first time.

Afterwards, the Brethren had saved him: brought him to Tiré Gand, where they'd applied the Chalice to his lips. He'd awoken in a tomb, thinking the Last Day had come. But then he recognised the thirst that raged in his body, registered that his heart barely beat at all. Then he knew what he'd become.

But now? Now he would die again, slowly, without blood to moisten his parched veins. It would only take a day or two until he was reduced to a dried husk, a mummy without animation.

How had he come here, buried under broken flagstones and bricks, buried so deep that even his dust-clogged eyes saw nothing but darkness? Dim memories of mazy corridors, zigzags of broken floors and crumbling pillars, ancient wall friezes, flaking paint, the blistered painted face of Marizian . . .

The tomb of Marizian—that was where he was. It had seemed so easy; he had been so near to his goal. Then the explosion of fire, fire that could kill, *had* killed.

Then why did he still live? He licked his parched tongue over his cracked lips and knew. Blood was the answer, blood that he could taste on his lips: not the dried blood of the undead, but the sweet blood of a living soul. Now he could feel the body against him: one of the Reapers, blown through the ceiling with him, his dismembered body leaking blood over his face, blood that he licked slowly into his dying body. It tasted sweeter than loganberries crushed on the end of his tongue. His very being bent to it; as a green shoot bends to the sun, so all his senses turned to that slowly oozing source of blood, the perfume of it pulling him back from the abyss of Hel and the second death.

He must have lost consciousness again, for the next thing he knew he heard a voice calling. It was muffled by the debris lying over him, but he recognised it: the voice of Golon. He croaked as best as he could in response. Golon must have heard, for there now came a scrabbling sound as bricks were thrown aside. Light flooded into his eyes, burning his sensitive retinas. When he opened them again, he saw the gaunt face of the sorcerer bending over him, examining his wound. He craned his head and saw what Golon saw, a shattered stump of yellow bone exiting from his shoulder socket. To his surprise he began to laugh, a dry throaty rattle. One hundred and fifty years, one hundred and fifty years of slow decay, a tailor's mannequin falling slowly to pieces; even immortality was not worth this indignity. Golon's face took on an even more worried aspect.

He started pulling away at more of the debris crushing Faran, but stopped again suddenly. Faran looked down and saw the three-foot-wide column lying across his midriff: curious, he hadn't even felt it, but there it was, its weight crushing his leathery guts against his spine.

He was still looking at it when the first of the giant vibrations struck the chamber. Faran's teeth juddered together, his eyeballs strained at the pressure, his eardrums felt as if they were popping. The noise seemed to come from everywhere and nowhere at the same time: an angry boom that sent showers of dust down from the shattered ceiling. The pillar shifted. He was surprised when unconsciousness stole over him again and he felt himself slipping back into the darkness. . . .

Golon looked about him wildly. The cave-in site was in a vast chamber lined with massive stone blocks. Dark twenty-foot-high tunnels disappeared into the distance on all four sides: the pile of rubble in which his master was buried was in the exact centre. He strained his eyes to see where the sound was coming from. There it was again, accompanied by such a violent shaking that his vision blurred from the vibration. Then there was a crack, as loud as a thunderclap, as the masonry blocks to one side of the chamber crashed inwards, filling it with yet more dust.

Then it cleared.

He saw with amazement a giant hand, as big as a door, grey as the stone through which it had broken, flexing slightly; then the boom came again and more masonry blocks came crashing in, revealing a massive muscled forearm, some six feet wide and twenty-five feet long. A human arm, but twenty times larger than any he'd seen. One of the giants who had built the city, maybe Adamanstor himself, stirring from centuries-old sleep. When Golon had thought of giants before he had thought of men eight or maybe ten feet tall. But whatever was on the end of this fist must be four times that size, or more. Something with the destructive power to bring the whole pyramid crashing down on itself.

Golon had not often been scared in his life: the secrets he'd unearthed in the library of the temple, the spells and summonings, had quickly distanced him from such emotions. All men had learned to quail before him and his knowledge. But as the giant arm moved again, bringing another section of the wall crashing into the chamber, he knew fear, naked and raw. This thing, this avatar of an older age, now awoken from its sleep, could destroy him and anything else. For had it not lived in another time, when magic, magic that had built this city, had been as common as air? When all men had had the power that Golon, alone of all his generation, had mastered? A desperate remedy, one that had not been invoked outside the walls of the temple, was required. A spell from the *Book of Worms,* a summoning more dreadful than any other known. But did he have time? He brushed the thought aside: what he was about to do was Faran's only chance.

There was just room on the floor next to the shattered masonry. Staring anxiously at the hand, now once more immobile, he quickly pulled a piece of chalk from the pouch at his belt, and cleared the dust and the mortar from the chamber floor, praying that no more dust would fall as he drew. His hand trembled slightly as he inscribed the form. It was a complex hieroglyph, like a many-petalled flower in which the lines, like Iss' devouring of his own tail, bent back into themselves in endless circles. His brow furrowed in concentration as he struggled to remember each subtle nuance of the form. Then the boom came again, a mighty roar, now identifiable as such. A fissure ran across the floor towards him like a giant snake, the chalk wavered in his hand. Should he run? He didn't have time to decide as the fissure sped right up to his feet then stopped just short of the circle he'd drawn. He started drawing frantically again, finishing the sign with a desperate scrawl. He leapt back, and threw his black cloak wide, holding his hands up to the ceiling. He tried not to hurry as he intoned the prayer, a prayer in an ancient tongue not heard for centuries outside the sanctuary of Iss' temples:

> "Oh lord most old, most venerable—
> You who consume the dust of which we are made,
> You whose eyes never see the sun your enemy,
> You whose vigil is dark and deep and invisible:

Hear your servant, mighty one
Whose heart is an endless circle
At the centre of the world,
Aid your servant now in this time
And we shall evermore praise thee."

He finished and there was left a mere ringing silence in the air, broken by another almighty boom from the rock. Another explosion of rubble followed, and a giant cheek and a red eyeball, some two feet wide, were thrust through the rock. The eyeball stared at him.

Golon was too scared to move. The summoning hadn't worked: he must have made a mistake in drawing the symbol. But then he felt a small vibration through the cracked floor, a tremor that came not from the buried form of the giant, but from elsewhere. Dust began falling from the ceiling again, first in tiny dribbles, then like rain. His jaw began to vibrate uncontrollably, and his eyes bulged in his head. It was as if all the air was being sucked from the tunnel at once. He became aware of the noise: the sound of an avalanche, the sound of a thousand stampeding horses, greater even than the giant's bellows. His eyes strained to see down the tunnel to the north from which the sound seemed to be coming, but even though he saw a long way down it, nothing was visible.

Then he looked back at the pattern of runes on the floor. A whirling column of dust had sprung up from its centre like a miniature typhoon. The dust began to take shape, form an outline. The first thing he noticed was an outsize skull, then a long carapaced body that ended in a scorpion tail. Purple light radiated from the creature, bathing the shattered walls and the giant's cheekbone before flooding down the corridors. The giant roared in pain as the violet light burned its eyes; the fist flailed up and down, smashing rock, throwing Golon to the ground. He screamed, but he couldn't hear himself think, let alone hear any external noise.

The demon reared up, over the rubble, sending spirals of dust flying off into the corridors. Its breath was the stink of an abattoir, its shrieking the sound of a thousand butchered animals.

The giant's face began melting as if it were wax; black bile streamed from its mouth and eyes; it roared again, the sound of a thousand rocks smashing together around Golon's head. His eardrums exploded. But perversely he still remained conscious, though his brain shrieked for blackness, oblivion from the horror before him.

He saw that the walls of the chamber were bulging with life. He saw the wriggling heads of worms emerging through the cracks towards the central nexus point of the summoning. But something more powerful was moving, too. Then the wall just to the left of where he was looking disappeared in a frenzied shower of bricks and mortar, and a mighty head thrust through, some ten feet wide, a thing of interlatticed teeth and blind rage that filled the chamber with an earth-shattering roar.

Alanda had stopped dead in her tracks when she heard the first booming repercussion coming from below them. "What was that?" she asked, turning to the others. They stood, like her, with their heads tilted to the side, listening to see if the sound came again. It wasn't long in coming. The ground quaked beneath their feet, and dust fell from the ceiling.

"It came from back near the tomb chamber," Thalassa answered.

"Golon," Urthred muttered.

"Then we must hurry," Alanda said, setting off as quickly as her old legs could carry her.

Further dust fell from the ceiling, and something slithered over Thalassa's foot. She screamed. Alanda turned and in the lantern light they saw a brown snake wriggling away into the darkness. The noise and vibration were increasing by the second.

Once more Urthred felt the cold mantle of fear fall on his shoulders and penetrate to his chest and heart: the Worm was close, closer than it had been all evening. It was as if Iss himself had arrived in the tomb. But with the fear came another sensation altogether. He'd first felt it when he'd passed through the trial by fire: a tingling over the burn scars on his body. Now the tingling became a warmth, combating the cold fear, melting it; the soul of fire had returned to help him. He wondered whether it was Dragonstooth, sheathed in his belt, which had brought it about, or whether it was the God's blessing. Whatever it was, he would need it: the three women and the old man were virtually helpless.

The vibration increased: something was following them. Whatever was coming after them was coming fast; the speed of its movement sent a cascade of dust and rubble down from the ceiling. There seemed no end to the tunnel in front. Only now and again were there side passages, like the ones he'd seen before, meeting up in a complex web of intersections.

A roar came from behind: a sound the like of which he'd never heard, as of metal being torn asunder. Bricks rained down from the ceiling, one striking off his shoulder. Alanda fell from the vibration, but struggled back up. Something large was thundering down the passage towards them. He thrust Furtal's unconscious body at Thalassa. "Go on!" he screamed over the noise.

Thalassa struggled with the body of the old man. "There's nothing you can do, come with us," she implored. But he shook his masked head.

"Go!" he yelled again, pushing her. She stumbled backwards, taking the old man's arm over her shoulder and dragging him after the others.

Urthred waited, his jaw juddering from the vibrations shaking the corridor. The end from which they'd just come was utterly dark, and without Alanda's lantern he could see nothing. Now was the time to use the power, the seed of fire. He swept his gloved hand in a wide arc and flame appeared like a glowing net flung in front of him. The sight of what it revealed froze him to the spot.

At first it looked as if, by a curious trick of the light, the tunnel was consuming itself, foreshortening and foreshortening. But then he realised that its entire circumference was occupied by a heaving worm some ten feet wide, its mouth a portico of barbed and glistening incisors. It was rushing towards him as fast as a man could run. It was only some fifty feet away, and he had little time.

In a flash, as he had done in the temple square, his arm came up and he sent a wall of fire rolling down the corridor. The flame burned the air from his lungs and he felt his cloak singeing. Then there came a thunderous roar as it met with its target in an explosion of orange. Part of the ceiling collapsed, knocking him to the ground. He struggled to see what had happened through the dust cloud, then rolled back in terror. The worm's forward progress had been slowed, but it was still coming on, its pink mouth area blackened and charred, laying even barer the row upon row of incisors in its mouth.

He gestured again, letting fly with another wall of fire, but his prone position hampered him, and this one was less powerful than the last, a mere spurt of fire as opposed to the roiling mass of his first effort. Nevertheless oily smoke issued from the creature's blind snout and it halted some three feet away from where he lay. For a brief second he thought he'd killed it, but then it pulsed forward to within inches of him, the teeth suspended over his outstretched leg. He drew in his breath, waiting for the killing bite.

It was at that moment that the figure appeared from the side passage to his right. Urthred had a split second to realise it was Jayal. He leant down and dragged Urthred back from the snapping jaws. The thing pulsed forward again, one of its barbed teeth snagging Urthred's cloak. But Jayal had drawn Dragonstooth from Urthred's belt. The weapon formed a sudden arc of light as it sliced deep into the blunt snout of the creature. The sword burned down and down, deep into its head until it must have met with the tiny bundle of nerve ganglions that served as its brain, for its heaving bulk spasmed, then lay utterly still.

Urthred stared first at the dead monster, then at his rescuer. "You saved my life," he managed over his gasps for air.

"It's nothing. Come, we must hurry. There will be others where this came from—Faran's sorcerer has summoned a demon."

"What of your double?"

Jayal smiled grimly. "Nothing will live long against the demon. The double is trapped in the maze; he will die if he appears, just as I would have died if I'd waited. That's why I came back."

"Then you'll stay with us?"

A struggle was apparent in Jayal's face. The matter was resolved as he saw Alanda cautiously coming back towards them down the tunnel. She was alone. She looked at the dead creature blocking the passage, then at Urthred and Jayal. She didn't question Illgill's reappearance.

"Malliana has gone—she fled down one of the side passages."

"And Thalassa?"

"She is with Furtal. I came back when the noise stopped to see what had happened."

"Jayal killed the creature—but there will be more."

Alanda now turned to Jayal. "Will you stay with us now?"

Jayal stared at her silently. "Very well," he said eventually. "My double may live, but only by a miracle. If he does, I'll kill him when we next meet."

"Your father will still have the Rod: we may be able to use it to banish him back to his own plane."

"Perhaps," Jayal answered. "But there's only one certainty now: if we don't hurry, we'll all be dead."

"Then let's go," Alanda said, leading them off into the darkness of the underworld.

The pit was now a wriggling mass of slithering life: tapeworms, blindworms, snakes and more of the giant ten-foot-wide ones which resembled giant millipedes. They were all congregated around the whirling purple mass of the demon. The rubble lying in the room was slowly being sucked into the purple vortex, which spun like a typhoon at the centre of the chamber. The pillar trapping Faran followed the blocks of stone as if it were virtually weightless. But the howling wind didn't touch Golon, or Faran, who by now was slowly coming back to his senses. Golon helped him to his feet. Broken bones grated in Faran's body, but he would have to wait to see what permanent damage had been done—he was immune to pain; only the cold air on the shattered arm stump bothered him.

Never before had either of them been so close to such power. A power that was beyond fear, beyond thought. Golon realised that they couldn't stay long, though for the moment they were safe from the creature's influence. Numbly he spread his cloak wide and uttered a phrase in the ancient language. Immediately both he and Faran began to float slowly up to the mouth of the cave-in, leaving the scene of chaos behind.

Snakes and worms spun past them through the air, into the demon's maw. As they rose up, the spinning form seemed to grow and grow, pushing farther and farther into the cavern, and as the demon assimilated more and more of the writhing life around it, so too did it assume a palpable form: a horned head with wriggling worms for skin, writhing snakes as arms and hair.

Then they rose above the level of the pit and alighted in the upper chamber. The noise below was deafening. From all corners came further slithering reptiles, tumbling over its lips into the pit below. White smoke began to billow up from it. Golon looked around him, disoriented, spotting the two dead guards almost immediately. So, the rebels had escaped, but he expected the demon would kill them soon enough. Now he would never know what was in the maze. Maybe that was just as well.

"Quickly, lord," he urged, tugging at Faran's sleeve.

"Where is Thalassa?"

"Gone—they've all gone."

Faran clamped his one remaining hand on Golon's shoulder with surprising strength. Even with only one arm, he was stronger than ten men, far stronger than the sorcerer. He fixed Golon with his glittering gaze; a gaze that had subdued princes and potentates, living and dead. "We will find them—we will kill the traitors, and then I will have Thalassa if it is the last thing I do!"

Golon looked around at the dust-choked passageway. The ceiling heaved with the force of the vibrations coming from below; it would collapse any moment. If it did, rescue of any kind would be out of the question. It was best to temporise. "They must have gone back to the City of the Dead."

"Then we must get there before the Brethren discover them." He set off as quickly as he could, though his injuries were clearly still troubling him.

But then a movement caught Golon's eye: a human form had stumbled out of the maze and looked around with shock at Faran and Golon and the mass of slithering life that was pouring into the pit. Golon recognised the man who had been skulking at the back of the party that had attacked them. After the initial shock, the man came to his senses and began running towards one of the side tunnels. But at a gesture from Golon, grave roots burst from cracks in the flagstoned floor and seized the man's ankles, bringing him to the ground. He writhed there, helpless to break the bonds.

Golon helped Faran to hobble over to him. The man was clawing frantically at the roots with his hands. He looked up in abject terror as the two figures loomed over him.

"So, the dog who caused us all the trouble!" Golon spat, resolving to leave him for the demon.

But Faran was inspecting the man's face intently. "Look what we have here! That is a face I'd recognise anywhere, despite the scars and beard."

"Who is it?" Golon asked, looking around nervously at the mist billowing up from the pit.

"Why, it's Jayal Illgill—the High Priestess was right!"

"I'm not Illgill's son!" the Doppelgänger fairly shrieked. "Spare me! I've got information; I can help you."

The floor vibrated with another tremor. They were running out of time. Faran made his mind up quickly.

"We'll take him with us, we can question him later," he decided. Golon looked doubtful, but with a flick of his wrists the bonds holding the Doppelgänger's feet flew off. He scrambled up.

"No tricks now!" Golon muttered, pushing him in front of him as he helped Faran along. The Doppelgänger complied, nursing his broken wrist. They stumbled along the passage, nearly losing their footing as the floor bucked and shuddered under them. Then a huge block of masonry tumbled down behind them with a roar. They reached the stairs, now covered by the flecks of paint that were flaking like snow from the frescoes on either side of the stairwell. They struggled upwards, crawling on their hands and knees for much of the way, dust covering them and choking the air, bricks tumbling to left and right. The secret door had fallen from its hinges; the room beyond was ankle deep in water from the pool, which had cracked and spilled its contents. In the outer chamber, where the demon of fire had been, there was only a thick white mist. They looked up and saw that the whole top of the pyramid had fallen away, revealing the night sky. An earth and rubble slope led up to safety. There was no sign of the makeshift tunnel down which they had come earlier.

They scrambled up, emerging on the lip of the cave-in, the air, though tinged with the marsh gas, like crystal after the fetid atmosphere of the tomb. The giant steps of the pyramid were covered by a hundred small avalanches of falling masonry and earth as its outer shell sloughed away. Above them, the city was ablaze with flame from the fires surrounding the Temples of Reh and Sutis. Over in the east there was the faintest hint of grey in the sky.

Even the merest glimmer was warning enough that the time of the undead was nearly over: soon the ageing sun would return, driving the Brethren underground again, sending those who had not drunk blood into an everlasting sleep.

A figure was standing on the topmost step, staring uncertainly at the sliding mass of masonry below. Her skirt was covered with grime and ripped to tatters, her dark hair falling in tendrils over her face, yet it was still easy to recognise the High Priestess of Sutis. She whirled towards them, suddenly sensing their presence behind her. Faran and Golon covered the steps between them before she could escape.

Faran glared at the High Priestess, who quailed visibly before him. "Where is Thalassa?" he growled, oblivious of the horror with which she stared at the stump of his arm. A blow from Golon brought her back to her senses.

"Th-they are still down there."

Faran turned in anguish. The edge of the top of the pyramid was slowly caving in. Cracks were opening up in its sides and all around them masonry blocks were falling into the chasm. A heavy cloud of dust eddied up from its centre, suggesting that soon the whole structure would collapse in on itself.

Malliana, sensing the effect of her words on him, tried to lessen the blow: "They spoke of finding another way out—they thought the Brethren would be waiting for them here."

Faran turned to Golon. "Are there other ways out?"

"None that have been used for centuries—but they probably exist."

"Where would they lead to?"

"Back into the city, or out onto the marshes."

"Then there's only one way they will be going—the marshes!" With a shout, he broke from Golon's grip and plunged down the precipitous steps towards the mist-filled City of the Dead, sliding with the falling rubble, careless of his wounds, or that he had only one arm to balance himself, or the speed of his breakneck descent.

CHAPTER FORTY-ONE

The Broken Lute

They found Thalassa crouching by Furtal next to a lime-covered pool. Ahead, over the pool, lay an arched entrance-way. Beyond it, the lantern light showed a tunnel leading off into the darkness. Water fell onto the surface with melancholy plops, disturbing the layer of lime.

Furtal's condition was obviously grave. Faran's glove had left a livid weal on the right front hemisphere of his bald head. Half his head was now one purple bruise. One of his eye sockets had filled with blood so that in the gloom he appeared to have one red and one white eye.

Thalassa looked up when she saw their light, but did not comment on the unexpected reappearance of Jayal: her gaze returned to Furtal. He was struggling back to consciousness. "He shouldn't be moved," she said quietly.

But the old man had obviously heard her; he reached out a skinny hand and grasped the sleeve of her dress. "Leave me," he mumbled.

"Nonsense!" Alanda said vehemently, kneeling by his side. "Remember what we said in the kitchen earlier? We'll be over the marshes by dawn!"

A thin smile played on Furtal's bloodied lips: "I remember well, my lady—we're going to the north."

"Yes—that's it! Come on, let's get you on your feet."

But Furtal shook his head slightly. "I'll never make the marshes. Leave me." His voice, though weak, was determined. Alanda looked around desperately; someone would have to carry Furtal. Urthred had done it before. Without being asked, he stepped forward readily when she looked at him. He reached his gloved hands under the old man's armpits and pulled him gently upright, before hoisting him over one shoulder. He had the leech gatherer's staff in the other. "Lead on," he said, a slight strain apparent in his voice from the extra burden, but the mask, as always, hid the weariness of his face. Another huge reverberation came from behind them in the corridor, sending the flagstones jumping under their feet. Urthred fought to stay upright. The sound of falling masonry echoed up from the interior of the tomb. They would have to hurry. There was no way around the pool: the only way forward was through it. Alanda took up the lantern, and gingerly put a slippered foot in the water.

There was a sudden explosion of water that blinded all of them. Alanda fell back onto the floor of the corridor. The hot metal of the lantern sizzled as the water sluiced around her. But her eyes were not on the flickering light, but the thing which had burst from the surface of the pool.

For a split second all of them stood paralysed, unable to move.

A serpent, some eight feet long, covered in green slimy scales the colour of the water, its neck arched in an S shape, its eyes red, yellow incisors dripping venom, towered over her, ready for her to strike.

Then another reverberation came from the depths of the tomb. Its neck lowered and it fell with an oily slap to the floor of the corridor. It slithered against Urthred's legs as it wound away into the darkness.

"Are you all right?" asked Thalassa, kneeling by her old friend.

"I'm fine, child—just wet, and that won't kill me." She got to her feet, and, undeterred by her narrow escape, stepped once more into the pool. There were steps under the surface and she went down them until they ended when she was waist deep in the water. She began to wade across, the lantern held high, her

cloak trailing behind her on the surface of the water like a wedding train.

The others followed, Urthred slipping slightly on the slick
steps, Thalassa steadying him, Jayal taking up the rear. They
passed through the arched entrance. Ahead they saw the tunnel
debouch into a much larger chamber. They waded forward, entering it. Beyond, as far as the lantern light would go, the whole
surface area was covered with black water. A gallery supported
by brick pillars ran around the rectangular area some twenty
feet above their heads. Slime-covered steps led up to it. In the
dim light of the lantern and the sword, other exits could be seen
disappearing into the darkness on each side of the room.

Alanda paused, uncertain which way to go. She clenched
her eyes shut, concentrating hard. She must seek the way in her
mind. She'd come through the catacombs once before, when
she'd dragged the remains of her husband from the battlefield.
Then she'd followed an ancient map. Now she had no such
aids, only what the inner sight might bring her. But as always
when she tried to predict an outcome involving her own fate,
the future that her inner vision conjured was a total blank. She
opened her eyes—there were so many passages. Some might
lead to safety, others to death. For the first time she began to
feel a savage hopelessness. But just as she felt the despair eating away at her resolve, Thalassa shouted out.

"Look!" She was pointing up to the gallery which ran
around the chamber. A lantern light had appeared on it directly
above where they were standing. At first Alanda could only see
a three-fingered hand holding the lantern in the pool of light,
but as her eyes adjusted she made out a reptilian head behind it.

"It's Sashel!" Urthred exclaimed.

"Who?" Jayal asked, recoiling from the sight of the creature
above them.

"He is a leech gatherer—a friend."

The creature was now making its way down a flight of steps
from the gallery, its lantern casting a wide beam of light. Jayal
stirred uneasily, adjusting his grip on Dragonstooth. But
Urthred waded towards Sashel, his back bowed by Furtal's
weight. The leech gatherer waited on the lowest step.

Once more its words came unbidden into Urthred's mind: "Where is Seresh?" it whispered.

"He died in the tomb."

The leech gatherer nodded its head solemnly. "He was too fierce to live long, the Flame protect his soul. And you, Mask— it is as I prophesied, we meet again before the night is done. The Elder saw you in the fire pot, saw where the staff was, that you needed help. And now I will repay the favour I owe you— I will lead your people to safety."

Another reverberation sent a shower of water droplets down from the ceiling of the chamber onto the placid surface of the lake. The water hissed on contact with the lanterns and the blade of Dragonstooth.

The leech gatherer seemed unperturbed: "Humanity's time is finished here on the rock you call Thrull. Centuries ago my people enjoyed peace here when the rock was a mere island in a sea. Then men came with their dead: since then, death is all you have brought us. But now you and she"—he nodded at Thalassa—"have come. She will repay all your debts: I have seen it in the fire globes at night when all the others slept. She will bring the Second Dawn."

"But what of the demon that Faran has summoned?" Urthred asked.

"It is a creature of the Worm—it can only live in the darkness of night and the catacombs. When it is light my people will go out with the dawn and see the sun. We will no longer be sick."

With this, it seemed his conversation was exhausted, and he turned and led the way upwards. Urthred gestured for the others to follow.

Myriad flooded corridors and dank tunnels succeeded one another as Sashel set a relentless pace away from the explosions. They passed through a cave where more of the leech gatherers were congregated, crouched by their fire pots. Urthred's mind filled with the noise of their fearful chatter as explosion after explosion shook the underworld. Their voices followed, even when they had passed down a flight of rock-hewn steps into an entrance.

Urthred saw beyond it the gloomy vastness of Stick's Hole

rearing up into the darkness. They emerged at the side of the ravine that ran along its bottom.

Sashel led the way along the side of the rushing torrent, and through the mighty arch at its end where the waters fell fifty feet down in a thundering waterfall. They descended a set of steps by its side. At the bottom, the air was dense with water vapour, forming a thick fog. They passed through, the lantern light ghostly in the mist, and emerged into a massive underground sewer. Rotting barges, sunk into the river and covered with green slime, were moored to the banks. Rats scuttled away at the light. Sashel paid no heed to the barges but led them on another half mile until their way was blocked by iron gates barring a massive arch. Beyond, they could see a slight lightening of the blackness. A waft of fetid marsh air came down the corridor. The gates must lead out to the moat surrounding Thrull.

Sashel stopped. "I must leave you here—my people need me. The gates are the only barrier left. You have the power to destroy them, Mask."

Urthred had put Furtal down. He bowed. "You saved us."

"I have told you," Sashel replied, "the girl will save all of us. Look after her." He fixed Urthred once more with his red eyes, then turned and disappeared into the darkness as abruptly as he'd appeared.

"What was all that about?" Jayal asked. He had obviously failed to pick up anything of the telepathic communication between the two.

Urthred shook his head. "He's a friend; he's led us to safety."

"My father hunted his like in the catacombs for their skins."

"Then it is a miracle he helped us. Now let us find a way past the gates."

He was about to pick up Furtal again, but Jayal stooped low, and lifted the old man over his shoulder, nodding for Urthred to proceed.

The shakings and tremors that had accompanied them on their journey through the underworld had grown suddenly weaker, as if whatever it was that was being born in the gloomy depths of Marizian's tomb had come to a chrysalis stage of development and now brooded, pondering its next move. Urthred was glad they were not lingering to find out what that might be.

The stink of the marsh gases became more and more pronounced as they approached the iron gates. Beyond them, they could now see the weed-covered surface of the moat and a blanket of white fog. The iron bars guarding the entrance were an arm's thickness wide. Urthred inspected the ones guarding the side of the path along which they'd approached. He seized one with his gloves and heaved, his muscles spasming with the effort. The ancient iron groaned, then bent, rust pouring off its surface. Urthred turned to the adjacent bar and forced that aside as well. He stepped through the gap, the others following.

They found themselves on a stone ledge overlooking the thirty-foot-wide moat. The moat had been built to defend the city against siege, but now it presented an unfordable obstacle for those trying to get out. Urthred looked up: the sheer cliff face reared up and up above them, revealing nothing of what lay at its top. Were they going to be trapped at the base of the walls?

Alanda had brushed past him, looking intently at the lilies and weeds that dotted the moat's surface. She began to inch along the narrow ledge, hugging the ancient lichen-covered walls. Urthred looked at Thalassa quizzically. She shrugged; the old lady obviously had a plan. They followed her. Eventually she found what she was looking for: a place where the plants had slowly intertwined over the years, forming a solid mat of vegetation from one bank to the other. Even so, Urthred could see that there was no way that the frail scum of weeds in front of them could hold a human weight. It bobbed slightly as a breeze came in off the marshes, rippling the surface of the moat. Alanda leant over the water, the lantern light hanging like a star over its surface. She stretched out her arms, her palms upwards. Immediately there was movement in the weeds and lilies, as if hidden life was twisting through their stems and leaves. Then the roots began to twist round each other, and the leaves furled around their neighbours, as if a hidden hand weaved them slowly together, plaiting the strands and stems so they became intertwined and strong. The unseen hand moved outward over the thirty-foot gap, and as it moved it left behind a solid mat of vegetation, a carpet of lilies and rushes that looked as strong as sandgrass.

Thalassa stared at Alanda. The old woman seemed to be in a trance. She had known her to be a master of divination and prophecy, but she had never even hinted at this magic.

The old lady started out of her reverie and noticed the others' astonished glances. She smiled as she straightened her back. "Come," she said, "it's perfectly safe." She stepped off onto the mat. It gave slightly under her feet, and she put her hands out for balance, then made her way across. The others glanced at one another and followed her. She had been right; the mat of weeds was very strong and swayed only slightly under their weight.

They reached the other side of the moat. The rushes grew man high and thick on this other bank. The air seemed fresh and sweet after the mustiness of the tomb and the stench of the city, though in truth the fog hung as thick and coiled and sulphurous here as it had done in Thrull. It was freedom they were scenting. The only movement was the bending of the reeds as another gust of air wafted over the marshes.

Alanda held out the lantern as Jayal began to cut a path through the reeds with his sword. Thalassa was holding Furtal, so Urthred had leisure to look behind him at the towering cliffs of the city. The light of the raging fires suffused the mists. Off to the right, where the cliffs descended to the City of the Dead, the tomb pyramid of Marizian loomed out of the fog, a black, implacable monolith, rising high above the fifty-foot outer walls of the city.

But despite the fog and the thickly congregated rushes, there was something else in the air, something which he couldn't put his finger on initially. Then he had it. Through the mist and the smoke over the city, the sky was lightening imperceptibly. Dawn was approaching; the night was nearly over. The others had now beaten a twenty-foot path into the reeds. He hurried after them.

He had entered Thrull twelve hours before, twelve hours that seemed twelve years, or aeons. Darkness had covered all the events that had followed his brother's murder and his revenge on Varash. Darkness in which he'd seen visions, refound his powers, fought with the undead, fallen under the spell of Thalassa, seen things in Marizian's tomb which only one other had seen for centuries. He had ridden a whirlwind. Now dawn promised a return to sanity, a glimmer of hope. He turned and caught up with Thalassa, who was helping Furtal through the passage that Jayal was making in front of them with his sword.

"It's nearly dawn," he whispered excitedly. Thalassa turned her face to his. Exhaustion and filth lined her face. Her hair hung in limp strands, and her body trembled with the cold. Just looking at her, Urthred remembered how tired he should be, but the tingling energy with which he'd blasted the serpent in the tomb still burned in his veins. He felt he could march all day. Just as well, as they would have to traverse the entire breadth of the causeway before night fell again and the vampires could pursue them. But Thalassa looked as if she could barely go another step.

"Let me take him," Urthred said, lifting Furtal again. The old man was once more delirious, each jarring movement making his condition appreciably worse.

Thalassa thanked him, then turned her eyes to Jayal as he hewed away at the rushes. Jayal had kept a resolute silence during their journey through the waterways under the tomb, though there had been plenty of opportunity to speak. As she looked at him once more, she couldn't get over the feeling of displacement she had had when she had seen him again. So like the other man, except for the scar. The latter had been evil and malicious. This Jayal was as she remembered the eighteen-year-old who had ridden out to battle that day seven years ago. Proud, silent, inflexible.

Had he come back for her? Yes and no, she suspected. There had been other factors in his return. But she remembered what an idealist he had been even at the age of eighteen. He had been dominated by his father, mocked by his peers who thought his ideas of virtue outmoded. In the days before Faran it had been these companions who had visited the brothels and the wineshops, not Jayal. She could imagine what he had thought when he'd discovered his betrothed had become part of that sordid world he had once scorned. The pride had always been there in his youth, smouldering below the surface.

She wished she had never seen him again. Her own idealism had ended seven years before, and with it the memory of him. Then she had believed his skull to have been one of the many thousands in the pyramid on the marshes.

And now, as fate would have it, they were approaching the area of the marshes where the battle had taken place. Jayal hewed at the reeds ahead of him with a fixity of purpose which betrayed the fact that he, too, realised where they were. He turned and she caught the haunted look in his eyes. There was no joy in Jayal's look, no sparkle in his eyes; the curse weighed him down. He might have been a dead man, come to haunt her and the other survivors for wanting to seize life once more when he himself could no longer enjoy it.

Urthred was struggling with Furtal, who had begun thrashing around in his delirium. He stumbled over a marsh root and fell to his knees, the old man rolling from his grasp. Furtal continued to strike out with his arms despite Urthred's attempts to quiet him. Thalassa and Alanda hurriedly knelt by his side. The old man was regaining consciousness.

"Where's my lute?" he asked querulously, realising that it was no longer strapped over his shoulder.

"You broke it over the head of a vampire," Thalassa said, trying to keep her tone light.

He must have heard her, for he quieted, his bloodied brow furrowing as he tried to recall what had happened. "Ah! I remember now . . . did I kill it?"

"No, someone else did."

"Seresh?"

Thalassa looked at Alanda. Should they tell him? The old lady squeezed Furtal's shoulder. "Seresh is dead," she said, as gently as possible.

Furtal's face creased in pain. "I remember now, we were outnumbered. Seresh fought, but . . ." His voice trailed off.

Jayal had now returned and was looking down at the dying man. "How is he?" he asked.

At his voice, Furtal's face took on a quizzical expression. "That voice—it sounds familiar."

Jayal knelt next to him: "As it should. It is I, Jayal Illgill, returned to Thrull."

A flash of animation crossed Furtal's bloodied features. "I knew you weren't dead! You've brought the sword?"

"Yes," Jayal said, raising the gleaming blade up to Furtal's blind eyes.

"I see something—a glimmer! Your father and I discussed it many times—now I'll die happy. Go to your father, tell him that I have sung the songs of the old times many times in my captivity—tell him I died thinking of him." The effort of talking seemed to have exhausted him, and he sank back into semiconsciousness. But, after a few moments, he rallied and spoke again: "Where is my lute?"

"I told you; it's broken," Thalassa whispered patiently, mopping his brow with the hem of her dress.

"How will I sing the lord's return?"

"There will be other lutes in the north."

"There are no lutes to be had for miles across the causeway. The best were hewed by ancient hand in the Forest of Lorn, in the north, where the Nations are." He blinked his eyes, trying to fight back the pain. "Take my hand, little one," he said to Thalassa. She held out her pale hand. To Urthred it seemed to glimmer in the pearly light of dawn like one of the white lilies of the marshes. The old man clutched it. "I've seen the future—where you will go: you will see the place where they made those lutes, those golden lutes . . ."

"You will be with us too!" Thalassa exclaimed, but the old man shook his head vehemently.

"No, the sands are running out—this is as much freedom as I could have hoped for—out here on the marshes, away from that dungeon . . ." He tilted his head, as if listening to the fugitive breeze moving through the rushes. As if on cue, a stronger gust of wind came from the west, driving back the bank of fog, and replacing the sulphurous stink with air that smelled of the mountains. He inhaled deeply, before turning his head slightly to Thalassa. "Listen, you must know something of the Nations, more than you have heard in ballads or old wives' saws. I travelled there once, many years ago . . ."

"But no one has ever been there!" Urthred protested.

The old man ignored him. "First, in the last days of the gods when they lived on earth, it is said they kept their palace there on Shandering Plain. I saw the place, when I could still see: their campfires still burn, night and day, sending pillars of smoke to the heavens." He shook his head, remembering the strangeness of the sight. "But do not go to the fires, though they will guide you well at night. You will see the pillars of fire, and a long way to the east the topless towers. Do not go there either—they are haunted by the ghosts of the gods. As for the creatures themselves, believe the ballads: it is as they tell us, they are implacable enemies of mankind. Only those who dwell about the Forge will help you and be your friends."

"But how will we know where to find this Forge?" Urthred asked.

"You saw it—in the tomb." Urthred wondered how the old man even knew they'd been to the tomb, but it was not for him to question his dying words. He remembered the Orb and the glowing spots of light. The first must be at the Forge.

But the old man had begun to lose consciousness again. They had to lean close to hear his words: "My lute is gone," he murmured. "I cannot sing without my lute." Then, with a dying fall, he said his last words: "I will never sing again." There came a dry rattle from his throat and he jerked from side to side. Thalassa tried to quiet him, but he spasmed violently once more, then lay still. Alanda's face was creased and tears coursed down her cheeks. She dropped her head to Furtal's chest, the old man's blind eyes staring at the mist-filled skies.

"He's gone," Urthred said, putting a comforting hand on her shoulder.

"Gone, and it was so close to dawn," Alanda moaned, looking up at the lightening sky.

Thalassa helped her to her feet. Urthred stood as well. Thalassa' body heaved with silent tears as she held Alanda, her eyes fixed on the grey band of light over the mountains to the east.

Urthred was too numb to feel anything. For a few seconds he stared at the old man's face in the lantern light. Then looked away. Jayal had already walked on, up the path he had cut in the reeds.

"We can't bury him out here," Urthred said eventually. The ground underfoot was spongy: the idea of burying any worshipper of Reh in watery ground was too unpalatable to be borne. The sacred birds did not come to marshy lowlands—Furtal's flesh would be lost to the Worm by the Day of Resurrection.

"Never fear, priest," Alanda said, choking back her tears. "We will raise him up where the waters will not corrupt him."

She broke away gently from Thalassa, pulling her cloak back straight. With the gesture she seemed to regain her composure. She turned to the bank of rushes and marsh weeds by her and held her hands, palms outward, to them. The plants started to twist and turn as if being shaped by an invisible force, slowly twining together to form four separate pillars a few feet apart in a rectangle. Tendrils of growth shot across the gap between them, intertwining. Thicker branches followed, so that soon there was a solid platform between the pillars. Then, in a final explosion of growth, dog roses and eglantine bloomed suddenly from the reeds and grasses forming the bier.

No words had been spoken during this time, and no words were needed now the bier was complete. Urthred knelt and lifted the old man's body up. He seemed to weigh no more than a newborn child; indeed his old bald head could have been that of a baby, so peacefully did he seem to sleep. He placed him reverently on the bier.

"Let the birds of Reh find you," he prayed. "Let them feed upon you and carry you up to Reh, who will hold your body until the Resurrection. And let the light of Reh make bright your days in Paradise. And may your lute be heard in the Palace of the White Rose."

He had not known him well, but the words of the funeral rite stuck in his throat. He turned away. The women's faces were tear-stained, and he couldn't bear to look at them. He stumbled up the path after Jayal, the optimism gone from his heart, a prayer for the swift arrival of dawn upon his lips.

CHAPTER FORTY-TWO

The Dawn

From his vantage point at the top of the temple pyramid of Iss, Lord Faran looked down at the mist-wreathed marshes, then back at the hint of grey in the sky. He had somehow escaped the descent of Marizian's tomb without further injury. Some of the Brethren had been waiting there, but there had been no sign of his human guards. Now there were watchers on all the city walls, undead watchers who could spot any movement below in the darkness. But, in the hour since he had got here, there had been no sightings of Thalassa's party. Soon it would be too late. In another hour light would flood over the plains from the mountains to the east: Iss' nightly imprisonment of Reh would be at an end, and he and the Brethren would have to seek the darkness of the crypts.

In that there was a blessing: the scenes that had greeted him as he had walked through the city reminded him of those seven years before. Corpses, drained white, littered the streets, body parts were scattered here and there. The air was full of sparks and smoke from the burning buildings. As he'd crossed the main square he'd been confused by a high keening sound he heard coming from the Temple of Reh, now enveloped in a maelstrom of flame. Then he recognised it for what it was: the screams of the thousands dying as they burned in the inner sanctum. The Brethren would not enjoy their blood. There would be many of the undead left unsatisfied.

The author of all the Brethren's woes, Malliana, had wrapped herself in a large cloak stolen from a corpse and cowered by his side throughout the journey to the top of the city. But the vampires who had not yet drunk had come sniffing at her, desperate to avoid the second death with a drop of her blood. He should have given her to them, but the revenge would have been too cheap—he had other plans for the High Priestess of Sutis. Once more Golon's sorcery had kept the undead at bay. The other man, Jayal's shadow, seemed to be without scent, and the vampires had ignored him, as if he were one of them rather than the living. This was a mystery, but one which he would only explore later, once they'd found Thalassa. Now he was away from the tomb, the man seemed above fear, a small smile playing over his scarred lips. But Faran had his book, Illgill's book. Again, he would have to wait until later to question him about it. First he must find Thalassa.

Now they were here, on the topmost platform of the Temple of Iss, the wind whipping in from the faraway mountains whose peaks were becoming more and more pronounced in the growing light. Faran's arm stump ached horribly, each gust of wind sending a razor of pain more acute than anything he had experienced since his first death through his nerves. But his eyes never gave up their quartering of the marshes around the city. Though the wind blew hard at the top of the temple, the marshes were still covered with a thick layer of the fog. The ignis fatuis wandered through the mists, the blue light of their lamps dimmer and dimmer in the growing grey of dawn.

He cursed again. Had Thalassa been killed in the tomb? He had seen the power of Golon's summoning, had no doubt that the demon was even now concentrating its strength for one last frenzy of destruction. She could have died, but he doubted it. The priest and the old witch she was with were too resourceful to die so easily.

Just as he was having these thoughts, a shout came up from one of the watchers on the parapet below. Faran hurried over to that side of the temple and peered into the darkness. Over to the southwest he first saw the glowing mass of the pyramid of skulls, then, moving imperceptibly slowly towards it, a tiny red glow. Illgill's sword, the weapon that had blown him into the pit! He glanced once more at the sky: in the east the grey over the Niasseh Range was shot through with bands of white. Dawn would catch any pursuers on the marshes. Thalassa was going to escape!

Once more an oath came to his lips. She was almost free of his grasp. It was too much to bear. Better she was ripped apart in the Brethren's last blood frenzy than she should enjoy a life of freedom without him.

He climbed up on the parapet, a mad song in his heart. He looked down into the temple square. The shadows away from the fires were thronged with the Brethren, all of them that had ever been in Thrull since the Worm's first bite. Once he had thought that only two thousand had slept in the catacombs, but the shadows were so full of them, so many who would die the second death at dawn now every drop of blood had been drunk. How many were there? Five thousand or more, and these were only the ones in the square. Doubtless there were thousands more scouring streets or catacombs, pursuing the last fugitive scent of blood before the dawn light slew them.

Faran still had strength enough to make his voice heard over the roar of the flames and the keening wind. It carried far and wide with the ashes of the dead and the burning buildings, giving those who heard it their last chance of an eternal life in death. "Brethren—there is no blood left in Thrull. Admit it— the moon is nearly set. Reh has once more slipped the bonds of Our Potentate. Yet over yonder—to the south of the city gate, where I extinguished the Flame on Thrull field—there still is blood. Go now, brothers, before the light. Drink your fill, spare none, in the name of Iss!"

A murmur came up from the assembled throng at his words, then a stirring, as the great black mass of vampires began to swarm towards the citadel gate.

Faran felt moisture in his eye, and with his one good hand he brushed at the offending drop. He looked at it. A tear. A tear 150 years in the making. He would never have Thalassa's marble white neck in his grasp, never crush the berry of her blood between his lips, never make her forever his. Another of the

Brethren would, in senseless bloodlust, tear at that which he held most dear. . . . He thought of following the Brethren, risk the growing light on the plain. What did it matter if the rising sun reduced him to a mist? It was better than this continuing mockery of nonlife, where nothing he truly desired would ever be his. He let out an inarticulate moan of anguish, grinding his teeth so hard that his mouth filled with ivory splinters.

Then he heard Golon talking to him, leading him down from the parapet. In a daze he allowed the sorcerer to take him into the pyramid. There was Calabas coming forward with a cloak to cover the stump of his arm. All was not lost. He had Illgill's book. Wherever his enemy had gone, he would find him. Seven years he had waited. Now he would go to him and forever snuff out the Flame.

Though he had lost Thalassa, there was a purpose to his existence still. He had eternity, or until the sun went out. He would not fail.

Out on the marshes the grey was becoming more and more pronounced. Urthred's party were out of the taller stands of bulrushes now, and the fog began to thin rapidly as the breeze over the marshes got up from the east. They could see the causeway: bone white near the bridge over the moat, earth brown farther back, where the bones ran out. To the left, the pyramid of skulls gleamed in the grey pearly light, as it had at dusk, its phosphorescence even more intense in this half-light of dawn than it had been then.

Jayal leant wearily against his sword. He had been hacking away at the reeds for more than half an hour. His sandy hair was matted to his face which in turn was streaked with grime. The front of his leather cuirass was stained with sweat, his shirt was wet beneath it, and the wounds on his arm and wrist ached abominably. By the early light of dawn he saw where he was: an odd twist of fate had brought him almost exactly to the place where his father had fought his last stand seven years before. Features in the landscape became more recognisable as the grey light intensified. The slight mound where his father's headquarters tent had stood, the grey circles of ash where the carrion pyres had been, the ground from which the undead had burst at dusk. Only the pyramid of skulls had been added to the scene of seven years before. He eyed the causeway some half a mile in front. It was still veiled by the remaining strands of fog. Nothing moved on it. The twin gates of the city, the same distance away to the right, were still shut, though a heavy pall of smoke made the fog even thicker in that direction.

He thought of Cloud. Cloud, who had carried him those seven years, abandoned at Skerrib's Inn. Though he had once more escaped the city, he felt incomplete. That part which carried Dragonstooth and possessed the knowledge which would take him to the two other artefacts was free. But with the loss of Cloud, he had lost his last contact with the past, the seven years of his quest.

He had regained his breath, and, nodding wearily at the others, began to move slowly over the boggy ground towards the causeway. It was then that he heard the noise: the noise he had last heard seven years before. Now as then, it froze the marrow in his blood. It was the long melancholy call of the Reapers' cow horns: a long dismal hoot consonant with the drifting fog and despair, with the pyramid of skulls and the causeway of bones. At first he wondered whether the ghosts had risen in the pearly light of dawn from the battlefield, but then the gates of the city began to open with an almighty groan that drifted, magnified in the stillness of the air, to where he stood. Figures, antlike at this distance, began pouring out from the opening; Jayal counted the first twenty or so, but they were followed by another twenty and another twenty after that: he gave up counting. There were hundreds of them, so many that their low moaning carried over the air, chilling his spine. Though their progress was slow and shambling, he could see that the vampires would cut them off well before they reached the causeway. They would have to go back into the marshes and take their chances there. With Alanda and Urthred and the coming dawn they might still be safe.

But then a shout of alarm came from behind them: Urthred was pointing with his gloved hand back in the direction they had come: the scene of the battle. It was as if Jayal had been transported back in time seven years. The ground churned with hidden life, just as it had when the vampires had burst from the ground. Now the marsh worked again, but this time it was skeletal hands which broke the surface of the peat, webs of purple light playing about their limbs. Limbs, and fragments of limbs, all those that the priests of Iss had missed when they'd built the causeway, reared up and scuttled to and fro like sinister insects. He whirled around: the causeway had changed in the few seconds since he'd last looked at it. Purple light glowed on its surface. Even at this distance, he saw its surface writhing as if it were alive. Unbalanced, several vampires fall off it into the marsh or the moat. The others were struggling down from it, like victims fleeing an earthquake.

Then his eyes went to the pyramid of skulls. It was as if a purple eldritch fire had been lit within each skull: the light burning from the eye sockets like lanterns.

His glance went finally to the tomb pyramid of Marizian. The fog was fleeing away from it in long fingers, and he could now see it clearly. Purple light pulsed up and down its four-hundred-foot height. Blocks of stone began to fall down its side. Then, like the eruption of a volcano, the whole top of the pyramid exploded, sending more ashlar blocks spinning through the air. A writhing purple mass emerged: some hundred feet tall, a faint outline of a horned skull head and a carapace could be seen in the whirling pattern. Its wings spread like a shadow over the City of the Dead, wafting the flames that played over the citadel area.

Jayal screamed; it was as if a vise had seized his right ankle. He looked down—a skeletal hand had grasped him just above his shoe. He kicked out, sending it flying through the air. It landed twenty feet away and scuttled away like a crab. There was more movement in the marshes all over the battlefield: weed-strung skulls rising up, skeletal claws breaking the surface: how had the priests missed so many bones? He waded back towards the others. The three of them were standing clustered on an island of dry land: the very hump on which his father had made his last stand. The water channel around it bubbled and heaved with reanimated bones. He leapt over it, and turned to assess their situation.

There was danger on every side. The vampires were still pouring across the causeway, despite the fact that its surface was alive with reknitting bones. The first wave of them were already swarming across the marshes, ignoring the waters that would rot their dried limbs. They would reach the mound within minutes. On every side bones clacked and scuttled hither and thither, gleaming with magical light. Then a chill shadow fell over them, and they saw the demon rear up, a hundred feet over the top of the pyramid, blocking out the dawn light with its body. It rose up and up, sucking masonry and dust into itself like a typhoon.

A flash of grey caught his eye by the city gate. There was a sudden turmoil in the heaving mass of vampires fighting to get out of the city. They split open as if an unseen hand was parting them. A grey form appeared in their midst. Then Jayal saw what it was: a galloping horse. But no ordinary horse; he would recognise those markings anywhere—it was Cloud. The gelding, as in its youth, when it had carried Baron Illgill to the hunt, was streaking down the causeway as if it were made of solid stone instead of chattering bone parts. As it came closer, Jayal recognised the figure bent low over the gelding's withers: Fazad the stableboy, riding like the wind. The vampires couldn't touch horse and rider, so fast was Cloud moving, as if once more it had heard his father's voice urging it to carry his son from the battle. Now Fazad alone of all those who lived in Thrull was going to get away.

Astride the horse, Fazad the stableboy clung to the gelding's grey-and-white mane. All night, since Skerrib's Inn had fallen to the vampires, Cloud had borne him round the city. They'd gone from one place of safety to another, the horse carrying him as if by instinct from where the vampires congregated. Even so, they'd been surrounded several times, but the horse had reared up, flailing at the undead with its hooves, clearing a path into which they'd galloped. It had been nearly dawn when Fazad had looked up wearily and seen they were in an alleyway near the city gates. He wondered why the horse had brought them there. But all had been quiet, and they'd seen no vampire for the past hour.

The light grew steadily in the sky behind them, and, for the first time, Fazad wondered whether they were going to escape after all. But then he'd heard a hubbub in front of him and to the sides. Shambling undead issued out of the side streets, flooding towards the gate like a tide. Miraculously they didn't scent his blood, but went to the beam barring the city gates and lifted it aside. The gates were prised open and the vampires flooded through, hundreds upon hundreds. Beyond, Fazad could see the bone causeway leading into the half-light of the dawn, but something strange was happening to it: it seemed to warp and writhe as if possessed of an unseen life beneath its surface. But whatever it was didn't deter Cloud. With a thunderous whinny, the horse reared up onto its haunches and raced for the opening. Vampires scattered to left and right as the charger bore down on them. Then they were out on the causeway, the horse oblivious of the bones that bucked and heaved under its hooves. Then the bones were left behind, and he heard the old horse's hooves drumming on the solid earth of the road. Ahead, to the south-west, his eyes fixed on the distant ring of the Fire Mountains. Cloud ran on and on—to freedom.

"Go, Cloud!" Jayal heard himself yell: it was as if he saw his own self escaping the battle those seven years before. And like those who had watched him go then, Manichee and the others who had congregated about the headquarters tent with his father, he knew that he would die and Fazad would live. Then horse and rider disappeared, swallowed up in a bank of fog. The charge had momentarily distracted the floods of vampires. Some made as if to follow horse and rider, but then, realising they had already escaped, rejoined the others wading over the marshes towards the knoll.

Jayal turned to Urthred: they had only a few minutes before the vampires reached them. His mind was paralysed, unable to think what they should do. The situation looked hopeless. The creature looming over Marizian's tomb turned its head slowly in their direction. A chill passed up Jayal's spine, a chill that began to freeze his marrow, further immoblising him. The activity of the bones in the marshes around them became even more frenzied. Skeletal hands began scuttling up the mound towards them, their fingers joints clacking with the speed of their movement.

But Urthred was not looking at the demon, but towards the monument of skulls over to their right some two hundred yards away, each skull in it aglow with purple light. A deafening chattering noise, like the sound of cicadas on a summer night, sounded from it, and he had to shout to be heard. "We must go to the pyramid."

Jayal kicked away the first of the scuttling crab hands. Had the priest taken leave of his senses? If the skulls had been reanimated like these hands, they were likely to be bitten to pieces. But the priest was shouting out something else, pointing to the east. Jayal followed the direction of his arm. Above the bleak granite cliffs of Thrull, and through the whirling body of the demon, the sky above the eastern mountains was flecked with red which glowed on the snow-covered peaks and the underside of the scudding cloud base. The sun was nearly risen. But where they stood was still in the deep shadows cast by the cliffs of Thrull. As long as there were shadows the vampires were safe. They would have to get up higher, to where the first of the sunbeams would strike. The only high ground was the skull pyramid.

Without thinking, the four of them began running towards it, splashing across the pool surrounding the knoll, kicking away the bones that snatched at their clothes. A skeleton suddenly rose from a clump of rushes in front of them, but Urthred swung a roundhouse blow at its skull, his gloves hitting it with explosive force, and smashing it into a hundred fragments.

Then they were at the base of the fifty-foot-high pyramid. The chattering din from the skulls was deafening, accompanied by a low moaning from each and every one of them as if each was reliving its dying agony on the battlefield: fragments of conversation, entreaties, endearments—the last thoughts of the dead. The four of them stared at the chattering mass, then behind them. The vampires were very close, splashing across the water channel around the knoll. The skeletons seemed to be hampering their movement as much as they had their own, but they were still coming on at a steady pace, thousands of them. They were so close they could make out their haggard faces and grave-soiled clothes, even the stench of embalming fluids as the breeze got up again, blowing away the fog.

He heard a rattle, and a scree of skulls came tumbling down the slopes of the pyramid. Alanda had begun to climb, but had slipped a few feet up her ascent. The skulls fell at Jayal's feet, muttering and cursing. Alanda started upwards again, followed by Thalassa and Urthred. Jayal slipped Dragonstooth through his belt and began to climb as well, whipping his hands away from the champing teeth, the skulls sliding under his feet, the ghostly protests loud, deafening. A slip was possible at any moment. A skull bounced down from above. He followed it as it fell. The first of the vampires had reached the base of the pyramid and was beginning to scramble up after them.

Jayal was now about halfway up, the other three were nearly at the summit. He glanced desperately at the mountains to the east. The crimson glow over them was even more pronounced, and, as he watched, a ray shot like an arrow through the sky and burst upon the red flanks of the Fire Mountains to the west. But still the looming bulk of Thrull hid the pyramid of skulls from the sun, and it was immersed in gloom. It looked as if their gamble had failed.

Jayal was nearly at the top, Urthred having already reached the summit: he could see the faces of the two women looking down. Then the skull his foot was resting on gave way, and he began to fall. Quick as a darting snake, Urthred's gloved hand shot out and grabbed his forearm: he nearly blanked out in pain as the steel talons drove into his arm despite the leather vambraces. He hung precariously, his feet sliding uselessly over the smooth skulls below, trying to get purchase. Then his ankle was seized. He looked down. A yellow-toothed mouth opened in triumph; he kicked at it, and the vampire tumbled back, taking two others with it. But now the whole face of the pyramid was swarming with the undead. Sobbing in desperation he pulled himself up on Urthred's arm, Alanda and Thalassa anchoring the priest's legs. Then he was over the lip of the pyramid.

Urthred stood rapidly, glancing up at the red sky as if taking inspiration from it, then chopped his hand down in a sharp movement. Fire blossomed, shimmering in the air, then rolled down the side of the pyramid, blackening the lichen-covered skulls. The fireball exploded in the mass of vampires at the bottom. Their dried skins ignited like dried papyrus, the flame ex-

panding outwards in an unstoppable tide that consumed all in
its wake.

Jayal looked around him desperately: the top of the pyramid
was truncated, making a platform some ten feet square, in the
middle of which was a single fire-blackened skull. But unlike
the others it didn't glow with the purple demon light. Straightaway he knew whose skull this was: Manichee's, placed on top
of the pyramid in lieu of the man who had escaped Faran's
grasp: his father.

A face appeared over the edge of the pyramid. He unsheathed Dragonstooth from his belt and brought it down on the
vampire's head, splitting it in two. Dried brain matter shot from
it like sawdust. He turned to face the next threat, but his movements were hampered by the narrowness of the platform. The
others were too near, allowing him only downward strokes. Another vampire appeared to his right: he tried to get his sword
into play, but the creature was already standing. He shoulder-
barged it over the side while it was still unbalanced, and it fell
back over the edge. Behind him, Urthred was pirouetting right
and left, his metal gloves punching and chopping at the swarm
of undead that had appeared on the other side of the platform.
He fell back, orange flame exploding from the gloves. When
the smoke cleared the vampires had disappeared. Then Thalassa screamed. A vampire had appeared from the opposite direction and was struggling with her on the platform. In an
instant, Urthred's gloves had clamped over its mouth and
throat, twisting its head round. Thalassa spun from its grip and
fell onto Manichee's skull. But now the platform was crowded
with milling figures. Jayal's sword arm was seized and he
swayed from side to side, beating off a bite with his forearm. A
vampire seized his leg and tried to pull him over; he kicked out,
but lost his balance, falling on his back. Sharp teeth glistened
above him, wide, ready for the bite. Then the world exploded in
red, the creature's face above him began to bubble away from
the bone as if it was being reduced in a boiling liquid. Steam
burst from its eye sockets. Its body twisted back, then fell like
a limp rag off the top of the pyramid. Jayal looked round
wildly: the other vampires were wreathed in fumes as they
burned away, their arms windmilling in the air as they fell.

The sun, the blessed sun, had arrived. A flat red beam had just crested the top of the city and bathed the pyramid in its glow. The body of the demon was shredding away into a thousand streamers under the effect of its rays, the mad chattering of the skulls grew dim, then suddenly stopped. He struggled to his feet: rejoicing in the hint of warmth in the sunbeam. He looked over the edge of the pyramid. Below the sun was rapidly travelling down the eastern face of the pyramid, catching the vampires in a fiery red tide, consuming them. On the lee side, the vampires hunched helplessly, unable to move, imprisoned in the shadows.

Then he heard a sob. He turned: Thalassa lay on the ground. Alanda and Urthred knelt to either side of her. A faint ribbon of blood had leaked from the corner of her mouth, and her face was even paler than usual. Her neck was twisted slightly to one side. In the middle of its white marble expanse was what could have been a love bite: except the lover had bitten hard and deep in his passion: blood welled from the teeth marks.

Jayal knew what it meant: one bite would be enough. Not to kill, but to change her forever. The virus would already be in her blood: within a month she would begin to change, her skin would become leathery, her eyes sensitive to the light. Even now she had begun to cross over, the infection spreading through her veins. Even the red glow of the sun could not save her.

A knife twisted in his heart. He had been rejoicing at living, but this woman he had once loved would soon be worse than dead.

He wondered dimly whether the priest would finish her now, as was his duty. Thalassa's end would be so different from her beginning. He knelt beside her too. Her breath was harsh and shallow. Alanda had laid her hands over the wound, repeating over and over some charm in a language he didn't recognise. When she removed her hands, the blood had stopped welling up, but the puncture marks were left.

"It's beyond my skill," she said, her voice breaking.

A strange noise came from behind the priest's mask, a half-strangled sob. He rose to his feet. The hideous mask tilted up towards the sun for a moment, then turned towards the fire-blackened skull lying next to Thalassa's body. It was if he communed with both the sun and the skull for several seconds.

"We need the sword," he said softly.

Jayal looked down at Dragonstooth. "What for?"

The priest's voice seemed to come from far away. "Manichee will help us one more time—he promised. He will take us to a place where there is rest, where Thalassa may recover."

"But Manichee is dead—look, there's only a skull!"

The priest fixed him with a level stare. In the light of the morning, Jayal for the first time sensed movement behind the eye slits of the mask.

"You must have faith," he said, holding out a gloved hand.

Jayal handed him the sword as if in a trance. "What are you going to do?"

"The sword will take us to the Forge, where the first artefact is."

"How can you be so sure?"

"My master promised: he never lied."

Jayal was going to speak again, but, before he could, the priest had raised the weapon to the sun, so its rays glinted off its blade. It coruscated with a rainbow of light. Jayal stared at the blinding light, feeling himself drawn deeply into its shining heart. Then the top of the pyramid of skulls began to whirl about him, slowly at first, then with ever-quicker revolutions. He felt dizzy and looked away briefly, catching a glimpse of the city. The rock of Thrull was blanketed with a thick pall of smoke and fog in which nothing moved. Despite the rising sun that had shredded its form, he knew the demon was in the mists, hunting out the souls of those who had survived the night. In the split second he watched, he saw tendrils of mist dart out across the plains towards the pyramid of skulls. The demon, once summoned, would not die, its powers were only dampened by the sun. He felt himself being drawn into the darkness that still covered the city, into the ancient soul of darkness and the earth. He wrested his gaze away, giving himself up to the vortex that spun around Manichee's skull. Immediately the top of the pyramid began to spin again. The figures of Urthred and Alanda and Thalassa were growing more indistinct, the sword a mere pinprick of light into which they were being sucked. Then he, too, was drawn into the ever diminishing light and he felt the void rushing by, ever faster. Then all became black.

He awoke to the sound of birds singing.

Coming Next Month From Roc

S. M. Stirling

On the Oceans of Eternity

Jim Butcher

Storm Front

Book One of the Dresden Files